Born in Kasauli, Himachal Pradesh, in 1934, Ruskin Bond grew up in Jamnagar (Gujarat), Dehradun and Simla. His first novel, *The Room on the Roof*, written when he was seventeen received the John Llewellyn Rhys Memorial Prize in 1957. Since then he has written over a hundred short stories, essays and novellas (including *Vagrants in the Valley* and *A Flight of Pigeons*) and more than thirty books for children. He has also published two volumes of autobiography, *Scenes from a Writer's Life*, which describes his formative years growing up in Anglo-India, and *The Lamp Is Lit*, a collection of essays and episodes from his journal. In 1992 he received the Sahitya Akademi Award for English writing in India. He was awarded the Padma Shree in 1999.

Ruskin Bond lives with his adopted family in Mussoorie.

RUSKIN BOND

Collected Fiction

PENGUIN BOOKS

PENGUIN BOOKS

Published by the Penguin Group

Penguin Books India Pvt Ltd, 11 Community Centre, Panchsheel Park, New Delhi 110 017, India

Penguin Group (USA) Inc., 375 Hudson Street, New York, New York 10014, USA

Penguin Group (Canada), 90 Eglinton Avenue East, Suite 700, Toronto, Ontario, M4P 2Y3, Canada (a division of Pearson Penguin Canada Inc.)

Penguin Books Ltd, 80 Strand, London WC2R 0RL, England

Penguin, Ireland, 25 St Stephen's Green, Dublin 2, Ireland (a division of Penguin Books Ltd)

Penguin Group (Australia), 250 Camberwell Road, Camberwell, Victoria 3124, Australia (a division of Pearson Australia Group Pty Ltd)

Penguin Group (NZ), cnr Airborne and Rosedale Roads, Albany, Auckland 1310, New Zealand (a division of Pearson New Zealand Ltd)

Penguin Group (South Africa) (Pty) Ltd, 24 Sturdee Avenue, Rosebank, Johannesburg 2196, South Africa

Penguin Books Ltd, Registered Offices: 80 Strand, London WC2R 0RL, England

First published in Viking as *Complete Short Stories and Novels* by Penguin Books India 1996
Published by Penguin Books 1999

Typeset in Palatino by FOLIO, New Delhi
Printed at Chaman Offset Printers, New Delhi

CONTENTS

NOVELS AND NOVELLAS

AUTHOR'S NOTE

It was 1986, and times were bad.

Bad for Ruskin Bond, writer, who had been pounding his typewriter for over thirty years without achieving fame, money or even critical approval.

And now he was in a hospital bed, doing his best to recover from a duodenal ulcer, surgery for haemorrhoids, and a bladder infection. The doctors (there were only two of them in Landour's Community Hospital) weren't making much headway, and a month had passed and the hospital bill was in excess of the author's bank balance. In such circumstances people often resort to religion. I would probably have done so myself if it wasn't for the copy of George and Weedon Grossmith's *Diary of a Nobody*, which I kept under my pillow. It has never failed to make me laugh at life's little vanities, pomposities and inanities. What are we humans, really—just absurd little creatures strutting about as though we owned the earth and everything upon it. An ill wind comes along, and we're finished. The graveyards are full of people who once thought they were indispensable.

Much as I loved *The Diary of a Nobody*, I did not want it to lose its freshness, so after the third reading I put it aside and tried a modern novel. But this only deepened my depression. And then a letter was placed on my bedside table, and I opened it and saw that it was from David Davidar, who had recently started editing and publishing Penguin Books in India. Could he reprint my first novel, published in England some thirty years earlier? The author sat up in bed; he *did* feel a little better. So people were publishing books again. And they wanted something of his, too.

Mind began exerting its dominance over matter. The author remembered that there was an old copy of *The Room on the Roof* lying around somewhere in his home. Forgetting ulcers and surgical dressings, he discharged himself from the hospital and made his way home to locate that precious copy before it vanished!

To David Davidar it went, reappearing under the Penguin India imprint a few months later, with a cover splendidly illustrated by Subroto Gangopadhyay and designed by Amiya Bhattacharya. These same artists—along with Bimal Das, Tapas Guha, Sunil Sil, Suddhasatwa Basu and others—were to embellish other Penguin books by Ruskin Bond, much to his delight. No one quite realizes how much a book owes to an attractive cover. This is one writer who values his illustrators, and he takes this opportunity to thank them.

Almost ten years have passed since Penguin began publishing in India, and among the hundreds of titles they have brought out, twelve have been mine. Now they do me the honour of including me among their more popular authors, with an omnibus volume of my adult fiction.

Sir Allen Lane's Penguins first appeared just over sixty years ago, a year before I was born. I read my first Penguin at school, in Simla. I think it was Compton Mackenzie's *Carnival*. I don't remember much about the story (except that it had something to do with the theatre), and I no longer have it; but for some strange reason I have always remembered the opening lines:

"Put out the lights, and then—put out the light!"

Maybe it had something to do with the dormitory lights which, as a school prefect, I was supposed to switch off at night. Or maybe it went deeper. Maybe I'll find out some day . . .

August 23, 1995   *Ruskin Bond*

SHORT STORIES

THE WOMAN ON PLATFORM No. 8

જ

IT WAS MY SECOND year at boarding-school, and I was sitting on platform No. 8 at Ambala station, waiting for the northern bound train. I think I was about twelve at the time. My parents considered me old enough to travel alone, and I had arrived by bus at Ambala early in the evening: now there was a wait till midnight before my train arrived. Most of the time I had been pacing up and down the platform, browsing at the bookstall, or feeding broken biscuits to stray dogs; trains came and went, and the platform would be quiet for a while and then, when a train arrived, it would be an inferno of heaving, shouting, agitated human bodies. As the carriage doors opened, a tide of people would sweep down upon the nervous little ticket-collector at the gate; and every time this happened I would be caught in the rush and swept outside the station. Now tired of this game and of ambling about the platform, I sat down on my suitcase and gazed dismally across the railway tracks.

Trolleys rolled past me, and I was conscious of the cries of the various vendors—the men who sold curds and lemon, the sweetmeat-seller, the newspaper boy—but I had lost interest in all that went on along the busy platform, and continued to stare across the railway tracks, feeling bored and a little lonely.

'Are you all alone, my son?' asked a soft voice close behind me.

I looked up and saw a woman standing near me. She was leaning over, and I saw a pale face, and dark kind eyes. She wore no jewels, and was dressed very simply in a white sari.

'Yes, I am going to school,' I said, and stood up respectfully.

She seemed poor, but there was a dignity about her that commanded respect.

'I have been watching you for some time,' she said. 'Didn't your parents come to see you off?'

'I don't live here,' I said. 'I had to change trains. Anyway, I can travel alone.'

'I am sure you can,' she said, and I liked her for saying that, and I also liked her for the simplicity of her dress, and for her deep, soft voice and the serenity of her face.

'Tell me, what is your name?' she asked.

'Arun,' I said.

'And how long do you have to wait for your train?'

'About an hour, I think. It comes at twelve o'clock.'

'Then come with me and have something to eat.'

I was going to refuse, out of shyness and suspicion, but she took me by the hand, and then I felt it would be silly to pull my hand away. She told a coolie to look after my suitcase, and then she led me away down the platform. Her hand was gentle, and she held mine neither too firmly nor too lightly. I looked up at her again. She was not young. And she was not old. She must have been over thirty, but had she been fifty, I think she would have looked much the same.

She took me into the station dining-room, ordered tea and samosas and jalebis, and at once I began to thaw and take a new interest in this kind woman. The strange encounter had little effect on my appetite. I was a hungry school boy, and I ate as much as I could in as polite a manner as possible. She took obvious pleasure in watching me eat, and I think it was the food that strengthened the bond between us and cemented our friendship, for under the influence of the tea and sweets I began to talk quite freely, and told her about my school, my friends, my likes and dislikes. She questioned me quietly from time to time, but preferred listening; she drew me out very well, and I had soon forgotten that we were strangers. But she did not ask me about my family or where I lived, and I did not ask her where she lived. I accepted her for what she had been to me—a quiet, kind and gentle woman who gave sweets to a lonely boy on a railway platform . . . .

After about half an hour we left the dining-room and began walking back along the platform. An engine was shunting up and down beside platform No. 8, and as it approached, a boy leapt off the platform and ran across the rails, taking a short cut to the next platform. He was at a safe distance from the engine, but as he leapt across the rails, the woman clutched my arm. Her fingers dug into my flesh, and I winced with pain. I caught her fingers and looked up at her, and I saw a spasm of pain and fear and sadness pass across her face. She watched the boy as he climbed the platform, and it was not until he had disappeared in the crowd that she relaxed her hold on my arm. She smiled at me reassuringly, and took my hand again; but her fingers trembled against mine.

'He was all right,' I said, feeling that it was she who needed reassurance.

She smiled gratefully at me and pressed my hand. We walked together in silence until we reached the place where I had left my suitcase. One of my schoolfellows, Satish, a boy of about my age, had turned up with his mother.

'Hello, Arun!' he called. 'The train's coming in late, as usual. Did you know we have a new headmaster this year?'

We shook hands, and then he turned to his mother and said: 'This is Arun, Mother. He is one of my friends, and the best bowler in the class.'

'I am glad to know that,' said his mother, a large imposing woman who wore spectacles. She looked at the woman who held my hand and said: 'And I suppose you're Arun's mother?'

I opened my mouth to make some explanation, but before I could say anything the woman replied: 'Yes, I am Arun's mother.'

I was unable to speak a word. I looked quickly up at the woman, but she did not appear to be at all embarrassed, and was smiling at Satish's mother.

Satish's mother said: 'It's such a nuisance having to wait for the train right in the middle of the night. But one can't let the child wait here alone. Anything can happen to a boy at a big station like this—there are so many suspicious characters hanging about. These days one has to be very careful of strangers.'

'Arun can travel alone though,' said the woman beside me, and somehow I felt grateful to her for saying that. I had already forgiven her for lying; and besides, I had taken an instinctive dislike to Satish's mother.

'Well, be very careful, Arun,' said Satish's mother looking sternly at me through her spectacles. 'Be very careful when your mother is not with you. And never talk to strangers!'

I looked from Satish's mother to the woman who had given me tea and sweets, and back at Satish's mother.

'I like strangers,' I said.

Satish's mother definitely staggered a little, as obviously she was not used to being contradicted by small boys. 'There you are, you see! If you don't watch over them all the time, they'll walk straight into trouble. Always listen to what your mother tells you,' she said, wagging a fat little finger at me. 'And never, never talk to strangers.'

I glared resentfully at her, and moved closer to the woman who had befriended me. Satish was standing behind his mother, grinning at me, and delighting in my clash with his mother. Apparently he was on my side.

The station bell clanged, and the people who had till now been squatting resignedly on the platform began bustling about.

'Here it comes,' shouted Satish, as the engine whistle shrieked and the front lights played over the rails.

The train moved slowly into the station, the engine hissing and sending out waves of steam. As it came to a stop, Satish jumped on the footboard of a lighted compartment and shouted, 'Come on, Arun, this one's empty!' and I picked up my suitcase and made a dash for the open door.

We placed ourselves at the open windows, and the two women stood outside on the platform, talking up to us. Satish's mother did most of the talking.

'Now don't jump on and off moving trains, as you did just now,' she said. 'And don't stick your heads out of the windows, and don't eat any rubbish on the way.' She allowed me to share the benefit of her advice, as she probably didn't think my 'mother' a very capable person. She handed Satish a bag of fruit, a cricket bat and a big box of chocolates, and told him to share the food with me. Then she stood back from the window to watch how my 'mother' behaved.

I was smarting under the patronizing tone of Satish's mother, who obviously thought mine a very poor family; and I did not intend giving the other woman away. I let her take my hand in hers, but I could think of nothing to say. I was conscious of

Satish's mother staring at us with hard, beady eyes, and I found myself hating her with a firm, unreasoning hate. The guard walked up the platform, blowing his whistle for the train to leave. I looked straight into the eyes of the woman who held my hand, and she smiled in a gentle, understanding way. I leaned out of the window then, and put my lips to her cheek, and kissed her.

The carriage jolted forward, and she drew her hand away.

'Good-bye, Mother!' said Satish, as the train began to move slowly out of the station. Satish and his mother waved to each other.

'Good-bye,' I said to the other woman, 'good-bye—Mother . . .'

I didn't wave or shout, but sat still in front of the window, gazing at the woman on the platform. Satish's mother was talking to her, but she didn't appear to be listening; she was looking at me, as the train took me away. She stood there on the busy platform, a pale sweet woman in white, and I watched her until she was lost in the milling crowd.

The Coral Tree

❧

THE NIGHT HAD BEEN hot, the rain frequent, and I slept on the veranda instead of in the house. I was in my twenties and I had begun to earn a living and felt I had certain responsibilities. In a short while a tonga would take me to a railway station, and from there a train would take me to Bombay, and then a ship would take me to England. There would be work, interviews, a job, a different kind of life; so many things, that this small bungalow of my grandfather's would be remembered fitfully, in rare moments of reflection.

When I awoke on the veranda I saw a grey morning, smelt the rain on the red earth, and remembered that I had to go away. A girl was standing in the veranda porch, looking at me very seriously. When I saw her, I sat up in bed with a start.

She was a small, dark girl, her eyes big and black, her pigtails tied up in a bright red ribbon; and she was fresh and clean like the rain and the red earth.

She stood looking at me, and she was very serious.

'Hallo,' I said, smiling, trying to put her at ease.

But the girl was businesslike. She acknowledged my greeting with a brief nod.

'Can I do anything for you?' I asked, stretching my limbs. 'Do you stay near here?'

She nodded again.

'With your parents?'

With great assurance she said, 'Yes. But I can stay on my own.'

'You're like me,' I said, and for a while I forgot about being an old man of twenty. 'I like to do things on my own. I'm going away today.'

'Oh,' she said, a little breathlessly.

'Would you care to go to England?'

'I want to go everywhere,' she said, 'to America and Africa and Japan and Honolulu.'

'Maybe you will,' I said. 'I'm going everywhere, and no one can stop me . . . But what is it you want? What did you come for?'

'I want some flowers but I can't reach them.' She waved her hand towards the garden. 'That tree, see?'

The coral tree stood in front of the house surrounded by pools of water and broken, fallen blossoms. The branches of the tree were thick with the scarlet, pea-shaped flowers.

'All right,' I said. 'Just let me get ready.'

The tree was easy to climb, and I made myself comfortable on one of the lower branches, smiling down at the serious upturned face of the girl.

'I'll throw them down to you,' I said.

I bent a branch but the wood was young and green, and I had to twist it several times before it snapped.

'I'm not sure that I ought to do this,' I said, as I dropped the flowering branch to the girl.

'Don't worry,' she said.

'Well, if you're ready to speak up for me—'

'Don't worry.'

I felt a sudden nostalgic longing for childhood and an urge to remain behind in my grandfather's house with its tangled memories and ghosts of yesteryear. But I was the only one left, and what could I do except climb coral and jackfruit trees?

'Have you many friends?' I asked.

'Oh, yes.'

'Who is the best?'

'The cook. He lets me stay in the kitchen, which is more interesting than the house. And I like to watch him cooking. And he gives me things to eat, and tells me stories . . .'

'And who is your second best friend?'

She inclined her head to one side, and thought very hard.

'I'll make you the second best,' she said.

I sprinkled coral blossoms over her head. 'That's very kind of you. I'm happy to be your second best.'

A tonga bell sounded at the gate, and I looked out from the tree and said, 'It's come for me. I have to go now.'

I climbed down.

'Will you help me with my suitcases?' I asked, as we walked together towards the veranda. 'There is no one here to help me. I am the last to go. Not because I want to go, but because I have to.'

I sat down on the cot and packed a few last things in a suitcase. All the doors of the house were locked. On my way to the station I would leave the keys with the caretaker. I had already given instructions to an agent to try and sell the house. There was nothing more to be done.

We walked in silence to the waiting tonga, thinking and wondering about each other.

'Take me to the station,' I said to the tonga driver.

The girl stood at the side of the path, on the damp red earth, gazing at me.

'Thank you,' I said. 'I hope I shall see you again.'

'I'll see you in London,' she said. 'Or America or Japan. I want to go everywhere.'

'I'm sure you will,' I said. 'And perhaps I'll come back and we'll meet again in this garden. That would be nice, wouldn't it?'

She nodded and smiled. We knew it was an important moment.

The tonga driver spoke to his pony, and the carriage set off down the gravel path, rattling a little. The girl and I waved to each other.

In the girl's hand was a sprig of coral blossom. As she waved, the blossoms fell apart and danced lightly in the breeze.

'Goodbye!' I called.

'Goodbye!' called the girl.

The ribbon had come loose from her pigtail and lay on the ground with the coral blossoms.

'I'm going everywhere,' I said to myself, 'and no one can stop me.'

And she was fresh and clean like the rain and the red earth.

THE PHOTOGRAPH

❧

I WAS TEN YEARS old. My grandmother sat on the string bed under the mango tree. It was late summer and there were sunflowers in the garden and a warm wind in the trees. My grandmother was knitting a woollen scarf for the winter months. She was very old, dressed in a plain white sari. Her eyes were not very strong now but her fingers moved quickly with the needles and the needles kept clicking all afternoon. Grandmother had white hair but there were very few wrinkles on her skin.

I had come home after playing cricket on the maidan. I had taken my meal and now I was rummaging in a box of old books and family heirlooms that had just that day been brought out of the attic by my mother. Nothing in the box interested me very much except for a book with colourful pictures of birds and butterflies. I was going through the book, looking at the pictures, when I found a small photograph between the pages. It was a faded picture, a little yellow and foggy. It was the picture of a girl standing against a wall and behind the wall there was nothing but sky. But from the other side a pair of hands reached up, as though someone was going to climb the wall. There were flowers growing near the girl but I couldn't tell what they were. There was a creeper too but it was just a creeper.

I ran out into the garden. 'Granny!' I shouted. 'Look at this picture! I found it in the box of old things. Whose picture is it?'

I jumped on the bed beside my grandmother and she walloped me on the bottom and said, 'Now I've lost count of my stitches and the next time you do that I'll make you finish the scarf yourself.'

Granny was always threatening to teach me how to knit which I thought was a disgraceful thing for a boy to do. It was a good deterrent for keeping me out of mischief. Once I had torn the drawing-room curtains and Granny had put a needle and thread in my hand and made me stitch the curtain together, even though I make long, two-inch stitches, which had to be taken out by my mother and done again.

She took the photograph from my hand and we both stared at it for quite a long time. The girl had long, loose hair and she wore a long dress that nearly covered her ankles, and sleeves that reached her wrists, and there were a lot of bangles on her hands. But despite all this drapery, the girl appeared to be full of freedom and movement. She stood with her legs apart and her hands on her hips and had a wide, almost devilish smile on her face.

'Whose picture is it?' I asked.

'A little girl's, of course,' said Grandmother. 'Can't you tell?'

'Yes, but did you know the girl?'

'Yes, I knew her,' said Granny, 'but she was a very wicked girl and I shouldn't tell you about her. But I'll tell you about the photograph. It was taken in your grandfather's house about sixty years ago. And that's the garden wall and over the wall there was a road going to town.'

'Whose hands are they,' I asked, 'coming up from the other side?'

Grandmother squinted and looked closely at the picture, and shook her head. 'It's the first time I've noticed,' she said. 'They must have been the sweeper boy's. Or maybe they were your grandfather's.'

'They don't look like Grandfather's hands,' I said. 'His hands are all bony.'

'Yes, but this was sixty years ago.'

'Didn't he climb up the wall after the photo?'

'No, nobody climbed up. At least, I don't remember.'

'And you remember well, Granny.'

'Yes, I remember . . . . I remember what is not in the photograph. It was a spring day and there was a cool breeze blowing, nothing like this. Those flowers at the girl's feet, they were marigolds, and the bougainvillaea creeper, it was a mass of purple. You cannot see these colours in the photo and even if you could, as nowadays, you wouldn't be able to smell the flowers or feel the breeze.'

'And what about the girl?' I said. 'Tell me about the girl.'

'Well, she was a wicked girl,' said Granny. 'You don't know the trouble they had getting her into those fine clothes she's wearing.'

'I think they are terrible clothes,' I said.

'So did she. Most of the time, she hardly wore a thing. She used to go swimming in a muddy pool with a lot of ruffianly boys, and ride on the backs of buffaloes. No boy ever teased her, though, because she could kick and scratch and pull his hair out!'

'She looks like it too,' I said. 'You can tell by the way she's smiling. At any moment something's going to happen.'

'Something did happen,' said Granny. 'Her mother wouldn't let her take off the clothes afterwards, so she went swimming in them, and lay for half an hour in the mud.'

I laughed heartily and Grandmother laughed too.

'Who was the girl?' I said. 'You must tell me who she was.'

'No, that wouldn't do,' said Grandmother, but I pretended I didn't know. I knew, because Grandmother still smiled in the same way, even though she didn't have as many teeth.

'Come on, Granny,' I said, 'tell me, tell me.'

But Grandmother shook her head and carried on with the knitting. And I held the photograph in my hand looking from it to my grandmother and back again, trying to find points in common between the old lady and the little pig-tailed girl. A lemon-coloured butterfly settled on the end of Grandmother's knitting needle and stayed there while the needles clicked away. I made a grab at the butterfly and it flew off in a dipping flight and settled on a sunflower.

'I wonder whose hands they were,' whispered Grandmother to herself, with her head bowed, and her needles clicking away in the soft warm silence of that summer afternoon.

THE WINDOW

⤫

I CAME IN THE spring, and took the room on the roof. It was a long low building which housed several families; the roof was flat, except for my room and a chimney. I don't know whose room owned the chimney, but my room owned the roof. And from the window of my room I owned the world.

But only from the window.

The banyan tree, just opposite, was mine, and its inhabitants my subjects. They were two squirrels, a few mina, a crow, and at night, a pair of flying-foxes. The squirrels were busy in the afternoons, the birds in the mornings and evenings, the foxes at night. I wasn't very busy that year; not as busy as the inhabitants of the banyan tree.

There was also a mango tree but that came later, in the summer, when I met Koki and the mangoes were ripe.

At first, I was lonely in my room. But then I discovered the power of my window. I looked out on the banyan tree, on the garden, on the broad path that ran beside the building, and out over the roofs of other houses, over roads and fields, as far as the horizon. The path was not a very busy one but it held variety: an ayah, with a baby in a pram; the postman, an event in himself; the fruit-seller, the toy-seller, calling their wares in high-pitched familiar cries; the rent-collector; a posse of cyclists; a long chain of schoolgirls; a lame beggar . . . all passed my way, the way of my window . . .

In the early summer, a tonga came rattling and jingling down the path and stopped in front of the house. A girl and an elderly lady climbed down, and a servant unloaded their baggage. They went into the house and the tonga moved off, the horse snorting a little.

The next morning the girl looked up from the garden and saw me at my window.

She had long black hair that fell to her waist, tied with a single red ribbon. Her eyes were black like her hair and just as shiny. She must have been about ten or eleven years old.

'Hallo,' I said with a friendly smile.

She looked suspiciously at me. 'Who are you?' she asked.

'I'm a ghost.'

She laughed, and her laugh had a gay, mocking quality. 'You look like one!'

I didn't think her remark particularly flattering, but I had asked for it. I stopped smiling anyway. Most children don't like adults smiling at them all the time.

'What have you got up there?' she asked.

'Magic,' I said.

She laughed again but this time without mockery. 'I don't believe you,' she said.

'Why don't you come up and see for yourself?'

She hesitated a little but came round to the steps and began climbing them, slowly, cautiously. And when she entered the room, she brought a magic of her own.

'Where's your magic?' she asked, looking me in the eye.

'Come here,' I said, and I took her to the window, and showed her the world.

She said nothing but stared out of the window uncomprehendingly at first, and then with increasing interest. And after some time she turned round and smiled at me, and we were friends.

I only knew that her name was Koki, and that she had come with her aunt for the summer months; I didn't need to know any more about her, and she didn't need to know anything about me except that I wasn't really a ghost—not the frightening sort anyway . . . .

She came up my steps nearly every day, and joined me at the window. There was a lot of excitement to be had in our world, especially when the rains broke.

At the first rumblings, women would rush outside to retrieve the washing on the clothesline and if there was a breeze, to chase a few garments across the compound. When the rain came, it came with a vengeance, making a bog of the garden and a river of the path. A cyclist would come riding furiously down the path, an elderly gentleman would be having difficulty with an umbrella, naked children would be frisking about in the rain. Sometimes Koki would run out on the roof, and shout and dance in the rain. And the rain would come through the open door and window of the room, flooding the floor and making an island of the bed.

But the window was more fun than anything else. It gave us the power of detachment: we were deeply interested in the life around us, but we were not involved in it.

'It is like a cinema,' said Koki. 'The window is the screen, the world is the picture.'

Soon the mangoes were ripe, and Koki was in the branches of the mango tree as often as she was in my room. From the window I had a good view of the tree, and we spoke to each other from the same height. We ate far too many mangoes, at least five a day.

'Let's make a garden on the roof,' suggested Koki. She was full of ideas like this.

'And how do you propose to do that?' I asked.

'It's easy. We bring up mud and bricks and make the flower-beds. Then we plant the seeds. We'll grow all sorts of flowers.'

'The roof will fall in,' I predicted.

But it didn't. We spent two days carrying buckets of mud up the steps to the roof and laying out the flower-beds. It was very hard work, but Koki did most of it. When the beds were ready, we had the opening ceremony. Apart from a few small plants collected from the garden below we had only one species of seeds—pumpkin . . . .

We planted the pumpkin seeds in the mud, and felt proud of ourselves.

But it rained heavily that night, and in the morning I discovered that everything—except the bricks—had been washed away.

So we returned to the window.

A mina had been in a fight—with a crow perhaps—and the feathers had been knocked off its head. A bougainvillaea that had been climbing the wall had sent a long green shoot in through the window.

Koki said, 'Now we can't shut the window without spoiling the creeper.'

'Then we will never close the window,' I said.

And we let the creeper into the room.

The rains passed, and an autumn wind came whispering through the branches of the banyan tree. There were red leaves on the ground, and the wind picked them up and blew them about, so that they looked like butterflies. I would watch the sun rise in the morning, the sky all red, until its first rays splashed the window-still and crept up the walls of the room. And in the evening Koki and I watched the sun go down in a sea of fluffy clouds; sometimes the clouds were pink, and sometimes orange; they were always coloured clouds. framed in the window.

'I'm going tomorrow,' said Koki one evening.

I was too surprised to say anything.

'You stay here for ever, don't you?' she said.

I remained silent.

'When I come again next year you will still be here, won't you?'

'I don't know,' I said. 'But the window will still be here.'

'Oh, do be here next year,' she said, 'or someone will close the window!'

In the morning the tonga was at the door, and the servant, the aunt and Koki were in it. Koki waved to me at my window. Then the driver flicked the reins, the wheels of the carriage creaked and rattled, the bell jingled. Down the path went the tonga, down the path and through the gate, and all the time Koki waved; and from the gate I must have looked like a ghost, standing alone at the high window, amongst the bougainvillaea.

When the tonga was out of sight I took the spray of bougainvillaea in my hand and pushed it out of the room. Then I closed the window. It would be opened only when the spring and Koki came again.

CHACHI'S FUNERAL

&

Chachi died at 6 p.m. on Wednesday the 5th of April, and came to life again exactly twenty minutes later. This is how it happened.

Chachi was, as a rule, a fairly tolerant, easy-going person, who waddled about the house without paying much attention to the swarms of small sons, daughters, nephews and nieces who poured in and out of the rooms. But she had taken a particular aversion to her ten-year-old nephew, Sunil. She was a simple woman and could not understand Sunil. He was a little brighter than her own sons, more sensitive, and inclined to resent a scolding or a cuff across the head. He was better looking than her own children. All this, in addition to the fact that she resented having to cook for the boy while both his parents went out to office jobs, led her to grumble at him a little more than was really necessary.

Sunil sensed his aunt's jealousy and fanned its flames. He was a mischievous boy, and did little things to annoy her, like bursting paperbags behind her while she dozed, or commenting on the width of her pyjamas when they were hung out to dry. On the evening of the 5th of April, he had been in particularly high spirits and, feeling hungry, entered the kitchen with the intention of helping himself to some honey. But the honey was on the top shelf, and Sunil wasn't quite tall enough to grasp the bottle. He got his fingers to it but as he tilted it towards him, it fell to the ground with a crash.

Chachi reached the scene of the accident before Sunil could slip away. Removing her slipper, she dealt him three or four furious blows across the head and shoulders. This done, she sat down on the floor and burst into tears.

Had the beating come from someone else, Sunil might have cried; but his pride was hurt and, instead of weeping, he muttered something under his breath and stormed out of the room.

Climbing the steps to the roof, he went to his secret hiding-place, a small hole in the wall of the unused barsati, where he kept his marbles, kite-string, tops, and a clasp-knife. Opening the knife, he plunged it thrice into the soft wood of the window-frame.

'I'll kill her!' he whispered fiercely, 'I'll kill her, I'll kill her!'

'Who are you going to kill, Sunil?'

It was his cousin Madhu, a dark, slim girl of twelve, who aided and abetted him in most of his exploits. Sunil's Chachi was her 'Mammi'. It was a very big family.

'Chachi,' said Sunil. 'She hates me, I know. Well, I hate her too. This time I'll kill her.'

'How are you going to do it?'

'I'll stab with this.' He showed her the knife. 'Three times, in the heart.'

'But you'll be caught. The C.I.D. is very clever. Do you want to go to jail?'

'Won't they hang me?'

'They don't hang small boys. They send them to boarding schools.'

'I don't want to go to a boarding school.'

'Then better not kill your Chachi. At least not this way. I'll show you how.'

Madhu produced pencil and paper, went down on her hands and knees, and screwing up her face in sharp concentration, made a rough drawing of Chachi. Then, with a red crayon, she sketched in a big heart in the region of Chachi's stomach.

'Now,' she said, 'stab her to death!'

Sunil's eyes shone with excitement. Here was a great new game. You could always depend on Madhu for something original. He held the drawing against the woodwork, and plunged his knife three times into Chachi's pastel breast.

'You have killed her,' said Madhu.

'Is that all?'

'Well, if you like, we can cremate her.'

'All right.'

She took the torn paper, crumpled it up, produced a box of matches from Sunil's hiding-place, lit a match, and set fire to the paper. In a few minutes all that remained of Chachi was a few ashes.

'Poor Chachi,' said Madhu.

'Perhaps we shouldn't have done it,' said Sunil beginning to feel sorry.

'I know, we'll put her ashes in the river!'

'What river?'

'Oh, the drain will do.'

Madhu gathered the ashes together, and leant over the balcony of the roof. She threw out her arms, and the ashes drifted downwards. Some of them settled on the pomegranate tree, a few reached the drain and were carried away by a sudden rush of kitchen water. She turned to face Sunil.

Big tears were rolling down Sunil's cheeks.

'What are you crying for?' asked Madhu.

'Chachi. I didn't hate her so much.'

'Then why did you want to kill her?'

'Oh, that was different.'

'Come on, then, let's go down. I have to do my homework.'

As they came down the steps from the roof, Chachi emerged from the kitchen.

'Oh Chachi!' shouted Sunil. He rushed to her and tried to get his arms around her ample waist.

'Now what's up?' grumbled Chachi. 'What is it this time?'

'Nothing, Chachi. I love you so much. Please don't leave us.'

A look of suspicion crossed Chachi's face. She frowned down at the boy. But she was reassured by the look of genuine affection that she saw in his eyes.

'Perhaps he *does* care for me, after all,' she thought and patting him gently on the head. She took him by the hand and led him back to the kitchen.

The Man Who Was Kipling

&

I was sitting on a bench in the Indian Section of the Victoria and Albert Museum in London, when a tall, stooping, elderly gentleman sat down beside me. I gave him a quick glance, noting his swarthy features, heavy moustache, and horn-rimmed spectacles. There was something familiar and disturbing about his face and I couldn't resist looking at him again.

I noticed that he was smiling at me.

'Do you recognize me?' he asked in a soft pleasant voice.

'Well, you do seem familiar,' I said. 'Haven't we met somewhere?'

'Perhaps. But if I seem familiar to you, that is at least something. The trouble these days is that people don't *know* me anymore—I'm a familiar, that's all. Just a name standing for a lot of outmoded ideas.'

A little perplexed, I asked. 'What is it you do?'

'I wrote books once. Poems and tales . . . . Tell me, whose books do you read?'

'Oh, Maugham, Priestley, Thurber. And among the older lot, Bennett and Wells . . . .' I hesitated, groping for an important name, and I noticed a shadow, a sad shadow, pass across my companion's face.

'Oh yes, and Kipling,' I said. 'I read a lot of Kipling.'

His face brightened up at once and the eyes behind the thick-lensed spectacles suddenly came to life.

'I'm Kipling,' he said.

I stared at him in astonishment. And then, realizing that he might perhaps be dangerous, I smiled feebly and said, 'Oh yes?'

'You probably don't believe me. I'm dead, of course.'

'So I thought,'

'And you don't believe in ghosts?'

'Not as a rule.'

'But you'd have no objection to talking to one if he came along?'

'I'd have no objection. But how do I know you're Kipling? How do I know you're not an impostor?'

'Listen, then:

> When my heavens were turned to blood,
> When the dark had filled my day,
> Furthest, but most faithful, stood
> That lone star I cast away.
> I had loved myself, and I
> Have not lived and dare not die.

'Once,' he said, gripping me by the arm and looking me straight in the eye. 'Once in life I watched a star but I whistled her to go.'

'Your star hasn't fallen yet,' I said, suddenly moved, suddenly quite certain that I sat beside Kipling. 'One day, when there is a new spirit of adventure abroad, we will discover you again.'

'Why have they heaped scorn on me for so long?'

'You were too militant, I suppose—too much of an Empire man. You were too patriotic for your own good.'

He looked a little hurt. 'I was never very political,' he said. 'I wrote over six hundred poems. And you could only call a dozen of them political. I have been abused for harping on the theme of the White Man's burden but my only aim was to show off the Empire to my audience—and I believed the Empire was a fine and noble thing. Is it wrong to believe in something? I never went deeply into political issues, that's true. You must remember, my seven years in India were very youthful years. I was in my twenties, a little immature if you like, and my interest in India was a boy's interest. Action appealed to me more than anything else. You must understand that.'

'No one has described action more vividly, or India so well.

I feel at one with Kim wherever he goes along the Grand Trunk Road, in the temples at Banaras, amongst the Saharanpur fruit gardens, on the snow-covered Himalayas. *Kim* has colour and movement and poetry.'

He sighed and a wistful look came into his eyes.

'I'm prejudiced, of course,' I continued. 'I've spent most of my life in India—not *your* India, but an India that does still have much of the colour and atmosphere that you captured. You know, Mr Kipling, you can still sit in a third-class railway carriage and meet the most wonderful assortment of people. In any village you will still find the same courtesy, dignity and courage that the Lama and Kim found on their travels.'

'And the Grand Trunk Road? Is it still a long winding procession of humanity?'

'Well, not exactly,' I said a little ruefully. 'It's just a procession of motor vehicles now. The poor Lama would be run down by a truck if he became too dreamy on the Grand Trunk Road. Times *have* changed. There are no more Mrs Hawksbees in Simla, for instance.'

There was a faraway look in Kipling's eyes. Perhaps he was imagining himself a boy again. Perhaps he could see the hills or the red dust of Rajputana. Perhaps he was having a private conversation with Privates Mulvaney and Ortheris, or perhaps he was out hunting with the Seonce wolf-pack. The sound of London's traffic came to us through the glass doors but we heard only the creaking of bullock-cart wheels and the distant music of a flute.

He was talking to himself, repeating a passage from one of his stories. 'And the last puff of the daywind brought from the unseen villages the scent of damp wood-smoke, hot cakes, dripping undergrowth, and rotting pine-cones. That is the true smell of the Himalayas and if once it creeps into the blood of a man, that man will at the last, forgetting all else, return to the hills to die.'

A mist seemed to have risen between us—or had it come in from the streets?—and when it cleared, Kipling had gone away.

I asked the gatekeeper if he had seen a tall man with a slight stoop, wearing spectacles.

'Nope,' said the gatekeeper. 'Nobody been by for the last ten minutes.'

'Did someone like that come into the gallery a little while ago?'

'No one that I recall. What did you say the bloke's name was?'

'Kipling,' I said.

'Don't know him.'

'Didn't you ever read *The Jungle Books*?'

'Sounds familiar. Tarzan stuff, wasn't it?'

I left the museum and wandered about the streets for a long time but I couldn't find Kipling anywhere. Was it the boom of London's traffic that I heard or the boom of the Sutlej river racing through the valleys?

The Eyes Have It

ھ

I HAD THE TRAIN compartment to myself up to Rohana, then a girl got in. The couple who saw her off were probably her parents. They seemed very anxious about her comfort and the woman gave the girl detailed instructions as to where to keep her things, when not to lean out of windows, and how to avoid speaking to strangers.

They called their goodbyes and the train pulled out of the station. As I was totally blind at the time, my eyes sensitive only to light and darkness, I was unable to tell what the girl looked like. But I knew she wore slippers from the way they slapped against her heels.

It would take me some time to discover something about her looks and perhaps I never would. But I liked the sound of her voice and even the sound of her slippers.

'Are you going all the way to Dehra? I asked.

I must have been sitting in a dark corner because my voice startled her. She gave a little exclamation and said, 'I didn't know anyone else was here.'

Well, it often happens that people with good eyesight fail to see what is right in front of them. They have too much to take in, I suppose. Whereas people who cannot see (or see very little) have to take in only the essentials, whatever registers tellingly on their remaining senses.

'I didn't see you either,' I said. 'But I heard you come in.'

I wondered if I would be able to prevent her from discovering that I was blind. Provided I keep to my seat, I thought, it shouldn't be too difficult.

The girl said, 'I'm getting off at Saharanpur. My aunt is meeting me there.'

'Then I had better not get too familiar,' I replied. 'Aunts are usually formidable creatures.'

'Where are you going?' she asked.

'To Dehra and then to Mussoorie.'

'Oh, how lucky you are. I wish I were going to Mussoorie. I love the hills. Especially in October.'

'Yes, this is the best time,' I said, calling on my memories. 'The hills are covered with wild dahlias, the sun is delicious, and at night you can sit in front of a log fire and drink a little brandy. Most of the tourists have gone and the roads are quiet and almost deserted. Yes, October is the best time.'

She was silent. I wondered if my words had touched her or whether she thought me a romantic fool. Then I made a mistake.

'What is it like outside?' I asked.

She seemed to find nothing strange in the question. Had she noticed already that I could not see? But her next question removed my doubts.

'Why don't you look out of the window?' she asked.

I moved easily along the berth and felt for the window ledge. The window was open and I faced it, making a pretence of studying the landscape. I heard the panting of the engine, the rumble of the wheels, and, in my mind's eye I could see telegraph posts flashing by.

'Have you noticed,' I ventured, 'that the trees seem to be moving while we seem to be standing still?'

'That always happens,' she said. 'Do you see any animals?'

'No,' I answered quite confidently. I knew that there were hardly any animals left in the forests near Dehra.

I turned from the window and faced the girl and for a while we sat in silence.

'You have an interesting face,' I remarked. I was becoming quite daring but it was a safe remark. Few girls can resist flattery. She laughed pleasantly—a clear, ringing laugh.

'It's nice to be told I have an interesting face. I'm tired of people telling me I have a pretty face.'

Oh, so you do have a pretty face, thought I. And aloud I said: 'Well, an interesting face can also be pretty.'

'You are a very gallant young man,' she said. 'But why are you so serious?'

I thought, then, that I would try to laugh for her, but the thought of laughter only made me feel troubled and lonely.

'We'll soon be at your station,' I said.

'Thank goodness it's a short journey. I can't bear to sit in a train for more than two or three hours.'

Yet I was prepared to sit there for almost any length of time, just to listen to her talking. Her voice had the sparkle of a mountain stream. As soon as she left the train she would forget our brief encounter. But it would stay with me for the rest of the journey and for some time after.

The engine's whistle shrieked, the carriage wheels changed their sound and rhythm, the girl got up and began to collect her things. I wondered if she wore her hair in a bun or if it was plaited. Perhaps it was hanging loose over her shoulders. Or was it cut very short?

The train drew slowly into the station. Outside, there was the shouting of porters and vendors and a high-pitched female voice near the carriage door. That voice must have belonged to the girl's aunt.

'Goodbye,' the girl said.

She was standing very close to me. So close that the perfume from her hair was tantalizing. I wanted to raise my hand and touch her hair but she moved away. Only the scent of perfume still lingered where she had stood.

There was some confusion in the doorway. A man, getting into the compartment, stammered an apology. Then the door banged and the world was shut out again. I returned to my berth. The guard blew his whistle and we moved off. Once again I had a game to play and a new fellow traveller.

The train gathered speed, the wheels took up their song, the carriage groaned and shook. I found the window and sat in front of it, staring into the daylight that was darkness for me.

So many things were happening outside the window. It could be a fascinating game guessing what went on out there.

The man who had entered the compartment broke into my reverie.

'You must be disappointed,' he said. 'I'm not nearly as attractive a travelling companion as the one who just left.'

'She was an interesting girl,' I said. 'Can you tell me—did she keep her hair long or short?'

'I don't remember,' he said sounding puzzled. 'It was her eyes I noticed, not her hair. She had beautiful eyes but they were of no use to her. She was completely blind. Didn't you notice?'

THE THIEF

&

I WAS STILL A thief when I met Arun and though I was only fifteen I was an experienced and fairly successful hand.

Arun was watching the wrestlers when I approached him. He was about twenty, a tall, lean fellow, and he looked kind and simple enough for my purpose. I hadn't had much luck of late and thought I might be able to get into this young person's confidence. He seemed quite fascinated by the wrestling. Two well-oiled men slid about in the soft mud, grunting and slapping their thighs. When I drew Arun into conversation he didn't seem to realize I was a stranger.

'You look like a wrestler yourself,' I said.

'So do you,' he replied, which put me out of my stride for a moment because at the time I was rather thin and bony and not very impressive physically.

'Yes,' I said. 'I wrestle sometimes.'

'What's your name?'

'Deepak,' I lied.

Deepak was about my fifth name. I had earlier called myself Ranbir, Sudhir, Trilok and Surinder.

After this preliminary exchange Arun confined himself to comments on the match, and I didn't have much to say. After a while he walked away from the crowd of spectators. I followed him.

'Hallo,' he said. 'Enjoying yourself?'

I gave him my most appealing smile. 'I want to work for you,' I said.

He didn't stop walking. 'And what makes you think I want someone to work for me?'

'Well,' I said, 'I've been wandering about all day looking for the best person to work for. When I saw you I knew that no one else had a chance.'

'You flatter me,' he said.

'That's all right.'

'But you can't work for me.'

'Why not?'

'Because I can't pay you.'

I thought that over for a minute. Perhaps I had misjudged my man.

'Can you feed me?' I asked.

'Can you cook?' he countered.

'I can cook,' I lied.

'If you can cook,' he said, 'I'll feed you.'

He took me to his room and told me I could sleep in the verandah. But I was nearly back on the street that night. The meal I cooked must have been pretty awful because Arun gave it to the neighbour's cat and told me to be off. But I just hung around smiling in my most appealing way and then he couldn't help laughing. He sat down on the bed and laughed for a full five minutes and later patted me on the head and said, never mind, he'd teach me to cook in the morning.

Not only did he teach me to cook but he taught me to write my name and his and said he would soon teach me to write whole sentences and add money on paper when you didn't have any in your pocket!

It was quite pleasant working for Arun. I made the tea in the morning and later went out shopping. I would take my time buying the day's supplies and make a profit of about twenty-five paise a day. I would tell Arun that rice was fifty-six paise a pound (it generally was), but I would get it at fifty paise a pound. I think he knew I made a little this way but he didn't mind. He wasn't giving me a regular wage.

I was really grateful to Arun for teaching me to write. I knew that once I could write like an educated man there would be no limit to what I could achieve. It might even be an incentive to be honest.

Arun made money by fits and starts. He would be borrowing one week, lending the next. He would keep worrying about his next cheque but as soon as it arrived he would go out and celebrate lavishly.

One evening he came home with a wad of notes and at night I saw him tuck the bundles under his mattress at the head of the bed.

I had been working for Arun for nearly a fortnight and, apart from the shopping hadn't done much to exploit him. I had every opportunity for doing so. I had a key to the front door which meant I had access to the room whenever Arun was out. He was the most trusting person I had ever met. And that was why I couldn't make up my mind to rob him.

It's easy to rob a greedy man because he deserves to be robbed. It's easy to rob a rich man because he can afford to be robbed. But it's difficult to rob a poor man, even one who really doesn't care if he's robbed. A rich man or a greedy man or a careful man wouldn't keep his money under a pillow or mattress. He'd lock it up in a safe place. Arun had put his money where it would be child's play for me to remove it without his knowledge.

It's time I did some real work, I told myself. I'm getting out of practice . . . . If I don't take the money, he'll only waste it on his friends . . . . He doesn't even pay me . . . .

Arun was asleep. Moonlight came in from the veranda and fell across the bed. I sat up on the floor, my blanket wrapped round me, considering the situation. There was quite a lot of money in that wad and if I took it I would have to leave town—I might make the 10.30 express to Amritsar . . . .

Slipping out of the blanket, I crept on all fours through the door and up to the bed and peeped at Arun. He was sleeping peacefully with a soft and easy breathing. His face was clear and unlined. Even I had more markings on my face, though mine were mostly scars.

My hand took on an identity of its own as it slid around under the mattress, the fingers searching for the notes. They found them and I drew them out without a crackle.

Arun sighed in his sleep and turned on his side, towards me. My free hand was resting on the bed and his hair touched my fingers.

I was frightened when his hair touched my fingers, and crawled quickly and quietly out of the room.

When I was in the street I began to run. I ran down the bazaar road to the station. The shops were all closed but a few lights were on in the upper windows. I had the notes at my waist, held there by the string of my pyjamas. I felt I had to stop and count the notes though I knew it might make me late for the train. It was already 10.20 by the clock tower. I slowed down to a walk and my fingers flicked through the notes. There were about a hundred rupees in fives. A good haul. I could live like a prince for a month or two.

When I reached the station I did not stop at the ticket office (I had never bought a ticket in my life) but dashed straight onto the platform. The Amritsar Express was just moving out. It was moving slowly enough for me to be able to jump on the footboard of one of the carriages but I hesitated for some urgent, unexplainable reason.

I hesitated long enough for the train to leave without me.

When it had gone and the noise and busy confusion of the platform had subsided, I found myself standing alone on the deserted platform. The knowledge that I had a hundred stolen rupees in my pyjamas only increased my feeling of isolation and loneliness. I had no idea where to spend the night. I had never kept any friends because sometimes friends can be one's undoing. I didn't want to make myself conspicuous by staying at a hotel. And the only person I knew really well in town was the person I had robbed!

Leaving the station, I walked slowly through the bazaar keeping to dark, deserted alleys. I kept thinking of Arun. He would still be asleep, blissfully unaware of his loss.

I have made a study of men's faces when they have lost something of material value. The greedy man shows panic, the rich man shows anger, the poor man shows fear. But I knew that neither panic nor anger nor fear would show on Arun's face when he discovered the theft; only a terrible sadness not for the loss of the money but for my having betrayed his trust.

I found myself on the maidan and sat down on a bench with my feet tucked up under my haunches. The night was a little cold and I regretted not having brought Arun's blanket along. A light drizzle added to my discomfort. Soon it was raining heavily. My shirt and pyjamas stuck to my skin and a cold wind brought the rain whipping across my face. I told myself that sleeping on a bench was something I should have been used to by now but the veranda had softened me.

I walked back to the bazaar and sat down on the steps of a closed shop. A few vagrants lay beside me, rolled up tight in thin blankets. The clock showed midnight. I felt for the notes. They were still with me but had lost their crispness and were damp with rainwater.

Arun's money. In the morning he would probably have given me a rupee to go to the pictures but now I had it all. No more cooking his meals, running to the bazaar, or learning to write whole sentences. Whole sentences . . . .

They were something I had forgotten in the excitement of a hundred rupees. Whole sentences, I knew, could one day bring me more than a hundred rupees. It was a simple matter to steal (and sometimes just as simple to be caught) but to be a really big man, a wise and successful man, that was something. I should go back to Arun, I told myself, if only to learn how to write.

Perhaps it was also concern for Arun that drew me back. A sense of sympathy is one of my weaknesses, and through hesitation over a theft I had often been caught. A successful thief must be pitiless. I was fond of Arun. My affection for him, my sense of sympathy, but most of all my desire to write whole sentences, drew me back to the room.

I hurried back to the room extremely nervous, for it is easier to steal something than to return it undetected. If I was caught beside the bed now, with the money in my hand, or with my hand under the mattress, there could be only one explanation: that I was actually stealing. If Arun woke up I would be lost.

I opened the door clumsily and stood in the doorway in clouded moonlight. Gradually my eyes became accustomed to the darkness of the room. Arun was still asleep. I went on all fours again and crept noiselessly to the head of the bed. My hand came up with the notes. I felt his breath on my fingers. I was fascinated by his tranquil features and easy breathing and remained motionless for a minute. Then my hand explored the mattress, found the edge, slipped under it with the notes.

I awoke late next morning to find that Arun had already made the tea. I found it difficult to face him in the harsh light of day. His hand was stretched out towards me. There was a five-rupee note between his fingers. My heart sank.

'I made some money yesterday,' he said. 'Now you'll get paid regularly.' My spirit rose as rapidly as it had fallen. I congratulated myself on having returned the money.

But when I took the note, I realized that he knew everything. The note was still wet from last night's rain.

'Today I'll teach you to write a little more than your name,' he said.

He knew but neither his lips nor his eyes said anything about their knowing.

I smiled at Arun in my most appealing way. And the smile came by itself, without my knowing it.

THE BOY WHO BROKE THE BANK

ॐ

NATHU GRUMBLED TO HIMSELF as he swept the steps of the Pipalnagar Bank, owned by Seth Govind Ram. He used the small broom hurriedly and carelessly, and the dust, after rising in a cloud above his head, settled down again on the steps. As Nathu was banging his pan against a dustbin, Sitaram, the washerman's son, passed by.

Sitaram was on his delivery round. He had a bundle of freshly pressed clothes balanced on his head.

'Don't raise such dust!' he called out to Nathu. 'Are you annoyed because they are still refusing to pay you an extra two rupees a month?'

'I don't wish to talk about it,' complained the sweeper boy. 'I haven't even received my regular pay. And this is the 20th of the month. Who would think a bank would hold up a poor man's salary? As soon as I get my money, I'm off! Not another week do I work in this place.' And Nathu banged the pan against the dustbin several times, just to emphasize his point and give himself confidence.

'Well, I wish you luck,' said Sitaram. 'I'll keep a look-out for any jobs that might suit you.' And he plodded barefoot along the road, the big bundle of clothes hiding most of his head and shoulders.

At the fourth home he visited, Sitaram heard the lady of the house mention that she was in need of a sweeper. Tying his bundle together, he said, 'I know of a sweeper boy who's looking for work. He can start from next month. He's with the bank just now but they aren't giving him his pay, and he wants to leave.'

'Is that so?' said Mrs Srivastava. 'Well, tell him to come and see me tomorrow.'

And Sitaram, glad that he had been of service to both a customer and his friend, hoisted his bag on his shoulders and went his way.

Mrs Srivastava had to do some shopping. She gave instructions to the ayah about looking after the baby, and told the cook not to be late with the midday meal. Then she set out for the Pipalnagar market-place, to make her customary tour of the cloth shops.

A large, shady tamarind tree grew at one end of the bazaar, and it was here that Mrs Srivastava found her friend Mrs Bhushan sheltering from the heat. Mrs Bhushan was fanning herself with a large handkerchief. She complained of the summer which, she affirmed, was definitely the hottest in the history of Pipalnagar. She then showed Mrs Srivastava a sample of the cloth she was going to buy, and for five minutes they discussed its shade, texture and design. Having exhausted this topic, Mrs Srivastava said, 'Do you know, my dear, that Seth Govind Ram's bank can't even pay its employees? Only this morning I heard a complaint from their sweeper, who hasn't received his wages for over a month!'

'Shocking!' remarked Mrs Bhushan. 'If they can't pay the sweeper they must be in a bad way. None of the others could be getting paid either.'

She left Mrs Srivastava at the tamarind tree and went in search of her husband, who was sitting in front of Kamal Kishore's photographic shop, talking to the owner.

'So there you are!' cried Mrs Bhushan. 'I've been looking for you for almost an hour. Where did you disappear?'

'Nowhere,' replied Mr Bhushan. 'Had you remained stationary in one shop, I might have found you. But you go from one shop to another, like a bee in a flower garden.'

'Don't start grumbling. The heat is trying enough. I don't know what's happening to Pipalnagar. Even the bank's about to go bankrupt.'

'What's that?' said Kamal Kishore, sitting up suddenly. 'Which bank?'

'Why the Pipalnagar Bank of course. I hear they have

stopped paying employees. Don't tell me you have an account there, Mr Kishore?'

'No, but my neighbour has!' he exclaimed; and he called out over the low partition to the keeper of the barber shop next door. 'Deep Chand, have you heard the latest? The Pipalnagar Bank is about to collapse. You'd better get your money out as soon as you can!'

Deep Chand, who was cutting the hair of an elderly gentleman, was so startled that his hand shook and he nicked his customer's right ear. The customer yelped in pain and distress: pain, because of the cut and distress because of the awful news he had just heard. With one side of his neck still unshaven, he sped across the road to the general merchant's store where there was a telephone. He dialled Seth Govind Ram's number. The Seth was not at home. Where was he, then? The Seth was holidaying in Kashmir. Oh, was that so? The elderly gentleman did not believe it. He hurried back to the barber's shop and told Deep Chand: 'The bird has flown! Seth Govind Ram has left town. Definitely, it means a collapse.' And then he dashed out of the shop, making a beeline for his office and chequebook.

The news spread through the bazaar with the rapidity of forest fire. At the general merchant's it circulated amongst the customers, and then spread with them in various directions, to the betel-seller, the tailor, the free vendor, the jeweller, the beggar sitting on the pavement.

Old Ganpat, the beggar, had a crooked leg. He had been squatting on the pavement for years, calling for alms. In the evening someone would come with a barrow and take him away. He had never been known to walk. But now, on learning that the bank was about to collapse, Ganpat astonished everyone by leaping to his feet and actually running at top speed in the direction of the bank. It soon became known that he had a thousand rupees in savings!

Men stood in groups at street corners discussing the situation. Pipalnagar seldom had a crisis, seldom or never had floods, earthquakes or drought; and the imminent crash of the Pipalnagar Bank set everyone talking and speculating and rushing about in a frenzy. Some boasted of their farsightedness, congratulating themselves on having already taken out their money, or on never having put any in; others speculated on the reasons for the crash, putting it all down to excesses indulged in by Seth Govind Ram. The Seth had fled the state, said one. He had fled the country, said another. He was hiding in Pipalnagar, said a third. He had hanged himself from the tamarind tree, said a fourth, and had been found that morning by the sweeper boy.

By noon the small bank had gone through all its ready cash, and the harassed manager was in a dilemma. Emergency funds could only be obtained from another bank some thirty miles distant, and he wasn't sure he could persuade the crowd to wait until then. And there was no way of contacting Seth Govind Ram on his houseboat in Kashmir.

People were turned back from the counters and told to return the following day. They did not like the sound of that. And so they gathered outside, on the steps of the bank, shouting 'Give us our money or we'll break in!' and 'Fetch the Seth, we know he's hiding in a safe deposit locker!' Mischief makers who didn't have a paisa in the bank joined the crowd and aggravated the mood. The manager stood at the door and tried to placate them. He declared that the bank had plenty of money but no immediate means of collecting it; he urged them to go home and come back the next day.

'We want it now!' chanted some of the crowd. 'Now, now, now!'

And a brick hurtled through the air and crashed through the plate glass window of the Pipalnagar Bank.

Nathu arrived next morning to sweep the steps of the bank. He saw the refuse and the broken glass and the stones cluttering the steps. Raising his hands in a gesture of horror and disgust he cried: 'Hooligans! Sons of donkeys! As though it isn't bad enough to be paid late, it seems my work has also to be increased!' He smote the steps with his broom scattering the refuse.

'Good morning, Nathu,' said the washerman's boy, getting down from his bicycle. 'Are you ready to take up a new job from the first of next month? You'll have to I suppose, now that the bank is going out of business.'

'How's that?' said Nathu.

'Haven't you heard? Well you'd better wait here until half

the population of Pipalnagar arrives to claim their money.' And he waved cheerfully—he did not have a bank account—and sped away on his cycle.

Nathu went back to sweeping the steps, muttering to himself. When he had finished his work, he sat down on the highest step, to await the arrival of the manager. He was determined to get his pay.

'Who would have thought the bank would collapse!' he said to himself, and looked thoughtfully into the distance. 'I wonder how it could have happened . . . .'

HIS NEIGHBOUR'S WIFE

❧

No (SAID ARUN, AS we waited for dinner to be prepared), I did not fall in love with my neighbour's wife. It is not that kind of story.

Mind you, Leela was a most attractive woman. She was not beautiful or pretty but she was handsome. Hers was the firm, athletic body of a sixteen-year-old boy, free of any surplus flesh. She bathed morning and evening, oiling herself well, so that her skin glowed a golden-brown in the winter sunshine. Her lips were often coloured with paan-juice, but her teeth were perfect.

I was her junior by about five years, and she called me her 'younger brother'. Her husband, who was forty to her thirty-two, was an official in the Customs and Excise Department: an extrovert, a hard-drinking, backslapping man, who spent a great deal of time on tour. Leela knew that he was not always faithful to her during these frequent absences but she found solace in her own loyalty and in the well-being of her one child, a boy called Chandu.

I did not care for the boy. He had been well spoilt, and took great delight in disturbing me whenever I was at work. He entered my rooms uninvited, knocked my books about, and, if guests were present, made insulting remarks about them to their faces.

Leela, during her lonely evenings, would often ask me to sit on her verandah and talk to her. The day's work done, she would relax with a hookah. Smoking a hookah was a habit she had brought with her from her village near Agra, and it was a habit she refused to give up. She liked to talk and, as I was a good listener, she soon grew fond of me. The fact that I was twenty-six years old and still a bachelor, never failed to astonish her.

It was not long before she took upon herself the responsibility for getting me married. I found it useless to protest. She did not believe me when I told her that I could not afford to marry, that I preferred a bachelor's life. A wife, she insisted, was an asset to any man. A wife reduced expenses. Where did I eat? At a hotel, of course. That must cost me at least sixty rupees a month, even on a vegetarian diet. But if I had a simple homely wife to do the cooking, we could both eat well for less than that.

Leela fingered my shirt, observing that a button was missing and that the collar was frayed. She remarked on my pale face and general look of debility and told me that I would fall victim to all kinds of diseases if I did not find someone to look after me. What I needed, she declared between puffs at the hookah, was a woman—a young, healthy, buxom woman, preferably from a village near Agra.

'If I could find someone like you,' I said slyly, 'I would not mind getting married.'

She appeared neither flattered nor offended by my remark.

'Don't marry an older woman,' she advised. 'Never take a wife who is more experienced in the ways of the world than you are. You just leave it to me, I'll find a suitable bride for you.'

To please Leela, I agreed to this arrangement, thinking she would not take it seriously. But, two days later, when she suggested that I accompany her to a certain distinguished home for orphan girls, I became alarmed. I refused to have anything to do with her project.

'Don't you have confidence in me?' she asked. 'You said you would like a girl who resembled me. I know one who looks just as I did ten years ago.'

'I like you as you are now,' I said. 'Not as you were ten years ago.'

'Of course. We shall arrange for you to see the girl first.'

'You don't understand,' I protested. 'It's not that I feel I have to be in love with someone before marrying her—I know you would choose a fine girl, and I would really prefer someone who is homely and simple to an M.A. with Honours in Psychology—it's just that I'm not ready for it. I want another year or two of freedom. I don't want to be chained down. To be frank, I don't want the responsibility.'

'A little responsibility will make a man of you,' said Leela; but she did not insist on my accompanying her to the orphanage, and the matter was allowed to rest for a few days.

I was beginning to hope that Leela had reconciled herself to allowing one man to remain single in a world full of husbands when, one morning, she accosted me on the verandah with an open newspaper, which she thrust in front of my nose.

'There!' she said triumphantly. 'What do you think of that? I did it to surprise you.'

She had certainly succeeded in surprising me. Her henna-stained forefinger rested on an advertisement in the matrimonial columns.

Bachelor journalist, age 25, seeks attractive young wife well-versed in household duties. Caste, religion no bar. Dowry optional.

I must admit that Leela had made a good job of it. In a few days the replies began to come in, usually from the parents of the girls concerned. Each applicant wanted to know how much money I was earning. At the same time, they took the trouble to list their own connections and the high positions occupied by relatives. Some parents enclosed their daughters' photographs. They were very good photographs, though there was a certain amount of touching-up employed.

I studied the pictures with interest. Perhaps marriage wasn't such a bad proposition, after all. I selected the photographs of the three girls I most fancied and showed them to Leela.

To my surprise, she disapproved of all three. One of the girls she said, had a face like a hermaphrodite; another obviously suffered from tuberculosis; and the third was undoubtedly an adventuress. Leela decided that the whole idea of the advertisement had been a mistake. She was sorry she had inserted it; the only replies we were likely to get would be from fortune-hunters. And I had no fortune.

So we destroyed the letters. I tried to keep some of the photographs, but Leela tore them up too.

And so, for some time, there were no more attempts at getting me married.

Leela and I met nearly every day, but we spoke of other things. Sometimes, in the evenings, she would make me sit on the charpoy opposite her, and then she would draw up her hookah and tell me stories about her village and her family. I was getting used to the boy, too, and even growing rather fond of him.

All this came to an end when Leela's husband went and got himself killed. He was shot by a bootlegger who had decided to get rid of the excise man rather than pay him an exorbitant sum of money. It meant that Leela had to give up her quarters and return to her village near Agra. She waited until the boy's school-term had finished, and then she packed their things and bought two tickets, third-class to Agra.

Something, I could see, had been troubling her, and when I saw her off at the station I realized what it was. She was having a fit of conscience about my continued bachelorhood.

'In my village,' she said confidently, leaning out from the carriage window, 'there is a very comely young girl, a distant relative of mine, I shall speak to the parents.'

And then I said something which I had not considered before; which had never, until that moment, entered my head. And I was no less surprised than Leela when the words came tumbling out of my mouth: 'Why don't *you* marry me now?'

Arun didn't have time to finish his story because, just at this interesting stage, the dinner arrived.

But the dinner brought with it the end of his story.

It was served by his wife, a magnificent woman, strong and handsome, who could only have been Leela. And a few minutes later, Chandu, Arun's stepson, charged into the house, complaining that he was famished.

Arun introduced me to his wife, and we exchanged the usual formalities.

'But why hasn't your friend brought his family with him?' she asked.

'Family? Because he's still a bachelor!'

And then as he watched his wife's expression change from a look of mild indifference to one of deep concern, he hurriedly changed the subject.

THE NIGHT TRAIN AT DEOLI

❧

Wᴀʜᴇɴ I ᴡᴀꜱ ᴀᴛ college I used to spend my summer vacations in Dehra, at my grandmother's place. I would leave the plains early in May and return late in July. Deoli was a small station about thirty miles from Dehra. It marked the beginning of the heavy jungles of the Indian Terai.

The train would reach Deoli at about five in the morning when the station would be dimly lit with electric bulbs and oil lamps and the jungle across the railway tracks would just be visible in the faint light of dawn. Deoli had only one platform, an office for the stationmaster and a waiting room. The platform boasted a tea stall, a fruit vendor, and a few stray dogs; not much else because the train stopped there for only ten minutes before rushing on into the forests.

Why it stopped at Deoli, I don't know. Nothing ever happened there. Nobody got off the train and nobody got in. There were never any coolies on the platform. But the train would halt there a full ten minutes and then a bell would sound, the guard would blow his whistle, and presently Deoli would be left behind and forgotten.

I used to wonder what happened in Deoli behind the station walls. I always felt sorry for that lonely little platform and for the place that nobody wanted to visit. I decided that one day I would get off the train at Deoli and spend the day there just to please the town.

I was eighteen, visiting my grandmother, and the night train stopped at Deoli. A girl came down the platform selling baskets.

It was a cold morning and the girl had a shawl thrown

across her shoulders. Her feet were bare and her clothes were old but she was a young girl, walking gracefully and with dignity.

When she came to my window, she stopped. She saw that I was looking at her intently but at first she pretended not to notice. She had a pale skin, set off by shiny black hair and dark, troubled eyes. And then those eyes, searching and eloquent, met mine.

She stood by my window for some time and neither of us said anything. But when she moved on, I found myself leaving my seat and going to the carriage door. I stood waiting on the platform looking the other way. I walked across to the tea stall. A kettle was boiling over on a small fire but the owner of the stall was busy serving tea somewhere on the train. The girl followed me behind the stall.

'Do you want to buy a basket?' she asked. 'They are very strong, made of the finest cane . . . .'

'No,' I said, 'I don't want a basket.'

We stood looking at each other for what seemed a very long time and she said, 'Are you sure you don't want a basket?'

'All right, give me one,' I said and took the one on top and gave her a rupee, hardly daring to touch her fingers.

As she was about to speak, the guard blew his whistle. She said something but it was lost in the clanging of the bell and the hissing of the engine. I had to run back to my compartment. The carriage shuddered and jolted forward.

I watched her as the platform slipped away. She was alone on the platform and she did not move, but she was looking at me and smiling. I watched her until the signal-box came in the way and then the jungle hid the station. But I could still see her standing there alone . . . .

I stayed awake for the rest of the journey. I could not rid my mind of the picture of the girl's face and her dark, smouldering eyes.

But when I reached Dehra the incident became blurred and distant, for there were other things to occupy my mind. It was only when I was making the return journey, two months later, that I remembered the girl.

I was looking out for her as the train drew into the station and I felt an unexpected thrill when I saw her walking up the platform. I sprang off the footboard and waved to her.

When she saw me, she smiled. She was pleased that I remembered her. I was pleased that she remembered me. We were both pleased and it was almost like a meeting of old friends.

She did not go down the length of the train selling baskets but came straight to the tea stall. Her dark eyes were suddenly filled with light. We said nothing for some time but we couldn't have been more eloquent.

I felt the impulse to put her on the train there and then and take her away with me. I could not bear the thought of having to watch her recede into the distance of Deoli station. I took the baskets from her hand and put them down on the ground. She put out her hand for one of them but I caught her hand and held it.

'I have to go to Delhi,' I said.

She nodded. 'I do not have to go anywhere.'

The guard blew his whistle for the train to leave and how I hated the guard for doing that.

'I will come again,' I said. 'Will you be here?'

She nodded again and, as she nodded, the bell clanged and the train slid forward. I had to wrench my hand away from the girl and run for the moving train.

This time I did not forget her. She was with me for the remainder of the journey and for long after. All that year she was a bright, living thing. And when the college term finished I packed in haste and left for Dehra earlier than usual. My grandmother would be pleased at my eagerness to see her.

I was nervous and anxious as the train drew into Deoli because I was wondering what I should say to the girl and what I should do. I was determined that I wouldn't stand helplessly before her, hardly able to speak or do anything about my feelings.

The train came to Deoli and I looked up and down the platform but I could not see the girl anywhere.

I opened the door and stepped off the footboard. I was deeply disappointed and overcome by a sense of foreboding. I felt I had to do something and so I ran up to the stationmaster and said, 'Do you know the girl who used to sell baskets here?'

'No, I don't,' said the stationmaster. 'And you'd better get on the train if you don't want to be left behind.'

But I paced up and down the platform and stared over the railings at the station yard. All I saw was a mango tree and a dusty road leading into the jungle. Where did the road go? The train was moving out of the station and I had to run up the platform and jump for the door of my compartment. Then, as the train gathered speed and rushed through the forests, I sat brooding in front of the window.

What could I do about finding a girl I had seen only twice, who had hardly spoken to me, and about whom I knew nothing—absolutely nothing—but for whom I felt a tenderness and responsibility that I had never felt before?

My grandmother was not pleased with my visit after all because I didn't stay at her place more than a couple of weeks. I felt restless and ill at ease. So I took the train back to the plains, meaning to ask further questions of the stationmaster at Deoli.

But at Deoli there was a new stationmaster. The previous man had been transferred to another post within the past week. The new man didn't know anything about the girl who sold baskets. I found the owner of the tea stall, a small, shrivelled-up man, wearing greasy clothes, and asked him if he knew anything about the girl with the baskets.

'Yes, there was such a girl here. I remember quite well,' he said. 'But she has stopped coming now.'

'Why?' I asked. 'What happened to her?'

'How should I know?' said the man. 'She was nothing to me.'

And once again I had to run for the train.

As Deoli platform receded, I decided that one day I would have to break journey there, spend a day in the town, make enquiries, and find the girl who had stolen my heart with nothing but a look from her dark, impatient eyes.

With this thought I consoled myself throughout my last term in college. I went to Dehra again in the summer and when, in the early hours of the morning, the night train drew into Deoli station, I looked up and down the platform for signs of the girl, knowing I wouldn't find her but hoping just the same.

Somehow, I couldn't bring myself to break journey at Deoli
and spend a day there. (If it was all fiction or a film, I reflected,
I would have got down and cleaned up the mystery and
reached a suitable ending for the whole thing). I think I was
afraid to do this. I was afraid of discovering what really
happened to the girl. Perhaps she was no longer in Deoli,
perhaps she was married, perhaps she had fallen ill . . . .

In the last few years I have passed through Deoli many
times and I always look out of the carriage window half
expecting to see the same unchanged face smiling up at me. I
wonder what happens in Deoli, behind the station walls. But I
will never break my journey there. It may spoil my game. I
prefer to keep hoping and dreaming and looking out of the
window up and down that lonely platform, waiting for the girl
with the baskets.

I never break my journey at Deoli but I pass through as
often as I can.

THE GARLANDS ON HIS BROW

🐌

*Fame has but a fleeting hold
on the reins in our fast-paced society;
so many of yesterday's
heroes crumble.*

Shortly after my return from England, I was walking down the
main road of my old home town of Dehra, gazing at the shops
and passers-by to see what changes, if any, had taken place
during my absence. I had been away three years. Still a boy
when I went abroad, I was twenty-one when I returned with
some mediocre qualifications to flaunt in the faces of my
envious friends. (I did not tell them of the loneliness of those
years in exile; it would not have impressed them.) I was
nearing the clock tower when I met a beggar coming from the
opposite direction. In one respect, Dehra had not changed. The
beggars were as numerous as ever, though I must admit they
looked healthier.

This beggar had a straggling beard, a hunch, a cavernous
chest, and unsteady legs on which a number of purple sores
were festering. His shoulders looked as though they had once
been powerful, and his hands thrusting a begging-bowl at me,
were still strong.

He did not seem sufficiently decrepit to deserve of my
charity, and I was turning away when I thought I discerned a
gleam of recognition in his eyes. There was something slightly
familiar about the man; perhaps he was a beggar who
remembered me from earlier years. He was even attempting a

smile; showing me a few broken yellow fangs; and to get away from him, I produced a coin, dropped it in his bowl, and hurried away.

I had gone about a hundred yards when, with a rush of memory, I knew the identity of the beggar. He was the hero of my childhood, Hassan, the most magnificent wrestler in the entire district.

I turned and retraced my steps, half hoping I wouldn't be able to catch up with the man and he had indeed got lost in the bazaar crowd. Well, I would doubtless be confronted by him again in a day or two . . . . Leaving the road, I went into the Municipal gardens and stretching myself out on the fresh green February grass, allowed my memory to journey back to the days when I was a boy of ten, full of health and optimism, when my wonder at the great game of living had yet to give way to disillusionment at its shabbiness.

On those precious days when I played truant from school— and I would have learnt more had I played truant more often— I would sometimes make my way to the akhara at the corner of the gardens to watch the wrestling pit. My chin cupped in my hands, I would lean against a railing and gaze in awe at their rippling muscles, applauding with the other watchers whenever one of the wrestlers made a particularly clever move or pinned an opponent down on his back.

Amongst these wrestlers the most impressive and engaging young man was Hassan, the son of a kite-maker. He had a magnificent build, with great wide shoulders and powerful legs, and what he lacked in skill he made up for in sheer animal strength and vigour. The idol of all small boys, he was followed about by large numbers of us, and I was a particular favourite of his. He would offer to lift me on to his shoulders and carry me across the akhara to introduce me to his friends and fellow-wrestlers.

From being Dehra's champion, Hassan soon became the outstanding representative of his art in the entire district. His technique improved, he began using his brain in addition to his brawn, and it was said by everyone that he had the making of a national champion.

It was during a large fair towards the end of the rains that destiny took a hand in the shaping of his life. The Rani of —— was visiting the fair, and she stopped to watch the wrestling bouts. When she saw Hassan stripped and in the ring, she began to take more than a casual interest in him. It has been said that she was a woman of a passionate and amoral nature, who could not be satisfied by her weak and ailing husband. She was struck by Hassan's perfect manhood, and through an official offered him the post of her personal bodyguard.

The Rani was rich and, in spite of having passed her fortieth summer, was a warm and attractive woman. Hassan did not find it difficult to make love according to the bidding, and on the whole he was happy in her service. True, he did not wrestle as often as in the past; but when he did enter a competition, his reputation and his physique combined to overawe his opponents, and they did not put up much resistance. One or two well-known wrestlers were invited to the district. The Rani paid them liberally, and they permitted Hassan to throw them out of the ring. Life in the Rani's house was comfortable and easy, and Hassan, a simple man, felt himself secure. And it is to the credit of the Rani (and also of Hassan) that she did not tire of him as quickly as she had of others.

But Ranis, like washerwomen, are mortal; and when a long-standing and neglected disease at last took its toll, robbing her at once of all her beauty, she no longer struggled against it, but allowed it to poison and consume her once magnificent body.

It would be wrong to say that Hassan was heart-broken when she died. He was not a deeply emotional or sensitive person. Though he could attract the sympathy of others, he had difficulty in producing any of his own. His was a kindly but not compassionate nature.

He had served the Rani well, and what he was most aware of now was that he was without a job and without any money. The Raja had his own personal amusements and did not want a wrestler who was beginning to sag a little about the waist.

Times had changed. Hassan's father was dead, and there was no longer a living to be had from making kites; so Hassan returned to doing what he had always done: wrestling. But there was no money to be made at the akhara. It was only in the professional arena that a decent living could be made. And so, when a travelling circus of professionals—a Negro, a Russian, a Cockney-Chinese and a giant Sikh—came to town and offered a hundred rupees and a contract to the challenger who could stay five minutes in the ring with any one of them, Hassan took up the challenge.

He was pitted against the Russian, a bear of a man, who wore a black mask across his eyes; and in two minutes Hassan's Dehra supporters saw their hero slung about the ring, licked in the head and groin, and finally flung unceremoniously through the ropes.

After this humiliation, Hassan did not venture into competitive bouts again. I saw him sometimes at the akhara, where he made a few rupees giving lessons to children. He had a paunch, and folds were beginning to accumulate beneath his chin. I was no longer a small boy, but he always had a smile and a hearty back-slap reserved for me.

I remember seeing him a few days before I went abroad. He was moving heavily about the akhara; he had lost the lightning swiftness that had once made him invincible. Yes, I told myself.

The garlands wither on your brow;
Then boast no more your mighty deeds . . .

That had been over three years ago. And for Hassan to have been reduced to begging was indeed a sad reflection of both the passing of time and the changing times. Fifty years ago a popular local wrestler would never have been allowed to fall into a state of poverty and neglect. He would have been fed by his old friends and stories would have been told of his legendary prowess. He would not have been forgotten. But those were more leisurely times, when the individual had his place in society, when a man was praised for his past achievement and his failures were tolerated and forgiven. But life had since become fast and cruel and unreflective, and people were too busy counting their gains to bother about the idols of their youth.

It was a few days after my last encounter with Hassan that I found a small crowd gathered at the side of the road, not far from the clock tower. They were staring impassively at something in the drain, at the same time keeping a discreet

distance. Joining the group, I saw that the object of their
disinterested curiosity was a corpse, its head hidden under a
culvert, legs protruding into the open drain. It looked as
though the man had crawled into the drain to die, and had
done so with his head in the culvert so the world would not
witness his last unavailing struggle.

When the municipal workers came in their van, and lifted
the body out of the gutter, a cloud of flies and bluebottles rose
from the corpse with an angry buzz of protest. The face was
muddy, but I recognized the beggar who was Hassan.

In a way, it was a consolation to know that he had been
forgotten, that no one present could recognize the remains of
the man who had once looked like a young god. I did not come
forward to identify the body. Perhaps I saved Hassan from one
final humiliation.

A Guardian Angel

I CAN STILL PICTURE the little Dilaram bazaar as I first saw it twenty years ago. Hanging on the hem of Aunt Mariam's sari, I had followed her along the sunlit length of the dusty road and up the wooden staircase to her rooms above the barber's shop.

There were a number of children playing on the road and they all stared at me. They must have wondered what my dark, black-haired aunt was doing with a strange child who was fairer than most. She did not bother to explain my presence and it was several weeks before the bazaar people learned something of my origins.

Aunt Mariam, my mother's younger sister, was at that time about thirty. She came from a family of Christian converts, originally Muslims of Rampur. My mother had married an Englishman who died while I was still a baby. She herself was not a strong woman and fought a losing battle with tuberculosis while bringing me up.

My sixth birthday was approaching when she died, in the middle of the night, without my being aware of it. And I woke up to experience, for a day, all the terrors of abandonment.

But that same evening Aunt Mariam arrived. Her warmth, worldliness and carefree chatter gave me the reassurance I needed so badly. She slept beside me that night and the next morning, after the funeral, took me with her to her rooms in the bazaar. This small flat was to be my home for the next year and a half.

Before my mother's death I had seen very little of my aunt.

From the remarks I occasionally overheard, it appeared that Aunt Mariam had, in some indefinable way, disgraced the family. My mother was cold towards her and I could not help wondering why because a more friendly and cheerful extrovert than Aunt Mariam could hardly be encountered.

There were other relatives but they did not come to my rescue with the same readiness. It was only later, when the financial issues became clearer, that innumerable uncles and aunts appeared on the scene.

The age of six is the beginning of an interesting period in the life of a boy and the months I spent with Aunt Mariam are not difficult to recall. She was a joyous, bubbling creature—a force of nature rather than a woman—and every time I think of her I am tempted to put down on paper some aspect of her conversation, or her gestures, or her magnificent physique.

She was a strong woman, taller than most men in the bazaar, but this did not detract from her charms. Her voice was warm and deep, her face was a happy one, broad and unlined, and her teeth gleamed white in the dark brilliance of her complexion.

She had large soft breasts, long arms and broad thighs. She was majestic and at the same time graceful. Above all, she was warm and full of understanding and it was this tenderness of hers that overcame resentment and jealousy in other women.

She called me Ladla, her darling, and told me she had always wanted to look after me. She had never married. I did not, at that age, ponder the reasons for her single state. At six, I took all things for granted and accepted Mariam for what she was—my benefactress and guardian angel.

Her rooms were untidy compared with the neatness of my mother's house. Mariam revelled in untidiness. I soon grew accustomed to the topsy-turviness of her rooms and found them comfortable. Beds (hers a very large and soft one) were usually left unmade, while clothes lay draped over chairs and tables.

A large water-colour hung on a wall but Mariam's bodice and knickers were usually suspended from it and I cannot recall the subject of the painting. The dressing table was a fascinating place, crowded with all kinds of lotions, mascaras, paints, oils and ointments.

Mariam would spend much time sitting in front of the mirror running a comb through her long black hair or preferably having young Mulia, a servant girl, comb it for her. Though a Christian, my aunt retained several Muslim superstitions and never went into the open with her hair falling loose.

Once Mulia came into the rooms with her own hair open. 'You ought not to leave your hair open. Better knot it,' said Aunt Mariam.

'But I have not yet oiled it, Aunty,' replied Mulia. 'How can I put it up?'

'You are too young to understand. There are jinns—aerial spirits—who are easily attracted by long hair and pretty black eyes like yours.'

'Do jinns visit human beings, Aunty?'

'Learned people say so. Though I have never seen a jinn myself, I have seen the effect they can have on one.'

'Oh, do tell about them,' said Mulia.

'Well, there was once a lovely girl like you who had a wealth of black hair,' said Mariam. 'Quite unaccountably she fell ill and in spite of every attention and the best medicines she kept getting worse. She grew as thin as a whipping post, her beauty decayed, and all that remained of it till her dying day was her wonderful head of hair.'

It did not take me long to make friends in the Dilaram bazaar. At first I was an object of curiosity, and when I came down to play in the street both women and children would examine me as though I was a strange marine creature.

'How fair he is,' observed Mulia.

'And how black his aunt,' commented the washerman's wife, whose face was riddled with the marks of smallpox.

'His skin is very smooth,' pointed out Mulia, who took considerable pride in having been the first to see me at close quarters. She pinched my cheeks with obvious pleasure.

'His hair and eyes are black,' remarked Mulia's ageing mother.

'Is it true that his father was an Englishman?'

'Mariam-bi says so,' said Mulia. 'She never lies.'

'True,' said the washerman's wife. 'Whatever her faults—

and there are many—she has never been known to lie.'

My aunt's other 'faults' were a deep mystery to me. Nor did anyone try to enlighten me about them.

Some nights she had me sleep with her, other nights (I often wondered why) she gave me a bed in an adjoining room, although I much preferred remaining with her—especially since, on cold January nights, she provided me with considerable warmth.

I would curl up into a ball just below her soft tummy. On the other side, behind her knees, slept Leila, an enchanting Siamese cat given to her by an American businessman whose house she would sometimes visit. Every night, before I fell asleep, Mariam would kiss me, very softly, on my closed eyelids. I never fell asleep until I had received this phantom kiss.

At first I resented the nocturnal visitors that Aunt Mariam frequently received. Their arrival meant that I had to sleep in the spare room with Leila. But when I found that these people were impermanent creatures, mere ships that passed in the night, I learned to put up with them.

I seldom saw those men, though occasionally I caught a glimpse of a beard or an expensive waistcoat or white pyjamas. They did not interest me very much though I did have a vague idea that they provided Aunt Mariam with some sort of income, thus enabling her to look after me.

Once, when one particular visitor was very drunk, Mariam had to force him out of the flat. I glimpsed this episode through a crack in the door. The man was big but no match for Aunt Mariam.

She thrust him out onto the landing and then he lost his footing and went tumbling downstairs. No damage was done and the man called on Mariam again a few days later, very sober and contrite, and was readmitted to my aunt's favours.

Aunt Mariam must have begun to worry about the effect these comings and goings might have on me because after a few months she began to make arrangements for sending me to a boarding-school in the hills.

I had not the slightest desire to go to school and raised many objections. We had long arguments in which she tried vainly to impress upon me the desirability of receiving an education.

'To make a living, my Ladla,' she said, 'you must have an education.'

'But you have no education,' I said, 'and you have no difficulty in making a living!'

Mariam threw up her arms in mock despair. 'Ten years from now I will not be able to make such a living. Then who will support and help me? An illiterate young fellow or an educated gentleman? When I am old, my son, when I am old . . . .'

Finally, I succumbed to her arguments and agreed to go to a boarding school. And when the time came for me to leave, both Aunt Mariam and I broke down and wept at the railway station.

I hung out of the window as the train moved away from the platform and saw Mariam, her bosom heaving, being helped from the platform by Mulia and some of our neighbours.

My incarceration in a boarding-school was made more unbearable by the absence of any letters from Aunt Mariam. She could write little more than her name.

I was looking forward to my winter holidays and my return to Aunt Mariam and the Dilaram bazaar, but this was not to be. During my absence there had been some litigation over my custody and my father's relatives claimed that Aunt Mariam was not a fit person to be a child's guardian.

And so when I left school, it was not to Aunt Mariam's place that I was sent but to a strange family living in a railway colony near Moradabad. I remained with these relatives until I finished school. But that is a different story.

I did not see Aunt Mariam again. The Dilaram bazaar and my beautiful aunt and the Siamese cat all became part of the receding world of my childhood.

I would often think of Mariam, but as time passed she became more remote and inaccessible in my memory. It was not until many years later, when I was a young man, that I visited the Dilaram bazaar again. I knew from my foster parents that Aunt Mariam was dead. Her heart, it seemed, had always been weak.

I was anxious to see the Dilaram bazaar and its residents again but my visit was a disappointment. The place had disappeared. Or rather, it had been swallowed up by a growing city.

It was lost in the complex of a much larger market which had sprung up to serve a new government colony. The older people had died and the young ones had gone to colleges or factories or offices in different towns. Aunt Mariam's rooms had been pulled down.

I found her grave in the little cemetery on the town's outskirts. One of her more devoted admirers had provided a handsome gravestone surmounted by a sculptured angel. One of the wings had broken off and the face was chipped which gave the angel a slightly crooked smile.

But in spite of the broken wing and the smile it was a very ordinary stone angel and could not hold a candle to my Aunt Mariam the very special guardian angel of my childhood.

DEATH OF A FAMILIAR

❧

WHEN I LEARNT FROM a mutual acquaintance that my friend Sunil had been killed, I could not help feeling a little surprised, even shocked. Had Sunil killed somebody, it would not have surprised me in the least; he did not greatly value the lives of others. But for him to have been the victim was a sad reflection of his rapid decline.

He was twenty-one at the time of his death. Two friends of his had killed him, stabbing him several times with their knives. Their motive was said to have been revenge. Apparently he had seduced their wives. They had invited him to a bar in Meerut, had plied him with country liquor, and had then accompanied him out into the cold air of a December night. It was drizzling a little. Near the bridge over the canal, one of his companions seized him from behind, while the other plunged a knife first into his stomach and then into his chest. When Sunil slumped forward, the other friend stabbed him in the back. A passing cyclist saw the little group, heard a cry and a groan, saw a blade flash in the light from his lamp. He pedalled furiously into town, burst into the kotwali, and roused the sergeant on duty. Accompanied by two constables, they ran to the bridge but found the area deserted. It was only as the rising sun drew an open wound across the sky that they found Sunil's body on the canal-back, his head and shoulders on the sand, his legs in running water.

The bar-keeper was able to describe Sunil's companions, and they were arrested that same morning in their homes. They had not found time to get rid of their blood-soaked clothes. As they were not known to me, I took very little interest in the proceedings against them; but I understand that they have appealed against their sentences of life imprisonment.

I was in Delhi at the time of the murder, and it was almost a year since I had last seen Sunil. We had both lived in Shahganj and had left the place for jobs; I to work in a newspaper office, he in a paper factory owned by an uncle. It had been hoped that he would in time acquire a sense of responsibility and some stability of character. But I had known Sunil for over two years, and in that time it had been made abundantly clear that he had not been torn to fit in with the conventions. And as for character, his had the stability of a grasshopper. He was forever in search of new adventures and sensations, and this appetite of his for every novelty led him into some awkward situations.

He was a product of Partition, of the frontier provinces, of Anglo-Indian public schools, of films Indian and American, of medieval India, knights in armour, hippies, drugs, sex-magazines and the subtropical Terai. Had he lived in the time of the Moghuls, he might have governed a province with saturnine and spectacular success. Being born into the 20th century, he was but a juvenile delinquent.

It must be said to his credit that he was a delinquent of charm and originality. I realized this when I first saw him, sitting on the wall of the football stadium, his long legs—looking even longer and thinner because of the tight trousers he wore—dangling over the wall, his chappals trailing in the dust of the road, while his white bush-shirt lay open, unbuttoned, showing his smooth brown chest. He had a smile on his long face, which, with its high cheekbones, gave his cheeks a cavernous look, an impression of unrequited hunger.

We were both watching the wrestling. Two practice bouts were in progress—one between two thin, undernourished boys, and the other between the master of the akhara and a bearded Sikh who drove trucks for a living. They struggled in the soft mud of the wrestling pit, their well-oiled bodies glistening in the sunlight that filtered through a massive banyan tree. I had been standing near the akhara for a few minutes when I became conscious of the young man's gaze. When I turned round to look at him, he smiled satanically.

'Are you a wrestler, too?' he asked.

'Do I look like one?' I countered.

'No, you look more like an athlete,' he said. 'I mean a long-distance runner. Very thin.'

'I'm a writer. Like long-distance runners most writers are very thin.'

'You're an Anglo-Indian, aren't you?'

'My family history is very complicated, otherwise I'd be delighted to give you all the details.'

'You could pass for a European, you know. You're quite fair. But you have an Indian accent.'

'An Indian accent is very similar to a Welsh accent,' I observed. 'I might pass for Welsh, but not many people in India have met Welshmen!'

He chuckled at my answer; then stared at me speculatively. 'I say,' he said at length, as though an idea of great weight and importance had occurred to him. 'Do you have any magazines with pictures of dames?'

'Well, I may have some old *Playboys*. You can have them if you like.'

'Thanks,' he said, getting down from the wall. 'I'll come and fetch them. This wresting is boring, anyway.'

He slipped his hand into mine (a custom of no special significance), and began whistling snatches of Hindi film tunes and the latest American hits.

I was living at the time in a small flat above the town's main shopping centre. Below me there were shops, restaurants and a cinema. Behind the building lay a junkyard littered with the framework of vintage cars and broken-down tongas. I was paying thirty rupees a month for my two rooms, and sixty to the Punjabi restaurant where I took my meals. My earnings as a freelance writer were something like a hundred and fifty rupees a month, sufficient to enable me to make both ends meet, provided I remained in the backwater, that was Shahganj.

Sunil (I had learnt his name during our walk from the stadium), made himself at home in my flat as soon as he entered it. He went through all my magazines, books and photographs with the thoroughness of an executor of a will. In India, it is customary for people to try and find out all there is to know about you, and Sunil went through the formalities with considerable thoroughness. While he spoke, his roving eyes made a mental inventory of all my belongings. These were few—a typewriter, a small radio, and a cupboard full of books and clothes, besides the furniture that went with the flat. I had no valuables. Was he disappointed? I could not be sure. He wore good clothes and spoke fluent English, but good clothes and good English are no criterion of honesty. He was a little too glib to inspire confidence. Apparently, he was still at college. His father owned a cloth shop; a strict man who did not give his son much spending money.

But Sunil was not seriously interested in money, as I was shortly to discover. He was interested in experience, and searched for it in various directions.

'You have a nice view,' he said, leaning over my balcony and looking up and down the street. 'You can see everyone on parade. Girls! They're becoming quite modern now. Short hair and small blouses. Tight salwars. Maxis, minis. Falsies. Do you like girls?'

'Well . . . .' I began, but he did not really expect an answer to his question.

'What are little girls made of? That's an English poem, isn't it? "Sugar and spice and everything nice . . . ." And I don't remember the rest.' He lowered his voice to a confidential undertone. 'Have you had any girls?'

'Well . . . .'

'I had fun with a girl, you know, my cousin. She came to stay with us last summer. Then there's a girl in college who's stuck on me. But this is such a backward country. We can't be seen together in public and I can't invite her to my house. Can I bring her here some day?'

'Well, I don't know . . . .' I hadn't lived in a small town like Shahganj for some time, and wasn't sure if morals had changed along with the fashions.

'Oh, not now,' he said. 'There's no hurry. I'll give you plenty of warning, don't worry.' He put an arm around my shoulders and looked at me with undisguised affection. 'We are going to be great friends, you and I.'

After that I began to receive almost daily visits from Sunil. His college classes got over at three in the afternoon, and though it was seldom that he attended them, he would stop at my place after putting in a brief appearance at the study hall. I could hardly blame him for neglecting his books: Shakespeare and Chaucer were prescribed for students who had but a rudimentary knowledge of Modern English usage. Vast numbers of graduates were produced every year, and most of them became clerks or bus-conductors or, perhaps, schoolteachers. But Sunil's father wanted the best for his son. And in Shahganj that meant as many degrees as possible.

Sunil would come stamping into my rooms, waking me from the siesta which had become a habit during summer afternoons. When he found that I did not relish being woken up, he would leave me to sleep while he took a bath under the tap. After making liberal use of my hair-cream and after-shave lotion (he had just begun shaving, but used the lotion on his body), he would want to go to a picture or restaurant, and would sprinkle me with cold water so that I leapt off the bed.

One afternoon he felt more than usually ebullient, and poured a whole bucket of water over me, soaking the sheets and mattress. I retaliated by flinging the water-jug at his head. It missed him and shattered itself against the wall. Sunil then went berserk and started splashing water all over the room, while I threatened and shouted. When I tried restraining him by force, we rolled over on the ground, and I banged my head against the bedstead and almost lost consciousness. He was then full of contrition and massaged the lump on my head with hair-cream and refused to borrow any money from me that day.

Sunil's 'borrowing' consisted of extracting a few rupees from my wallet, saying he needed the money for books or a tailor's bill or a shopkeeper who was threatening him with violence, and then spending it on something quite different. Before long I gave up asking him to return anything, just as I had given up asking him to stop seeing me.

Sunil was one of those people best loved from a distance. He was born with a special talent for trouble. I think it pleased his vanity when he was pursued by irate creditors, shopkeepers, brothers whose sisters he had insulted, and husbands whose wives he had molested. My association with him did nothing to improve my own reputation in Shahganj.

My landlady, a protective, motherly, Punjabi widow said:

'Son, you are in bad company. Do you know that Sunil has already been expelled from one school for stealing, and from another for sexual offences?'

'He's only a boy,' I said. 'And he's taking longer than most boys to grow up. He doesn't realize the seriousness of what he does. He will learn as he grows older.'

'If he grows older,' said my landlady darkly. 'Do you know that he nearly killed a man last year? When a fruit-seller who had been cheated threatened to report Sunil to the police, he threw a brick at the man's head. The poor man was in hospital for three weeks. If Sunil's father did not have political influence, the boy would be in jail now, instead of climbing your stairs every afternoon.'

Once again I suggested to Sunil that he come to see me less often.

He looked hurt and offended.

'Don't you like me any more?'

'I like you immensely. But I have work to do . . . .'

'I know. You think I am a crook. Well, I am a crook.' He spoke with all the confidence of a young man who has never been hurt or disillusioned; he had romantic notions about swindlers and gangsters. 'I'll be a big crook one day, and people will be scared of me. But don't worry, old boy, you're my friend. I wouldn't harm you in any way. In fact, I'll protect you.'

'Thank you, but I don't require protection, I want to be left alone. I have work, and you are a worry and a distraction.'

'Well, I'm not going to leave you alone,' he said, assuming the posture of a spoilt child. 'Why should you be left alone? Who do you think you are? If we're friends now, it's your fault. I'm not going to buzz off just to suit your convenience.'

'Come less often, that's all.'

'I'll come more often, you old snob! I know, you're thinking of your reputation—as if you had any. Well, you don't have to worry, *mon ami*—as they say in Hollywood. I'll be very discreet, Daddyji!'

Whenever I complained or became querulous, Sunil would call me daddy or uncle or sometimes mum, and make me feel more ridiculous. If he was in a good mood, he would use the Hindi word chacha (uncle). All it did was to make me feel much older than my twenty-five years.

Sunil turned up one afternoon with blood streaming from his nose and from a gash across his forehead: He sat down at the foot of the bed and began dabbing his face with the bedsheet.

'What have you done to yourself?' I asked in some alarm.

'Some fellows beat me up. There were three of them. They followed me on their cycles.'

'Who were they?' I asked, looking for iodine on the dressing-table.

'Just some fellows . . .'

'They must have had a reason.'

'Well, a sister of one of them had been talking to me.'

'Well, that isn't a reason, even in Shahganj. You must have said or done something to offend her.'

'No, she likes me,' he said, wincing as I dabbed iodine on his forehead. 'We went to the guava orchard near my uncle's farm.'

'She went out there alone with you?'

'Sure. I took her on my bike. They must have followed us. Anyway, we weren't doing much except kissing and fooling around. But some people seem to think that's worse than . . .'

Both he and the other boys of Shahganj had grown up to look upon girls as strange, exotic animals, who must be seized at the first opportunity. Experimenting in sex was like playing a surreptitious game of marbles.

Sunil produced a clasp-knife from his pocket, opened it, and held the blade against the flat of his hand.

'Don't worry, Uncle, I can look after myself. The next fellow who tries to interfere with me will get this in his guts.'

'Don't be silly,' I said. 'You will go to prison for ten years. Listen, I'm going up to Simla for a couple of weeks, just for a change. Why don't you come with me? It will be a pleasant change from Shahganj, and in the meantime all this fuss will die down.'

It was one of those invitations which I make so readily and instantly regret. As soon as I had made the suggestion, I realized that Sunil in Simla might be even more of a problem than Sunil in Shahganj. But it was too late for me to back out.

'Simla! Why not? The college is closing for the summer holidays, and my father won't mind my going with you. He believes you're the only respectable friend I've got. Boy! We'll have a good time in Simla.'

'You'll have to behave yourself there, if you want to come with me. No girls, Sunil.'

'No girls, sir. I'll be very good, Chachaji. Please take me to Simla.'

'I think two hundred rupees should be enough for a fortnight for both of us,' I said.

'Oh, too much,' said Sunil modestly.

And a week later we were actually in Simla, putting up at a moderately priced, middle-class hotel.

Our first few days in the hill station were pleasant enough. We went for long walks, tired ourselves out, and acquired enormous appetites. Sunil, in the hills for the first time in his life, declared that they were wonderful, and thanked me a score of times for bringing him up. He took a genuine interest in exploring remote valleys, forest and waterfalls, and seemed to be losing some of his self-centredness. I believe that mountains do affect one's personality, if one can remain among them long enough; and if Sunil had grown up in the hills instead of in a refugee township, I have no doubt he would have been a completely different person.

There was one small waterfall I rather liked. It was down a ravine, in a rather inaccessible spot, where very few people ever went. The water fell about thirty feet into a small pool. We bathed here on two occasions, and Sunil quite forgot the attractions of the town. And we would have visited the spot again had I not slipped and sprained my ankle. This accident confined me to the hotel balcony for several days, and I was afraid that Sunil, for want of companionship, would go in search of more mundane distractions. But though he went out often enough, he came back dusty and sunburnt; and the fact that he asked me for very little money was evidence enough of his fondness for the outdoors. Striding through forests of oak and pine, with all the world stretched out far below, was no doubt a new and exhilarating experience for him. But how long would it be before the spell was broken?

'Don't you need any money?' I asked him uneasily, on the third day of his Thoreau-like activities.

'What for, Uncle? Fresh air costs nothing. And besides, I

don't owe money to anyone in Simla. We haven't been here long enough.'

'Then perhaps we should be going,' I said.

'Shahganj is a miserable little dump.'

'I know, but it's your home. And for the time being, it's mine.'

'Listen, Uncle,' he said, after a moment of reflection, 'yesterday, on one of my walks, I met a schoolteacher. She's over thirty so don't get nervous. She doesn't have any brothers or relatives who will come chasing after me. And she's much fairer than you, Uncle. Is it all right if I'm friendly with her?'

'I suppose so,' I said uncertainly. Schoolteachers can usually take care of themselves (if they want to), and, besides, an older woman might have a sobering influence on Sunil.

He brought her over to see me that same evening, and seemed quite proud of his new acquisition. She was indeed fair, perhaps insipidly so, with blonde hair and light blue eyes. She had a young face and a healthy body, but her voice was peculiarly toneless and flat, giving an impression of boredom, of lassitude. I wondered what she found attractive in Sunil apart from his obvious animal charm. They had hardly anything in common; but perhaps the absence of similar interests was an attraction in itself. In six or seven years of teaching Maureen must have been tired of the usual scholastic types. Sunil was refreshingly free from all classroom associations.

Maureen let her hair down at the first opportunity. She switched on the bedroom radio and found Ceylon. Soon she was teaching Sunil to dance. This was amusing, because Sunil, with his long legs, had great difficulty in taking small steps; nor could Maureen cope with his great strides. But he was very earnest about it all, and inserting an unlighted cigarette between his lips, did his best to move rhythmically around the bedroom. I think he was convinced that by learning to dance he would reach the high-water mark of western culture. Maureen stood for all that was remote and romantic, and for all the films that he had seen. To conquer her would, for Sunil, be a voyage of discovery, not a mere gratification of his senses. And for Maureen, this new unconventional friendship must have been a refreshing diversion from the dreariness of her school routine. She was old enough to realize that it was only a diversion. The intensity of emotional attachments had faded with her early youth, and love could wound her heart no more. But for Sunil, it was only the beginning of something that stirred him deeply, moved him inexorably towards manhood.

It was unfortunate that I did not then notice this subtle change in my friend. I had known him only as a shallow creature, and was certain that this new infatuation would disappear as soon as the novelty of it wore off. As Maureen had no encumbrances, no relations that she would speak of, I saw no harm in encouraging the friendship and seeing how it would develop.

'I think we'd better have something to drink,' I said, and ringing the bell for the room-bearer, ordered several bottles of beer.

Sunil gave me an odd, whimsical look. I had never before encouraged him to drink. But he did not hesitate to open the bottles; and, before long, Maureen and he were drinking from the same glass.

'Let's make love,' said Sunil, putting his arm round Maureen's shoulders and gazing adoringly into her dreamy blue eyes.

They seemed unconcerned by my presence; but I was embarrassed, and getting up, said I would be going for a walk.

'Enjoy yourself,' said Sunil, winking at me over Maureen's shoulder.

'You ought to get yourself a girl friend,' said the young woman in a conciliatory tone.

'True,' I said, and moved guiltily out of the room I was paying for.

Our stay in Simla lasted several days longer than we had planned. I saw little of Sunil and Maureen during this time. As Sunil had no desire to return to Shahganj any earlier than was absolutely necessary, he avoided me during the day but I managed to stay awake late enough one night to confront him when he crept quietly into the room.

'Dear friend and familiar,' I said. 'I hate to spoil your beautiful romance, but I have absolutely no money left, and unless you have resources of your own—or if Maureen can support you—I suggest that you accompany me back to Shahganj the day after tomorrow.'

'How mean you are, Chachaji. This is something serious. I mean Maureen and me. Do you think we should get married?'

'No.'

'But why not?'

'Because she cannot support you on a teacher's salary. And she probably isn't interested in a permanent relationship—like ours.'

'Very funny. And you think I'd let my wife slave for me?'

'I do. And besides . . .'

'And besides,' he interrupted, grinning, 'she's old enough to be my mother.'

'Are you really in love with her?' I asked him. 'I've never known you to be serious about anything.'

'Honestly, Uncle.'

'And what about her?'

'Oh, she loves me terribly, really she does. She's ready to come down with us if it's possible. Only I've told her that I'll first have to break the news to my father, otherwise he might kick me out of the house.'

'Well, then,' I said shrewdly, 'the sooner we return to Shahganj and get your father's blessings, the sooner you and Maureen can get married, if that's what both of you really want.'

Early next morning Sunil disappeared, and I knew he would be gone all day. My foot was better, and I decided to take a walk on my own to the waterfall I had liked so much. It was almost noon when I reached the spot and began descending the steep path to the ravine. The stream was hidden by dense foliage, giant fens and dahlias, but the water made a tremendous noise as it tumbled over the rocks. When I reached a sharp promontory, I was able to look down on the pool. Two people were lying on the grass.

I did not recognize them at first. They looked very beautiful together, and I had not expected Sunil and Maureen to look so beautiful. Sunil, on whom no surplus flesh had as yet gathered, possessed all the sinuous grace and power of a young god; and the woman, her white flesh pressed against young grass, reminded me of a painting by Titian that I had seen in a gallery in Florence. Her full, mature body was touched with a tranquil intoxication, her breasts rose and fell slowly, and waves of muscle merged into the shadows of her broad thighs. It was as though I had stumbled into another age, and had found two lovers in a forest glade. Only a fool would have wished to disturb them. Sunil had for once in his life risen above mediocrity, and I hurried away before the magic was lost.

The human voice often shatters the beauty of the most tender passions; and when we left Simla the next day, and Maureen and Sunil used all the stock clichés to express their love, I was a little disappointed. But the poetry of life was in their bodies, not in their tongues.

Back in Shahganj, Sunil actually plucked up the courage to speak to his father. This, to me, was a sign that he took the affair very seriously, for he seldom approached his father for anything. But all the sympathy that he received was a box on the ears. I received a curt note suggesting that I was having a corrupting influence on the boy and that I should stop seeing him. There was little I could do in the matter, because it had always been Sunil who had insisted on seeing me.

He continued to visit me, bring me Maureen's letters (strange, how lovers cannot bear that the world should not know their love), and his own to her, so that I could correct his English!

It was at about this time that Sunil began speaking to me about his uncle's paper factory, and the possibility of working in it. Once he was getting a salary, he pointed out, Maureen would be able to leave her job and join him.

Unfortunately Sunil's decision to join the paper factory took months to crystallize into a definite course of action, and in the meantime he was finding a panacea for lovesickness in rum and sometimes cheap country spirit. The money that he now borrowed was used not to pay his debts, or to incur new ones, but to drink himself silly. I regretted having been the first person to have offered him a drink. I should have known that Sunil was a person who could do nothing in moderation.

He pestered me less often now, but the purpose of his occasional visits became all too obvious. I was having a little success, and thoughtlessly gave Sunil the few rupees he usually demanded. At the same time I was beginning to find other friends, and I no longer found myself worrying about Sunil, as

I had so often done in the past. Perhaps this was treachery on my part . . . .

When finally I decided to leave Shahganj for Delhi, I went in search of Sunil to say goodbye. I found him in a small bar, alone at a table with a bottle of rum. Though barely twenty, he no longer looked a boy. He was a completely different person from the handsome, cocksure youth I had met at the wrestling pit a year previously. His cheeks were hollow and he had not shaved for days. I knew that when I first met him he had been without scruples, a shallow youth, the product of many circumstances. He was no longer so shallow and he had stumbled upon love, but his character was too weak to sustain the weight of disillusionment. Perhaps I should have left him severely alone from the beginning. Before me sat a ruin, and I had helped to undermine the foundations. None of us can really avoid seeing the outcome of our smallest actions . . . .

'I'm off to Delhi, Sunil.'

He did not look up from the table.

'Have a good time,' he said.

'Have you heard from Maureen?' I asked, certain that he had not.

He nodded, but for once did not offer to show me the letter.

'What's wrong?' I asked.

'Oh, nothing,' he said, looking up and forcing a smile. 'These dames are all the same, Uncle. We shouldn't take them too seriously, you know.'

'Why, what has she done, got married to someone else?'

'Yes,' he said scornfully. 'To a bloody teacher.'

'Well, she wasn't young,' I said. 'She couldn't wait for you for ever, I suppose.'

'She could if she had really loved me. But there's no such thing as love, is there, Uncle?'

I made no reply. Had he really broken his heart over a woman? Were there, within him, unsuspected depths of feeling and passion? You find love when you least expect to and lose it when you are sure that it is in your grasp.

'You're a lucky beggar,' he said. 'You're a philosopher. You find a reason for every stupid thing, and so you are able to ignore all stupidity.'

I laughed. 'You're becoming a philosopher yourself. But don't think too hard, Sunil, you might find it painful.'

'Not I, Chachaji,' he said, emptying his glass. 'I'm not going to think. I'm going to work in a paper factory. I shall become respectable. What an adventure that will be!'

And that was the last time I saw Sunil.

He did not become respectable. He was still searching like a great discoverer for something new, someone different, when he met his pitiful end in the cold rain of a December night.

Though murder cases usually get reported in the papers, Sunil was a person of such little importance that his violent end was not considered newsworthy. It went unnoticed, and Maureen could not have known about it. The case has already been forgotten, for in the great human mass that is India, hundreds of people disappear every day and are never heard of again. Sunil will be quickly forgotten by all except those to whom he owed money.

The Kitemaker

❦

There was but one tree in the street known as Gali Ram Nath—an ancient banyan that had grown through the cracks of an abandoned mosque—and little Ali's kite had caught in its branches. The boy, barefoot and clad only in a torn shirt, ran along the cobbled stones of the narrow street to where his grandfather sat nodding dreamily in the sunshine of their back courtyard.

'Grandfather,' shouted the boy. 'My kite has gone!'

The old man woke from his daydream with a start and, raising his head, displayed a beard that would have been white had it not been dyed red with mehendi leaves.

'Did the twine break?' he asked. 'I know that kite twine is not what it used to be.'

'No, Grandfather, the kite is stuck in the banyan tree.'

The old man chuckled. 'You have yet to learn how to fly a kite properly, my child. And I am too old to teach you, that's the pity of it. But you shall have another.'

He had just finished making a new kite from bamboo paper and thin silk, and it lay in the sun, firming up. It was a pale pink kite, with a small green tail. The old man handed it to Ali, and the boy raised himself on his toes and kissed his grandfather's hollowed-out cheek.

'I will not lose this one,' he said. 'This kite will fly like a bird.' And he turned on his heels and skipped out of the courtyard.

The old man remained dreaming in the sun. His kite shop was gone, the premises long since sold to a junk dealer; but he still made kites, for his own amusement and for the benefit of his grandson, Ali. Not many people bought kites these days. Adults disdained them, and children preferred to spend their money at the cinema. Moreover, there were not many open spaces left for the flying of kites. The city had swallowed up the open grassland that had stretched from the old fort's walls to the river bank.

But the old man remembered a time when grown men flew kites, and great battles were fought, the kites swerving and swooping in the sky, tangling with each other until the string of one was severed. Then the defeated but liberated kite would float away into the blue unknown. There was a good deal of betting, and money frequently changed hands.

Kite-flying was then the sport of kings, and the old man remembered how the Nawab himself would come down to the riverside with his retinue to participate in this noble pastime. There was time, then, to spend an idle hour with a gay, dancing strip of paper. Now everyone hurried, in a heat of hope, and delicate things like kites and daydreams were trampled underfoot.

He, Mehmood the kitemaker, had in the prime of his life been well known throughout the city. Some of his more elaborate kites once sold for as much as three or four rupees each.

At the request of the Nawab he had once made a very special kind of kite, unlike any that had been seen in the district. It consisted of a series of small, very light paper disks trailing on a thin bamboo frame. To the end of each disk he fixed a sprig of grass, forming a balance on both sides. The surface of the foremost disk was slightly convex, and a fantastic face was painted on it, having two eyes made of small mirrors. The disks, decreasing in size from head to tail, assumed an undulatory form and gave the kite the appearance of a crawling serpent. It required great skill to raise this cumbersome device from the ground, and only Mehmood could manage it.

Everyone had heard of the 'Dragon Kite' that Mehmood had built, and word went round that it possessed supernatural powers. A large crowd assembled in the open to watch its first public launching in the presence of the Nawab.

At the first attempt it refused to leave the ground. The disks made a plaintive, protesting sound, and the sun was trapped in the little mirrors, making of the kite a living, complaining creature. Then the wind came from the right direction, and the Dragon Kite soared into the sky, wriggling its way higher and higher, the sun still glinting in its devil-eyes. And when it went very high, it pulled fiercely on the twine, and Mehmood's young sons had to help him with the reel. Still the kite pulled, determined to be free, to break loose, to live a life of its own. And eventually it did so.

The twine snapped, the kite leaped away toward the sun, sailing on heavenward until it was lost to view. It was never found again, and Mehmood wondered afterwards if he made too vivid, too living a thing of the great kite. He did not make another like it. Instead he presented to the Nawab a musical kite, one that made a sound like a violin when it rose in the air.

Those were more leisurely, more spacious days. But the Nawab had died years ago, and his descendants were almost as poor as Mehmood himself. Kitemakers, like poets, once had their patrons; but no one knew Mehmood, simply because there were too many people in the Gali, and they could not be bothered with their neighbours.

When Mehmood was younger and had fallen sick, everyone in the neighbourhood had come to ask after his health; but now, when his days were drawing to a close, no one visited him. Most of his old friends were dead and his sons had grown up: one was working in a local garage and the other, who was in Pakistan at the time of the Partition, had not been able to rejoin his relatives.

The children who had bought kites from him ten years ago were now grown men, struggling for a living; they did not have time for the old man and his memories. They had grown up in a swiftly changing and competitive world, and they looked at the old kitemaker and the banyan tree with the same indifference.

Both were taken for granted—permanent fixtures that were of no concern to the raucous, sweating mass of humanity that surrounded them. No longer did people gather under the banyan tree to discuss their problems and their plans; only in the summer months did a few seek shelter from the fierce sun.

But there was the boy, his grandson. It was good that Mehmood's son worked close by, for it gladdened the old man's heart to watch the small boy at play in the winter sunshine, growing under his eyes like a young and well-nourished sapling putting forth new leaves each day. There is a great affinity between trees and men. We grow at much the same pace, if we are not hurt or starved or cut down. In our youth we are resplendent creatures, and in our declining years we stoop a little, we remember, we stretch our brittle limbs in the sun, and then, with a sigh, we shed our last leaves.

Mehmood was like the banyan, his hands gnarled and twisted like the roots of the ancient tree. Ali was like the young mimosa planted at the end of the courtyard. In two years both he and the tree would acquire the strength and confidence of their early youth.

The voices in the street grew fainter, and Mehmood wondered if he was going to fall asleep and dream, as he so often did, of a kite so beautiful and powerful that it would resemble the great white bird of the Hindus—Garuda, God Vishnu's famous steed. He would like to make a wonderful new kite for little Ali. He had nothing else to leave the boy.

He heard Ali's voice in the distance, but did not realize that the boy was calling him. The voice seemed to come from very far away.

Ali was at the courtyard door, asking if his mother had as yet returned from the bazaar. When Mehmood did not answer, the boy came forward repeating his question. The sunlight was slanting across the old man's head, and a small white butterfly rested on his flowing beard. Mehmood was silent; and when Ali put his small brown hand on the old man's shoulder, he met with no response. The boy heard a faint sound, like the rubbing of marbles in his pocket.

Suddenly afraid, Ali turned and moved to the door, and then ran down the street shouting for his mother. The butterfly left the old man's beard and flew to the mimosa tree, and a sudden gust of wind caught the torn kite and lifted it in the air, carrying it far above the struggling city into the blind blue sky.

THE MONKEYS

❧

I COULDN'T BE SURE, next morning, if I had been dreaming or if I had really heard dogs barking in the night and had seen them scampering about on the hillside below the cottage. There had been a Golden Cocker, a Retriever, a Peke, a Dachshund, a black Labrador, and one or two nondescripts. They had woken me with their barking shortly after midnight, and made so much noise that I got out of bed and looked out of the open window. I saw them quite plainly in the moonlight, five or six dogs rushing excitedly through the bracket and long monsoon grass.

It was only because there had been so many breeds among the dogs that I felt a little confused. I had been in the cottage only a week, and I was already on nodding or speaking terms with most of my neighbours. Colonel Fanshawe, retired from the Indian Army, was my immediate neighbour. He did keep a Cocker, but it was black. The elderly Anglo-Indian spinsters who lived beyond the deodars kept only cats. (Though why cats should be the prerogative of spinsters, I have never been able to understand.) The milkman kept a couple of mongrels. And the Punjabi industrialist who had bought a former prince's palace—without ever occupying it—left the property in charge of a watchman who kept a huge Tibetan mastiff.

None of these dogs looked like the ones I had seen in the night.

'Does anyone here keep a Retriever?' I asked Colonel Fanshawe, when I met him taking his evening walk.

'No one that I know of,' he said and gave me a swift, penetrating ook from under his bushy eyebrows. 'Why, have you seen one around?'

'No, I just wondered. There are a lot of dogs in the area, aren't there?'

'Oh, yes. Nearly everyone keeps a dog here. Of course every now and then a panther carries one off. Lost a lovely little terrier myself, only last winter.'

Colonel Fanshawe, tall and red-faced, seemed to be waiting for me to tell him something more—or was he just taking time to recover his breath after a stiff uphill climb?'

That night I heard the dogs again. I went to the window and looked out. The moon was at the full, silvering the leaves of the oak trees.

The dogs were looking up into the trees, and barking. But I could see nothing in the trees, not even an owl.

I gave a shout, and the dogs disappeared into the forest.

Colonel Fanshawe looked at me expectantly when I met him the following day. He knew something about those dogs, of that I was certain; but he was waiting to hear what I had to say. I decided to oblige him.

'I saw at least six dogs in the middle of the night,' I said. 'A Cocker, a Retriever, a Peke, a Dachshund, and two mongrels. Now, Colonel, I'm sure you must know whose they are.'

The Colonel was delighted. I could tell by the way his eyes glinted that he was going to enjoy himself at my expense.

'You've been seeing Miss Fairchild's dogs,' he said with smug satisfaction.

'Oh, and where does she live?'

'She doesn't, my boy. Died fifteen years ago.'

'Then what are her dogs doing here?'

'Looking for monkeys,' said the Colonel. And he stood back to watch my reaction.

'I'm afraid I don't understand,' I said.

'Let me put it this way,' said the Colonel. 'Do you believe in ghosts?'

'I've never seen any,' I said.

'But you have, my boy, you have. Miss Fairchild's dogs died years ago—a Cocker, a Retriever, a Dachshund, a Peke, and two mongrels. They were buried on a little knoll under the oaks. Nothing odd about their deaths, mind you. They were all quite old, and didn't survive their mistress very long. Neighbours looked after them until they died.'

'And Miss Fairchild lived in the cottage where I stay? Was she young?'

'She was in her mid-forties, an athletic sort of woman, fond of the outdoors. Didn't care much for men. I thought you knew about her.'

'No, I haven't been here very long, you know. But what was it you said about monkeys? Why were the dogs looking for monkeys?'

'Ah, that's the interesting part of the story. Have you seen the langur monkeys that sometimes come to eat oak leaves?'

'No.'

'You will, sooner or later. There has always been a band of them roaming these forests. They're quite harmless really, except that they'll ruin a garden if given half a chance . . . . Well, Miss Fairchild fairly loathed those monkeys. She was very keen on her dahlias—grew some prize specimens—but the monkeys would come at night, dig up the plants, and eat the dahlia bulbs. Apparently they found the bulbs much to their liking. Miss Fairchild would be furious. People who are passionately fond of gardening often go off balance when their best plants are ruined—that's only human, I suppose. Miss Fairchild set her dogs on the monkeys, whenever she could, even if it was in the middle of the night. But the monkeys simply took to the trees and left the dogs barking.'

'Then one day—or rather, one night—Miss Fairchild took desperate measures. She borrowed a shotgun, and sat up near a window. And when the monkeys arrived, she shot one of them dead.'

The Colonel paused and looked out over the oak trees which were shimmering in the warm afternoon sun.

'She shouldn't have done that,' he said.

'Never shoot a monkey. It's not only that they're sacred to Hindus—but they are rather human, you know. Well, I must be getting on. Good day!' And the Colonel, having ended his story rather abruptly, set off at a brisk pace through the deodars.

I didn't hear the dogs that night. But the next day I saw the monkeys—the real ones, not ghosts. There were about twenty of them, young and old, sitting in the trees munching oak leaves. They didn't pay much attention to me, and I watched them for some time.

They were handsome creatures, their fur a silver-grey, their tails long and sinuous. They leapt gracefully from tree to tree, and were very polite and dignified in their behaviour towards each other—unlike the bold, rather crude red monkeys of the plains. Some of the younger ones scampered about on the hillside, playing and wrestling with each other like schoolboys.

There were no dogs to molest them—and no dahlias to tempt them into the garden.

But that night, I heard the dogs again. They were barking more furiously than ever.

'Well, I'm not getting up for them this time,' I mumbled, and pulled the blanket over my ears.

But the barking grew louder, and was joined by other sounds, a squealing and a scuffling.

Then suddenly the piercing shriek of a woman rang through the forest. It was an unearthly sound, and it made my hair stand up.

I leapt out of bed and dashed to the window.

A woman was lying on the ground, three or four huge monkeys were on top of her, biting her arms and pulling at her throat. The dogs were yelping and trying to drag the monkeys off, but they were being harried from behind by others. The woman gave another bloodcurdling shriek, and I dashed back into the room, grabbed hold of a small axe, and ran into the garden.

But everyone—dogs, monkeys and shrieking woman—had disappeared, and I stood alone on the hillside in my pyjamas, clutching an axe and feeling very foolish.

The Colonel greeted me effusively the following day.

'Still seeing those dogs?' he asked in a bantering tone.

'I've seen the monkeys too,' I said.

'Oh, yes, they've come around again. But they're real enough, and quite harmless.'

'I know—but I saw them last night with the dogs.'

'Oh, did you really? That's strange, very strange.'

The Colonel tried to avoid my eye, but I hadn't quite finished with him.

'Colonel,' I said. 'You never did get around to telling me how Miss Fairchild died.'

'Oh, didn't I? Must have slipped my memory. I'm getting old, don't remember people as well as I used to. But of course I remember about Miss Fairchild, poor lady. The monkeys killed her. Didn't you know? They simply tore her to pieces . . . .'

His voice trailed off, and he looked thoughtfully at a caterpillar that was making its way up his walking stick.

'She shouldn't have shot one of them,' he said. 'Never shoot a monkey—they're rather human, you know . . . .'

THE PROSPECT OF FLOWERS

❧

FERN HILL, THE OAKS, Hunter's Lodge, The Parsonage, The Pines, Dumbarnie, Mackinnon's Hall and Windermere. These are the names of some of the old houses that still stand on the outskirts of one of the smaller Indian hill stations. Most of them have fallen into decay and ruin. They are very old, of course— built over a hundred years ago by Britishers who sought relief from the searing heat of the plains. Today's visitors to the hill stations prefer to live near the markets and cinemas and many of the old houses, set amidst oak and maple and deodar, are inhabited by wild cats, bandicoots, owls, goats, and the occasional charcoal-burner or mule-driver.

But amongst these neglected mansions stands a neat, white-washed cottage called Mulberry Lodge. And in it, up to a short time ago, lived an elderly English spinster named Miss Mackenzie.

In years Miss Mackenzie was more than 'elderly,' being well over eighty. But no one would have guessed it. She was clean, sprightly, and wore old-fashioned but well-preserved dresses. Once a week, she walked the two miles to town to buy butter and jam and soap and sometimes a small bottle of *eau-de-Cologne*.

She had lived in the hill station since she had been a girl in her teens, and that had been before the First World War. Though she had never married, she had experienced a few love affairs and was far from being the typical frustrated spinster of fiction. Her parents had been dead thirty years; her brother and sister were also dead. She had no relatives in India, and she lived on a small pension of forty rupees a month and the gift parcels that were sent out to her from New Zealand by a friend of her youth.

Like other lonely old people, she kept a pet, a large black cat with bright yellow eyes. In her small garden she grew dahlias, chrysanthemums, gladioli and a few rare orchids. She knew a great deal about plants, and about wild flowers, trees, birds and insects. She had never made a serious study of these things, but having lived with them for so many years, had developed an intimacy with all that grew and flourished around her.

She had few visitors. Occasionally the padre from the local church called on her, and once a month the postman came with a letter from New Zealand or her pension papers. The milkman called every second day with a litre of milk for the lady and her cat. And sometimes she received a couple of eggs free, for the egg-seller remembered a time when Miss Mackenzie, in her earlier prosperity bought eggs from him in large quantities. He was a sentimental man. He remembered her as a ravishing beauty in her twenties when he had gazed at her in round-eyed, nine-year-old wonder and consternation.

Now it was September and the rains were nearly over and Miss Mackenzie's chrysanthemums were coming into their own. She hoped the coming winter wouldn't be too severe because she found it increasingly difficult to bear the cold.

One day, as she was pottering about in her garden, she saw a schoolboy plucking wild flowers on the slope about the cottage.

'Who's that?' she called. 'What are you up to, young man?'

The boy was alarmed and tried to dash up the hillside, but he slipped on pine needles and came slithering down the slope into Miss Mackenzie's nasturtium bed.

When he found there was no escape, he gave a bright disarming smile and said, 'Good morning, Miss.'

He belonged to the local English-medium school, and wore a bright red blazer and a red and black striped tie. Like most polite Indian schoolboys, he called every woman 'Miss.'

'Good morning,' said Miss Mackenzie severely. 'Would you mind moving out of my flower-bed?'

The boy stepped gingerly over the nasturtiums and looked up at Miss Mackenzie with dimpled cheeks and appealing eyes. It was impossible to be angry with him.

'You're trespassing,' said Miss Mackenzie.

'Yes, Miss.'

'And you ought to be in school at this hour.'

'Yes, Miss.'

'Then what are you doing here?'

'Picking flowers, Miss.' And he held up a bunch of ferns and wild flowers.

'Oh,' Miss Mackenzie was disarmed. It was a long time since she had seen a boy taking an interest in flowers, and, what was more, playing truant from school in order to gather them.

'Do you like flowers?' she asked.

'Yes, Miss. I'm going to be a botan—a botantist?'

'You mean a botanist.'

'Yes, Miss.'

'Well, that's unusual. Most boys at your age want to be pilots or soldiers or perhaps engineers. But you want to be a botanist. Well, well. There's still hope for the world, I see. And do you know the names of these flowers?'

'This is a bukhilo flower,' he said, showing her a small golden flower. 'That's a Pahari name. It means puja, or prayer. The flower is offered during prayers. But I don't know what this is . . . .'

He held out a pale pink flower with a soft, heart-shaped leaf.

'It's a wild begonia,' said Miss Mackenzie. 'And that purple stuff is salvia, but it isn't wild. It's a plant that escaped from my garden. Don't you have any books on flowers?'

'No, Miss.'

'All right, come in and I'll show you a book.'

She led the boy into a small front room, which was crowded with furniture and books and vases and jam-jars and offered him a chair. He sat awkwardly on its edge. The black cat immediately leapt on to his knees, and settled down on them, purring loudly.

'What's your name?' asked Miss Mackenzie, as she rummaged among her books.

'Anil, Miss.'

'And where do you live?'

'When school closes, I go to Delhi. My father has a business.'

'Oh, and what's that?'

'Bulbs, Miss.'

'Flower bulbs?'

'No, electric bulbs.'

'Electric bulbs! You might send me a few, when you get home. Mine are always fusing, and they're so expensive, like everything else these days. Ah, here we are!' She pulled a heavy volume down from the shelf and laid it on the table. 'Flora Himaliensis, published in 1892, and probably the only copy in India. This is a very valuable book, Anil. No other naturalist has recorded so many wild Himalayan flowers. And let me tell you this, there are many flowers and plants which are still unknown to the fancy botanists who spend all their time with microscopes instead of in the mountains. But perhaps, you'll do something about that, one day.'

'Yes, Miss.'

They went through the book together, and Miss Mackenzie pointed out many flowers that grew in and around the hill station, while the boy made notes of their names and seasons. She lit a stove, and put the kettle on for tea. And then the old English lady and the small Indian boy sat side by side over cups of hot sweet tea, absorbed in a book of wild flowers.

'May I come again?' asked Anil, when finally he rose to go.

'If you like,' said Miss Mackenzie. 'But not during school hours. You mustn't miss your classes.'

After that, Anil visited Miss Mackenzie about once a week, and nearly always brought a wildflower for her to identify. She found herself looking forward to the boy's visits—and sometimes, when more than a week passed and he didn't come, she was disappointed and lonely and would grumble at the black cat.

Anil reminded her of her brother, when the latter had been a boy. There was no physical resemblance. Andrew had been fair-haired and blue-eyed. But it was Anil's eagerness, his alert, bright look and the way he stood—legs apart, hands on hips, a picture of confidence—that reminded her of the boy who had shared her own youth in these same hills.

And why did Anil come to see her so often?

Partly because she knew about wild flowers, and he really did want to become a botanist. And partly because she smelt of freshly baked bread, and that was a smell his own grandmother had possessed. And partly because she was lonely and sometimes a boy of twelve can sense loneliness better than an adult. And partly because he was a little different from other children.

By the middle of October, when there was only a fortnight left for the school to close, the first snow had fallen on the distant mountains. One peak stood high above the rest, a white pinnacle against the azure-blue sky. When the sun set, this peak turned from orange to gold to pink to red.

'How high is that mountain?' asked Anil.

'It must be over 12,000 feet,' said Miss Mackenzie. 'About thirty miles from here, as the crow flies. I always wanted to go there, but there was no proper road. At that height, there'll be flowers that you don't get here—the blue gentian and the purple columbine, the anemone and the edelweiss.'

'I'll go there one day,' said Anil.

'I'm sure you will, if you really want to.'

The day before his school closed, Anil came to say goodbye to Miss Mackenzie.

'I don't suppose you'll be able to find many wild flowers in Delhi,' she said. 'But have a good holiday.'

'Thank you, Miss.'

As he was about to leave, Miss Mackenzie, on an impulse, thrust the *Flora Himaliensis* into his hands.

'You keep it,' she said. 'It's a present for you.'

'But I'll be back next year, and I'll be able to look at it then. It's so valuable.'

'I know it's valuable and that's why I've given it to you. Otherwise it will only fall into the hands of the junk-dealers.'

'But, Miss . . .'

'Don't argue. Besides, I may not be here next year.'

'Are you going away?'

'I'm not sure. I may go to England.'

She had no intention of going to England; she had not seen

the country since she was a child, and she knew she would not fit in with the life of post-war Britain. Her home was in these hills, among the oaks and maples and deodars. It was lonely, but at her age it would be lonely anywhere.

The boy tucked the book under his arm, straightened his tie, stood stiffly to attention, and said, 'Goodbye, Miss Mackenzie.'

It was the first time he had spoken her name.

Winter set in early, and strong winds brought rain and sleet, and soon there were no flowers in the garden or on the hillside. The cat stayed indoors, curled up at the foot of Miss Mackenzie's bed.

Miss Mackenzie wrapped herself up in all her old shawls and mufflers, but still she felt the cold. Her fingers grew so stiff that she took almost an hour to open a can of baked beans. And then it snowed and for several days the milkman did not come. The postman arrived with her pension papers, but she felt too tired to take them up to town to the bank.

She spent most of the time in bed. It was the warmest place. She kept a hot-water bottle at her back, and the cat kept her feet warm. She lay in bed, dreaming of the spring and summer months. In three months' time the primroses would be out and with the coming of spring the boy would return.

One night the hot-water bottle burst and the bedding was soaked through. As there was no sun for several days, the blanket remained damp. Miss Mackenzie caught a chill and had to keep to her cold, uncomfortable bed. She knew she had a fever but there was no thermometer with which to take her temperature. She had difficulty in breathing.

A strong wind sprang up one night, and the window flew open and kept banging all night. Miss Mackenzie was too weak to get up and close it, and the wind swept the rain and sleet into the room. The cat crept into the bed and snuggled close to its mistress's warm body. But towards morning that body had lost its warmth and the cat left the bed and started scratching about on the floor.

As a shaft of sunlight streamed through the open window, the milkman arrived. He poured some milk into the cat's saucer on the doorstep and the cat leapt down from the window-sill and made for the milk.

The milkman called a greeting to Miss Mackenzie, but received no answer. Her window was open and he had always known her to be up before sunrise. So he put his head in at the window and called again. But Miss Mackenzie did not answer. She had gone away to the mountain where the blue gentian and purple columbine grew.

A Case for Inspector Lal

I MET INSPECTOR KEEMAT Lal about two years ago, while I was living in the hot, dusty town of Shahpur in the plains of northern India.

Keemat Lal had charge of the local police station. He was a heavily built man, slow and rather ponderous, and inclined to be lazy; but, like most lazy people, he was intelligent. He was also a failure. He had remained an inspector for a number of years, and had given up all hope of further promotion. His luck was against him, he said. He should never have been a policeman. He had been born under the sign of Capricorn and should really have gone into the restaurant business but now it was too late to do anything about it.

The Inspector and I had little in common. He was nearing forty, and I was twenty-five. But both of us spoke English, and in Shahpur there were very few people who did. In addition, we were both fond of beer. There were no places of entertainment in Shahpur. The searing heat, the dust that came whirling up from the east, the mosquitoes (almost as numerous as the flies), and the general monotony gave one a thirst for something more substantial than stale lemonade.

My house was on the outskirts of the town, where we were not often disturbed. On two or three evenings in the week, just as the sun was going down and making it possible for one to emerge from the *khas*-cooled confines of a dark, high-ceilinged bedroom, Inspector Keemat Lal would appear on the veranda steps, mopping the sweat from his face with a small towel, which he used instead of a handkerchief. My only servant, excited at the prospect of serving an Inspector of Police, would hurry out with glasses, a bucket of ice and several bottles of the best Indian beer.

One evening, after we had overtaken our fourth bottle, I said, 'You must have had some interesting cases in your career, Inspector.'

'Most of them were rather dull,' he said. 'At least the successful ones were. The sensational cases usually went unsolved—otherwise I might have been a superintendent by now. I suppose you are talking of murder cases. Do you remember the shooting of the Minister of the Interior? I was on that one, but it was political murder and we never solved it.'

'Tell me about a case you solved,' I said. 'An interesting one.' When I saw him looking uncomfortable, I added, 'You don't have to worry, Inspector. I'm a very discreet person, in spite of all the beer I consume.'

'But how can you be discreet? You are a writer.'

I protested: 'Writers are usually very discreet. They always change the names of people and places.'

He gave me one of his rare smiles. 'And how would you describe me, if you were to put me in a story?'

'Oh, I'd leave you as you are. No one would believe in you, anyway.'

He laughed indulgently and poured out more beer. 'I suppose I can change names, too . . . I will tell you of a very interesting case. The victim was an unusual person, and so was the killer. But you must promise not to write this story.'

'I promise,' I lied.

'Do you know Panauli?'

'In the hills? Yes, I have been there once or twice.'

'Good, then you will follow me without my having to be too descriptive. This happened about three years ago, shortly after I had been stationed at Panauli. Nothing much ever happened there. There were a few cases of theft and cheating, and an occasional fight during the summer. A murder took place about once every ten years. It was therefore quite an event when the Rani of —— was found dead in her sitting-room, her head split open with an axe. I knew that I would have to solve the case if I wanted to stay in Panauli.

'The trouble was, anyone could have killed the Rani, and

there were some who made no secret of their satisfaction that she was dead. She had been an unpopular woman. Her husband was dead, her children were scattered, and her money—for she had never been a very wealthy Rani—had been dwindling away. She lived alone in an old house on the outskirts of the town, ruling the locality with the stern authority of a matriarch. She had a servant, and he was the man who found the body and came to the police, dithering and tongue-tied. I arrested him at once, of course. I knew he was probably innocent, but a basic rule is to grab the first man on the scene of crime, especially if he happens to be a servant. But we let him go after a beating. There was nothing much he could tell us, and he had a sound alibi.

'The axe with which the Rani had been killed must have been a small woodcutter's axe—so we deduced from the wound. We couldn't find the weapon. It might have been used by a man or a woman, and there were several of both sexes who had a grudge against the Rani. There were bazaar rumours that she had been supplementing her income by trafficking in young women: she had the necessary connections. There were also rumours that she possessed vast wealth, and that it was stored away in her godowns. We did not find any treasure. There were so many rumours darting about like battered shuttlecocks that I decided to stop wasting my time in trying to follow them up. Instead I restricted my enquiries to those people who had been close to the Rani—either in their personal relationships or in actual physical proximity.

'To begin with, there was Mr Kapur, a wealthy businessman from Bombay who had a house in Panauli. He was supposed to be an old admirer of the Rani's. I discovered that he had occasionally lent her money, and that, in spite of his professed friendship for her, he had charged a high rate of interest.

'Then there were her immediate neighbours—an American missionary and his wife, who had been trying to convert the Rani to Christianity; an English spinster of seventy who made no secret of the fact that she and the Rani had hated each other with great enthusiasm; a local councillor and his family, who did not get on well with their aristocratic neighbour; and a tailor, who kept his shop close by. None of these people had any powerful motive for killing the Rani—or none that I could discover. But the tailor's daughter interested me.

'Her name was Kusum. She was twelve or thirteen years old—a thin, dark girl, with lovely black eyes and a swift, disarming smile. While I was making my routine enquiries in the vicinity of the Rani's house, I noticed that the girl always tried to avoid me. When I questioned her about the Rani, and about her own movements on the day of the crime, she pretended to be very vague and stupid.

'But I could see she was not stupid, and I became convinced that she knew something unusual about the Rani. She might even know something about the murder. She could have been protecting someone, and was afraid to tell me what she knew. Often, when I spoke to her of the violence of the Rani's death, I saw fear in her eyes. I began to think the girl's life might be in danger, and I had a close watch kept on her. I liked her. I liked her youth and freshness, and the innocence and wonder in her eyes. I spoke to her whenever I could, kindly and paternally, and though I knew she rather liked me and found me amusing—the ups and downs of Panauli always left me panting for breath—and though I could see that she *wanted* to tell me something, she always held back at the last moment.

'Then, one afternoon while I was in the Rani's house going through her effects, I saw something glistening in a narrow crack near the doorstep. I would not have noticed it if the sun had not been pouring through the window, glinting off the little object. I stooped and picked up a piece of glass. It was part of a broken bangle.

'I turned the fragment over in my hand. There was something familiar about its colour and design. Didn't Kusum wear similar glass bangles? I went to look for the girl but she was not at her father's shop. I was told that she had gone down the hill, to gather firewood.

'I decided to take the narrow path down the hill. It went round some rocks and cactus, and then disappeared into a forest of oak trees. I found Kusum sitting at the edge of the forest, a bundle of twigs beside her.

'"You are always wandering about alone," I said. "Don't you feel afraid?"

'"It is safer when I am alone," she replied. "Nobody comes here."

'I glanced quickly at the bangles on her wrist, and noticed that their colour matched that of the broken piece. I held out the bit of broken glass and said, "I found it in the Rani's house. It must have fallen . . ."

'She did not wait for me to finish what I was saying. With a look of terror, she sprang up from the grass and fled into the forest.

'I was completely taken aback. I had not expected such a reaction. Of what significance was the broken bangle? I hurried after the girl, slipping on the smooth pine needles that covered the slopes. I was searching amongst the trees when I heard someone sobbing behind me. When I turned round, I saw the girl standing on a boulder, facing me with an axe in her hands.

'When Kusum saw me staring at her, she raised the axe and rushed down the slope towards me.

'I was too bewildered to be able to do anything but stare with open mouth as she rushed at me with the axe. The impetus of her run would have brought her right up against me, and the axe, coming down, would probably have crushed my skull, thick though it is. But while she was still six feet from me, the axe flew out of her hands. It sprang into the air as though it had a life of its own and came curving towards me.

'In spite of my weight, I moved swiftly aside. The axe grazed my shoulder and sank into the soft bark of the tree behind me. And Kusum dropped at my feet weeping hysterically.'

Inspector Keemat Lal paused in order to replenish his glass. He took a long pull at the beer and the froth glistened on his moustache.

'And then what happened?' I prompted him.

'Perhaps it could only have happened in India—and to a person like me,' he said. 'This sudden compassion for the person you are supposed to destroy. Instead of being furious and outraged, instead of seizing the girl and marching her off to the police station, I stroked her head and said silly comforting things.'

'And she told you that she had killed the Rani?'

'She told me how the Rani had called her to her house and given her tea and sweets. Mr Kapur had been there. After some time he began stroking Kusum's arms and squeezing her knees. She had drawn away, but Kapur kept pawing her. The Rani was telling Kusum not to be afraid, that no harm would come to her. Kusum slipped away from the man and made a rush for the door. The Rani caught her by the shoulders and pushed her back into the room. The Rani was getting angry. Kusum saw the axe lying in a corner of the room. She seized it, raised it above her head and threatened Kapur. The man realized that he had gone too far, and, valuing his neck, backed away. But the Rani, in a great rage, sprang at the girl. And Kusum, in desperation and panic, brought the axe down across the Rani's head.'

'The Rani fell to the ground. Without waiting to see what Kapur might do, Kusum fled from the house. Her bangle must have broken when she stumbled against the door. She ran into the forest and, after concealing the axe amongst some tall ferns, lay weeping on the grass until it grew dark. But such was her nature, and such the resilience of youth, that she recovered sufficiently to be able to return home looking her normal self. And during the following days she managed to remain silent about the whole business.'

'What did you do about it?' I asked.

Keemat Lal looked me straight in my beery eye.

'Nothing,' he said. 'I did absolutely nothing. I couldn't have the girl put away in a remand home. It would have crushed her spirit.'

'And what about Kapur?'

'Oh, he had his own reasons for remaining quiet, as you may guess. No, the case was closed—or perhaps I should say the file was put in my pending tray. My promotion, too, went into the pending tray.'

'It didn't turn out very well for you,' I said.

'No. Here I am in Shahpur, and still an inspector. But, tell me, what would you have done if you had been in my place?'

I considered his question carefully for a moment or two, then said, 'I suppose it would have depended on how much sympathy the girl evoked in me. She had killed in innocence . . . .'

'Then you would have put your personal feeling above your duty to uphold the law?'

'Yes. But I would not have made a very good policeman.'

'Exactly.'

'Still, it's a pity that Kapur got off so easily.'

'There was no alternative if I was to let the girl go. But he didn't get off altogether. He found himself in trouble later on for swindling some manufacturing concern, and went to jail for a couple of years.'

'And the girl—did you see her again?'

'Well, before I was transferred from Panauli, I saw her occasionally on the road. She was usually on her way to school. She would greet me with folded hands, and call me Uncle.'

The beer bottles were all empty, and Inspector Keemat Lal got up to leave. His final words to me were, 'I should never have been a policeman.'

A FACE IN THE DARK

ৼ

Mr Oliver, an Anglo-Indian teacher, was returning to his school late one night, on the outskirts of the hill station of Simla. From before Kipling's time, the school had been run on English public school lines and the boys, most of them from wealthy Indian families, wore blazers, caps and ties. *Life* magazine, in a feature on India, had once called it the 'Eton of the East'. Mr Oliver had been teaching in the school for several years.

The Simla Bazaar, with its cinemas and restaurants, was about three miles from the school and Mr Oliver, a bachelor, usually strolled into the town in the evening, returning after dark, when he would take a short cut through the pine forest.

When there was a strong wind the pine trees made sad, eerie sounds that kept most people to the main road. But Mr Oliver was not a nervous or imaginative man. He carried a torch and its gleam—the batteries were running down—moved fitfully down the narrow forest path. When its flickering light fell on the figure of a boy, who was sitting alone on a rock, Mr Oliver stopped. Boys were not supposed to be out after dark.

'What are you doing out here, boy?' asked Mr Oliver sharply, moving closer so that he could recognize the miscreant. But even as he approached the boy, Mr Oliver sensed that something was wrong. The boy appeared to be crying. His head hung down, he held his face in his hands, and his body shook convulsively. It was a strange, soundless weeping and Mr Oliver felt distinctly uneasy.

'Well, what's the matter?' he asked, his anger giving way to

concern. 'What are you crying for?' The boy would not answer
or look up. His body continued to be racked with silent
sobbing. 'Come on, boy, you shouldn't be out here at this hour.
Tell me the trouble. Look up!' The boy looked up. He took his
hands from his face and looked up at his teacher. The light
from Mr Oliver's torch fell on the boy's face—if you could call
it a face.

It had no eyes, ears, nose or mouth. It was just a round
smooth head—with a school cap on top of it! And that's where
the story should end. But for Mr Oliver it did not end here.

The torch fell from his trembling hand. He turned and
scrambled down the path, running blindly through the trees
and calling for help. He was still running towards the school
buildings when he saw a lantern swinging in the middle of the
path. Mr Oliver stumbled up to the watchman, gasping for
breath. 'What is it, sahib?' asked the watchman. 'Has there
been an accident? Why are you running?'

'I saw something—something horrible—a boy weeping in
the forest—and he had no face!'

'No face, sahib?'

'No eyes, nose, mouth—nothing!'

'Do you mean it was like this, sahib?' asked the watchman
and raised the lamp to his own face. The watchman had no
eyes, no ears, no features at all—not even an eyebrow! And
that's when the wind blew the lamp out.

THE STORY OF MADHU

&

I MET LITTLE MADHU several years ago, when I lived alone in an obscure town near the Himalayan foothills. I was in my late twenties then, and my outlook on life was still quite romantic; the cynicism that was to come with the thirties had not yet set in.

I preferred the solitude of the small district town to the kind of social life I might have found in the cities; and in my books, my writing and the surrounding hills, there was enough for my pleasure and occupation.

On summer mornings I would often sit beneath an old mango tree, with a notebook or a sketch pad on my knees. The house which I had rented (for a very nominal sum) stood on the outskirts of the town; and a large tank and a few poor houses could be seen from the garden wall. A narrow public pathway passed under the low wall.

One morning, while I sat beneath the mango tree, I saw a young girl of about nine, wearing torn clothes, darting about on the pathway and along the high banks of the tank.

Sometimes she stopped to look at me; and, when I showed that I noticed her, she felt encouraged and gave me a shy, fleeting smile. The next day I discovered her leaning over the garden wall, following my actions as I paced up and down on the grass.

In a few days an acquaintance had been formed. I began to take the girl's presence for granted, and even to look for her; and she, in turn, would linger about on the pathway until she saw me come out of the house.

One day, as she passed the gate, I called her to me.

'What is your name?' I asked. 'And where do you live?'

'Madhu,' she said, brushing back her long untidy black hair and smiling at me from large black eyes. She pointed across the road: 'I live with my grandmother.'

'Is she very old?' I asked.

Madhu nodded confidingly and whispered: 'A hundred years . . .'

'We will never be that old,' I said. She was very slight and frail, like a flower growing in a rock, vulnerable to wind and rain.

I discovered later that the old lady was not her grandmother but a childless woman who had found the baby girl on the banks of the tank. Madhu's real parentage was unknown; but the wizened old woman had, out of compassion, brought up the child as her own.

My gate once entered, Madhu included the garden in her circle of activities. She was there every morning, chasing butterflies, stalking squirrels and mina, her voice brimming with laughter, her slight figure flitting about between the trees.

Sometimes, but not often, I gave her a toy or a new dress; and one day she put aside her shyness and brought me a present of a nosegay, made up of marigolds and wild blue-cotton flowers.

'For you,' she said, and put the flowers in my lap.

'They are very beautiful,' I said, picking out the brightest marigold and putting it in her hair. 'But they are not as beautiful as you.'

More than a year passed before I began to take more than a mildly patronizing interest in Madhu.

It occurred to me after some time that she should be taught to read and write, and I asked a local teacher to give her lessons in the garden for an hour every day. She clapped her hands with pleasure at the prospect of what was to be for her a fascinating new game.

In a few weeks Madhu was surprising us with her capacity for absorbing knowledge. She always came to me to repeat the lessons of the day, and pestered me with questions on a variety of subjects. How big was the world? And were the stars really like our world? Or were they the sons and daughters of the sun and the moon?

My interest in Madhu deepened, and my life, so empty till then, became imbued with a new purpose. As she sat on the grass beside me, reading aloud, or listening to me with a look of complete trust and belief, all the love that had been lying dormant in me during my years of self-exile surfaced in a sudden surge of tenderness.

Three years glided away imperceptibly, and at the age of thirteen Madhu was on the verge of blossoming into a woman. I began to feel a certain responsibility towards her.

It was dangerous, I knew, to allow a child so pretty to live almost alone and unprotected, and to run unrestrained about the grounds. And in a censorious society she would be made to suffer if she spent too much time in my company.

She could see no need for any separation but I decided to send her to a mission school in the next district, where I could visit her from time to time.

'But why?' said Madhu. 'I can learn more from you, and from the teacher who comes. I am so happy here.'

'You will meet other girls and make many friends,' I told her. 'I will come to see you. And, when you come home, we will be even happier. It is good that you should go.'

It was the middle of June, a hot and oppressive month in the Siwaliks. Madhu had expressed her readiness to go to school, and when, one evening, I did not see her as usual in the garden, I thought nothing of it; but the next day I was informed that she had fever and could not leave the house.

Illness was something Madhu had not known before, and for this reason I felt afraid. I hurried down the path which led to the old woman's cottage. It seemed strange that I had never once entered it during my long friendship with Madhu.

It was a humble mud hut, the ceiling just high enough to enable me to stand upright, the room dark but clean. Madhu was lying on a string cot, exhausted by fever, her eyes closed, her long hair unkempt, one small hand hanging over the side.

It struck me then how little, during all this time, I had thought of her physical comforts. There was no chair; I knelt down, and took her hand in mine. I knew, from the fierce heat of her body, that she was seriously ill.

She recognized my touch, and a smile passed across her

face before she opened her eyes. She held on to my hand, then laid it across her cheek.

I looked round the little room in which she had grown up. It had scarcely an article of furniture apart from two string cots, on one of which the old woman sat and watched us, her white, wizened head nodding like a puppet's.

In a corner lay Madhu's little treasures. I recognized among them the presents which during the past four years I had given her. She had kept everything. On her dark arm she still wore a small piece of ribbon which I had playfully tied there about a year ago. She had given her heart, even before she was conscious of possessing one, to a stranger unworthy of the gift.

As the evening drew on, a gust of wind blew open the door of the dark room, and a gleam of sunshine streamed in, lighting up a portion of the wall. It was the time when every evening she would join me under the mango tree. She had been quiet for almost an hour, and now a slight pressure of her hand drew my eyes back to her face.

'What will we do now?' she said. 'When will you send me to school?'

'Not for a long time. First you must get well and strong. That is all that matters.'

She didn't seem to hear me. I think she knew she was dying, but she did not resent it happening.

'Who will read to you under the tree?' she went on. 'Who will look after you?' she asked, with the solicitude of a grown woman.

'You will, Madhu. You are grown up now. There will be no one else to look after me.'

The old woman was standing at my shoulder. A hundred years—and little Madhu was slipping away. The woman took Madhu's hand from mine, and laid it gently down. I sat by the cot a little longer, and then I rose to go, all the loneliness in the world pressing upon my heart.

A JOB WELL DONE

❧

DHUKI, THE GARDENER, WAS clearing up the weeds that grew in profusion around the old disused well. He was an old man, skinny and bent and spindly-legged but he had always been like that. His strength lay in his wrists and in his long, tendril-like fingers. He looked as frail as a petunia but he had the tenacity of a vine.

'Are you going to cover the well?' I asked. I was eight, and a great favourite of Dhuki's. He had been the gardener long before my birth, had worked for my father until my father died and now worked for my mother and stepfather.

'I must cover it, I suppose,' said Dhuki. 'That's what the Major Sahib wants. He'll be back any day and if he finds the well still uncovered he'll get into one of his raging fits and I'll be looking for another job!'

The 'Major Sahib' was my stepfather, Major Summerskill. A tall, hearty, back-slapping man, who liked polo and pig-sticking. He was quite unlike my father. My father had always given me books to read. The Major said I would become a dreamer if I read too much and took the books away. I hated him and did not think much of my mother for marrying him.

'The boy's too soft,' I heard him tell my mother. 'I must see that he gets riding lessons.'

But before the riding lessons could be arranged the Major's regiment was ordered to Peshawar. Trouble was expected from some of the frontier tribes. He was away for about two months. Before leaving, he had left strict instructions for Dhuki to cover up the old well.

'Too damned dangerous having an open well in the middle of the garden,' my stepfather had said. 'Make sure that it's completely covered by the time I get back.'

Dhuki was loth to cover up the old well. It had been there for over fifty years, long before the house had been built. In its walls lived a colony of pigeons. Their soft cooing filled the garden with a lovely sound. And during the hot dry summer months, when taps ran dry, the well was always a dependable source of water. The bhisti still used it, filling his goatskin bag with the cool clear water and sprinkling the paths around the house to keep the dust down.

Dhuki pleaded with my mother to let him leave the well uncovered.

'What will happen to the pigeons?' he asked.

'Oh, surely they can find another well,' said my mother. 'Do close it up soon, Dhuki. I don't want the Sahib to come back and find that you haven't done anything about it.'

My mother seemed just a little bit afraid of the Major. How can we be afraid of those we love? It was a question that puzzled me then and puzzles me still.

The Major's absence made life pleasant again. I returned to my books, spent long hours in my favourite banyan tree, ate buckets of mangoes and dawdled in the garden talking to Dhuki.

Neither he nor I were looking forward to the Major's return. Dhuki had stayed on after my mother's second marriage only out of loyalty to her and affection for me. He had really been my father's man. But my mother had always appeared deceptively frail and helpless and most men, Major Summerskill included, felt protective towards her. She liked people who did things for her.

'Your father liked this well,' said Dhuki. 'He would often sit here in the evenings with a book in which he made drawings of birds and flowers and insects.'

I remembered those drawings and I remembered how they had all been thrown away by the Major when he had moved into the house. Dhuki knew about it too. I didn't keep much from him.

'It's a sad business closing this well,' said Dhuki again. 'Only a fool or a drunkard is likely to fall into it.'

But he had made his preparations. Planks of sal wood, bricks and cement were neatly piled up around the well.

'Tomorrow,' said Dhuki. 'Tomorrow I will do it. Not today. Let the birds remain for one more day. In the morning, baba, you can help me drive the birds from the well.'

On the day my stepfather was expected back, my mother hired a tonga and went to the bazaar to do some shopping. Only a few people had cars in those days. Even colonels went about in tongas. Now, a clerk finds it beneath his dignity to sit in one.

As the Major was not expected before evening, I decided I would make full use of my last free morning. I took all my favourite books and stored them away in an outhouse where I could come for them from time to time. Then, my pockets bursting with mangoes, I climbed into the banyan tree. It was the darkest and coolest place on a hot day in June.

From behind the screen of leaves that concealed me, I could see Dhuki moving about near the well. He appeared to be most unwilling to get on with the job of covering it up.

'Baba!' he called several times. But I did not feel like stirring from the banyan tree. Dhuki grasped a long plank of wood and placed it across one end of the well. He started hammering. From my vantage point in the banyan tree, he looked very bent and old.

A jingle of tonga bells and the squeak of unoiled wheels told me that a tonga was coming in at the gate. It was too early for my mother to be back. I peered through the thick, waxy leaves of the tree and nearly fell off my branch in surprise. It was my stepfather, the Major! He had arrived earlier than expected.

I did not come down from the tree. I had no intention of confronting my stepfather until my mother returned.

The Major had climbed down from the tonga and was watching his luggage being carried onto the veranda. He was red in the face and the ends of his handlebar moustache were stiff with brilliantine. Dhuki approached with a half-hearted salaam.

'Ah, so there you are, you old scoundrel!' exclaimed the Major, trying to sound friendly and jocular. 'More jungle than garden, from what I can see. You're getting too old for this sort of work, Dhuki. Time to retire! And where's the memsahib?'

'Gone to the bazaar,' said Dhuki.

'And the boy?'

Dhuki shrugged. 'I have not seen the boy today, Sahib.'

'Damn!' said the Major. 'A fine homecoming, this. Well, wake up the cook-boy and tell him to get some sodas.'

'Cook-boy's gone away,' said Dhuki.

'Well, I'll be double-damned,' said the Major.

The tonga went away and the Major started pacing up and down the garden path. Then he saw Dhuki's unfinished work at the well. He grew purple in the face, strode across to the well, and started ranting at the old gardener.

Dhuki began making excuses. He said something about a shortage of bricks, the sickness of a niece, unsatisfactory cement, unfavourable weather, unfavourable gods. When none of this seemed to satisfy the Major, Dhuki began mumbling about something bubbling up from the bottom of the well and pointed down into its depths. The Major stepped onto the low parapet and looked down. Dhuki kept pointing. The Major leant over a little.

Dhuki's hand moved swiftly, like a conjurer making a pass. He did not actually push the Major. He appeared merely to tap him once on the bottom. I caught a glimpse of my stepfather's boots as he disappeared into the well. I couldn't help thinking of Alice in Wonderland, of Alice disappearing down the rabbit hole.

There was a tremendous splash and the pigeons flew up, circling the well thrice before settling on the roof of the bungalow.

By lunchtime—or tiffin, as we called it then—Dhuki had the well covered over with the wooden planks.

'The Major will be pleased,' said my mother when she came home. 'It will be quite ready by evening, won't it, Dhuki?'

By evening the well had been completely bricked over. It was the fastest bit of work Dhuki had ever done.

Over the next few weeks, my mother's concern changed to anxiety, her anxiety to melancholy, and her melancholy to resignation. By being gay and high-spirited myself, I hope I did something to cheer her up. She had written to the Colonel of the Regiment and had been informed that the Major had gone home on leave a fortnight previously. Somewhere, in the vastness of India, the Major had disappeared.

It was easy enough to disappear and never be found. After seven months had passed without the Major turning up, it was presumed that one of two things must had happened. Either he had been murdered on the train and his corpse flung into a river. Or, he had run away with a tribal girl and was living in some remote corner of the country.

Life had to carry on for the rest of us. The rains were over and the guava season was approaching.

My mother was receiving visits from a colonel of His Majesty's 32nd Foot. He was an elderly, easygoing, seemingly absent-minded man, who didn't get in the way at all but left slabs of chocolate lying around the house.

'A good sahib,' observed Dhuki as I stood beside him behind the bougainvillaea, watching the Colonel saunter up the veranda steps. 'See how well he wears his sola topi! It covers his head completely.'

'He's bald underneath,' I said.

'No matter. I think he will be all right.'

'And if he isn't,' I said, 'we can always open up the well again.'

Dhuki dropped the nozzle of the hose pipe and water gushed out over our feet. But he recovered quickly and taking me by the hand led me across to the old well now surmounted by a three-tired cement platform which looked rather like a wedding cake.

'We must not forget our old well,' he said. 'Let us make it beautiful, baba. Some flower pots, perhaps.'

And together we fetched pots and decorated the covered well with ferns and geraniums. Everyone congratulated Dhuki on the fine job he'd done. My only regret was that the pigeons had gone away.

THE CHERRY TREE

❧

ONE DAY, WHEN RAKESH was six, he walked home from the Mussoorie bazaar eating cherries. They were a little sweet, a little sour; small, bright red cherries, which had come all the way from the Kashmir Valley.

Here in the Himalayan foothills where Rakesh lived, there were not many fruit trees. The soil was stony, and the dry cold winds stunted the growth of most plants. But on the more sheltered slopes there were forests of oak and deodar.

Rakesh lived with his grandfather on the outskirts of Mussoorie, just where the forest began. His father and mother lived in a small village fifty miles away, where they grew maize and rice and barley in narrow terraced fields on the lower slopes of the mountain. But there were no schools in the village, and Rakesh's parents were keen that he should go to school. As soon as he was of school-going age, they sent him to stay with his grandfather in Mussoorie.

Grandfather was a retired forest ranger. He had a little cottage outside the town.

Rakesh was on his way home from school when he bought the cherries. He paid fifty paise for the bunch. It took him about half an hour to walk home, and by the time he reached the cottage there were only three cherries left.

'Have a cherry, Grandfather,' he said, as soon as he saw his grandfather in the garden.

Grandfather took one cherry and Rakesh promptly ate the other two. He kept the last seed in this mouth for some time, rolling it round and round on his tongue until all the tang had gone. Then he placed the seed on the palm of his hand and studied it.

'Are cherry seeds lucky?' asked Rakesh.

'Of course.'

'Then I'll keep it.'

'Nothing is lucky if you put it away. If you want luck, you must put it to some use.'

'What can I do with a seed?'

'Plant it.'

So Rakesh found a small spade and began to dig up a flower-bed.

'Hey, not there,' said Grandfather. 'I've sown mustard in that bed. Plant it in that shady corner, where it won't be disturbed.'

Rakesh went to a corner of the garden where the earth was soft and yielding. He did not have to dig. He pressed the seed into the soil with his thumb and it went right in.

Then he had his lunch and ran off to play cricket with his friends and forgot all about the cherry seed.

When it was winter in the hills, a cold wind blew down from the snows and went *whoo-whoo-whoo* in the deodar trees, and the garden was dry and bare. In the evenings Grandfather told Rakesh stories—stories, about people who turned into animals, and ghosts who lived in trees, and beans that jumped and stones that wept—and in turn Rakesh would read to him from the newspaper, Grandfather's eyesight being rather weak. Rakesh found the newspaper very dull—especially after the stories—but Grandfather wanted all the news . . . .

They knew it was spring when the wild duck flew north again, to Siberia. Early in the morning, when he got up to chop wood and light a fire, Rakesh saw the V-shaped formation streaming northwards, the calls of the birds carrying clearly through the thin mountain air.

One morning in the garden he bent to pick up what he thought was a small twig and found to his surprise that it was well rooted. He stared at it for a moment, then ran to fetch Grandfather, calling, 'Dada, come and look, the cherry tree has come up!'

'What cherry tree?' asked Grandfather, who had forgotten about it.

'The seed we planted last year—look, it's come up!'

Rakesh went down on his haunches, while Grandfather bent almost double and peered down at the tiny tree. It was about four inches high.

'Yes, it's a cherry tree,' said Grandfather. 'You should water it now and then.'

Rakesh ran indoors and came back with a bucket of water.

'Don't drown it!' said Grandfather.

Rakesh gave it a sprinkling and circled it with pebbles.

'What are the pebbles for?' asked Grandfather.

'For privacy,' said Rakesh.

He looked at the tree every morning but it did not seem to be growing very fast. So he stopped looking at it—except quickly, out of the corner of his eye. And, after a week or two, when he allowed himself to look at it properly, he found that it had grown—at least an inch!

That year the monsoon rains came early and Rakesh plodded to and from school in raincoat and gum boots. Ferns sprang from the trunks of trees, strange looking lilies came up in the long grass, and even when it wasn't raining the trees dripped and mist came curling up the valley. The cherry tree grew quickly in this season.

It was about two feet high when a goat entered the garden and ate all the leaves. Only the main stem and two thin branches remained.

'Never mind,' said Grandfather, seeing that Rakesh was upset. 'It will grow again, cherry trees are tough.'

Towards the end of the rainy season new leaves appeared on the tree. Then a woman cutting grass scrambled down the hillside, her scythe swishing through the heavy monsoon foliage. She did not try to avoid the tree: one sweep, and the cherry tree was cut in two.

When Grandfather saw what had happened, he went after the woman and scolded her; but the damage could not be repaired.

'Maybe it will die now,' said Rakesh.

'Maybe,' said Grandfather.

But the cherry tree had no intention of dying.

By the time summer came round again, it had sent out several new shoots with tender green leaves. Rakesh had grown taller too. He was eight now, a sturdy boy with curly black hair and deep black eyes. Blackberry eyes, Grandfather called them.

That monsoon Rakesh went home to his village, to help his father and mother with the planting and ploughing and sowing. He was thinner but stronger when he came back to Grandfather's house at the end of the rains, to find that the cherry tree had grown another foot. It was now up to his chest.

Even when there was rain, Rakesh would sometimes water the tree. He wanted it to know that he was there.

One day he found a bright green praying-mantis perched on a branch, peering at him with bulging eyes. Rakesh let it remain there. It was the cherry tree's first visitor.

The next visitor was a hairy caterpillar, who started making a meal of the leaves. Rakesh removed it quickly and dropped it on a heap of dry leaves.

'They're pretty leaves,' said Rakesh. 'And they are always ready to dance. If there's a breeze.'

After Grandfather had come indoors, Rakesh went into the garden and lay down on the grass beneath the tree. He gazed up through the leaves at the great blue sky; and turning on his side, he could see the mountain striding away into the clouds. He was still lying beneath the tree when the evening shadows crept across the garden. Grandfather came back and sat down beside Rakesh, and they waited in silence until the stars came out and the nightjar began to call. In the forest below, the crickets and cicadas began tuning up; and suddenly the tree was full of the sound of insects.

'There are so many trees in the forest,' said Rakesh. 'What's so special about this tree? Why do we like it so much?'

'We planted it ourselves,' said Grandfather. 'That's why it's special.'

'Just one small seed,' said Rakesh, and he touched the smooth bark of the tree that had grown. He ran his hand along the trunk of the tree and put his finger to the tip of a leaf. 'I wonder,' he whispered, 'is this what it feels to be God?

My Father's Trees In Dehra

&

OUR TREES STILL GROW in Dehra. This is one part of the world
where trees are a match for man. An old pipal may be cut
down to make way for a new building; two pipal trees will
sprout from the walls of the building. In Dehra the air is moist,
the soil hospitable to seeds and probing roots. The valley of
Dehra Dun lies between the first range of the Himalayas and
the smaller but older Siwalik range. Dehra is an old town, but
it was not in the reign of Rajput princes or Mughal kings that
it really grew and flourished; it acquired a certain size and
importance with the coming of British and Anglo-Indian settlers.
The English have an affinity with trees, and in the rolling hills
of Dehra they discovered a retreat which, in spite of snakes and
mosquitoes, reminded them, just a little bit, of England's green
and pleasant land.

The mountains to the north are austere and inhospitable;
the plains to the south are flat, dry and dusty. But Dehra is
green. I look out of the train window at daybreak to see the sal
and shisham trees sweep by majestically, while trailing vines
and great clumps of bamboo give the forest a darkness and
density which add to its mystery. There are still a few tigers
in these forests; only a few, and perhaps they will survive, to
stalk the spotted deer and drink at forest pools.

I grew up in Dehra. My grandfather built a bungalow on
the outskirts of the town at the turn of the century. The house
was sold a few years after independence. No one knows me
now in Dehra, for it is over twenty years since I left the place,
and my boyhood friends are scattered and lost. And although

the India of Kim is no more, and the Grand Trunk Road is now a procession of trucks instead of a slow-moving caravan of horses and camels, India is still a country in which people are easily lost and quickly forgotten.

From the station I can take either a taxi or a snappy little scooter-rickshaw (Dehra had neither before 1950), but, because I am on an unashamedly sentimental pilgrimage, I take a tonga, drawn by a lean, listless pony, and driven by a tubercular old Muslim in a shabby green waistcoat. Only two or three tongas stand outside the station. There were always twenty or thirty here in the nineteen-forties when I came home from boarding-school to be met at the station by my grandfather; but the days of the tonga are nearly over, and in many ways this is a good thing, because most tonga ponies are overworked and underfed. Its wheels squeaking from lack of oil and its seat slipping out from under me, the tonga drags me through the bazaars of Dehra. A couple of miles at this slow, funereal pace makes me impatient to use my own legs, and I dismiss the tonga when we get to the small Dilaram Bazaar.

It is a good place from which to start walking.

The Dilaram Bazaar has not changed very much. The shops are run by a new generation of bakers, barbers and banias, but professions have not changed. The cobblers belong to the lower castes, the bakers are Muslims, the tailors are Sikhs. Boys still fly kites from the flat rooftops, and women wash clothes on the canal steps. The canal comes down from Rajpur and goes underground here, to emerge about a mile away.

I have to walk only a furlong to reach my grandfather's house. The road is lined with eucalyptus, jacaranda and laburnum trees. In the compounds there are small groves of mangoes, lichis and papayas. The poinsettia thrusts its scarlet leaves over garden walls. Every veranda has its bougainvillaea creeper, every garden its bed of marigolds. Potted palms, those symbols of Victorian snobbery, are popular with Indian housewives. There are a few houses, but most of the bungalows were built by 'old India hands' on their retirement from the army, the police or the railways. Most of the present owners are Indian businessmen or government officials.

I am standing outside my grandfather's house. The wall has been raised, and the wicket-gate has disappeared; I cannot get a clear view of the house and garden. The name-plate identifies the owner as Major General Saigal; the house has had more than one owner since my grandparents sold it in 1949.

On the other side of the road there is an orchard of lichi trees. This is not the season for fruit, and there is no one looking after the garden. By taking a little path that goes through the orchard, I reach higher ground and gain a better view of our old house.

Grandfather built the house with granite rocks taken from the foothills. It shows no sign of age. The lawn has disappeared; but the big jackfruit tree, giving shade to the side veranda, is still there. In this tree I spent my afternoons, absorbed in my Magnets, Champions and Hotspurs, while sticky mango juice trickled down my chin. (One could not eat the jackfruit unless it was cooked into a vegetable curry.) There was a hole in the bole of the tree in which I kept my pocket-knife, top, catapult and any badges or buttons that could be saved from my father's RAF tunics when he came home on leave. There was also an Iron Cross, a relic of the First World War, given to me by my grandfather. I have managed to keep the Iron Cross; but what did I do with my top and catapult? Memory fails me. Possibly they are still in the hole in the jackfruit tree; I must have forgotten to collect them when we went away after my father's death. I am seized by a whimsical urge to walk in at the gate, climb into the branches of the jackfruit tree, and recover my lost possessions. What would the present owner, the Major General (retired), have to say if I politely asked permission to look for a catapult left behind more than twenty years ago?

An old man is coming down the path through the lichi trees. He is not a Major General but a poor street vendor. He carries a small tin trunk on his head, and walks very slowly. When he sees me he stops and asks me if I will buy something. I can think of nothing I need, but the old man looks so tired, so very old, that I am afraid he will collapse if he moves any further along the path without resting. So I ask him to show me his wares. He cannot get the box off his head by himself, but together we manage to set it down in the shade, and the old man insists on spreading its entire contents on the grass; bangles, combs, shoelaces, safety-ins, cheap stationery, buttons, pomades, elastic and scores of other household necessities.

When I refuse buttons because there is no one to sew them on for me, he piles me with safety-pins. I say no; but as he moves from one article to another, his querulous, persuasive voice slowly wears down my resistance, and I end up by buying envelopes, a letter pad (pink roses on bright blue paper), a one-rupee fountain pen guaranteed to leak and several yards of elastic. I have no idea what I will do with the elastic, but the old man convinces me that I cannot live without it.

Exhausted by the effort of selling me a lot of things I obviously do not want, he closes his eyes and leans back against the trunk of a lichi tree. For a moment I feel rather nervous. Is he going to die sitting here beside me? He sinks to his haunches and puts his chin on his hands. He only wants to talk.

'I am very tired, *hazoor*,' he says. 'Please do not mind if I sit here for a while.'

'Rest for as long as you like,' I say. 'That's a heavy load you've been carrying.'

He comes to life at the chance of a conversation and says, 'When I was a young man, it was nothing. I could carry my box up from Rajpur to Mussoorie by the bridle-path—seven steep miles! But now I find it difficult to cover the distance from the station to the Dilaram Bazaar.'

'Naturally. You are quite old.'

'I am seventy, sahib.'

'You look very fit for your age.' I say this to please him; he looks frail and brittle. 'Isn't there someone to help you?' I ask.

'I had a servant boy last month, but he stole my earnings and ran off to Delhi. I wish my son was alive—he would not have permitted me to work like a mule for a living—but he was killed in the riots in forty-seven.'

'Have you no other relatives?'

'I have outlived them all. That is the curse of a healthy life. Your friends, your loved ones, all go before you, and at the end you are left alone. But I must go too, before long. The road to the bazaar seems to grow longer every day. The stones are harder. The sun is hotter in the summer, and the wind much colder in the winter. Even some of the trees that were there in my youth have grown old and have died. I have outlived the trees.'

He has outlived the trees. He is like an old tree himself, gnarled and twisted. I have the feeling that if he falls asleep in the orchard, he will strike root here, sending out crooked branches. I can imagine a small bent tree wearing a black waist-coat; a living scarecrow.

He closes his eyes again, but goes on talking.

'The English memsahibs would buy great quantities of elastic. Today it is ribbons and bangles for the girls, and combs for the boys. But I do not make much money. Not because I cannot walk very far. How many houses do I reach in a day? Ten, fifteen. But twenty years ago I could visit more than fifty houses. *That* makes a difference.'

'Have you always been here?'

'Most of my life, *hazoor*. I was here before they built the motor road to Mussoorie. I was here when the sahibs had their own carriages and ponies and the memsahibs their own rickshaws. I was here before there were any cinemas. I was here when the Prince of Wales came to Dehra Dun . . . . Oh, I have been here a long time, *hazoor*. I was here when that house was built,' he says pointing with his chin towards my grandfather's house. 'Fifty, sixty years ago it must have been. I cannot remember exactly. What is ten years when you have lived seventy? But it was a tall, red-bearded sahib who built that house. He kept many creatures as pets. A *kachwa* (turtle) was one of them. And there was a python, which crawled into my box one day and gave me a terrible fright. The sahib used to keep it hanging from his shoulders, like a garland. His wife, the *burra-mem*, always bought a lot from me—lots of elastic. And there were sons, one a teacher, another in the Air Force, and there were always children in the house. Beautiful children. But they went away many years ago. Everyone has gone away.'

I do not tell him that I am one of the 'beautiful children'. I doubt if he will believe me. His memories are of another age, another place, and for him there are no strong bridges into the present.

'But others have come,' I say.

'True, and that is as it should be. That is not my complaint. My complaint—should God be listening—is that I have been left behind.'

He gets slowly to his feet and stands over his shabby tin

box, gazing down at it with a mixture of disdain and affection. I help him to lift and balance it o1n the flattened cloth on his head. He does not have the energy to turn and make a salutation of any kind; but, setting his sights on the distant hills, he walks down the path with steps that are shaky and slow but still wonderfully straight.

I wonder how much longer he will live. Perhaps a year or two, perhaps a week, perhaps an hour. It will be an end of living, but it will not be death. He is too old for death; he can only sleep; he can only fall gently, like an old, crumpled brown leaf.

I leave the orchard. The bend in the road hides my grandfather's house. I reach the canal again. It emerges from under a small culvert, where ferns and maidenhair grow in the shade. The water, coming from a stream in the foothills, rushes along with a familiar sound; it does not lose its momentum until the canal has left the gently sloping streets of the town.

There are new buildings on this road, but the small police station is housed in the same old limewashed bungalow. A couple of off-duty policemen, partly uniformed but with their pyjamas on, stroll hand in hand on the grass verge. Holding hands (with persons of the same sex of course) is common practice in northern India, and denotes no special relationship.

I cannot forget this little police station. Nothing very exciting ever happened in its vicinity until, in 1947, communal riots broke out in Dehra. Then, bodies were regularly fished out of the canal and dumped on a growing pile in the station compound. I was only a boy, but when I looked over the wall at that pile of corpses, there was no one who paid any attention to me. They were too busy to send me away. At the same time they knew that I was perfectly safe; while Hindus and Muslims were at each other's throats, a white boy could walk the streets in safety. No one was any longer interested in the Europeans.

The people of Dehra are not violent by nature, and the town has no history of communal discord. But when refugees from the partitioned Punjab poured into Dehra in their thousands, the atmosphere became charged with tension. These refugees, many of them Sikhs, had lost their homes and livelihoods; many had seen their loved ones butchered. They were in a fierce and vengeful frame of mind. The calm, sleepy atmosphere of Dehra was shattered during two months of looting and murder. Those Muslims who could get away, fled. The poorer members of the community remained in a refugee camp until the holocaust was over; then they returned to their former occupations, frightened and deeply mistrustful. The old boxman was one of them.

I cross the canal and take the road that will lead me to the river-bed. This was one of my father's favourite walks. He, too, was a walking man. Often, when he was home on leave, he would say, 'Ruskin, let's go for a walk,' and we would slip off together and walk down to the river-bed or into the sugar-cane fields or across the railway lines and into the jungle.

On one of these walks (this was before Independence), I remember him saying, 'After the war is over, we'll be going to England. Would you like that?'

'I don't know,' I said. 'Can't we stay in India?'

'It won't be ours any more.'

'Has it always been ours?' I asked.

'For a long time,' he said, 'over two hundred years. But we have to give it back now.'

'Give it back to whom?' I asked. I was only nine.

'To the Indians,' said my father.

The only Indians I had known till then were my ayah and the cook and the gardener and their children, and I could not imagine them wanting to be rid of us. The only other Indian who came to the house was Dr Ghose, and it was frequently said of him that he was more English than the English. I could understand my father better when he said, 'After the war, there'll be a job for me in England. There'll be nothing for me here.'

The war had at first been a distant event; but somehow it kept coming closer. My aunt, who lived in London with her two children, was killed with them during an air-raid; then my father's younger brother died of dysentery on the long walk out from Burma. Both these tragic events depressed my father. Never in good health (he had been prone to attacks of malaria), he looked more worn and wasted every time he came home. His personal life was far from being happy, as he and my mother had separated, she to marry again. I think he looked forward a great deal to the days he spent with me; far more than I could have realized at the time. I was someone to come back to; someone for whom things could be planned; someone who could learn from him.

Dehra suited him. He was always happy when he was among trees, and this happiness communicated itself to me. I felt like drawing close to him. I remember sitting beside him on the veranda steps when I noticed the tendril of a creeping vine that was trailing near my feet. As we sat there, doing nothing in particular—in the best gardens, time has no meaning—I found that the tendril was moving almost imperceptibly away from me and towards my father. Twenty minutes later it had crossed the veranda steps and was touching his feet. This, in India, is the sweetest of salutations.

There is probably a scientific explanation for the plant's behaviour—something to do with the light and warmth on the veranda steps—but I like to think that its movements were motivated simply by an affection for my father. Sometimes, when I sat alone beneath a tree, I felt a little lonely or lost. As soon as my father rejoined me, the atmosphere lightened, the tree itself became more friendly.

Most of the fruit trees round the house were planted by Father; but he was not content with planting trees in the garden. On rainy days we would walk beyond the river-bed, armed with cuttings and saplings, and then we would amble through the jungle, planting flowering shrubs between the sal and shisham trees.

'But no one ever comes here,' I protested the first time. 'Who is going to see them?'

'Some day,' he said, '*someone* may come this way . . . . If people keep cutting trees, instead of planting them, there'll soon be no forests left at all, and the world will be just one vast desert.'

The prospect of a world without trees became a sort of nightmare for me (and one reason why I shall never want to live on a treeless moon), and I assisted my father in his tree-planting with great enthusiasm.

'One day the trees will move again,' he said. 'They've been standing still for thousands of years. There was a time when they could walk about like people, but someone cast a spell on them and rooted them to one place. But they're always trying to move—see how they reach out with their arms!'

We found an island, a small rocky island in the middle of a dry river-bed. It was one of those river-beds, so common in the foot-hills, which are completely dry in the summer but flooded during the monsoon rains. The rains had just begun, and the stream could still be crossed on foot, when we set out with a number of tamarind, laburnum and coral-tree saplings and cuttings. We spent the day planting them on the island, then ate our lunch there, in the shelter of a wild plum.

My father went away soon after that tree-planting. Three months later, in Calcutta, he died.

I was sent to boarding-school. My grandparents sold the house and left Dehra. After school, I went to England. The years passed, my grandparents died, and when I returned to India I was the only member of the family in the country.

And now I am in Dehra again, on the road to the river-bed.

The houses with their trim gardens are soon behind me, and I am walking through fields of flowering mustard, which make a carpet of yellow blossom stretching away towards the jungle and the foothills.

The river-bed is dry at this time of the year. A herd of skinny cattle graze on the short brown grass at the edge of the jungle. The sal trees have been thinned out. Could our trees have survived? Will our island be there, or has some flash-flood during a heavy monsoon washed it away completely?

As I look across the dry water-course, my eye is caught by the spectacular red plumes of the coral blossom. In contrast with the dry, rocky river-bed, the little island is a green oasis. I walk across to the trees and notice that a number of parrots have come to live in them. A koel challenges me with a rising *who-are-you, who-are-you* . . . .

But the trees seem to know me. They whisper among themselves and beckon me nearer. And looking around, I find that other trees and wild plants and grasses have sprung up under the protection of the trees we planted.

They have multiplied. They are moving. In this small forgotten corner of the world, my father's dreams are coming true, and the trees are moving again.

PANTHER'S MOON

৯৯

I

IN THE ENTIRE VILLAGE, he was the first to get up. Even the dog, a big hill mastiff called Sheroo, was asleep in a corner of the dark room, curled up near the cold embers of the previous night's fire. Bisnu's tousled head emerged from his blanket. He rubbed the sleep from his eyes and sat up on his haunches. Then, gathering his wits, he crawled in the direction of the loud ticking that came from the battered little clock which occupied the second most honoured place in a niche in the wall. The most honoured place belonged to a picture of Ganesh, the god of learning, who had an elephant's head and a fat boy's body.

Bringing his face close to the clock, Bisnu could just make out the hands. It was five o'clock. He had half an hour in which to get ready and leave.

He got up, in vest and underpants, and moved quietly towards the door. The soft tread of his bare feet woke Sheroo, and the big black dog rose silently and padded behind the boy. The door opened and closed, and then the boy and the dog were outside in the early dawn. The month was June, and the nights were warm, even in the Himalayan valleys; but there was fresh dew on the grass. Bisnu felt the dew beneath his feet. He took a deep breath and began walking down to the stream.

The sound of the stream filled the small valley. At that early hour of the morning, it was the only sound; but Bisnu was hardly conscious of it. It was a sound he lived with and took for granted. It was only when he has crossed the hill, on his way to the town—and the sound of the stream grew distant—that he really began to notice it. And it was only when the stream was too far away to be heard that he really missed its sound.

He slipped out of his underclothes, gazed for a few moments at the goose-pimples rising on his flesh, and then dashed into the shallow stream. As he went further in, the cold mountain water reached his loins and navel, and he gasped with shock and pleasure. He drifted slowly with the current, swam across to a small inlet which formed a fairly deep pool, and plunged beneath the water. Sheroo hated cold water at this early hour. Had the sun been up, he would not have hesitated to join Bisnu. Now he contented himself with sitting on a smooth rock and gazing placidly at the slim brown boy splashing about in the clear water, in the widening light of dawn.

Bisnu did not stay long in the water. There wasn't time. When he returned to the house, he found his mother up, making tea and chapattis. His sister, Puja, was still asleep. She was a little older than Bisnu, a pretty girl with large black eyes, good teeth and strong arms and legs. During the day, she helped her mother in the house and in the fields. She did not go to the school with Bisnu. But when he came home in the evenings, he would try teaching her some of the things he had learnt. Their father was dead. Bisnu, at twelve, considered himself the head of the family.

He ate two chapattis, after spreading butter-oil on them. He drank a glass of hot sweet tea. His mother gave two thick chapattis to Sheroo, and the dog wolfed them down in a few minutes. Then she wrapped two chapattis and a gourdcurry in some big green leaves, and handed these to Bisnu. This was his lunch packet. His mother and Puja would take their meal afterwards.

When Bisnu was dressed, he stood with folded hands before the picture of Ganesh. Ganesh is the god who blesses all beginnings. The author who begins to write a new book, the banker who opens a new ledger, the traveller who starts on a journey, all invoke the kindly help of Ganesh. And as Bisnu made a journey every day, he never left without the goodwill of the elephant-headed god.

How, one might ask, did Ganesh get his elephant's head? When born, he was a beautiful child. Parvati, his mother, was so proud of him that she went about showing him to everyone. Unfortunately she made the mistake of showing the child to that envious planet, Saturn, who promptly burnt off poor Ganesh's head. Parvati in despair went to Brahma, the Creator, for a new head for her son. He had no head to give her but advised her to search for some man or animal caught in a sinful or wrong act. Parvati wandered about until she came upon an elephant sleeping with its head the wrong way, that is, to the south. She promptly removed the elephant's head and planted it on Ganesh's shoulders, where it took root.

Bisnu knew this story. He had heard it from his mother.

Wearing a white shirt and black shorts, and a pair of worn white keds, he was ready for his long walk to school, five miles up the mountain.

His sister woke up just as he was about to leave. She pushed the hair away from her face and gave Bisnu one of her rare smiles.

'I hope you have not forgotten,' she said.

'Forgotten?' said Bisnu, pretending innocence. 'Is there anything I am supposed to remember?'

'Don't tease me. You promised to buy me a pair of bangles, remember? I hope you won't spend the money on sweets, as you did last time.'

'Oh yes, your bangles,' said Bisnu. 'Girls have nothing better to do than waste money on trinkets. Now, don't lose your temper! I'll get them for you. Red and gold are the colours you want?'

'Yes, brother,' said Puja gently, pleased that Bisnu had remembered the colours. 'And for your dinner tonight we'll make you something special. Won't we, Mother?'

'Yes. But hurry up and dress. There is some ploughing to be done today. The rains will soon be here, if the gods are kind.'

'The monsoon will be late this year,' said Bisnu. 'Mr Nautiyal, our teacher, told us so. He said it had nothing to do with the gods.'

'Be off, you are getting late,' said Puja, before Bisnu could begin an argument with his mother. She was diligently winding the old clock. It was quite light in the room. The sun would be up any minute.

Bisnu shouldered his school-bag, kissed his mother, pinched his sister's cheeks, and left the house. He started climbing the steep path up the mountain-side. Sheroo bounded ahead; for he, too, always went with Bisnu to school.

Five miles to school. Every day, except Sunday, Bisnu walked five miles to school; and in the evening, he walked home again. There was no school in his own small village of Manjari, for the village consisted of only five families. The nearest school was at Kemptee, a small township on the bus route through the district of Garhwal. A number of boys walked to school, from distances of two or three miles; their villages were not quite as remote as Manjari. But Bisnu's village lay right at the bottom of the mountain, a drop of over two thousand feet from Kemptee. There was no proper road between the village and the town.

In Kemptee, there was a school, a small mission hospital, a post office and several shops. In Manjari village there were none of these amenities. If you were sick, you stayed at home until you got well; if you were *very* sick, you walked or were carried to the hospital, up the five-mile path. If you wanted to buy something, you went without it; but if you wanted it very badly, you could walk the five miles to Kemptee.

Manjari was known as the Five-mile Village.

Twice a week, if there were any letters, a postman came to the village. Bisnu usually passed the postman on his way to and from school.

There were other boys in Manjari village, but Bisnu was the only one who went to school. His mother would not have fussed if he had stayed at home and worked in the fields. That was what the other boys did; all except lazy Chittru, who preferred fishing in the stream or helping himself to the fruit off other people's trees. But Bisnu went to school. He went because he wanted to. No one could force him to go; and no one could stop him from going. He had set his heart on receiving a good schooling. He wanted to read and write as well as anyone in the big world, the world that seemed to begin only where the mountains ended. He felt cut off from the world in his small valley. He would rather live at the top of a mountain than at the bottom of one. That was why he liked climbing to Kemptee, it took him to the top of the mountain; and from its ridge he could look down on his own valley, to the north, and on the wide endless plains stretching towards the south.

The plainsman looks to the hills for the needs of his spirit but the hill man looks to the plains for a living.

Leaving the village and the fields below him, Bisnu climbed steadily up the bare hillside, now dry and brown. By the time the sun was up, he had entered the welcome shade of an oak and rhododendron forest. Sheroo went bounding ahead, chasing squirrels and barking at langoors.

A colony of langoors lived in the oak forest. They fed on oak leaves, acorns, and other green things, and usually remained in the trees, coming down to the ground only to play or bask in the sun. They were beautiful, supple-limbed animals, with black faces and silver-grey coats and long, sensitive tails. They leapt from tree to tree with great agility. The young ones wrestled on the grass like boys.

A dignified community, the langoors did not have the cheekiness or dishonest habits of the red monkeys of the plains; they did not approach dogs or humans. But they had grown used to Bisnu's comings and goings, and did not fear him. Some of the older ones would watch him quietly, a little puzzled. They did not go near the town, because the Kemptee boys threw stones at them. And anyway, the oak forest gave them all the food they required.

Emerging from the trees, Bisnu crossed a small brook. Here he stopped to drink the fresh clean water of a spring. The brook tumbled down the mountain and joined the river a little below Bisnu's village. Coming from another direction was a second path, and at the junction of the two paths Sarru was waiting for him.

Sarru came from a small village about three miles from Bisnu's and closer to the town. He had two large milk cans slung over his shoulders. Every morning he carried this milk to town, selling one can to the school and the other to Mrs Taylor, the lady doctor at the small mission hospital. He was a little older than Bisnu but not as well-built.

They hailed each other, and Sarru fell into step beside

Bisnu. They often met at this spot, keeping each other company for the remaining two miles to Kemptee.

'There was a panther in our village last night,' said Sarru.

This information interested but did not excite Bisnu. Panthers were common enough in the hills and did not usually present a problem except during the winter months, when their natural prey was scarce. Then, occasionally, a panther would take to haunting the outskirts of a village, seizing a careless dog or a stray goat.

'Did you lose any animals?' asked Bisnu.

'No. It tried to get into the cowshed but the dogs set up an alarm. We drove it off.'

'It must be the same one which came around last winter. We lost a calf and two dogs in our village.'

'Wasn't that the one the shikaris wounded? I hope it hasn't became a cattle-lifter.'

'It could be the same. It has a bullet in its leg. These hunters are the people who cause all the trouble. They think it's easy to shoot a panther. It would be better if they missed altogether, but they usually wound it.'

'And then the panther's too slow to catch the barking-deer, and starts on our own animals.'

'We're lucky it didn't become a man-eater. Do you remember the man-eater six years ago? I was very small then. My father told me all about it. Ten people were killed in our valley alone. What happened to it?'

'I don't know. Some say it poisoned itself when it ate the headman of another village.'

Bisnu laughed. 'No one liked that old villain. He must have been a man-eater himself in some previous existence!' They linked arms and scrambled up the stony path. Sheroo began barking and ran ahead. Someone was coming down the path.

It was Mela Ram, the postman.

II

'Any letters for us?' asked Bisnu and Sarru together.

They never received any letters but that did not stop them from asking. It was one way of finding out who had received letters.

'You're welcome to all of them,' said Mela Ram, 'if you'll carry my bag for me.'

'Not today,' said Sarru. 'We're busy today. Is there a letter from Corporal Ghanshyam for his family?'

'Yes, there is a postcard for his people. He is posted on the Ladakh border now and finds it very cold there.'

Postcards, unlike sealed letters, were considered public property and were read by everyone. The senders knew that too, and so Corporal Ghanshyam Singh was careful to mention that he expected a promotion very soon. He wanted everyone in his village to know it.

Mela Ram, complaining of sore feet, continued on his way, and the boys carried on up the path. It was eight o'clock when they reached Kemptee. Dr Taylor's out-patients were just beginning to trickle in at the hospital gate. The doctor was trying to prop up a rose creeper which had blown down during the night. She liked attending to her plants in the mornings, before starting on her patients. She found this helped her in her work. There was a lot in common between ailing plants and ailing people.

Dr Taylor was fifty, white-haired but fresh in the face and full of vitality. She had been in India for twenty years, and ten of these had been spent working in the hill regions.

She saw Bisnu coming down the road. She knew about the boy and his long walk to school and admired him for his keenness and sense of purpose. She wished there were more like him.

Bisnu greeted her shyly. Sheroo barked and put his paws up on the gate.

'Yes, there's a bone for you,' said Dr Taylor. She often put aside bones for the big black dog, for she knew that Bisnu's people could not afford to give the dog a regular diet of meat—though he did well enough on milk and chapattis.

She threw the bone over the gate and Sheroo caught it before it fell. The school bell began ringing and Bisnu broke into a run. Sheroo loped along behind the boy.

When Bisnu entered the school gate, Sheroo sat down on the grass of the compound. He would remain there until the lunchbreak. He knew of various ways of amusing himself during school hours and had friends among the bazaar dogs.

But just then he didn't want company. He had his bone to get on with.

Mr Nautiyal, Bisnu's teacher, was in a bad mood. He was a keen rose grower and only that morning on getting up and looking out of his bedroom window, had been horrified to see a herd of goats in his garden. He had chased them down the road with a stick but the damage had already been done. His prize roses had all been consumed.

Mr Nautiyal had been so upset that he had gone without his breakfast. He had also cut himself whilst shaving. Thus, his mood had gone from bad to worse. Several times during the day he brought down his ruler on the knuckles of any boy who irritated him. Bisnu was one of his best pupils. But even Bisnu irritated him by asking too many questions about a new sum which Mr Nautiyal didn't feel like explaining.

That was the kind of day it was for Mr Nautiyal. Most schoolteachers know similar days.

'Poor Mr Nautiyal,' thought Bisnu. 'I wonder why he's so upset. It must be because of his pay. He doesn't get much money. But he's a good teacher. I hope he doesn't take another job.'

But after Mr Nautiyal had eaten his lunch, his mood improved (as it always did after a meal), and the rest of the day passed serenely. Armed with a bundle of homework, Bisnu came out from the school compound at four o'clock, and was immediately joined by Sheroo. He proceeded down the road in the company of several of his classfellows. But he did not linger long in the bazaar. There were five miles to walk and he did not like to get home too late. Usually he reached his house just as it was beginning to get dark.

Sarru had gone home long ago and Bisnu had to make the return journey on his own. It was a good opportunity to memorize the words of an English poem he had been asked to learn.

Bisnu had reached the little brook when he remembered the bangles he had promised to buy for his sister.

'Oh, I've forgotten them again,' he said aloud. 'Now I'll catch it—and she's probably made something special for my dinner!'

Sheroo, to whom these words were addressed, paid no

attention but bounded off into the oak forest. Bisnu looked around for the monkeys but they were nowhere to be seen.

'Strange,' he thought, 'I wonder why they have disappeared.'

He was startled by a sudden sharp cry, followed by a fierce yelp. He knew at once that Sheroo was in trouble. The noise came from the bushes down the khud, into which the dog had rushed but a few seconds previously.

Bisnu jumped off the path and ran down the slope towards the bushes. There was no dog and not a sound. He whistled and called but there was no response. Then he saw something lying on the dry grass. He picked it up. It was a portion of a dog's collar, stained with blood. It was Sheroo's collar and Sheroo's blood.

Bisnu did not search further. He knew, without a doubt, that Sheroo had been seized by a panther. No other animal could have attacked so silently and swiftly and carried off a big dog without a struggle. Sheroo was dead—must have been dead within seconds of being caught and flung into the air. Bisnu knew the danger that lay in wait for him if he followed the blood trail through the trees. The panther would attack anyone who interfered with its meal.

With tears starting in his eyes, Bisnu carried on down the path to the village. His fingers still clutched the little bit of bloodstained collar that was all that was left to him of his dog.

III

Bisnu was not a very sentimental boy but he sorrowed for his dog who had been his companion on many a hike into the hills and forests. He did not sleep that night, but turned restlessly from side to side moaning softly. After some time he felt Puja's hand on his head. She began stroking his brow. He took her hand in his own and the clasp of her rough, warm familiar hand gave him a feeling of comfort and security.

Next morning, when he went down to the stream to bathe, he missed the presence of his dog. He did not stay long in the water. It wasn't as much fun when there was no Sheroo to watch him.

When Bisnu's mother gave him his food she told him to be careful and hurry home that evening. A panther, even if it is only a cowardly lifter of sheep or dogs, is not to be trifled with.

And this particular panther had shown some daring by seizing the dog even before it was dark.

Still, there was no question of staying away from school. If Bisnu remained at home every time a panther put in an appearance, he might just as well stop going to school altogether.

He set off even earlier than usual and reached the meeting of the paths long before Sarru. He did not wait for his friend because he did not feel like talking about the loss of his dog. It was not the day for the postman and so Bisnu reached Kemptee without meeting anyone on the way. He tried creeping past the hospital gate unnoticed but Dr Taylor saw him and the first thing she said was: 'Where's Sheroo? I've got something for him.'

When Dr Taylor saw the boy's face, she knew at once that something was wrong.

'What is it, Bisnu?' she asked. She looked quickly up and down the road. 'Is it Sheroo?'

He nodded gravely.

'A panther took him,' he said.

'In the village?'

'No, while we were walking home through the forest. I did not see anything—but I heard.'

Dr Taylor knew that there was nothing she could say that would console him and she tried to conceal the bone which she had brought out for the dog, but Bisnu noticed her hiding it behind her back and the tears welled up in his eyes. He turned away and began running down the road.

His schoolfellows noticed Sheroo's absence and questioned Bisnu. He had to tell them everything. They were full of sympathy but they were also quite thrilled at what had happened and kept pestering Bisnu for all the details. There was a lot of noise in the classroom and Mr Nautiyal had to call for order. When he learnt what had happened, he patted Bisnu on the head and told him that he need not attend school for the rest of the day. But Bisnu did not want to go home. After school, he got into a fight with one of the boys and that helped him forget.

IV

The panther that plunged the village into an atmosphere of gloom and terror may not have been the same panther that took Sheroo. There was no way of knowing, and it would have made no difference, because the panther that came by night and struck at the people of Manjari was that most feared of wild creatures, a man-eater.

Nine-year-old Sanjay, son of Kalam Singh, was the first child to be attacked by the panther.

Kalam Singh's house was the last in the village and nearest the stream. Like the other house, it was quite small, just a room above and a stable below, with steps leading up from outside the house. He lived there with his wife, two sons (Sanjay was the youngest) and little daughter Basanti who had just turned three.

Sanjay had brought his father's cows home after grazing them on the hillside in the company of other children. He had also brought home an edible wild plant which his mother cooked into a tasty dish for their evening meal. They had their food at dusk, sitting on the floor of their single room, and soon after settled down for the night. Sanjay curled up in his favourite spot, with his head near the door, where he got a little fresh air. As the nights were warm, the door was usually left a little ajar. Sanjay's mother piled ash on the embers of the fire and the family was soon asleep.

No one heard the stealthy padding of a panther approaching the door, pushing it wider open. But suddenly there were sounds of a frantic struggle and Sanjay's stifled cries were mixed with the grunts of the panther. Kalam Singh leapt to his feet with a shout. The panther had dragged Sanjay out of the door and was pulling him down the steps when Kalam Singh started battering at the animal with a large stone. The rest of the family screamed in terror, rousing the entire village. A number of men came to Kalam Singh's assistance and the panther was driven off. But Sanjay lay unconscious.

Someone brought a lantern and the boy's mother screamed when she saw her small son with his head lying in a pool of blood. It looked as if the side of his head had been eaten off by the panther. But he was still alive and as Kalam Singh plastered ash on the boy's head to stop the bleeding, he found that though the scalp had been torn off one side of the head, the bare bone was smooth and unbroken.

'He won't live through the night,' said a neighbour. 'We'll have to carry him down to the river in the morning.'

The dead were always cremated on the banks of a small river which flowed past Manjari village.

Suddenly the panther, still prowling about the village, called out in rage and frustration and the villagers rushed to their homes in panic and barricaded themselves in for the night.

Sanjay's mother sat by the boy for the rest of the night, weeping and watching. Towards dawn he started to moan and show signs of coming round. At this sign of returning consciousness, Kalam Singh rose determinedly and looked around for his stick.

He told his elder son to remain behind with the mother and daughter as he was going to take Sanjay to Dr Taylor at the hospital.

'See, he is moaning and in pain,' said Kalam Singh. 'That means he has a chance to live if he can be treated at once.'

With a stout stick in his hand, and Sanjay on his back, Kalam Singh set off on the two miles of hard mountain track to the hospital at Kemptee. His son, a blood-stained cloth around his head, was moaning but still unconscious. When at last Kalam Singh climbed up through the last fields below the hospital, he asked for the doctor and stammered out an account of what had happened.

It was a terrible injury, as Dr Taylor discovered. The bone over almost one-third of the head was bare and the scalp was torn all round. As the father told his story, the doctor cleaned and dressed the wound and then gave Sanjay a shot of penicillin to prevent sepsis. Later, Kalam Singh carried the boy home again.

V

After this, the panther went away for some time. But the people of Manjari could not be sure of its whereabouts. They kept to their houses after dark and shut their doors. Bisnu had to stop going to school because there was no one to accompany him and it was dangerous to go alone. This worried him, because his final exam was only a few weeks off and he would be missing important classwork. When he wasn't in the fields, helping with the sowing of rice and maize, he would be sitting in the shade of a chestnut tree, going through his well-thumbed second-hand school books. He had no other reading, except for a copy of the *Ramayana* and a Hindi translation of *Alice in Wonderland*. These were well-preserved, read only in fits and starts, and usually kept locked in his mother's old tin trunk.

Sanjay had nightmares for several nights and woke up screaming. But with the resilience of youth, he quickly recovered. At the end of the week he was able to walk to the hospital, though his father always accompanied him. Even a desperate panther will hesitate to attack a party of two. Sanjay, with his thin little face and huge bandaged head, looked a pathetic figure but he was getting better and the wound looked healthy.

Bisnu often went to see him and the two boys spent long hours together near the stream. Sometimes Chittru would join them and they would try catching fish with a home-made net. They were often successful in taking home one or two mountain trout. Sometimes Bisnu and Chittru wrestled in the shallow water or on the grassy banks of the stream. Chittru was a chubby boy with a broad chest, strong legs and thighs and when he used his weight he got Bisnu under him. But Bisnu was hard and wiry and had very strong wrists and fingers. When he had Chittru in a vice, the bigger boy would cry out and give up the struggle. Sanjay could not join in these games.

He had never been a very strong boy and he needed plenty of rest if his wounds were to heal well.

The panther had not been seen for over a week and the people of Manjari were beginning to hope that it might have moved on over the mountain or further down the valley.

'I think I can start going to school again,' said Bisnu. 'The panther has gone away.'

'Don't be too sure,' said Puja. 'The moon is full these days and perhaps it is only being cautious.'

'Wait a few days,' said their mother. 'It is better to wait. Perhaps you could go the day after tomorrow when Sanjay goes to the hospital with his father. Then you will not be alone.'

And so, two days later, Bisnu went up to Kemptee with Sanjay and Kalam Singh. Sanjay's wound had almost healed over. Little islets of flesh had grown over the bone. Dr Taylor told him that he need come to see her only once a fortnight, instead of every third day.

Bisnu went to his school and was given a warm welcome by his friends and by Mr Nautiyal.

'You'll have to work hard,' said his teacher. 'You have to catch up with the others. If you like, I can give you some extra time after classes.'

'Thank you sir, but it will make me late,' said Bisnu. 'I must get home before it is dark, otherwise my mother will worry. I think the panther has gone but nothing is certain.'

'Well, you mustn't take risks. Do your best, Bisnu. Work hard and you'll soon catch up with your lessons.'

Sanjay and Kalam Singh were waiting for him outside the school. Together they took the path down to Manjari, passing the postman on the way. Mela Ram said he had heard that the panther was in another district and that there was nothing to fear. He was on his rounds again.

Nothing happened on the way. The langoors were back in their favourite part of the forest. Bisnu got home just as the kerosene lamp was being lit. Puja met him at the door with a winsome smile.

'Did you get the bangles?' she asked.

But Bisnu had forgotten again.

VI

There had been a thunderstorm and some rain—a short, sharp shower which gave the villagers hope that the monsoon would arrive on time. It brought out the thunder-lilies—pink, crocus-like flowers which sprang up on the hillsides immediately after a summer shower.

Bisnu, on his way home from school, was caught in the rain. He knew the shower would not last so he took shelter in a small cave and, to pass the time, began doing sums, scratching figures in the damp earth with the end of a stick.

When the rain stopped, he came out from the cave and continued down the path. He wasn't in a hurry. The rain had made everything smell fresh and good. The scent from fallen pine needles rose from wet earth. The leaves of the oak trees had been washed clean and a light breeze turned them about, showing their silver undersides. The birds, refreshed and high-spirited, set up a terrific noise. The worst offenders were the yellow-bottomed bulbuls who squabbled and fought in the blackberry bushes. A barbet, high up in the branches of a deodar, set up its querulous, plaintive call. And a flock of bright green parrots came swooping down the hill to settle in a wild plum tree and feast on the unripe fruit. The langoors, too, had been revived by the rain. They leapt friskily from tree to tree greeting Bisnu with little grunts.

He was almost out of the oak forest when he heard a faint bleating. Presently a little goat came stumbling up the path towards him. The kid was far from home and must have strayed from the rest of the herd. But it was not yet conscious of being lost. It came to Bisnu with a hop, skip and a jump and started nuzzling against his legs like a cat.

'I wonder who you belong to,' mused Bisnu, stroking the little creature. 'You'd better come home with me until someone claims you.'

He didn't have to take the kid in his arms. It was used to humans and followed close at his heels. Now that darkness was coming on, Bisnu walked a little faster.

He had not gone very far when he heard the sawing grunt of a panther.

The sound came from the hill to the right and Bisnu judged the distance to be anything from a hundred to two hundred yards. He hesitated on the path, wondering what to do. Then he picked the kid up in his arms and hurried on in the direction of home and safety.

The panther called again, much closer now. If it was an ordinary panther, it would go away on finding that the kid was with Bisnu. If it was the man-eater it would not hesitate to attack the boy, for no man-eater fears a human. There was no time to lose and there did not seem much point in running. Bisnu looked up and down the hillside. The forest was far behind him and there were only a few trees in his vicinity. He chose a spruce.

The branches of the Himalayan spruce are very brittle and snap easily beneath a heavy weight. They were strong enough to support Bisnu's light frame. It was unlikely they would take the weight of a full-grown panther. At least that was what Bisnu hoped.

Holding the kid with one arm, Bisnu gripped a low branch

and swung himself up into the tree. He was a good climber. Slowly but confidently he climbed half-way up the tree, until he was about twelve feet above the ground. He couldn't go any higher without risking a fall.

He had barely settled himself in the crook of a branch when the panther came into the open, running into the clearing at a brisk trot. This was no stealthy approach, no wary stalking of its prey. It was the man-eater, all right. Bisnu felt a cold shiver run down his spine. He felt a little sick.

The panther stood in the clearing with a slight thrusting forward of the head. This gave it the appearance of gazing intently and rather short-sightedly at some invisible object in the clearing. But there is nothing short-sighted about a panther's vision. Its sight and hearing are acute.

Bisnu remained motionless in the tree and sent up a prayer to all the gods he could think of. But the kid began bleating. The panther looked up and gave its deep-throated, rasping grunt—a fearsome sound, calculated to strike terror in any tree-borne animal. Many a monkey, petrified by a panther's roar, has fallen from its perch to make a meal for Mr Spots. The man-eater was trying the same technique on Bisnu. But though the boy was trembling with fright, he clung firmly to the base of the spruce tree.

The panther did not make any attempt to leap into the tree. Perhaps it knew instinctively that this was not the type of tree that it could climb. Instead it described a semi-circle round the tree, keeping its face turned towards Bisnu. Then it disappeared into the bushes.

The man-eater was cunning. It hoped to put the boy off his guard, perhaps entice him down from the tree. For, a few seconds later, with a half-humorous growl, it rushed back into the clearing and then stopped, staring up at the boy in some surprise. The panther was getting frustrated. It snarled and putting its forefeet up against the tree-trunk began scratching at the bark in the manner of an ordinary domestic cat. The tree shook at each thud of the beast's paw.

Bisnu began shouting for help.

The moon had not yet come up. Down in Manjari village, Bisnu's mother and sister stood in their lighted doorway, gazing anxiously up the pathway. Every now and then Puja would turn to take a look at the small clock.

Sanjay's father appeared in a field below. He had a kerosene lantern in his hand.

'Sister, isn't your boy home as yet?' he asked.

'No, he hasn't arrived. We are very worried. He should have been home an hour ago. Do you think the panther will be about tonight? There's going to be a moon.'

'True, but it will be dark for another hour. I will fetch the other menfolk and we will go up the mountain for your boy. There may have been a landslide during the rain. Perhaps the path has been washed away.'

'Thank you, brother. But arm yourselves, just in case the panther is about.'

'I will take my spear,' said Kalam Singh. 'I have sworn to spear that devil when I find him. There is some evil spirit dwelling in the beast and it must be destroyed!'

'I am coming with you,' said Puja.

'No, you cannot go,' said her mother. 'It's bad enough that Bisnu is in danger. You stay at home with me. This is work for men.'

'I shall be safe with them,' insisted Puja. 'I am going, Mother!' And she jumped down the embankment into the field and followed Sanjay's father through the village.

Ten minutes later, two men armed with axes had joined Kalam Singh in the courtyard of his house and the small party moved silently and swiftly up the mountain path. Puja walked in the middle of the group, holding the lantern. As soon as the village lights were hidden by a shoulder of the hill, the men began to shout—both to frighten the panther, if it was about, and to give themselves courage.

Bisnu's mother closed the front door and turned to the image of Ganesh, the god for comfort and help.

Bisnu's calls were carried on the wind and Puja and the men heard him while they were still half a mile away. Their own shouts increased in volume and, hearing their voices, Bisnu felt strength return to his shaking limbs. Emboldened by the approach of his own people, he began shouting insults at the snarling panther, then throwing twigs and small branches at the enraged animal. The kid added its bleats to the boy's shouts, the birds took up the chorus. The langoors squealed and grunted, the searchers shouted themselves hoarse, and the panther howled with rage. The forest had never before been so noisy.

As the search party drew near, they could hear the panther's savage snarls, and hurried, fearing that perhaps Bisnu had been seized. Puja began to run.

'Don't rush ahead, girl,' said Kalam Singh. 'Stay between us.'

The panther, now aware of the approaching humans, stood still in the middle of the clearing, head thrust forward in a familiar stance. There seemed too many men for one panther. When the animal saw the light of the lantern dancing between the trees, it turned, snarled defiance and hate, and without another look at the boy in the tree, disappeared into the bushes. It was not yet ready for a showdown.

VII

Nobody turned up to claim the little goat so Bisnu kept it. A goat was a poor substitute for a dog but, like Mary's lamb, it followed Bisnu wherever he went and the boy couldn't help being touched by its devotion. He took it down to the stream where it would skip about in the shallows and nibble the sweet grass that grew on the banks.

As for the panther, frustrated in its attempt on Bisnu's life, it did not wait long before attacking another human.

It was Chittru who came running down the path one afternoon, bubbling excitedly about the panther and the postman.

Chittru, deeming it safe to gather ripe bilberries in the daytime, had walked about half a mile up the path from the village when he had stumbled across Mela Ram's mail-bag lying on the ground. Of the postman himself there was no sign. But a trail of blood led through the bushes.

Once again, a party of men headed by Kalam Singh and accompanied by Bisnu and Chittru, went out to look for the postman. But though they found Mela Ram's bloodstained clothes, they could not find his body. The panther had made no mistake this time.

It was to be several weeks before Manjari had a new postman.

A few days after Mela Ram's disappearance, an old woman was sleeping with her head near the open door of her house. She had been advised to sleep inside with the door closed but the nights were hot and anyway the old woman was a little deaf and in the middle of the night, an hour before moonrise, the panther seized her by the throat. Her strangled cry woke her grown-up son and all the men in the village woke up at his shouts and came running.

The panther dragged the old woman out of the house and down the steps but left her when the men approached with their axes and spears and made off into the bushes. The old woman was still alive and the men made a rough stretcher of bamboo and vines and started carrying her up the path. But hey had not gone far when she began to cough and because of her terrible throat wounds her lungs collapsed and she died.

It was the 'dark of the month'—the week of the new moon when nights are darkest.

Bisnu, closing the front door and lighting the kerosene lantern, said, 'I wonder where that panther is tonight!'

The panther was busy in another village: Sarru's village.

A woman and her daughter had been out in the evening bedding the cattle down in the stable. The girl had gone into the house and the woman was following. As she bent down to go in at the low door, the panther sprang from the bushes. Fortunately, one of its paws hit the door-post and broke the force of the attack, or the woman would have been killed. When she cried out, the men came round shouting and the panther slunk off. The woman had deep scratches on her back and was badly shocked.

The next day a small party of villagers presented themselves in front of the magistrate's office at Kemptee and demanded that something be done about the panther. But the magistrate was away on tour and there was no one else in Kemptee who had gun. Mr Nautiyal met the villagers and promised to write to a well-known shikari, but said that it would be at least a fortnight before the shikari would be able to come.

Bisnu was fretting because he could not go to school. Most boys would be only too happy to miss school but when you are living in a remote village in the mountains and having an education is the only way of seeing the world, you look forward to going to school, even if it is five miles from home. Bisnu's exams were only two weeks off and he didn't want to remain in the same class while the others were promoted. Besides, he knew he could pass even though he had missed a number of lessons. But he had to sit for the exams. He couldn't miss them.

'Cheer up, Bhaiya,' said Puja, as they sat drinking glasses of hot tea after their evening meal. 'The panther may go away once the rains break.'

'Even the rains are late this year,' said Bisnu. 'It's so hot and dry. Can't we open the door?'

'And be dragged down the steps by the panther?' said his mother. 'It isn't safe to have the window open, let alone the door.' And she went to the small window—through which a cat would have found difficulty in passing—and bolted it firmly.

With a sigh of resignation Bisnu threw off all his clothes except his underwear and stretched himself out on the earthen floor.

'We will be rid of the beast soon,' said his mother. 'I know it in my heart. Our prayers will be heard and you shall go to school and pass your exams.'

To cheer up her children, she told them a humorous story which had been handed down to her by her grandmother. It was all about a tiger, a panther and a bear, the three of whom were made to feel very foolish by a thief hiding in the hollow trunk of a banyan tree. Bisnu was sleepy and did not listen very attentively. He dropped off to sleep before the story was finished.

When he woke it was dark and his mother and sister were asleep on the cot. He wondered what it was that had woken him. He could hear his sister's easy breathing and the steady ticking of the clock. Far away an owl hooted—an unlucky sign, his mother would have said; but she was asleep and Bisnu was not superstitious.

And then he heard something scratching at the door and the hair on his head felt tight and prickly. It was like a cat scratching, only louder. The door creaked a little whenever it felt the impact of the paw—a heavy paw, as Bisnu could tell from the dull sound it made.

'It's the panther,' he muttered under his breath, sitting up on the hard floor.

The door, he felt, was strong enough to resist the panther's weight. And if he set up an alarm, he could rouse the village. But the middle of the night was no time for the bravest of men to tackle a panther.

In a corner of the room stood a long bamboo stick with a sharp knife tied to one end which Bisnu sometimes used for spearing fish. Crawling on all fours across the room, he grasped the home-made spear and then, scrambling on to a cupboard, he drew level with the skylight window. He could get his head and shoulders through the window.

'What are you doing up there?' said Puja, who had woken up at the sound of Bisnu shuffling about the room.

'Be quiet,' said Bisnu. 'You'll wake Mother.'

Their mother was awake by now. 'Come down from there, Bisnu. I can hear a noise outside.'

'Don't worry,' said Bisnu, who found himself looking down on the wriggling animal which was trying to get its paw in under the door. With his mother and Puja awake, there was no time to lose. He had got the spear through the window, and though he could not manoeuvre it so as to strike the panther's head, he brought the sharp end down with considerable force on the animal's rump.

With a roar of pain and rage the man-eater leapt down from the steps and disappeared into the darkness. It did not pause to see what had struck it. Certain that no human could have come upon it in that fashion, it ran fearfully to its lair, howling until the pain subsided.

VIII

A panther is an enigma. There are occasions when he proves himself to be the most cunning animal under the sun and yet the very next day he will walk into an obvious trap that no self-respecting jackal would ever go near. One day a panther will prove himself to be a complete coward and run like a hare from a couple of dogs and the very next he will dash in amongst half a dozen men sitting round a camp fire and inflict terrible injuries on them.

It is not often that a panther is taken by surprise, as his power of sight and hearing are very acute. He is a master at the art of camouflage and his spotted coat is admirably suited for the purpose. He does not need heavy jungle to hide in. A couple of bushes and the light and shade from surrounding trees are enough to make him almost invisible.

Because the Manjari panther had been fooled by Bisnu, it did not mean that he was a stupid panther. It simply meant that he had been a little careless. And Bisnu and Puja, growing in confidence since their midnight encounter with the animal, became a little careless themselves.

Puja was hoeing the last field above the house and Bisnu, at the other end of the same field, was chopping up several branches of green oak, prior to leaving the wood to dry in the loft. It was late afternoon and the descending sun glinted in patches on the small river. It was a time of day when only the most desperate and daring of man-eaters would be likely to show itself.

Pausing for a moment to wipe the sweat from his brow, Bisnu glanced up at the hillside and his eye caught sight of a rock on the brown of the hill which seemed unfamiliar to him. Just as he was about to look elsewhere, the round rock began to grow and then alter its shape and Bisnu watching in fascination was at last able to make out the head and forequarters of the panther. It looked enormous from the angle at which he saw it and for a moment he thought it was a tiger. But Bisnu knew instinctively that it was the man-eater.

Slowly the wary beast pulled itself to its feet and began to walk round the side of the great rock. For a second it disappeared and Bisnu wondered if it had gone away. Then it reappeared and the boy was all excitement again. Very slowly and silently the panther walked across the face of the rock until it was in direct line with the corner of the field where Puja was working.

With a thrill of horror Bisnu realized that the panther was stalking his sister. He shook himself free from the spell which had woven itself round him and shouting hoarsely ran forward.

'Run, Puja, run!' he called. 'It's on the hill above you!'

Puja turned to see what Bisnu was shouting about. She saw him gesticulate to the hill behind her, looked up just in time to see the panther crouching for his spring.

With great presence of mind, she leapt down the banking of the field and tumbled into an irrigation ditch.

The springing panther missed its prey, lost its foothold on the slippery shale banking and somersaulted into the ditch a few feet away from Puja. Before the animal could recover from its surprise, Bisnu was dashing down the slope, swinging his axe and shouting 'Maro, maro!' (Kill, kill!).

Two men came running across the field. They, too, were armed with axes. Together with Bisnu they made a half-circle around the snarling animal which turned at bay and plunged at them in order to get away. Puja wriggled along the ditch on her stomach. The men aimed their axes at the panther's head and Bisnu had the satisfaction of getting in a well-aimed blow between the eyes. The animal then charged straight at one of the men, knocked him over, and tried to get at his throat. Just then Sanjay's father arrived with his long spear. He plunged the end of the spear into the panther's neck.

The panther left its victim and ran into the bushes, dragging the spear through the grass and leaving a trail of blood on the ground. The men followed cautiously—all except the man who had been wounded and who lay on the ground while Puja and the other womenfolk rushed up to help him.

The panther had made for the bed of the stream and Bisnu, Sanjay's father, and their companion were able to follow it quite easily. The water was red where the panther had crossed the stream, and the rocks were stained with blood. After they had gone downstream for about a furlong, they found the panther lying still on its side at the edge of the water. It was mortally wounded. but it continued to wave its tail like an angry cat. Then even the tail lay still.

'It is dead,' said Bisnu. 'It will not trouble us again in *this* body.'

'Let us be certain,' said Sanjay's father and he bent down and pulled the panther's tail.

There was no response.

'It is dead,' said Kalam Singh. 'No panther would suffer such an insult were it alive!'

They cut down a long piece of thick bamboo and tied the panther to it by its feet. Then, with their enemy hanging upside down from the bamboo pole, they started back for the village.

'There will be a feast at my house tonight,' said Kalam Singh. 'Everyone in the village must come. And tomorrow we will visit all the villages in the valley and show them the dead panther so that they may move about again without fear.'

'We can sell the skin in Kemptee,' said their companion. 'It will fetch a good price.'

'But the claws we will give to Bisnu,' said Kalam Singh, putting his arm around the boy's shoulders. 'He has done a man's work today. He deserves the claws.'

A panther's or tiger's claws are considered to be lucky charms.

'I will take only three claws,' said Bisnu. 'One each for my mother and sister, and one for myself. You may give the others to Sanjay and Chittru and the smaller children.'

As the sun set, a big fire was lit in the middle of the village of Manjari and the people gathered round it, singing and laughing. Kalam Singh killed his fattest goat and there was meat for everyone.

IX

Bisnu was on his way home. He had just handed in his first paper, arithmetic, which he had found quite easy. Tomorrow it would be algebra and when he got home he would have to practice square roots and cube roots and fractional coefficients.

Mr Nautiyal and the entire class had been happy that he had been able to sit for the exams. He was also a hero to them for his part in killing the panther. The story had spread through the villages with the rapidity of a forest fire, a fire which was now raging in Kemptee town.

When he walked past the hospital, he was whistling cheerfully. Dr Taylor waved to him from the veranda steps.

'How is Sanjay now?' she asked.

'He is well,' said Bisnu.

'And your mother and sister?'

'They are well,' said Bisnu.

'Are you going to get yourself a new dog?'

'I am thinking about it,' said Bisnu. 'At present I have a baby goat—I am teaching it to swim!'

He started down the path to the valley. Dark clouds had gathered and there was a rumble of thunder. A storm was imminent.

'Wait for me!' shouted Sarru, running down the path behind Bisnu, his milk-pails clanging against each other. He fell into step beside Bisnu.

'Well, I hope we don't have any more man-eaters for some time,' he said. 'I've lost a lot of money by not being able to take milk up to Kemptee.'

'We should be safe as long as a shikari doesn't wound another panther. There was an old bullet wound in the man-eater's thigh. That's why it couldn't hunt in the forest. The deer were too fast for it.'

'Is there a new postman yet?'

'He starts tomorrow. A cousin of Mela Ram's.'

When they reached the parting of their ways it had begun to rain a little.

'I must hurry,' said Sarru. 'It's going to get heavier any minute.'

'I feel like getting wet,' said Bisnu. 'This time it's the monsoon, I'm sure.'

Bisnu entered the forest on his own and at the same time the rain came down in heavy opaque sheets. The trees shook in the wind and the langoors chattered with excitement.

It was still pouring when Bisnu emerged from the forest, drenched to the skin. But the rain stopped suddenly, just as the village of Manjari came in view. The sun appeared through a rift in the clouds. The leaves and the grass gave out a sweet, fresh smell.

Bisnu could see his mother and sister in the field transplanting the rice seedlings. The menfolk were driving the yoked oxen through the thin mud of the fields, while the children hung on to the oxen's tails, standing on the plain wooden harrows and with weird cries and shouts sending the animals almost at a gallop along the narrow terraces.

Bisnu felt the urge to be with them, working in the fields. He ran down the path, his feet falling softly on the wet earth.

Puja saw him coming and waved to him. She met him at the edge of the field.

'How did you find your paper today?' she asked.

'Oh, it was easy.' Bisnu slipped his hand into hers and together they walked across the field. Puja felt something smooth and hard against her fingers and before she could see what Bisnu was doing, he had slipped a pair of bangles over her wrist.

'I remembered,' he said with a sense of achievement.

Puja looked at the bangles and burst out: 'But they are blue, Bhai, and I wanted red and gold bangles!' And then, when she saw him looking crestfallen, she hurried on: 'But they are very pretty and you did remember . . . . Actually, they're just as nice as red and gold bangles! Come into the house when you are ready. I have made something special for you.'

'I am coming,' said Bisnu, turning towards the house. 'You don't know how hungry a man gets, walking five miles to reach home!'

THE LEOPARD

෫

I FIRST SAW THE leopard when I was crossing the small stream at the bottom of the hill.

The ravine was so deep that for most of the day it remained in shadow. This encouraged many birds and animals to emerge from cover during the daylight hours. Few people ever passed that way: only milkmen and charcoal-burners from the surrounding villages. As a result, the ravine had become a little haven of wildlife, one of the few natural sanctuaries left near Mussoorie, a hill station in northern India.

Below my cottage was a forest of oak and a maple and Himalayan rhododendron. A narrow path twisted its way down through the trees, over an open ridge where red sorrel grew wild, and then steeply down through a tangle of wild raspberries, creeping vines and slender bamboo. At the bottom of the hill the path led on to a grassy verge, surrounded by wild dog roses. (It is surprising how closely the flora of the lower Himalayas, between 5,000 to 8,000 feet, resembles that of the English countryside.)

The stream ran close by the verge, tumbling over smooth pebbles, over rocks worn yellow with age, on its way to the plains and to the little Song River and finally to the sacred Ganga.

When I first discovered the stream it was early April and the wild roses were flowering—small white blossoms lying in clusters.

I walked down to the stream almost every day after two or three hours of writing. I had lived in cities too long and had returned to the hills to renew myself, both physically and mentally. Once you have lived with mountains for any length of time you belong to them, and must return again and again.

Nearly every morning, and sometimes during the day, I heard the cry of the barking deer. And in the evening, walking through the forest, I disturbed parties of pheasant. The birds went gliding down the ravine on open, motionless wings. I saw pine martens and a handsome red fox, and I recognized the footprints of a bear.

As I had not come to take anything from the forest, the birds and animals soon grew accustomed to my presence; or possibly they recognized my footsteps. After some time, my approach did not disturb them.

The langurs in the oak and rhododendron trees, who would at first go leaping through the branches at my approach, now watched me with some curiosity as they munched the tender green shoots of the oak. The young ones scuffled and wrestled like boys while their parents groomed each other's coats, stretching themselves out on the sunlit hillside.

But one evening, as I passed, I heard them chattering in the trees, and I knew I was not the cause of their excitement. As I crossed the stream and began climbing the hill, the grunting and chattering increased, as though the langurs were trying to warn me of some hidden danger. A shower of pebbles came rattling down the steep hillside, and I looked up to see a sinewy, orange-gold leopard poised on a rock about twenty feet above me.

It was not looking towards me but had its head thrust attentively forward, in the direction of the ravine. Yet it must have sensed my presence because it slowly turned its head and looked down at me.

It seemed a little puzzled at my presence there; and when, to give myself courage, I clapped my hands sharply, the leopard sprang away into the thickets, making absolutely no sound as it melted into the shadows.

I had disturbed the animal in its quest for food. But a little after I heard the quickening cry of a barking deer as it fled through the forest. The hunt was still on.

The leopard, like other members of the cat family, is nearing extinction in India, and I was surprised to find one so close to

Mussoorie. Probably the deforestation that had been taking place in the surrounding hills had driven the deer into this green valley; and the leopard, naturally, had followed.

It was some weeks before I saw the leopard again, although I was often made aware of its presence. A dry, rasping cough sometimes gave it away. At times I felt almost certain that I was being followed.

Once, when I was late getting home, and the brief twilight gave way to a dark moonless night, I was startled by a family of porcupines running about in a clearing. I looked around nervously and saw two bright eyes staring at me from a thicket. I stood still, my heart banging away against my ribs. Then the eyes danced away and I realized that they were only fireflies.

In May and June, when the hills were brown and dry, it was always cool and green near the stream, where ferns and maidenhair and long grasses continued to thrive.

Downstream I found a small pool where I could bathe, and a cave with water dripping from the roof, the water spangled gold and silver in the shafts of sunlight that pushed through the slits in the cave roof.

'He maketh me to lie down in green pastures: he leadeth me beside the still waters.' Perhaps David had discovered a similar paradise when he wrote those words; perhaps I, too, would write good words. The hill station's summer visitors had not discovered this haven of wild and green things. I was beginning to feel that the place belonged to me, that dominion was mine.

The stream had at least one other regular visitor, a spotted forktail, and though it did not fly away at my approach it became restless if I stayed too long, and then it would move from boulder to boulder uttering a long complaining cry.

I spent an afternoon trying to discover the bird's nest, which I was certain contained young ones, because I had seen the forktail carrying grubs in her bill. The problem was that when the bird flew upstream I had difficulty in following her rapidly enough as the rocks were sharp and slippery.

Eventually I decorated myself with bracken fronds and, after slowly making my way upstream, hid myself in the hollow stump of a tree at a spot where the forktail often disappeared. I had no intention of robbing the bird. I was simply curious to see its home.

By crouching down, I was able to command a view of a small stretch of the stream and the side of the ravine; but I had done little to deceive the forktail, who continued to object strongly to my presence so near her home.

I summoned up my reserves of patience and sat perfectly still for about ten minutes. The forktail quietened down. Out of sight, out of mind. But where had she gone? Probably into the walls of the ravine where, I felt sure, she was guarding her nest.

I decided to take her by surprise and stood up suddenly, in time to see not the forktail on her doorstep but the leopard bounding away with a grunt of surprise! Two urgent springs, and it had crossed the stream and plunged into the forest.

I was as astonished as the leopard, and forgot all about the forktail and her nest. Had the leopard been following me again? I decided against this possibility. Only man-eaters follow humans and, as far as I knew, there had never been a man-eater in the vicinity of Mussoorie.

During the monsoon the stream became a rushing torrent, bushes and small trees were swept away, and the friendly murmur of the water became a threatening boom. I did not visit the place too often as there were leeches in the long grass.

One day I found the remains of a barking deer which had only been partly eaten. I wondered why the leopard had not hidden the rest of his meal, and decided that it must have been disturbed while eating.

Then, climbing the hill, I met a party of hunters resting beneath the oaks. They asked me if I had seen a leopard. I said I had not. They said they knew there was a leopard in the forest.

Leopard skins, they told me, were selling in Delhi at over 1,000 rupees each. Of course there was a ban on the export of skins, but they gave me to understand that there were ways and means . . . . I thanked them for their information and walked on, feeling uneasy and disturbed.

The hunters had seen the carcass of the deer, and they had seen the leopard's pug-marks, and they kept coming to the forest. Almost every evening I heard their guns banging away; for they were ready to fire at almost anything.

'There's a leopard about,' they always told me. 'You should carry a gun.'

'I don't have one,' I said.

There were fewer birds to be seen, and even the langurs had moved on. The red fox did not show itself; and the pine martens, who had become quite bold, now dashed into hiding at my approach. The smell of one human is like the smell of any other.

And then the rains were over and it was October; I could lie in the sun, on sweet-smelling grass, and gaze up through a pattern of oak leaves into a blinding blue heaven. And I would praise God for leaves and grass and the smell of things—the smell of mint and bruised clover—and the touch of things—the touch of grass and air and sky, the touch of the sky's blueness.

I thought no more of the men. My attitude towards them was similar to that of the denizens of the forest. These were men, unpredictable, and to be avoided if possible.

On the other side of the ravine rose Pari Tibba, Hill of the Fairies; a bleak, scrub-covered hill where no one lived.

It was said that in the previous century Englishmen had tried building their houses on the hill, but the area had always attracted lightning, due to either the hill's location or due to its mineral deposits; after several houses had been struck by lightning, the settlers had moved on to the next hill, where the town now stands.

To the hillmen it is Pari Tibba, haunted by the spirits of a pair of ill-fated lovers who perished there in a storm; to others it is known as Burnt Hill, because of its scarred and stunted trees.

One day, after crossing the stream, I climbed Pari Tibba—a stiff undertaking, because there was no path to the top and I had to scramble up a precipitous rock-face with the help of rocks and roots that were apt to come loose in my groping hand.

But at the top was a plateau with a few pine trees, their upper branches catching the wind and humming softly. There I found the ruins of what must have been the houses of the first settlers—just a few piles of rubble, now overgrown with weeds, sorrel, dandelions and nettles.

As I walked though the roofless ruins, I was struck by the silence that surrounded me, the absence of birds and animals, the sense of complete desolation.

The silence was so absolute that it seemed to be ringing in my ears. But there was something else of which I was becoming increasingly aware: the strong feline odour of one of the cat family. I paused and looked about. I was alone. There was no movement of dry leaf or loose stone.

The ruins were for the most part open to the sky. Their rotting rafters had collapsed, jamming together to form a low passage like the entrance to a mine; and this dark cavern seemed to lead down into the ground. The smell was stronger when I approached this spot, so I stopped again and waited there, wondering if I had discovered the lair of the leopard, wondering if the animal was now at rest after a night's hunt.

Perhaps he was crouching there in the dark, watching me, recognizing me, knowing me as the man who walked alone in the forest without a weapon.

I like to think that he was there, that he knew me, and that he acknowledged my visit in the friendliest way: by ignoring me altogether.

Perhaps I had made him confident—too confident, too careless, too trusting of the human in his midst. I did not venture any further; I was not out of my mind. I did not seek physical contact, or even another glimpse of that beautiful sinewy body, springing from rock to rock. It was his trust I wanted, and I think he gave it to me.

But did the leopard, trusting one man, make the mistake of bestowing his trust on others? Did I, by casting out all fear—my own fear, and the leopard's protective fear—leave him defenceless?

Because next day, coming up the path from the stream, shouting and beating drums, were the hunters. They had a long bamboo pole across their shoulders; and slung from the pole, feet up, head down, was the lifeless body of the leopard, shot in the neck and in the head.

'We told you there was a leopard!' they shouted, in great good humour. 'Isn't he a fine specimen?'

'Yes,' I said. 'He was a beautiful leopard.'

I walked home through the silent forest. It was very silent, almost as though the birds and animals knew that their trust had been violated.

I remembered the lines of a poem by D.H. Lawrence; and, as I climbed the steep and lonely path to my home, the words beat out their rhythm in my mind: 'There was room in the world for a mountain lion and me.'

SITA AND THE RIVER

෪

The Island in the River

IN THE MIDDLE OF the river, the river that began in the mountains of the Himalayas and ended in the Bay of Bengal, there was a small island. The river swept round the island, sometimes clawing at its banks but never going right over it. The river was still deep and swift at this point, because the foothills were only forty miles distant. More than twenty years had passed since the river had flooded the island and at that time no one had lived there. But then years ago a small family had came to live on the island and now a small hut stood on it, a mud-walled hut with a sloping thatched roof. The hut had been built into a huge rock. Only three of its walls were mud, the fourth was rock.

A few goats grazed on the short grass and the prickly leaves of the thistle. Some hens followed them about. There was a melon patch and a vegetable patch and a small field of marigolds. The marigolds were sometimes made into garlands, and the garlands were sold during weddings or festivals in the nearby town.

In the middle of the islands stood a peepul tree. It was the only tree on this tongue of land. But peepul trees will grow anywhere—through the walls of old temples, through gravestones, even from rooftops. It is usually the buildings, and not the trees, that give way!

Even during the great flood, which had occurred twenty years back, the peepul tree had stood firm.

It was an old tree, much older than the old man on the island, who was only seventy. The peepul was about three hundred. It also provided shelter for the birds who sometimes visited it from the mainland.

Three hundred years ago, the land on which the peepul tree stood had been part of the mainland; but the river had changed its course and the bit of land with the tree on it had become an island. The tree had lived alone for many years. Now it gave shade and shelter to a small family who were grateful for its presence.

The people of India love peepul trees, especially during the hot summer month when the heart-shaped leaves catch the least breath of air and flutter eagerly, fanning those who sit beneath.

A sacred tree, the peepul, the abode of spirits, good and bad.

'Do not yawn when you are sitting beneath the tree,' Grandmother would warn Sita, her ten-year-old granddaughter. 'And if you must yawn always snap your fingers in front of your mouth. If you forget to do that, a demon might jump down your throat!'

'And then what will happen?' asked Sita.

'He will probably ruin your digestion,' said Grandfather, who didn't take demons very seriously.

The peepul had beautiful leaves and Grandmother likened it to the body of the mighty god Krishna—broad at the shoulders, then tapering down to a very slim waist.

The tree attracted birds and insects from across the river. On some nights it was full of fireflies.

Whenever Grandmother saw the fireflies, she told her favourite story.

'When we first came here,' she said, 'we were greatly troubled by mosquitoes. One night your grandfather rolled himself up in his sheet so that they couldn't get at him. After a while he peeped out of his bedsheet to make sure they were gone. He saw a firefly and said, you clever mosquito! You could not see in the dark, so you got a lantern!'

Grandfather was mending a fishing-net. He had fished in the river for ten years, and he was a good fisherman. He knew where to find to slim silver chilwa and the big, beautiful mahseer and the singhara with its long whiskers; he knew where the river was deep and where it was shallow; he knew which baits to use—when to use worms and when to use gram. He had taught his son to fish but his son had gone to work in a factory in a city nearly a hundred miles away. He had no grandson but he had a granddaughter, Sita, and she could do all the things a boy could do and sometimes she could do them better. She had lost her mother when she was two or three. Grandmother had taught her all that a girl should know—cooking, sewing, grinding spices, cleaning the house, feeding the birds—and Grandfather had taught her other things, like taking a small boat across the river, cleaning a fish, repairing a net, or catching a snake by the tail! And some things she had learnt by herself—like climbing the peepul tree, or leaping from rock to rock in shallow water, or swimming in an inlet where the water was calm.

Neither grandparent could read or write and as a result Sita couldn't read or write.

There was a school in one of the villages across the river, but Sita had never seen it. She had never been further than Shahganj, the small market town near the river. She had never seen a city. She had never been in a train. The river cut her off from many things but she could not miss what she had never known and, besides, she was much too busy.

While Grandfather mended his net, Sita was inside the hut, pressing her grandmother's forehead which was hot with fever. Grandmother had been ill for three days and could not eat. She had been ill before but she had never been so bad. Grandfather had brought her some sweet oranges but she couldn't take anything else.

She was younger than Grandfather but, because she was sick, she looked much older. She had never been very strong. She coughed a lot and sometimes she had difficulty in breathing.

When Sita noticed that Grandmother was sleeping, she left the bedside and tip-toed out of the room on her bare feet.

Outside, she found the sky dark with monsoon clouds. It had rained all night, and, in a few hours, it would rain again. The monsoon rains had come early at the end of June. Now it was the end of July and already the river was swollen. Its rushing sound seemed nearer and more menacing than usual.

Sita went to her grandfather and sat down beside him.

'When you are hungry, tell me,' she said, 'and I will make the bread.'

'Is your Grandmother asleep?'

'Yes. But she will wake soon. The pain is deep.'

The old man stared out across the river, at the dark green of the forest, at the leaden sky, and said, 'If she is not better by morning, I will take her to the hospital in Shahganj. They will know how to make her well. You may be on your own for two or three days. You have been on your own before.'

Sita nodded gravely—she had been alone before; but not in the middle of the rains with the river so high. But she knew that someone must stay behind. She wanted Grandmother to get well and she knew that only Grandfather could take the small boat across the river when the current was so strong.

Sita was not afraid of being left alone but she did not like the look of the river. That morning, when she had been fetching water, she had noticed that the lever suddenly disappeared.

'Grandfather, if the river rises higher, what will I do?'

'You must keep to the high ground.'

'And if the water reaches the high ground?'

'Then go into the hut and take the hens with you.'

'And if the water comes into the hut?'

'Then climb into the peepul tree. It is a strong tree. It will not fall. And the water cannot rise higher than the tree.'

'And the goats, Grandfather?'

'I will be taking them with me. I may have to sell them, to pay for good food and medicine for your Grandmother. As for the hens, you can put them on the roof if the water enters the hut. But do not worry too much,' and he patted Sita's head, the water will not rise so high. Has it ever done so? I will be back soon, remember that.'

'And won't Grandmother come back?'

'Yes—but they may keep her in the hospital for some time.'

The Sound of the River

That evening it began to rain again. Big pellets of rain, scarring the surface of the river. But it was warm rain and Sita could move about in it. She was not afraid of getting wet, she rather liked it. In the previous month, when the first monsoon shower had arrived, washing the dusty leaves of the tree and bringing up the good smell of the earth, she had exulted in it, had run about shouting for joy. She was used to it now, even a little tired of the rain, but she did not mind getting wet. It was steamy indoors and her thin dress would soon dry in the heat from the kitchen fire.

She walked about barefooted, barelegged. She was very sure on her feet. Her toes had grown accustomed to gripping all kinds of rocks, slippery or sharp, and though thin, she was surprisingly strong.

Black hair, streaming across her face. Black eyes. Slim brown arms. A scar on her thigh: when she was small, visiting her mother's village, a hyaena had entered the house where she was sleeping, fastened on to her leg and tried to drag her away but her screams had roused the villagers and the hyena had run off.

She moved about in the pouring rain, chasing the hens into a shelter behind the hut. A harmless brown snake, flooded out of its hole, was moving across the open ground. Sita took a stick, picked the snake up with it, and dropped it behind a cluster of rocks. She had no quarrel with snakes. They kept down the rats and the frogs. She wondered how the rats had first come to the island—probably in someone's boat or in a sack of grain.

She disliked the huge black scorpions who left their waterlogged dwellings and tried to take shelter in the hut. It was so easy to step on one and the sting could be very painful. She had been bitten by a scorpion the previous monsoon and for a day and a night she had known fever and great pain. Sita had never killed living creatures but now, whenever she found a scorpion, she crushed it with a rock! When, finally, she went indoors, she was hungry. She ate some parched gram and warmed up some goat's milk.

Grandmother woke once and asked for water and Grandfather held the brass tumbler to her lips.

It rained all night.

The roof was leaking and a small puddle formed on the floor. Grandfather kept the kerosene lamps alight. They did not need the light but somehow it made them feel safer.

The sound of the river had always been with them, although they seldom noticed it. But that night they noticed a change in its sound. There was something like a moan, like a wind in the tops of tall trees, and a swift hiss as the water swept round the rocks and carried away pebbles. And sometimes there was a rumble as loose earth fell into the water. Sita could not sleep.

She had a rag doll made with Grandmother's help out of bits of old clothing. She kept it by her side every night. The doll was someone to talk to when the nights were long and sleep, elusive. Her grandparents were often ready to talks but sometimes Sita wanted to have secrets, and, though there were no special secrets in her life, she made up a few because it was fun to have them. And if you have secrets, you must have a friend to share them with. Since there were no other children on the island, Sita shared her secrets with the rag doll whose name was Mumta.

Grandfather and Grandmother were asleep, though the sound of Grandmother's laboured breathing was almost as persistent as the sound of the river.

'Mumta,' whispered Sita in the dark, starting one of her private conversations, 'do you think Grandmother will get well again?'

Mumta always answered Sita's questions, even though the answers were really Sita's answers.

'She is very old,' said Mumta.

'Do you think the river will reach the hut?' asked Sita.

'If it keeps raining like this, and the river keeps rising, it will reach the hut.'

'I am afraid of the river, Mumta. Aren't you afraid?'

'Don t be afraid. The river has always been good to us.'

'What will we do if it comes into the hut?'

'We will climb on the roof.'

'And if it reaches the roof?'

'We will climb the peepul tree. The river has never gone higher than the peepul tree.'

As soon as the first light showed through the little skylight, Sita got up and went outside. It wasn't raining hard, it was drizzling, but it was the sort of drizzle that could continue for days, and it probably meant that heavy rain was falling in the hills where the river began.

Sita went down to the water's edge. She couldn't find her favourite rock, the one on which she often sat dangling her feet in the water, watching the little chilwa fish swim by. It was still there, no doubt, but the river had gone over it.

She stood on the sand and she could feel the water oozing and bubbling beneath her feet.

The river was no longer green and blue and flecked with white. It was a muddy colour.

Sita milked the goat thinking that perhaps it was the last time she would be milking it. But she did not care for the goat in the same way that she cared for Mumta.

The sun was just coming up when Grandfather pushed off in the boat. Grandmother lay in the prow. She was staring hard at Sita, trying to speak, but the words would not come. She raised her hand in blessing.

Sita bent and touched her Grandmother's feet and then Grandfather pushed off. The little boat—with its two old people and three goats—rode swiftly on the river, edging its way towards the opposite bank. The current was very swift and the boat would be carried about half a mile downstream before Grandfather would be able to get it to dry land.

It bobbed about on the water, getting small and smaller, until it was just a speck on the broad river.

And suddenly Sita was alone.

There was a wind, whipping the raindrops against her face; and there was the water, rushing past the island; and there was the distant shore, blurred by rain; and there was the small hut; and there was the tree.

Sita got busy. The hens had to be fed. They weren't concerned about anything except food. Sita threw them a handful of coarse grain, potato-peels and peanut-shells.

Then she took the broom and swept out the hut; lit the charcoal-burner, warmed some milk, and thought, 'Tomorrow there will be no milk . . . .' She began peeling onions. Soon her eyes started smarting, and, pausing for a few moments and glancing round the quiet room, she became aware again that she was alone. Grandfather's hookah-pipe stood by itself in one corner. It was a beautiful old hookah, which had belonged to Sita's great-grandfather. The bowl was made out of a coconut encased in silver. The long winding stem was at least four feet long. It was their most treasured possession. Grandmother's sturdy shisham-wood walking stick stood in another corner.

Sita looked around for Mumta, found the doll beneath the light wooden charpoy, and placed her within sight and hearing.

Thunder rolled down from the hills. Boom—boom—boom . . .

'The Gods of the mountains are angry,' said Sita. 'Do you think they are angry with me?'

'Why should they be angry with you?' asked Mumta.

'They don't need a reason for being angry. They are angry with everything and we are in the middle of everything. We are so small—do you think they know we are here?'

'Who knows what the gods think?'

'But I made you,' said Sita, 'and I know you are here.'

'And will you save me if the river rises?'

'Yes, of course. I won't go anywhere without you, Mumta.'

The Water Rises

Sita couldn't stay indoors for long. She went out, taking Mumta with her, and stared out across the river, to the safe land on the other side. But was it really safe there? The river looked much wider now. It had crept over its banks and spread far across the flat plain. Far away, people were driving their cattle through waterlogged, flooded fields, carrying their belongings in bundles on their heads or shoulders, leaving their homes, making for high land. It wasn't safe anywhere.

Sita wondered what had happened to Grandfather and Grandmother. If they had reached the shore safely, Grandfather would have had to engage a bullock-cart or a pony-drawn ekka to get Grandmother to the district hospital, five or six miles away. Shahganj had a market, a court, a jail, a cinema and a hospital.

She wondered if she would ever see Grandmother again. She had done her best to look after the old lady, remembering the times when Grandmother had looked after her, had gently touched her fevered brow, and had told her stories—stories about the gods—about the young Krishna, friend of birds and animals, so full of mischief, always causing confusion among the other gods. He made the god Indra angry by shifting a mountain without permission. Indra was the god of the clouds, who made the thunder and lightning, and when he was angry he sent down a deluge such as this one.

The island looked much smaller now. Some of its mud banks had dissolved quickly, sinking into the river. But in the middle of the island there was rocky ground, and the rocks would never crumble, they could only be submerged.

Sita climbed into the tree to get a better view of the flood. She had climbed the tree many times and it took her only a few seconds to reach the higher branches. She put her hand to her eyes as a shield from the rain and gazed upstream.

There was water everywhere. The world had become one vast river. Even the trees on the forested side of the river looked as though they had grown out of the water, like mangroves. The sky was banked with massive, moisture-laden clouds. Thunder rolled down from the hills and the river seemed to take it up with a hollow booming sound.

Something was floating down the river, something big and bloated. It was closer now and Sita could make out its bulk—a drowned bullock being carried downstream.

So the water had already flooded the villages further upstream. Or perhaps the bullock had strayed too close to the rising river.

Sita's worst fears were confirmed when, a little later, she saw planks of wood, small trees and bushes, and then a wooden bedstead, floating past the island.

As she climbed down from the tree, it began to rain more heavily. She ran indoors, shooing the hens before her. They few into the hut and huddled under Grandmother's cot. Sita thought it would be best to keep them together now.

There were three hens and a cockbird. The river did not bother them. They were interested only in food and Sita kept them content by throwing them a handful of onion-skins.

She would have liked to close the door and shut out the swish of the rain and the boom of the river but then she would have no way of knowing how fast the water rose.

She took Mumta in her arms and began praying for the rain to stop and the river to fall. She prayed to the God Indra, and, just in case he was busy elsewhere, she prayed to other gods too. She prayed for the safety of her grandparents and for her own safety. She put herself last—but only after an effort!

Finally Sita decided to make herself a meal. So she chopped up some onions, fried them, then added turmeric and red chilli-powder, salt and water, and stirred until she had everything sizzling; and then she added a cup of lentils and covered the pot.

Doing this took her about ten minutes. It would take about half an hour for the dish to cook.

When she looked outside, she saw pools of water among the rocks. She couldn't tell if it was rain water or the overflow from the river.

She had an idea.

A big tin trunk stood in a corner of the room. In it Grandmother kept an old single-thread sewing-machine. It had belonged once to an English lady, had found its way to a Shahganj junk-yard, and had been rescued by Grandfather who had paid fifteen rupees for it. It was just over a hundred years old but it could still be used.

The trunk also contained an old sword. This had originally belonged to Sita's great-grandfather, who had used it to help defend his village against marauding Rohilla soldiers more than a century ago. Sita could tell that it had been used to fight with because there were several small dents in the steel blade.

But there was no time for Sita to start admiring family heirlooms. She decided to stuff the trunk with everything useful or valuable. There was a chance that it wouldn't be carried away by the water.

Grandfather's hookah went into the trunk. Grandmother's walking-stick went in, too. So did a number of small tins containing the spices used in cooking—nutmeg, caraway seed, cinnamon, coriander, pepper—also a big tin of flour and another of molasses. Even if she had to spend several hours in the tree, there would be something to eat when she came down again.

A clean white cotton dhoti of Grandfather's, and Grandmother's only spare sari also went into the trunk. Never mind if they got stained with curry powder! Never mind if they got the smell of slated fish—some of that went in, too.

Sita was so busy packing the trunk that she paid no attention to the lick of cold water at her heels. She locked the trunk, dropped the key into a crack in the rock wall and turned to give her attention to the food. It was only then that she discovered that she was walking about on a watery floor.

She stood still, horrified by what she saw. The water was oozing over the threshold, pushing its way into the room.

In her fright, Sita forgot about her meal and everything else. Darting out of the hut, she ran splashing through ankle-deep water toward the safety of the peepul tree. If the tree hadn't been there, such a well-known landmark, she might have floundered into deep water, into the river.

She climbed swiftly into the strong arms of the tree, made herself comfortable on a familiar branch and thrust her wet hair away from her eyes.

The Tree

She was glad she had hurried. The hut was now surrounded by water. Only the higher parts of the island could still be seen—a few rocks, the big rock into which the hut was built, a hillock on which some brambles and thorn-apples grew.

The hens hadn't bothered to leave the hut. Instead, they were perched on the wooden bedstead.

'Will the river rise still higher?' wondered Sita. She had never seen it like this before. With a deep, muffled roar it swirled around her, stretching away in all directions.

The most unusual things went by on the water—an aluminium kettle, a cane-chair, a tin of tooth-powder, an empty cigarette packet, a wooden slipper, a plastic doll . . . .

A doll!

With a sinking feeling, Sita remembered Mumta.

Poor Mumta, she had been left behind in the hut. Sita, in her hurry, had forgotten her only companion.

She climbed down from the tree and ran splashing through the water towards the hut. Already the current was pulling at her legs. When she reached the hut, she found it full of water. The hens had gone and so had Mumta.

Sita struggled back to the tree. She was only just in time, for the waters were higher now, the island fast disappearing.

She crouched miserably in the fork of the tree, watching her world disappear.

She had always loved the river. Why was it threatening her

now? She remembered the doll and thought, 'If I can be so careless with someone I have made, how can I expect the gods to notice me?'

Something went floating past the tree. Sita caught a glimpse of a stiff, upraised arm and long hair streaming behind on the water. The body of a drowned woman. It was soon gone but it made Sita feel very small and lonely, at the mercy of great and cruel forces. She began to shiver and then to cry.

She stopped crying when she saw an empty kerosene tin, with one of the hens perched on top. The tin came bobbing along on the water and sailed slowly past the tree. The hen looked a bit ruffled but seemed secure on its perch.

A little later Sita saw the remaining hens fly up to the rock-ledge to huddle there in a small recess.

The water was still rising. All that remained of the island was the big rock behind the hut and the top of the hut and the peepul tree.

She climbed a little higher into the crook of a branch. A jungle-crow settled in the branches above her. Sita saw the nest, the crow's nest, an untidy platform of twigs wedged in the fork of a branch.

In the nest were four speckled eggs. The crow sat on them and cawed disconsolately. But though the bird sounded miserable, its presence brought some cheer to Sita. At least she was not alone. Better to have a crow for company than no one at all.

Other things came floating out of the hut—a large pumpkin; a red turban belonging to Grandfather, unwinding in the water like a long snake; and then—Mumta!

The doll, being filled with straw and wood shavings, moved quite swiftly on the water, too swiftly for Sita to do anything about rescuing it. Sita wanted to call out, to urge her friend to make for the tree but she knew that Mumta could not swim— the doll could only float, travel with the river, and perhaps be washed ashore many miles downstream.

The trees shook in the wind and rain. The crow cawed and flew up, circled the tree a few times, then returned to the nest. Sita clung to the branch.

The tree trembled throughout its tall frame. To Sita it felt like an earthquake tremor. She felt the shudder of the tree in her own bones.

The river swirled all around her now. It was almost up to the roof of the hut. Soon the mud walls would crumble and vanish. Except for the big rock and some trees very far away, there was only water to be seen. Water and grey weeping sky.

In the distance, a boat with several people in it moved sluggishly away from the ruins of a flooded village. Someone looked out across the flooded river and said, 'See, there is a tree right in the middle of the river! How could it have got there? Isn't someone moving in the tree?'

But the others thought he was imagining things. It was only a tree carried down by the flood, they said. In worrying about their own distress, they had forgotten about the island in the middle of the river.

The river was very angry now, rampaging down from the hills and thundering across the plain, bringing with it dead animals, uprooted trees, household goods, and huge fish choked to death by the swirling mud.

The peepul tree groaned. Its long, winding roots still clung tenaciously to the earth from which it had sprung many, many years ago. But the earth was softening, the stones were being washed away. The roots of the tree were rapidly losing their hold.

The crow must have known that something was wrong because it kept flying up and circling the tree, reluctant to settle in it, yet unwilling to fly away. As long as the nest was there, the crow would remain too.

Sita's wet cotton dress clung to her thin body. The rain streamed down from her long black hair. It poured from every leaf of the tree. The crow, too, was drenched and groggy.

The tree groaned and moved again.

There was a flurry of leaves, then a surge of mud from below. To Sita it seemed as though the river was rising to meet the sky. The tree tilted, swinging Sita from side to side. Her feet were in the water but she clung tenaciously to her branch.

And then, she found the tree moving, moving with the river, rocking her about, dragging its roots along the ground as it set out on the first and last journey of its life.

And as the tree moved out on the river and the little island was lost in the swirling waters, Sita forgot her fear and her loneliness. The tree was taking her with it. She was not alone.

It was as though one of the gods had remembered her after all.

Taken with the Flood

The branches swung Sita about, but she did not lose her grip. The tree was her friend. It had known her all these years and now it held her in its old and dying arms as though it were determined to keep her from the river.

The crow kept flying around the moving tree. The bird was in a great rage. Its nest was still up there—but not for long! The tree lurched and twisted and the nest fell into the water. Sita saw the eggs sink.

The crow swooped low over the water but there was nothing it could do. In a few moments the nest had disappeared.

The bird followed the tree for sometime. Then, flapping its wings, it rose high into the air and flew across the river until it was out of sight.

Sita was alone once more. But there was no time for feeling lonely. Everything was in motion—up and down and sideways and forwards.

She saw a turtle swimming past—a great big river turtle, the kind that feeds on decaying flesh. Sita turned her face away. In the distance she saw a flooded village and people in flat-bottomed boats; but they were very far.

Because of its great size, the tree did not move very swiftly on the river. Sometimes, when it reached shallow water, it stopped, its roots catching in the rocks. But not for long, the river's momentum soon swept it on.

At one place, where there was a bend in the river, the tree struck a sandbank and was still. It would not move again.

Sita felt very tired. Her arms were aching and she had to cling tightly to her branch to avoid slipping into the water. The rain blurred her vision. She wondered if she should brave the current and try swimming to safety. But she did not want to leave the tree. It was all that was left to her now and she felt safe in its branches.

Then, above the sound of the river, she heard someone calling. The voice was faint and seemed very far but, looking upriver through the curtain of rain, Sita was able to make out a small boat coming towards her.

There was a boy in the boat. He seemed quite at home in the turbulent river, and he was smiling at Sita as he guided his boat towards the tree. He held on to one of the branches to steady himself and gave his free hand to Sita.

She grasped the outstretched hand and slipped into the boat beside the boy.

He placed his bare foot against the trunk of the tree and pushed away.

The little boat moved swiftly down the river. Sita looked back and saw the big tree lying on its side on the sandbank, while the river swirled round it and pulled at its branches, carrying away its beautiful slender leaves.

And then the tree grew smaller and was left far behind. A new journey had begun.

The Boy in the Boat

She lay stretched out in the boat, too tired to talk, too tired to move. The boy looked at her but did not say anything. He just kept smiling. He leant on his two small oars, stroking smoothly, rhythmically, trying to keep from going into the middle of the river. He wasn't strong enough to get the boat right out of the swift current but he kept trying.

A small boat on a big river—a river that had broken its bounds and reached across the plains in every direction—the boat moved swiftly on the wild brown water, and the girl's home and the boy's home were both left far behind.

The boy wore only a loincloth. He was a slim, wiry boy, with a hard flat belly. He had high cheekbones and strong white teeth. He was a little darker than Sita.

He did not speak until they reached a broader, smoother stretch of river, and then, resting on his oars and allowing the boat to drift a little, he said, 'You live on the island. I have seen you sometimes from my boat. But where are the others?'

'My grandmother was sick,' said Sita. 'Grandfather took her to the hospital in Shahganj.'

'When did they leave?'

'Early this morning.'

Early that morning—and already Sita felt as though it had been many mornings ago!

'Where are you from?' she asked.

'I am from a village near the foothills. About six miles from your home. I was in my boat, trying to get across the river with the news that our village was badly flooded. The current was too strong. I was swept down and past your island. We cannot fight the river when it is like this, we must go where it takes us.'

'You must be tired,' said Sita. 'Give me the oars.'

'No. There is not much to do now. The river has gone wherever it wanted to go—it will not drive us before it any more.'

He brought in one oar and with his free hand felt under the seat where there was a small basket. He produced two mangoes and gave one to Sita.

'I was supposed to sell these in Shahganj,' he said. 'My father is very strict. Even if I return home safely, he will ask me what I got for the mangoes!'

'And what will you tell him?'

'I will say they are at the bottom of the river!'

They bit deep into the ripe fleshy mangoes, using their teeth to tear the skin away. The sweet juice trickled down their skins. The good smell—like the smell of the leaves of the cosmos flower when crushed between the palms—helped to revive Sita. The flavour of the fruit was heavenly—truly the nectar of the gods!

Sita hadn't tasted a mango for over a year. For a few moments she forgot about everything else. All that mattered was the sweet, dizzy flavour of the mango.

The boat drifted, but slowly now, for as they went further downstream, the river gradually lost its power and fury. It was late afternoon when the rain stopped but the clouds did not break up.

'My father has many buffaloes,' said the boy, 'but several have been lost in the flood.'

'Do you go to school?' asked Sita.

'Yes, I am supposed to go to school. I don't always go. At least not when the weather is fine! There is a school near our village. I don't think you go to school?'

'No. There is too much work at home.'

'Can you read and write?'

'Only a little . . .'

'Then you should go to a school.'

'It is too far away.'

'True. But you should know how to read and write. Otherwise you will be stuck on your island for the rest of your life—that is, if your island is still there!'

'But I like the island,' protested Sita.

'Because you are with people you love,' said the boy. 'But your grandparents, they are old, they must die some day—and then you will be alone, and will you like the island then?'

Sita did not answer. She was trying to think of what life would be like without her grandparents. It would be an empty island, that was true. She would be imprisoned by the river.

'I can help you,' said the boy. 'When we get back—if we get back—I will come to see you sometimes and I will teach you to read and write. All right?'

'Yes,' said Sita, nodding thoughtfully. 'When we get back . . .'

The boy smiled.

'My name is Vijay,' he said.

Towards evening the river changed colour. The sun, low in the sky, broke through a rift in the clouds and the river changed slowly from grey to gold, from gold to a deep orange, and then, as the sun were down, all these colours were drowned in the river, and the river took the colour of night.

The moon was almost at the full and they could see a belt of forest along the line of the river.

'I will try to reach the trees,' said Vijay.

He pulled for the trees and after ten minutes of strenuous rowing reached a bend in the river and was able to escape the pull of the main current.

Soon they were in a forest, rowing between tall trees, sal and shisham.

The boat moved slowly as Vijay took it in and out of the trees, while the moonlight made a crooked silver path over the water.

'We will tie the boat to a tree,' he said. 'Then we can rest. Tomorrow, we will have to find a way out of the forest.'

He produced a length of rope from the bottom of the boat,

tied one end to the boat's stern, and threw the other end over a stout branch which hung only a few feet above the water. The boat came to rest against the trunk of the tree.

It was a tall, sturdy tree, The Indian mahogany. It was a safe place for there was no rush of water in the forest and the trees grew close together, making the earth firm and unyielding.

But those who lived in the forest were on the move. The animals had been flooded out of their homes, caves and lairs, and were looking for shelter and high ground.

Sita and Vijay had just finished tying the boat to the tree when they saw a huge python gliding over the water towards them.

'Do you think it will try to get into the boat?' asked Sita.

'I don't think so,' said Vijay, although he took the precaution of holding an oar ready to fend off the snake.

But the python went past them, its head above water, its great length trailing behind, until it was lost in the shadows.

Vijay had more mangoes in the basket and he and Sita sucked hungrily on them while they sat in the boat.

A big sambhur-stag came threshing through the water. He did not have to swim. He was so tall that his head and shoulders remained well above the water. His antlers were big and beautiful.

'There will be other animals,' said Sita. 'Should we climb onto the tree?'

'We are quite safe in the boat,' said Vijay. 'The animals will not be dangerous tonight. They will not even hunt each other. They are only interested in reaching dry land. For once, the deer are safe from the tiger and the leopard. You lie down and sleep. I will keep watch.'

Sita stretched herself out in the boat and closed her eyes. She was very tired and the sound of the water lapping against the side of the boat soon lulled her to sleep.

She woke once, when a strange bird called overhead. She raised herself on one elbow but Vijay was awake, sitting beside her, his legs drawn up and his chin resting on his knees. He was gazing out across the water. He looked blue in the moonlight, the colour of the young god Krishna, and for a few moments Sita was confused and wondered if the boy was actually Krishna. But when she thought about it, she decided that it wasn't possible, he was just a village boy and she had seen hundreds like him—well, not exactly like him, he was a little different . . . .

And when she slept again, she dreamt that the boy and Krishna were one, and that she was sitting beside him on a great white bird, which flew over the mountains, over the snow peaks of the Himalayas, into the cloud-land of the gods. And there was a great rumbling sound, as though the gods were angry about the whole thing, and she woke up to this terrible sound and looked about her, and there in the moonlit glade, up to his belly in water, stood a young elephant, his trunk raised as he trumpeted his predicament to the forest—for he was a young elephant, and he was lost, and was looking for his mother.

He trumpeted again, then lowered his head and listened. And presently, from far away, came the shrill trumpeting of another elephant. It must have been the young one's mother, because he gave several excited trumpet calls, and then went stamping and churning through the water toward a gap in the trees. The boat rocked in the waves made by his passing.

'It is all right,' said Vijay. 'You can go to sleep again.'

'I don't think I will sleep now,' said Sita.

'Then I will play my flute for you and the time will pass quickly.'

He produced a flute from under the seat and putting it to his lips began to play. And the sweetest music that Sita had ever heard came pouring from the little flute, and it seemed to fill the forest with its beautiful sound. And the music carried her away again, into the land of dreams, and they were riding on the bird once more, Sita and the blue god. And they were passing through cloud and mist, until suddenly the sun shot through the clouds. And at that moment Sita opened her eyes and saw the sky through the branches of the mahogany tree, the shiny green leaves making a bold pattern against the blinding blue of an open sky.

The forest was drenched with sunshine. Clouds were gathering again, but for an hour or- wo there would be hot sun on a steamy river.

Vijay was fast asleep in the bottom of the boat. His flute lay in the palm of his half-open hand. The sun came slanting across his bare brown legs. A leaf had fallen on his face, but it had not woken him. It lay on his cheek as though it had grown there.

Sita did not move about as she did not want to wake the boy. Instead she looked around her, and she thought the water level had fallen in the night, but she couldn't be sure.

Vijay woke at last. He yawned, stretched his limbs, and sat up beside Sita.

'I am hungry,' he said.

'So am I,' said Sita.

'The last mangoes, he said, emptying the basket of its last two mangoes.

After they had finished the fruit, they sucked the big seeds until they were quite dry. The discarded seeds floated well on the water. Sita had always preferred them to paper-boats.

'We had better move on,' said Vijay.

He rowed the boat through the trees and then for about an hour they were passing through the flooded forest, under the dripping branches of rain washed trees. Sometimes they had to use the oars to push away vines and creepers. Sometimes submerged bushes hampered them. But they were out of the forest before ten o'clock.

The water was no longer very deep and they were soon gliding over flooded fields. In the distance they saw a village standing on high ground. In the old days, people had built their villages on hill tops as a better defence against bandits and the soldiers of invading armies. This was an old village and, though its inhabitant had long ago exchanged their swords for pruning-forks, the hill on which it stood gave it protection from the flood waters.

A Bullock-Cart Ride

The people of the village were at first reluctant to help Sita and Vijay.

'They are strangers,' said an old woman. 'They are not of our people.

'They are of low-caste,' said another. 'They cannot remain with us.'

'Nonsense!' said a tall, turbaned farmer, twirling his long white moustaches. 'They are children, not robbers. They will come into my house.'

The people of the village—long-limbed, sturdy men and women of the Jat race—were generous by nature and once the elderly farmer had given them the lead they were friendly and helpful.

Sita was anxious to get to her grandparents and the farmer, who had business to transact at a village fair some twenty miles distant, offered to take Sita and Vijay with him.

The fair was being held at a place called Karauli and at Karauli there was a railway station from which a train went to Shahganj.

It was a journey that Sita would always remember. The bullock-cart was so slow on the waterlogged roads that there was plenty of time in which to see things, to notice one another, to talk, to think, to dream.

Vijay couldn't sit still in the cart. He was used to the swift, gliding movements of his boat (which he had had to leave behind in the village), and every now and then he would jump off the cart and walk beside it, often ankle-deep in water.

There were four of them in the cart. Sita and Vijay, Hukam Singh, the Jat farmer and his son, Phambiri, a mountain of a man who was going to take part in the wrestling-matches at the fair.

Hukam Singh, who drove the bullocks, liked to talk. He had been a soldier in the British Indian Army during the First World War and had been with his regiment to Italy and Mesopotamia.

'There is nothing to compare with soldiering,' he said, 'except, of course, farming. If you can't be a farmer, be a soldier. Are you listening, boy? Which will you be—farmer or soldier?'

'Neither,' said Vijay. 'I shall be an engineer!'

Hukam Singh's long moustaches seemed almost to bristle with indignation.

'An engineer! What next! What does your father do, boy?'

'He keeps buffaloes.'

'Ah! And his son would be an engineer? . . . Well, well, the world isn't what it used to be! No one knows his rightful place any more. Men send their children to schools and what is the result? Engineers! And who will look after the buffaloes while you are engineering?'

'I will sell the buffaloes,' said Vijay, adding rather cheekily, 'perhaps you will buy one of them, Subedar-Sahib!'

He took the cheek out of his remark by adding 'Subedar-Sahib,' the rank of a non-commissioned officer in the old army. Hukam Singh, who had never reached this rank, was naturally flattered.

'Fortunately, Phambiri hasn't been to school. He'll be a farmer and a fine one too.'

Phambiri simply grunted, which could have meant anything. He hadn't studied further than class six, which was just as well, as he was a man of muscle, not brain.

Phambiri loved putting his strength to some practical and useful purpose. Whenever the cart wheels got stuck in the mud, he would get off, remove his shirt and put his shoulder to the side of the cart, while his muscles bulged and the sweat glistened on his broad back.

'Phambiri is the strongest man in our district,' said Hukam Singh proudly. 'And clever, too! It takes quick thinking to win a wrestling match.'

'I have never seen one,' said Sita.

'Then stay with us tomorrow morning, and you will see Phambiri wrestle. He has been challenged by the Karauli champion. It will be a great fight!'

'We must see Phambiri win,' said Vijay.

'Will there be time?' asked Sita.

'Why not? The train for Shahganj won't come in till evening. The fair goes on all day and the wrestling bouts will take place in the morning.'

'Yes, you must see me win!' exclaimed Phambiri, thumping himself on the chest as he climbed back on to the cart after freeing the wheels. 'No one can defeat me!'

'How can you be so certain?' asked Vijay.

'He *has* to be certain,' said Hukam Singh. 'I have taught him to be certain! You can't win anything if you are uncertain . . . Isn't that right, Phambiri? You *know* you are going to win!'

'I know,' said Phambiri with a grunt of confidence.

'Well, someone has to lose,' said Vijay.

'Very true,' said Hukam Singh smugly. 'After all, what would we do without losers? But for Phambiri, it is win, win, all the time!'

'And *if* he loses?' persisted Vijay.

'Then he will just forget that it happened and will go on to win his next fight!'

Vijay found Hukam Singh's logic almost unanswerable, but Sita, who had been puzzled by the argument, now saw everything very clearly and said, 'Perhaps he hasn't won any fights as yet. Did he lose the last one?'

'Hush!' said Hukam Singh looking alarmed. 'You must not let him remember. You do not remember losing a fight, do you, my son?'

'I have never lost a fight,' said Phambiri with great simplicity and confidence.

'How strange,' said Sita. 'If you lose, how can you win?'

'Only a soldier can explain that,' sad Hukam Singh. 'For a man who fights, there is no such thing as defeat. You fought against the river, did you not?'

'I went with the river,' said Sita. 'I went where it took me.'

'Yes, and you would have gone to the bottom if the boy had not come along to help you. He fought the river, didn't he?'

'Yes, he fought the river,' said Sita.

'You helped me to fight it,' said Vijay.

'So you both fought,' said the old man with a nod of satisfaction. 'You did not go with the river. You did not leave *everything* to the gods.'

'The gods were with us,' said Sita.

And so they talked, while the bullock-cart trundled along the muddy village roads. Both bullocks were white and were decked out for the fair with coloured bead necklaces and bells hanging from their necks. They were patient, docile beasts. But the cart-wheels which were badly in need of oiling, protested loudly, creaking and groaning as though all the demons in the world had been trapped within them.

Sita noticed a number of birds in the paddy fields. There were black and white curlews and cranes with pink coat-tails. A good monsoon means plenty of birds. But Hukam Singh was not happy about the cranes.

'They do great damage in the wheat fields,' he said. Lighting up a small hand-held hookah pipe, he puffed at it and became philosophical again: 'Life is one long struggle for the farmer. When he has overcome the drought, survived the flood, hunted off the pig, killed the crane, and reaped the crop, then comes that blood-sucking ghoul, the moneylender. There is no escaping him! Is your father in debt to a moneylender, boy?'

'No,' said Vijay.

'That is because he doesn't have daughters who must be married! I have two. As they resemble Phambiri, they will need generous dowries.'

In spite of his grumbling, Hukam Singh seemed fairly content with his lot. He'd had a good maize crop and the front of his cart was piled high with corn. He would sell the crop at the fair, along with some cucumbers, eggplants and melons.

The bad road had slowed them down so much that when darkness came they were still far from Karauli. In India there is hardly any twilight. Within a short time of the sun's going down, the stars come out.

'Six miles to go,' said Hukam Singh. 'In the dark our wheels may get stuck again. Let us spend the night here. If it rains, we can pull an old tarpaulin over the cart.'

Vijay made a fire in the charcoal-burner which Hukam Singh had brought along, and they had a simple meal, roasting the corn over the fire and flavouring it with salt and spices and a squeeze of lemon. There was some milk, but not enough for everyone because Phambiri drank three tumblers by himself.

'If I win tomorrow,' he said, 'I will give all of you a feast!'

They settled down to sleep in the bullock-cart and Phambiri and his father were soon snoring. Vijay lay awake, his arms crossed behind his head, staring up at the stars. Sita was very tired but she couldn't sleep. She was worrying about her grandparents and wondering when she would see them again.

The night was full of sounds. The loud snoring that came from Phambiri and his father seemed to be taken up by invisible sleepers all around them, and Sita, becoming alarmed, turned to Vijay and asked, 'What is that strange noise?'

He smiled in the darkness, and she could see his white teeth and the glint of laughter in his eyes.

'Only the spirits of lost demons,' he said and then laughed. 'Can't you recognize the music of the frogs?'

And that was what they heard—a sound more hideous than the wail of demons, a rising crescendo of noise—*wurrk, wurrk, wurrk*—coming from the flooded ditches on either side of the road. All the frogs in the jungle seemed to have gathered at the one spot, and each one appeared to have something to say for himself. The speeches continued for about an hour. Then the meeting broke up and silence returned to the forest.

A jackal slunk across the road. A puff of wind brushed through the trees. The bullocks, freed from the cart, were asleep beside it. The men's snores were softer now. Vijay slept, a half-smile on his face. Only Sita lay awake, worried and waiting for the dawn.

At the Fair

Already, at nine o'clock, the fairground was crowded. Cattle were being sold or auctioned. Stalls had opened, selling everything from pins to ploughs. Foodstuffs were on sale—hot food, spicy food, sweets and ices. A merry-go-round, badly oiled, was squeaking and groaning, while a loudspeaker blared popular film music across the grounds.

While Phambiri was preparing for his wrestling match, Hukam Singh was busy haggling over the price of pumpkins. Sita and Vijay wandered on their own among the stalls, gazing at toys and kites and bangles and clothing, at brightly coloured, syrupy sweets. Some of the rural people had transistor-radios dangling by straps from their shoulders, the radio music competing with the loudspeaker. Occasionally a buffalo bellowed, drowning all other sounds.

Various people were engaged in roadside professions. There was the fortune-teller. He had slips of paper, each of them covered with writing, which he kept in little trays along with some grain. He had a tame sparrow. When you gave the fortune-teller your money, he allowed the little bird to hop in and out among the trays until it stopped at one and started pecking at the grain. From this tray the fortune-teller took the slip of paper and presented it to his client. The writing told you what to expect over the next few months or years.

A harassed, middle-aged man, who was surrounded by six noisy sons and daughters, was looking a little concerned, because his slip of paper said: 'Do not lose hope. You will have a child soon.'

Some distance away sat a barber, and near him a professional ear-cleaner. Several children clustered around a peepshow, which was built into an old gramophone cabinet. While one man wound up the gramophone and placed a well-worn record on the turn-table, his partner pushed coloured pictures through a slide-viewer.

A young man walked energetically up and down the fairground, beating a drum and announcing the day's attractions. The wrestling bouts were about to start. The main attraction was going to be the fight between Phambiri, described as a man 'whose thighs had the thickness of an elephant's trunk', and the local champion, Sher Dil (tiger's heart)—a wild-looking man, with hairy chest and beetling brow. He was heavier than Phambiri but not so tall.

Sita and Vijay joined Hukam Singh at one corner of the akhara, the wrestling-pit. Hukam Singh was massaging his son's famous thighs.

A gong sounded and Sher Dil entered the ring, slapping himself on the chest and grunting like a wild boar. Phambiri advanced slowly to meet him.

They came to grips immediately, and stood swaying from side to side, two giants pitting their strength against each other. The sweat glistened on their well-oiled bodies.

Sher Dil got his arms round Phambiri's waist and tried to lift him off his feet but Phambiri had twined one powerful leg around his opponent's thigh, and they both came down together with a loud squelch, churning up the soft mud of the wrestling pit. But neither wrestler had been pinned down.

Soon they were so covered with mud that it was difficult to distinguish one from the other. There was a flurry of arms and legs. The crowd was cheering and Sita and Vijay were cheering too, but the wrestlers were too absorbed in their struggle to be aware of their supporters. Each sought to turn the other on to his back. That was all that mattered. There was no count.

For a few moments Sher Dil had Phambiri almost helpless, but Phambiri wriggled out of a crushing grip and, using his legs once again, sent Sher Dil rocketing across the akhara. But Sher Dil landed on his belly, and even with Phambiri on top of him, it wasn't victory.

Nothing happened for several minutes, and the crowd became restless and shouted for more action. Phambiri thought of twisting his opponent's ear but he realized that he might get disqualified for doing that so he restrained himself. He relaxed his grip slightly and this gave Sher Dil a chance to heave himself up and sent Phambiri spinning across the akhara. Phambiri was still in a sitting position when the other took a flying leap at him. But Phambiri dived forward, taking his opponent between the legs, and then rising, flung him backwards with a resounding thud. Sher Dil was helpless and Phambiri sat on his opponent's chest to remove all doubts as to who was the winner. Only when the applause of the spectators told him that he had won did he rise and leave the ring.

Accompanied by his proud father, Phambiri accepted the prize money, thirty rupees, and then went in search of a tap. After he had washed the oil and mud from his body, he put on fresh clothes. Then, putting his arms around Vijay and Sita he said, 'You have brought me luck, both of you. Now let us celebrate!' And he led the way to the sweet shops.

They ate syrupy rasgollas (made from milk and sugar) and almond-filled fudge, and little pies filled with minced meat, and washed everything down with a fizzy orange drink.

'Now I will buy each of you a small present,' said Phambiri.

He bought a bright blue sports' shirt for Vijay. He bought a new hookah-bowl for his father. And he took Sita to a stall where dolls were sold, and asked her to choose one.

There were all kinds of dolls—cheap plastic dolls, and beautiful dolls made by hand, dressed in the traditional costumes of different regions of the country. Sita was immediately reminded of Mumta, her own rag doll, who had been made at home with Grandmother's help. And she remembered Grandmother, and Grandmother's sewing-machine, and the home that had been swept away, and the tears started to her eyes.

The dolls seemed to smile at Sita. The shopkeeper held them up one by one, and they appeared to dance, to twirl their wide skirts, to stamp their jingling feet on the counter. Each doll made her own special appeal to Sita. Each one wanted her love.

'Which one will you have?' asked Phambiri. 'Choose the prettiest, never mind the price!'

But Sita could say nothing. She could only shake her head.

No doll, no matter how beautiful, could replace Mumta. She would never keep a doll again. That part of her life was over.

So instead of a doll Phambiri bought her bangles-coloured glass bangles which slipped easily over Sita's thin wrists. And then he took them into a temporary cinema, a large shed made of corrugated tin sheets.

Vijay had been in a cinema before—the towns were full of cinemas—but for Sita it was another new experience. Many things that were common enough for other boys and girls were strange and new for a girl who had spent nearly all her life on a small island in the middle of a big river.

As they found seats, a curtain rolled up and a white sheet came into view. The babble of talk dwindled into silence. Sita became aware of a whirring noise somewhere not far behind her. But, before she could turn her head to see what it was, the sheet became a rectangle of light and colour. It came to life. People moved and spoke. A story unfolded.

But, long afterwards, all that Sita could remember of her first film was a jumble of images and incidents. A train in danger, the audience murmuring with anxiety, a bridge over a river (but smaller than hers), the bridge being blown to pieces, the engine plunging into the river, people struggling in the water, a woman rescued by a man who immediately embraced her, the lights coming on again, and the audience rising slowly and drifting out of the theatre, looking quite unconcerned and even satisfied. All those people struggling in the water were now quite safe, back in the little black box in the projection room.

Catching the Train

And now a real engine, a stream-engine belching smoke and fire, was on its way towards Sita.

She stood with Vijay on the station platform along with over a hundred other people waiting for the Shahganj train.

The platform was littered with the familiar bedrolls (or holdalls) without which few people in India ever travel. On these rolls sat women, children, great-aunts and great-uncles, grandfathers, grandmothers and grandchildren, while the more active adults hovered at the edge of the platform, ready to leap onto the train as soon as it arrived and reserve a space for the family. In India, people do not travel alone if they can help it. The whole family must be taken along—especially if the reason for the journey is a marriage, a pilgrimage, or simply a visit to friends or relations.

Moving among the piles of bedding and luggage were coolies, vendors of magazines, sweetmeats, tea, and betel-leaf preparation; also stray dogs, stray people and sometimes a stray station-master. The cries of the vendors mingled with the general clamour of the station and the shunting of a steam-engine in the yard. 'Tea, hot tea!,' 'Fresh limes!' Sweets, papads, hot stuff, cold drinks, mangoes, toothpowder, photos of film stars, bananas, balloons, wooden toys! The platform had become a bazaar. What a blessing for those vendors that trains ran late and that people had to wait, and waiting, drank milky tea, bought toys for children, cracked peanut shells, munched bananas and chose little presents for the friends or relations on whom they were going to descend very shortly.

But there came the train!

The signal was down. The crowd surged forward, swamping an assistant station-master. Vijay took Sita by the hand and led her forward. If they were too slow, they would not get a place on the crowded train. In front of them was a tall, burly, bearded Sikh from the Punjab. Vijay decided it would be a wise move to stand behind him and move forward at the same time.

The station bell clanged and a big, puffing, black steam-engine appeared in the distance. A stray dog, with a lifetime's experience of trains, darted away across the railway lines. As the train came alongside the platform, doors opened, window shutters fell, eager faces appeared in the openings, and, even before the train had come to a stop, people were trying to get in or out.

For a few moments there was chaos. The crowd surged backwards and forwards. No one could get out. No one could get in! Fifty people were leaving the train, a hundred were catching it! No one wanted to give way. But every problem has a solution somewhere, provided one looks for it. And this particular problem was solved by a man climbing out of a window. Others followed his example. The pressure at the doors eased and people started squeezing into their compartments.

Vijay stayed close to the Sikh who forged a way through the throng. The Sikh reached an open doorway and was through. Vijay and Sita were through! They found somewhere to sit and were then able to look down at the platform, into the whirlpool, and enjoy themselves a little. The vendors had abandoned the people on the platform and had started selling their wares at the windows. Hukam Singh, after buying their tickets, had given Vijay and Sita a rupee to spend on the way. Vijay bought a freshly split coconut, and Sita bought a comb for her hair. She had never bothered with her hair before.

They saw a worried man rushing along the platform searching for his family; but they were already in the compartment, having beaten him to it, and eagerly helped him in at the door. A whistle shrilled and they were off! A couple of vendors made last-minute transactions, then jumped from the slow-moving train. One man did this expertly with a tray of teacups balanced on one hand.

The train gathered speed.

'What will happen to all those people still on the platform?' asked Sita anxiously. 'Will they all be left behind?'

She put her head out of the window and looked back at the receding platform. It was strangely empty. Only the vendors and the coolies and the stray dogs and the dishevelled railway staff were in evidence. A miracle had happened. No one— absolutely no one—had been left behind!

Then the train was rushing through the night, the engine throwing out bright sparks that danced away like fireflies. Sometimes the train had to slow down, as flood water had weakened the embankments. Sometimes it stopped at brightly-lit stations.

When the train started again and moved on into the dark countryside, Sita would stare through the glass of the window, at the bright lights of a town or the quiet glow of village lamps. She thought of Phambiri and Hukam Singh, and wondered if she would ever see them again. Already they were like people in a fairy-tale, met briefly on the road and never seen again.

There was no room in the compartment in which to lie down; but Sita soon fell asleep, her head resting against Vijay's shoulder.

A Meeting and a Parting

Sita did not know where to look for her grandfather. For an hour she and Vijay wandered through the Shahganj bazaar, growing hungrier all the time. They had no money left and they were hot and thirsty.

Outside the bazaar, near a small temple, they saw a tree in which several small boys were helping themselves to the sour, purple fruit.

It did not take Vijay long to join the boys in the tree. They did not object to his joining them. It wasn't their tree, anyway.

Sita stood beneath the tree while Vijay threw the jamuns down to her. They soon had a small pile of the fruit. They were on the road again, their faces stained with purple juice.

They were asking the way to the Shahganj hospital when Sita caught a glimpse of her grandfather on the road.

At first the old man did not recognize her. He was walking stiffly down the road, looking straight ahead, and would have walked right past the dusty, dishevelled girl, had she not charged straight at his thin, shaky legs and clasped him round the waist.

'Sita!' he cried, when he had recovered his wind and his balance. 'Why are you here? How did you get off the island? I have been very worried—it has been bad, these last two days. . .'

'Is Grandmother all right?' asked Sita.

But even as she spoke, she knew that Grandmother was no longer with them. The dazed look in the old man's eyes told her as much. She wanted to cry—not for Grandmother, who could suffer no more, but for Grandfather, who looked so helpless and bewildered. She did not want him to be unhappy. She forced back her tears and took his gnarled and trembling hand and with Vijay walking beside her, led the old man down the crowded street.

She knew, then, that it would be on her shoulder that Grandfather would lean in the years to come.

They decided to remain in Shahganj for a couple of days, staying at a dharamsala—a wayside rest-house—until the flood waters subsided. Grandfather still had two of the goats—it had not been necessary to sell more than one—but he did not want to take the risk of rowing a crowded boat across to the island. The river was still fast and dangerous.

But Vijay could not stay with Sita any longer.

'I must go now,' he said. 'My father and mother will be very worried and they will not know where to look for me. In a day or two the water will go down and you will be able to go back to your home.'

'Perhaps the island has gone forever,' said Sita.

'It will be there,' said Vijay. 'It is a rocky island. Bad for crops but good for a house!'

'Will you come?' asked Sita.

What she really wanted to say was, 'Will you come to see me?' but she was too shy to say it; and besides, she wasn't sure if Vijay would want to see her again.

'I will come,' said Vijay. 'That is, if my father gets me another boat!'

As he turned to go, he gave her his flute.

'Keep it for me,' he said. 'I will come for it one day.' When he saw her hesitate, he smiled and said, 'It is a good flute!'

The Return

There was more rain, but the worst was over, and when Grandfather and Sita returned to the island, the river was no longer in spate.

Grandfather could hardly believe his eyes when he saw that the tree had disappeared—the tree that had seemed as permanent as the island, as much a part of his life as the river itself had been. He marvelled at Sita's escape.

'It was the tree that saved you,' he said.

'And the boy,' said Sita.

'Yes, and the boy.'

She thought about Vijay and wondered if she would ever see him again. Would he, like Phambiri and Hukam Singh, be one of those people who arrived as though out of a fairy-tale and then disappeared silently and mysteriously? She did not know it then, but some of the moving forces of our lives are meant to touch us briefly and go their way . . . .

And because Grandmother was no longer with them, life on the island was quite different. The evenings were sad and lonely.

But there was a lot of work to be done and Sita did not have much time to think of Grandmother or Vijay or the world she had glimpsed during her journey.

For three nights they slept under a crude shelter made out of gunny-bags. During the day Sita helped Grandfather rebuild the mud-hut. Once again they used the big rock for support.

The trunk which Sita had packed so carefully had not been swept off the island, but water had got into it and the food and clothing had been spoilt. But Grandfather's hookah had been saved, and, in the evenings after work was done and they had eaten their light meal which Sita prepared, he would smoke with a little of his old contentment and tell Sita about other floods which he had experienced as a boy. And he would tell her about the wrestling matches he had won, and the kites he had flown.

Sita planted a mango seed in the same spot where the peepul tree had stood. It would be many years before it grew into a big tree, but Sita liked to imagine herself sitting in the branches, picking the mangoes straight from the tree and feasting on them all day.

Grandfather was more particular about making a vegetable garden, putting down peas, carrots, gram and mustard.

One day, when most of the hard work had been done and the new hut was ready, Sita took the flute which had been given to her by Vijay, and walked down to the water's edge and tried to play it. But all she could produce were a few broken notes, and even the goats paid no attention to her music.

Sometimes Sita thought she saw a boat coming down the river, and she would run to meet it; but usually there was no boat, or, if there was, it belonged to a stranger or to another fisherman. And so she stopped looking out for boats.

Slowly, the rains came to an end. The flood waters had receded, and in the villages people were beginning to till the land again and sow crops for the winter months. There were more cattle fairs and wrestling matches. The days were warm and sultry. The water in the river was no longer muddy, and one evening Grandfather brought home a huge mahseer, and Sita made it into a delicious curry.

Deep River

Grandfather sat outside the hut, smoking his hookah. Sita was at the far end of the island, spreading clothes on the rocks to dry. One of the goats had followed her. It was the friendlier of the two and often followed Sita about the island. She had made it a necklace of coloured beads.

She sat down on a smooth rock, and, as she did so, she noticed a small bright object in the sand near her feet. She picked it up. It was a little wooden toy—a coloured peacock, the god Krishna's favourite bird—it must have come down on the river and been swept ashore on the island. Some of the paint had been rubbed off; but for Sita, who had no toys, it was a great find.

There was a soft footfall behind her. She looked round, and there was Vijay, barefoot, standing over her and smiling.

'I thought you wouldn't come,' said Sita.

'There was much work in my village. Did you keep my flute?'

'Yes, but I cannot play it properly.'

'I will teach you,' said Vijay.

He sat down beside her and they cooled their feet in the water, which was clear now, taking in the blue of the sky. They could see the sand and the pebbles of the riverbed.

'Sometimes the river is angry and sometimes it is kind,' said Sita.

'We are part of the river,' said Vijay.

It was a good river, deep and strong, beginning in the mountains and ending in the sea.

Along its banks, for hundreds of miles, lived millions of people, and Sita was only one small girl among them, and no one had ever heard of her, no one knew her—except for the old man, and the boy, and the water that was blue and white and wonderful.

LOVE IS A SAD SONG

❧

I SIT AGAINST THIS grey rock, beneath a sky of pristine blueness, and think of you, Sushila. It is November and the grass is turning brown and yellow. Crushed, it still smells sweet. The afternoon sun shimmers on the oak leaves and turns them a glittering silver. A cricket sizzles its way through the long grass. The stream murmurs at the bottom of the hill—that stream where you and I lingered on a golden afternoon in May.

I sit here and think of you and try to see your slim brown hand resting against this rock, feeling its warmth. I am aware again of the texture of your skin, the coolness of your feet, the sharp tingle of your fingertips. And in the pastures of my mind I run my hand over your quivering mouth and crush your tender breasts. Remembered passion grows sweeter with the passing of time.

You will not be thinking of me now, as you sit in your home in the city, cooking or sewing or trying to study for examinations. There will be men and women and children circling about you, in that crowded house of your grandmother's, and you will not be able to think of me for more than a moment or two. But I know you do think of me sometimes, in some private moment which cuts you off from the crowd. You will remember how I wondered what it is all about, this loving, and why it should cause such an upheaval. You are still a child, Sushila—and yet you found it so easy to quieten my impatient heart.

On the night you came to stay with us, the light from the street lamp shone through the branches of the peach tree and made leaf patterns on the walls. Through the glass panes of the front door I caught a glimpse of little Sunil's face, bright and questing, and then—a hand—a dark, long-fingered hand that could only have belonged to you.

It was almost a year since I had seen you, my dark and slender girl. And now you were in your sixteenth year. And Sunil was twelve; and your uncle, Dinesh, who lived with me, was twenty-three. And I was almost thirty—a fearful and wonderful age, when life becomes dangerous for dreamers.

I remember that when I left Delhi last year, you cried. At first I thought it was because I was going away. Then I realized that it was because you could not go anywhere yourself. Did you envy my freedom—the freedom to live in a poverty of my own choosing, the freedom of the writer? Sunil, to my surprise, did not show much emotion at my going away. This hurt me a little, because during that year he had been particularly close to me, and I felt for him a very special love. But separations cannot be of any significance to small boys of twelve who live for today, tomorrow, and—if they are very serious—the day after.

Before I went away with Dinesh, you made us garlands of marigolds. They were orange and gold, fresh and clean and kissed by the sun. You garlanded me as I sat talking to Sunil. I remember you both as you looked that day—Sunil's smile dimpling his cheeks, while you gazed at me very seriously, your expression very tender. I loved you even then . . . .

Our first picnic.

The path to the little stream took us through the oak forest, where the flashy blue magpies played follow-my-leader with their harsh, creaky calls. Skirting an open ridge (the place where I now sit and write), the path dipped through oak, rhododendron and maple, until it reached a little knoll above the stream. It was a spot unknown to the tourists and summer visitors. Sometimes a milkman or woodcutter crossed the stream on the way to town or village but no one lived beside it. Wild roses grew on the banks.

I do not remember much of that picnic. There was a lot of dull conversation with our neighbours, the Kapoors, who had come along too. You and Sunil were rather bored. Dinesh looked preoccupied. He was fed up with college. He wanted to start earning a living: wanted to paint. His restlessness often made him moody, irritable.

Near the knoll the stream was too shallow for bathing, but I told Sunil about a cave and a pool further downstream and promised that we would visit the pool another day.

That same night, after dinner, we took a walk along the dark road that goes past the house and leads to the burning ghat. Sunil, who had already sensed the intimacy between us, took my hand and put it in yours. An odd, touching little gesture!

'Tell us a story,' you said.

'Yes, tell us,' said Sunil.

I told you the story of the pure in heart. A shepherd boy found a snake in the forest and the snake told the boy that it was really a princess who had been bewitched and turned into a snake and that it could only recover its human form if someone who was truly pure in heart gave it three kisses on the mouth. The boy put his lips to the mouth of the snake and kissed it thrice. And the snake was transformed into a beautiful princess. But the boy lay cold and dead.

'You always tell sad stories,' complained Sunil.

'I like sad stories,' you said. 'Tell us another.'

'Tomorrow night. I'm sleepy.'

We were woken in the night by a strong wind which went whistling round the old house and came rushing down the chimney, humming and hawing and finally choking itself.

Sunil woke up and cried out, 'What's that noise, Uncle?'

'Only the wind,' I said.

'Not a ghost?'

'Well, perhaps the wind is made up of ghosts. Perhaps this wind contains the ghosts of all the people who have lived and died in this old house and want to come in again from the cold.'

You told me about a boy who had been fond of you in Delhi. Apparently he had visited the house on a few occasions, and had sometimes met you on the street while you were on your way home from school. At first, he had been fond of another girl but later he switched his affections to you. When you told me that he had written to you recently, and that before coming up you had replied to his letter, I was consumed by jealousy—an emotion which I thought I had grown out of long ago. It did not help to be told that you were not serious about the boy, that you were sorry for him because he had already been disappointed in love.

'If you feel sorry for everyone who has been disappointed in love,' I said, 'you will soon be receiving the affections of every young man over ten.'

'Let them give me their affections,' you said, 'and I will give them my chappal over their heads.'

'But spare my head,' I said.

'Have *you* been in love before?'

'Many times. But this is the first time.'

'And who is your love?'

'Haven't you guessed?'

Sunil, who was following our conversation with deep interest, seemed to revel in the situation. Probably he fancied himself playing the part of Cupid, or Kamadeva, and delighted in watching the arrows of love strike home. No doubt I made it more enjoyable for him. Because I could not hide my feelings. Soon Dinesh would know, too—and then?

A year ago my feelings about you were almost paternal! Or so I thought . . . . But you are no longer a child and I am a little older too. For when, the night after the picnic, you took my hand and held it against your soft warm cheek, it was the first time that a girl had responded to me so readily, so tenderly. Perhaps it was just innocence but that one action of yours, that acceptance of me, immediately devastated my heart.

Gently, fervently, I kissed your eyes and forehead, your small round mouth, and the lobes of your ears, and your long smooth throat; and I whispered, 'Sushila, I love you, I love you, I love you,' in the same way that millions and millions of love-smitten young men have whispered since time immemorial. What else can one say? I love you, I love you. There is nothing simpler; nothing that can be made to mean any more than that. And what else did I say? That I would look after you and work for you and make you happy; and that too had been said before, and I was in no way different from anyone. I was a man and yet I was a boy again.

We visited the stream again, a day or two later, early in the morning. Using the rocks as stepping-stones, we wandered downstream for about a furlong until we reached a pool and a small waterfall and a cool dark cave. The rocks were mostly grey but some were yellow with age and some were cushioned with moss. A forktail stood on a boulder in the middle of the stream, uttering its low pleasant call. Water came dripping down from the sides of the cave, while sunlight filtered through a crevice in the rock ceiling, dappling your face. A spray of water was caught by a shaft of sunlight and at intervals it reflected the colours of the rainbow.

'It is a beautiful place,' you said.

'Come, then,' I said, 'let us bathe.'

Sunil and I removed our clothes and jumped into the pool while you sat down in the shade of a walnut tree and watched us disport ourselves in the water. Like a frog, Sunil leapt and twisted about in the clear, icy water; his eyes shone, his teeth glistened white, his body glowed with sunshine, youth, and the jewels made by drops of water glistening in the sun.

Then we stretched ourselves out beside you and allowed the sun to sink deep into our bodies.

Your feet, laved with dew, stood firm on the quickening grass. There was a butterfly between us: its wings red and gold and heavy with dew. It could not move because of the weight of moisture. And as your foot came nearer and I saw that you would crush it, I said, 'Wait. Don't crush the butterfly, Sushila. It has only a few days in the sun and we have many.'

'And if I spare it,' you said, laughing, 'what will you do for me, what will you pay?'

'Why, anything you say.'

'And will you kiss my foot?'

'Both feet,' I said and did so willingly. For they were no less than the wings of butterflies.

Later, when you ventured near the water, I dragged you in with me. You cried out, not in alarm but with the shock of the cold water, and then, wrenching yourself from my arms, clambered on to the rocks, your thin dress clinging to your thighs, your feet making long patterns on the smooth stone.

Though we tired ourselves out that day, we did not sleep at night. We lay together, you and Sunil on either side of me. Your head rested on my shoulders, your hair lay pressed against my cheek. Sunil had curled himself up into a ball but he was far from being asleep. He took my hand, and he took yours, and he placed them together. And I kissed the tender inside of your hand.

I whispered to you, 'Sushila, there has never been anyone I've loved so much. I've been waiting all these years to find you. For a long time I did not even like women. But you are so different. You care for me, don't you?'

You nodded in the darkness. I could see the outline of your face in the faint moonlight that filtered through the skylight. You never replied directly to a question. I suppose that was feminine quality; coyness, perhaps.

'Do you love me, Sushila?'

No answer.

'Not now. When you are a little older. In a year or two.'

Did she nod in the darkness or did I imagine it?

'I know it's too early,' I continued. 'You are still too young. You are still at school. But already you are much wiser than me. I am finding it too difficult to control myself, but I will, since you wish it so. I'm very impatient, I know that, but I'll wait for as long as you make me—two or three or a hundred years. Yes, Sushila, a hundred years!'

Ah, what a pretty speech I made! Romeo could have used some of it; Majnu, too.

And your answer? Just a nod, a little pressure on my hand.

I took your fingers and kissed them one by one. Long fingers, as long as mine.

After some time I became aware of Sunil nudging me.

'You are not talking to me,' he complained. 'You are only talking to her. You only love her.'

'I'm terribly sorry. I love you too, Sunil.'

Content with this assurance, he fell asleep; but towards morning, thinking himself in the middle of the bed, he rolled over and landed with a thump on the floor. He didn't know how it had happened and accused me of pushing him out.

'I know you don't want me in the bed,' he said.

It was a good thing Dinesh, in the next room, didn't wake up.

*

'Have you done any work this week?' asked Dinesh with a look of reproach.

'Not much,' I said.

'You are hardly ever in the house. You are never at your desk. Something seems to have happened to you.'

'I have given myself a holiday, that's all. Can't writers take holidays too?'

'No. You have said so yourself. And anyway, you seem to have taken a permanent holiday.'

'Have you finished that painting of the Tibetan woman?' I asked, trying to change the subject.

'That's the third time you've asked me that question, even though you saw the completed painting a week ago. You're getting very absent-minded.'

There was a letter from your old boy-friend; I mean your young boy-friend. It was addressed to Sunil, but I recognized the sender's name and knew it was really for you.

I assumed a look of calm detachment and handed the letter to you. But both you and Sunil sensed my dismay. At first you teased me and showed me the boy's photograph, which had been enclosed (he was certainly good-looking in a flashy way); then, finding that I became gloomier every minute, you tried to make amends, assuring me that the correspondence was one-sided and that you no longer replied to his letters.

And that night, to show me that you really cared, you gave me your hand as soon as the lights were out. Sunil was fast asleep.

We sat together at the foot of your bed. I kept my arm about you, while you rested your head against my chest. Your feet lay in repose upon mine. I kept kissing you. And when we lay down together, I loosened your blouse and kissed your small firm breasts, and put my lips to your nipples and felt them grow hard against my mouth.

The shy responsiveness of your kisses soon turned to passion. You clung to me. We had forgotten time and place and circumstance. The light of your eyes had been drowned in that lost look of a woman who desires. For a space we both struggled against desire. Suddenly I had become afraid of myself—afraid for you. I tried to free myself from your clasping arms. But you cried in a low voice, 'Love me! Love me! I want you to love me.'

Another night you fell asleep with your face in the crook of my arm, and I lay awake a long time, conscious of your breathing, of the touch of your hair on my cheek, of the soft warm soles of your feet, of your slim waist and legs.

And in the morning, when the sunshine filled the room, I watched you while you slept—your slim body in repose, your face tranquil, your thin dark hands like sleeping butterflies and then, when you woke, the beautiful untidiness of your hair and the drowsiness in your eyes. You lay folded up like a kitten, your limbs as untouched by self-consciousness as the limbs of a young and growing tree. And during the warmth of the day a bead of sweat rested on your brow like a small pearl.

I tried to remember what you looked like as a child. Even then, I had always been aware of your presence. You must have been nine or ten when I first saw you—thin, dark, plain-faced, always wearing the faded green skirt that was your school uniform. You went about barefoot. Once, when the monsoon arrived, you ran out into the rain with the other children, naked, exulting in the swish of the cool rain. I remembered your beautiful straight legs and thighs, your swift smile, your dark eyes. You say you do not remember playing naked in the rain but that is because you did not see yourself.

I did not notice you growing. Your face did not change very much. You must have been thirteen when you gave up skirts and started wearing the salwar-kameez. You had few clothes but the plainness of your dress only seemed to bring out your own radiance. And as you grew older, your eyes became more expressive, your hair longer and glossier, your gestures more graceful. And then, when you came to me in the hills, I found that you had been transformed into a fairy princess of devastating charm.

We were idling away the afternoon on our beds and you were reclining in my arms when Dinesh came in unexpectedly. He said nothing, merely passed through the room and entered his studio. Sunil got a fright and you were momentarily confused. Then you said, 'He knows already,' and I said, 'yes, he must know.'

Later I spoke to Dinesh. I told him that I wanted to marry;

that I knew I would have to wait until you were older and had finished school—probably two or three years—and that I was prepared to wait although I knew it would be a long and difficult business. I asked him to help me.

He was upset at first, probably because he felt I had been deceptive (which was true), and also because of his own responsibility in the matter. You were his niece and I had made love to you while he had been preoccupied with other things. But after a little while when he saw that I was sincere and rather confused he relented.

'It has happened too soon,' he said. 'She is too young for all this. Have you told her that you love her?'

'Of course. Many times.'

'You're a fool, then. Have you told her that you want to marry her?'

'Yes.'

'Fool again. That's not the way it is done. Haven't you lived in India long enough to know that?'

'But I love her.'

'Does she love you?'

'I think so.'

'You think so. Desire isn't love, you must know that. Still, I suppose she does love you, otherwise she would not be holding hands with you all day. But you are quite mad, falling in love with a girl half your age.'

'Well, I'm not exactly an old man. I'm thirty.'

'And she's a schoolgirl.'

'She isn't a girl any more, she's too responsive.'

'Oh, you've found that out, have you?'

'Well . . .' I said, covered in confusion. 'Well, she has shown that she cares a little. You know that it's years since I took any interest in a girl. You called it unnatural on my part, remember? Well, they simply did not exist for me, that's true.'

'Delayed adolescence,' muttered Dinesh.

'But Sushila is different. She puts me at ease. She doesn't turn away from me. I love her and I want to look after her. I can only do that by marrying her.'

'All right, but take it easy. Don't get carried away. And don't, for God's sake, give her a baby. Not while she's still at school! I will do what I can to help you. But you will have to be patient. And no one else must know of this or I will be blamed for everything. As it is Sunil knows too much, and he's too small to know so much.'

'Oh, he won't tell anyone.'

'I wish you had fallen in love with her two years from now. You will have to wait that long, anyway. Getting married isn't a simple matter. People will wonder why we are in such a hurry, marrying her off as soon as she leaves school. They'll think the worst!'

'Well, people do marry for love you know, even in India. It's happening all the time.'

'But it doesn't happen in *our* family. You know how orthodox most of them are. They wouldn't appreciate your outlook. You may marry Sushila for love but it will have to *look* like an arranged marriage!'

Little things went wrong that evening.

First, a youth on the road passed a remark which you resented; and you, most unlady-like, but most Punjabi-like, picked up a stone and threw it at him. It struck him on the leg. He was too surprised to say anything and limped off. I remonstrated with you, told you that throwing stones at people often resulted in a fight, then realized that you had probably wanted to see me fighting on your behalf.

Later you were annoyed because I said you were a little absent-minded. Then Sunil sulked because I spoke roughly to him (I can't remember why), and refused to talk to me for three hours, which was a record. I kept apologizing but neither of you would listen. It was all part of a game. When I gave up trying and turned instead to my typewriter and my unfinished story, you came and sat beside me and started playing with my hair. You were jealous of my story, of the fact that it was possible for me to withdraw into my work. And I reflected that a woman had to be jealous of something. If there wasn't another woman, then it was a man's work, or his hobby, or his best friend, or his favourite sweater, or his pet mongoose that made her resentful. There is a story in Kipling about a woman who grew insanely jealous of a horse's saddle because her husband spent an hour every day polishing it with great care and loving kindness.

Would it be like that in marriage, I wondered—an eternal triangle: you, me and the typewriter?

But there were only a few days left before you returned to the plains, so I gladly pushed away the typewriter and took you in my arms instead. After all, once you had gone away, it would be a long, long time before I could hold you in my arms again. I might visit you in Delhi but we would not be able to enjoy the same freedom and intimacy. And while I savoured the salt kiss of your lips, I wondered how long I would have to wait until I could really call you my own.

Dinesh was at college and Sunil had gone roller-skating and we were alone all morning. At first you avoided me, so I picked up a book and pretended to read. But barely five minutes had passed before you stole up from behind and snapped the book shut.

'It is a warm day,' you said. 'Let us go down to the stream.

Alone together for the first time, we took the steep path down to the stream, and there, hand in hand, scrambled over the rocks until we reached the pool and the waterfall.

'I will bathe today,' you said; and in a few moments you stood beside me, naked, caressed by sunlight and a soft breeze coming down the valley. I put my hand out to share in the sun's caress, but you darted away, laughing, and ran to the waterfall as though you would hide behind a curtain of gushing water. I was soon beside you. I took you in my arms and kissed you, while the water crashed down upon our heads. Who yielded—you or I? All I remember is that you had entwined yourself about me like a clinging vine, and that a little later we lay together on the grass, on bruised and broken clover, while a whistling-thrush released its deep sweet secret on the trembling air.

Blackbird on the wing, bird of the forest shadows, black rose in the long ago of summer, this was your song. It isn't time that's passing by, it is you and I.

It was your last night under my roof. We were not alone but when I woke in the middle of the night and stretched my hand out, across the space between our beds, you took my hand, for you were awake too. Then I pressed the ends of your fingers, one by one, as I had done so often before, and you dug your nails into my flesh. And our hands made love, much as our bodies might have done. They clung together, warmed and caressed each other, each finger taking on an identity of its own and seeking its opposite. Sometimes the tips of our fingers merely brushed against each other, teasingly, and sometimes our palms met with a rush, would tremble and embrace, separate, and then passionately seek each other out. And when sleep finally overcame you, your hand fell listlessly between our beds, touching the ground. And I lifted it up, and after putting it once to my lips, returned it gently to your softly rising bosom.

And so you went away, all three of you, and I was left alone with the brooding mountain. If I could not pass a few weeks without you how was I to pass a year, two years? This was the question I kept asking myself. Would I have to leave the hills and take a flat in Delhi? And what use would it be— looking at you and speaking to you but never able to touch you? Not to be able to touch that which I had already possessed would have been the subtlest form of torture.

The house was empty but I kept finding little things to remind me that you had been there—a handkerchief, a bangle, a length of ribbon—and these remnants made me feel as though you had gone for ever. No sound at night, except the rats scurrying about on the rafters.

The rain had brought out the ferns, which were springing up from tree and rock. The murmur of the stream had become an angry rumble. The honeysuckle creeper winding over the front windows was thick with scented blossom. I wish it had flowered a little earlier, before you left. Then you could have put the flowers in your hair.

At night I drank brandy, wrote listlessly, listened to the wind in the chimney, and read poetry in bed. There was no one to tell stories to and no hand to hold.

I kept remembering little things—the soft hair hiding your ears, the movement of your hands, the cool touch of your feet, the tender look in your eyes and the sudden stab of mischief that sometimes replaced it.

Mrs Kapoor remarked on the softness of your expression. I was glad that someone had noticed it. In my diary I wrote: 'I have looked at Sushila so often and so much that perhaps I have overlooked her most compelling qualities—her kindness (or is it just her easy-goingness?), her refusal to hurt anyone's feelings (or is it just her indifference to everything?), her wide tolerance (or is it just her laziness?) . . . . Oh, how absolutely ignorant I am of women!'

Well, there was a letter from Dinesh and it held out a lifeline, one that I knew I must seize without any hesitation. He said he might be joining an art school in Delhi and asked me if I would like to return to Delhi and share a flat with him. I had always dreaded the possibility of leaving the hills and living again in a city as depressing as Delhi but love, I considered, ought to make any place habitable . . . .

And then I was on a bus on the road to Delhi.

The first monsoon showers had freshened the fields and everything looked much greener than usual. The maize was just shooting up and the mangoes were ripening fast. Near the larger villages, camels and bullock-carts cluttered up the road, and the driver cursed, banging his fist on the horn.

Passing through small towns, the bus-driver had to contend with cycle-rickshaws, tonga-ponies, trucks, pedestrians, and other buses. Coming down from the hills for the first time in over a year, I found the noise, chaos, dust and dirt a little unsettling.

As my taxi drew up at the gate of Dinesh's home, Sunil saw me and came running to open the car door. Other children were soon swarming around me. Then I saw you standing near the front door. You raised your hand to your forehead in a typical Muslim form of greeting—a gesture you had picked up, I suppose, from a film.

For two days Dinesh and I went house-hunting, for I had decided to take a flat if it was at all practicable. Either it was very hot, and we were sweating, or it was raining and we were drenched. (It is difficult to find a flat in Delhi, even if one is in a position to pay an exorbitant rent, which I was not. It is especially difficult for bachelors. No one trusts bachelors, especially if there are grown-up daughters in the house. Is this because bachelors are wolves or because girls are so easily seduced these days?)

Finally, after several refusals, we were offered a flat in one of those new colonies that sprout like mushrooms around the capital. The rent was two hundred rupees a month and although I knew I couldn't really afford so much, I was so sick of refusals and already so disheartened and depressed that I took the place and made out a cheque to the landlord, an elderly gentleman with his daughters all safely married in other parts of the country.

There was no furniture in the flat except for a couple of beds, but we decided we would fill the place up gradually. Everyone at Dinesh's home—brothers, sister-in-law, aunts, nephews and nieces—helped us to move in. Sunil and his younger brother were the first arrivals. Later the other children, some ten of them, arrived. You, Sushila, came only in the afternoon, but I had gone out for something and only saw you when I returned at tea-time. You were sitting on the first-floor balcony and smiled down at me as I walked up the road.

I think you were pleased with the flat; or at any rate, with my courage in taking one. I took you up to the roof, and there, in a corner under the stairs, kissed you very quickly. It had to be quick, because the other children were close on our heels. There wouldn't be much opportunity for kissing you again. The mountains were far and in a place like Delhi, and with a family like yours, private moments would be few and far between.

Hours later, when I sat alone on one of the beds, Sunil came to me, looking rather upset. He must have had a quarrel with you.

'I want to tell you something,' he said.

'Is anything wrong?'

To my amazement he burst into tears.

'Now you must not love me any more,' he said.

'Why not?'

'Because you are going to marry Sushila, and if you love me too much it will not be good for you.'

I could think of nothing to say. It was all too funny and all too sad.

But a little later he was in high spirits, having apparently forgotten the reasons for his earlier dejection. His need for affection stemmed perhaps from his father's long and unnecessary absence from the country.

Dinesh and I had no sleep during our first night in the new flat. We were near the main road and traffic roared past all night. I thought of the hills, so silent that the call of a nightjar startled one in the stillness of the night.

I was out most of the next day and when I got back in the evening it was to find that Dinesh had had a rumpus with the landlord. Apparently the landlord had really wanted bachelors, and couldn't understand or appreciate a large number of children moving in and out of the house all day.

'I thought landlords preferred having families,' I said.

'He wants to know how a bachelor came to have such a large family!'

'Didn't you tell him that the children were only temporary, and wouldn't be living here?'

'I did, but he doesn't believe me.'

'Well, anyway, we're not going to stop the children from coming to see us,' I said indignantly. (No children, no Sushila!) 'If he doesn't see reason, he can have his flat back.'

'Did he cash my cheque?'

'No, he's given it back.'

'That means he really wants us out. To hell with his flat! It's too noisy here anyway. Let's go back to your place.'

We packed our bedding, trunks and kitchen utensils once more; hired a bullock-cart and arrived at Dinesh's home (three miles distant) late at night, hungry and upset.

Everything seemed to be going wrong.

Living in the same house as you, but unable to have any real contact with you (except for the odd, rare moment when we were left alone in the same room and were able to exchange a word or a glance) was an exquisite form of self-inflicted torture: self-inflicted, because no one was forcing me to stay in Delhi. Sometimes you had to avoid me and I could not stand that. Only Dinesh (and of course Sunil and some of the children) knew anything about the affair—adults are much slower than children at sensing the truth—and it was still too soon to reveal the true state of affairs and my own feelings, to anyone else in the family. If I came out with the declaration that I was in love with you, it would immediately become obvious that something had happened during your holiday in the hill station. It would be said that I had taken advantage of the situation (which I had), and that I had seduced you—even though I was beginning to wonder if it was you who had seduced me! And if a marriage was suddenly arranged, people would say: 'It's been arranged so quickly. And she's so young. He must have got her into trouble.' Even though there were no signs of your having got into that sort of trouble.

And yet I could not help hoping that you would become my wife sooner than could be foreseen. I *wanted* to look after you. I did not want others to be doing it for me. Was that very selfish? Or was it a true state of being in love?

There were times—times when you kept at a distance and did not even look at me—when I grew desperate. I knew you could not show your familiarity with me in front of others and yet, knowing this, I still tried to catch your eye, to sit near you, to touch you fleetingly. I could not hold myself back. I became morose, I wallowed in self-pity. And self-pity, I realized, is a sign of failure, especially of failure in love.

It was time to return to the hills.

Sushila, when I got up in the morning to leave, you were still asleep and I did not wake you. I watched you stretched out on your bed, your dark face tranquil and untouched by care, your black hair spread over the white pillow, your long thin hands and feet in repose. You were so beautiful when you were asleep.

And as I watched, I felt a tightening around my heart, a sudden panic that I might somehow lose you.

The others were up and there was no time to steal a kiss. A taxi was at the gate. A baby was bawling. Your grandmother was giving me advice. The taxi driver kept blowing his horn.

Goodbye, Sushila!

We were in the middle of the rains. There was a constant drip and drizzle and drumming on the corrugated tin roof. The walls were damp and there was mildew on my books and even on the pickle that Dinesh had made.

Everything was green, the foliage almost tropical, especially near the stream. Great stagferns grew from the trunks of trees, fresh moss covered the rocks, and the maidenhair fern was at its loveliest. The water was a torrent, rushing through the ravine and taking with it bushes and small trees. I could not remain out for long, for at any moment it might start raining. And there were also the leeches who lost no time in fastening themselves on to my legs and fattening themselves on my blood.

Once, standing on some rocks, I saw a slim brown snake swimming with the current. It looked beautiful and lonely.

I dreamt a dream, a very disturbing dream, which troubled me for days.

In the dream, Sunil suggested that we go down to the stream.

We put some bread and butter into an airbag, along with a long bread knife, and set off down the hill. Sushila was barefoot, wearing the old cotton tunic which she had worn as a child, Sunil had on a bright yellow T-shirt and black jeans. He looked very dashing. As we took the forest path down to the stream, we saw two young men following us. One of them, a dark, slim youth, seemed familiar. I said, 'Isn't that Sushila's boy-friend?' But they denied it. The other youth wasn't anyone I knew.

When we reached the stream, Sunil and I plunged into the pool, while Sushila sat on the rock just above us. We had been bathing for a few minutes when the two young men came down the slope and began fondling Sushila. She did not resist but Sunil climbed out of the pool and began scrambling up the slope. One of the youths, the less familiar one, had a long knife in his hand. Sunil picked up a stone and flung it at the youth, striking him on the shoulder. I rushed up and grabbed the hand that held the knife. The youth kicked me on the shins and thrust me away and I fell beneath him. The arm with the knife was raised over me, but I still held the wrist. And then I saw Sushila behind him, her face framed by a passing cloud. She had the bread knife in her hand, and her arm swung up and down, and the knife cut through my adversary's neck as though it were passing through a ripe melon.

I scrambled to my feet to find Sushila gazing at the headless corpse with the detachment and mild curiosity of a child who has just removed the wings from a butterfly.

The other youth, who looked like Sushila's boy-friend, began running away. He was chased by the three of us. When he slipped and fell, I found myself beside him, the blade of the knife poised beneath his left shoulder-blade. I couldn't push the knife in. Then Sunil put his hand over mine and the blade slipped smoothly into the flesh.

At all times of the day and night I could hear the murmur of the stream at the bottom of the hill. Even if I didn't listen, the sound was there. I had grown used to it. But whenever I went away, I was conscious of something missing and I was lonely without the sound of running water.

I remained alone for two months and then I had to see you again, Sushila. I could not bear the long-drawn-out uncertainty of the situation. I wanted to do something that would bring everything nearer to a conclusion. Merely to stand by and wait was intolerable. Nor could I bear the secrecy to which Dinesh had sworn me. Someone else would have to know about my intentions—*someone* would have to help. I needed another ally to sustain my hopes; only then would I find the waiting easier.

You had not been keeping well and looked thin, but you were as cheerful, as serene as ever.

When I took you to the pictures with Sunil, you wore a sleeveless kameez made of purple silk. It set off your dark beauty very well. Your face was soft and shy and your smile hadn't changed. I could not keep my eyes off you.

Returning home in the taxi, I held your hand all the way.

Sunil (in Punjabi): 'Will you give your children English or Hindi names?'

Me: 'Hindustani names.'

Sunil (in Punjabi): 'Ah, that is the right answer, Uncle!'

And first I went to your mother.

She was a tiny woman and looked very delicate. But she'd had six children—a seventh was on the way—and they had all come into the world without much difficulty and were the healthiest in the entire joint family.

She was on her way to see relatives in another part of the city and I accompanied her part of the way. As she was pregnant, she was offered a seat in the crowded bus. I managed to squeeze in beside her. She had always shown a liking for me and I did not find it difficult to come to the point.

'At what age would you like Sushila to get married?' I asked casually, with almost paternal interest.

'We'll worry about that when the time comes. She has still to finish school. And if she keeps failing her exams, she will never finish school.'

I took a deep breath and made the plunge.

'When the time comes,' I said, 'when the time comes, I would like to marry her.' And without waiting to see what her reaction would be, I continued: 'I know I must wait, a year or two, even longer. But I am telling you this, so that it will be in your mind. You are her mother and so I want you to be the first to know.' (Liar that I was! She was about the fifth to know. But what I really wanted to say was, 'Please don't be looking for any other husband for her just yet.')

She didn't show much surprise. She was a placid woman. But she said, rather sadly, 'It's all right but I don't have much say in the family. I do not have any money, you see. It depends on the others, especially her grandmother.'

'I'll speak to them when the time comes. Don't worry about that. And you don't have to worry about money or anything—what I mean is, I don't believe in dowries—I mean, you don't have to give me a Godrej cupboard and a sofa-set and that sort of thing. All I want is Sushila . . .'

'She is still very young.'

But she was pleased—pleased that her flesh and blood, her own daughter, could mean so much to a man.

'Don't tell anyone else just now,' I said.

'I won't tell anyone,' she said with a smile.

So now the secret—if it could be called that—was shared by at least five people.

The bus crawled on through the busy streets and we sat in silence, surrounded by a press of people but isolated in the intimacy of our conversation.

I warmed towards her—towards that simple, straightforward, uneducated woman (she had never been to school, could not read or write), who might still have been young and pretty had her circumstances been different. I asked her when the baby was due.

'In two months,' she said. She laughed. Evidently she found it unusual and rather amusing for a young man to ask her such a question.

'I'm sure it will be a fine baby,' I said. And I thought: That makes six brothers-in-law!

I did not think I would get a chance to speak to your Uncle Ravi (Dinesh's elder brother) before I left. But on my last evening in Delhi, I found myself alone with him on the Karol Bagh road. At first we spoke of his own plans for marriage, and, to please him, I said the girl he'd chosen was both beautiful and intelligent.

He warmed towards me.

Clearing my throat, I went on. 'Ravi, you are five years younger than me and you are about to get married.'

'Yes, and it's time you thought of doing the same thing.'

'Well, I've never thought seriously about it before—I'd always scorned the institution of marriage—but now I've changed my mind. Do you know whom I'd like to marry?'

To my surprise Ravi unhesitatingly took the name of Asha, a distant cousin I'd met only once. She came from Ferozepur, and her hips were so large that from a distance she looked like an oversized pear.

'No, no,' I said. 'Asha is a lovely girl but I wasn't thinking of her. I would like to marry a girl like Sushila. To be frank, Ravi, I would like to marry Sushila.'

There was a long silence and I feared the worst. The noise of cars, scooters and buses seemed to recede into the distance and Ravi and I were alone together in a vacuum of silence.

So that the awkwardness would not last too long, I stumbled on with what I had to say. 'I know she's young and that I will have to wait for some time.' (Familiar words!) 'But if you approve, and the family approves, and Sushila approves, well then, there's nothing I'd like better than to marry her.'

Ravi pondered, scratched himself, and then, to my delight, said: 'Why not? It's a fine idea.'

The traffic sounds returned to the street, and I felt as though I could set fire to a bus or do something equally in keeping with my high spirits.

'It would bring you even closer to us,' said Ravi. 'We would like to have you in our family. At least I would like it.'

'That makes all the difference,' I said. 'I will do my best for her, Ravi. I'll do everything to make her happy.'

'She is very simple and unspoilt.'

'I know. That's why I care so much for her.'

'I will do what I can to help you. She should finish school by the time she is seventeen. It does not matter if you are older. Twelve years difference in age is not uncommon. So don't worry. Be patient and all will be arranged.'

And so I had three strong allies—Dinesh, Ravi and your mother. Only your grandmother remained, and I dared not approach her on my own. She was the most difficult hurdle because she was the head of the family and she was autocratic and often unpredictable. She was not on good terms with your mother and for that very reason I feared that she might oppose my proposal. I had no idea how much she valued Ravi's and Dinesh's judgement. All I knew was that they bowed to all her decisions.

How impossible it was for you to shed the burden of your relatives! Individually, you got on quite well with all of them; but because they could not live without bickering among themselves, you were just a pawn in the great Joint Family Game.

You put my hand to your cheek and to your breast. I kissed your closed eyes and took your face in my hands, and touched your lips with mine; a phantom kiss in the darkness of a veranda. And then, intoxicated, I stumbled into the road and walked the streets all night.

I was sitting on the rocks above the oak forest when I saw a young man walking towards me down the steep path. From his careful manner of walking, and light clothing, I could tell that he was a stranger, one who was not used to the hills. He was about my height, slim, rather long in the face; good-looking in a delicate sort of way. When he came nearer, I recognized him as the young man in the photograph, the youth of my dream—your late admirer! I wasn't too surprised to see him. Somehow, I had always felt that we would meet one day.

I remembered his name and said, 'How are you, Pramod?'

He became rather confused. His eyes were already clouded with doubt and unhappiness; but he did not appear to be an aggressive person.

'How did you know my name?' he asked.

'How did you know where to find me?' I countered.

'Your neighbours, the Kapoors, told me. I could not wait for you to return to the house. I have to go down again tonight.'

'Well then, would you like to walk home with me, or would you prefer to sit here and talk? I know who you are but I've no idea why you've come to see me.'

'It's all right here,' he said, spreading his handkerchief on the grass before sitting down on it. 'How did you know my name?'

I stared at him for a few moments and got the impression that he was a vulnerable person—perhaps more vulnerable than myself. My only advantage was that I was older and therefore better able to conceal my real feelings.

'Sushila told me,' I said.

'Oh. I did not think you would know.'

I was a little puzzled but said, 'I knew about you, of course. And you must have known that or you would hardly have come here to see me.'

'You knew about Sushila and me?' he asked, looking even more confused.

'Well, I know that you are supposed to be in love with her.'

He smote himself on the forehead. 'My God! Do the others know, too?'

'I don't think so.' I deliberately avoided mention of Sunil.

In his distraction he started plucking at tufts of grass. 'Did she tell you?' he asked.

'Yes.'

'Girls can't keep secrets. But in a way I'm glad she told you. Now I don't have to explain everything. You see, I came here for your help. I know you are not her real uncle but you are very close to her family. Last year in Delhi he often spoke about you. She said you were very kind.'

It then occurred to me that Pramod knew nothing about my relationship with you, other than that I was supposed to be the most benevolent of 'uncles.' He knew that you had spent your summer holidays with me—but so had Dinesh and Sunil. And now, aware that I was a close friend of the family, he had come to make an ally of me—in much the same way that I had gone about making allies!

'Have you seen Sushila recently?' I asked.

'Yes. Two days ago, in Delhi. But I had only a few minutes alone with her. We could not talk much. You see, Uncle—you will not mind if I also call you Uncle?—I want to marry her but there is no one who can speak to her people on my behalf. My own parents are not alive. If I go straight to her family, most probably I will be thrown out of the house. So I want you to help me. I am not well off but I will soon have a job and then I can support her.'

'Did you tell her all this?'

'Yes.'

'And what did she say?'

'She told me to speak to you about it.'

Clever Sushila! Diabolical Sushila!

'To me?' I repeated.

'Yes, she said it would be better than talking to her parents.'

I couldn't help laughing. And a long-tailed blue magpie, disturbed by my laughter, set up a shrill creaking and chattering of its own.

'Don't laugh, I'm serious, Uncle,' said Pramod. He took me by the hand and looked at me appealingly.

'Well, it ought to be serious,' I said. 'How old are you, Pramod?'

'Twenty-three.'

'Only seven years younger than me. So please don't call me uncle. It makes me feel prehistoric. Use my first name, if you like. And when do you hope to marry Sushila?'

'As soon as possible. I know she is still very young for me.'

'Not at all,' I said. 'Young girls are marrying middle-aged men every day! And you're still quite young yourself. But she can't get married as yet, Pramod, I know that for a certainty.'

'That's what I feared. She will have to finish school, I suppose.'

'That's right. But tell me something. It's obvious that you are in love with her and I don't blame you for it. Sushila is the kind of girl we all fall in love with! But do you know if she loves you? Did she say she would like to marry you?'

'She did not say—I do not know . . . . There was a haunted, hurt look in his eyes and my heart went out to him. 'But I love her—isn't that enough?'

'It *could* be enough—provided she doesn't love someone else.'

'Does she, Uncle?'

'To be frank, I don't know.'

He brightened up at that. 'She likes me,' he said. 'I know that much.'

'Well, I like you too but that doesn't mean I'd marry you.'

He was despondent again. 'I see what you mean . . . . But what is love, how can I recognize it?'

And that was one question I couldn't answer. How do we recognize it?

I persuaded Pramod to stay the night. The sun had gone down and he was shivering. I made a fire, the first of the winter, using oak and thorn branches. Then I shared my brandy with him.

I did not feel any resentment against Pramod. Prior to meeting him, I had been jealous. And when I first saw him coming along the path, I remembered my dream, and thought, 'Perhaps I am going to kill him, after all. Or perhaps he's going to kill me.' But it had turned out differently. If dreams have any meaning at all, the meaning doesn't come within our limited comprehension.

I had visualized Pramod as being rather crude, selfish and irresponsible, an unattractive college student, the type who has never known or understood girls very well and looks on them as strange exotic creatures who are to be seized and plundered at the first opportunity. Such men do exist but Pramod was not one of them. He did not know much about women; neither did

I. He was gentle, polite, unsure of himself. I wondered if I should tell him about my own feelings for you.

After a while he began to talk about himself and about you. He told me how he fell in love with you. At first he had been friendly with another girl, a classfellow of yours but a year or two older. You had carried messages to him on the girl's behalf. Then the girl had rejected him. He was terribly depressed and one evening he drank a lot of cheap liquor. Instead of falling dead, as he had been hoping, he lost his way and met you near your home. He was in need of sympathy and you gave him that. You let him hold your hand. He told you how hopeless he felt and you comforted him. And when he said the world was a cruel place, you consented. You *agreed* with him. What more can a man expect from a woman? Only fourteen at the time, you had no difficulty in comforting a man of twenty-two. No wonder he fell in love with you!

Afterwards you met occasionally on the road and spoke to each other. He visited the house once or twice, on some pretext or other. And when you came to the hills, he wrote to you.

That was all he had to tell me. That was all there was to tell. You had touched his heart once and touching it, had no difficulty in capturing it.

Next morning I took Pramod down to the stream. I wanted to tell him everything and somehow I could not do it in the house.

He was charmed by the place. The water flowed gently, its music subdued, soft chamber music after the monsoon orchestration. Cowbells tinkled on the hillside and an eagle soared high above.

'I did not think water could be so clear,' said Pramod. 'It is not muddy like the streams and rivers of the plains.'

'In the summer you can bathe here,' I said. 'There is a pool further downstream.'

He nodded thoughtfully. 'Did she come here too?'

'Yes, Sushila and Sunil and I . . . . We came here on two or three occasions.' My voice trailed off and I glanced at Pramod standing at the edge of the water. He looked up at me and his eyes met mine.

'There is something I want to tell you,' I said.

He continued staring at me and a shadow seemed to pass

across his face—a shadow of doubt, fear, death, eternity, was it one or all of these, or just a play of light and shade? But I remembered my dream and stepped back from him. For a moment both of us looked at each other with distrust and uncertainty. Then the fear passed. Whatever had happened between us, dream or reality, had happened in some other existence. Now he took my hand and held it, held it tight, as though seeking assurance, as though identifying himself with me.

'Let us sit down,' I said. 'There is something I must tell you.'

We sat down on the grass and when I looked up through the branches of the banj-oak, everything seemed to have been tilted and held at an angle, and the sky shocked me with its blueness, and the leaves were no longer green but purple in the shadows of the ravine. They were your colour, Sushila. I remembered you wearing purple—dark smiling Sushila, thinking your own thoughts and refusing to share them with anyone.

'I love Sushila too,' I said.

'I know,' he said naively. 'That is why I came to you for help.'

'No, you don't know,' I said. 'When I say I love Sushila, I mean just that. I mean caring for her in the same way that you care for her. I mean I want to marry her.'

'You, Uncle?'

'Yes. Does it shock you very much?'

'No, no.' He turned his face away and stared at the worn face of an old grey rock and perhaps he drew some strength from its permanency. 'Why should you not love her? Perhaps, in my heart, I really knew it, but did not want to know—did not want to believe. Perhaps that is why I really came here— to find out. Something that Sunil said . . . . But why didn't you tell me before?'

'Because you were telling me!'

'Yes, I was too full of my own love to think that any other was possible. What do we do now? Do we both wait and then let her make her choice?'

'If you wish.'

'You have the advantage, Uncle. You have more to offer.'

'Do you mean more security or more love? Some women place more value on the former.'

'Not Sushila.'
'Not Sushila.'
'I mean you can offer her a more interesting life. You are a writer. Who knows, you may be famous one day.'
'You have your youth to offer, Pramod. I have only a few years of youth left to me—and two or three of them will pass in waiting.'
'Oh, no,' he said. 'You will always be young. If you have Sushila, you will always be young.'
Once again I heard the whistling-thrush. Its song was a crescendo of sweet notes and variations that rang clearly across the ravine. I could not see the bird but its call emerged from the forest like some dark sweet secret and again it was saying, 'It isn't time that's passing by, my friend. It is you and I.'

Listen. Sushila, the worst has happened. Ravi has written to say that a marriage will not be possible—not now, not next year; never. Of course he makes a lot of excuses—that you must receive a complete college education ('higher studies'), that the difference in our age is too great, that you might change your mind after a year or two—but reading between the lines, I can guess that the real reason is your grandmother. She does not want it. Her word is law and no one, least of all Ravi, would dare oppose her.

But I do not mean to give in so easily. I will wait my chance. As long as I know that you are with me, I will wait my chance.

I wonder what the old lady objects to in me. Is it simply that she is conservative and tradition-bound? She has always shown a liking for me and I don't see why her liking should change because I want to marry her grandniece. Your mother has no objection. Perhaps that's why your grandmother objects.

Whatever the reason, I am coming down to Delhi to find out how things stand.

Of course the worst part is that Ravi has asked me—in the friendliest terms and in a most roundabout manner—not to come to the house for some time. He says this will give the affair a chance to cool off and die a natural (I would call it an unnatural) death. He assumes, of course, that I will accept the old lady's decision and simply forget all about you. Ravi has yet to fall in love.

Dinesh was in Lucknow. I could not visit the house. So I sat on a bench in the Talkatora Gardens and watched a group of children playing gulli-danda. Then I recalled that Sunil's school got over at three o'clock and that if I hurried I would be able to meet him outside St Columba's gate.

I reached the school on time. Boys were streaming out of the compound and as they were all wearing green uniforms—a young forest on the move—I gave up all hope of spotting Sunil. But he saw me first. He ran across the road, dodged a cyclist, evaded a bus and seized me about the waist.

'I'm so happy to see you, Uncle!'

'As I am to see you, Sunil.'

'You want to see Sushila?'

'Yes, but you too. I can't come to the house, Sunil. You probably know that. When do you have to be home?'

'About four o'clock. If I'm late, I'll say the bus was too crowded and I couldn't get in.'

'That gives us an hour or two. Let's go to the exhibition grounds. Would you like that?'

'All right, I haven't seen the exhibition yet.'

We took a scooter-rickshaw to the exhibition grounds on Mathura Road. It was an industrial exhibition and there was little to interest either a schoolboy or a lovesick author. But a cafe was at hand, overlooking an artificial lake, and we sat in the sun consuming hot dogs and cold coffee.

'Sunil, will you help me?' I asked.

'Whatever you say, Uncle.'

'I don't suppose I can see Sushila this time. I don't want to hang about near the house or her school like a disreputable character. It's all right lurking outside a boy's school; but it wouldn't do to be hanging about the Kanyadevi Pathshala or wherever it is she's studying. It's possible the family will change their minds about us later. Anyway, what matters now is Sushila's attitude. Ask her this, Sunil. Ask her if she wants me to wait until she is eighteen. She will be free then to do what she wants, even to run away with me if necessary—that is, if she really wants to. I was ready to wait two years. I'm prepared to wait three. But it will help if I know she's waiting too. Will you ask her that, Sunil?'

'Yes, I'll ask her.'

'Ask her tonight. Then tomorrow we'll meet again outside your school.'

We met briefly the next day. There wasn't much time. Sunil had to be home early and I had to catch the night train out of Delhi. We stood in the generous shade of a pipal tree and I asked, 'What did she say?'

'She said to keep waiting.'

'All right, I'll wait.'

'But when she is eighteen, what if she changes her mind? You know what girls are like.'

'You're a cynical chap, Sunil.'

'What does that mean?'

'It means you know too much about life. But tell me—what makes you think she might change her mind?'

'Her boy-friend.'

'Pramod? She doesn't care for him, poor chap.'

'Not Pramod. Another one.'

'Another! You mean a new one?'

'New,' said Sunil. 'An officer in a bank. He's got a car.'

'Oh,' I said despondently. 'I can't compete with a car.'

'No,' said Sunil. 'Never mind, Uncle. You still have me for your friend. Have you forgotten that?'

I had almost forgotten but it was good to be reminded.

'It is time to go,' he said. 'I must catch the bus today. When will you come to Delhi again?'

'Next month. Next year. Who knows? But I'll come. Look after yourself, my friend.'

He ran off and jumped on to the footboard of a moving bus. He waved to me until the bus went round the bend in the road.

It was lonely under the pipal tree. It is said that only ghosts live in pipal trees. I do not blame them, for pipal trees are cool and shady and full of loneliness.

I may stop loving you, Sushila but I will never stop loving the days I loved you.

WHEN YOU CAN'T CLIMB TREES ANY MORE

&

He stood on the grass verge by the side of the road and looked over the garden wall at the old house. It hadn't changed much. There's little anyone can do to alter a house built with solid blocks of granite brought from the riverbed. But there was a new outhouse and there were fewer trees. He was pleased to see that the jackfruit tree still stood at the side of the building, casting its shade on the wall. He remembered his grandmother saying: 'A blessing rests on the house where falls the shadow of a tree.' And so the present owners must also be the recipients of the tree's blessings.

At the spot where he stood there had once been a turnstile, and as a boy he would swing on it, going round and round until he was quite dizzy. Now the turnstile had gone and the opening walled up. Tall hollyhocks grew on the other side of the wall.

'What are you looking at?'

It was a disembodied voice at first. Moments later a girl stood framed between dark red hollyhocks, staring at the man.

It was difficult to guess her age. She might have been twelve or she might have been sixteen: slim and dark, with lovely eyes and long black hair.

'I'm looking at the house,' he said.

'Why? Do you want to buy it?'

'Is it your house?'

'It's my father's.'

'And what does your father do?'

'He's only a Colonel.'

'*Only* a Colonel?'

'Well, he should have been a Brigadier by now.'

The man burst out laughing.

'It's not funny,' she said. 'Even mummy says he should have been a Brigadier.'

It was on the tip of his tongue to make a witty remark ('Perhaps that's why he's still a Colonel'), but he did not want to give offence. They stood on either side of the wall, appraising each other.

'Well,' she said finally. 'If you don't want to buy the house, what are you looking at?'

'I used to live here once.'

'Oh.'

'Twenty-five years ago. When I was a boy. And then again, when I was a young man . . . until my grandmother died and then we sold the house and went away.'

She was silent for a while, taking in this information. Then she said, 'And you'd like to buy it back now, but you don't have the money?' He did not look very prosperous.

'No, I wasn't thinking of buying it back. I wanted to see it again, that's all. How long have you lived here?'

'Only three years,' She smiled. She'd been eating a melon and there was still juice at the corners of her mouth. 'Would you like to come in—and look—once more?'

'Wouldn't your parents mind?'

'They've gone to the Club. They won't mind. I'm allowed to bring my friends home.'

'Even adult friends?'

'How old are you?'

'Oh, just middle-aged, but feeling young today.' And to prove it he decided he'd climb over the wall instead of going round by the gate. He got up on the wall all right, but had to rest there, breathing heavily. 'Middle-aged man on the flying trapeze,' he muttered to himself.

'Let me help you,' she said and gave him her hand.

He slithered down into a flower-bed, shattering the stem of a hollyhock.

As they walked across the grass he noticed a stone bench under a mango tree. It was the bench on which his grandmother used to sit when she tired of pruning rose bushes and bougainvillaea.

'Let's sit here,' he said. 'I don't want to go inside.'

She sat beside him on the bench. It was March and the mango tree was in bloom. A sweet, heavy fragrance drenched the garden.

They were silent for some time. The man closed his eyes and remembered other times—the music of a piano, the chiming of a grandfather clock, the constant twitter of budgerigars on the veranda, his grandfather cranking up the old car . . . .

'I used to climb the jackfruit tree,' he said, opening his eyes. 'I didn't like the jackfruit, though. Do you?'

'It's all right in pickles.'

'I suppose so . . . . The tree was easy to climb. I spent a lot of time in it.'

'Do you want to climb it again? My parents won't mind.'

'No, I don't think so. Not after climbing the wall! Let's just sit here for a few minutes and talk. I mention the jackfruit tree because it was my favourite place. Do you see that thick branch stretching out over the roof? Half-way along it there's a small hollow in which I used to keep some of my treasures.'

'What kind of treasures?'

'Oh, nothing very valuable. Marbles I'd won. A book I wasn't supposed to read. A few old coins I'd collected. Things came and went. There was my Grandfather's medal, well not his exactly, because he was British and the Iron Cross was a German decoration, awarded for bravery during the War—that's the first World War—when Grandfather fought in France. He got it from a German soldier.'

'Dead or alive?'

'Pardon?' Oh, you mean the German. I never asked. Dead, I suppose. Or perhaps he was a prisoner. I never asked Grandfather. Isn't that strange?'

'And the Iron Cross? Do you still have it?'

'No,' he said, looking her in the eye. 'I left it in the jackfruit tree.'

'You left it in the tree!'

'Yes, I was so busy at the time—packing, and saying goodbye to friends, and thinking about the ship I was going to sail on—that I just forgot all about it.'

She was silent, considering, her finger on her lips, her gaze fixed on the jackfruit tree.

Then, quietly, she said, 'It may still be there. In the hollow of the branch.'

'Yes,' he said. 'After twenty-five years, it may still be there. Unless someone else found it.'

'Would you like to take a look?'

'I can't climb trees any more.'

'I can! I'll go and see. You just sit here and wait for me.'

She sprang up and ran across the grass, swift and sweet of limb. Soon she was in the jackfruit tree, crawling along the projecting branch. A warm wind brought little eddies of dust along the road. Summer was in the air. Ah, if only he could learn to climb trees again!

'I've found something!' she cried.

And now, barefoot, she runs breathlessly towards him, in her outstretched hand a rusty old medal.

He takes it from her and turns it over on his palm.

'Is it the Iron Cross?' she asks eagerly.

'Yes, this is it.'

'Now I know why you came. You wanted to see if it was still in the tree.'

'I don't know. I'm not really sure why I came. But you can keep the Cross. You found it, after all.'

'No, you keep it. It's yours.'

'But it might have remained in the tree for a hundred years if you hadn't gone to look for it.'

'Only because you came back—'

'On the right day, at the right time, and with the right person.' Getting up, he squeezed the hard rusty medal into her soft palm. 'No, it wasn't the Cross I came for. It was my lost youth.'

She understood this, even though her own youth still lay ahead of her, she understood it, not as an adult, but with the wisdom of the child that was still part of her. She walked with him to the gate and stood there gazing after him as he walked away. Where the road turned, he glanced back and waved to her. Then he quickened his step and moved briskly towards the bus stop. There was a spring in his step. Something cried aloud in his heart.

A Love of Long Ago

&

Last week, as the taxi took me to Delhi, I passed through the small town in the foothills where I had lived as a young man.

Well, it's the only road to Delhi and one must go that way, but I seldom travel beyond the foothills. As the years go by, my visits to the city—any city—are few and far between. But whenever I am on the road, I look out of the window of my bus or taxi, to catch a glimpse of the first-floor balcony where a row of potted plants lend colour to an old and decrepit building. Ferns, a palm, a few bright marigolds, zinnias and nasturtiums—they made that balcony stand out from others. It was impossible to miss it.

But last week, when I looked out of the taxi window, the balcony garden had gone. A few broken pots remained but the ferns had crumpled into dust, the palm had turned brown and yellow, and of the flowers nothing remained.

All these years I had taken that balcony garden for granted and now it had gone. It shook me. I looked back at the building for signs of life but saw none. The taxi sped on. On my way back, I decided, I would look again. But it was as though a part of my life had come to an abrupt end. The link between youth and middle-age, the bridge that spanned that gap, had suddenly been swept away.

And what had happened to Kamla, I wondered. Kamla, who had tended those plants all these years, knowing I would be looking out for them even though I might not see her, even though she might never see me.

Chance gives and takes away and gives again. But I would

have to look elsewhere now for the memories of my love, my young love, the girl who came into my life for a few blissful weeks and then went out of it for the remainder of our lives.

Was it almost thirty years ago that it all happened? How old was I then? Twenty-two at the most! And Kamla could not have been more than seventeen.

She had a laughing face, mischievous, always ready to break into smiles or peals of laughter. Sparkling brown eyes. How can I ever forget those eyes? Peeping at me from behind a window curtain, following me as I climbed the steps to my room—the room that was separated from her quarters by a narrow wooden landing that creaked loudly if I tried to move quietly across it. The trick was to *dash* across, as she did so neatly on her butterfly feet.

She was always on the move—flitting about on the veranda, running errands of no consequence, dancing on the steps, singing on the rooftop as she hung out the family washing. Only once was she still. That was when we met on the steps in the dark and I stole a kiss, a sweet phantom kiss. She was very still then, very close, a butterfly drawing out nectar, and then she broke away from me and ran away laughing.

'What is your work?' she asked me one day.

'I write stories.'

'Will you write one about me?'

'Some day.'

I was living in a room above Moti-Bibi's grocery shop near the cinema. At night I could hear the sound-track from the film. The songs did not help me much with my writing, nor with my affair, for Kamla could not come out at night. We met in the afternoons when the whole town took a siesta and expected us to do the same. Kamla had a young brother who worked for Moti-Bibi (a widow who was also my landlady) and it was through the boy that I had first met Kamla.

Moti-Bibi always a sent me a glass of Kanji or sugarcane juice or lime juice (depending on the season) around noon. Usually the boy brought me the drink but one day I looked up from my typewriter to see what at first I thought was an apparition hovering over me. She seemed to shimmer before me in the hot sunlight that came slashing through the open door. I looked up into her face and our eyes met over the rim of the glass. I forgot to take it from her.

What I liked about her was her smile. It dropped over her face slowly, like sunshine moving over brown hills. She seemed to give out some of the glow that was in her face. I felt it pour over me. And this golden feeling did not pass when she left the room. That was how I knew she was going to mean something special to me.

They were poor, but in time I was to realize that I was even poorer. When I discovered that plans were afoot to marry her to a widower of forty, I plucked up enough courage to declare that I would marry her myself. But my youth was no consideration. The widower had land and a generous gift of money for Kamla's parents. Not only was this offer attractive, it was customary. What had I to offer? A small rented room, a typewriter, and a precarious income of two to three hundred rupees a month from freelancing. I told the brother that I would be famous one day, that I would be rich, that I would be writing bestsellers! He did not believe me. And who can blame him? I never did write bestsellers or become rich. Nor did I have parents or relatives to speak on my behalf.

I thought of running away with Kamla. When I mentioned it to her, her eyes lit up. She thought it would be great fun. Women in love can be more reckless than men! But I had read too many stories about runaway marriages ending in disaster and I lacked the courage to go through with such an adventure. I must have known instinctively that it would not work. Where would we go and how would we live? There would be no home to crawl back to for either of us.

Had I loved more passionately, more fiercely, I might have felt compelled to elope with Kamla, regardless of the consequences. But it never became an intense relationship. We had so few moments together. Always stolen moments—on the stairs, on the roof, in the deserted junk-yard behind the shops. She seemed to enjoy every moment of this secret affair. I fretted and longed for something more permanent. Her responses, so sweet and generous, only made my longing greater. But she seemed content with the immediate moment and what it offered.

And so the marriage took place and she did not appear to be too dismayed about her future. But before she left for her husband's house, she asked me for some of the plants that I had owned and nourished on my small balcony.

'Take them all,' I said. 'I am leaving, anyway.'

'Where are you going?'

'To Delhi—to find work. But I shall come this way sometimes.'

'My husband's house is on the Delhi road. You will pass that way. I will keep these flowers where you can see them.'

We did not touch each other in parting. Her brother came and collected the plants. Only the cactii remained. Not a lover's plant, the cactus! I gave the cactii to my landlady and went to live in Delhi.

And whenever I passed through the old place, summer or winter, I looked out of the window of my bus or taxi and saw the garden flourishing on Kamla's balcony. Leaf and fern abounded and the flowers grew rampant on the sunny ledge.

Once I saw her, leaning over the balcony railing. I stopped the taxi and waved to her. She waved back, smiling like the sun breaking through clouds. She called to me to come up but I said I would come another time. I never did visit her home and I never saw her husband. Her parents had gone back to their village. Her brother had vanished into the great grey spaces of India.

In recent years, after leaving Delhi and making my home in the hills, I have passed through the town less often, but the flowers have always been there, bright and glowing in their increasingly shabby surroundings. Except on this last journey of mine . . . .

And on the return trip, only yesterday, I looked again, but the house was empty and desolate. I got out of the car and looked up at the balcony and called Kamla's name—called it after so many years—but there was no answer.

I asked questions in the locality. The old man had died, his wife had gone away, probably to her village. There had been no children. Would she return? No one could say. The house had been sold. It would be pulled down to make way for a block of flats.

I glanced once more at the deserted balcony, the withered, drooping plants. A butterfly flitted about the railing, looking in vain for a flower on which to alight. It settled briefly on my hand before opening its wings and fluttering away into the blue.

THE FUNERAL

&

'I DON'T THINK HE should go,' said Aunt M.

'He's too small,' concurred Aunt B. 'He'll get upset and probably throw a tantrum. And you know Padre Lal doesn't like having children at funerals.'

The boy said nothing. He sat in the darkest corner of the darkened room, his face revealing nothing of what he thought and felt. His father's coffin lay in the next room, the lid fastened forever over the tired, wistful countenance of the man who had meant so much to the boy. Nobody else had mattered—neither uncles nor aunts nor fond grandparents. Least of all the mother who was hundreds of miles away with another husband. He hadn't seen her since he was four—that was just over five years ago—and he did not remember her very well.

The house was full of people—friends, relatives, neighbours. Some had tried to fuss over him but had been discouraged by his silence, the absence of tears. The more understanding of them had kept their distance.

Scattered words of condolence passed back and forth like dragonflies on the wind. 'Such a tragedy!' . . . . 'Only forty' . . . . 'No one realized how serious it was' . . . . 'Devoted to the child' . . . .

It seemed to the boy that everyone who mattered in the hill station was present. And for the first time they had the run of the house for his father had not been a sociable man. Books, music, flowers and his stamp collection had been his main preoccupations, apart from the boy.

A small hearse, drawn by a hill pony, was led in at the gate and several able-bodied men lifted the coffin and manoeuvred it into the carriage. The crowd drifted away. The cemetery was about a mile down the road and those who did not have cars would have to walk the distance.

The boy stared through a window at the small procession passing through the gate. He'd been forgotten for the moment— left in care of the servants, who were the only ones to say behind. Outside it was misty. The mist had crept up the valley and settled like a damp towel on the face of the mountain. Everyone was wet although it hadn't rained.

The boy waited until everyone had gone and then he left the room and went out on the veranda. The gardener, who had been sitting in a bed of nasturtiums, looked up and asked the boy if he needed anything. But the boy shook his head and retreated indoors. The gardener, looking aggrieved because of the damage done to the flower-beds by the mourners, shambled off to his quarters. The sahib's death meant that he would be out of a job very soon. The house would pass into other hands. The boy would go to an orphanage. There weren't many people who kept gardeners these days. In the kitchen, the cook was busy preparing the only big meal ever served in the house. All those relatives, and the Padre too, would come back famished, ready for a sombre but nevertheless substantial meal. He too would be out of a job soon; but cooks were always in demand.

The boy slipped out of the house by a back-door and made his way into the lane through a gap in a thicket of dog-roses. When he reached the main road, he could see the mourners wending their way round the hill to the cemetery. He followed at a distance.

It was the same road he had often taken with his father during their evening walks. The boy knew the name of almost every plant and wildflower that grew on the hillside. These, and various birds and insects, had been described and pointed out to him by his father.

Looking northwards, he could see the higher ranges of the Himalayas and the eternal snows. The graves in the cemetery were so laid out that if their incumbents did happen to rise one day, the first thing they would see would be the glint of the sun on those snow-covered peaks. Possibly the site had been chosen for the view. But to the boy it did not seem as if anyone would be able to thrust aside those massive tombstones and rise from their graves to enjoy the view. Their rest seemed as eternal as the snows. It would take an earthquake to burst those stones asunder and thrust the coffins up from the earth. The boy wondered why people hadn't made it easier for the dead to rise. They were so securely entombed that it appeared as though no one really wanted them to get out.

'God has need of your father . . . .' With those words a well-meaning missionary had tried to console him.

And had God, in the same way, laid claim to the thousands of men, women and children who had been put to rest here in these neat and serried rows? What could he have wanted them for? Of what use are we to God when we are dead, wondered the boy.

The cemetery gate stood open but the boy leant against the old stone wall and stared down at the mourners as they shuffled about with the unease of a batsman about to face a very fast bowler. Only this bowler was invisible and would come up stealthily and from behind.

Padre Lal's voice droned on through the funeral service and then the coffin was lowered—down, deep down—the boy was surprised at how far down it seemed to go! Was that other, better world down in the depths of the earth? How could anyone, even a Samson, push his way back to the surface again? Superman did it in comics but his father was a gentle soul who wouldn't fight too hard against the earth and the grass and the roots of tiny trees. Or perhaps he'd grow into a tree and escape that way! 'If ever I'm put away like this,' thought the boy, 'I'll get into the root of a plant and then I'll become a flower and then maybe a bird will come and carry my seed away . . . . I'll get out somehow!'

A few more words from the Padre and then some of those present threw handfuls of earth over the coffin before moving away.

Slowly, in twos and threes, the mourners departed. The mist swallowed them up. They did not see the boy behind the wall. They were getting hungry.

He stood there until they had all gone. Then he noticed that the gardeners or caretakers were filling in the grave. He did not know whether to go forward or not. He was a little afraid. And it was too late now. The grave was almost covered.

He turned and walked away from the cemetery. The road stretched ahead of him, empty, swathed in mist. He was alone. What had his father said to him once? 'The strongest man in the world is he who stands alone.'

Well, he was alone, but at the moment he did not feel very strong.

For a moment he thought his father was beside him, that they were together on one of their long walks. Instinctively he put out his hand, expecting his father's warm, comforting touch. But there was nothing there, nothing, no one . . . .

He clenched his fists and pushed them deep down into his pockets. He lowered his head so that no one would see his tears. There were people in the mist but he did not want to go near them for they had put his father away.

'He'll find a way out,' the boy said fiercely to himself. 'He'll get out somehow!'

THE ROOM OF MANY COLOURS

&

LAST WEEK I WROTE a story, and all the time I was writing it I thought it was a good story; but when it was finished and I had read it through, I found that there was something missing, that it didn't ring true. So I tore it up. I wrote a poem, about an old man sleeping in the sun, and this was true, but it was finished quickly, and once again I was left with the problem of what to write next. And I remembered my father, who taught me to write; and I thought, why not write about my father, and about the trees we planted, and about the people I knew while growing up and about what happened on the way to growing up . . .

And so, like Alice, I must begin at the beginning, and in the beginning there was this red insect, just like a velvet button, which I found on the front lawn of the bungalow. The grass was still wet with overnight rain.

I placed the insect on the palm of my hand and took it into the house to show my father.

'Look, Dad,' I said, 'I haven't seen an insect like this before. Where has it come from?'

'Where did you find it?' he asked.

'On the grass.'

'It must have come down from the sky,' he said. 'It must have come down with the rain.'

Later he told me how the insect really happened but I preferred his first explanation. It was more fun to have it dropping from the sky.

I was seven at the time, and my father was thirty-seven,

but, right from the beginning, he made me feel that I was old enough to talk to him about everything—insects, people, trees, steam engines, King George, comics, crocodiles, the Mahatma, the Viceroy, America, Mozambique and Timbuctoo. We took long walks together, explored old ruins, chased butterflies and waved to passing trains.

My mother had gone away when I was four, and I had very dim memories of her. Most other children had their mothers with them, and I found it a bit strange that mine couldn't stay. Whenever I asked my father why she'd gone, he'd say, 'You'll understand when you grow up.' And if I asked him *where* she'd gone, he'd look troubled and say, 'I really don't know.' This was the only question of mine to which he didn't have an answer.

But I was quite happy living alone with my father; I had never known any other kind of life.

We were sitting on an old wall, looking out to sea at a couple of Arab dhows and a tram steamer, when my father said, 'Would you like to go to sea one day?'

'Where does the sea go?' I asked.

'It goes everywhere.'

'Does it go to the end of the world?'

'It goes right round the world. It's a round world.'

'It can't be.'

'It is. But it's so big, you can't see the roundness. When a fly sits on a water-melon, it can't see right round the melon, can it? The melon must seem quite flat to the fly. Well, in comparison to the world, we're much, much smaller than the tiniest of insects.'

'Have you been around the world?' I asked.

'No, only as far as England. That's where your grandfather was born.'

'And my grandmother?'

'She came to India from Norway when she was quite small. Norway is a cold land, with mountains and snow, and the sea cutting deep into the land. I was there as a boy. It's very beautiful, and the people are good and work hard.'

'I'd like to go there.'

'You will, one day. When you are older, I'll take you to Norway.'

'Is it better than England?'

'It's quite different.'

'Is it better than India?'

'It's quite different.'

'Is India like England?'

'No, it's different.'

'Well, what does "different" mean?'

'It means things are not the same. It means people are different. It means the weather is different. It means tree and birds and insects are different.'

'Are English crocodiles different from Indian crocodiles?'

'They don't have crocodiles in England.'

'Oh, then it must be different.'

'It would be a dull world if it was the same everywhere,' said my father.

He never lost patience with my endless questioning. If he wanted a rest, he would take out his pipe and spend a long time lighting it. If this took very long I'd find something else to do. But sometimes I'd wait patiently until the pipe was drawing, and then return to the attack.

'Will we always be in India?' I asked.

'No, we'll have to go away one day. You see, it's hard to explain, but it isn't really our country.'

'Ayah says it belongs to the King of England, and the jewels in his crown were taken from India, and that when the Indians get their jewels back the King will lose India! But first they have to get the crown from the King, but this is very difficult, she says, because the crown is always on his head. He even sleeps wearing his crown!'

Ayah was my nanny. She loved me deeply, and was always filling my head with strange and wonderful stories.

My father did not comment on Ayah's views. All he said was, 'We'll have to go away some day.'

'How long have we been here?' I asked.

'Two hundred years.'

'No, I mean us.'

'Well, you were born in India, so that's seven years for you.'

'Then can't I stay here?'

'Do you want to?'

'I want to go across the sea. But can we take Ayah with us?'

'I don't know, son. Let's walk along the beach.'

We lived in an old palace beside a lake. The palace looked like a ruin from the outside, but the rooms were cool and comfortable. We lived in one wing, and my father organized a small school in another wing. His pupils were the children of the Raja and the Raja's relatives. My father had started life in India as a tea-planter, but he had been trained as a teacher and the idea of starting a school in a small state facing the Arabian Sea had appealed to him. The pay wasn't much, but we had a palace to live in, the latest 1938-model Hillman to drive about in, and a number of servants. In those days, of course, everyone had servants (although the servants did not have any!). Ayah was our own; but the cook, the bearer, the gardener, and the bhisti were all provided by the state.

Sometimes I sat in the schoolroom with the other children (who were all much bigger than me), sometimes I remained in the house with Ayah, sometimes I followed the gardener, Dukhi, about the spacious garden.

Dukhi means 'sad', and though I never could discover if the gardener had anything to feel sad about, the name certainly suited him. He had grown to resemble the drooping weeds that he was always digging up with a tiny spade. I seldom saw him standing up. He always sat on the ground with his knees well up to his chin, and attacked the weeds from this position. He could spend all day on his haunches, moving about the garden simply by shuffling his feet along the grass.

I tried to imitate his posture, sitting down on my heels and putting my knees into my armpits, but could never hold the position for more than five minutes.

Time had no meaning in a large garden, and Dukhi never hurried. Life, for him, was not a matter of one year succeeding another, but of five seasons—winter, spring, hot weather, monsoon and autumn—arriving and departing. His seedbeds had always to be in readiness for the coming season, and he did not look any further than the next monsoon. It was impossible to tell his age. He may have been thirty-six or eighty-six. He was either very young for his years or very old for them.

Dukhi loved bright colours, especially reds and yellows. He liked strongly scented flowers, like jasmine and honeysuckle. He couldn't understand my father's preference for the more delicately perfumed petunias and sweetpeas. But I shared Dukhi's fondness for the common bright orange marigold, which is offered in temples and is used to make garlands and nosegays. When the garden was bare of all colour, the marigold would still be there, gay and flashy, challenging the sun.

Dukhi was very fond of making nosegays, and I liked to watch him at work. A sunflower formed the centrepiece. It was surrounded by roses, marigolds and oleander, fringed with green leaves, and bound together with silver thread. The perfume was overpowering. The nosegays were presented to me or my father on special occasions, that is, on a birthday or to guests of my father's who were considered important.

One day I found Dukhi making a nosegay, and said, 'No one is coming today, Dukhi. It isn't even a birthday.'

'It is a birthday, chhota sahib,' he said. 'Little sahib' was the title he had given me. It wasn't much of a title compared to Raja sahib, Diwan sahib or Burra sahib, but it was nice to have a title at the age of seven.

'Oh,' I said. 'And is there a party, too?'

'No party.'

'What's the use of a birthday without a party? What's the use of a birthday without presents?'

'This person doesn't like presents—just flowers.'

'Who is it?' I asked, full of curiosity.

'If you want to find out, you can take these flowers to her. She lives right at the top of that far side of the palace. There are twenty-two steps to climb. Remember that, chhota sahib, you take twenty-three steps and you will go over the edge and into the lake!'

I started climbing the stairs.

It was a spiral staircase of wrought iron, and it went round and round and up and up, and it made me quite dizzy and tired.

At the top I found myself on a small balcony, which looked out over the lake and another palace, at the crowded city and the distant harbour. I heard a voice, a rather high, musical voice, saying (in English), 'Are you a ghost?' I turned to see who had spoken but found the balcony empty. The voice had come from a dark room.

I turned to the stairway, ready to flee, but the voice said, 'Oh, don't go, there's nothing to be frightened of!'

And so I stood still, peering cautiously into the darkness of the room.

'First, tell me—are you a ghost?'

'I'm a boy,' I said.

'And I'm a girl. We can be friends. I can't come out there, so you had better come in. Come along, I'm not a ghost either—not yet, anyway!'

As there was nothing very frightening about the voice, I stepped into the room. It was dark inside, and, coming in from the glare, it took me some time to make out the tiny, elderly lady seated on a cushioned gilt chair. She wore a red sari, lots of coloured bangles on her wrists, and golden earrings. Her hair was streaked with white, but her skin was still quite smooth and unlined, and she had large and very beautiful eyes.

'You must be Master Bond!' she said. 'Do you know who I am?'

'You're a lady with a birthday,' I said, 'but that's all I know. Dukhi didn't tell me any more.'

'If you promise to keep it secret, I'll tell you who I am. You see, everyone thinks I'm mad. Do you think so too?'

'I don't know.'

'Well, you must tell me if you think so,' she said with a chuckle. Her laugh was the sort of sound made by the gecko, a little wall-lizard, coming from deep down in the throat. 'I have a feeling you are a truthful boy. Do you find it very difficult to tell the truth?'

'Sometimes.'

'Sometimes. Of course, there are times when I tell lies—lots of little lies—because they're such fun! But would you call me a liar? I wouldn't, if I were you, but *would* you?'

'Are you a liar?'

'I'm asking you! If I were to tell you that I was a queen—that I *am* a queen—would you believe me?'

I thought deeply about this, and then said, 'I'll try to believe you.'

'Oh, but you *must* believe me. I'm a real queen, I'm a Rani! Look, I've got diamonds to prove it!' And she held out her hands, and there was a ring on each finger, the stones glowing and glittering in the dim light. 'Diamonds, rubies, pearls and emeralds! Only a queen can have these!' She was most anxious that I should believe her.

'You must be a queen,' I said.

'Right!' she snapped. 'In that case, would you mind calling me "Your Highness"?'

'Your Highness,' I said.

She smiled. It was a slow, beautiful smile. Her whole face lit up.

'I could love you,' she said. 'But better still, I'll give you something to eat. Do you like chocolates?'

'Yes, Your Highness.'

'Well,' she said, taking a box from the table beside her, 'these have come all the way from England. Take two. Only two, mind, otherwise the box will finish before Thursday, and I don't want that to happen because I won't get any more till Saturday. That's when Captain MacWhirr's ship gets in, the S.S. Lucy, loaded with boxes and boxes of chocolates!'

'All for you?' I asked in considerable awe.

'Yes, of course. They have to last at least three months. I get them from England. I get only the best chocolates. I like them with pink, crunchy fillings, don't you?'

'Oh, yes!' I exclaimed, full of envy.

'Never mind,' she said. 'I may give you one, now and then—if you're *very* nice to me! Here you are, help yourself . . .' She pushed the chocolate box towards me.

I took a silver-wrapped chocolate, and then just as I was thinking of taking a second, she quickly took the box away.

'No more!' she said. 'They have to last till Saturday.'

'But I took only *one*,' I said with some indignation.

'Did you?' She gave me a sharp look, decided I was telling the truth, and said graciously, 'Well, in that case you can have another.'

Watching the Rani carefully, in case she snatched the box away again, I selected a second chocolate, this one with a green wrapper. I don't remember what kind of day it was outside, but I remember the bright green of the chocolate wrapper.

I thought it would be rude to eat the chocolates in front of a queen, so I put them in my pocket and said, 'I'd better go now. Ayah will be looking for me.'

'And when will you be coming to see me again?'

'I don't know,' I said.

'Your Highness.'

'Your Highness.'

'There's something I want you to do for me,' she said, placing one finger on my shoulder and giving me a conspiratorial look. 'Will you do it?'

'What is it, Your Highness?'

'What is it? Why do you ask? A real prince never asks where or why or whatever, he simply does what the princess asks of him. When I was a princess—before I became a queen, that is—I asked a prince to swim across the lake and fetch me a lily growing on the other bank.'

'And did he get it for you?'

'He drowned half way across. Let *that* be a lesson to you. Never agree to do something without knowing what it is.'

'But I thought you said . . .'

'Never mind what I *said*. It's what I *say* that matters!'

'Oh, all right,' I said, fidgeting to be gone. 'What is it you want me to do?'

'Nothing.' Her tiny rosebud lips pouted and she stared sullenly at a picture on the wall. Now that my eyes had grown used to the dim light in the room, I noticed that the walls were hung with portraits of stout Rajas and Ranis turbaned and bedecked in fine clothes. There were also portraits of Queen Victoria and King George V of England. And, in the centre of all this distinguished company, a large picture of mickey mouse.

'I'll do it if it isn't too dangerous,' I said.

'Then listen.' She took my hand and drew me towards her—what a tiny hand she had!—and whispered, 'I want a *red* rose. From the palace garden. But be careful! Don't let Dukhi the gardener catch you. He'll know it's for me. He knows I love roses. And he hates me! I'll tell you why, one day. But if he catches you, he'll do something terrible.'

'To me?'

'No, to himself. That's much worse, isn't it? He'll tie himself into knots, or lie naked on a bed of thorns, or go on a long fast with nothing to eat but fruit, sweets and chicken! So you will be careful, won't you?'

'Oh, but he doesn't hate you,' I cried in protest, remembering the flowers he'd sent for her, and looking around I found that I'd been sitting on them. 'Look, he sent these flowers for your birthday!'

'Well, if he sent them for my birthday, you can take them back,' she snapped. 'But if he sent them for *me* . . .' and she suddenly softened and looked coy, 'then I might keep them. Thank you, my dear, it was a very sweet thought.' And she learnt forward as though to kiss me.

'It's late, I must go!' I said in alarm, and turning on my heels, ran out of the room and down the spiral staircase.

Father hadn't started lunch, or rather tiffin, as we called it then. He usually waited for me if I was late. I don't suppose he enjoyed eating alone.

For tiffin we usually had rice, a mutton curry (koftas or meat balls, with plenty of gravy, was my favourite curry), fried dal and a hot lime or mango pickle. For supper we had English food—a soup, roast pork and fried potatoes, a rich gravy made by my father, and a custard or caramel pudding. My father enjoyed cooking, but it was only in the morning that he found time for it. Breakfast was his own creation. He cooked eggs in a variety of interesting ways, and favoured some Italian recipes which he had collected during a trip to Europe, long before I was born.

In deference to the feelings of our Hindu friends, we did not eat beef; but, apart from mutton and chicken, there was a plentiful supply of other meats—partridge, venison, lobster, and even porcupine!

'And where have you been?' asked my father, helping himself to the rice as soon as he saw me come in.

'To the top of the old palace,' I said.

'Did you meet anyone there?'

'Yes, I met a tiny lady who told me she was a Rani. She gave me chocolates.'

'As a rule, she doesn't like visitors.'

'Oh, she didn't mind me. But is she really a queen?'

'Well, she's the daughter of a Maharaja. That makes her a princess. She never married. There's a story that she fell in love with a commoner, one of the palace servants, and wanted to marry him, but of course they wouldn't allow that. She became very melancholic, and started living all by herself in the old palace. They give her everything she needs, but she doesn't go out or have visitors. Everyone says she's mad.'

'How do they know?' I asked.

'Because she's different from other people, I suppose.'

'Is that being mad?'

'No. Not really I suppose madness is not *seeing* things as others see them.'

'Is that very bad?'

'No,' said Father, who for once was finding it very difficult to explain something to me. 'But people who are like that—people whose minds are so different that they don't think, step by step, as we do, whose thoughts jump all over the place—such people are very difficult to live with . . .'

'Step by step,' I repeated. 'Step by step . . .'

'You aren't eating,' said my father. 'Hurry up, and you can come with me to school today.'

I always looked forward to attending my father's classes. He did not take me to the schoolroom very often, because he wanted school to be a treat, to begin with, and then, later, the routine wouldn't be so unwelcome.

Sitting there with older children, understanding only half of what they were learning, I felt important and part grownup. And of course I did learn to read and write, although I first learnt to read upside-down, by means of standing in front of the others' desks and peering across at their books. Later, when I went to school, I had some difficulty in learning to read the right way up; and even today I sometimes read upside-down, for the sake of variety. I don't mean that I read standing on my head; simply that I held the book upside-down.

I had at my command a number of rhymes and jingles, the most interesting of these being 'Solomon Grundy'.

> *Solomon Grundy,*
> *Born on a Monday,*
> *Christened on Tuesday,*
> *Married on Wednesday,*
> *Took ill on Thursday,*
> *Worse on Friday,*
> *Died on Saturday,*
> *Buried on Sunday:*
> *This is the end of*
> *Solomon Grundy.*

Was that all that life amounted to, in the end? And were we all Solomon Grundies? These were questions that bothered me at the time.

Another puzzling rhyme was the one that went:

> *Hark, hark,*
> *The dogs do bark,*
> *The beggars are coming to town;*
> *Some in rags,*
> *Some in bags,*
> *And some in velvet gowns.*

This rhyme puzzled me for a long time. There were beggars aplenty in the bazaar, and sometimes they came to the house, and some of them did wear rags and bags (and some nothing at all) and the dogs did bark at them, but the beggar in the velvet gown never came our way.

'Who's this beggar in a velvet gown?' I asked my father.

'Not a beggar at all,' he said.

'Then why call him one?'

And I went to Ayah and asked her the same question, 'Who is the beggar in the velvet gown?'

'Jesus Christ,' said Ayah.

Ayah was a fervent Christian and made me say my prayers at night, even when I was very sleepy. She had, I think, Arab and Negro blood in addition to the blood of the Koli fishing community to which her mother had belonged. Her father, a sailor on an Arab dhow, had been a convert to Christianity. Ayah was a large, buxom woman, with heavy hands and feet and a slow, swaying gait that had all the grace and majesty of a royal elephant. Elephants for all their size are nimble creatures; and Ayah, too, was nimble, sensitive, and gentle with her big hands. Her face was always sweet and childlike.

Although a Christian, she clung to many of the beliefs of her parents, and loved to tell me stories about mischievous spirits and evil spirits, humans who changed into animals, and snakes who had been princes in their former lives.

There was the story of the snake who married a princess. At first the princess did not wish to marry the snake, whom she had met in a forest, but the snake insisted, saying, 'I'll kill you if you won't marry me,' and of course that settled the question. The snake led his bride away and took her to a great treasure. 'I was a prince in my former life,' he explained. 'This treasure is yours.' And then the snake very gallantly disappeared.

'Snakes,' declared Ayah, 'were very lucky omens if seen early in the morning.'

'But what if the snake bites the lucky person?' I asked.

'He will be lucky all the same,' said Ayah with a logic that was all her own.

Snakes! There were a number of them living in the big garden, and my father had advised me to avoid the long grass. But I had seen snakes crossing the road (a lucky omen, according to Ayah) and they were never aggressive.

'A snake won't attack you,' said Father, 'provided you leave it alone. Of course, if you step on one it will probably bite.'

'Are all snakes poisonous?'

'Yes, but only a few are poisonous enough to kill a man. Others use their poison on rats and frogs. A good thing, too, otherwise during the rains the house would be taken over by the frogs.'

One afternoon, while Father was at school, Ayah found a snake in the bath-tub. It wasn't early morning and so the snake couldn't have been a lucky one. Ayah was frightened and ran into the garden calling for help. Dukhi came running. Ayah ordered me to stay outside while they went after the snake.

And it was while I was alone in the garden—an unusual circumstance, since Dukhi was nearly always there—that I remembered the Rani's request. On an impulse, I went to the nearest rose bush and plucked the largest rose, pricking my thumb in the process.

And then, without waiting to see what had happened to the snake (it finally escaped), I started up the steps to the top of the old palace.

When I got to the top, I knocked on the door of the Rani's room. Getting no reply, I walked along the balcony until I reached another doorway. There were wooden panels around the door, with elephants, camels and turbaned warriors carved into it. As the door was open, I walked boldly into the room then stood still in astonishment. The room was filled with a strange light.

There were windows going right round the room, and each small window-pane was made of a different coloured glass. The sun that came through one window flung red and green and purple colours on the figure of the little Rani who stood there with her face pressed to the glass.

She spoke to me without turning from the window. 'This is my favourite room. I have all the colours here. I can see a different world through each pane of glass. Come, join me!' And she beckoned to me, her small hand fluttering like a delicate butterfly.

I went up to the Rani. She was only a little taller than me, and we were able to share the same window-pane.

'See, it's a red world!' she said.

The garden below, the palace and the lake, were all tinted red. I watched the Rani's world for a little while and then touched her on the arm and said, 'I have brought you a rose!'

She started away from me, and her eyes looked frightened. She would not look at the rose.

'Oh, why did you bring it?' she cried, wringing her hands. 'He'll be arrested now!'

'Who'll be arrested?'

'The prince, of course!'

'But I took it,' I said. 'No one saw me. Ayah and Dukhi were inside the house, catching a snake.'

'Did they catch it?' she asked, forgetting about the rose.

'I don't know. I didn't wait to see!'

'They should follow the snake, instead of catching it. It may lead them to a treasure. All snakes have treasures to guard.'

This seemed to confirm what Ayah had been telling me, and I resolved that I would follow the next snake that I met.

'Don't you like the rose, then?' I asked.

'Did you steal it?'

'Yes.'

'Good. Flowers should always be stolen. They're more fragrant then.'

Because of a man called Hitler war had been declared in Europe and Britain was fighting Germany.

In my comic papers, the Germans were usually shown as blundering idiots; so I didn't see how Britain could possibly lose the war, nor why it should concern India, nor why it should be necessary for my father to join up. But I remember his showing me a newspaper headline which said:

BOMBS FALL ON BUCKINGHAM PALACE—
KING AND QUEEN SAFE

I expect that had something to do with it.

He went to Delhi for an interview with the RAF and I was left in Ayah's charge.

It was a week I remember well, because it was the first time I had been left on my own. That first night I was afraid—afraid of the dark, afraid of the emptiness of the house, afraid of the howling of the jackals outside. The loud ticking of the clock was the only reassuring sound: clocks really made themselves heard in those days! I tried concentrating on the ticking, shutting out other sounds and the menace of the dark, but it wouldn't work. I thought I heard a faint hissing near the bed, and sat up, bathed in perspiration, certain that a snake was in the room. I shouted for Ayah and she came running, switching on all the lights.

'A snake!' I cried. 'There's a snake in the room!'

'Where, baba?'

'I don't know where, but I *heard* it.'

Ayah looked under the bed, and behind the chairs and

tables, but there was no snake to be found. She persuaded me that I must have heard the breeze whispering in the mosquito-curtains.

But I didn't want to be left alone.

'I'm coming to you,' I said and followed her into her small room near the kitchen.

Ayah slept on a low string cot. The mattress was thin, the blanket worn and patched up; but Ayah's warm and solid body made up for the discomfort of the bed. I snuggled up to her and was soon asleep.

I had almost forgotten the Rani in the old palace and was about to pay her a visit when, to my surprise, I found her in the garden.

I had risen early that morning, and had gone running barefoot over the dew-drenched grass. No one was about, but I startled a flock of parrots and the birds rose screeching from a banyan tree and wheeled away to some other corner of the palace grounds. I was just in time to see a mongoose scurrying across the grass with an egg in its mouth. The mongoose must have been raiding the poultry farm at the palace.

I was trying to locate the mongoose's hideout, and was on all fours in a jungle of tall cosmos plants when I heard the rustle of clothes, and turned to find the Rani staring at me.

She didn't ask me what I was doing there, but simply said: 'I don't think he could have gone in there.'

'But I saw him go this way,' I said.

'Nonsense! He doesn't live in this part of the garden. He lives in the roots of the banyan tree.'

'But that's where the snake lives,' I said.

'You mean the snake who was a prince. Well, that's who I'm looking for!'

'A snake who was a prince!' I gaped at the Rani.

She made a gesture of impatience with her butterfly hands, and said, 'Tut, you're only a child, you can't *understand*. The prince lives in the roots of the banyan tree, but he comes out early every morning. Have you seen him?'

'No. But I saw a mongoose.'

The Rani became frightened. 'Oh dear, is there a mongoose in the garden? He might kill the prince!'

'How can a mongoose kill a prince?' I asked.

'You don't understand, Master Bond. Princes, when they die, are born again as snakes.'

'*All* princes?'

'No, only those who die before they can marry.'

'Did your prince die before he could marry you?'

'Yes. And he returned to this garden in the form of a beautiful snake.'

'Well,' I said, 'I hope it wasn't the snake the water-carrier killed last week.'

'He killed a snake!' The Rani looked horrified. She was quivering all over. 'It might have been the prince!'

'It was a brown snake,' I said.

'Oh, then it wasn't him.' She looked very relieved. 'Brown snakes are only ministers and people like that. It has to be a green snake to be a prince.'

'I haven't seen any green snakes here.'

'There's one living in the roots of the banyan tree. You won't kill it, will you?'

'Not if it's really a prince.'

'And you won't let others kill it?'

'I'll tell Ayah.'

'Good. You're on my side. But be careful of the gardener. Keep him away from the banyan tree. He's always killing snakes. I don't trust him at all.'

She came nearer and, leaning forward a little, looked into my eyes.

'Blue eyes—I trust them. But don't trust green eyes. And yellow eyes are evil.'

'I've near seen yellow eyes.'

'That's because you're pure,' she said, and turned away and hurried across the lawn as though she had just remembered a very urgent appointment.

The sun was up, slanting through the branches of the banyan tree, and Ayah's voice could be heard calling me for breakfast.

'Dukhi,' I said, when I found him in the garden later that day, 'Dukhi, don't kill the snake in the banyan tree.'

'A snake in the banyan tree!' he exclaimed, seizing his hose.

'No, no!' I said. 'I haven't seen it. But the Rani says there's one. She says it was a prince in its former life, and that we shouldn't kill it.'

'Oh,' said Dukhi, smiling to himself. 'The Rani says so. All right, you tell her we won't kill it.'

'Is it true that she was in love with a prince but that he died before she could marry him?'

'Something like that,' said Dukhi. 'It was a long time ago—before I came here.'

'My father says it wasn't a prince, but a commoner. Are you a commoner, Dukhi?'

'A commoner? What's that, chhota sahib?'

'I'm not sure. Someone very poor, I suppose.'

'Then I must be a commoner,' said Dukhi.

'Were *you* in love with the Rani?' I asked.

Dukhi was so startled that he dropped his hose and lost his balance; the first time I'd seen him lose his poise while squatting on his haunches.

'Don't say such things, chhota sahib!'

'Why not?'

'You'll get me into trouble.'

'Then it must be true.'

Dukhi threw up his hands in mock despair and started collecting his implements.

'It's true, it's true!' I cried, dancing round him, and then I ran indoors to Ayah and said, 'Ayah, Dukhi was in love with the Rani!'

Ayah gave a shriek of laughter, then looked very serious and put her finger against my lips.

'Don't say such things,' she said. 'Dukhi is of a very low caste. People won't like it if they hear what you say. And besides, the Rani told you her prince died and turned into a snake. Well, Dukhi hasn't become a snake as yet, has he?'

True, Dukhi didn't look as though he could be anything but a gardener; but I wasn't satisfied with his denials or with Ayah's attempts to still my tongue. Hadn't Dukhi sent the Rani a nosegay?

When my father came home, he looked quite pleased with himself.

'What have you brought for me?' was the first question I asked.

He had brought me some new books, a dart-board, and a

train set; and in my excitement over examining these gifts, I forgot to ask about the result of his trip.

It was during tiffin that he told me what had happened—and what was going to happen.

'We'll be going away soon,' he said. 'I've joined the Royal Air Force. I'll have to work in Delhi.'

'Oh! Will you be in the war, Dad? Will you fly a plane?'

'No, I'm too old to be flying planes. I'll be forty years in July. The RAF will be giving me what they call intelligence work—decoding secret messages and things like that and I don't suppose I'll be able to tell you much about it.'

This didn't sound as exciting as flying planes, but it sounded important and rather mysterious.

'Well, I hope it's interesting,' I said. 'Is Delhi a good place to live in?'

'I'm not sure. It will be very hot by the middle of April. And you won't be able to stay with me, Ruskin—not at first, anyway, not until I can get married quarters and then, only if your mother returns . . . . Meanwhile, you'll stay with your grandmother in Dehra.' He must have seen the disappointment in my face, because he quickly added: 'Of course I'll come to see you often. Dehra isn't far from Delhi—only a night's train journey.'

But I was dismayed. It wasn't that I didn't want to stay with my grandmother, but I had grown so used to sharing my father's life and even watching him at work, that the thought of being separated from him was unbearable.

'Not as bad as going to boarding-school,' he said. 'And that's the only alternative.'

'Not boarding-school,' I said quickly, 'I'll run away from boarding-school.'

'Well, you won't want to run away from your grandmother. She's very fond of you. And if you come with me to Delhi, you'll be alone all day in a stuffy little hut while I'm away at work. Sometimes I may have to go on tour—then what happens?'

'I don't mind being on my own.' And this was true. I had already grown accustomed to having my own room and my own trunk and my own bookshelf and I felt as though I was about to lose these things.

'Will Ayah come too?' I asked.

My father looked thoughtful. 'Would you like that?'

'Ayah must come,' I said firmly. 'Otherwise I'll run away.'

'I'll have to ask her,' said my father.

Ayah, it turned out, was quite ready to come with us. In fact, she was indignant that Father should have considered leaving her behind. She had brought me up since my mother went away, and she wasn't going to hand over charge to any upstart aunt or governess. She was pleased and excited at the prospect of the move, and this helped to raise my spirits.

'What is Dehra like?' I asked my father.

'It's a green place,' he said. 'It lies in a valley in the foothills of the Himalayas, and it's surrounded by forests. There are lots of trees in Dehra.'

'Does Grandmother's house have trees?'

'Yes. There's a big jackfruit tree in the garden. Your grandmother planted it when I was a boy. And there's an old banyan tree, which is good to climb. And there are fruit trees, lichis, mangoes, papayas.'

'Are there any books?'

'Grandmother's books won't interest you. But I'll be bringing you books from Delhi whenever I come to see you.'

I was beginning to look forward to the move. Changing houses had always been fun. Changing towns ought to be fun, too.

A few days before we left, I went to say goodbye to the Rani.

'I'm going away,' I said.

'How lovely!' said the Rani. 'I wish I could go away!'

'Why don't you?'

'They won't let me. They're afraid to let me out of the palace.'

'What are they afraid of, Your Highness?'

'That I might run away. Run away, far far away, to the land where the leopards are learning to pray.'

Gosh, I thought, she's really quite crazy . . . . But then she was silent, and started smoking a small hookah.

She drew on the hookah, looked at me, and asked: 'Where is your mother?'

'I haven't one.'

'Everyone has a mother. Did yours die?'

'No. She went away.'

She drew on her hookah again and then said, very sweetly, 'Don't go away . . .'

'I must,' I said. 'It's because of the war.'

'What war? Is there a war on? You see, no one tells me anything.'

'It's between us and Hitler,' I said.

'And who is Hitler?'

'He's a German.'

'I knew a German once, Dr Schreinherr, he had beautiful hands.'

'Was he an artist?'

'He was a dentist.'

The Rani got up from her couch and accompanied me out on to the balcony. When we looked down at the garden, we could see Dukhi weeding a flower-bed. Both of us gazed down at him in silence, and I wondered what the Rani would say if I asked her if she had ever been in love with the palace gardener. Ayah had told me it would be an insulting question, so I held my peace. But as I walked slowly down the spiral staircase, the Rani's voice came after me.

'Thank him,' she said. 'Thank him for the beautiful rose.'

Time Stops at Shamli

&

The Dehra Express usually drew into Shamli at about five o'clock in the morning at which time the station would be dimly lit and the jungle across the tracks would just be visible in the faint light of dawn. Shamli is a small station at the foot of the Siwalik hills and the Siwaliks lie at the foot of the Himalayas which in turn lie at the feet of God.

The station, I remember, had only one platform, an office for the station-master, and a waiting-room. The platform boasted a tea stall, a fruit vendor, and a few stray dogs. Not much else was required because the train stopped at Shamli for only five minutes before rushing on into the forests.

Why it stopped at Shamli, I never could tell. Nobody got off the train and nobody got in. There were never any coolies on the platform. But the train would stand there a full five minutes and the guard would blow his whistle and presently Shamli would be left behind and forgotten . . . until I passed that way again.

I was paying my relations in Saharanpur an annual visit when the night train stopped at Shamli. I was thirty-six at the time and still single.

On this particular journey, the train came into Shamli just as I awoke from a restless sleep. The third-class compartment was crowded beyond capacity and I had been sleeping in an upright position with my back to the lavatory door. Now someone was trying to get into the lavatory. He was obviously hard pressed for time.

'I'm sorry, brother,' I said, moving as much as I could to one side.

He stumbled into the closet without bothering to close the door.

'Where are we now?' I asked the man sitting beside me. He was smoking a strong aromatic bidi.

'Shamli station,' he said, rubbing the palm of a large calloused hand over the frosted glass of the window.

I let the window down and stuck my head out. There was a cool breeze blowing down the platform, a breeze that whispered of autumn in the hills. As usual there was no activity except for the fruit-vendor walking up and down the length of the train with his basket of mangoes balanced on his head. At the tea stall, a kettle was steaming, but there was no one to mind it. I rested my forehead on the window-ledge and let the breeze play on my temples. I had been feeling sick and giddy but there was a wild sweetness in the wind that I found soothing.

'Yes,' I said to myself, 'I wonder what happens in Shamli behind the station walls.'

My fellow passenger offered me a beedi. He was a farmer, I think, on his way to Dehra. He had a long, untidy, sad moustache.

We had been more than five minutes at the station. I looked up and down the platform, but nobody was getting on or off the train. Presently the guard came walking past our compartment.

'What's the delay?' I asked him.

'Some obstruction further down the line,' he said.

'Will we be here long?'

'I don't know what the trouble is. About half an hour at the least.'

My neighbour shrugged and throwing the remains of his beedi out of the window, closed his eyes and immediately fell asleep. I moved restlessly in my seat and then the man came out of the lavatory, not so urgently now, and with obvious peace of mind. I closed the door for him.

I stood up and stretched and this stretching of my limbs seemed to set in motion a stretching of the mind and I found myself thinking: 'I am in no hurry to get to Saharanpur and I have always wanted to see Shamli behind the station walls. If I get down now, I can spend the day here. It will be better than sitting in this train for another hour. Then in the evening I can catch the next train home.'

In those days I never had the patience to wait for second thoughts and so I began pulling my small suitcase out from under the seat.

The farmer woke up and asked, 'What are you doing, brother?'

'I'm getting out,' I said.

He went to sleep again.

It would have taken at least fifteen minutes to reach the door as people and their belongings cluttered up the passage. So I let my suitcase down from the window and followed it onto the platform.

There was no one to collect my ticket at the barrier because there was obviously no point in keeping a man there to collect tickets from passengers who never came. And anyway, I had a through-ticket to my destination which I would need in the evening.

I went out of the station and came to Shamli.

Outside the station there was a neem tree and under it stood a tonga. The pony was nibbling at the grass at the foot of the tree. The youth in the front seat was the only human in sight. There were no signs of inhabitants or habitation. I approached the tonga and the youth stared at me as though he couldn't believe his eyes.

'Where is Shamli?' I asked.

'Why, friend, this is Shamli,' he said.

I looked around again but couldn't see any sign of life. A dusty road led past the station and disappeared into the forest.

'Does anyone live here?' I asked.

'I live here,' he said with an engaging smile. He looked an amiable, happy-go-lucky fellow. He wore a cotton tunic and dirty white pyjamas.

'Where?' I asked.

'In my tonga, of course,' he said. 'I have had this pony five years now. I carry supplies to the hotel. But today the manager has not come to collect them. You are going to the hotel? I will take you.'

'Oh, so there's a hotel?'

'Well, friend, it is called that. And there are a few houses too and some shops, but they are all about a mile from the station. If they were not a mile from here, I would be out of business.'

I felt relieved but I still had the feeling of having walked into a town consisting of one station, one pony and one man.

'You can take me,' I said. 'I'm staying till this evening.'

He heaved my suitcase into the seat beside him and I climbed in at the back. He flicked the reins and slapped his pony on the buttocks and, with a roll and a lurch, the buggy moved off down the dusty forest road.

'What brings you here?' asked the youth.

'Nothing,' I said. 'The train was delayed. I was feeling bored. And so I got off.'

He did not believe that but he didn't question me further. The sun was reaching up over the forest but the road lay in the shadow of tall trees—eucalyptus, mango and neem.

'Not many people stay in the hotel,' he said. 'So it is cheap. You will get a room for five rupees.'

'Who is the manager?'

'Mr Satish Dayal. It is his father's property. Satish Dayal could not pass his exams or get a job so his father sent him here to look after the hotel.'

The jungle thinned out and we passed a temple, a mosque, a few small shops. There was a strong smell of burnt sugar in the air and in the distance I saw a factory chimney. That, then, was the reason for Shamli's existence. We passed a bullock-cart laden with sugarcane. The road went through fields of cane and maize, and then, just as we were about to re-enter the jungle, the youth pulled his horse to a side road and the hotel came in sight.

It was a small white bungalow with a garden in the front, banana trees at the sides and an orchard of guava trees at the back. We came jingling up to the front veranda. Nobody appeared, nor was there any sign of life on the premises.

'They are all asleep,' said the youth.

I said, 'I'll sit in the veranda and wait.' I got down from the tonga and the youth dropped my case on the veranda steps. Then he stooped in front of me, smiling amiably, waiting to be paid.

'Well, how much?' I asked.

'As a friend, only one rupee.'

'That's too much,' I complained. 'This is not Delhi.'

'This is Shamli,' he said. 'I am the only tonga in Shamli. You may not pay me anything, if that is your wish. But then, I will not take you back to the station this evening. You will have to walk.'

I gave him the rupee. He had both charm and cunning, an effective combination.

'Come in the evening at about six,' I said.

'I will come,' he said with an infectious smile. 'Don't worry.' I waited till the tonga had gone round the bend in the road before walking up the verandah steps.

The doors of the house were closed and there were no bells to ring. I didn't have a watch but I judged the time to be a little past six o'clock. The hotel didn't look very impressive. The whitewash was coming off the walls and the cane-chairs on the verandah were old and crooked. A stag's head was mounted over the front door but one of its glass eyes had fallen out. I had often heard hunters speak of how beautiful an animal looked before it died, but how could anyone with true love of the beautiful care for the stuffed head of an animal, grotesquely mounted, with no resemblance to its living aspect?

I felt too restless to take any of the chairs. I began pacing up and down the verandah, wondering if I should start banging on the doors. Perhaps the hotel was deserted. Perhaps the tonga-driver had played a trick on me. I began to regret my impulsiveness in leaving the train. When I saw the manager I would have to invent a reason for coming to his hotel. I was good at inventing reasons. I would tell him that a friend of mine had stayed here some years ago and that I was trying to trace him. I decided that my friend would have to be a little eccentric (having chosen Shamli to live in), that he had become a recluse, shutting himself off from the world. His parents—no, his sister—for his parents would be dead—had asked me to find him if I could and, as he had last been heard of in Shamli, I had taken the opportunity to enquire after him. His name would be Major Roberts, retired.

I heard a tap running at the side of the building and walking around found a young man bathing at the tap. He was strong and well-built and slapped himself on the body with great enthusiasm. He had not seen me approaching so I waited until he had finished bathing and had begun to dry himself.

'Hallo,' I said.

He turned at the sound of my voice and looked at me for a few moments with a puzzled expression. He had a round cheerful face and crisp black hair. He smiled slowly. But it was a more genuine smile than the tonga-driver's. So far I had met two people in Shamli and they were both smilers. That should have cheered me, but it didn't. 'You have come to stay?' he asked in a slow easygoing voice.

'Just for the day,' I said. 'You work here?'

'Yes, my name is Daya Ram. The manager is asleep just now but I will find a room for you.'

He pulled on his vest and pyjamas and accompanied me back to the verandah. Here he picked up my suitcase and, unlocking a side door, led me into the house. We went down a passageway. Then Daya Ram stopped at the door on the right, pushed it open and took me into a small, sunny room that had a window looking out onto the orchard. There was a bed, a desk, a couple of cane chairs, and a frayed and faded red carpet.

'Is it all right?' said Daya Ram.

'Perfectly all right.'

'They have breakfast at eight o'clock. But if you are hungry, I will make something for you now.'

'No, it's all right. Are you the cook too?'

'I do everything here.'

'Do you like it?'

'No,' he said. And then added, in a sudden burst of confidence, 'There are no women for a man like me.'

'Why don't you leave, then?'

'I will,' he said with a doubtful look on his face. 'I will leave . . . .'

After he had gone I shut the door and went into the bathroom to bathe. The cold water refreshed me and made me feel one with the world. After I had dried myself, I sat on the bed, in front of the open window. A cool breeze, smelling of rain, came through the window and played over my body. I thought I saw a movement among the trees.

And getting closer to the window, I saw a girl on a swing. She was a small girl, all by herself, and she was swinging to and fro and singing, and her song carried faintly on the breeze.

I dressed quickly and left my room. The girl's dress was billowing in the breeze, her pigtails flying about. When she saw me approaching, she stopped swinging and stared at me. I stopped a little distance away.

'Who are you?' she asked.

'A ghost,' I replied.

'You look like one,' she said.

I decided to take this as a compliment, as I was determined to make friends. I did not smile at her because some children dislike adults who smile at them all the time.

'What's your name?' I asked.

'Kiran,' she said. 'I'm ten.'

'You are getting old.'

'Well, we all have to grow old one day. Aren't you coming any closer?'

'May I?' I asked.

'You may. You can push the swing.'

One pigtail lay across the girl's chest, the other behind her shoulder. She had a serious face and obviously felt she had responsibilities. She seemed to be in a hurry to grow up, and I suppose she had no time for anyone who treated her as a child. I pushed the swing until it went higher and higher and then I stopped pushing so that she came lower each time and we could talk.

'Tell me about the people who live here,' I said.

'There is Heera,' she said. 'He's the gardener. He's nearly a hundred. You can see him behind the hedges in the garden. You can't see him unless you look hard. He tells me stories, a new story every day. He's much better than the people in the hotel and so is Daya Ram.'

'Yes, I met Daya Ram.'

'He's my bodyguard. He brings me nice things from the kitchen when no one is looking.'

'You don't stay here?'

'No, I live in another house. You can't see it from here. My father is the manager of the factory.'

'Aren't there any other children to play with?' I asked.

'I don't know any,' she said.

'And the people staying here?'

'Oh, *they*.' Apparently Kiran didn't think much of the hotel guests. 'Miss Deeds is funny when she's drunk. And Mr Lin is the *strangest*.'

'And what about the manager, Mr Dayal?'

'He's mean. And he gets frightened of the slightest things. But Mrs Dayal is nice. She lets me take flowers home. But she doesn't talk much.'

I was fascinated by Kiran's ruthless summing up of the guests. I brought the swing to a standstill and asked, 'And what do you think of me?'

'I don't know as yet,' said Kiran quite seriously. 'I'll think about you.'

As I came back to the hotel, I heard the sound of a piano in one of the front rooms. I didn't know enough about music to be able to recognize the piece but it had sweetness and melody though it was played with some hesitancy. As I came nearer, the sweetness deserted the music, probably because the piano was out of tune.

The person at the piano had distinctive Mongolian features and so I presumed he was Mr Lin. He hadn't seen me enter the room and I stood beside the curtains of the door, watching him play. He had full round lips and high, slanting cheekbones. His eyes were large and round and full of melancholy. His long, slender fingers hardly touched the keys.

I came nearer and then he looked up at me, without any show of surprise or displeasure, and kept on playing.

'What are you playing?' I asked.

'Chopin,' he said.

'Oh, yes. It's nice but the piano is fighting it.'

'I know. This piano belonged to one of Kipling's aunts. It hasn't been tuned since the last century.'

'Do you live here?'

'No, I come from Calcutta,' he answered readily. 'I have some business here with the sugarcane people, actually, though I am not a businessman.' He was playing softly all the time so that our conversation was not lost in the music. 'I don't know anything about business. But I have to do something.'

'Where did you learn to play the piano?'

'In Singapore. A French lady taught me. She had great hopes of my becoming a concert pianist when I grew up. I would have toured Europe and America.'

'Why didn't you?'

'We left during the War and I had to give up my lessons.'

'And why did you go to Calcutta?'

'My father is a Calcutta businessman. What do you do and why do you come here?' he asked. 'If I am not being too inquisitive.'

Before I could answer, a bell rang, loud and continuously, drowning the music and conversation.

'Breakfast,' said Mr Lin.

A thin dark man, wearing glasses, stepped nervously into the room and peered at me in an anxious manner.

'You arrived last night?'

'That's right,' I said. 'I just want to stay the day. I think you're the manager?'

'Yes. Would you like to sign the register?'

I went with him past the bar and into the office. I wrote my name and Mussoorie address in the register and the duration of my stay. I paused at the column marked 'Profession', thought it would be best to fill it with something and wrote 'Author'.

'You are here on business?' asked Mr Dayal.

'No, not exactly. You see, I'm looking for friend of mine who was last heard of in Shamli, about three years ago. I thought I'd make a few enquiries in case he's still here.'

'What was his name? Perhaps he stayed here.'

'Major Roberts,' I said. 'An Anglo-Indian.'

'Well, you can look through the old registers after breakfast.'

He accompanied me into the dining-room. The establishment was really more of a boarding-house than a hotel because Mr Dayal ate with his guests. There was a round mahogany dining-table in the centre of the room and Mr Lin was the only one seated at it. Daya Ram hovered about with plates and trays. I took my seat next to Lin and, as I did so, a door opened from the passage and a woman of about thirty-five came in.

She had on a skirt and blouse which accentuated a firm, well-rounded figure, and she walked on high heels, with a rhythmical swaying of the hips. She had an uninteresting face, camouflaged with lipstick, rouge and powder—the powder so thick that it had become embedded in the natural lines of her face—but her figure compelled admiration.

'Miss Deeds,' whispered Lin.

There was a false note to her greeting.

'Hallo, everyone,' she said heartily, straining for effect. 'Why are you all so quiet? Has Mr Lin been playing the Funeral March again?' She sat down and continued talking. 'Really, we must have a dance or something to liven things up. You must know some good numbers, Lin, after your experience of Singapore night-clubs. What's for breakfast? Boiled eggs. Daya Ram, can't you make an omelette for a change? I know you're not a professional cook but you don't have to give us the same thing every day, and there's absolutely no reason why you should burn the toast. You'll have to do something about a cook, Mr Dayal.' Then she noticed me sitting opposite her. 'Oh, hallo,' she said, genuinely surprised. She gave me a long appraising look.

'This gentleman,' said Mr Dayal introducing me, 'is an author.'

'That's nice,' said Miss Deeds. 'Are you married?'

'No,' I said. 'Are you?'

'Funny, isn't it,' she said, without taking offence, 'no one in this house seems to be married.'

'I'm married,' said Mr Dayal.

'Oh, yes, of course,' said Miss Deeds. 'And what brings you to Shamli?' she asked, turning to me.

'I'm looking for a friend called Major Roberts.'

Lin gave an exclamation of surprise. I thought he had seen through my deception.

But another game had begun.

'I knew him,' said Lin. 'A great friend of mine.'

'Yes,' continued Lin. 'I knew him. A good chap, Major Roberts.'

Well, there I was, inventing people to suit my convenience, and people like Mr Lin started inventing relationships with them. I was too intrigued to try and discourage him. I wanted to see how far he would go.

'When did you meet him?' asked Lin, taking the initiative.

'Oh, only about three years back. Just before he disappeared. He was last heard of in Shamli.'

'Yes, I heard he was here,' said Lin. 'But he went away, when he thought his relatives had traced him. He went into the mountains near Tibet.'

'Did he?' I said, unwilling to be instructed further. 'What part of the country? I come from the hills myself. I know the Mana and Niti passes quite well. If you have any idea of exactly where he went, I think I could find him.' I had the advantage in this exchange because I was the one who had originally invented Roberts. Yet I couldn't bring myself to end his deception, probably because I felt sorry for him. A happy man wouldn't take the trouble of inventing friendships with people who didn't exist. He'd be too busy with friends who did.

'You've had a lonely life, Mr Lin?' I asked.

'Lonely?' said Mr Lin, with forced incredulousness. 'I'd never been lonely till I came here a month ago. When I was in Singapore . . . .'

'You never get any letters though, do you?' asked Miss Deeds suddenly.

Lin was silent for a moment. Then he said: 'Do you?'

Miss Deeds lifted her head a little, as a horse does when it is annoyed, and I thought her pride had been hurt, but then she laughed unobtrusively and tossed her head.

'I never write letters,' she said. 'My friends gave me up as hopeless years ago. They know it's no use writing to me because they rarely get a reply. They call me the Jungle Princess.'

Mr Dayal tittered and I found it hard to suppress a smile. To cover up my smile I asked, 'You teach here?'

'Yes, I teach at the girl's school,' she said with a frown. 'But don't talk to me about teaching. I have enough of it all day.'

'You don't like teaching?'

She gave me an aggressive look. 'Should I?' she asked.

'Shouldn't you?' I said.

She paused, and then said, 'Who are you, anyway, the Inspector of Schools?'

'No,' said Mr Dayal who wasn't following very well, 'he's a journalist.'

'I've heard they are nosey,' said Miss Deeds.

Once again Lin interrupted to steer the conversation away from a delicate issue.

'Where's Mrs Dayal this morning?' asked Lin.

'She spent the night with our neighbours,' said Mr Dayal. 'She should be here after lunch.'

It was the first time Mrs Dayal had been mentioned. Nobody spoke either well or ill of her. I suspected that she kept her distance from the others, avoiding familiarity. I began to wonder about Mrs Dayal.

Daya Ram came in from the veranda looking worried.

'Heera's dog has disappeared,' he said. 'He thinks a leopard took it.'

Heera, the gardener, was standing respectfully outside on the veranda steps. We all hurried out to him, firing questions which he didn't try to answer.

'Yes. It's a leopard,' said Kiran appearing from behind Heera. 'It's going to come into the hotel,' she added cheerfully.

'Be quiet,' said Satish Dayal crossly.

'There are pug marks under the trees,' said Daya Ram.

Mr Dayal, who seemed to know little about leopards or pug marks, said, 'I will take a look,' and led the way to the orchard, the rest of us trailing behind in an ill-assorted procession.

There were marks on the soft earth in the orchard (they could have been a leopard's) which went in the direction of the riverbed. Mr Dayal paled a little and went hurrying back to the hotel. Heera returned to the front garden, the least excited, the most sorrowful. Everyone else was thinking of a leopard but he was thinking of the dog.

I followed him and watched him weeding the sunflower beds. His face was wrinkled like a walnut but his eyes were clear and bright. His hands were thin and bony but there was a deftness and power in the wrist and fingers and the weeds flew fast from his spade. He had a cracked, parchment-like skin. I could not help thinking of the gloss and glow of Daya Ram's limbs as I had seen them when he was bathing and wondered if Heera's had once been like that and if Daya Ram's would ever be like this, and both possibilities—or were they probabilities—saddened me. Our skin, I thought, is like the leaf of a tree, young and green and shiny. Then it gets darker and heavier, sometimes spotted with disease, sometimes eaten away. Then fading, yellow and red, then falling, crumbling into dust or feeding the flames of fire. I looked at my own skin, still smooth, not coarsened by labour. I thought of Kiran's fresh rose-tinted complexion; Miss Deed's skin, hard and dry; Lin's pale taut skin, stretched tightly across his prominent cheeks and forehead; and Mr Dayal's grey skin growing thick hair. And I wondered about Mrs Dayal and the kind of skin she would have.

'Did you have the dog for long?' I asked Heera.

He looked up with surprise for he had been unaware of my presence.

'Six years, sahib,' he said. 'He was not a clever dog but he was very friendly. He followed me home one day when I was coming back from the bazaar. I kept telling him to go away but he wouldn't. It was a long walk and so I began talking to him. I liked talking to him and I have always talked to him and we have understood each other. That first night, when I came home, I shut the gate between us. But he stood on the other side looking at me with trusting eyes. Why did he have to look at me like that?'

'So you kept him?'

'Yes, I could never forget the way he looked at me. I shall feel lonely now because he was my only companion. My wife and son died long ago. It seems I am to stay here forever, until everyone has gone, until there are only ghosts in Shamli. Already the ghosts are here . . . .'

I heard a light footfall behind me and turned to find Kiran. The barefoot girl stood beside the gardener and with her toes began to pull at the weeds.

'You are a lazy one,' said the old man. 'If you want to help me sit down and use your hands.'

I looked at the girl's fair round face and in her bright eyes I saw something old and wise. And I looked into the old man's wise eyes, and saw something forever bright and young. The skin cannot change the eyes. The eyes are the true reflection of a man's age and sensibilities. Even a blind man has hidden eyes.

'I hope we find the dog,' said Kiran. 'But I would like a leopard. Nothing ever happens here.'

'Not now,' sighed Heera. 'Not now . . . . Why, once there was a band and people danced till morning, but now . . . .' He paused, lost in thought and then said: 'I have always been here. I was here before Shamli.'

'Before the station?'

'Before there was a station, or a factory, or a bazaar. It was a village then, and the only way to get here was by bullock-cart. Then a bus service was started, then the railway lines were laid and a station built, then they started the sugar factory, and for a few years Shamli was a town. But the jungle was bigger than the town. The rains were heavy and malaria was everywhere. People didn't stay long in Shamli. Gradually, they went back into the hills. Sometimes I too wanted to go back to the hills, but what is the use when you are old and have no one left in the world except a few flowers in a troublesome garden. I had to choose between the flowers and the hills, and I chose the flowers. I am tired now, and old, but I am not tired of flowers.'

I could see that his real world was the garden; there was more variety in his flower-beds than there was in the town of Shamli. Every month, every day, there were new flowers in the garden, but there were always the same people in Shamli.

I left Kiran with the old man, and returned to my room. It must have been about eleven o'clock.

I was facing the window when I heard my door being opened. Turning, I perceived the barrel of a gun moving slowly round the edge of the door. Behind the gun was Satish Dayal, looking hot and sweaty. I didn't know what his intentions were; so, deciding it would be better to act first and reason later, I grabbed a pillow from the bed and flung it in his face. I then threw myself at his legs and brought him crashing down to the ground.

When we got up, I was holding the gun. It was an old Enfield rifle, probably dating back to Afghan wars, the kind that goes off at the least encouragement.

'But—but—why?' stammered the dishevelled and alarmed Mr Dayal.

'I don't know,' I said menacingly. 'Why did you come in here pointing this at me?'

'I wasn't pointing it at you. It's for the leopard.'

'Oh, so you came into my room looking for a leopard? You have, I presume been stalking one about the hotel?' (By now I was convinced that Mr Dayal had taken leave of his senses and was hunting imaginary leopards.)

'No, no,' cried the distraught man, becoming more confused. 'I was looking for you. I wanted to ask you if you could use a gun. I was thinking we should go looking for the leopard that took Heera's dog. Neither Mr Lin nor I can shoot.'

'Your gun is not up-to-date,' I said. 'It's not at all suitable for hunting leopards. A stout stick would be more effective. Why don't we arm ourselves with lathis and make a general assault?'

I said this banteringly, but Mr Dayal took the idea quite seriously. 'Yes, yes,' he said with alacrity, 'Daya Ram has got one or two lathis in the godown. The three of us could make an expedition. I have asked Mr Lin but he says he doesn't want to have anything to do with leopards.'

'What about our Jungle Princess?' I said. 'Miss Deeds should be pretty good with a lathi.'

'Yes, yes,' said Mr Dayal humourlessly, 'but we'd better not ask her.'

Collecting Daya Ram and two lathis, we set off for the orchard and began following the pug marks through the trees. It took us ten minutes to reach the riverbed, a dry hot rocky place; then we went into the jungle, Mr Dayal keeping well to the rear. The atmosphere was heavy and humid, and there was not a breath of air amongst the trees. When a parrot squawked suddenly, shattering the silence, Mr Dayal let out a startled exclamation and started for home.

'What was that?' he asked nervously.

'A bird,' I explained.

'I think we should go back now,' he said. 'I don't think the leopard's here.'

'You never know with leopards,' I said, 'they could be anywhere.'

Mr Dayal stepped away from the bushes. 'I'll have to go,' he said. 'I have a lot of work. You keep a lathi with you, and I'll send Daya Ram back later.'

'That's very thoughtful of you,' I said.

Daya Ram scratched his head and reluctantly followed his employer back through the trees. I moved on slowly, down the little used path, wondering if I should also return. I saw two monkeys playing on the branch of a tree, and decided that there could be no danger in the immediate vicinity.

Presently I came to a clearing where there was a pool of fresh clear water. It was fed by a small stream that came suddenly, like a snake, out of the long grass. The water looked cool and inviting. Laying down the lathi and taking off my clothes, I ran down the bank until I was waist-deep in the middle of the pool. I splashed about for some time before emerging, then I lay on the soft grass and allowed the sun to dry my body. I closed my eyes and gave myself up to beautiful thoughts. I had forgotten all about leopards.

I must have slept for about half-an-hour because when I awoke, I found that Daya Ram had come back and was vigorously threshing about in the narrow confines of the pool. I sat up and asked him the time.

'Twelve o'clock,' he shouted, coming out of the water, his dripping body all gold and silver in sunlight. 'They will be waiting for dinner.'

'Let them wait,' I said.

It was a relief to talk to Daya Ram, after the uneasy conversations in the lounge and dining-room.

'Dayal sahib will be angry with me.'

'I'll tell him we found the trail of the leopard, and that we went so far into the jungle that we lost our way. As Miss Deeds is so critical of the food, let her cook the meal.'

'Oh, she only talks like that,' said Daya Ram. 'Inside she is very soft. She is too soft in some ways.'

'She should be married.'

'Well, she would like to be. Only there is no one to marry her. When she came here she was engaged to be married to an English army captain. I think she loved him, but she is the sort of person who cannot help loving many men all at once, and the captain could not understand that—it is just the way she is made, I suppose. She is always ready to fall in love.'

'You seem to know,' I said.

'Oh, yes.'

We dressed and walked back to the hotel. In a few hours, I thought, the tonga will come for me and I will be back at the station. The mysterious charm of Shamli will be no more, but whenever I pass this way I will wonder about these people, about Miss Deeds and Lin and Mrs Dayal.

Mrs Dayal . . . . She was the one person I had yet to meet. It was with some excitement and curiosity that I looked forward to meeting her; she was about the only mystery left in Shamli, now, and perhaps she would be no mystery when I met her. And yet . . . . I felt that perhaps she would justify the impulse that made me get down from the train.

I could have asked Daya Ram about Mrs Dayal, and so satisfied my curiosity; but I wanted to discover her for myself. Half the day was left to me, and I didn't want my game to finish too early.

I walked towards the veranda, and the sound of the piano came through the open door.

'I wish Mr Lin would play something cheerful,' said Miss Deeds. 'He's obsessed with the Funeral March. Do you dance?'

'Oh, no,' I said.

She looked disappointed. But when Lin left the piano, she went into the lounge and sat down on the stool. I stood at the door watching her, wondering what she would do. Lin left the room somewhat resentfully.

She began to play an old song which I remembered having heard in a film or on a gramophone record. She sang while she played, in a slightly harsh but pleasant voice:

Rolling round the world
Looking for the sunshine
I know I'm going to find some day . . . .

Then she played 'Am I blue?' and 'Darling, Je Vous Aime Beaucoup.' She sat there singing in a deep husky voice, her eyes a little misty, her hard face suddenly kind and sloppy. When the dinner gong rang, she broke off playing and shook off her sentimental mood, and laughed derisively at herself.

I don't remember that lunch. I hadn't slept much since the previous night and I was beginning to feel the strain of my journey. The swim had refreshed me, but it had also made me drowsy. I ate quite well, though, of rice and kofta curry, and then, feeling sleepy, made for the garden to find a shady tree.

There were some books on the shelf in the lounge, and I ran my eye over them in search of one that might condition sleep. But they were too dull to do even that. So I went into the garden, and there was Kiran on the swing, and I went to her tree and sat down on the grass.

'Did you find the leopard?' she asked.

'No,' I said, with a yawn.

'Tell me a story.'

'You tell me one,' I said.

'All right. Once there was a lazy man with long legs, who was always yawning and wanting to fall asleep . . . .'

I watched the swaying motions of the swing and the movements of the girl's bare legs, and a tiny insect kept buzzing about in front of my nose . . .

'. . . and fall asleep, and the reason for this was that he liked to dream.'

I blew the insect away, and the swing became hazy and distant, and Kiran was a blurred figure in the trees . . .

'. . . liked to dream, and what do you think he dreamt about . . . .' Dreamt about, dreamt about . . .

When I awoke there was that cool rain-scented breeze blowing across the garden. I remember lying on the grass with my eyes closed, listening to the swishing of the swing. Either I had not slept long, or Kiran had been a long time on the swing; it was moving slowly now, in a more leisurely fashion, without much sound. I opened my eyes and saw that my arm was stained with the juice of the grass beneath me. Looking up, I expected to see Kiran's legs waving above me. But instead I saw dark slim feet and above them the folds of a sari. I straightened up against the trunk of the tree to look closer at Kiran, but Kiran wasn't there. It was someone else in the swing, a young woman in a pink sari, with a red rose in her hair.

She had stopped the swing with her foot on the ground, and she was smiling at me.

It wasn't a smile you could see, it was a tender fleeting movement that came suddenly and was gone at the same time, and its going was sad. I thought of the others' smiles, just as I had thought of their skins: the tonga-driver's friendly, deceptive smile; Daya Ram's wide sincere smile; Miss Deed's cynical, derisive smile. And looking at Sushila, I knew a smile could never change. She had always smiled that way.

'You haven't changed,' she said.

I was standing up now, though still leaning against the tree for support. Though I had never thought much about the *sound* of her voice, it seemed as familiar as the sounds of yesterday.

'You haven't changed either,' I said. 'But where did you come from?' I wasn't sure yet if I was awake or dreaming.

She laughed as she had always laughed at me.

'I came from behind the tree. The little girl has gone.'

'Yes, I'm dreaming,' I said helplessly.

'But what brings you here?'

'I don't know. At least I didn't know when I came. But it must have been you. The train stopped at Shamli and I don't know why, but I decided I would spend the day here, behind the station walls. You must be married now, Sushila.'

'Yes, I am married to Mr Dayal, the manager of the hotel. And what has been happening to you?'

'I am still a writer, still poor, and still living in Mussoorie.'

'When were you last in Delhi?' she asked. 'I don't mean Delhi, I mean at home.'

'I have not been to your home since you were there.'

'Oh, my friend,' she said, getting up suddenly and coming to me, 'I want to talk about our home and Sunil and our friends and all those things that are so far away now. I have been here two years, and I am already feeling old. I keep remembering our home—how young I was, how happy—and I am all alone with memories. But now you are here! It was a bit of magic. I came through the trees after Kiran had gone, and there you were, fast asleep under the tree. I didn't wake you then, because I wanted to see you wake up.'

'As I used to watch you wake up . . .'

She was near me and I could look at her more closely. Her cheeks did not have the same freshness—they were a little pale—and she was thinner now, but her eyes were the same, smiling the same way. Her fingers, when she took my hand, were the same warm delicate fingers.

'Talk to me,' she said. 'Tell me about yourself.'

'You tell me,' I said.

'I am here,' she said. 'That is all there is to say about myself.'

'Then let us sit down and I'll talk.'

'Not here,' she took my hand and led me through the trees. 'Come with me.'

I heard the jingle of a tonga-bell and a faint shout. I stopped and laughed.

'My tonga,' I said. 'It has come to take me back to the station.'

'But you are not going,' said Sushila, immediately downcast.

'I will tell him to come in the morning,' I said. 'I will spend the night in your Shamli.'

I walked to the front of the hotel where the tonga was waiting. I was glad no one else was in sight. The youth was smiling at me in his most appealing manner.

'I'm not going today,' I said. 'Will you come tomorrow morning?'

'I can come whenever you like, friend. But you will have to pay for every trip, because it is a long way from the station even if my tonga is empty. Usual fare, friend, one rupee.'

I didn't try to argue but resignedly gave him the rupee. He cracked his whip and pulled on the reins, and the carriage moved off.

'If you don't leave tomorrow,' the youth called out after me, 'you'll never leave Shamli!'

I walked back through the trees, but I couldn't find Sushila.

'Sushila, where are you?' I called, but I might have been speaking to the trees, for I had no reply. There was a small path going through the orchard, and on the path I saw a rose petal. I walked a little further and saw another petal. They were from Sushila's red rose. I walked on down the path until I had skirted the orchard, and then the path went along the fringe of the jungle, past a clump of bamboos, and here the grass was a lush green as though it had been constantly watered. I was still finding rose petals. I heard the chatter of seven-sisters, and the call of a hoopoe. The path bent to meet a stream, there was a willow coming down to the water's edge, and Sushila was waiting there.

'Why didn't you wait?' I said.

'I wanted to see if you were as good at following me as you used to be.'

'Well, I am,' I said, sitting down beside her on the grassy bank of the stream. 'Even if I'm out of practice.'

'Yes, I remember the time you climbed up an apple tree to pick some fruit for me. You got up all right but then you couldn't come down again. I had to climb up myself and help you.'

'I don't remember that,' I said.

'Of course you do.'

'It must have been your other friend, Pramod.'

'I never climbed trees with Pramod.'

'Well, I don't remember.'

I looked at the little stream that ran past us. The water was no more than ankle-deep, cold and clear and sparking, like the mountain-stream near my home. I took off my shoes, rolled up my trousers, and put my feet in the water. Sushila's feet joined mine.

At first I had wanted to ask about her marriage, whether she was happy or not, what she thought of her husband; but now I couldn't ask her these things. They seemed far away and of little importance. I could think of nothing she had in common with Mr Dayal. I felt that her charm and attractiveness and warmth could not have been appreciated, or even noticed, by that curiously distracted man. He was much older than her, of course, probably older than me. He was obviously not her choice but her parents', and so far they were childless. Had there been children, I don't think Sushila would have minded Mr Dayal as her husband. Children would have made up for the absence of passion—or was there passion in Satish Dayal? . . . . I remembered having heard that Sushila had been married to a man she didn't like. I remembered having shrugged off the news, because it meant she would never come my way again, and I have never yearned after something that has been irredeemably lost. But she *had* come my way again. And was she still lost? That was what I wanted to know . . . .

'What do you do with yourself all day?' I asked.

'Oh, I visit the school and help with the classes. It is the only interest I have in this place. The hotel is terrible. I try to keep away from it as much as I can.'

'And what about the guests?'

'Oh, don't let us talk about them. Let us talk about ourselves. Do you have to go tomorrow?'

'Yes, I suppose so. Will you always be in this place?'

'I suppose so.'

That made me silent. I took her hand, and my feet churned up the mud at the bottom of the stream. As the mud subsided, I saw Sushila's face reflected in the water, and looking up at her again, into her dark eyes, the old yearning returned and I wanted to care for her and protect her. I wanted to take her away from that place, from sorrowful Shamli. I wanted her to live again. Of course, I had forgotten all about my poor finances, Sushila's family, and the shoes I wore, which were my last pair. The uplift I was experiencing in this meeting with Sushila, who had always, throughout her childhood and youth, bewitched me as no other had ever bewitched me, made me reckless and impulsive.

I lifted her hand to my lips and kissed her on the soft of her palm.

'Can I kiss you?' I said.

'You have just done so.'

'Can I kiss you?' I repeated.

'It is not necessary.'

I leaned over and kissed her slender neck. I knew she would like this, because that was where I had kissed her often before. I kissed her on the soft of the throat, where it tickled.

'It is not necessary,' she said, but she ran her fingers through my hair and let them rest there. I kissed her behind the ear then, and kept my mouth to her ear and whispered, 'Can I kiss you?'

She turned her face to me so that we looked deep into each other's eyes, and I kissed her again. And we put our arms around each other and lay together on the grass with the water running over our feet. We said nothing at all, simply lay there for what seemed like several years, or until the first drop of rain.

It was a big wet drop, and it splashed on Sushila's cheek just next to mine, and ran down to her lips so that I had to kiss her again. The next big drop splattered on the tip of my nose, and Sushila laughed and sat up. Little ringlets were forming on the stream where the raindrops hit the water, and above us there was a pattering on the banana leaves.

'We must go,' said Sushila.

We started homewards, but had not gone far before it was raining steadily, and Sushila's hair came loose and streamed down her body. The rain fell harder, and we had to hop over pools and avoid the soft mud. Sushila's sari was plastered to her body, accentuating her ripe, thrusting breasts, and I was excited to passion. I pulled her beneath a big tree, crushed her in my arms and kissed her rain-kissed mouth. And then I thought she was crying, but I wasn't sure, because it might have been the raindrops on her cheeks.

'Come away with me,' I said. 'Leave this place. Come away with me tomorrow morning. We will go somewhere where nobody will know us or come between us.'

She smiled at me and said, 'You are still a dreamer, aren't you?'

'Why can't you come?'

'I am married. It is as simple as that.'

'If it is that simple you can come.'

'I have to think of my parents, too. It would break my father's heart if I were to do what you are proposing. And you are proposing it without a thought for the consequences.'

'You are too practical,' I said.

'If women were not practical, most marriages would be failures.'

'So your marriage is a success?'

'Of course it is, as a marriage. I am not happy and I do not love him, but neither am I so unhappy that I should hate him. Sometimes, for our own sakes, we have to think of the happiness of others. What happiness would we have living in hiding from everyone we once knew and cared for. Don't be a fool. I am always here and you can come to see me, and nobody will be made unhappy by it. But take me away and we will only have regrets.'

'You don't love me,' I said foolishly.

'That sad word love,' she said, and became pensive and silent.

I could say no more. I was angry again and rebellious, and there was no one and nothing to rebel against. I could not understand someone who was afraid to break away from an unhappy existence lest that existence should become unhappier. I had always considered it an admirable thing to break away from security and respectability. Of course, it is easier for a man to do this. A man can look after himself, he can do without neighbours and the approval of the local society. A woman, I reasoned, would do anything for love provided it was not at the price of security; for a woman loves security as much as a man loves independence.

'I must go back now,' said Sushila. 'You follow a little later.'

'All you wanted to do was talk,' I complained.

She laughed at that and pulled me playfully by the hair. Then she ran out from under the tree, springing across the grass, and the wet mud flew up and flecked her legs. I watched her through the thin curtain of rain until she reached the veranda. She turned to wave to me, and then skipped into the hotel.

The rain had lessened, but I didn't know what to do with myself. The hotel was uninviting, and it was too late to leave Shamli. If the grass hadn't been wet I would have preferred to sleep under a tree rather than return to the hotel to sit at that alarming dining-table.

I came out from under the trees and crossed the garden. But instead of making for the veranda I went round to the back of the hotel. Smoke issuing from the barred window of a back room told me I had probably found the kitchen. Daya Ram was inside, squatting in front of a stove, stirring a pot of stew. The stew smelt appetizing. Daya Ram looked up and smiled at me.

'I thought you had gone,' he said.

'I'll go in the morning,' I said, pulling myself up on an empty table. Then I had one of my sudden ideas and said, 'Why don't you come with me? I can find you a good job in Mussoorie. How much do you get paid here?'

'Fifty rupees a month. But I haven't been paid for three months.'

'Could you get your pay before tomorrow morning?'

'No, I won't get anything until one of the guests pays a bill. Miss Deeds owes about fifty rupees on whisky alone. She will pay up, she says, when the school pays her salary. And the school can't pay her until they collect the children's fees. That is how bankrupt everyone is in Shamli.'

'I see,' I said, though I didn't see. 'But Mr Dayal can't hold back your pay just because his guests haven't paid their bills.'

'He can if he hasn't got any money.'

'I see,' I said. 'Anyway, I will give you my address. You can come when you are free.'

'I will take it from the register,' he said.

I edged over to the stove and leaning over, sniffed at the stew. 'I'll eat mine now,' I said. And without giving Daya Ram a chance to object, I lifted a plate off the shelf, took hold of the stirring-spoon and helped myself from the pot.

'There's rice too,' said Daya Ram.

I filled another plate with rice and then got busy with my fingers. After ten minutes I had finished. I sat back comfortably, in a ruminative mood. With my stomach full I could take a more tolerant view of life and people. I could understand Sushila's apprehensions, Lin's delicate lying and Miss Deed's aggressiveness. Daya Ram went out to sound the dinner-gong, and I trailed back to my room.

From the window of my room I saw Kiran running across the lawn and I called to her, but she didn't hear me. She ran down the path and out of the gate, her pigtails beating against the wind.

The clouds were breaking and coming together again, twisting and spiralling their way across a violet sky. The sun was going down behind the Siwaliks. The sky there was bloodshot. The tall slim trunks of the eucalyptus tree were tinged with an orange glow; the rain had stopped, and the wind was a soft, sullen puff, drifting sadly through the trees. There was a steady drip of water from the eaves of the roof onto the window-still. Then the sun went down behind the old, old hills, and I remembered my own hills, far beyond these.

The room was dark but I did not turn on the light. I stood near the window, listening to the garden. There was a frog warbling somewhere and there was a sudden flap of wings overhead. Tomorrow morning I would go, and perhaps I would come back to Shamli one day, and perhaps not. I could always come here looking for Major Roberts, and who knows, one day I might find him. What should he be like, this lost man? A romantic, a man with a dream, a man with brown skin and blue eyes, living in a hut on a snowy mountain-top, chopping wood and catching fish and swimming in cold mountain streams; a rough, free man with a kind heart and a shaggy beard, a man who owed allegiance to no one, who gave a damn for money and politics, and cities and civilizations, who was his own master, who lived at one with nature knowing no fear. But that was not Major Roberts—that was the man I wanted to be. He was not a Frenchman or an Englishman, he was me, a dream of myself. If only I could find Major Roberts.

When Daya Ram knocked on the door and told me the others had finished dinner, I left my room and made for the lounge. It was quite lively in the lounge. Satish Dayal was at the bar, Lin at the piano, and Miss Deeds in the centre of the room, executing a tango on her own. It was obvious she had been drinking heavily.

'All on credit,' complained Mr Dayal to me. 'I don't know when I'll be paid, but I don't dare refuse her anything for fear she starts breaking up the hotel.'

'She could do that, too,' I said. 'It would come down without much encouragement.'

Lin began to play a waltz (I think it was a waltz), and then I found Miss Deeds in front of me, saying, 'Wouldn't you like to dance, old boy?'

'Thank you,' I said, somewhat alarmed. 'I hardly know how to.'

'Oh, come on, be a sport,' she said, pulling me away from the bar. I was glad Sushila wasn't present. She wouldn't have minded, but she'd have laughed as she always laughed when I made a fool of myself.

We went around the floor in what I suppose was waltz-time, though all I did was mark time to Miss Deeds' motions. We were not very steady—this because I was trying to keep her at arm's length, while she was determined to have me crushed to her bosom. At length Lin finished the waltz. Giving him a grateful look, I pulled myself free. Miss Deeds went over to the piano, leaned right across it and said, 'Play something lively, dear Mr Lin, play some hot stuff.'

To my surprise Mr Lin without so much as an expression of distaste or amusement, began to execute what I suppose was the frug or the jitterbug. I was glad she hadn't asked me to dance that one with her.

It all appeared very incongruous to me: Miss Deeds letting herself go in crazy abandonment, Lin playing the piano with great seriousness, and Mr Dayal watching from the bar with an anxious frown. I wondered what Sushila would have thought of them now.

Eventually Miss Deeds collapsed on the couch breathing heavily. 'Give me a drink,' she cried.

With the noblest of intentions I took her a glass of water. Miss Deeds took a sip and made a face. 'What's this stuff?' she asked. 'It is different.'

'Water,' I said.

'No,' she said, 'now don't joke, tell me what it is.'

'It's water, I assure you,' I said.

When she saw that I was serious, her face coloured up and I thought she would throw the water at me. But she was too tired to do this and contented herself with throwing the glass over her shoulder. Mr Dayal made a dive for the flying glass, but he wasn't in time to rescue it and it hit the wall and fell to pieces on the floor.

Mr Dayal wrung his hands. 'You'd better take her to her room,' he said, as though I were personally responsible for her behaviour just because I'd danced with her.

'I can't carry her alone,' I said, making an unsuccessful attempt at helping Miss Deeds up from the couch.

Mr Dayal called for Daya Ram, and the big amiable youth came lumbering into the lounge. We took an arm each and helped Miss Deeds, feet dragging, across the room. We got her to her room and onto her bed. When we were about to withdraw she said, 'Don't go, my dear, stay with me a little while.'

Daya Ram had discreetly slipped outside. With my hand on the door-knob I said, 'Which of us?'

'Oh, are there two of you?' said Miss Deeds, without a trace of disappointment.

'Yes, Daya Ram helped me carry you here.'

'Oh, and who are you?'

'I'm the writer. You danced with me, remember?'

'Of course. You dance divinely, Mr Writer. Do stay with me. Daya Ram can stay too if he likes.'

I hesitated, my hand on the door-knob. She hadn't opened her eyes all the time I'd been in the room, her arms hung loose, and one bare leg hung over the side of the bed. She was fascinating somehow, and desirable, but I was afraid of her. I went out of the room and quietly closed the door.

As I lay awake in bed I heard the jackal's 'Pheau', the cry of fear which it communicates to all the jungle when there is danger about, a leopard or a tiger. It was a weird howl, and between each note there was a kind of low gurgling. I switched off the light and peered through the closed window. I saw the jackal at the edge of the lawn. It sat almost vertically on its haunches, holding its head straight up to the sky, making the neighbourhood vibrate with the eerie violence of its cries. Then suddenly it started up and ran off into the trees.

Before getting back into bed I made sure the window was shut. The bull-frog was singing again, 'ing-ong, ing-ong', in some foreign language. I wondered if Sushila was awake too, thinking about me. It must have been almost eleven o'clock. I thought of Miss Deeds with her leg hanging over the edge of the bed. I tossed restlessly and then sat up. I hadn't slept for two nights but I was not sleepy. I got out of bed without turning on the light and slowly opening my door, crept down the passage-way. I stopped at the door of Miss Deed's room. I stood there listening, but I heard only the ticking of the big clock that might have been in the room or somewhere in the passage. I put my hand on the door-knob, but the door was bolted. That settled the matter.

I would definitely leave Shamli the next morning. Another day in the company of these people and I would be behaving like them. Perhaps I was already doing so! I remembered the tonga-driver's words: 'Don't stay too long in Shamli or you will never leave!'

When the rain came, it was not with a preliminary patter or shower, but all at once, sweeping across the forest like a massive wall, and I could hear it in the trees long before it reached the house. Then it came crashing down on the corrugated roof, and the hailstones hit the window panes with a hard metallic sound so that I thought the glass would break. The sound of thunder was like the booming of big guns and the lightning kept playing over the garden. At every flash of lightning I sighted the swing under the tree, rocking and leaping in the air as though some invisible, agitated being was sitting on it. I wondered about Kiran. Was she sleeping through all this, blissfully unconcerned, or was she lying awake in bed, starting at every clash of thunder as I was? Or was she up and about, exulting in the storm? I half expected to see her come running through the trees, through the rain, to stand on the swing with her hair blowing wild in the wind, laughing at the thunder and the angry skies. Perhaps I did see her, perhaps she was there. I wouldn't have been surprised if she were some forest nymph living in the hole of a tree, coming out sometimes to play in the garden.

A crash, nearer and louder than any thunder so far, made me sit up in bed with a start. Perhaps lightning had struck the house. I turned on the switch but the light didn't come on. A tree must have fallen across the line.

I heard voices in the passage—the voices of several people. I stepped outside to find out what had happened, and started at the appearance of a ghostly apparition right in front of me. It was Mr Dayal standing on the threshold in an oversized pyjama suit, a candle in his hand.

'I came to wake you,' he said. 'This storm . . . .'

He had the irritating habit of stating the obvious.

'Yes, the storm,' I said. 'Why is everybody up?'

'The back wall has collapsed and part of the roof has fallen in. We'd better spend the night in the lounge—it is the safest room. This is a very old building,' he added apologetically.

'All right,' I said. 'I am coming.'

The lounge was lit by two candles. One stood over the piano, the other on a small table near the couch. Miss Deeds was on the couch, Lin was at the piano-stool, looking as though he would start playing Stravinsky any moment, and Dayal was fussing about the room. Sushila was standing at a window, looking out at the stormy night. I went to the window and touched her but she didn't look around or say anything. The lightning flashed and her dark eyes were pools of smouldering fire.

'What time will you be leaving?' she asked.

'The tonga will come for me at seven.'

'If I come,' she said, 'if I come with you, I will be at the station before the train leaves.'

'How will you get there?' I asked, and hope and excitement rushed over me again.

'I will get there,' she said. 'I will get there before you. But if I am not there, then do not wait, do not come back for me. Go on your way. It will mean I do not want to come. Or I will be there.'

'But are you sure?'

'Don't stand near me now. Don't speak to me unless you have to.' She squeezed my fingers, then drew her hand away. I sauntered over to the next window, then back into the centre of the room. A gust of wind blew through a cracked window-pane and put out the candle near the couch.

'Damn the wind,' said Miss Deeds.

The window in my room had burst open during the night and there were leaves and branches strewn about the floor. I sat down on the damp bed and smelt eucalyptus. The earth was red, as though the storm had bled it all night.

After a little while I went into the veranda with my suitcase to wait for the tonga. It was then that I saw Kiran under the trees. Kiran's long black pigtails were tied up in a red ribbon, and she looked fresh and clean like the rain and the red earth. She stood looking seriously at me.

'Did you like the storm?' she asked.

'Some of the time,' I said. 'I'm going soon. Can I do anything for you?'

'Where are you going?'

'I'm going to the end of the world. I'm looking for Major Roberts, have you seen him anywhere?'

'There is no Major Roberts,' she said perceptively. 'Can I come with you to the end of the world?'

'What about your parents?'

'Oh, we won't take them.'

'They might be annoyed if you go off on your own.'

'I can stay on my own. I can go anywhere.'

'Well, one day I'll come back here and I'll take you everywhere and no one will stop us. Now is there anything else I can do for you?'

'I want some flowers, but I can't reach them,' she pointed to a hibiscus tree that grew against the wall. It meant climbing the wall to reach the flowers. Some of the red flowers had fallen during the night and were floating in a pool of water.

'All right,' I said and pulled myself up on the wall. I smiled down into Kiran's serious, upturned face. 'I'll throw them to you and you can catch them.'

I bent a branch, but the wood was young and green and I had to twist it several times before it snapped.

'I hope nobody minds,' I said, as I dropped the flowering branch to Kiran.

'It's nobody's tree,' she said.

'Sure?'

She nodded vigorously. 'Sure, don't worry.'

I was working for her and she felt immensely capable of protecting me. Talking and being with Kiran, I felt a nostalgic longing for childhood—emotions that had been beautiful because they were never completely understood.

'Who is your best friend?' I said.

'Daya Ram,' she replied. 'I told you so before.'

She was certainly faithful to her friends.

'And who is the second best?'

She put her finger in her mouth to consider the question, and her head dropped sideways.

'I'll make you the second best,' she said.

I dropped the flowers over her head. 'That is so kind of you. I'm proud to be your second best.'

I heard the tonga bell, and from my perch on the wall saw the carriage coming down the driveway. 'That's for me,' I said. 'I must go now.'

I jumped down the wall. And the sole of my shoe came off at last.

'I knew that would happen,' I said.

'Who cares for shoes,' said Kiran.

'Who cares,' I said.

I walked back to the veranda and Kiran walked beside me, and stood in front of the hotel while I put my suitcase in the tonga.

'You nearly stayed one day too late,' said the tonga-driver. 'Half the hotel has come down and tonight the other half will come down.'

I climbed into the back seat. Kiran stood on the path, gazing intently at me.

'I'll see you again,' I said.

'I'll see you in Iceland or Japan,' she said. 'I'm going everywhere.'

'Maybe,' I said, 'maybe you will.'

We smiled, knowing and understanding each other's importance. In her bright eyes I saw something old and wise. The tonga-driver cracked his whip, the wheels creaked, the carriage rattled down the path. We kept waving to each other. In Kiran's hand was a spring of hibiscus. As she waved, the blossoms fell apart and danced a little in the breeze.

Shamli station looked the same as it had the day before. The same train stood at the same platform and the same dogs prowled beside the fence. I waited on the platform till the bell clanged for the train to leave, but Sushila did not come.

Somehow, I was not disappointed. I had never really expected her to come. Unattainable, Sushila would always be more bewitching and beautiful than if she were mine.

Shamli would always be there. And I could always come back, looking for Major Roberts.

MOST BEAUTIFUL

ক্ষ

I DON'T QUITE KNOW why I found that particular town so heartless. Perhaps because of its crowded, claustrophobic atmosphere, its congested and insanitary lanes, its weary people . . . . One day I found the children of the bazaar tormenting a deformed, retarded boy.

About a dozen boys, between the ages of eight and fourteen, were jeering at the retard, who was making things worse for himself by confronting the gang and shouting abuses at them. The boy was twelve or thirteen, judging by his face, but had the height of an eight- or nine-year-old. His legs were thick, short and bowed. He had a small chest but his arms were long, making him rather ape-like in his attitude. His forehead and cheeks were pitted with the scars of small-pox. He was ugly by normal standards, and the gibberish he spoke did nothing to discourage his tormentors. They threw mud and stones at him, while keeping well out of his reach. Few can be more cruel than a gang of schoolboys in high spirits.

I was an uneasy observer of the scene. I felt that I ought to do something to put a stop to it, but lacked the courage to interfere. It was only when a stone struck the boy on the face, cutting open his cheek, that I lost my normal discretion and ran in amongst the boys, shouting at them and clouting those I could reach. They scattered like defeated soldiery.

I was surprised at my own daring, and rather relieved when the boys did not return. I took the frightened, angry boy by the hand, and asked him where he lived. He drew away from me, but I held on to his fat little fingers and told him I would take him home. He mumbled something incoherent and pointed down a narrow lane. I led him away from the bazaar.

I said very little to the boy because it was obvious that he had some defect of speech. When he stopped outside a door set in a high wall, I presumed that we had come to his house.

The door was opened by a young woman. The boy immediately threw his arms around her and burst into tears. I had not been prepared for the boy's mother. Not only did she look perfectly normal physically, but she was also strikingly handsome. She must have been about thirty-five.

She thanked me for bringing her son home, and asked me into the house. The boy withdrew into a corner of the sitting-room, and sat on his haunches in gloomy silence, his bow legs looking even more grotesque in this posture. His mother offered me tea, but I asked for a glass of water. She asked the boy to fetch it, and he did so, thrusting the glass into my hands without looking me in the face.

'Suresh is my only son,' she said. 'My husband is disappointed in him, but I love my son. Do you think he is very ugly?'

'Ugly is just a word,' I said. 'Like beauty. They mean different things to different people. What did the poet say?— "Beauty is truth, truth is beauty." But if beauty and truth are the same thing, why have different words? There are no absolutes except birth and death.'

The boy squatted down at her feet, cradling his head in her lap. With the end of her sari, she began wiping his face.

'Have you tried teaching him to talk properly?' I asked.

'He has been like this since childhood. The doctors can do nothing.'

While we were talking the father came in, and the boy slunk away to the kitchen. The man thanked me curtly for bringing the boy home, and seemed at once to dismiss the whole matter from his mind. He seemed preoccupied with business matters. I got the impression that he had long since resigned himself to having a deformed son, and his early disappointment had changed to indifference. When I got up to leave, his wife accompanied me to the front door.

'Please do not mind if my husband is a little rude,' she said. 'His business is not going too well. If you would like to come again, please do. Suresh does not meet many people who treat him like a normal person.'

I knew that I wanted to visit them again—more out of sympathy for the mother than out of pity for the boy. But I realized that she was not interested in me personally, except as a possible mentor for her son.

After about a week I went to the house again.

Suresh's father was away on a business trip, and I stayed for lunch. The boy's mother made some delicious parathas stuffed with ground radish, and served it with pickle and curds. If Suresh ate like an animal, gobbling his food, I was not far behind him. His mother encouraged him to overeat. He was morose and uncommunicative when he ate, but when I suggested that he come with me for a walk, he looked up eagerly. At the same time a look of fear passed across his mother's face.

'Will it be all right?' she asked. 'You have seen how other children treat him. That day he slipped out of the house without telling anyone.'

'We won't go towards the bazaar,' I said. 'I was thinking of a walk in the fields.'

Suresh made encouraging noises and thumped the table with his fists to show that he wanted to go. Finally his mother consented, and the boy and I set off down the road.

He could not walk very fast because of his awkward legs, but this gave me a chance to point out to him anything that I thought might arouse his interest—parrots squabbling in a banyan tree, buffaloes wallowing in a muddy pond, a group of hermaphrodite musicians strolling down the road. Suresh took a keen interest in the hermaphrodites, perhaps because they were grotesque in their own way: tall, masculine-looking people dressed in women's garments, ankle-bells jingling on their heavy feet, and their long, gaunt faces made up with rouge and mascara. For the first time, I heard Suresh laugh. Apparently he had discovered that there were human beings even odder than he. And like any human being, he lost no time in deriding them.

'Don't laugh,' I said. 'They were born that way, just as you were born the way you are.'

But he did not take me seriously and grinned, his wide mouth revealing surprisingly strong teeth.

We reached the dry riverbed on the outskirts of the town and crossing it entered a field of yellow mustard flowers. The mustard stretched away towards the edge of a sub-tropical forest. Seeing trees in the distance, Suresh began to run towards them, shouting and clapping his hands. He had never been out of town before. The courtyard of his house and, occasionally, the road to the bazaar, were all that he had seen of the world. Now the trees beckoned him.

We found a small stream running through the forest and I took off my clothes and leapt into the cool water, inviting Suresh to join me. He hesitated about taking off his clothes, but after watching me for a while, his eagerness to join me overcame his self-consciousness, and he exposed his misshapen little body to the soft spring sunshine.

He waded clumsily towards me. The water which came only to my knees reached up to his chest.

'Come, I'll teach you to swim,' I said. And lifting him up from the waist, I held him afloat. He spluttered and thrashed around, but stopped struggling when he found that he could stay afloat.

Later, sitting on the banks of the stream, he discovered a small turtle sitting over a hole in the ground in which it had laid its eggs. He had never watched a turtle before, and watched it in fascination, while it drew its head into its shell and then thrust it out again with extreme circumspection. He must have felt that the turtle resembled him in some respects, with its squat legs, rounded back, and tendency to hide its head from the world.

After that I went to the boy's house about twice a week, and we nearly always visited the stream. Before long Suresh was able to swim a short distance. Knowing how to swim—this was something the bazaar boys never learnt—gave him a certain confidence, made his life something more than a one-dimensional existence.

The more I saw Suresh, the less conscious was I of his deformities. For me, he was fast becoming the norm; while the children of the bazaar seemed abnormal in their very similarity to each other. That he was still conscious of his ugliness—and how could he ever cease to be—was made clear to me about two months after our first meeting.

We were coming home through the mustard fields, which had turned from yellow to green, when I noticed that we were being followed by a small goat. It appeared to have been separated from its mother, and now attached itself to us. Though I tried driving the kid away, it continued tripping along at out heels, and when Suresh found that it persisted in accompanying us, he picked it up and took it home.

The kid became his main obsession during the next few days. He fed it with his own hands and allowed it to sleep at the foot of his bed. It was a pretty little kid, with fairy horns and an engaging habit of doing a hop, skip and jump when moving about the house. Everyone admired the pet, and the boy's mother and I both remarked on how pretty it was.

His resentment against the animal began to show when others started admiring it. He suspected that they found it better-looking than its owner. I remember finding him squatting in front of a low mirror, holding the kid in his arms, and studying their reflections in the glass. After a few minutes of this, Suresh thrust the goat away. When he noticed that I was watching him, he got up and left the room without looking at me.

Two days later, when I called at the house, I found his mother looking very upset. I could see that she had been crying. But she seemed relieved to see me, and took me into the sitting room. When Suresh saw me, he got up from the floor and ran to the veranda.

'What's wrong?' I asked.

'It was the little goat,' she said. 'Suresh killed it.'

She told me how Suresh, in a sudden and uncontrollable rage, had thrown a brick at the kid, breaking its skull. What had upset her more than the animal's death was the fact that Suresh had shown no regret for what he had done.

'I'll talk to him,' I said, and went out to the veranda, but the boy had disappeared.

'He must have gone to the bazaar,' said his mother anxiously. 'He does that when he's upset. Sometimes I think he likes to be teased and beaten.'

He was not in the bazaar. I found him near the stream, lying flat on his belly in the soft mud, chasing tadpoles with a stick.

'Why did you kill the goat?' I asked.

He shrugged his shoulders.

'Did you enjoy killing it?'

He looked at me and smiled and nodded his head vigorously.

'How very cruel,' I said. But I did not mean it. I knew that his cruelty was no different from mine or anyone else's; only his was an untrammelled cruelty, primitive, as yet undisguised by civilizing restraints.

He took a pen-knife from his shirt pocket, opened it, and held it out to me by the blade. He pointed to his bare stomach and motioned me to thrust the blade into his belly. He had such a mournful look on his face (the result of having offended me and not in remorse for the goat-sacrifice) that I had to burst out laughing.

'You are a funny fellow,' I said, taking the knife from him and throwing it into the stream. 'Come, let's have a swim.'

We swam all afternoon, and Suresh went home smiling. His mother and I conspired to keep the whole affair a secret from his father—who had not in any case been aware of the goat's presence.

Suresh seemed quite contented during the following weeks. And then I received a letter offering me a job in Delhi and I knew that I would have to take it, as I was earning very little by my writing at the time.

The boy's mother was disappointed, even depressed, when I told her I would be going away. I think she had grown quite fond of me. But the boy, always unpredictable, displayed no feeling at all. I felt a little hurt by his apparent indifference. Did our weeks of companionship mean nothing to him? I told myself that he probably did not realize that he might never see me again.

On the evening my train was to leave, I went to the house to say goodbye. The boy's mother made me promise to write to them, but Suresh seemed cold and distant, and refused to sit near me or take my hand. He made me feel that I was an outsider again—one of the mob throwing stones at odd and frightening people.

At eight o'clock that evening I entered a third-class compartment and, after a brief scuffle with several other travellers, succeeded in securing a seat near a window. It enabled me to look down the length of the platform.

The guard had blown his whistle and the train was about to leave, when I saw Suresh standing near the station turnstile, looking up and down the platform.

'Suresh!' I shouted and he heard me and came hobbling along the platform. He had run the gauntlet of the bazaar during the busiest hour of the evening.

'I'll be back next year,' I called.

The train had begun moving out of the station, and as I waved to Suresh, he broke into a stumbling run, waving his arms in frantic, restraining gestures.

I saw him stumble against someone's bedding-roll and fall sprawling on the ground. The engine picked up speed and the platform receded.

And that was the last I saw of Suresh, lying alone on the crowded platform, alone in the great grey darkness of the world, crooked and bent and twisted—the most beautiful boy in the world.

DUST ON THE MOUNTAIN

~

I

WINTER CAME AND WENT, without so much as a drizzle. The hillside was brown all summer and the fields were bare. The old plough that was dragged over the hard ground by Bisnu's lean oxen made hardly any impression. Still, Bisnu kept his seeds ready for sowing. A good monsoon, and there would be plenty of maize and rice to see the family through the next winter.

Summer went its scorching way, and a few clouds gathered on the south-western horizon.

'The monsoon is coming,' announced Bisnu.

His sister Puja was at the small stream, washing clothes. 'If it doesn't come soon, the stream will dry up,' she said. 'See, it's only a trickle this year. Remember when there were so many different flowers growing here on the banks of the stream? This year there isn't one.'

'The winter was dry. It did not even snow,' said Bisnu.

'I cannot remember another winter when there was no snow,' said his mother. 'The year your father died, there was so much snow the villagers could not light his funeral pyre for hours . . . . And now there are fires everywhere.' She pointed to the next mountain, half-hidden by the smoke from a forest fire.

At night they sat outside their small house, watching the fire spread. A red line stretched right across the mountain.

Thousands of Himalayan trees were perishing in the flames. Oaks, deodars, maples, pines; trees that had taken hundreds of years to grow. And now a fire started carelessly by some campers had been carried up the mountain with the help of the dry grass and strong breeze. There was no one to put it out. It would take days to die down by itself.

'If the monsoon arrives tomorrow, the fire will go out,' said Bisnu, ever the optimist. He was only twelve, but he was the man in the house; he had to see that there was enough food for the family and for the oxen, for the big black dog and the hens.

There were clouds the next day but they brought only a drizzle.

'It's just the beginning,' said Bisnu as he placed a bucket of muddy water on the steps.

'It usually starts with a heavy downpour,' said his mother.

But there were to be no downpours that year. Clouds gathered on the horizon but they were white and puffy and soon disappeared. True monsoon clouds would have been dark and heavy with moisture. There were other signs—or lack of them—that warned of a long dry summer. The birds were silent, or simply absent. The Himalayan barbet, who usually heralded the approach of the monsoon with strident calls from the top of a spruce tree, hadn't been seen or heard. And the cicadas, who played a deafening overture in the oaks at the first hint of rain, seemed to be missing altogether.

Puja's apricot tree usually gave them a basket full of fruit every summer. This year it produced barely a handful of apricots, lacking juice and flavour. The tree looked ready to die, its leaves curled up in despair. Fortunately there was a store of walnuts, and a binful of wheat-grain and another of rice stored from the previous year, so they would not be entirely without food; but it looked as though there would be no fresh fruit or vegetables. And there would be nothing to store away for the following winter. Money would be needed to buy supplies in Tehri, some thirty miles distant. And there was no money to be earned in the village.

'I will go to Mussoorie and find work,' announced Bisnu.

'But Mussoorie is a two-day journey by bus,' said his mother. 'There is no one there who can help you. And you may not get any work.'

'In Mussoorie there is plenty of work during the summer. Rich people come up from the plains for their holidays. It is full of hotels and shops and places where they can spend their money.'

'But they won't spend any money on *you*.'

'There is money to be made there. And if not, I will come home. I can walk back over the Nag Tibba mountain. It will take only two and a half days and I will save the bus fare!'

'Don't go, bhai,' pleaded Puja. 'There will be no one to prepare your food—you will only get sick.'

But Bisnu had made up his mind so he put a few belongings in a cloth shoulder-bag, while his mother prised several rupee-coins out of a cache in the wall of their living room. Puja prepared a special breakfast of parathas and an egg scrambled with onions, the hen having laid just one for the occasion. Bisnu put some of the parathas in his bag. Then, waving goodbye to his mother and sister, he set off down the road from the village.

After walking for a mile, he reached the highway where there was a hamlet with a bus stop. A number of villagers were waiting patiently for a bus. It was an hour late but they were used to that. As long as it arrived safely and got them to their destination, they would be content. They were patient people. And although Bisnu wasn't quite so patient, he too had learnt how to wait—for late buses and late monsoon.

II

Along the valley and over the mountains went the little bus with its load of frail humans. A little misjudgement on the part of the driver, and they would all be dashed to pieces on the rocks far below.

'How tiny we are,' thought Bisnu, looking up at the towering peaks and the immensity of the sky. 'Each of us no more than a raindrop . . . . And I wish we had a few raindrops!'

There were still fires burning to the north but the road went south, where there were no forests anyway, just bare brown hillsides. Down near the river there were small paddy fields but unfortunately rivers ran downhill and not uphill, and there was no inexpensive way in which the water could be brought up the steep slopes to the fields that depended on rainfall.

Bisnu stared out of the bus window at the river running far below. On either bank huge boulders lay exposed, for the level of the water had fallen considerably during the past few months.

'Why are there no trees here?' he asked aloud, and received the attention of a fellow passenger, an old man in the next seat who had been keeping up a relentless dry coughing. Even though it was a warm day, he wore a woollen cap and had an old muffler wrapped about his neck.

'There were trees here once,' he said. 'But the contractors took the deodars for furniture and houses. And the pines were tapped to death for resin. And the oaks were stripped of their leaves to feed the cattle—you can still see a few tree-skeletons if you look hard—and the bushes that remained were finished off by the goats!'

'When did all this happen?' asked Bisnu.

'A few years ago. And it's still happening in other areas, although it's forbidden now to cut trees. The only forests that remain are in remote places where there are no roads.' A fit of coughing came over him, but he had found a good listener and was eager to continue. 'The road helps you and me to get about but it also makes it easier for others to do mischief. Rich men from the cities come here and buy up what they want—land, trees, people!'

'What takes you to Mussoorie, Uncle?' asked Bisnu politely. He always addressed elderly people as uncle or aunt.

'I have a cough that won't go away. Perhaps they can do something for it at the hospital in Mussoorie. Doctors don't like coming to villages, you know—there's no money to be made in villages. So we must go to the doctors in the towns. I had a brother who could not be cured in Mussoorie. They told him to go to Delhi. He sold his buffaloes and went to Delhi, but there they told him it was too late to do anything. He died on the way back. I won't go to Delhi. I don't wish to die amongst strangers.'

'You'll get well, Uncle,' said Bisnu.

'Bless you for saying so. And you—what takes you to the big town?'

'Looking for work—we need money at home.'

'It is always the same. There are many like you who must go out in search of work. But don't be led astray. Don't let your friends persuade you to go to Bombay to become a film star! It is better to be hungry in your village than to be hungry on the streets of Bombay. I had a nephew who went to Bombay. The smugglers put him to work selling afeem (opium) and now he is in jail. Keep away from the big cities, boy. Earn your money and go home.'

'I'll do that, Uncle. My mother and sister will expect me to return before the summer season is over.'

The old man nodded vigorously and began coughing again. Presently he dozed off. The interior of the bus smelt of tobacco smoke and petrol fumes and as a result Bisnu had a headache. He kept his face near the open window to get as much fresh air as possible, but the dust kept getting into his mouth and eyes.

Several dusty hours later the bus got into Mussoorie, honking its horn furiously at everything in sight. The passengers, looking dazed, got down and went their different ways. The old man trudged off to the hospital.

Bisnu had to start looking for a job straightaway. He needed a lodging for the night and he could not afford even the cheapest of hotels. So he went from one shop to another, and to all the little restaurants and eating-places, asking for work— anything in exchange for a bed, a meal, and a minimum wage. A boy at one of the sweet shops told him there was a job at the Picture Palace, one of the town's three cinemas. The hill station's main road was crowded with people, for the season was just starting. Most of them were tourists who had come up from Delhi and other large towns.

The street lights had come on, and the shops were lighting up, when Bisnu presented himself at the Picture Palace.

III

The man who ran the cinema's tea stall had just sacked the previous helper for his general clumsiness. Whenever he engaged a new boy (which was fairly often) he started him off with the warning:

'I will be keeping a record of all the cups and plates you break, and their cost will be deducted from your salary at the end of the month.'

As Bisnu's salary had been fixed at fifty rupees a month, he would have to be very careful if he was going to receive any of it.

'In my first month,' said Chittru, one of the three tea stall boys, 'I broke six cups and five saucers, and my pay came to three rupees! Better be careful!'

Bisnu's job was to help prepare the tea and samosas, serve these refreshments to the public during intervals in the film, and later wash up the dishes. In addition to his salary, he was allowed to drink as much tea as he wanted or could hold in his stomach. But the sugar supply was kept to a minimum.

Bisnu went to work immediately and it was not long before he was as well-versed in his duties as the other two tea-boys, Chittru and Bali. Chittru was an easy-going, lazy boy who always tried to place the brunt of his work on someone else's shoulders. But he was generous and lent Bisnu five rupees during the first week. Bali, besides being a tea-boy, had the enviable job of being the poster-boy. As the cinema was closed during the mornings, Bali would be busy either pushing the big poster-board around Mussoorie, or sticking posters on convenient walls.

'Posters are very useful,' he claimed. 'They prevent old walls from falling down.'

Chittru had relatives in Mussoorie and slept at their house. But both Bisnu and Bali were on their own and had to sleep at the cinema. After the last show the hall was locked up, so they could not settle down in the expensive seats as they would have liked! They had to sleep on a dirty mattress in the foyer, near the ticket-office, where they were often at the mercy of icy Himalayan winds.

Bali made things more comfortable by setting his poster-board at an angle to the wall, which gave them a little alcove where they could sleep protected from the wind. As they had only one blanket each, they placed their blankets together and rolled themselves into a tight warm ball.

During shows, when Bisnu took the tea around, there was nearly always someone who would be rude and offensive. Once when he spilt some tea on a college student's shoes, he received a hard kick on the shin. He complained to the tea stall owner, but his employer said, 'The customer is always right. You should have got out of the way in time!'

As he began to get used to this life, Bisnu found himself taking an interest in some of the regular customers.

There was, for instance, the large gentleman with the soup-strainer moustache, who drank his tea from the saucer. As he drank, his lips worked like a suction pump, and the tea, after a brief agitation in the saucer, would disappear in a matter of seconds. Bisnu often wondered if there was something lurking in the forests of that gentleman's upper lip, something that would suddenly spring out and fall upon him! The boys took great pleasure in exchanging anecdotes about the peculiarities of some of the customers.

Bisnu had never seen such bright, painted women before. The girls in his village, including his sister Puja, were good-looking and often sturdy; but they did not use perfumes or make-up like these more prosperous women from the towns of the plains. Wearing expensive clothes and jewellery, they never gave Bisnu more than a brief, bored glance. Other women were more inclined to notice him, favouring him with kind words and a small tip when he took away the cups and plates. He found he could make a few rupees a month in tips; and when he received his first month's pay, he was able to send some of it home.

Chittru accompanied him to the post office and helped him to fill in the money order form. Bisnu had been to the village school, but be wasn't used to forms and official paperwork. Chittru, a town boy, knew all about them, even though he could just about read and write.

Walking back to the cinema, Chittru said, 'We can make more money at the limestone quarries.'

'All right, let's try them,' said Bisnu.

'Not now,' said Chittru, who enjoyed the busy season in the hill station. 'After the season—after the monsoon.'

But there was still no monsoon to speak of, just an occasional drizzle which did little to clear the air of the dust that blew up from the plains. Bisnu wondered how his mother and sister were faring at home. A wave of homesickness swept over him. The hill station, with all its glitter, was just a pretty gift box with nothing inside.

One day in the cinema Bisnu saw the old man who had been with him on the bus. He greeted him like a long lost friend. At first the old man did not recognize the boy, but when Bisnu asked him if he had recovered from his illness, the old man remembered and said, 'So you are still in Mussoorie, boy. That is good. I thought you might have gone down to Delhi to make more money.' He added that he was a little better and that he was undergoing a course of treatment at the hospital. Bisnu brought him a cup of tea and refused to take any money for it; it could be included in his own quota of free tea. When the show was over, the old man went his way and Bisnu did not see him again.

In September the town began to empty. The taps were running dry or giving out just a trickle of muddy water. A thick mist lay over the mountain for days on end, but there was no rain. When the mists cleared, an autumn wind came whispering through the deodars.

At the end of the month the manager of the Picture Palace gave everyone a week's notice, a week's pay, and announced that the cinema would be closing for the winter.

IV

Bali said, 'I'm going to Delhi to find work. I'll come back next summer. What about you, Bisnu, why don't you come with me? It's easier to find work in Delhi.'

'I'm staying with Chittru,' said Bisnu. 'We may work at the quarries.'

'I like the big towns,' said Bali. 'I like shops and people and lots of noise. I will never go back to my village. There is no money there, no fun.'

Bali made a bundle of his things and set out for the bus stand. Bisnu bought himself a pair of cheap shoes, for his old ones had fallen to pieces. With what was left of his money, he sent another money order home. Then he and Chittru set out for the limestone quarries, an eight-mile walk from Mussoorie.

They knew they were nearing the quarries when they saw clouds of limestone dust hanging in the air. The dust hid the next mountain from view. When they did see the mountain, they found that the top of it was missing—blasted away by dynamite to enable the quarries to get at the rich strata of limestone rock below the surface.

The skeletons of a few trees remained on the lower slopes. Almost everything else had gone—grass, flowers, shrubs, birds, butterflies, grasshoppers, ladybirds . . . . A rock lizard popped its head out of a crevice to look at the intruders. Then, like some prehistoric survivor, it scuttled back into its underground shelter.

'I used to come here when I was small,' announced Chittru cheerfully.

'Were the quarries here then?'

Oh, no. My friends and I—we used to come for the strawberries. They grew all over this mountain. Wild strawberries, but very tasty.'

'Where are they now?' asked Bisnu, looking around at the devastated hillside.

'All gone,' said Chittru. 'Maybe there are some on the next mountain.'

Even as they approached the quarries, a blast shook the hillside. Chittru pulled Bisnu under an overhanging rock to avoid the shower of stones that pelted down on the road. As the dust enveloped them, Bisnu had a fit of coughing. When the air cleared a little, they saw the limestone dump ahead of them.

Chittru, who was older and bigger than Bisnu, was immediately taken on as a labourer; but the quarry foreman took one look at Bisnu and said, 'You're too small. You won't be able to break stones or lift those heavy rocks and load them into the trucks. Be off, boy. Find something else to do.'

He was offered a job in the labourers' canteen, but he'd had enough of making tea and washing dishes. He was about to turn round and walk back to Mussoorie when he felt a heavy hand descend on his shoulder. He looked up to find a grey-bearded, turbanned Sikh looking down at him in some amusement.

'I need a cleaner for my truck,' he said. 'The work is easy, but the hours are long!'

Bisnu responded immediately to the man's gruff but jovial manner.

'What will you pay?' he asked.

'Fifteen rupees a day, and you'll get food and a bed at the depot.'

'As long as I don't have to cook the food,' said Bisnu.

The truck driver laughed. 'You might prefer to do so, once you've tasted the depot food. Are you coming on my truck? Make up your mind.'

'I'm your man,' said Bisnu; and waving goodbye to Chittru, he followed the Sikh to his truck.

V

A horn blared, shattering the silence of the mountains, and the truck came round a bend in the road. A herd of goats scattered to left and right.

The goatherds cursed as a cloud of dust enveloped them, and then the truck had left them behind and was rattling along the bumpy, unmetalled road to the quarries.

At the wheel of the truck, stroking his grey moustache with one hand, sat Pritam Singh. It was his own truck. He had never allowed anyone else to drive it. Every day he made two trips to the quarries, carrying truckloads of limestone back to the depot at the bottom of the hill. He was paid by the trip and he was always anxious to get in two trips every day.

Sitting beside him was Bisnu, his new cleaner. In less than a month Bisnu had become an experienced hand at looking after trucks, riding in them, and even sleeping in them. He got on well with Pritam, the grizzled, fifty-year-old Sikh, who boasted of two well-off sons—one a farmer in Punjab, the other a wine merchant in far-off London. He could have gone to live with either of them, but his sturdy independence kept him on the road in his battered old truck.

Pritam pressed hard on his horn. Now there was no one on the road—neither beast nor man—but Pritam was fond of the sound of his horn and liked blowing it. He boasted that it was the loudest horn in northern India. Although it struck terror into the hearts of all who heard it—for it was louder than the trumpeting of an elephant—it was music to Pritam's ears.

Pritam treated Bisnu as an equal and a friendly banter had grown between them during their many trips together.

'One more year on this bone-breaking road,' said Pritam, 'and then I'll sell my truck and retire.'

'But who will buy such a shaky old truck?' asked Bisnu. 'It will retire before you do!'

'Now don't be insulting, boy. She's only twenty years old—there are still a few years left in her!' And as though to prove it, he blew the horn again. Its strident sound echoed and re-echoed down the mountain gorge. A pair of wildfowl burst from the bushes and fled to more silent regions.

Pritam's thoughts went to his dinner.

'Haven't had a good meal for days.'

'Haven't had a good meal for weeks,' said Bisnu, although in fact he looked much healthier than when he had worked at the cinema's tea stall.

'Tonight I'll give you a dinner in a good hotel. Tandoori chicken and rice pillau.'

He sounded his horn again as though to put a seal on his promise. Then he slowed down, because the road had become narrow and precipitous, and trotting ahead of them was a train of mules.

As the horn blared, one mule ran forward, another ran backward. One went uphill, another went downhill. Soon there were mules all over the place. Pritam cursed the mules and the mule drivers cursed Pritam; but he had soon left them far behind.

Along this range, all the hills were bare and dry. Most of the forest had long since disappeared.

'Are your hills as bare as these?' asked Pritam.

'No, we still have some trees,' said Bisnu. 'Nobody has started blasting the hills as yet. In front of our house there is a walnut tree which gives us two baskets of walnuts every year. And there is an apricot tree. But it was a bad year for fruit. There was no rain. And the stream is too far away.'

'It will rain soon,' said Pritam. 'I can smell rain. It is coming from the north. The winter will be early.'

'It will settle the dust.'

Dust was everywhere. The truck was full of it. The leaves of the shrubs and the few trees were thick with it. Bisnu could feel the dust under his eyelids and in his mouth. And as they approached the quarries, the dust increased. But it was a different kind of dust now—whiter, stinging the eyes, irritating the nostrils.

They had been blasting all morning.

'Let's wait here,' said Pritam, bringing the truck to a halt.

They sat in silence, staring through the windscreen at the scarred cliffs a little distance down the road. There was a sharp crack of explosives and the hillside blossomed outwards. Earth and rocks hurtled down the mountain.

Bisnu watched in awe as shrubs and small trees were flung into the air. It always frightened him—not so much the sight of the rocks bursting asunder, as the trees being flung aside and destroyed. He thought of the trees at home—the walnut, the chestnuts, the pines—and wondered if one day they would suffer the same fate, and whether the mountains would all become a desert like this particular range. No trees, no grass, no water—only the choking dust of mines and quarries.

VI

Pritam pressed hard on his horn again, to let the people at the site know that he was approaching. He parked outside a small shed where the contractor and the foreman were sipping cups of tea. A short distance away, some labourers, Chittru among them, were hammering at chunks of rock, breaking them up into manageable pieces. A pile of stones stood ready for loading, while the rock that had just been blasted lay scattered about the hillside.

'Come and have a cup of tea,' called out the contractor.

'I can't hang about all day,' said Pritam. 'There's another trip to make—and the days are getting shorter. I don't want to be driving by night.'

But he sat down on a bench and ordered two cups of tea from the stall. The foreman strolled over to the group of labourers and told them to start loading. Bisnu let down the grid at the back of the truck. Then, to keep himself warm, he began helping Chittru and the men with the loading.

'Don't expect to be paid for helping,' said Sharma, the contractor, for whom every rupee spent was a rupee off his profits.

'Don't worry,' said Bisnu. 'I don't work for contractors, I work for friends.'

'That's right,' called out Pritam. 'Mind what you say to Bisnu—he's no one's servant!'

Sharma wasn't happy until there was no space left for a

single stone. Then Bisnu had his cup of tea and three of the
men climbed on the pile of stones in the open truck.

'All right, let's go!' said Pritam. 'I want to finish early
today—Bisnu and I are having a big dinner!'

Bisnu jumped in beside Pritam, banging the door shut. It
never closed properly unless it was slammed really hard. But it
opened at a touch.

'This truck is held together with sticking plaster,' joked
Pritam. He was in good spirits. He started the engine, and blew
his horn just as he passed the foreman and the contractor.

'They are deaf in one ear from the blasting,' said Pritam.
'I'll make them deaf in the other ear!'

The labourers were singing as the truck swung round the
sharp bends of the winding road. The door beside Bisnu rattled
on its hinges. He was feeling quite dizzy.

'Not too fast,' he said.

'Oh,' said Pritam. 'And since when did you become nervous
about my driving?'

'It's just today,' said Bisnu uneasily. 'It's a feeling, that's
all.'

'You're getting old,' said Pritam. 'That's your trouble.'

'I suppose so,' said Bisnu.

Pritam was feeling young, exhilarated. He drove faster.

As they swung round a bend, Bisnu looked out of his
window. All he saw was the sky above and the valley below.
They were very near the edge; but it was usually like that on
this narrow mountain road.

After a few more hairpin bends, the road descended steeply
to the valley. Just then a stray mule ran into the middle of the
road. Pritam swung the steering wheel over to the right to
avoid the mule, but here the road turned sharply to the left.
The truck went over the edge.

As it tipped over, hanging for a few seconds on the edge of
the cliff, the labourers leapt from the back of the truck. It
pitched forward, and as it struck a rock outcrop, the loose door
burst open. Bisnu was thrown out.

The truck hurtled forward, bouncing over the rocks, turning
over on its side and rolling over twice before coming to rest
against the trunk of a scraggly old oak tree. But for the tree, the
truck would have plunged several hundred feet down to the

bottom of the gorge.

Two of the labourers sat on the hillside, stunned and badly shaken. The third man had picked himself up and was running back to the quarry for help.

Bisnu had landed in a bed of nettles. He was smarting all over, but he wasn't really hurt; the nettles had broken his fall.

His first impulse was to get up and run back to the road. Then he realized that Pritam was still in the truck.

Bisnu skidded down the steep slope, calling out, 'Pritam Uncle, are you all right?'

There was no answer.

VII

When Bisnu saw Pritam's arm and half his body jutting out of the open door of the truck, he feared the worst. It was a strange position, half in and half out. Bisnu was about to turn away and climb back up the hill, when he noticed that Pritam had opened a bloodied and swollen eye. It looked straight up at Bisnu.

'Are you alive?' whispered Bisnu, terrified.

'What do you think?' muttered Pritam. He closed his eye again.

When the contractor and his men arrived, it took them almost an hour to get Pritam Singh out of the wreckage of the truck, and another hour to get him to the hospital in the next big town. He had broken bones and fractured ribs and a dislocated shoulder. But the doctors said he was repairable—which was more than could be said for the truck.

'So the truck's finished,' said Pritam, between groans when Bisnu came to see him after a couple of days. 'Now I'll have to go home and live with my son. And what about you, boy? I can get you a job on a friend's truck.'

'No,' said Bisnu, 'I'll be going home soon.'

'And what will you do at home?'

'I'll work on my land. It's better to grow things on the land than to blast things out of it.'

They were silent for some time.

'There is something to be said for growing things,' said Pritam. 'But for that tree, the truck would have finished up at the foot of the mountain, and I wouldn't be here, all bandaged up and talking to you. It was the tree that saved me. Remember that, boy.'

'I'll remember, and I won't forget the dinner you promised me, either.'

It snowed during Bisnu's last night at the quarries. He slept on the floor with Chittru, in a large shed meant for the labourers. The wind blew the snowflakes in at the entrance; it whistled down the deserted mountain pass. In the morning Bisnu opened his eyes to a world of dazzling whiteness. The snow was piled high against the walls of the shed, and they had some difficulty getting out.

Bisnu joined Chittru at the tea stall, drank a glass of hot sweet tea, and ate two stale buns. He said goodbye to Chittru and set out on the long march home. The road would be closed to traffic because of the heavy snow, and he would have to walk all the way.

He trudged over the hills all day, stopping only at small villages to take refreshment. By nightfall he was still ten miles from home. But he had fallen in with other travellers, and with them he took shelter at a small inn. They built a fire and crowded round it, and each man spoke of his home and fields and all were of the opinion that the snow and rain had come just in time to save the winter crops. Someone sang, and another told a ghost story. Feeling at home already, Bisnu fell asleep listening to their tales. In the morning they parted and went their different ways.

It was almost noon when Bisnu reached his village.

The fields were covered with snow and the mountain stream was in spate. As he climbed the terraced fields to his house, he heard the sound of barking, and his mother's big black mastiff came bounding towards him over the snow. The dog jumped on him and licked his arms and then went bounding back to the house to tell the others.

Puja saw him from the courtyard and ran indoors shouting, 'Bisnu has come, my brother has come!'

His mother ran out of the house, calling 'Bisnu, Bisnu!'

Bisnu came walking through the fields, and he did not

hurry, he did not run; he wanted to savour the moment of his
return, with his mother and sister smiling, waiting for him in
front of the house.

There was no need to hurry now. He would be with them
for a long time, and the manager of the Picture Palace would
have to find someone else for the summer season . . . . It was
his home, and these were his fields! Even the snow was his.
When the snow melted he would clear the fields, and nourish
them, and make them rich.

He felt very big and very strong as he came striding over
the land he loved.

THE FIGHT

Ranji had been less than a month in Rajpur when he discovered the pool in the forest. It was the height of summer, and his school had not yet opened, and, having as yet made no friends in this semi-hill station, he wandered about a good deal by himself into the hills and forests that stretched away interminably on all sides of the town. It was hot, very hot, at that time of year, and Ranji walked about in his vest and shorts, his brown feet white with the chalky dust that flew up from the ground. The earth was parched, the grass brown, the trees listless, hardly stirring, waiting for a cool wind or a refreshing shower of rain.

It was on such a day—a hot, tired day—that Ranji found the pool in the forest. The water had a gentle translucency, and you could see the smooth round pebbles at the bottom of the pool. A small stream emerged from a cluster of rocks to feed the pool. During the monsoon, this stream would be a gushing torrent, cascading down from the hills, but during the summer it was barely a trickle. The rocks, however, held the water in the pool, and it did not dry up like the pools in the plains.

When Ranji saw the pool, he did not hesitate to get into it. He had often gone swimming, alone or with friends, when he had lived with his parents in a thirsty town in the middle of the Rajputana desert. There, he had known only sticky, muddy pools, where buffaloes wallowed and women washed clothes. He had never seen a pool like this—so clean and cold and inviting. He threw off all his clothes, as he had done when he went swimming in the plains, and leapt into the water. His limbs were supple, free of any fat, and his dark body glistened in patches of sunlit water.

The next day he came again to quench his body in the cool waters of the forest pool. He was there for almost an hour, sliding in and out of the limpid green water, or lying stretched out on the smooth yellow rocks in the shade of broad-leaved sal trees. It was while he lay thus, naked on a rock, that he noticed another boy standing a little distance away, staring at him in a rather hostile manner. The other boy was a little older than Ranji, taller, thick-set, with a broad nose and thick, red lips. He had only just noticed Ranji, and he stood at the edge of the pool, wearing a pair of bathing shorts, waiting for Ranji to explain himself.

When Ranji did not say anything, the other called out, 'What are you doing here, Mister?'

Ranji, who was prepared to be friendly, was taken aback at the hostility of the other's tone.

'I am swimming,' he replied. 'Why don't you join me?'

'I always swim alone,' said the other. 'This is my pool, I did not invite you here. And why are you not wearing any clothes?'

'It is not your business if I do not wear clothes. I have nothing to be ashamed of.'

'You skinny fellow, put on your clothes.'

'Fat fool, take yours off.'

This was too much for the stranger to tolerate. He strode up to Ranji, who still sat on the rock and, planting his broad feet firmly on the sand, said (as though this would settle the matter once and for all), 'Don't you know I am a Punjabi? I do not take replies from villagers like you!'

'So you like to fight with villagers?' said Ranji. 'Well, I am not a villager. I am a Rajput!'

'I am a Punjabi!'

'I am a Rajput!'

They had reached an impasse. One had said he was a Punjabi, the other had proclaimed himself a Rajput. There was little else that could be said.

'You understand that I am a Punjabi?' said the stranger, feeling that perhaps this information had not penetrated Ranji's head.

'I have heard you say it three times,' replied Ranji.

'Then why are you not running away?'

'I am waiting for *you* to run away!'

'I will have to beat you,' said the stranger, assuming a violent attitude, showing Ranji the palm of his hand.

'I am waiting to see you do it,' said Ranji.

'You will see me do it,' said the other boy.

Ranji waited. The other boy made a strange, hissing sound. They stared each other in the eye for almost a minute. Then the Punjabi boy slapped Ranji across the face with all the force he could muster. Ranji staggered, feeling quite dizzy. There were thick red finger marks on his cheek.

'There you are!' exclaimed his assailant. 'Will you be off now?'

For answer, Ranji swung his arm up and pushed a hard, bony fist into the other's face.

And then they were at each other's throats, swaying on the rock, tumbling on to the sand, rolling over and over, their legs and arms locked in a desperate, violent struggle. Gasping and cursing, clawing and slapping, they rolled right into the shallows of the pool.

Even in the water the fight continued as, spluttering and covered with mud, they groped for each other's head and throat. But after five minutes of frenzied, unscientific struggle, neither boy had emerged victorious. Their bodies heaving with exhaustion, they stood back from each other, making tremendous efforts to speak.

'Now—now do you realize—I am a Punjabi?' gasped the stranger.

'Do you know I am a Rajput?' said Ranji with difficulty.

They gave a moment's consideration to each other's answers, and in that moment of silence there was only their heavy breathing and the rapid beating of their hearts.

'Then you will not leave the pool?' said the Punjabi boy.

'I will not leave it,' said Ranji.

'Then we shall have to continue the fight,' said the other.

'All right,' said Ranji.

But neither boy moved, neither took the initiative.

The Punjabi boy had an inspiration.

'We will continue the fight tomorrow,' he said. 'If you dare to come here again tomorrow, we will continue this fight, and I will not show you mercy as I have done today.'

'I will come tomorrow,' said Ranji. 'I will be ready for you.'

They turned from each other then and, going to their respective rocks, put on their clothes, and left the forest by different routes.

When Ranji got home, he found it difficult to explain the cuts and bruises that showed on his face, leg and arms. It was difficult to conceal the fact that he had been in an unusually violent fight, and his mother insisted on his staying at home for the rest of the day. That evening, though, he slipped out of the house and went to the bazaar, where he found comfort and solace in a bottle of vividly coloured lemonade and a banana-leaf full of hot, sweet jalebis. He had just finished the lemonade when he saw his adversary coming down the road. His first impulse was to turn away and look elsewhere, his second to throw the lemonade bottle at his enemy. But he did neither of these things. Instead, he stood his ground and scowled at his passing adversary. And the Punjabi boy said nothing either, but scowled back with equal ferocity.

The next day was as hot as the previous one. Ranji felt weak and lazy and not at all eager for a fight. His body was stiff and sore after the previous day's encounter. But he could not refuse the challenge. Not to turn up at the pool would be an acknowledgement of defeat. From the way he felt just then, he knew he would be beaten in another fight. But he could not acquiesce in his own defeat. He must defy his enemy to the last, or outwit him, for only then could he gain his respect. If he surrendered now, he would be beaten for all time; but to fight and be beaten today left him free to fight and be beaten again. As long as he fought, he had a right to the pool in the forest.

He was half hoping that the Punjabi boy would have forgotten the challenge, but these hopes were dashed when he saw his opponent sitting, stripped to the waist, on a rock on the other side of the pool. The Punjabi boy was rubbing oil on his body, massaging it into his broad thighs. He saw Ranji beneath the sal trees, and called a challenge across the waters of the pool.

'Come over on this side and fight!' he shouted.

But Ranji was not going to submit to any conditions laid down by his opponent.

'Come *this* side and fight!' he shouted back with equal vigour.

'Swim across and fight me here!' called the other. 'Or perhaps you cannot swim the length of this pool?'

But Ranji could have swum the length of the pool a dozen times without tiring, and here he would show the Punjabi boy his superiority. So, slipping out of his vest and shorts, he dived straight into the water, cutting through it like a knife, and surfaced with hardly a splash. The Punjabi boy's mouth hung open in amazement.

'You can dive!' he exclaimed.

'It is easy,' said Ranji, treading water, waiting for a further challenge. 'Can't you dive?'

'No,' said the other. 'I jump straight in. But if you will tell me how, I will make a dive.'

'It is easy,' said Ranji. 'Stand on the rock, stretch your arms out and allow your head to displace your feet.'

The Punjabi boy stood up, stiff and straight, stretched out his arms, and threw himself into the water. He landed flat on his belly, with a crash that sent the birds screaming out of the trees.

Ranji dissolved into laughter.

'Are you trying to empty the pool?' he asked, as the Punjabi boy came to the surface, spouting water like a small whale.

'Wasn't it good?' asked the boy, evidently proud of his feat.

'Not very good,' said Ranji. 'You should have more practice. See, I will do it again.'

And pulling himself up on a rock, he executed another perfect dive. The other boy waited for him to come up, but, swimming under water, Ranji circled him and came upon him from behind.

'How did you do that?' asked the astonished youth.

'Can't you swim under water?' asked Ranji.

'No, but I will try it.'

The Punjabi boy made a tremendous effort to plunge to the

bottom of the pool and indeed he thought he had gone right down, though his bottom, like a duck's, remained above the surface.

Ranji, however, did not discourage him.

'It was not bad,' he said. 'But you need a lot of practice.'

'Will you teach me?' asked his enemy.

'If you like, I will teach you.'

'You must teach me. If you do not teach me, I will beat you. Will you come here every day and teach me?'

'If you like,' said Ranji. They had pulled themselves out of the water, and were sitting side by side on a smooth grey rock.

'My name is Suraj,' said the Punjabi boy. 'What is yours?'

'It is Ranji.'

'I am strong, am I not?' asked Suraj, bending his arm so that a ball of muscle stood up stretching the white of his flesh.

'You are strong,' said Ranji. 'You are a real *pahelwan*.'

'One day I will be the world's champion wrestler,' said Suraj, slapping his thighs, which shook with the impact of his hand. He looked critically at Ranji's hard thin body. 'You are quite strong yourself,' he conceded. 'But you are too bony. I know, you people do not eat enough. You must come and have your food with me. I drink one seer of milk every day. We have got our own cow! Be my friend, and I will make you a *pahelwan* like me! I know—if you teach me to dive and swim underwater, I will make you a *pahelwan*! That is fair, isn't it?'

'That is fair!' said Ranji, though he doubted if he was getting the better of the exchange.

Suraj put his arm around the younger boy and said, 'We are friends now, yes?'

They looked at each other with honest, unflinching eyes, and in that moment love and understanding were born.

'We are friends,' said Ranji.

The birds had settled again in their branches, and the pool was quiet and limpid in the shade of the sal trees.

'It is our pool,' said Suraj. 'Nobody else can come here without our permission. Who would dare?'

'Who would dare?' said Ranji, smiling with the knowledge that he had won the day.

The Tunnel

৯

It was almost noon, and the jungle was very still, very silent. Heat waves shimmered along the railway embankment where it cut a path through the tall evergreen trees. The railway lines were two straight black serpents disappearing into the tunnel in the hillside.

Ranji stood near the cutting, waiting for the mid-day train. It wasn't a station and he wasn't catching a train. He was waiting so he could watch the stream-engine come roaring out of the tunnel.

He had cycled out of town and taken the jungle path until he had come to a small village. He had left the cycle there, and walked over a low, scrub-covered hill and down to the tunnel exit.

Now he looked up. He had heard, in the distance, the shrill whistle of the engine. He couldn't see anything, because the train was approaching from the other side of the hill, but presently a sound like distant thunder came from the tunnel, and he knew the train was coming through.

A second or two later the steam-engine shot out of the tunnel, snorting and puffing like some green, black and gold dragon, some beautiful monster out of Ranji's dreams. Showering sparks right and left, it roared a challenge to the jungle.

Instinctively Ranji stepped back a few paces. Waves of hot steam struck him in the face. Even the trees seemed to flinch from the noise and heat. And then the train had gone, leaving only a plume of smoke to drift lazily over the tall shisham trees.

The jungle was still again. No one moved.

Ranji turned from watching the drifting smoke and began walking along the embankment towards the tunnel. It grew darker the further he walked, and when he had gone about twenty yards it became pitch black. He had to turn and look back at the opening to make sure that there was a speck of daylight in the distance.

Ahead of him, the tunnel's other opening was also a small round circle of light.

The walls of the tunnel were damp and sticky. A bat flew past. A lizard scuttled between the lines. Coming straight from the darkness into the light, Ranji was dazzled by the sudden glare. He put a hand up to shade his eyes and looked up at the scrub-covered hillside, and he thought he saw something moving between the trees.

It was just a flash of gold and black, and a long swishing tail. It was there between the trees for a second or two, and then it was gone.

About fifty feet from the entrance to the tunnel stood the watchman's hut. Marigolds grew in front of the hut, and at the back there was a small vegetable patch. It was the watchman's duty to inspect the tunnel and keep it clear of obstacles.

Every day, before the train came through, he would walk the length of the tunnel. If all was well, he would return to his hut and take a nap. If something was wrong, he would walk back up the line and wave a red flag and the engine-driver would slow down.

At night, the watchman lit an oil-lamp and made a similar inspection. If there was any danger to the train, he'd go back up the line and wave his lamp to the approaching engine. If all was well, he'd hang his lamp at the door of his hut and go to sleep.

He was just settling down on his cot for an afternoon nap when he saw the boy come out of the tunnel. He waited until the boy was only a few feet away and then said, 'Welcome, welcome. I don't often get visitors. Sit down for a while, and tell me why you were inspecting my tunnel.'

'Is it your tunnel?' asked Ranji.

'It is,' said the watchman. 'It is truly my tunnel, since no one else will have anything to do with it. I have only lent it to the Government.'

Ranji sat down on the edge of the cot.

'I wanted to see the train come through,' he said. 'And then, when it had gone, I decided to walk through the tunnel.'

'And what did you find in it?'

'Nothing. It was very dark. But when I came out, I thought I saw an animal—up on the hill—but I'm not sure, it moved off very quickly.'

'It was a leopard you saw,' said the watchman. 'My leopard.'

'Do you own a leopard too?'

'I do.'

'And do you lend it to the Government?'

'I do not.'

'Is it dangerous?'

'Not if you leave it alone. It comes this way for a few days every month, because there are still deer in this jungle, and the deer is its natural prey. It keeps away from people.'

'Have you been here a long time?' asked Ranji.

'Many years. My name is Kishan Singh.'

'Mine is Ranji.'

'There is one train during the day. And there is one train during the night. Have you seen the Night Mail come through the tunnel?'

'No. At what time does it come?'

'About nine o'clock, if it isn't late. You could come and sit here with me, if you like. And, after it has gone, I will take you home.'

'I'll ask my parents,' said Ranji. 'Will it be safe?'

'It is safer in the jungle than in the town. No rascals out here. Only last week, when I went into the town, I had my pocket picked! Leopards don't pick pockets.'

Kishan Singh stretched himself out on his cot. 'And now I am going to take a nap, my friend. It is too hot to be up and about in the afternoon.'

'Everyone goes to sleep in the afternoon,' complained Ranji. 'My father lies down as soon as he's had his lunch.'

'Well, the animals also rest in the heat of the day. It is only the tribe of boys who cannot, or will not, rest.'

Kishan Singh placed a large banana-leaf over his face to keep away the flies, and was soon snoring gently. Ranji stood up, looking up and down the railway tracks. Then he began walking back to the village.

The following evening, towards dusk, as the flying-foxes swooped silently out of the trees, Ranji made his way to the watchman's hut.

It had been a long hot day, but now the earth was cooling and a light breeze was moving through the trees. It carried with it the scent of mango blossom, the promise of rain.

Kishan Singh was waiting for Ranji. He had watered his small garden and the flowers looked cool and fresh. A kettle was boiling on an oil-stove.

'I am making tea,' he said. 'There is nothing like a glass of hot sweet tea while waiting for a train.'

They drank their tea, listening to the sharp notes of the tailor-bird and the noisy chatter of the seven-sisters. As the brief twilight faded, most of the birds fell silent. Kishan lit his oil-lamp and said it was time for him to inspect the tunnel. He moved off towards the dark entrance, while Ranji sat on the cot, sipping tea.

In the dark, the trees seemed to move closer. And the night life of the forest was conveyed on the breeze—the sharp call of a barking-deer, the cry of a fox, the quaint tonk-tonk of a nightjar.

There were some sounds that Ranji would not recognize—sounds that came from the trees. Creakings, and whisperings, as though the trees were coming alive, stretching their limbs in the dark, shifting a little, flexing their fingers.

Kishan Singh stood outside the tunnel, trimming his lamp. The night sounds were familiar to him· and he did not give them much thought; but something else—a padded footfall, a rustle of dry leaves—made him stand still for a few seconds, peering into the darkness. Then, humming softly, he returned to where Ranji was waiting. Ten minutes remained for the Night Mail to arrive.

As the watchman sat down on the cot beside Ranji, a new sound reached both of them quite distinctly—a rhythmic sawing sound, as of someone cutting through the branch of a tree.

'What's that?' whispered Ranji.

'It's the leopard,' said Kishan Singh. 'I think it's in the tunnel.'

'The train will soon be here.'

'Yes, my friend. And if we don't drive the leopard out of the tunnel, it will be run over by the engine.'

'But won't it attack us if we try to drive it out?' asked Ranji, beginning to share the watchman's concern.

'It knows me well. We have seen each other many times. I don't think it will attack. Even so, I will take my axe along. You had better stay here, Ranji.'

'No, I'll come too. It will be better than sitting here alone in the dark.'

'All right, but stay close behind me. And remember, there is nothing to fear.'

Raising his lamp, Kishan Singh walked into the tunnel, shouting at the top of his voice to try and scare away the animal. Ranji followed close behind. But he found he was unable to do any shouting; his throat had gone quite dry.

They had gone about twenty paces into the tunnel when the light from the lamp fell upon the leopard. It was crouching between the tracks, only fifteen feet away from them. Baring its teeth and snarling, it went down on its belly, tail twitching. Ranji felt sure it was going to spring at them.

Kishan Singh and Ranji both shouted together. Their voices rang through the tunnel. And the leopard, uncertain as to how many terrifying humans were there in front of him, turned swiftly and disappeared into the darkness.

To make sure it had gone, Ranji and the watchman walked the length of the tunnel. When they returned to the entrance, the rails were beginning to hum. They knew the train was coming.

Ranji put his hand to one of the rails and felt its tremor. He heard the distant rumble of the train. And then the engine came round the bend, hissing at them, scattering sparks into the darkness, defying the jungle as it roared through the steep sides of the cutting. It charged straight into the tunnel, thundering past Ranji like the beautiful dragon of his dreams.

And when it had gone, the silence returned and the forest

seemed to breathe, to live again. Only the rails still trembled with the passing of the train.

They trembled again to the passing of the same train, almost a week later, when Ranji and his father were both travelling in it.

Ranji's father was scribbling in a notebook, doing his accounts. How boring of him, thought Ranji as he sat near an open window staring out at the darkness. His father was going to Delhi on a business trip and had decided to take the boy along.

'It's time you learnt something about the business,' he had said, to Ranji's dismay.

The Night Mail rushed through the forest with its hundreds of passengers. The carriage wheels beat out a steady rhythm on the rails. Tiny flickering lights came and went, as they passed small villages on the fringe of the jungle.

Ranji heard the rumble as the train passed over a small bridge. It was too dark to see the hut near the cutting, but he knew they must be approaching the tunnel. He strained his eyes, looking out into the night; and then, just as the engine let out a shrill whistle, Ranji saw the lamp.

He couldn't see Kishan Singh, but he saw the lamp, and he knew that his friend was out there.

The train went into the tunnel and out again, it left the jungle behind and thundered across the endless plains. And Ranji stared out at the darkness, thinking of the lonely cutting in the forest, and the watchman with the lamp who would always remain a firefly for those travelling thousands, as he lit up the darkness for steam-engines and leopards.

GOING HOME

❧

THE TRAIN CAME PANTING through the forest and into the flat brown plain. The engine whistled piercingly, and a few cows moved off the track. In a swaying third-class compartment two men played cards; a woman held a baby to an exposed breast; a Sikh labourer, wearing brief pants, lay asleep on an upper bunk, snoring fitfully; an elderly unshaven man chewed the last of his pan and spat the red juice out of the window. A small boy, mischief in his eyes, jingled a bag of coins in front of an anxious farmer.

Daya Ram, the farmer, was going home; home to his rice fields, his buffalo and his wife. A brother had died recently, and Daya Ram had taken the ashes to Hardwar to immerse them in the holy waters of the Ganga, and now he was on the train to Dehra and soon he would be home. He was looking anxious because he had just remembered his wife's admonition about being careful with money. Ten rupees was what he had left with him, and it was all in the bag the boy held.

'Let me have it now,' said Daya Ram, 'before the money falls out.' He made a grab at the little bag that contained his coins, notes and railway ticket, but the boy shrieked with delight and leapt out of the way.

Daya Ram stroked his moustache; it was a long drooping moustache that lent a certain sadness to his somewhat kind and foolish face. He reflected that it was his own fault for having started the game. The child had been sulky and morose, and to cheer him up Daya Ram had begun jingling his money. Now the boy was jingling the money, right in front of the open window.

'Come now, give it back,' pleaded Daya Ram, 'or I shall tell your mother.'

The boy's mother had her back to them, and it was a large back, almost as forbidding as her front. But the boy was enjoying his game and would not give up the bag. He was exploiting to the full Daya Ram's easy-going tolerant nature, and kept bobbing up and down on the seat, waving the bag in the poor man's face.

Suddenly the boy's mother, who had been engrossed in conversation with another woman, turned and saw what was happening. She walloped the boy over the head and the suddenness of the blow (it was more of a thump than a slap) made him fall back against the window, and the cloth bag fell from his hand on to the railway embankment outside.

Now Daya Ram's first impulse was to leap out of the moving train. But when someone shouted, 'Pull the alarm cord!' he decided on this course of action. He plunged for the alarm cord, but just at the moment someone else shouted, 'Don't pull the cord!' and Daya Ram who usually listened to others, stood in suspended animation, waiting for further directions.

'Too many people are stopping trains every day all over India,' said one of the card players, who wore large thick-rimmed spectacles over a pair of tiny humourless eyes, and was obviously a post office counter-clerk. 'You people are becoming a menace to the railways.'

'Exactly,' said the other card-player. 'You stop the train on the most trifling excuses. What is your trouble?'

'My money has fallen out,' said Daya Ram.

'Why didn't you say so!' exclaimed the clerk, jumping up. 'Stop the train!'

'Sit down,' said his companion, 'it's too late now. The train cannot wait here until he walks half a mile back down the line. How much did you lose?' he asked Daya Ram.

'Ten rupees.'

'And you have no more?'

Daya Ram shook his head.

'Then you had better leave the train at the next station and go back for it.'

The next station, Harrawala, was about ten miles from the

spot where the money had fallen. Daya Ram got down from the train and started back along the railway track. He was a well-built man, with strong legs and a dark, burnished skin. He wore a vest and dhoti, and had a red cloth tied round his head. He walked with long, easy steps, but the ground had been scorched by the burning sun, and it was not long before his feet were smarting. His eyes too were unaccustomed to the glare of the plains, and he held a hand up over them, or looked at the ground. The sun was high in the sky, beating down on his bare arms and legs. Soon his body was running with sweat, his vest was soaked through and sticking to his skin.

There were no trees anywhere near the lines, which ran straight to the hazy blue horizon. There were fields in the distance, and cows grazed on short grass, but there were no humans in sight. After an hour's walk, Daya Ram felt thirsty; his tongue was furred, his gums dry, his lips like parchment. When he saw a buffalo wallowing in a muddy pool, he hurried to the spot and drank thirstily of the stagnant water.

Still, his pace did not slacken. He knew of only one way to walk, and that was at this steady long pace. At the end of another hour he felt sure he had passed the place where the bag had fallen. He had been inspecting the embankment very closely, and now he felt discouraged and dispirited. But still he walked on. He was worried more by the thought of his wife's attitude than by the loss of the money or the problem of the next meal.

Rather than turn back, he continued walking until he reached the next station. He kept following the lines, and after half an hour dragged his aching feet on to Raiwala platform. To his surprise and joy, he saw a note in Hindi on the notice board: 'Anyone having lost a bag containing some notes and coins may enquire at the station-master's office.' Some honest man or woman or child had found the bag and handed it in. Daya Ram felt that his faith in the goodness of human nature had been justified.

He rushed into the office and, pushing aside an indignant clerk, exclaimed: 'You have found my money!'

'What money?' snapped the harassed-looking official. 'And

don't just charge in here shouting at the top of your voice, this is not a hotel!'

'The money I lost on the train,' said Daya Ram. 'Ten rupees.'

'In notes or in coins?' asked the station-master, who was not slow in assessing a situation.

'Six one-rupee notes,' said Daya Ram. 'The rest in coins.'

'Hmmm . . . and what was the purse like?'

'White cloth,' said Daya Ram. 'Dirty white cloth,' he added for clarification.

The official put his hand in a drawer, took out the bag and flung it across the desk. Without further parley, Daya Ram scooped up the bag and burst through the swing doors, completely revived after his fatiguing march.

Now he had only one idea: to celebrate, in his small way, the recovery of his money.

So, he left the station and made his way through a sleepy little bazaar to the nearest tea shop. He sat down at a table and asked for tea and a hookah. The shopkeeper placed a record on a gramophone, and the shrill music shattered the afternoon silence of the bazaar.

A young man sitting idly at the next table smiled at Daya Ram and said, 'You are looking happy, brother.'

Daya Ram beamed. 'I lost my money and found it,' he said simply.

'Then you should celebrate with something stronger than tea,' said the friendly stranger with a wink. 'Come on into the next room.' He took Daya Ram by the arm and was so comradely that the older man felt pleased and flattered. They went behind a screen, and the shopkeeper brought them two glasses and a bottle of country-made rum.

Before long, Daya Ram had told his companion the story of his life. He had also paid for the rum and was prepared to pay for more. But two of the young man's friends came in and suggested a card game and Daya Ram, who remembered having once played a game of cards in his youth, showed enthusiasm. He lost sportingly, to the tune of five rupees; the rum had such a benevolent effect on his already genial nature that he was quite ready to go on playing until he had lost everything, but the shopkeeper came in hurriedly with the information that a policeman was hanging about outside. Daya Ram's table companions promptly disappeared.

Daya Ram was still happy. He paid for the hookah and the cup of tea he hadn't had, and went lurching into the street. He had some vague intention of returning to the station to catch a train, and had his ticket in his hand; by now his sense of direction was so confused that he turned down a side-alley and was soon lost in a labyrinth of tiny alley-ways. Just when he thought he saw trees ahead, his attention was drawn to a man leaning against a wall and groaning wretchedly. The man was in rags, his hair was tousled, and his face looked bruised.

Daya Ram heard his groans and stumbled over to him.

'What is wrong?' he asked with concern. 'What is the matter with you?'

'I have been robbed,' said the man, speaking with difficulty. 'Two thugs beat me and took my money. Don't go any further this way.'

'Can I do anything for you?' said Daya Ram. 'Where do you live?'

'No, I will be all right,' said the man, leaning heavily on Daya Ram. 'Just help me to the corner of the road, and then I can find my way.'

'Do you need anything?' said Daya Ram. 'Do you need any money?'

'No, no just help me to those steps.'

Daya Ram put an arm around the man and helped him across the road, seating him on a step.

'Are you sure I can do nothing for you?' persisted Daya Ram.

The man shook his head and closed his eyes, leaning back against the wall. Daya Ram hesitated a little, and then left. But as soon as Daya Ram turned the corner, the man opened his eyes. He transferred the bag of money from the fold of his shirt to the string of his pyjamas. Then, completely recovered, he was up and away.

Daya Ram discovered his loss when he had gone about

fifty yards, and then it was too late. He was puzzled, but was not upset. So many things had happened to him today, and he was confused and unaware of his real situation. He still had his ticket, and that was what mattered most.

The train was at the station, and Daya Ram got into a half-empty compartment. It was only when the train began to move that he came to his senses and realized what had befallen him. As the engine gathered speed, his thoughts came faster. He was not worried (except by the thought of his wife) and he was not unhappy, but he was puzzled. He was not angry or resentful, but he was a little hurt. He knew he had been tricked, but he couldn't understand why. He had really liked those people he had met in the tea shop of Raiwala, and he still could not bring himself to believe that the man in rags had been putting on an act.

'Have you got a bidi?' asked a man beside him, who looked like another farmer.

Daya Ram had a bidi. He gave it to the other man and lit it for him. Soon they were talking about crops and rainfall and their respective families, and although a faint uneasiness still hovered at the back of his mind, Daya Ram had almost forgotten the day's misfortunes. He had his ticket to Dehra and from there he had to walk only three miles, and then he would be home, and there would be hot milk and cooked vegetables waiting for him. He and the other farmer chattered away, as the train went panting across the wide brown plain.

MASTERJI

❧

I WAS STROLLING ALONG the platform, waiting for the arrival of
the Amritsar Express, when I saw Mr Khushal, handcuffed to
a policeman.

I hadn't recognized him at first—a paunchy gentleman with
a lot of grey in his beard and a certain arrogant amusement in
his manner. It was only when I came closer, and we were
almost face to face, that I recognized my old Hindi teacher.

Startled, I stopped and stared. And he stared back at me, a
glimmer of recognition in his eyes. It was over twenty years
since I'd last seen him, standing jauntily before the classroom
blackboard, and now here he was tethered to a policeman and
looking as jaunty as ever . . .

'Good—good evening, sir,' I stammered, in my best public
school manner. (You must always respect your teacher, no
matter what the circumstances.)

Mr Khushal's face lit up with pleasure. 'So you remember
me! It's nice to see you again, my boy.'

Forgetting that his right hand was shackled to the
policeman's left, I made as if to shake hands. Mr Khushal
thoughtfully took my right hand in his left and gave it a rough
squeeze. A faint odour of cloves and cinnamon reached me,
and I remembered how he had always been redolent of spices
when standing beside my desk, watching me agonize over my
Hindi-English translation.

He had joined the school in 1948, not long after the Partition.
Until then there had been no Hindi teacher; we'd been taught
Urdu and French. Then came a ruling that Hindi was to be a

compulsory subject, and at the age of sixteen I found myself struggling with a new script. When Mr Khushal joined the staff (on the recommendation of a local official), there was no one else in the school who knew Hindi, or who could assess Mr Khushal's abilities as a teacher . . .

And now once again he stood before me, only this time he was in the custody of the law.

I was still recovering from the shock when the train drew in, and everyone on the platform began making a rush for the compartment doors. As the policeman elbowed his way through the crowd, I kept close behind him and his charge, and as a result I managed to get into the same third-class compartment. I found a seat right opposite Mr Khushal. He did not seem to be the least bit embarrassed by the handcuffs, or by the stares of his fellow-passengers. Rather, it was the policeman who looked unhappy and ill-at-ease.

As the train got under way, I offered Mr Khushal one of the parathas made for me by my Ferozepur landlady. He accepted it with alacrity. I offered one to the constable as well, but although he looked at it with undisguised longing, he felt duty-bound to decline.

'Why have they arrested you, sir?' I asked. 'Is it very serious?'

'A trivial matter,' said Mr Khushal. 'Nothing to worry about. I shall be at liberty soon.'

'But what did you *do*?'

Mr Khushal leant forward. 'Nothing to be ashamed of,' he said in a confiding tone. 'Even a great teacher like Socrates fell foul of the law.'

'You mean—one of your pupil's—made a complaint?'

'And why should one of my pupils make a complaint?' Mr Khushal looked offended. 'They were the beneficiaries—it was for *them*.' He noticed that I looked mystified, and decided to come straight to the point: 'It was simply a question of false certificates.'

'Oh,' I said, feeling deflated. Public school boys are always prone to jump to the wrong conclusions . . .

'*Your* certificates, sir?'

'Of course not. Nothing wrong with my certificates—I had them printed in Lahore, in 1946.'

'With age comes respectability,' I remarked. 'In that case, whose . . .?'

'Why, the matriculation certificates I've been providing all these years to the poor idiots who would never have got through on their own!'

'You mean you gave them your own certificates?'

'That's right. And if it hadn't been for so many printing mistakes, no one would have been any wiser. You can't find a good press these days, that's the trouble . . . . It was a public service, my boy, I hope you appreciate that . . . . It isn't fair to hold a boy back in life simply because he can't get through some puny exam . . . . Mind you, I don't give my certificates to *anyone*. They come to me only after they have failed two or three times.'

'And I suppose you charge something?'

'Only if they can pay. There's no fixed sum. Whatever they like to give me. I've never been greedy in these matters, and you know I am not unkind . . . .'

Which is true enough, I thought, looking out of the carriage window at the green fields of Moga and remembering the half-yearly Hindi exam when I had stared blankly at the question paper, knowing that I was totally incapable of answering any of it. Mr Khushal had come walking down the line of desks and stopped at mine, breathing cloves all over me. 'Come on, boy, why haven't you started?'

'Can't do it sir,' I'd said. 'It's too difficult.'

'Never mind,' he'd urged in a whisper. 'Do *something*. Copy it out, copy it out!'

And so, to pass the time, I'd copied out the entire paper, word for word. And a fortnight later, when the results were out, I found I had passed!

'But, sir,' I had stammered, approaching Mr Khushal when I found him alone, 'I never answered the paper. I couldn't translate the passage. All I did was copy it out!'

'That's why I gave you pass-marks,' he'd answered imperturbably. 'You have such neat handwriting. If ever you *do* learn Hindi, my boy, you'll write a beautiful script!'

And remembering that moment, I was now filled with compassion for my old teacher; and leaning across, I placed my hand on his knee and said: 'Sir, if they convict you, I hope it

won't be for long. And when you come out, if you happen to
be in Delhi or Ferozepur, please look me up. You see, I'm still
rather hopeless at Hindi, and perhaps you could give me
tuition. I'd be glad to pay . . . .'

Mr Khushal threw back his head and laughed, and the
entire compartment shook with his laughter.

'Teach you Hindi!' he cried. 'My dear boy, what gave you
the idea that I ever knew any Hindi?'

'But, sir—if not Hindi what were you teaching us all the
time at school?'

'Punjabi!' he shouted, and everyone jumped in their seats.
'Pure Punjabi! But how were *you* to know the difference?'

LISTEN TO THE WIND

❧

MARCH IS PROBABLY THE most uncomfortable month in the hills. The rain is cold, often accompanied by sleet and hail, and the wind from the north comes tearing down the mountain-passes with tremendous force. Those few people who pass the winter in the hill station remain close to their fires. If they can't afford fires, they get into bed.

I found old Miss Mackenzie tucked up in bed with three hot-water bottles for company. I took the bedroom's single easy chair, and for some time Miss Mackenzie and I listened to the thunder and watched the play of lightning. The rain made a tremendous noise on the corrugated tin roof, and we had to raise our voices in order to be heard. The hills looked blurred and smudgy when seen through the rain-spattered windows. The wind battered at the doors and rushed round the cottage, determined to make an entry; it slipped down the chimney, but stuck there choking and gurgling and protesting helplessly.

'There's a ghost in your chimney and he can't get out,' I said.

'Then let him stay there,' said Miss Mackenzie.

A vivid flash of lightning lit up the opposite hill, showing me for a moment a pile of ruins which I never knew were there.

'You're looking at Burnt Hill,' said Miss Mackenzie. 'It always gets the lightning when there's a storm.'

'Possibly there are iron deposits in the rocks,' I said.

'I wouldn't know. But it's the reason why no one ever lived there for long. Almost every dwelling that was put up was struck by lightning and burnt down.'

'I thought I saw some ruins just now.'

'Nothing but rubble. When they were first settling in the hills they chose that spot. Later they moved to the site where the town now stands. Burnt Hill was left to the deer and the leopards and the monkeys—and to its ghosts, of course . . .'

'Oh, so it's haunted, too.'

'So they say. On evenings such as these. But you don't believe in ghosts, do you?'

'No. Do you?'

'No. But you'll understand why they say the hill is haunted when you hear its story. Listen.'

I listened, but at first I could hear nothing but the wind and the rain. Then Miss Mackenzie's clear voice rose above the sound of the elements, and I heard her saying:

'. . . it's really the old story of ill-starred lovers, only it's true. I'd met Robert at his parent's house some weeks before the tragedy took place. He was eighteen, tall and fresh-looking, and full of manhood. He'd been born out here, but his parents were hoping to return to England when Robert's father retired. His father was a magistrate, I think—but that hasn't any bearing on the story.

'Their plans didn't work out the way they expected. You see, Robert fell in love. Not with an English girl, mind you, but with a hill girl, the daughter of a landholder from the village behind Burnt Hill. Even today it would be unconventional. Twenty-five years ago, it was almost unheard of! Robert liked walking, and he was hiking through the forest when he saw or rather heard her. It was said later that he fell in love with her voice. She was singing, and the song—low and sweet and strange to his ears—struck him to the heart. When he caught sight of the girl's face, he was not disappointed. She was young and beautiful. She saw him and returned his awestruck gaze with a brief, fleeting smile.

'Robert, in his impetuousness, made enquiries at the village, located the girl's father, and without much ado asked for her hand in marriage. He probably thought that a sahib would not be refused such a request. At the same time, it was really quite gallant on his part, because any other young man might simply have ravished the girl in the forest. But Robert was in love and, therefore, completely irrational in his behaviour.

'Of course the girl's father would have nothing to do with the proposal. He was a Brahmin, and he wasn't going to have the good name of his family ruined by marrying off his only daughter to a foreigner. Robert did not argue with the father; nor did he say anything to his own parents, because he knew their reaction would be one of shock and dismay. They would do everything in their power to put an end to his madness.

'But Robert continued to visit the forest—you see it there, that heavy patch of oak and pine—and he often came across the girl, for she would be gathering fodder or fuel. She did not seem to resent his attentions, and, as Robert knew something of the language, he was soon able to convey his feelings to her. The girl must at first have been rather alarmed, but the boy's sincerity broke down her reserve. After all, she was young too—young enough to fall in love with a devoted swain, without thinking too much of his background. She knew her father would never agree to a marriage—and *he* knew his parents would prevent anything like that happening. So they planned to run away together. Romantic, isn't it? But it did happen. Only they did *not* live happily ever after.'

'Did their parents come after them?'

'No. They had agreed to meet one night in the ruined building on Burnt Hill—the ruin you saw just now; it hasn't changed much, except that there was a bit of roof to it then. They left their homes and made their way to the hill without any difficulty. After meeting, they planned to take the little path that followed the course of a stream until it reached the plains. After that—but who knows what they had planned, what dreams of the future they had conjured up? The storm broke soon after they'd reached the ruins. They took shelter under the dripping ceiling. It was a storm just like this one—a high wind and great torrents of rain and hail, and the lightning flitting about and crashing down almost every minute. They must have been soaked, huddled together in a corner of that crumbling building, when lightning struck. No one knows at what time it happened. But next morning their charred bodies were found on the worn yellow stones of the old building.'

Miss Mackenzie stopped speaking, and I noticed that the thunder had grown distant and the rain had lessened; but the chimney was still coughing and clearing its throat.

'That's true, every word of it,' said Miss Mackenzie. 'But as to Burnt Hill being haunted, that's another matter. I've no experience of ghosts.'

'Anyway, you need a fire to keep them out of the chimney,' I said, getting up to go. I had my raincoat and umbrella, and my own cottage was not far away.

Next morning, when I took the steep path up to Burnt Hill, the sky was clear, and though there was still a stiff wind, it was no longer menacing. An hour's climb brought me to the old ruin—now nothing but a heap of stones, as Miss Mackenzie had said. Part of a wall was left, and the corner of a fireplace. Grass and weeds had grown up through the floor, and primroses and wild saxifrage flowered amongst the rubble.

Where had they sheltered, I wondered, as the wind tore at them and fire fell from the sky.

I touched the cold stones, half expecting to find in them some traces of the warmth of human contact. I listened, waiting for some ancient echo, some returning wave of sound, that would bring me nearer to the spirits of the dead lovers; but there was only the wind coughing in the lovely pines.

I thought I heard voices in the wind; and perhaps I did. For isn't the wind the voice of the undying dead?

THE HAUNTED BICYCLE

❧

I WAS LIVING AT the time in a village about five miles out of Shahganj, a district in east Uttar Pradesh, and my only means of transport was a bicycle. I could of course have gone into Shahganj on any obliging farmer's bullock-cart, but, in spite of bad roads and my own clumsiness as a cyclist, I found the bicycle a trifle faster. I went into Shahganj almost every day, collected my mail, bought a newspaper, drank innumerable cups of tea, and gossiped with the tradesmen. I cycled back to the village at about six in the evening, along a quiet, unfrequented forest road. During the winter months it was dark by six, and I would have to use a lamp on the bicycle.

One evening, when I had covered about half the distance to the village, I was brought to a halt by a small boy who was standing in the middle of the road. The forest at that late hour was no place for a child: wolves and hyenas were common in the district. I got down from my bicycle and approached the boy, but he didn't seem to take much notice of me.

'What are you doing here on your own?' I asked.

'I'm waiting,' he said, without looking at me.

'Waiting for whom? Your parents?'

'No, I am waiting for my sister.'

'Well, I haven't passed her on the road,' I said. 'She may be further ahead. You had better come along with me, we'll soon find her.'

The boy nodded and climbed silently on to the crossbar in front of me. I have never been able to recall his features. Already it was dark and besides, he kept his face turned away from me.

The wind was against us, and as I cycled on, I shivered with the cold, but the boy did not seem to feel it. We had not gone far when the light from my lamp fell on the figure of another child who was standing by the side of the road. This time it was a girl. She was a little older than the boy, and her hair was long and wind-swept, hiding most of her face.

'Here's your sister,' I said. 'Let's take her along with us.'

The girl did not respond to my smile, and she did no more than nod seriously to the boy. But she climbed up on to my back carrier, and allowed me to pedal off again. Their replies to my friendly questions were monosyllabic, and I gathered that they were wary of strangers. Well, when I got to the village, I would hand them over to the headman, and he could locate their parents.

The road was level, but I felt as though I was cycling uphill. And then I noticed that the boy's head was much closer to my face, that the girl's breathing was loud and heavy, almost as though she was doing the riding. Despite the cold wind, I began to feel hot and suffocated.

'I think we'd better take a rest,' I suggested.

'No!' cried the boy and girl together. 'No rest!'

I was so surprised that I rode on without any argument; and then, just as I was thinking of ignoring their demand and stopping, I noticed that the boy's hands, which were resting on the handle-bar, had grown long and black and hairy.

My hands shook and the bicycle wobbled about on the road.

'Be careful!' shouted the children in unison. 'Look where you're going!'

Their tone now was menacing and far from childlike. I took a quick glance over my shoulder and had my worst fears confirmed. The girl's face was huge and bloated. Her legs, black and hairy, were trailing along the ground.

'Stop!' ordered the terrible children. 'Stop near the stream!'

But before I could do anything, my front wheel hit a stone and the bicycle toppled over. As I sprawled in the dust, I felt something hard, like a hoof, hit me on the back of the head, and then there was total darkness.

When I recovered consciousness, I noticed that the moon had risen and was sparkling on the waters of a stream. The children were not to be seen anywhere. I got up from the ground and began to brush the dust from my clothes. And then, hearing the sound of splashing and churning in the stream, I looked up again.

Two small black buffaloes gazed at me from the muddy, moonlit water.

Dead Man's Gift

❧

'A DEAD MAN IS no good to anyone,' said Nathu, the old shikari, as he stared into the glowing embers of the camp-fire and wrapped a thin blanket around his thin shoulders.

We had spent a rewarding but tiring day in the Terai forests near Haldwani, where I had been photographing swamp-deer. On our return to the forest resthouse, Nathu had made a log-fire near the front veranda, and we had gathered round it—Nathu, myself and Ghanshyam Singh, the chowkidar—discussing a suicide that had taken place in a neighbouring village. I forget the details of the suicide—it was connected with a disappointed bridegroom—but the discussion led to some interesting reminiscences on the part of Ghanshyam Singh.

We had all agreed with Nathu's sentiments about dead men, when Ghanshyam interrupted to say, 'I don't know about that, brother. At least one dead man brought considerable good fortune to a friend of mine.'

'How was that?' I asked.

'Well, about twenty years ago,' said Ghanshyam Singh, 'I was a policeman, one of the six constables at a small police post in the village of Ahirpur near the hills. A small stream ran past the village. Fed by springs, it contained a few feet of water even during the hottest of seasons, while after heavy rain it became a roaring torrent. The head constable in charge of our post was Dilawar Singh, who came from a good family which had fallen on evil days. He was a handsome fellow, very well-dressed, always spending his money before he received it. He was passionately fond of good horseflesh, and the mare he rode was a beautiful creature named Leila. He had obtained the mare by paying two hundred and fifty rupees down and promising to pay the remaining two hundred and fifty in six months time. If he failed to do so, he would have to return the mare and forfeit the deposit. But Dilawar Singh expected to be able to borrow the balance from Lala Ram Das, the wealthy bania of Ahirpur.

'The bania of Ahirpur was one of the meanest alive. You know the sort, fat and flabby from overeating and sitting all day in his shop, but very wealthy. His house was a large one, situated near the stream, at some distance from the village.'

'But why did he live outside the village, away from his customers?' I asked.

'It made no difference to him,' said Ghanshyam. 'Everyone was in his debt and, whether they liked it or not, were compelled to deal with him. His father had lived inside the village but had been looted by dacoits, whose ill-treatment had left him a cripple for life. Not a single villager had come to his assistance on that occasion. He had never forgotten it. He built himself another house outside the village, with a high wall and only one entrance. Inside the wall was a courtyard with a stable for a pony and a byre for two cows, the house itself forming one side of the enclosure. When the heavy door of the courtyard was closed, the bania's money bags were safe within his little fort. It was only after the old man's death that a police post was established at Ahirpur.'

'So Ram Das had a police post as well as a fort?'

'The police offered him no protection. He was so mean that not a litre of oil or pinch of salt ever came from him to the police post. Naturally, we wasted no love on him. The people of Ahirpur hated and feared him, for most of them were in his debt and practically his slaves.

'Now when the time came for Dilawar Singh to pay the remaining two hundred and fifty rupees for his mare Leila, he went to Ram Das for a loan. He expected to be well squeezed in the way of interest, but to his great surprise and anger the bania refused to let him have the money on any terms. It looked as though Dilawar would have to return the mare and be content with some knock-kneed *ekka*-pony.

'A few days before the date of payment, Dilawar Singh had

to visit a village some five miles downstream to investigate a case. He took me with him. On our return journey that night a terrific thunderstorm compelled us to take shelter in a small hut in the forest. When at last the storm was over, we continued on our way, I on foot, and Dilawar Singh riding Leila. All the way he cursed his ill-luck at having to part with Leila, and called down curses on Ram Das. We were not far from the bania's house when the full moon, high in the sky, came out from behind the passing storm-clouds, and suddenly Leila shied violently at something white on the bank of the stream.

'It was the naked body of a dead man. It had either been pushed into the stream without burning or swept off the pyre by the swollen torrent. I was about to push it off into the stream when Dilawar stopped me, saying that the corpse which had frightened Leila might yet be able to save her.'

'Together we pulled the body a little way up the bank. Then, after tying the mare to a tree, we carried the corpse up to the bania's house and propped it against the main doorway. Returning to the stream, Dilawar remounted Leila, and we concealed ourselves in the forest. Like everyone else in the village, we knew the bania was an early riser, always the first to leave his house and complete his morning ablutions.

'We sat and waited. The faint light of dawn was just beginning to make things visible when we heard the bania's courtyard door open. There was a thud, an exclamation, and then a long silence.'

'What had happened?'

'Ram Das had opened the door, and the corpse had fallen upon him! He was frightened almost out of his wits. That some enemy was responsible for the presence of the corpse he quickly realized, but how to rid himself of it? The stream! Even to touch the corpse was defilement, but, as the saying goes, "Where there are no eyes, there is no caste"—and he began to drag the body along the river bank, panting and perspiring, yet cold with terror. He had almost reached the stream when we emerged casually from our shelter.

' "Ah, bania-ji, you are up early this morning!" called Dilawar Singh. "Hallo, what's this? Is this one of your unfortunate debtors? Have you taken his life as well as his clothes?"

'Ram Das fell on his knees. His voice failed, and he went as pale as the corpse he still held by the feet. Dilawar Singh dismounted, caught him roughly by the arm and dragged him to his feet.

' "Thanedar sahib, I will let you have the money," gasped Ram Das.

' "What money?"

' "The two hundred and fifty rupees you wanted last week."

' "Then hurry up," said Dilawar Singh, "or someone will come, and I shall be compelled to arrest you. Run!"

'The unfortunate Ram Das realized that he was in an evil predicament. True, he was innocent, but before he could prove this he would be arrested by the police whom he had scorned and flouted. Lawyers would devour his savings. He would be torn from his family and deprived of his comforts. And worst of all, his clients would delay repayments! After only a little hesitation, he ran to his house and returned with two hundred and fifty rupees, which he handed over to Dilawar Singh. And, as far as I know—for I was transferred from Ahirpur a few weeks later—he never asked Dilawar Singh for its return.'

'And what of the body?' I asked.

'We pushed it back into the stream,' said Ghanshyam. 'It had served its purpose well. So Nathu, do you still insist that a dead man is no good to anyone?'

'No good at all,' said Nathu, spitting into the fire's fast fading glow. 'For I came to Ahirpur not long after you were transferred. I had the pleasure of meeting thanedar Dilawar Singh, and seeing his fine mare. It is true that he had the bania under his thumb, for Ram Das provided all the feed for the mare, at no charge. But one day the mare had a fit while Dilawar Singh was riding her, and plunging about in the street she flung her master to the ground. Dilawar Singh broke his neck, and died. She was indeed a dead man's gift!'

'The bania must have been quite pleased at the turn of events,' I said.

'Some say he poisoned the mare's feed. Anyway, he kept the police happy by providing the oil to light poor Dilawar Singh's funeral pyre, and generously refused to accept any payment for it!'

WHISPERING IN THE DARK

ॐ

A WILD NIGHT. WIND moaning, trees lashing themselves in a frenzy, rain beating down on the road, thunder over the mountains. Loneliness stretched ahead of me, a loneliness of the heart as well as a physical loneliness. The world was blotted out by a mist that had come up from the valley, a thick, white, clammy shroud.

I groped through the forest, groped in my mind for the memory of a mountain path, some remembered rock or ancient deodar. Then a streak of blue lightning gave me a glimpse of a barren hillside and a house cradled in mist.

It was an old-world house, built of limestone rock on the outskirts of a crumbling hill station. There was no light in its windows; probably the electricity had been disconnected long ago. But if I could get in it would do for the night.

I had no torch, but at times the moon shone through the wild clouds, and trees loomed out of the mist like primeval giants. I reached the front door and found it locked from within. I walked round to the side and broke a window-pane, put my hand through shattered glass and found the bolt.

The window, warped by over a hundred monsoons, resisted at first. Then it yielded, and I climbed into the mustiness of a long-closed room, and the wind came in with me, scattering papers across the floor and knocking some unidentifiable object off a table. I closed the window, bolted it again; but the mist crawled through the broken glass, and the wind rattled in it like a pair of castanets.

There were matches in my pocket. I struck three before a light flared up.

I was in a large room, crowded with furniture. Pictures on the walls. Vases on the mantelpiece. A candlestand. And, strangely enough, no cobwebs. For all its external look of neglect and dilapidation, the house had been cared for by someone. But before I could notice anything else, the match burnt out.

As I stepped further into the room, the old deodar flooring creaked beneath my weight. By the light of another match I reached the mantlepiece and lit the candle, noticing at the same time that the candlestick was a genuine antique with cutglass hangings. A deserted cottage with good furniture and glass. I wondered why no one had ever broken in. And then realized that I had just done so.

I held the candlestick high and glanced round the room. The walls were hung with several water-colours and portraits in oils. There was no dust anywhere. But no one answered my call, no one responded to my hesitant knocking. It was as though the occupants of the house were in hiding, watching me obliquely from dark corners and chimneys.

I entered a bedroom and found myself facing a full-length mirror. My reflection stared back at me as though I were a stranger, as though my reflection belonged to the house, while I was only an outsider.

As I turned from the mirror, I thought I saw someone, something, some reflection other than mine, move behind me in the mirror. I caught a glimpse of whiteness, a pale oval face, burning eyes, long tresses, golden in the candlelight. But when I looked in the mirror again there was nothing to be seen but my own pallid face.

A pool of water was forming at my feet. I set the candle down on a small table, found the edge of the bed—a large old four-poster—sat down, and removed my soggy shoes and socks. Then I took off my clothes and hung them over the back of a chair.

I stood naked in the darkness, shivering a little. There was no one to see me—and yet I felt oddly exposed, almost as though I had stripped in a room full of curious people.

I got under the bedclothes—they smelt slightly of eucalyptus and lavender—but found there was no pillow. That was odd. A perfectly made bed, but no pillow! I was too tired to hunt for one. So I blew out the candle—and the darkness closed in around me, and the whispering began . . .

The whispering began as soon as I closed my eyes. I couldn't tell where it came from. It was all around me, mingling with the sound of the wind coughing in the chimney, the stretching of old furniture, the weeping of trees outside in the rain.

Sometimes I could hear what was being said. The words came from a distance: a distance not so much of space as of time . . .

'Mine, mine, he is all mine . . .'

'He is ours, dear, ours.'

Whispers, echoes, words hovering around me with bats' wings, saying the most inconsequential things with a logical urgency. 'You're late for supper . . .'

'He lost his way in the mist.'

'Do you think he has any money?'

'To kill a turtle you must first tie its legs to two posts.'

'We could tie him to the bed and pour boiling water down his throat.'

'No, it's simpler this way.'

I sat up. Most of the whispering had been distant, impersonal, but this last remark had sounded horribly near.

I relit the candle and the voices stopped. I got up and prowled around the room, vainly looking for some explanation for the voices. Once again I found myself facing the mirror, staring at my own reflection and the reflection of that other person, the girl with the golden hair and shining eyes. And this time she held a pillow in her hands. She was standing behind me.

I remembered then the stories I had heard as a boy, of two spinster sisters—one beautiful, one plain—who lured rich, elderly gentlemen into their boarding-house and suffocated them in the night. The deaths had appeared quite natural, and they had got away with it for years. It was only the surviving sister's death-bed confession that had revealed the truth—and even then no one had believed her.

But that had been many, many years ago, and the house had long since fallen down . . .

When I turned from the mirror, there was no one behind me. I looked again, and the reflection had gone.

I crawled back into the bed and put the candle out. And I slept and dreamt (or was I awake and did it really happen?) that the woman I had seen in the mirror stood beside the bed, leant over me, looked at me with eyes flecked by orange flames. I saw people moving in those eyes. I saw myself. And then her lips touched mine, lips so cold, so dry, that a shudder ran through my body.

And then, while her face became faceless and only the eyes remained, something else continued to press down upon me, something soft, heavy and shapeless, enclosing me in a suffocating embrace. I could not turn my head or open my mouth. I could not breathe.

I raised my hands and clutched feebly at the thing on top of me. And to my surprise it came away. It was only a pillow that had somehow fallen over my face, half suffocating me while I dreamt of a phantom kiss.

I flung the pillow aside. I flung the bedclothes from me. I had had enough of whispering, of ownerless reflections, of pillows that fell on me in the dark. I would brave the storm outside rather than continue to seek rest in this tortured house.

I dressed quickly. The candle had almost guttered out. The house and everything in it belonged to the darkness of another time; I belonged to the light of day.

I was ready to leave. I avoided the tall mirror with its grotesque rococo design. Holding the candlestick before me, I moved cautiously into the front room. The pictures on the walls sprang to life.

One, in particular, held my attention, and I moved closer to examine it more carefully by the light of the dwindling candle. Was it just my imagination, or was the girl in the portrait the woman of my dream, the beautiful pale reflection in the mirror? Had I gone back in time, or had time caught up with me? Is it time that's passing by, or is it you and I?

I turned to leave, and the candle gave one final sputter and went out, plunging the room in darkness. I stood still for a moment, trying to collect my thoughts, to still the panic that came rushing upon me. Just then there was a knocking on the door.

'Who's there?' I called.

Silence. And then, again, the knocking, and this time a voice, low and insistent: 'Please let me in, please let me in . . .'

I stepped forward, unbolted the door, and flung it open.

She stood outside in the rain. Not the pale, beautiful one, but a wizened old hag with bloodless lips and flaring nostrils and—but where were the eyes? No eyes, no eyes!

She swept past me on the wind, and at the same time I took advantage of the open doorway to run outside, to run gratefully into the pouring rain, to be lost for hours among the dripping trees, to be glad for all the leeches clinging to my flesh.

And when, with the dawn, I found my way at last, I rejoiced in birdsong and the sunlight piercing and scattering the clouds.

And today if you were to ask me if the old house is still there or not, I would not be able to tell you, for the simple reason that I haven't the slightest desire to go looking for it.

HE SAID IT WITH ARSENIC

❧

IS THERE SUCH A person as a born murderer—in the sense that there are born writers and musicians, born winners and losers? One can't be sure. The urge to do away with troublesome people is common to most of us but only a few succumb to it.

If ever there was a born murderer, he must surely have been William Jones. The thing came so naturally to him. No extreme violence, no messy shootings or hacking or throttling. Just the right amount of poison, administered with skill and discretion.

A gentle, civilized sort of person was Mr Jones. He collected butterflies and arranged them systematically in glass cases. His ether bottle was quick and painless. He never stuck pins into the beautiful creatures.

Have you ever heard of the Agra Double Murder? It happened, of course, a great many years ago, when Agra was a far-flung outpost of the British Empire. In those days, William Jones was a male nurse in one of the city's hospitals. The patients—especially terminal cases—spoke highly of the care and consideration he showed them. While most nurses, both male and female, preferred to attend to the more hopeful cases, Nurse William was always prepared to stand duty over a dying patient.

He felt a certain empathy for the dying. He liked to see them on their way. It was just his good nature, of course.

On a visit to nearby Meerut, he met and fell in love with Mrs Browning, the wife of the local stationmaster. Impassioned love letters were soon putting a strain on the Agra-Meerut postal service. The envelopes grew heavier—not so much because the letters were growing longer but because they contained little packets of a powdery white substance, accompanied by detailed instructions as to its correct administration.

Mr Browning, an unassuming and trustful man—one of the world's born losers, in fact—was not the sort to read his wife's correspondence. Even when he was seized by frequent attacks of colic, he put them down to an impure water supply. He recovered from one bout of vomitting and diarrhoea only to be racked by another.

He was hospitalized on a diagnosis of gastroenteritis. And, thus freed from his wife's ministrations, soon got better. But on returning home and drinking a glass of nimbu-pani brought to him by the solicitous Mrs Browning, he had a relapse from which he did not recover.

Those were the days when deaths from cholera and related diseases were only too common in India and death certificates were easier to obtain than dog licences.

After a short interval of mourning (it was the hot weather and you couldn't wear black for long) Mrs Browning moved to Agra where she rented a house next door to William Jones.

I forgot to mention that Mr Jones was also married. His wife was an insignificant creature, no match for a genius like William. Before the hot weather was over, the dreaded cholera had taken her too. The way was clear for the lovers to unite in holy matrimony.

But Dame Gossip lived in Agra too and it was not long before tongues were wagging and anonymous letters were being received by the Superintendent of Police. Enquiries were instituted. Like most infatuated lovers, Mrs Browning had hung on to her beloved's letters and billet-doux, and these soon came to light. The silly woman had kept them in a box beneath her bed.

Exhumations were ordered in both Agra and Meerut. Arsenic keeps well, even in the hottest of weather, and there was no dearth of it in the remains of both victims.

Mr Jones and Mrs Browning were arrested and charged with murder.

'Is Uncle Bill really a murderer?' I asked from the drawing-room sofa in my grandmother's house in Dehra. (It's time I told you that William Jones was my uncle, my mother's half-brother.)

I was eight or nine at the time. Uncle Bill had spent the previous summer with us in Dehra and had stuffed me with bazaar sweets and pastries, all of which I had consumed without suffering any ill effects.

'Who told you that about Uncle Bill?' asked Grandmother.

'I heard it in school. All the boys are asking me the same question—"Is your uncle a murderer?" They say he poisoned both his wives.'

'He had only one wife,' snapped Aunt Mabel.

'Did he poison her?'

'No, of course not. How can you say such a thing!'

'Then why is Uncle Bill in goal?'

'Who says he's in goal?'

'The boys at school. They heard it from their parents. Uncle Bill is to go on trial in the Agra fort.'

There was a pregnant silence in the drawing room, then Aunt Mabel burst out: 'It was all that awful woman's fault.'

'Do you mean Mrs Browning?' asked Grandmother.

'Yes, of course. She must have put him up to it. Bill couldn't have thought of anything so—so diabolical!'

'But he sent her the powders, dear. And don't forget—Mrs Browning has since . . . .'

Grandmother stopped in mid-sentence and both she and Aunt Mabel glanced surreptitiously at me.

'Committed suicide,' I filled in. 'There were still some powders with her.'

Aunt Mabel's eyes rolled heavenwards. 'This boy is impossible. I don't know what he will be like when he grows up.'

'At least I won't be like Uncle Bill,' I said. 'Fancy poisoning people! If I kill anyone, it will be in a fair fight. I suppose they'll hang Uncle?'

'Oh, I hope not!'

Grandmother was silent. Uncle Bill was her stepson but she did have a soft spot for him. Aunt Mabel, his sister, thought he was wonderful. I had always considered him to be a bit soft but had to admit that he was generous. I tried to imagine him dangling at the end of a hangman's rope but somehow he didn't fit the picture.

As things turned out, he didn't hang. White people in India seldom got the death sentence, although the hangman was pretty busy disposing of dacoits and political terrorists. Uncle Bill was given a life sentence and settled down to a sedentary job in the prison library at Naini, near Allahabad. His gifts as a male nurse went unappreciated. They did not trust him in the hospital.

He was released after seven or eight years, shortly after the country became an independent republic. He came out of gaol to find that the British were leaving, either for England or the remaining colonies. Grandmother was dead. Aunt Mabel and her husband had settled in South Africa. Uncle Bill realized that there was little future for him in India and followed his sister out to Johannesburg. I was in my last year at boarding-school. After my father's death my mother had married an Indian and now my future lay in India.

I did not see Uncle Bill after his release from prison and no one dreamt that he would ever turn up again in India.

In fact fifteen years were to pass before he came back, and by then I was in my early thirties, the author of a book that had become something of a bestseller. The previous fifteen years had been a struggle—the sort of struggle that every young freelance writer experiences—but at last the hard work was paying off and the royalties were beginning to come in.

I was living in a small cottage on the outskirts of the hill station of Fosterganj, working on another book, when I received an unexpected visitor.

He was a thin, stooped, grey-haired man in his late fifties with a straggling moustache and discoloured teeth. He looked feeble and harmless but for his eyes which were a pale cold blue. There was something slightly familiar about him.

'Don't you remember me?' he asked. 'Not that I really expect you to, after all these years . . . .'

'Wait a minute. Did you teach me at school?'

'No—but you're getting warm.' He put his suitcase down and I glimpsed his name on the airlines label. I looked up in astonishment. 'You're not—you couldn't be . . . .'

'Your Uncle Bill,' he said with a grin and extended his hand. 'None other!' And he sauntered into the house.

I must admit that I had mixed feelings about his arrival. While I had never felt any dislike for him, I hadn't exactly approved of what he had done. Poisoning, I felt, was a particularly reprehensible way of getting rid of inconvenient people. Not that I could think of any commendable ways of getting rid of them! Still, it had happened a long time ago, he'd been punished, and presumably he was a reformed character.

'And what have you been doing all these years?' he asked me, easing himself into the only comfortable chair in the room.

'Oh just writing,' I said.

'Yes, I heard about your last book. It's quite a success, isn't it?'

'It's doing quite well. Have you read it?'

'I don't do much reading.'

'And what have you been doing all these years, Uncle Bill?'

'Oh, knocking about here and there. Worked for a soft drink company for some time. And then with a drug firm. My knowledge of chemicals was useful.'

'Weren't you with Aunt Mabel in South Africa?'

'I saw quite a lot of her until she died a couple of years ago. Didn't you know?'

'No. I've been out of touch with relatives.' I hoped he'd take that as a hint. 'And what about her husband?'

'Died too, not long after. Not many of us left, my boy. That's why, when I saw something about you in the papers, I thought—why not go and see my only nephew again?'

'You're welcome to stay a few days,' I said quickly. 'Then I have to go to Bombay.' (This was a lie but I did not relish the prospect of looking after Uncle Bill for the rest of his days.)

'Oh, I won't be staying long,' he said. 'I've got a bit of money put by in Johannesburg. It's just that—so far as I know—you're my only living relative and I thought it would be nice to see you again.'

Feeling relieved, I set about trying to make Uncle Bill as comfortable as possible. I gave him my bedroom and turned the window-seat into a bed for myself. I was a hopeless cook but, using all my ingenuity, I scrambled some eggs for supper. He waved aside my apologies. He'd always been a frugal eater, he said. Eight years in gaol had given him a cast-iron stomach.

He did not get in my way but left me to my writing and my lonely walks. He seemed content to sit in the spring sunshine and smoke his pipe.

It was during our third evening together that he said, 'Oh, I almost forgot. There's a bottle of sherry in my suitcase. I brought it especially for you.'

'That was very thoughtful of you, Uncle Bill. How did you know I was fond of sherry?'

'Just my intuition. You do like it, don't you?'

'There's nothing like a good sherry.'

He went to his bedroom and came back with an unopened bottle of South African sherry.

'Now you just relax near the fire,' he said agreeably. 'I'll open the bottle and fetch glasses.'

He went to the kitchen while I remained near the electric fire, flipping through some journals. It seemed to me that Uncle Bill was taking rather a long time. Intuition must be a family trait because it came to me quite suddenly— the thought that Uncle Bill might be intending to poison me.

After all, I thought, here he is after nearly fifteen years, apparently for purely sentimental reasons. But I had just published a bestseller. And I was his nearest relative. If I was to die Uncle Bill could lay claim to my estate and probably live comfortably on my royalties for the next five or six years!

What had really happened to Aunt Mabel and her husband, I wondered. And where did Uncle Bill get the money for an air ticket to India?

Before I could ask myself any more questions, he reappeared with the glasses on a tray. He set the tray on a small table that stood between us. The glasses had been filled. The sherry sparkled.

I stared at the glass nearest me, trying to make out if the liquid in it was cloudier than that in the other glass. But there appeared to be no difference.

I decided I would not take any chances. It was a round tray, made of smooth Kashmiri walnut wood. I turned it round with my index finger, so that the glasses changed places.

'Why did you do that?' asked Uncle Bill.

'It's a custom in these parts. You turn the tray with the sun, a complete revolution. It brings good luck.'

Uncle Bill looked thoughtful for a few moments, then said, 'Well, let's have some more luck,' and turned the tray around again.

'Now you've spoilt it,' I said. 'You're not supposed to keep revolving it! That's bad luck. I'll have to turn it about again to cancel out the bad luck.'

The tray swung round once more and Uncle Bill had the glass that was meant for me.

'Cheers!' I said and drank from my glass.

It was good sherry.

Uncle Bill hesitated. Then he shrugged, said 'Cheers' and drained his glass quickly.

But he did not offer to fill the glasses again.

Early next morning he was taken violently ill. I heard him retching in his room and I got up and went to see if there was anything I could do. He was groaning, his head hanging over the side of the bed. I brought him a basin and a jug of water.

'Would you like me to fetch a doctor?' I asked.

He shook his head. 'No, I'll be all right. It must be something I ate.'

'It's probably the water. It's not too good at this time of year. Many people come down with gastric trouble during their first few days in Fosterganj.'

'Ah, that must be it,' he said and doubled up as a fresh spasm of pain and nausea swept over him.

He was better by evening—whatever had gone into the glass must have been by way of the preliminary dose and a day later he was well enough to pack his suitcase and announce his departure. The climate of Fosterganj did not agree with him, he told me.

Just before he left, I said: 'Tell me, Uncle, why did you drink it?

'Drink what? The water?'

'No, the glass of sherry into which you'd slipped one of your famous powders.'

He gaped at me, then gave a nervous whinnying laugh. 'You will have your little joke, won't you?'

'No, I mean it,' I said. 'Why did you drink the stuff? It was meant for me, of course.'

He looked down at his shoes, then gave a little shrug and turned away.

'In the circumstances,' he said, 'it seemed the only decent thing to do.'

I'll say this for Uncle Bill: he was always the perfect gentleman.

THE MOST POTENT MEDICINE OF ALL

LIKE MOST MEN, WANG Chei was fond of being his own doctor. He studied the book of the ancient physician Lu Fei whenever he felt slightly indisposed. Had he really been familiar with the peculiarities of his digestion, he would have avoided eating too many pickled prawns. But he ate pickled prawns first, and studied Lu Fei afterwards.

Lu Fei, a physician of renown in Yunnan during the twelfth century, had devoted eight chapters to disorders of the belly, and there are many in western China who still swear by his methods—just as there are many in England who still swear by Culpepper's Herbal.

The great physician was a firm believer in the potency of otters' tails, and had Wang Chei taken a dose of otters' tails the morning after the prawns, his pain and cramps might soon have disappeared.

But otters' tails are both rare and expensive. In order to obtain a tail, one must catch an otter; in order to catch an otter, one must find a river; and there were no rivers in the region where Wang Chei lived.

Wang grew potatoes to sell in the market twelve miles away, and sometimes he traded in opium. But what interested him most was the practice of medicine, and he had some reputation as a doctor among those villagers who regarded the distant hospital with suspicion.

And so, in the absence of otters' tails, he fell back upon the gall of bear, the fat of python, the whiskers of tiger, the blood of rhino, and the horn of sambar in velvet. He tried all these (he had them in stock), mixing them—as directed by the book of Lu Fei—in the water of melted hailstones.

Wang took all these remedies in turn, anxiously noting the reactions that took place in his system. Unfortunately, neither he nor his mentor, Lu Fei, had given much thought to diagnosis, and he did not associate his trouble with the pickled prawns.

Life would hardly have been worth living without a few indulgences, especially as Wang's wife excelled at making pickles. This was his misfortune. Her pickles were such that no man could refuse them.

She was devoted to Wang Chei and indulged his tastes and his enormous appetite. Like him, she occasionally dipped into the pages of Lu Fei. From them she had learned that mutton fat was good for the eyebrows and that raspberry-leaf tea was just the thing for expectant mothers.

Her faith in this physician of an earlier century was as strong as her husband's. And now, with Wang Chei groaning and tossing on his bed, she studied the chapters on abdominal complaints.

It appeared to her that Wang was very ill indeed, and she did not connect his woeful condition with over-indulgence. He had been in bed for two days. Had he not dosed himself so liberally with python's fat and rhino's blood, it is possible that he might have recovered on the morning following his repast. Now he was too ill to mix himself any further concoctions. Fortunately—as he supposed—his wife was there to continue the treatment.

She was a small pale woman who moved silently about the house on little feet. It was difficult to believe that this frail creature had brought eleven healthy children into the world. Her husband had once been a strong, handsome man; but now the skin under his eyes was crinkling, his cheeks were hollow, his once well-proportioned body was sagging with loose flesh.

Nevertheless, Wang's wife loved him with the same intensity as on the day they first fell in love, twenty years ago. Anxiously, she turned the pages of Lu Fei.

Wang was not as critically ill as she imagined; but she was frightened by his distorted features, his sweating body, his groans of distress. Watching him lying there, helpless and in agony, she could not help remembering the slim, virile husband of her youth; she was overcome with pity and compassion.

And then she discovered, in the book of Lu Fei, a remedy for his disorder that could be resorted to when all else had failed.

It was around midnight when she prepared the vital potion—a potion prepared with selfless love and compassion. And it was almost dawn when, weak and exhausted, she brought him the potion mixed in a soup.

Wang felt no inclination for a bowl of soup at 5 a.m. He had with difficulty snatched a few hours of sleep, and his wife's interruption made him irritable.

'Must I drink this filth?' he complained. 'What is it anyway?'

'Never mind what it is,' she coaxed. 'It will give you strength and remove your pain.'

'But what's in it?' persisted Wang. 'Of what is it made?'

'Of love,' said his wife. 'It is recommended in the book of Lu Fei. He says it is the best of all remedies, and cannot fail.' She held the bowl to her husband's lips.

He drank hurriedly to get it over with, and only when he was halfway through the bowl did he suspect that something was wrong. It was his wife's terrible condition that made him sit up in bed, thrusting the bowl away. A terrible suspicion formed in his mind.

'Do not deceive me,' he demanded. 'Tell me at once—what is this potion made of?'

She told him then; and when Wang Chei heard her confession, he knelt before his wife who had by now collapsed on the floor. Seizing the hurricane lantern, he held it to her. Her body was wrapped in a towel, but from her left breast, the region of the heart, blood was oozing through the heavy cloth.

She had read in the book of Lu Fei that only her own flesh and blood could cure her husband; and these she had unflinchingly taken from her soft and generous bosom.

You were right, Lu Fei, old sage. What more potent ingredients are there than love and compassion?

HANGING AT THE MANGO-TOPE

❧

THE TWO CAPTIVE POLICEMEN, Inspector Hukam Singh and Sub-Inspector Guler Singh, were being pushed unceremoniously along the dusty, deserted, sun-drenched road. The people of the village had made themselves scarce. They would reappear only when the dacoits went away.

The leader of the dacoit gang was Mangal Singh Bundela, great-grandson of a Pindari adventurer who had been a thorn in the side of the British. Mangal was doing his best to be a thorn in the flesh of his own government. The local police force had been strengthened recently but it was still inadequate for dealing with the dacoits who knew the ravines better than any surveyor. The dacoit Mangal had made a fortune out of ransom. His chief victims were the sons of wealthy industrialists, money-lenders and landowners. But today he had captured two police officials; of no value as far as ransom went, but prestigious prisoners who could be put to other uses . . . .

Mangal Singh wanted to show off in front of the police. He would kill at least one of them—his reputation demanded it but he would let the other go, in order that his legendary power and ruthlessness be given maximum publicity. A legend is always a help!

His red and green turban was tied rakishly to one side. His dhoti extended right down to his ankles. His slippers were embroidered with gold and silver thread. His weapon was not ancient matchlock but a well-greased .303 rifle. Two of his men had similar rifles. Some had revolvers. Only the smaller fry carried swords or country-made pistols. Mangal Singh's gang, though traditional in many ways, was up-to-date in the matter of weapons. Right now they had the policemen's guns too.

'Come along, Inspector Sahib,' said Mangal Singh, in tones of police barbarity, tugging at the rope that encircled the stout Inspector's midriff. 'Had you captured me today, you would have been a hero. You would have taken all the credit even though you could not keep up with your men in the ravines. Too bad you chose to remain sitting in your jeep with the Sub-Inspector. The jeep will be useful to us. You will not. But I would like you to be a hero all the same and there is none better than a dead hero!'

Mangal Singh's followers doubled up with laughter. They loved their leader's cruel sense of humour.

'As for you, Guler Singh,' he continued, giving his attention to the Sub-Inspector, 'you are a man from my own village. You should having joined me long ago. But you were never to be trusted. You thought there would be better pickings in the police, didn't you?'

Guler Singh said nothing, simply hung his head and wondered what his fate would be. He felt certain that Mangal Singh would devise some diabolical and fiendish method of dealing with his captives. Guler Singh's only hope was Constable Ghanshyam, who hadn't been caught by the dacoits because, at the time of the ambush, he had been in the bushes relieving himself.

'To the mango-tope,' said Mangal Singh, prodding the policemen forward.

'Listen to me, Mangal,' said the perspiring Inspector, who was ready to try anything to get out of his predicament. 'Let me go and I give you my word there'll be no trouble for you in this area as long as I am posted here. What could be more convenient than that?'

'Nothing,' said Mangal Singh. 'But your word isn't good. *My* word is different. I have told my men that I will hang you at the mango-tope and I mean to keep my word. But I believe in fair play—I like a little sport! You may yet go free if your friend here, Sub-Inspector Guler Singh, has his wits about him.'

The Inspector and his subordinate exchanged doubtful puzzled looks. They were not to remain puzzled for long. On reaching the mango-tope, the dacoits produced a good strong

hempen rope, one end looped into a slip-knot. Many a garland
of marigolds had the Inspector received during his mediocre
career. Now, for the first time, he was being garlanded with a
hangman's noose. He had seen hangings, he had rather enjoyed
them, but he had no stomach for his own. The Inspector
begged for mercy. Who wouldn't have in his position?

'Be quiet,' commanded Mangal Singh. 'I do not want to
know about your wife and your children and the manner in
which they will starve. You shot my son last year.'

'Not I!' cried the Inspector. 'It was some other.'

'You led the party. But now, just to show you that I'm a
sporting fellow, I am going to have you strung up from this
tree and then I am going to give Guler Singh six shots with a
rifle, and if he can sever the rope that suspends you before you
are dead, well then, you can remain alive and I will let you go!
For your sake I hope the Sub-Inspector's aim is good. He will
have to shoot fast. My man Phambiri, who has made this
noose, was once executioner in a city jail. He guarantees that
you won't last more than fifteen seconds at the end of *his* rope.'

Guler Singh was taken to a spot about forty yards away. A
rifle was thrust into his hands. Two dacoits clambered into the
branches of the mango tree. The Inspector, his hands tied
behind, could only gaze at them in horror. His mouth opened
and shut as though he already had need of more air. And then,
suddenly, the rope went taut, up went the Inspector, his throat
caught in a vice, while the branch of the tree shook and
mango-blossoms fluttered to the ground. The Inspector dangled
from the rope, his feet about three feet above the ground.

'You can shoot,' said Mangal Singh, nodding to the Sub-
Inspector.

And Guler Singh, his hands trembling a little, raised the
rifle to his shoulder and fired three shots in rapid succession.
But the rope was swinging violently and the Inspector's body
was jerking about like a fish on a hook. The bullets went wide.

Guler Singh found the magazine empty. He reloaded, wiped
the stinging sweat from his eyes, raised the rifle again, took
more careful aim. His hands were steadier now. He rested the
sights on the upper portion of the rope, where there was less
motion. Normally he was a good shot but he had never been
asked to demonstrate his skill in circumstances such as these.

The Inspector still gyrated at the end of his rope. There was life in him yet. His face was purple. The world, in those choking moments, was a medley of upside-down roofs and a red sun spinning slowly towards him.

Guler Singh's rifle cracked again. An inch or two wide this time. But the fifth shot found its mark, sending small tuffs of rope winging into the air.

The shot did not sever the rope; it was only a nick.

Guler Singh had one shot left. He was quite calm. The rifle-sight followed the rope's swing, less agitated now that the Inspector's convulsions were lessening. Guler Singh felt sure he could sever the rope this time.

And then, as his finger touched the trigger, an odd, disturbing thought slipped into his mind, stayed there, throbbing. 'Whose life are you trying to save? Hukam Singh has stood in the way of your promotion more than once. He had you charge-sheeted for accepting fifty rupees from an unlicensed rickshaw-puller. He makes you do all the dirty work, blames you when things go wrong, takes the credit when there is credit to be taken. But for him, you'd be an Inspector!'

The rope swayed slightly to the right. The rifle moved just a fraction to the left. The last shot rang out, clipping a sliver of bark from the mango tree.

The Inspector was dead when they cut him down.

'Bad luck,' said Mangal Singh Bundela. 'You nearly saved him. But the next time I catch up with you, Guler Singh, it will be your turn to hang from the mango tree. So keep well away! You know that I am a man of my word. I keep it now by giving you your freedom.'

A few minutes later the party of dacoits had melted away into the late afternoon shadows of the scrub forest. There was the sound of a jeep starting up. Then silence—a silence so profound that it seemed to be shouting in Guler Singh's ears.

As the village people began to trickle out of their houses, Constable Ghanshyam appeared as if from nowhere, swearing that he had lost his way in the jungle. Several people had seen the incident from their windows. They were unanimous in praising the Sub-Inspector for his brave attempt to save his superior's life. He had done his best.

'It is true,' thought Guler Singh. 'I did my best.'

That moment of hesitation before the last shot, the question that had suddenly reared up in the darkness of his mind, had already gone from his memory. We remember only what we want to remember.

'I did my best,' he told everyone.

And so he had.

EYES OF THE CAT

ஃ

HER EYES SEEMED FLECKED with gold when the sun was on them. And as the sun set over the mountains, drawing a deep red wound across the sky, there was more than gold in Binya's eyes. There was anger; for she had been cut to the quick by some remarks her teacher had made—the culmination of weeks of insults and taunts.

Binya was poorer than most of the girls in her class and could not afford the tuitions that had become almost obligatory if one was to pass and be promoted. 'You'll have to spend another year in the ninth,' said Madam. 'And if you don't like that, you can find another school—a school where it won't matter if your blouse is torn and your tunic is old and your shoes are falling apart.' Madam had shown her large teeth in what was supposed to be a good-natured smile, and all the girls had tittered dutifully. Sycophancy had become part of the curriculum in Madam's private academy for girls.

On the way home in the gathering gloom, Binya's two companions commiserated with her.

'She's a mean old thing,' said Usha. 'She doesn't care for anyone but herself.'

'Her laugh reminds me of a donkey braying,' said Sunita, who was more forthright.

But Binya wasn't really listening. Her eyes were fixed on some point in the far distance, where the pines stood in silhouette against a night sky that was growing brighter every moment. The moon was rising, a full moon, a moon that meant something very special to Binya, that made her blood tingle and her skin prickle and her hair glow and send out sparks. Her steps seemed to grow lighter, her limbs more sinewy as she moved gracefully, softly over the mountain path.

Abruptly she left her companions at a fork in the road.

'I'm taking the short cut through the forest,' she said.

Her friends were used to her sudden whims. They knew she was not afraid of being alone in the dark. But Binya's moods made them feel a little nervous, and now, holding hands, they hurried home along the open road.

The short cut took Binya through the dark oak forest. The crooked, tormented branches of the oaks threw twisted shadows across the path. A jackal howled at the moon; a nightjar called from the bushes. Binya walked fast, not out of fear but from urgency, and her breath came in short, sharp gasps. Bright moonlight bathed the hillside when she reached her home on the outskirts of the village.

Refusing her dinner, she went straight to her small room and flung the window open. Moonbeams crept over the window-sill and over her arms which were already covered with golden hair. Her strong nails had shredded the rotten wood of the window-sill.

Tail swishing and ears pricked, the tawny leopard came swiftly out of the window, crossed the open field behind the house, and melted into the shadows.

A little later it padded silently through the forest.

Although the moon shone brightly on the tin-roofed town, the leopard knew where the shadows were deepest and merged beautifully with them. An occasional intake of breath, which resulted in a short rasping cough, was the only sound it made.

Madam was returning from dinner at a ladies' club, called the Kitten Club as a sort of foil to the husbands' club affiliations. There were still a few people in the street, and while no one could help noticing Madam, who had the contours of a steam-roller, none saw or heard the predator who had slipped down a side alley and reached the steps of the teacher's house. It sat there silently, waiting with all the patience of an obedient schoolgirl.

When Madam saw the leopard on her steps, she dropped

her handbag and opened her mouth to scream; but her voice would not materialize. Nor would her tongue ever be used again, either to savour chicken biryani or to pour scorn upon her pupils, for the leopard had sprung at her throat, broken her neck, and dragged her into the bushes.

In the morning, when Usha and Sunita set out for school, they stopped as usual at Binya's cottage and called out to her.

Binya was sitting in the sun, combing her long black hair.

'Aren't you coming to school today, Binya?' asked the girls.

'No, I won't bother to go today,' said Binya. She felt lazy, but pleased with herself, like a contented cat.

'Madam won't be pleased,' said Usha. 'Shall we tell her you're sick?'

'It won't be necessary,' said Binya, and gave them one of her mysterious smiles. 'I'm sure it's going to be a holiday.'

A Crow for All Seasons

8◆

Eᴀʀʟʏ ᴛᴏ ʙᴇᴅ ᴀɴᴅ early to rise makes a crow healthy, wealthy and wise.

They say it's true for humans too. I'm not so sure about that. But for crows it's a must.

I'm always up at the crack of dawn, often the first crow to break the night's silence with a lusty caw. My friends and relatives, who roost in the same tree, grumble a bit and mutter to themselves, but they are soon cawing just as loudly. Long before the sun is up, we set off on the day's work.

We do not pause even for the morning wash. Later in the day, if it's hot and muggy, I might take a dip in some human's bath water; but early in the morning we like to be up and about before everyone else. This is the time when trash cans and refuse dumps are overflowing with goodies, and we like to sift through them before the dustmen arrive in their disposal trucks.

Not that we are afraid of a famine in refuse. As human beings multiply, so does their rubbish.

Only yesterday I rescued an old typewriter ribbon from the dustbin, just before it was emptied. What a waste that would have been! I had no use for it myself, but I gave it to one of my cousins who got married recently, and she tells me it's just right for her nest, the one she's building on a telegraph pole. It helps her bind the twigs together, she says.

My own preference is for toothbrushes. They're just a hobby, really, like stamp-collecting with humans. I have a small but select collection which I keep in a hole in the garden wall.

Don't ask me how many I've got—crows don't believe there's any point in counting beyond *two*—but I know there's more than *one*, that there's a whole lot of them in fact, because there isn't anyone living on this road who hasn't lost a toothbrush to me at some time or another.

We crows living in the jackfruit tree have this stretch of road to ourselves, but so that we don't quarrel or have misunderstandings we've shared the houses out. I picked the bungalow with the orchard at the back. After all, I don't eat rubbish and throwaways all the time. Just occasionally I like a ripe guava or the soft flesh of a papaya. And sometimes I like the odd beetle as an *hors d'oeuvre*. Those humans in the bungalow should be grateful to me for keeping down the population of fruit-eating beetles, and even for recycling their refuse; but no, humans are never grateful. No sooner do I settle in one of their guava trees than stones are whizzing past me. So I return to the dustbin on the back veranda steps. They don't mind my being there.

One of my cousins shares the bungalow with me, but he's a lazy fellow and I have to do most of the foraging. Sometimes I get him to lend me a claw, but most of the time he's preening his feathers and trying to look handsome for a pretty young thing who lives in the banyan tree at the next turning.

When he's in the mood he can be invaluable, as he proved recently when I was having some difficulty getting at the dog's food on the veranda.

This dog who is fussed over so much by the humans I've adopted is a great big fellow, a mastiff who pretends to a pedigree going back to the time of Genghis Khan—he likes to pretend one of his ancestors was the great Khan's watchdog—but, as often happens in famous families, animal or human, there is a falling off in quality over a period of time, and this huge fellow—Tiger, they call him—is a case in point. All brawn and no brain. Many's the time I've removed a juicy bone from his plate or helped myself to pickings from under his nose.

But of late he's been growing canny and selfish. He doesn't like to share any more. And the other day I was almost in his jaws when he took a sudden lunge at me. Snap went his great teeth; but all he got was one of my tail feathers. He spat it out in disgust. Who wants crow's meat, anyway?

All the same, I thought, I'd better not be too careless. It's not for nothing that a crow's IQ is way above that of all other birds. And it's higher than a dog's, I bet.

I woke Cousin Slow from his midday siesta and said, 'Hey, Slow, we've got a problem. If you want any of that delicious tripe today, you've got to lend a claw—or a beak. That dog's getting snappier day by day.'

Slow opened one eye and said, 'Well, if you insist. But you know how I hate getting into a scuffle. It's bad for the gloss on my feathers.'

'I don't insist,' I said politely, 'but I'm not foraging for both of us today. It's every crow for himself.'

'Okay, okay, I'm coming,' said Slow, and with barely a flap he dropped down from the tree to the wall.

'What's the strategy?' I asked.

'Simple. We'll just give him the old one-two.'

We flew across to the veranda. Tiger had just started his meal. He was a fast, greedy eater who made horrible slurping sounds while he guzzled his food. We had to move fast if we wanted to get something before the meal was over.

I sidled up to Tiger and wished him good afternoon.

He kept on gobbling—but quicker now.

Slow came up from behind and gave him a quick peck near the tail—a sensitive spot—and, as Tiger swung round, snarling, I moved in quickly and snatched up several tidbits.

Tiger went for me, and I flew free-style for the garden wall. The dish was untended, so Slow helped himself to as many scraps as he could stuff in his mouth.

He joined me on the garden wall, and we sat there feasting, while Tiger barked himself hoarse below.

'Go catch a cat,' said Slow, who is given to slang. 'You're in the wrong league, big boy.'

The great sage Pratyasataka—ever heard of him? I guess not—once said, 'Nothing can improve a crow.'

Like most human sages, he wasn't very clear in his thinking, so that there has been some misunderstanding about what he meant. Humans like to think that what he really meant was that crows were so bad as to be beyond improvement. But we crows know better. We interpret the saying as meaning that the crow is so perfect that no improvement is possible.

It's not that we aren't human—what I mean is, there are times when we fall from our high standards and do rather foolish things. Like at lunch time the other day.

Sometimes, when the table is laid in the bungalow, and before the family enters the dining room, I nip in through the open window and make a quick foray among the dishes. Sometimes I'm lucky enough to pick up a sausage or a slice of toast, or even a pat of butter, making off before someone enters and throws a bread knife at me. But on this occasion, just as I was reaching for the toast, a thin slouching fellow—Junior sahib they call him—entered suddenly and shouted at me. I was so startled that I leapt across the table seeking shelter. Something flew at me, and in an effort to dodge the missile I put my head through a circular object and then found it wouldn't come off.

It wasn't safe to hang around there, so I flew out the window with this dashed ring still round my neck.

Serviette or napkin rings, that's what they are called. Quite unnecessary objects, but some humans—particularly the well-to-do sort—seem to like having them on their tables, holding bits of cloth in place. The cloth is used for wiping the mouth. Have you ever heard of such nonsense?

Anyway, there I was with a fat napkin ring round my neck, and as I perched on the wall trying to get it off, the entire human family gathered on their veranda to watch me.

There was the Colonel sahib and his wife, the memsahib; there was the scrawny Junior sahib (worst of the lot); there was a mischievous boy (the Colonel sahib's grandson) known as the Baba; and there was the cook (who usually flung orange peels at me) and the gardener (who once tried to decapitate me with a spade), and the dog Tiger who, like most dogs, tries unsuccessfully to be human.

Today they weren't cursing and shaking their fists at me; they were just standing and laughing their heads off. What's so funny above a crow with its head stuck in a napkin ring?

Worse was to follow.

The noise had attracted the other crows in the area, and if there's one thing crows detest, it's a crow who doesn't look like a crow.

They swooped low and dived on me, hammering at the wretched napkin ring, until they had knocked me off the wall and into a flower-bed. Then six or seven toughs landed on me with every intention of finishing me off.

'Hey, boys!' I cawed. 'This is me, Speedy! What are you trying to do—kill me?'

'That's right! You don't look like Speedy to us. What have you done with him, hey?'

And they set upon me with even greater vigour.

'You're just like a bunch of lousy humans!' I shouted. 'You're no better than them—this is just the way they carry on amongst themselves!'

That brought them to a halt. They stopped trying to peck me to pieces, and stood back, looking puzzled. The napkin ring had been shattered in the onslaught and had fallen to the ground.

'Why, it's Speedy!' said one of the gang.

'None other!'

'Good old Speedy—what are you doing here? And where's the guy we were hammering just now?'

There was no point in trying to explain things to them. Crows are like that. They're all good pals—until one of them tries to look different. Then he could be just another bird.

'He took off for Tibet,' I said. 'It was getting unhealthy for him around here.'

Summertime is here again. And although I'm a crow for all seasons, I must admit to a preference for the summer months.

Humans grow lazy and don't pursue me with so much vigour. Garbage cans overflow. Food goes bad and is constantly being thrown away. Overripe fruit gets tastier by the minute. If fellows like me weren't around to mop up all these unappreciated riches, how would humans manage?

There's one character in the bungalow, the Junior sahib, who will never appreciate our services, it seems. He simply hates crows. The small boy may throw stones at us occasionally, but then, he's the sort who throws stones at almost anything. There's nothing personal about it. He just throws stones on principle.

The memsahib is probably the best of the lot. She often throws me scraps from the kitchen—onionskins, potato peels, crusts, and leftovers—and even when I nip in and make off with something *not* meant for me (like a jam tart or a cheese pakora) she is quite sporting about it. The Junior sahib looks outraged, but the lady of the house says, 'Well, we've all got to make a living somehow, and that's how crows make theirs. It's high time *you* thought of earning a living.' Junior sahib's her nephew—that's his occupation. He has never been known to work.

The Colonel sahib has a sense of humor but it's often directed at me. He thinks I'm a comedian.

He discovered I'd been making off with the occasional egg from the egg basket on the veranda, and one day, without my knowledge, he made a substitution.

Right on top of the pile I found a smooth round egg, and before anyone could shout 'Crow!' I'd made off with it. It was abnormally light. I put it down on the lawn and set about cracking it with my strong beak, but it would keep slipping away or bounding off into the bushes. Finally I got it between my feet and gave it a good hard whack. It burst open, to my utter astonishment there was nothing inside!

I looked up and saw the old man standing on the veranda, doubled up with laughter.

'What are you laughing at?' asked the memsahib, coming out to see what it was all about.

'It's that ridiculous crow!' guffawed the Colonel, pointing at me. 'You know he's been stealing our eggs. Well, I placed a ping pong ball on top of the pile, and he fell for it! He's been struggling with that ball for twenty minutes! That will teach him a lesson.'

It did. But I had my revenge later, when I pinched a brand new toothbrush from the Colonel's bathroom.

The Junior sahib has no sense of humour at all. He idles about the house and grounds all day, whistling or singing to himself.

'Even that crow sings better than Uncle,' said the boy.

A truthful boy; but all he got for his honesty was a whack on the head from his uncle.

Anyway, as a gesture of appreciation, I perched on the garden wall and gave the family a rendering of my favourite crow song, which is my own composition. Here it is, translated for your benefit:

> *Oh, for the life of a crow!*
> *A bird who's in the know.*
> *Although we are cursed,*
> *We are never dispersed—*
> *We're always on the go!*
>
> *I know I'm a bit of a rogue*
> *(And my voice wouldn't pass for a brogue),*
> *But there's no one as sleek*
> *Or as neat with his beak—*
> *So they're putting my picture in Vogue!*
>
> *Oh, for the life of a crow!*
> *I reap what I never sow,*
> *They call me a thief—*
> *Pray I'll soon come to grief—*
> *But there's no getting rid of a crow!*

I gave it everything I had, and the humans— all of them on the lawn to enjoy the evening breeze, listened to me in silence, struck with wonder at my performance.

When I had finished, I bowed and preened myself, waiting for the applause.

They stared at each other for a few seconds. Then the Junior sahib stooped, picked up a bottle opener, and flung it at me.

Well, I ask you!

What can one say about humans? I do my best to defend them from all kinds of criticism, and this is what I get for my pains.

Anyway, I picked up the bottle opener and added it to my collection of odds and ends.

It was getting dark, and soon everyone was stumbling around, looking for another bottle opener. Junior sahib's popularity was even lower than mine.

One day Junior sahib came home carrying a heavy shotgun. He pointed it at me a few times and I dived for cover. But he didn't fire. Probably I was out of range.

'He's only threatening you,' said Slow from the safety of the jamun tree, where he sat in the shadows. 'He probably doesn't known how to fire the thing.'

But I wasn't taking any chances. I'd seen a sly look on Junior sahib's face, and I decided that he was trying to make me careless. So I stayed well out of range.

Then one evening I received a visit from my cousin, Charm. He'd come to me for a loan. He wanted some new bottle tops for his collection and had brought me a mouldy old toothbrush to offer in exchange.

Charm landed on the garden wall, toothbrush in his break, and was waiting for me to join him there, when there was a flash and a tremendous bank. Charm was sent several feet into the air, and landed limp and dead in a flower-bed.

'I've got him, I've got him!' shouted Junior sahib. 'I've shot that blasted crow!'

Throwing away the gun, Junior sahib ran out into the garden, overcome with joy. He picked up my fallen relative, and began running around the bungalow with his trophy.

The rest of the family had collected on the veranda.

'Drop that thing at once!' called the memsahib.

'Uncle is doing a war dance,' observed the boy.

'It's unlucky to shoot a crow,' said the Colonel.

I thought it was time to take a hand in the proceedings and let everyone know that the *right* crow—the one and only Speedy—was alive and kicking. So I swooped down the jackfruit tree, dived through Junior sahib's window, and emerged with one of his socks.

Triumphantly flaunting his dead crow, Junior sahib came dancing up the garden path, then stopped dead when he saw me perched on the window-sill, a sock in my beak. His jaw fell, his eyes bulged; he looked like the owl in the banyan tree.

'You shot the wrong crow!' shouted the Colonel, and everyone roared with laughter.

Before Junior sahib could recover from the shock, I took off in a leisurely fashion and joined Slow on the wall.

Junior sahib came rushing out with the gun, but by now it

was too dark to see anything, and I heard the memsahib telling the Colonel, 'You'd better take that gun away before he does himself a mischief.' So the Colonel took Junior indoors and gave him a brandy.

I composed a new song for Junior sahib's benefit, and sang it to him outside his window early next morning:

> *I understand you want a crow*
> *To poison, shoot or smother;*
> *My fond salaams, but by your leave*
> *I'll substitute another;*
> *Allow me then, to introduce*
> *My most respected brother.*

Although I was quite understanding about the whole tragic mix-up—I was, after all, the family's very own house-crow—my fellow crows were outraged at what happened to Charm, and swore vengeance on Junior sahib.

'*Carvus splendens!*' they shouted with great spirit, forgetting that this title had been bestowed on us by a human.

In times of war, we forget how much we owe to our enemies.

Junior sahib had only to step into the garden, and several crows would swoop down on him, screeching and swearing and aiming lusty blows at his head and hands. He took to coming out wearing a sola-topee, and even then they knocked it off and drove him indoors. Once he tried lighting a cigarette on the veranda steps, when Show swooped low across the porch and snatched it from his lips.

Junior sahib shut himself up in his room, and smoked countless cigarettes—a sure sign that his nerves were going to pieces.

Every now and then the memsahib would come out and shoo us off; and because she wasn't an enemy, we obliged by retreating to the garden wall. After all, Slow and I depended on her for much of our board if not for our lodging. But Junior sahib had only to show his face outside the house, and all the crows in the area would be after him like avenging furies.

'It doesn't look as though they are going to forgive you,' said the memsahib.

'Elephants never forget, and crows never forgive,' said the Colonel.

'Would you like to borrow my catapult, Uncle?' asked the boy. 'Just for self-protection, you know.'

'Shut up,' said Junior sahib and went to bed.

One day he sneaked out of the back door and dashed across to the garage. A little later the family's old car, seldom used, came out of the garage with Junior sahib at the wheel. He'd decided that if he couldn't take a walk in safety he'd go for a drive. All the windows were up.

No sooner had the car turned into the driveway than about a dozen crows dived down on it, crowding the bonnet and flapping in front of the windscreen. Junior sahib couldn't see a thing. He swung the steering wheel left, right and centre, and the car went off the driveway, ripped through a hedge, crushed a bed of sweetpeas and came to a stop against the trunk of a mango tree.

Junior sahib just sat there, afraid to open the door. The family had to come out of the house and rescue him.

'Are you all right?' asked the Colonel.

'I've bruised my knees,' said Junior sahib.

'Never mind your knees,' said the memsahib, gazing around at the ruin of her garden. 'What about my sweetpeas?'

'I think your uncle is going to have a nervous breakdown,' I heard the Colonel saying.

'What's that?' asked the boy. 'Is it the same as a car having a breakdown?'

'Well—not exactly . . . . . But you could call it a mind breaking up.'

Junior sahib had been refusing to leave his room or take his meals. The family was worried about him. I was worried, too. Believe it or not, we crows are among the very few who sincerely desire the preservation of the human species.

'He needs a change,' said the memsahib.

'A rest cure,' said the Colonel sarcastically. 'A rest from doing nothing.'

'Send him to Switzerland,' suggested the boy.

'We can't afford that. But we can take him up to a hill station.'

The nearest hill station was some fifty miles as the human

drives (only ten as the crow flies). Many people went up during the summer months. It wasn't fancied much by crows. For one thing, it was a tidy sort of place, and people lived in houses that were set fairly far apart. Opportunities for scavenging were limited. Also it was rather cold and the trees were inconvenient and uncomfortable. A friend of mine who had spent a night in a pine tree said he hadn't been able to sleep because of prickly pine needles and the wind howling through the branches.

'Let's all go up for a holiday,' said the memsahib. 'We can spend a week in a boarding house. All of us need a change.'

A few days later the house was locked up, and the family piled into the old car and drove off to the hills.

I had the grounds to myself.

The dog had gone too, and the gardener spent all day dozing in his hammock. There was no one around to trouble me.

'We've got the whole place to ourselves,' I told Slow.

'Yes, but what good is that? With everyone gone, there are no throwaways, give-aways and take-aways!'

'We'll have to try the house next door.'

'And be driven off by the other crows? That's not our territory, you know. We can go across to help them, or to ask for their help, but we're not supposed to take their pickings. It just isn't cricket, old boy.'

We could have tried the bazaar or the railway station, where there is always a lot of rubbish to be found, but there is also a lot of competition in those places. The station crows are gangsters. The bazaar crows are bullies. Slow and I had grown soft. We'd have been no match for the bad boys.

'I've just realized how much we depend on humans,' I said.

'We could go back to living in the jungle,' said Slow.

'No, that would be too much like hard work. We'd be living on wild fruit most of the time. Besides, the jungle crows won't have anything to do with us now. Ever since we took up with humans, we became the outcasts of the bird world.'

'That means we're almost human.'

'You might say we have all their vices and none of their virtues.'

'Just a different set of values, old boy.'

'Like eating hens' eggs instead of crows' eggs. That's *something* in their favour. And while you're hanging around here waiting for the mangoes to fall, I'm off to locate our humans.'

Slow's beak fell open. He looked like—well, a hungry crow.

'Don't tell me you're going to follow them up to the hill station? You don't even know where they are staying.'

'I'll soon find out,' I said, and took off for the hills.

You'd be surprised at how simple it is to be a good detective, if only you put your mind to it. Of course, if Ellery Queen had been able to fly, he wouldn't have required fifteen chapters and his father's assistance to crack a case.

Swooping low over the hill station, it wasn't long before I spotted my humans' old car. It was parked outside a boarding house called the Climber's Rest. I hadn't seen anyone climbing, but dozing in an armchair in the garden was my favourite human.

I perched on top of a colourful umbrella and waited for Junior sahib to wake up. I decided it would be rather inconsiderate of me to disturb his sleep, so I waited patiently on the brolly, looking at him with one eye and keeping one eye on the house. He stirred uneasily, as though he'd suddenly had a bad dream; then he opened his eyes. I must have been the first thing he saw.

'Good morning,' I cawed, in a friendly tone—always ready to forgive and forget, that's Speedy!

He leapt out of the armchair and ran into the house, hollering at the top of his voice.

I supposed he hadn't been able to contain his delight at seeing me again. Humans can be funny that way. They'll hate you one day and love you the next.

Well, Junior sahib ran all over the boarding house, screaming: 'It's that crow, it's that crow! He's following me everywhere!'

Various people, including the family, ran outside to see what the commotion was about, and I thought it would be better to make myself scarce. So I flew to the top of a spruce tree and stayed very still and quiet.

'Crow! What crow?' said the Colonel.

'Our crow!' cried Junior sahib. 'The one that persecutes me.

I was dreaming of it just now, and when I opened my eyes, there it was, on the garden umbrella!'

'There's nothing there now,' said the memsahib. 'You probably hadn't woken up completely.'

'He is having illusions again,' said the boy.

'Delusions,' corrected the Colonel.

'Now look here,' said the memsahib, 'you'll have to pull yourself together. You'll take leave of your senses if you don't.'

'I tell you, it's here!' sobbed Junior sahib. 'It's following me everywhere.'

'It's grown fond of Uncle,' said the boy. 'And it seems Uncle can't live without crows.'

Junior sahib looked up with a wild glint in his eye.

'That's it!' he cried. 'I can't live without them. That's the answer to my problem. I don't hate crows—I love them!'

Everyone just stood around goggling at Junior sahib.

'I'm feeling fine now,' he carried on. 'What a difference it makes if you can just do the opposite of what you've been doing before! I thought I hated crows. But all the time I really loved them!' And flapping his arms, and trying to caw like a crow, he went prancing about the garden.

'Now he thinks he's a crow,' said the boy. 'Is he still having delusions?'

'That's right,' said the memsahib. 'Delusions of grandeur.'

After that, the family decided that there was no point in staying on in the hill station any longer. Junior sahib had completed his rest cure. And even if he was the only one who believed himself cured, that was all right, because after all he was the one who mattered . . . . If you're feeling fine, can there be anything wrong with you?

No sooner was everyone back in the bungalow than Junior sahib took to hopping barefoot on the grass early every morning, all the time scattering food about for the crows. Bread, chappattis, cooked rice, curried eggplants, the memsahib's homemade toffee—you name it, we got it!

Slow and I were the first to help ourselves to these dawn offerings, and soon the other crows had joined us on the lawn. We didn't mind. Junior sahib brought enough for everyone.

'We ought to honour him in some way,' said Slow.

'Yes, why not?' said I. 'There was someone else, hundreds

of years ago, who fed the birds. They followed him wherever he went.'

'That's right. They made him a saint. But as far as I know, he didn't feed any crows. At least, you don't see any crows in the pictures—just sparrows and robins and wagtails.'

'Small fry. *Our* human is dedicated exclusively to crows. Do you realize that, Slow?'

'Sure. We ought to make him the patron saint of crows. What do you say, fellows?'

'Caw, caw, caw!' All the crows were in agreement.

'St Corvus!' said Slow, as Junior sahib emerged from the house, laden with good things to eat.

'Corvus, corvus, corvus!' we cried.

And what a pretty picture he made—a crow eating from his hand, another perched on his shoulder, and about a dozen of us on the grass, forming a respectful ring around him.

From persecutor to protector; from beastliness to saintliness. And sometimes it can be the other way round: you never know with humans!

A Tiger in the House

TIMOTHY, THE TIGER-CUB, WAS discovered by Grandfather on a hunting expedition in the Terai jungle near Dehra.

Grandfather was no shikari, but as he knew the forests of the Siwalik hills better than most people, he was persuaded to accompany the party—it consisted of several Very Important Persons from Delhi—to advise on the terrain and the direction the beaters should take once a tiger had been spotted.

The camp itself was sumptuous—seven large tents (one for each shikari), a dining-tent, and a number of servants' tents. The dinner was very good, as Grandfather admitted afterwards; it was not often that one saw hot-water plates, finger-glasses, and seven or eight courses, in a tent in the jungle! But that was how things were done in the days of the Viceroys . . . . There were also some fifteen elephants, four of them with howdahs for the shikaris, and the others specially trained for taking part in the beat.

The sportsmen never saw a tiger, nor did they shoot anything else, though they saw a number of deer, peacock, and wild boar. They were giving up all hope of finding a tiger, and were beginning to shoot at jackals, when Grandfather, strolling down the forest path at some distance from the rest of the party, discovered a little tiger about eighteen inches long, hiding among the intricate roots of a banyan tree. Grandfather picked him up, and brought him home after the camp had broken up. He had the distinction of being the only member of the party to have bagged any game, dead or alive.

At first the tiger cub, who was named Timothy by

Grandmother, was brought up entirely on milk given to him in a feeding-bottle by our cook, Mahmoud. But the milk proved too rich for him, and he was put on a diet of raw mutton and cod liver oil, to be followed later by a more tempting diet of pigeons and rabbits.

Timothy was provided with two companions—Toto the monkey, who was bold enough to pull the young tiger by the tail, and then climb up the curtains if Timothy lost his temper; and a small mongrel puppy, found on the road by Grandfather.

At first Timothy appeared to be quite afraid of the puppy, and darted back with a spring if it came too near. He would make absurd dashes at it with his large forepaws, and then retreat to a ridiculously safe distance. Finally, he allowed the puppy to crawl on his back and rest there!

One of Timothy's favourite amusements was to stalk anyone who would play with him, and so, when I came to live with Grandfather, I became one of the tiger's favourites. With a crafty look in his glittering eyes, and his body crouching, he would creep closer and closer to me, suddenly making a dash for my feet, rolling over on his back and kicking with delight, and pretending to bite my ankles.

He was by this time the size of a full-grown retriever, and when I took him out for walks, people on the road would give us a wide berth. When he pulled hard on his chain, I had difficulty in keeping up with him. His favourite place in the house was the drawing-room, and he would make himself comfortable on the long sofa, reclining there with great dignity, and snarling at anybody who tried to get him off.

Timothy had clean habits, and would scrub his face with his paws exactly like a cat. He slept at night in the cook's quarters, and was always delighted at being let out by him in the morning.

'One of these days,' declared Grandmother in her prophetic manner, 'we are going to find Timothy sitting on Mahmoud's bed, and no sign of the cook except his clothes and shoes!'

Of course, it never came to that, but when Timothy was about six months old a change came over him; he grew steadily less friendly. When out for a walk with me, he would try to steal away to stalk a cat or someone's pet Pekinese. Sometimes at night we would hear frenzied cackling from the poultry house, and in the morning there would be feathers lying all over the veranda. Timothy had to be chained up more often. And finally, when he began to stalk Mahmoud about the house with what looked like villainous intent, Grandfather decided it was time to transfer him to a zoo.

The nearest zoo was at Lucknow, two hundred miles away. Reserving a first class compartment for himself and Timothy— no one would share a compartment with them—Grandfather took him to Lucknow where the zoo authorities were only too glad to receive as a gift a well-fed and fairly civilized tiger.

About six months later, when my grandparents were visiting relatives in Lucknow, Grandfather took the opportunity of calling at the zoo to see how Timothy was getting on. I was not there to accompany him, but I heard all about it when he returned to Dehra.

Arriving at the zoo, Grandfather made straight for the particular cage in which Timothy had been interned. The tiger was there, crouched in a corner, full-grown and with a magnificent striped coat.

'Hello Timothy!' said Grandfather and, climbing the railing with ease, he put his arm through the bars of the cage.

The tiger approached the bars, and allowed Grandfather to put both hands around his head. Grandfather stroked the tiger's forehead and tickled his ear, and, whenever he growled, smacked him across the mouth, which was his old way of keeping him quiet.

He licked Grandfather's hands and only sprang away when a leopard in the next cage snarled at him. Grandfather 'shooed' the leopard away, and the tiger returned to lick his hands; but every now and then the leopard would rush at the bars, and the tiger would slink back to his corner.

A number of people had gathered to watch the reunion when a keeper pushed his way through the crowd and asked Grandfather what he was doing.

'I'm talking to Timothy,' said Grandfather. 'Weren't you here when I gave him to the zoo six months ago?'

'I haven't been here very long,' said the surprised keeper. 'Please continue your conversation. But I have never been able to touch him myself, he is always very bad tempered.'

'Why don't you put him somewhere else?' suggested Grandfather. 'That leopard keeps frightening him. I'll go and see the Superintendent about it.'

Grandfather went in search of the Superintendent of the zoo, but found that he had gone home early; and so, after wandering about the zoo for a little while, he returned to Timothy's cage to say goodbye. It was beginning to get dark.

He had been stroking and slapping Timothy for about five minutes when he found another keeper observing him with some alarm. Grandfather recognized him as the keeper who had been there when Timothy had first come to the zoo.

'*You* remember me,' said Grandfather. 'Now why don't you transfer Timothy to another cage, away from this stupid leopard?'

'But—sir—' stammered the keeper, 'it is not your tiger.'

'I know, I know,' said Grandfather testily. 'I realize he is no longer mine. But you might at least take a suggestion or two from me.'

'I remember your tiger very well,' said the keeper. 'He died two months ago.'

'Died!' exclaimed Grandfather.

'Yes, sir, of pneumonia. This tiger was trapped in the hills only last month, and he is very dangerous!'

Grandfather could think of nothing to say. The tiger was still licking his arm, with increasing relish. Grandfather took what seemed to him an age to withdraw his hand from the cage.

With his face near the tiger's he mumbled, 'Goodnight, Timothy,' and giving the keeper a scornful look, walked briskly out of the zoo.

TIGER, TIGER, BURNING BRIGHT

ॐ

On the left bank of the Ganga, where it emerges from the Himalayan foothills, there is a long stretch of heavy forest. These are villages on the fringe of the forest, inhabited by bamboo-cutters and farmers, but there are few signs of commerce or pilgrimage. Hunters, however, have found the area an ideal hunting-ground during the last seventy years, and as a result the animals are not as numerous as they used to be. The trees, too, have been disappearing slowly; and, as the forest recedes, the animals lose their food and shelter and move on further into the foothills. Slowly, they are being denied the right to live.

Only the elephant can cross the river. And two years ago, when a large area of forest was cleared to make way for a refugee resettlement camp, a herd of elephants—finding their favourite food, the green shoots of the bamboo, in short supply—waded across the river. They crashed through the suburbs of Hardwar, knocked down a factory wall, pulled down several tin roofs, held up a train, and left a trail of devastation in their wake until they found a new home in a new forest which was still untouched. Here, they settled down to a new life—but an unsettled, wary life. They did not know when men would appear again, with tractors, bulldozers and dynamite.

There was a time when the forest on the banks of the Ganga had provided food and shelter for some thirty or forty tigers; but men in search of trophies had shot them all, and now there remained only one old tiger in the jungle. Many hunters had tried to get him, but he was a wise and crafty old tiger, who knew the ways of men, and he had so far survived all attempts on his life.

Although the tiger had passed the prime of his life, he had lost none of his majesty. His muscles rippled beneath the golden yellow of his coat, and he walked through the long grass with the confidence of one who knew that he was still a king, even though his subjects were fewer. His great head pushed through the foliage, and it was only his tail, swinging high, that showed occasionally above the sea of grass.

In late spring he would head for the large *jheel*, the only water in the forest (if you don't count the river, which was several miles away), which was almost a lake during the rainy season, but just a muddy marsh at this time of the year.

Here, at different times of the day and night, all the animals came to drink—the long-horned sambhar, the delicate chital, the swamp deer, the hyenas and jackals, the wild boar, the panthers—and the lone tiger. Since the elephants had gone, the water was usually clear except when buffaloes from the nearest village came to wallow in it, and then it was very muddy. These buffaloes, though they were not wild, were not afraid of the panther or even of the tiger. They knew the panther was afraid of their massive horns and that the tiger preferred the flesh of the deer.

One day, there were several sambhars at the water's edge; but they did not stay long. The scent of the tiger came with the breeze, and there was no mistaking its strong feline odour. The deer held their heads high for a few moments, their nostrils twitching, and then scattered into the forest, disappearing behind a screen of leaf and bamboo.

When the tiger arrived, there was no other animal near the water. But the birds were still there. The egrets continued to wade in the shallows, and a kingfisher darted low over the water, dived suddenly, a flash of blue and gold, and made off with a slim silver fish, which glistened in the sun like a polished gem. A long brown snake glided in and out among the waterlilies and disappeared beneath a fallen tree which lay rotting in the shallows.

The tiger waited in the shelter of a rock, his ears pricked up for the least unfamiliar sound; he knew that it was at that place that men sometimes sat up for him with guns, for they coveted

his beauty—his stripes, and the gold of his body, his fine teeth,
his whiskers, and his noble head. They would have liked to
hang his skin on a wall, with his head stuffed and mounted,
and pieces of glass replacing his fierce eyes. Then they would
have boasted of their triumph over the king of the jungle.

The tiger had encountered hunters before, so he did not
usually show himself in the open during the day. But of late he
had heard no guns, and if there were hunters around, you
would have heard heir guns (for a man with a gun cannot
resist letting it off, even if it is only at a rabbit—or at another
man). And, besides, the tiger was thirsty.

He was also feeling quite hot. It was March; and the
shimmering dust-haze of summer had come early. Tigers—
unlike other cats—are fond of water, and on a hot day will
wallow in it for hours.

He walked into the water, in amongst the water-lilies, and
drank slowly. He was seldom in a hurry when he ate or drank.
Other animals might bolt down their food, but they are only
other animals. A tiger is a tiger; he has his dignity to preserve
even though he isn't aware of it!

He raised his head and listened, one paw suspended in the
air. A strange sound had come to him on the breeze, and he
was wary of strange sounds. So he moved swiftly into the
shelter of the tall grass that bordered the *jheel*, and climbed a
hillock until he reached his favourite rock. This rock was big
enough both to hide him and to give him shade. Anyone
looking up from the *jheel* would have thought it strange that
the rock had a round bump on the top. The bump was the
tiger's head. He kept it very still.

The sound he heard was only the sound of a flute, rendered
thin and reedy in the forest. It belonged to Ramu, a slim brown
boy who rode a buffalo. Ramu played vigorously on the flute.
Shyam, a slightly smaller boy, riding another buffalo, brought
up the rear of the herd.

There were about eight buffaloes in the herd, and they
belonged to the families of the two friends Ramu and Shyam.
Their people were Gujars, a nomadic community who earned a
livelihood by keeping buffaloes and selling milk and butter.
The boys were about twelve years old, but they could not have
told you exactly because in their village nobody thought

birthdays were important. They were almost the same age as the tiger, but he was old and experienced while they were still cubs.

The tiger had often seen them at the tank, and he was not worried by their presence. He knew the village people would do him no harm as long as he left their buffaloes alone. Once when he was younger and full of bravado, he had killed a buffalo—not because he was hungry, but because he was young and wanted to try out his strength—and after that the villagers had hunted him for days, with spears, bows and an old muzzle-loader. Now he left the buffaloes alone, even though the deer in the forest were not as numerous as before.

The boys knew that a tiger lived in the jungle, for they had often heard him roar; but they did not suspect that he was so near just then.

The tiger gazed down from his rock, and the sight of eight fat black buffaloes made him give a low, throaty moan. But the boys were there. Besides, a buffalo was not easy to kill.

He decided to move on and find a cool shady place in the heart of the jungle where he could rest during the warm afternoon and be free of the flies and mosquitoes that swarmed around the *jheel*. At night he would hunt.

With a lazy, half-humorous roar—'A-oonh!'—he got up off his haunches and sauntered off into the jungle.

Even the gentlest of the tiger's roars can be heard half a mile away, and the boys, who were barely fifty yards away, looked up immediately.

'There he goes!' said Ramu, taking the flute from his lips and pointing it towards the hillocks. He was not afraid, for he knew that this tiger was not interested in humans. 'Did you see him?'

'I saw his tail, just before he disappeared. He's a big tiger!'

'Do not call him tiger. Call him Uncle, or Maharaj.'

'Oh, why?'

'Don't you know that it's unlucky to call a tiger a tiger? My father always told me so. But if you meet a tiger, and call him Uncle, he will leave you alone.'

'I'll try and remember that,' said Shyam.

The buffaloes were now well inside the water, and some of them were lying down in the mud. Buffaloes love soft wet mud and will wallow in it for hours. The slushier the mud the better. Ramu, to avoid being dragged down into the mud with his buffalo, slipped off its back and plunged into the water. He waded to a small islet covered with reeds and water-lilies. Shyam was close behind him.

They lay down on their hard flat stomachs, on a patch of grass, and allowed the warm sun to beat down on their bare brown bodies.

Ramu was the more knowledgeable boy because he had been to Hardwar and Dehra Dun several times with his father. Shyam had never been out of the village.

Shyam said, 'The pool is not so deep this year.'

'We have had no rain since January,' said Ramu. 'If we do not get rain soon the *jheel* may dry up altogether.'

'And then what will we do?'

'We? I don't know. There is a well in the village. But even that may dry up. My father told me that it did once, just about the time I was born, and everyone had to walk ten miles to the river for water.'

'And what about the animals?'

'Some will stay here and die. Others will go to the river. But there are too many people near the river now—and temples, houses and factories—so the animals stay away. And the trees have been cut, so that between the jungle and the river there is no place to hide. Animals are afraid of the open—they are afraid of men with guns.'

'Even at night?'

'At night men come in jeeps, with searchlights. They kill the deer for meat, and sell the skins of tigers and panthers.'

'I didn't know a tiger's skin was worth anything.'

'It's worth more than our skins,' said Ramu knowingly. 'It will fetch six hundred rupees. Who would pay that much for one of us?'

'Our fathers would.'

'True—if they had the money.'

'If my father sold his fields, he would get more than six hundred rupees.'

'True—but if he sold his fields, none of you would have anything to eat. A man needs land as much as a tiger needs a jungle.'

'Yes,' said Shyam. 'And that reminds me—my mother asked me to take some roots home.'

'I will help you.'

They walked deeper into the *jheel* until the water was up to their waists, and began pulling up water-lilies by the roots. The flower is beautiful but the villagers value the root more. When it is cooked, it makes a delicious and nourishing dish. The plant multiples rapidly and is aways in good supply. In the year when famine hit the village, it was only the root of the water-lily that saved many from starvation.

When Shyam and Ramu had finished gathering roots, they emerged from the water and passed the time wrestling with each other, slipping about in the soft mud which soon covered them from head to toe.

To get rid of the mud, they dived into the water again and swam across to their buffaloes. Then, jumping on to their backs and digging their heels into the thick hides, the boys raced them across the *jheel*, shouting and hollering so much that all the birds flew away in fright, and the monkeys set up a shrill chattering of their own in the dhak trees.

In March, the Flame of the Forest, or dhak trees, are ablaze with bright scarlet and orange flowers.

It was evening, and the twilight was fading fast, when the buffalo-herd finally wandered its way homeward, to be greeted outside the village by the barking of dogs, the gurgle of hookah-pipes, and the homely smell of cow-dung smoke.

The tiger made a kill that night—a chital. He made his approach against the wind so that the unsuspecting spotted deer did not see him until it was too late. A blow on the deer's haunches from the tiger's paw brought it down, and then the great beast fastened his fangs on the deer's throat. It was all over in a few minutes. The tiger was too quick and strong, and the deer did not struggle much.

It was a violent end for so gentle a creature. But you must not imagine that in the jungle the deer live in permanent fear of death. It is only man, with his imagination and his fear of the hereafter, who is afraid of dying. In the jungle it is different. Sudden death appears at intervals. Wild creatures do not have to think about it, and so the sudden killing of one of their number by some predator of the forest is only a fleeting incident soon forgotten by the survivors.

The tiger feasted well, growling with pleasure as he ate his way up the body, leaving the entrails. When he had had his night's fill he left the carcass for the vultures and jackals. The cunning old tiger never returned to the same carcass, even if there was still plenty left to eat. In the past, when he had gone back to a kill he had often found a man sitting in a tree waiting up for him with a rifle.

His belly filled, the tiger sauntered over to the edge of the forest and looked out across the sandy wasteland and the deep, singing river at the twinkling lights of Rishikesh on the opposite bank, and raised his head and roared his defiance at mankind.

He was a lonesome bachelor. It was five or six years since he had a mate. She had been shot by the trophy-hunters, and her two cubs had been trapped by men who do trade in wild animals. One went to a circus, where he had to learn tricks to amuse men and respond to the crack of a whip; the other, more fortunate, went first to a zoo in Delhi and was later transferred to a zoo in America.

Sometimes, when the old tiger was very lonely, he gave a great roar, which could be heard throughout the forest. The villagers thought he was roaring in anger, but the jungle knew that he was really roaring out of loneliness. When the sound of his roar had died away, he paused, standing still, waiting for an answering roar; but it never came. It was taken up instead by the shrill scream of a barbet high up in a sal tree.

It was dawn now, dew-fresh and cool, and jungle-dwellers were on the move . . .

The black beady little eyes of a jungle rat were fixed on a small brown hen who was pecking around in the undergrowth near her nest. He had a large family to feed, this rat, and he knew that in the hen's nest was a clutch of delicious fawn-coloured eggs. He waited patiently for nearly an hour before he had the satisfaction of seeing the hen leave her nest and go off in search of food.

As soon as she had gone, the rat lost no time in making his raid. Slipping quietly out of his hole, he slithered along among the leaves; but, clever as he was, he did not realize that his own movements were being watched.

A pair of grey mongooses scouted about in the dry grass. They too were hungry, and eggs usually figured large on their menu. Now, lying still on an outcrop of rock, they watched the rat sneaking along, occasionally sniffing at the air and finally vanishing behind a boulder. When he reappeared, he was struggling to roll an egg uphill towards his hole.

The rat was in difficulty, pushing the egg sometimes with his paws, sometimes with his nose. The ground was rough, and the egg wouldn't move straight. Deciding that the must have help, he scuttled off to call his spouse. Even now the mongooses did not descend on the tantalizing egg. They waited until the rat returned with his wife, and then watched as the male rat took the egg firmly between his forepaws and rolled over on to his back. The female rat then grabbed her mate's tail and began to drag him along.

Totally absorbed in the struggle with the egg, the rat did not hear the approach of the mongooses. When these two large furry visitors suddenly bobbed up from behind a stone, the rats squealed with fright, abandoned the egg, and fled for their lives.

The mongooses wasted no time in breaking open the egg and making a meal of it. But just as, a few minutes ago, the rat had not noticed their approach, so now they did not notice the village boy, carrying a small bright axe and a net bag in his hands, creeping along.

Ramu too was searching for eggs, and when he saw the mongooses busy with one, he stood still to watch them, his eyes roving in search of the nest. He was hoping the mongooses would lead him to the nest; but, when they had finished their meal and made off into the undergrowth, Ramu had to do his own searching. He failed to find the nest, and moved further into the forest. The rat's hopes were just reviving when, to his disgust, the mother hen returned.

Ramu now made his way to a mahua tree.

The flowers of the mahua can be eaten by animals as well as by men. Bears are particularly fond of them and will eat large quantities of flowers which gradually start fermenting in their stomachs with the result that the animals get quite drunk. Ramu had often seen a couple of bears stumbling home to their cave, bumping into each other or into the trunks of trees. They are short-sighted to begin with, and when drunk can hardly see at all. But their sense of smell and hearing are so good that in the end they find their way home.

Ramu decided he would gather some mahua flowers, and climbed up the tree, which is leafless when it blossoms. He began breaking the white flowers and throwing them to the ground. He had been on the tree for about five minutes when he heard the whining grumble for a bear, and presently a young sloth bear ambled into the clearing beneath the tree.

He was a small bear, little more than a cub, and Ramu was not frightened; but, because he thought the mother might be in the vicinity, he decided to take no chances, and sat very still, waiting to see what the bear would do. He hoped it wouldn't choose the mahua tree for a meal.

At first the young bear put his nose to the ground and sniffed his way along until he came to a large ant-hill. Here he began huffing and puffing, blowing rapidly in and out of his nostrils, causing the dust from the ant-hill to fly in all directions. But he was a disappointed bear, because the ant-hill had been deserted long ago. And so, grumbling, he made his way across to a tall wild-plum tree, and shinning rapidly up the smooth trunk, was soon perched on its topmost branches. It was only then that he saw Ramu.

The bear at once scrambled several feet higher up the tree, and laid himself out flat on a branch. It wasn't a very thick branch and left a large expanse of bear showing on either side. The bear tucked his head away behind another branch, and so long as he could not see Ramu, seemed quite satisfied that he was well hidden, though he couldn't help grumbling with anxiety, for a bear, like most animals, is afraid of man.

Bears, however, are also very curious—and curiosity has often led them into trouble. Slowly, inch by inch, the young bear's black snout appeared over the edge of the branch; but immediately the eyes came into view and met Ramu's, he drew back with a jerk and the head was once more hidden. The bear did this two or three times, and Ramu, highly amused, waited until it wasn't looking, then moved some way down the tree. When the bear looked up again and saw that the boy was missing, he was so pleased with himself that he stretched right across to the next branch, to get a plum. Ramu chose this moment to burst into loud laughter. The startled bear tumbled out of the tree, dropped through the branches for a distance of some fifteen feet, and landed with a thud in a heap of dry leaves.

And then several things happened at almost the same time.

The mother bear came charging into the clearing. Spotting Ramu in the tree, she reared up on her hind legs, grunting fiercely. It was Ramu's turn to be startled. There are few animals more dangerous than a rampaging mother bear, and the boy knew that one blow from her clawed forepaws could rip his skull open.

But before the bear could approach the tree, there was a tremendous roar, and the old tiger bounded into the clearing. He had been asleep in the bushes not far away—he liked a good sleep after a heavy meal—and the noise in the clearing had woken him.

He was in a bad mood, and his loud 'A—Oonh!' made his displeasure quite clear. The bears turned and ran from the clearing, the youngster squealing with fright.

The tiger then came into the centre of the clearing, looked up at the trembling boy, and roared again.

Ramu nearly fell out of the tree.

'Good-day to you, Uncle,' he stammered, showing his teeth in a nervous grin.

Perhaps this was too much for the tiger. With a low growl, he turned his back on the mahua tree and padded off into the jungle, his tail twitching in disgust.

That night, when Ramu told his parents and his grandfather about the tiger and how it had saved him from a female bear, it started a round of tiger stories—about how some of them could be gentlemen, others rogues. Sooner or later the conversation came round to man-eaters, and Grandfather told two stories which he swore were true, although his listeners only half believed him.

The first story concerned the belief that a man-eating tiger is guided towards his next victim by the spirit of a human being previously killed and eaten by the tiger. Grandfather said that he actually knew three hunters who sat up in a machan over a human kill, and when the tiger came, the corpse sat up and pointed with his right hand at the men in the tree. The tiger then went away. But the hunters knew he would return, and one man was brave enough to get down from the tree and tie the right arm of the corpse to its side. Later, when the tiger returned, the corpse sat up and this time pointed out the men with his left hand. The enraged tiger sprang into the tree and killed his enemies in the machan.

'And then there was a bania,' said Grandfather, beginning another story, 'who lived in a village in the jungle. He wanted to visit a neighbouring village to collect some money that was owed to him, but as the road lay through heavy forest in which lived a terrible man-eating tiger, he did not know what to do. Finally, he went to a sadhu who gave him two powders. By eating the first powder he could turn into a huge tiger, capable of dealing with any other tiger in the jungle, and by eating the second he would become a bania again.

'Armed with his two powders, and accompanied by his pretty young wife, the bania set out on his journey. They had not gone far into the forest when they came upon the man-eater sitting in the middle of the road. Before swallowing the first powder, the bania told his wife to stay where she was, so that when he returned after killing the tiger, she could at once give him the second powder and enable him to resume his old shape.

'Well, the bania's plan worked, but only up to a point. He swallowed the first powder and immediately became a magnificent tiger. With a great roar, he bounded towards the man-eater, and after a brief, furious fight, killed his opponent. Then, with his jaws still dripping blood, he returned to his wife.

'The poor girl was terrified and spilt the second powder on the ground. The bania was so angry that he pounced on his wife and killed and ate her. And afterwards this terrible tiger was so enraged at not being able to become a human again that he killed and ate hundreds of people all over the country.'

'The only people he spared,' added Grandfather, with a twinkle in his eyes, 'were those who owed him money. A bania never gives up a loan as lost, and the tiger still hoped that one day he might become a human again and be able to collect his dues.'

Next morning, when Ramu came back from the well which was used to irrigate his father's fields, he found a crowd of curious children surrounding a jeep and three strangers with guns. Each of the strangers had a gun, and they were accompanied by two bearers and a vast amount of provisions.

They had heard that there was a tiger in the area, and they wanted to shoot it.

One of the hunters, who looked even more strange than the others, had come all the way from America to shoot a tiger, and he vowed that he would not leave the country without a tiger's skin in his baggage. One of his companions had said that he could buy a tiger's skin in Delhi, but the hunter said he preferred to get his own trophies.

These men had money to spend, and as most of the villagers needed money badly they were only too willing to go into the forest to construct a machan for the hunters. The platform, big enough to take the three men, was put up in the branches of a tall tun, or mahogany, tree.

It was the only night the hunters used the machan. At the end of March, though the days are warm, the nights are still cold. The hunters had neglected to bring blankets, and by midnight their teeth were chattering. Ramu, having tied up a buffalo calf for them at the foot of the tree, made as if to go home but instead circled the area, hanging up bits and pieces of old clothing on small trees and bushes. He thought he owed that much to the tiger. He knew the wily old king of the jungle would keep well away from the bait if he saw the bits of clothing—for where there were men's clothes, there would be men.

The vigil lasted well into the night but the tiger did not come near the tun tree. Perhaps he wasn't hungry; perhaps he got Ramu's message. In any case, the men in the tree soon gave themselves away.

The cold was really too much for them. A flask of rum was produced, and passed round, and it was not long before there was more purpose to finishing the rum than to finishing off a tiger. Silent at first, the men soon began talking in whispers; and to jungle creatures a human whisper is as telling as a trumpet-call.

Soon the men were quite merry, talking in loud voices. And

when the first morning light crept over the forest, and Ramu and his friends came back to fetch the great hunters, they found them fast asleep in the machan.

The hunters looked surly and embarrassed as they trudged back to the village.

'No game left in these parts,' said the American.

'Wrong time of the year for tiger,' said the second man.

'Don't know what the country's coming to,' said the third.

And complaining about the weather, the poor quality of cartridges, the quantity of rum they had drunk, and the perversity of tigers, they drove away in disgust.

It was not until the onset of summer that an event occurred which altered the hunting habits of the old tiger and brought him into conflict with the villagers.

There had been no rain for almost two months, and the tall jungle grass had become a sea of billowy dry yellow. Some refugee settlers, living in an area where the forest had been cleared, had been careless while cooking and had started a jungle fire. Slowly it spread into the interior, from where the acrid smell and the fumes smoked the tiger out toward the edge of the jungle. As night came on, the flames grew more vivid, and the smell stronger. The tiger turned and made for the *jheel*, where he knew he would be safe provided he swam across to the little island in the centre.

Next morning he was on the island, which was untouched by the fire. But his surroundings had changed. The slopes of the hills were black with burnt grass, and most of the tall bamboo had disappeared. The deer and the wild pig, finding that their natural cover had gone, fled further east.

When the fire had died down and the smoke had cleared, the tiger prowled through the forest again but found no game. Once he came across the body of a burnt rabbit, but he could not eat it. He drank at the *jheel* and settled down in a shady spot to sleep the day away. Perhaps, by evening, some of the animals would return. If not, he too would have to look for new hunting-grounds—or a new game.

The tiger spent five more days looking for a suitable game to kill. By that time he was so hungry that he even resorted to rooting among the dead leaves and burnt out stumps of trees, searching for worms and beetles. This was a sad come-down for the king of the jungle. But even now he hesitated to leave the area, for he had a deep suspicion and fear of the forest further east—forests that were fast being swallowed up by human habitation. He could have gone north, into high mountains, but they did not provide him with the long grass he needed. A panther could manage quite well up there, but not a tiger who loved the natural privacy of the heavy jungle. In the hills, he would have to hide all the time.

At break of day, the tiger came to the *jheel*. The water was now shallow and muddy, and a green scum had spread over the top. But it was still drinkable and the tiger quenched his thirst.

He lay down across his favourite rock, hoping for a deer but none came. He was about to get up and go away when he heard an animal approach.

The tiger at once leaped off his perch and flattened himself on the ground, his tawny striped skin merging with the dry grass. A heavy animal was moving through the bushes, and the tiger waited patiently.

A buffalo emerged and came to the water.

The buffalo was alone.

He was a big male, and his long curved horns lay right back across his shoulders. He moved leisurely towards the water, completely unaware of the tiger's presence.

The tiger hesitated before making his charge. It was a long time—many years—since he had killed a buffalo, and he knew the villagers would not like it. But the pangs of hunger overcame his scruples. There was no morning breeze, everything was still, and the smell of the tiger did not reach the buffalo. A monkey chattered on a nearby tree, but his warning went unheeded.

Crawling stealthily on his stomach, the tiger skirted the edge of the *jheel* and approached the buffalo from the rear. The water birds, who were used to the presence of both animals, did not raise an alarm.

Getting closer, the tiger glanced around to see if there were men, or other buffaloes, in the vicinity. Then, satisfied that he was alone, he crept forward. The buffalow was drinking, standing in shallow water at the edge of the tank, when the tiger charged from the side and bit deep into the animal's thigh.

The buffalo turned to fight, but the tendons of his right hind leg had been snapped, and he could only stragger forward a few paces. But he was a buffalo—the bravest of the domestic cattle. He was not afraid. He snorted, and lowered his horns at the tiger; but the great cat was too fast, and circling the buffalo, bit into the other hind leg.

The buffalo crashed to the ground, both hind legs crippled, and then the tiger dashed in, using both tooth and claw, biting deep into the buffalo's throat until the blood gushed out from the jugular vein.

The buffalo gave one long, last bellow before dying.

The tiger, having rested, now began to gorge himself, but, even though he had been starving for days, he could not finish the huge carcass. At least one good meal still remained when, satisfied and feeling his strength returning, he quenched his thirst at the *jheel*. Then he dragged the remains of the buffalow into the bushes to hide it from the vultures, and went off to find a place to sleep.

He would return to the kill when he was hungry.

The villagers were upset when they discovered that a buffalo was missing; and the next day, when Ramu and Shyam came running home to say that they had found the carcass near the *jheel*, half eaten by a tiger, the men were disturbed and angry. They felt that the tiger had tricked and deceived them. And they knew that once he got a taste for domestic cattle, he would make a habit of slaughtering them.

Kundan Singh, Shyam's father and the owner of the dead buffalo, said he would go after the tiger himself.

'It is all very well to talk about what you will do to the tiger,' said his wife, 'but you should never have let the buffalo go off on its own.'

'He had been out on his own before,' said Kundan. 'This is the first time the tiger has attacked one of our beasts. A devil must have entered the Maharaj.'

'He must have been very hungry,' said Shyam.

'Well, we are hungry too,' said Kundan Singh.

'Our best buffalo—the only male in our herd.'

'The tiger will kill again,' said Ramu's father.

'If we let him,' said Kundan.

'Should we send for the shikaris?'

'No. They were not clever. The tiger will escape them easily. Besides, there is no time. The tiger will return for another meal tonight. We must finish him off ourselves!'

'But how?'

Kundan Singh smiled secretively, played with the ends of his moustache for a few moments, and then, with great pride, produced from under his cot a double-barrelled gun of ancient vintage.

'My father bought it from an Englishman,' he said.

'How long ago was that?'

'At the time I was born.'

'And have you ever used it?' asked Ramu's father, who was not sure that the gun would work.

'Well, some years back I let it off at some bandits. You remember the time when those dacoits raided our village? They chose the wrong village, and were severely beaten for their pains. As they left, I fired my gun off at them. They didn't stop running until they crossed the Ganga!'

'Yes, but did you hit anyone?'

'I would have, if someone's goat hadn't got in the way at the last moment. But we had roast mutton that night! Don't worry, brother, I know how the thing fires.'

Accompanied by Ramu's father and some others, Kundan set out for the *jheel*, where, without shifting the buffalo's carcass—for they knew that the tiger would not come near them if he suspected a trap—they made another machan in the branches of a tall tree some thirty feet from the kill.

Later that evening Kundan Singh and Ramu's father settled down for the night on their crude platform in the tree.

Several hours passed, and nothing but a jackal was seen by the watchers. And then, just as the moon came up over the distant hills, Kundan and his companion were startled by a low 'A-ooonh', followed by a suppressed, rumbling growl.

Kundan grasped his old gun, whilst his friend drew closer to him for comfort. There was complete silence for a minute or two—time that was an agony of suspense for the watchers—and then the sound of stealthy footfalls on dead leaves under the trees.

A moment later the tiger walked out into the moonlight and stood over his kill.

At first Kundan could do nothing. He was completely overawed by the size of this magnificent tiger. Ramu's father had to nudge him, and then Kundan quickly put the gun to his shoulder, aimed at the tiger's head, and pressed the trigger.

The gun went off with a flash and two loud bangs, as Kundan fired both barrels. Then there was a tremendous roar. One of the bullets had grazed the tiger's head.

The enraged animal rushed at the tree and tried to leap up into the branches. Fortunately the machan had been built at a safe height, and the tiger was unable to reach it. It roared again and then bounded off into the forest.

'What a tiger!' exclaimed Kundan, half in fear and half in admiration. 'I feel as though my liver has turned to water.'

'You missed him completely,' said Ramu's father, 'Your gun makes a big noise; an arrow would have done more damage.'

'I did not miss him,' said Kundan, feeling offended, 'You heard him roar, didn't you? Would he have been so angry if he had not been hit? If I have wounded him badly, he will die.'

'And if you have wounded him slightly, he may turn into a man-eater, and then where will we be?'

'I don't think he will come back,' said Kundan. 'He will leave these forests.'

They waited until the sun was up before coming down from the tree. They found a few drops of blood on the dry grass but no trail led into the forest, and Ramu's father was convinced that the wound was only a slight one.

The bullet, missing the fatal spot behind the ear, had only grazed the back of the skull and cut a deep groove at its base. It took a few days to heal, and during this time the tiger lay low and did not go near the *jheel* except when it was very dark and he was very thirsty.

The villagers thought the tiger had gone away, and Ramu and Shyam—accompanied by some other youths, and always carrying axes and lathis—began bringing buffaloes to the tank again during the day; but they were careful not to let any of them stray far from the herd, and they returned home while it was still daylight.

It was some days since the jungle had been ravaged by the fire, and in the tropics the damage is repaired quickly. In spite of it being the dry season, new life was creeping into the forest.

While the buffaloes wallowed in the muddy water, and the boys wrestled on their grassy islet, a big tawny eagle soared high above them, looking for a meal—a sure sign that some of the animals were beginning to return to the forest. It was not long before his keen eyes detected a movement in the glade below.

What the eagle with his powerful eyesight saw was a baby hare, a small fluffy thing, its long pink-tinted ears laid flat along its sides. Had it not been creeping along between two large stones, it would have escaped notice. The eagle waited to see if the mother was about, and as he waited he realized that he was not the only one who coveted this juicy morsel. From the bushes there had appeared a sinuous yellow creature, pressed low to the ground and moving rapidly towards the hare. It was a yellow jungle cat, hardly noticeable in the scorched grass. With great stealth the jungle cat began to stalk the baby hare.

He pounced. The hare's squeal was cut short by the cat's cruel claws; but it had been heard by the mother hare, who now bounded into the glade and without the slightest hesitation went for the surprised cat.

There was nothing haphazard about the mother hare's attack. She flashed around behind the cat and jumped clean over him. As she landed, she kicked back, sending a stinging jet of dust shooting into the cat's face. She did this again and again.

The bewildered cat, crouching and snarling, picked up the kill and tried to run away with it. But the hare would not permit this. She continued her leaping and buffeting, till eventually the cat, out of sheer frustration, dropped the kill and attacked the mother.

The cat sprang at the hare a score of times, lashing out with his claws; but the mother hare was both clever and agile enough to keep just out of reach of those terrible claws, and drew the cat further and further away from her baby—for she did not as yet know that it was dead.

The tawny eagle saw his chance. Swift and true, he swooped. For a brief moment, as his wings overspread the furry little hare and his talons sank deep into it, he caught a glimpse of the cat racing towards him and the mother hare fleeing into the bushes. And then with a shrill 'kee-ee-ee' of triumph, he rose and whirled away with his dinner.

The boys had heard his shrill cry and looked up just in time to see the eagle flying over the *jheel* with the small little hare held firmly in his talons.

'Poor hare,' said Shyam. 'Its life was short.'

'That's the law of the jungle,' said Ramu. 'The eagle has a family too, and must feed it.'

'I wonder if we are any better than animals,' said Shyam.

'Perhaps we are a little better, in some ways,' said Ramu. 'Grandfather always says, "To be able to laugh and to be merciful are the only things that make man better than the beast." '

The next day, while the boys were taking the herd home, one of the buffaloes lagged behind. Ramu did not realize that the animal was missing until he heard an agonized bellow behind him. He glanced over his shoulder just in time to see the big striped tiger dragging the buffalow into a clump of young bamboo. At the same time the herd became aware of the danger, and the buffaloes snorted with fear as they hurried along the forest path. To urge them forward, and to warn his friends, Ramu cupped his hands to his mouth and gave vent to a yodelling call.

The buffaloes bellowed, the boys shouted, and the birds flew shrieking from the trees. It was almost a stampede by the time the herd emerged from the forest. The villagers heard the thunder of hoofs, and saw the herd coming home amidst clouds of dust and confusion, and knew that something was wrong.

'Then tiger!' shouted Ramu. 'He is here! He has killed one of the buffaloes.'

'He is afraid of us no longer,' said Shyam.

'Did you see where he went?' asked Kundan Singh, hurrying up to them.

'I remember the place,' said Ramu. 'He dragged the buffalo in amongst the bamboo.'

'Then there is no time to lose,' said his father. 'Kundan, you take your gun and two men, and wait near the suspension bridge, where the Garur stream joins the Ganga. The jungle is narrow there. We will beat the jungle from our side, and drive the tiger towards you. He will not escape us, unless he swims the river!'

'Good!' said Kundan, running into his house for his gun, with Shyam close at his heels. 'Was it one of our buffaloes again?' he asked.

'It was Ramu's buffalow this time,' said Shyam. 'A good milk buffalo.'

'Then Ramu's father will beat the jungle thoroughly. You boys had better come with me. It will not be safe for you to accompany the beaters.'

Kundan Singh, carrying his gun and accompanied by Ramu, Shyam and two men, headed for the river junction, while Ramu's father collected about twenty men from the village and, guided by one of the boys who had been with Ramu, made for the spot where the tiger had killed the buffalo.

The tiger was still eating when he heard the men coming. He had not expected to be disturbed so soon. With an angry 'whoof!' he bounded into a bamboo thicket and watched the men through a screen of leaves and tall grass.

The men did not seem to take much notice of the dead buffalo, but gathered round their leader and held a consultation. Most of them carried hand-drums slung from their shoulders. They also carried sticks, spears and axes.

After a hurried conversation, they entered the denser part of the jungle, beating their drums with the palms of their hands. Some of the men banged empty kerosene tins. These made even more noise than the drums.

The tiger did not like the noise and retreated deeper into the jungle. But he was surprised to find that the men, instead of going away, came after him into the jungle, banging away on their drums and tins, and shouting at the top of their voices. They had separated now, and advanced single or in pairs, but nowhere were they more than fifteen yards apart. The tiger could easily have broken through this slowly advancing semi-circle of men—one swift blow from his paw would have felled the strongest of them—but his main aim was to get away from the noise. He hated and feared noise made by men.

He was not a man-eater and he would not attack a man unless he was very angry or frightened or very desperate; and he was none of these things as yet. He had eaten well, and he would have liked to rest in peace—but there would be no rest for any animal until the men ceased their tremendous clatter and din.

For an hour Ramu's father and others beat the jungle, calling, drumming and trampling the undergrowth. The tiger had no rest. Whenever he was able to put some distance between himself and the men, he would sink down in some shady spot to rest; but, within five or ten minutes, the trampling and drumming would sound nearer, and the tiger, with an angry snarl, would get up and pad north, pad silently north along the narrowing strip of jungle, towards the junction of the Garur stream and the Ganga. Ten years back, he would have had the jungle on his right in which to hide; but the trees had been felled long ago to make way for humans and houses, and now he could only move to the left, towards the river.

It was about noon when the tiger finally appeared in the open. He longed for the darkness and security of the night, for the sun was his enemy. Kundan and the boys had a clear view of him as he stalked slowly along, now in the open with the sun glinting on his glossy hide, now in the shade or passing through the shorter reeds. He was still out of range of Kundan's gun, but there was no fear of his getting out of the beat, as the 'stops' were all picked men from the village. He disappeared among some bushes but soon reappeared to retrace his steps, the beaters having done their work well. He was now only one hundred and fifty yards from the rocks where Kundan Singh waited, and he looked very big.

The beat had closed in, and the exit along the bank downstream was completely blocked, so the tiger turned and disappeared into a belt of reeds, and Kundan Singh expected that the head would soon peer out of the cover a few yards away. The beaters were now making a great noise, shouting and beating their drums, but nothing moved; and Ramu, watching from a distance, wondered, 'Has he slipped through the beaters?' And he half hoped so.

Tins clashed, drums beat, and some of the men poked into the reeds with their spears or long bamboos. Perhaps one of these thrusts found a mark, because at last the tiger was roused, and with an angry desperate snarl he charged out of the reeds, splashing his way through an inlet of mud and water. Kundan Singh fired, and his bullet struck the tiger on the thigh.

The mighty animal stumbled; but he was up in a minute, and rushing through a gap in the narrowing line of beaters, he made straight for the only way across the river—the suspension bridge that passed over the Ganga here, providing a route into the high hills beyond.

'We'll get him now,' said Kundan, priming his gun again. 'He's right in the open!'

The suspension bridge swayed and trembled as the wounded tiger lurched across it. Kundan fired, and this time the bullet grazed the tiger's shoulder. The animal bounded forward, lost his footing on the unfamiliar, slippery planks of the swaying bridge, and went over the side, falling headlong into the strong, swirling waters of the river.

He rose to the surface once, but the current took him under and away, and only a thin streak of blood remained on the river's surface.

Kundan and others hurried downstream to see if the dead tiger had been washed up on the river's banks; but though they searched the riverside several miles, they did not find the king of the forest.

He had not provided anyone with a trophy. His skin would not be spread on a couch, nor would his head be hung up on a wall. No claw of his would be hung up on a wall. No claw of his would be hung as a charm round the neck of a child. No villager would use his fat as a cure for rheumatism.

At first the villagers were glad because they felt their buffaloes were safe. Then the men began to feel that something had gone out of their lives, out of the life of the forest; they began to feel that the forest was no longer a forest. It had been shrinking year by year, but, as long as the tiger had been there and the villagers had heard it roar at night, they had known that they were still secure from the intruders and newcomers who came to fell the trees and eat up the land and let the flood waters into the village. But now that the tiger had gone, it was as though a protector had gone, leaving the forest open and vulnerable, easily destroyable. And once the forest was destroyed they too would be in danger . . .

There was another thing that had gone with the tiger, another thing that had been lost, a thing that was being lost everywhere—something called 'nobility'.

Ramu remembered something that his grandfather had once said. 'The tiger is the very soul of India, and when the last tiger goes, so will the soul of the country.'

The boys lay flat on their stomachs on their little mud island and watched the monsoon clouds gathering overhead.

'The king of our forest is dead,' said Shyam. 'There are no more tigers.'

'There must be tigers,' said Ramu. 'How can there be an India without tigers?'

The river had carried the tiger many miles away from his home, from the forest he had always known, and brought him ashore on a strip of warm yellow sand, where he lay in the sun, quite still, but breathing.

Vultures gathered and waited at a distance, some of them perching on the branches of nearby trees.

But the tiger was more drowned than hurt, and as the river water oozed out of his mouth, and the warm sun made new life throb through his body, he stirred and stretched, and his glazed eyes came into focus. Raising his head, he saw trees and tall grass.

Slowly he heaved himself off the ground and moved at a crouch to where the grass waved in the afternoon breeze. Would he be harried again, and shot at? There was no smell of man. The tiger moved forward with greater confidence.

There was, however, another smell in the air—a smell that

reached back to the time when he was young and fresh and full of vigour—a smell that he had almost forgotten but could never quite forget—the smell of a tigress!

He raised his head high, and new life surged through his tired limbs. He gave a full-throated roar and moved purposefully through the tall grass. And the roar came back to him, calling him, calling him forward—a roar that meant there would be more tigers in the land!

ESCAPE FROM JAVA

🐦

IT ALL HAPPENED WITHIN the space of a few days. The cassia tree had barely come into flower when the first bombs fell on Batavia (now called Jakarta) and the bright pink blossoms lay scattered over the wreckage in the streets.

News had reached us that Singapore had fallen to the Japanese. My father said: 'I expect it won't be long before they take Java. With the British defeated, how can the Dutch be expected to win!' He did not mean to be critical of the Dutch; he knew they did not have the backing of the Empire that Britain had. Singapore had been called the Gibraltar of the East. After its surrender there could only be retreat, a vast exodus of Europeans from South-East Asia.

It was World War II. What the Javanese thought about the war is now hard for me to say, because I was only nine at the time and knew very little of worldly matters. Most people knew they would be exchanging their Dutch rulers for Japanese rulers; but there were also many who spoke in terms of freedom for Java when the war was over.

Our neighbour, Mr Hartono, was one of those who looked ahead to a time when Java, Sumatra and the other islands would make up one independent nation. He was a college professor and spoke Dutch, Chinese, Javanese and a little English. His son, Sono, was about my age. He was the only boy I knew who could talk to me in English, and as a result we spent a lot of time together. Our favourite pastime was flying kites in the park.

The bombing soon put an end to kite flying. Air raid alerts

sounded at all hours of the day and night and, although in the beginning most of the bombs fell near the docks, a couple of miles from where we lived, we had to stay indoors. If the planes sounded very near, we dived under beds or tables. I don't remember if there were any trenches. Probably there hadn't been time for trench digging, and now there was time only for digging graves. Events had moved all too swiftly, and everyone (except of course the Javanese) was anxious to get away from Java.

'When are you going?' asked Sono, as we sat on the veranda steps in a pause between air raids.

'I don't know,' I said. 'It all depends on my father.'

'My father says the Japs will be here in a week. And if you're still here then, they'll put you to work building a railway.'

'I wouldn't mind building a railway,' I said.

'But they won't give you enough to eat. Just rice with worms in it. And if you don't work properly, they'll shoot you.'

'They do that to soldiers,' I said. 'We're civilians.'

'They do it to civilians, too,' said Sono.

What were my father and I doing in Batavia, when our home had been first in India and then in Singapore? He worked for a firm dealing in rubber, and six months earlier he had been sent to Batavia to open a new office in partnership with a Dutch business house. Although I was so young, I accompanied my father almost everywhere. My mother left when I was very small, and my father had always looked after me. After the war was over he was going to take me to England.

'Are we going to win the war?' I asked.

'It doesn't look it from here,' he said.

No, it didn't look as though we were winning. Standing at the docks with my father, I watched the ships arrive from Singapore crowded with refugees—men, women and children, all living on the decks in the hot tropical sun; they looked pale and worn-out and worried. They were on their way to Colombo or Bombay. No one came ashore at Batavia. It wasn't British territory; it was Dutch, and everyone knew it wouldn't be Dutch for long.

'Aren't we going too?' I asked. 'Sono's father says the Japs will be here any day.'

'We've still got a few days,' said my father. He was a short, stocky man, who seldom got excited. If he was worried, he didn't show it. 'I've got to wind up a few business matters, and then we'll be off.'

'How will we go? There's no room for us on those ships.'

'There certainly isn't. But we'll find a way, lad, don't worry.'

I didn't worry. I had complete confidence in my father's ability to find a way out of difficulties. He used to say, 'Every problem has a solution hidden away somewhere, and if only you look hard enough you will find it.'

There were British soldiers in the streets but they did not make us feel much safer. They were just waiting for troop ships to come and take them away. No one, it seemed, was interested in defending Java, only in getting out as fast as possible.

Although the Dutch were unpopular with the Javanese people, there was no ill-feeling against individual Europeans. I could walk safely through the streets. Occasionally small boys in the crowded Chinese quarter would point at me and shout, 'Orang Balandi!' (Dutchman!) but they did so in good humour, and I didn't know the language well enough to stop and explain that the English weren't Dutch. For them, all white people were the same, and understandably so.

My father's office was in the commercial area, along the canal banks. Our two-storied house, about a mile away, was an old building with a roof of red tiles and a broad balcony which had stone dragons at either end. There were flowers in the garden almost all the year round. If there was anything in Batavia more regular than the bombing, it was the rain, which came pattering down on the roof and on the banana fronds almost every afternoon. In the hot and steamy atmosphere of Java, the rain was always welcome.

There were no anti-aircraft guns in Batavia—at least we never heard any—and the Jap bombers came over at will, dropping their bombs by daylight. Sometimes bombs fell in the town. One day the building next to my father's office received a direct hit and tumbled into the river. A number of office workers were killed.

The schools closed, and Sono and I had nothing to do all day except sit in the house, playing darts or carrom, wrestling on the carpets, or playing the gramophone. We had records by Gracie Fields, Harry Lauder, George Formby and Arthur Askey, all popular British artists of the early 1940s. One song by Arthur Askey made fun of Adolph Hitler, with the words, 'Adolph, we're gonna hang up your washing on the Siegfried Line, if the Siegfried Line's still there!' It made us feel quite cheerful to know that back in Britain people were confident of winning the war!

One day Sono said, 'The bombs are falling on Batavia, not in the countryside. Why don't we get cycles and ride out of town?'

I fell in with the idea at once. After the morning all-clear had sounded, we mounted our cycles and rode out of town. Mine was a hired cycle, but Sono's was his own. He'd had it since the age of five, and it was constantly in need of repair. 'The soul has gone out of it,' he used to say.

Our fathers were at work; Sono's mother had gone out to do her shopping (during air raids she took shelter under the most convenient shop counter) and wouldn't be back for at least an hour. We expected to be back before lunch.

We were soon out of town, on a road that passed through rice fields, pineapple orchards and cinchona plantations. On our right lay dark green hills; on our left, groves of coconut palms and, beyond them, the sea. Men and women were working in the rice fields, knee-deep in mud, their broad-brimmed hats protecting them from the fierce sun. Here and there a buffalo wallowed in a pool of brown water, while a naked boy lay stretched out on the animal's broad back.

We took a bumpy track through the palms. They grew right down to the edge of the sea. Leaving our cycles on the shingle, we ran down a smooth, sandy beach and into the shallow water.

'Don't go too far in,' warned Sono. 'There may be sharks about.'

Wading in amongst the rocks, we searched for interesting shells, then sat down on a large rock and looked out to sea, where a sailing ship moved placidly on the crisp, blue waters. It was difficult to imagine that half the world was at war, and that Batavia, two or three miles away, was right in the middle of it.

On our way home we decided to take a short cut through the rice fields, but soon found that our tyres got bogged down in the soft mud. This delayed our return; and to make things worse, we got the roads mixed up and reached an area of the town that seemed unfamiliar. We had barely entered the outskirts when the siren sounded, followed soon after by the drone of approaching aircraft.

'Should we get off our cycles and take shelter somewhere?' I called out.

'No, let's race home!' shouted Sono. 'The bombs won't fall here.'

But he was wrong. The planes flew in very low. Looking up for a moment, I saw the sun blotted out by the sinister shape of a Jap fighter-bomber. We pedalled furiously; but we had barely covered fifty yards when there was a terrific explosion on our right, behind some houses. The shock sent us spinning across the road. We were flung from our cycles. And the cycles, still propelled by the blast, crashed into a wall.

I felt a stinging sensation in my hands and legs, as though scores of little insects had bitten me. Tiny droplets of blood appeared here and there on my flesh. Sono was on all fours, crawling beside me, and I saw that he too had the same small scratches on his hands and forehead, made by tiny shards of flying glass.

We were quickly on our feet, and then we began running in the general direction of our homes. The twisted cycles lay forgotten on the road.

'Get off the street, you two!' shouted someone from a window; but we weren't going to stop running until we got home. And we ran faster than we'd ever run in our lives.

My father and Sono's parents were themselves running about the street, calling for us, when we came rushing around the corner and tumbled into their arms.

'Where have you been?'

'What happened to you?'

'How did you get those cuts?'

All superfluous questions but before we could recover our breath and start explaining, we were bundled into our respective homes. My father washed my cuts and scratches, dabbed at my face and legs with iodine—ignoring my yelps—and then stuck plaster all over my face.

Sono and I had had a fright, and we did not venture far from the house again.

That night my father said: 'I think we'll be able to leave in a day or two.'

'Has another ship come in?'

'No.'

'Then how are we going? By plane?'

'Wait and see, lad. It isn't settled yet. But we won't be able to take much with us—just enough to fill a couple of travelling bags.'

'What about the stamp collection?' I asked.

My father's stamp collection was quite valuable and filled several volumes.

'I'm afraid we'll have to leave most of it behind,' he said. 'Perhaps Mr Hartono will keep it for me, and when the war is over—if it's over—we'll come back for it.'

'But we can take one or two albums with us, can't we?'

'I'll take one. There'll be room for one. Then if we're short of money in Bombay, we can sell the stamps.'

'Bombay? That's in India. I thought we were going back to England.'

'First we must go to India.'

The following morning I found Sono in the garden, patched up like me, and with one foot in a bandage. But he was as cheerful as ever and gave me his usual wide grin.

'We're leaving tomorrow,' I said.

The grin left his face.

'I will be sad when you go,' he said. 'But I will be glad too, because then you will be able to escape from the Japs.'

'After the war, I'll come back.'

'Yes, you must come back. And then, when we are big, we will go round the world together. I want to see England and America and Africa and India and Japan. I want to go everywhere.'

'We can't go everywhere.'

'Yes, we can. No one can stop us!'

We had to be up very early the next morning. Our bags had been packed late at night. We were taking a few clothes, some of my father's business papers, a pair of binoculars, one stamp album, and several bars of chocolate. I was pleased about the stamp album and the chocolates, but I had to give up several of my treasures—favourite books, the gramophone and records, an old Samurai sword, a train set and a dartboard. The only consolation was that Sono, and not a stranger, would have them.

In the first faint light of dawn a truck drew up in front of the house. It was driven by a Dutch businessman, Mr Hookens, who worked with my father. Sono was already at the gate, waiting to say goodbye.

'I have a present for you,' he said.

He took me by the hand and pressed a smooth hard object into my palm. I grasped it and then held it up against the light. It was a beautiful little sea horse, carved out of pale blue jade.

'It will bring you luck,' said Sono.

'Thank you,' I said. 'I will keep it forever.'

And I slipped the little sea horse into my pocket.

'In you get, lad,' said my father, and I got up on the front seat between him and Mr Hookens.

As the truck started up, I turned to wave to Sono. He was sitting on his garden wall, grinning at me. He called out: 'We will go everywhere, and no one can stop us!'

He was still waving when the truck took us round the bend at the end of the road.

We drove through the still, quiet streets of Batavia, occasionally passing burnt-out trucks and shattered buildings. Then we left the sleeping city far behind and were climbing into the forested hills. It had rained during the night, and when the sun came up over the green hills, it twinkled and glittered on the broad, wet leaves. The light in the forest changed from dark green to greenish gold, broken here and there by the flaming red or orange of a trumpet-shaped blossom. It was impossible to know the names of all those fantastic plants! The road had been cut through dense tropical forest, and on either side the trees jostled each other, hungry for the sun; but they were chained together by the liana creepers and vines that fed upon the struggling trees.

Occasionally a Jelarang, a large Javan squirrel, frightened by the passing of the truck, leapt through the trees before disappearing into the depths of the forest. We saw many birds: peacocks, jungle-fowl, and once, standing majestically at the side of the road, a crowned pigeon, its great size and splendid crest making it a striking object even at a distance. Mr Hookens slowed down so that we could look at the bird. It bowed its head so that its crest swept the ground; then it emitted a low hollow boom rather than the call of a turkey.

When we came to a small clearing, we stopped for breakfast. Butterflies, black, green and gold, flitted across the clearing. The silence of the forest was broken only by the drone of airplanes. Japanese Zeros heading for Batavia on another raid. I thought about Sono, and wondered what he would be doing at home: probably trying out the gramophone!

We ate boiled eggs and drank tea from a thermos, then got back into the truck and resumed our journey.

I must have dozed off soon after, because the next thing I remember is that we were going quite fast down a steep, winding road, and in the distance I could see a calm blue lagoon.

'We've reached the sea again,' I said.

'That's right,' said my father. 'But we're now nearly a hundred miles from Batavia, in another part of the island. You're looking out over the Sunda Straits.'

Then he pointed towards a shimmering white object resting on the waters of the lagoon.

'There's our plane,' he said.

'A seaplane!' I exclaimed. 'I never guessed. Where will it take us?'

'To Bombay, I hope. There aren't many other places left to go to!'

It was a very old seaplane, and no one, not even the captain—the pilot was called the captain—could promise that it would take off. Mr Hookens wasn't coming with us; he said the plane would be back for him the next day. Besides my father and me, there were four other passengers, and all but one were Dutch. The odd man out was a Londoner, a motor mechanic who'd been left behind in Java when his unit was evacuated. (He told us later that he'd fallen asleep at a bar in the Chinese quarter, waking up some hours after his regiment had moved off!) He looked rather scruffy. He'd lost the top button of his shirt, but, instead of leaving his collar open, as we did, he'd kept it together with a large safety pin, which thrust itself out from behind a bright pink tie.

'It's a relief to find you here, guvnor,' he said, shaking my father by the hand. 'Knew you for a Yorkshireman the minute I set eyes on you. It's the *song-fried* that does it, if you know what I mean.' (He meant *sang-froid*, French for a 'cool look.') 'And here I was, with all these flippin' forriners, and me not knowing a word of what they've been yattering about. Do you think this old tub will get us back to Blighty?'

'It does look a bit shaky,' said my father. 'One of the first flying boats, from the looks of it. If it gets us to Bombay, that's far enough.'

'Anywhere out of Java's good enough for me,' said our new companion. 'The name's Muggeridge.'

'Pleased to know you, Mr Muggeridge,' said my father. 'I'm Bond. This is my son.'

Mr Muggeridge rumpled my hair and favoured me with a large wink.

The captain of the seaplane was beckoning to us to join him in a small skiff which was about to take us across a short stretch of water to the seaplane.

'Here we go,' said Mr Muggeridge. 'Say your prayers and keep your fingers crossed.'

The seaplane was a long time getting airborne. It had to make several runs before it finally took off. Then, lurching drunkenly, it rose into the clear blue sky.

'For a moment I thought we were going to end up in the briny,' said Mr Muggeridge, untying his seat belt. 'And talkin' of fish, I'd give a week's wages for a plate of fish an' chips and a pint of beer.'

'I'll buy you a beer in Bombay,' said my father.

'Have an egg,' I said, remembering we still had some boiled eggs in one of the travelling bags.

'Thanks, mate,' said Mr Muggeridge, accepting an egg with alacrity. 'A real egg, too! I've been livin' on egg powder these last six months. That's what they give you in the Army. And it ain't hens' eggs they make it from, let me tell you. It's either gulls' or turtles' eggs!'

'No,' said my father with a straight face. 'Snakes' eggs.'

Mr Muggeridge turned a delicate shade of green; but he soon recovered his poise, and for about an hour kept talking about almost everything under the sun, including Churchill, Hitler, Roosevelt, Mahatma Gandhi, and Betty Grable. (The last-named was famous for her beautiful legs.) He would have gone on talking all the way to Bombay had he been given a chance; but suddenly a shudder passed through the old plane, and it began lurching again.

'I think an engine is giving trouble,' said my father.

When I looked through the small glassed-in window, it seemed as though the sea was rushing up to meet us.

The copilot entered the passenger cabin and said something in Dutch. The passengers looked dismayed, and immediately began fastening their seat belts.

'Well, what did the blighter say?' asked Mr Muggeridge.

'I think he's going to have to ditch the plane,' said my father, who knew enough Dutch to get the gist of anything that was said.

'Down in the drink!' exclaimed Mr Muggeridge. 'Gawd 'elp us! and how far are we from Bombay, guv?'

'A few hundred miles,' said my father.

'Can you swim, mate?' asked Mr Muggeridge looking at me.

'Yes,' I said. 'But not all the way to Bombay. How far can you swim?'

'The length of a bathtub,' he said.

'Don't worry,' said my father. 'Just make sure your life-jacket's properly tied.'

We looked to our life-jackets; my father checked mine twice, making sure that it was properly fastened.

The pilot had now cut both engines, and was bringing the plane down in a circling movement. But he couldn't control the speed, and it was tilting heavily to one side. Instead of landing smoothly on its belly, it came down on a wing tip, and this caused the plane to swivel violently around in the choppy sea. There was a terrific jolt when the plane hit the water, and if it hadn't been for the seat belts we'd have been flung from our seats. Even so, Mr Muggeridge struck his head against the seat in front, and he was now holding a bleeding nose and using some shocking language.

As soon as the plane came to a standstill, my father undid my seat belt. There was no time to lose. Water was already filling the cabin, and all the passengers—except one, who was dead in his seat with a broken neck—were scrambling for the exit hatch. The copilot pulled a lever and the door fell away to reveal high waves slapping against the sides of the stricken plane.

Holding me by the hand, my father was leading me towards the exit.

'Quick lad,' he said. 'We won't stay afloat for long.'

'Give us a hand!' shouted Mr Muggeridge, still struggling with his life-jacket. 'First this bloody bleedin' nose, and now something's gone and stuck.'

My father helped him fix the life-jacket, then pushed him out of the door ahead of us.

As we swam away from the seaplane (Mr Muggeridge splashing fiercely alongside us), we were aware of the other passengers in the water. One of them shouted to us in Dutch to follow him.

We swam after him towards the dinghy, which had been released the moment we hit the water. That yellow dinghy, bobbing about on the waves, was as welcome as land.

All who had left the plane managed to climb into the dinghy. We were seven altogether—a tight fit. We had hardly settled down in the well of the dinghy when Mr Muggeridge, still holding his nose, exclaimed: 'There she goes!' And as we looked on helplessly, the seaplane sank swiftly and silently beneath the waves.

The dinghy had shipped a lot of water, and soon everyone was busy bailing it out with mugs (there were a couple in the dinghy), hats, and bare hands. There was a light swell, and every now and then water would roll in again and half fill the dinghy. But within half an hour we had most of the water out, and then it was possible to take turns, two men doing the bailing while the others rested. No one expected me to do this work, but I gave a hand anyway, using my father's sola topi for the purpose.

'Where are we?' asked one of the passengers.

'A long way from anywhere,' said another.

'There must be a few islands in the Indian Ocean.'

'But we may be at sea for days before we come to one of them.'

'Days or even weeks,' said the captain. 'Let us look at our supplies.'

The dinghy appeared to be fairly well provided with emergency rations: biscuits, raisins, chocolates (we'd lost our own), and enough water to last a week. There was also a first aid box, which was put to immediate use, as Mr Muggeridge's nose needed attention. A few others had cuts and bruises. One of the passengers had received a hard knock on the head and appeared to be suffering from a loss of memory. He had no idea how we happened to be drifting about in the middle of the Indian Ocean; he was convinced that we were on a pleasure cruise a few miles off Batavia.

The unfamiliar motion of the dinghy, as it rose and fell in the troughs between the waves, resulted in almost everyone getting seasick. As no one could eat anything, a day's rations were saved.

The sun was very hot, but my father covered my head with a large spotted handkerchief. He'd always had a fancy for bandanna handkerchiefs with yellow spots, and seldom carried fewer than two on his person; so he had one for himself too. The sola topi, well soaked in seawater, was being used by Mr Muggeridge.

It was only when I had recovered to some extent from my seasickness that I remembered the valuable stamp album, and sat up, exclaiming, 'The stamps! Did you bring the stamp album, Dad?'

He shook his head ruefully. 'It must be at the bottom of the sea by now,' he said. 'But don't worry, I kept a few rare stamps in my wallet.' And looking pleased with himself, he tapped the pocket of his bush shirt.

The dinghy drifted all day, with no one having the least idea where it might be taking us.

'Probably going round in circles,' said Mr Muggeridge pessimistically.

There was no compass and no sail, and paddling wouldn't have got us far even if we'd had paddles; we could only resign ourselves to the whims of the current and hope it would take us towards land or at least to within hailing distance of some passing ship.

The sun went down like an overripe tomato dissolving slowly in the sea. The darkness pressed down on us. It was a moonless night, and all we could see was the white foam on the crests of the waves. I lay with my head on my father's shoulder, and looked up at the stars which glittered in the remote heavens.

'Perhaps your friend Sono will look up at the sky tonight and see those same stars,' said my father. 'The world isn't so big after all.'

'All the same, there's a lot of sea around us,' said Mr Muggeridge from out of the darkness.

Remembering Sono, I put my hand in my pocket and was reassured to feel the smooth outline of the jade sea horse.

'I've still got Sono's sea horse,' I said, showing it to my father.

'Keep it carefully,' he said. 'It may bring us luck.'

'Are sea horses lucky?'

'Who knows? But he gave it to you with love, and love is like a prayer. So keep it carefully.'

I didn't sleep much that night. I don't think anyone slept. No one spoke much either, except of course Mr Muggeridge, who kept muttering something about cold beer and salami.

I didn't feel so sick the next day. By ten o'clock I was quite hungry; but breakfast consisted of two biscuits, a piece of chocolate, and a little drinking water. It was another hot day, and we were soon very thirsty, but everyone agreed that we should ration ourselves strictly.

Two or three still felt ill, but the others, including Mr Muggeridge, had recovered their appetites and normal spirits, and there was some discussion about the prospects of being picked up.

'Are there any distress rockets in the dinghy?' asked my father. 'If we see a ship or a plane, we can fire a rocket and hope to be spotted. Otherwise there's not much chance of our being seen from a distance.'

A thorough search was made in the dinghy, but there were no rockets.

'Someone must have used them last Guy Fawkes Day,' commented Mr Muggeridge.

'They don't celebrate Guy Fawkes Day in Holland,' said my father. 'Guy Fawkes was an Englishman.'

'Ah,' said Mr Muggeridge, not in the least put out. 'I've always said, most great men are Englishmen. And what did this chap Guy Fawkes do?'

'Tried to blow up Parliament,' said my father.

That afternoon we saw our first sharks. They were enormous creatures, and as they glided backward and forward under the boat it seemed they might hit and capsize us. They went away for some time, but returned in the evening.

At night, as I lay half asleep beside my father, I felt a few drops of water strike my face. At first I thought it was the sea spray; but when the sprinkling continued, I realized that it was raining lightly.

'Rain!' I shouted, sitting up. 'It's raining!'

Everyone woke up and did his best to collect water in mugs, hats or other containers. Mr Muggeridge lay back with his mouth open, drinking the rain as it fell.

'This is more like it,' he said. 'You can have all the sun an' sand in the world. Give me a rainy day in England!'

But by early morning the clouds had passed, and the day turned out to be even hotter than the previous one. Soon we were all red and raw from sunburn. By midday even Mr Muggeridge was silent. No one had the energy to talk.

Then my father whispered, 'Can you hear a plane, lad?'

I listened carefully, and above the hiss of the waves I heard what sounded like the distant drone of a plane; but it must have been very far away, because we could not see it. Perhaps it was flying into the sun, and the glare was too much for our sore eyes; or perhaps we'd just imagined the sound.

Then the Dutchman who'd lost his memory thought he saw land, and kept pointing towards the horizon and saying, 'That's Batavia, I told you we were close to shore!' No one else saw anything. So my father and I weren't the only ones imagining things.

Said my father, 'It only goes to show that a man can see what he wants to see, even if there's nothing to be seen!'

The sharks were still with us. Mr Muggeridge began to resent them. He took off one of his shoes and hurled it at the nearest shark; but the big fish ignored the shoe and swam on after us.

'Now, if your leg had been in that shoe, Mr Muggeridge, the shark might have accepted it,' observed my father.

'Don't throw your shoes away,' said the captain. 'We might land on a deserted coastline and have to walk hundreds of miles!'

A light breeze sprang up that evening, and the dinghy moved more swiftly on the choppy water.

'At last we're moving forward,' said the captain.

'In circles,' said Mr Muggeridge.

But the breeze was refreshing; it cooled our burning limbs, and helped us to get some sleep. In the middle of the night I woke up feeling very hungry.

'Are you all right?' asked my father, who had been awake all the time.

'Just hungry,' I said.

'And what would you like to eat?'

'Oranges!'

He laughed. 'No oranges on board. But I kept a piece of my chocolate for you. And there's a little water, if you're thirsty.'

I kept the chocolate in my mouth for a long time, trying to make it last. Then I sipped a little water.

'Aren't you hungry?' I asked.

'Ravenous! I could eat a whole turkey. When we get to Bombay or Madras or Colombo, or wherever it is we get to, we'll go to the best restaurant in town and eat like—like—'

'Like shipwrecked sailors!' I said.

'Exactly.'

'Do you think we'll ever get to land, Dad?'

'I'm sure we will. You're not afraid, are you?'

'No. Not as long as you're with me.'

Next morning, to everyone's delight, we saw seagulls. This was a sure sign that land couldn't be far away; but a dinghy could take days to drift a distance of thirty or forty miles. The birds wheeled noisily above the dinghy. Their cries were the first familiar sounds we had heard for three days and three nights, apart from the wind and the sea and our own weary voices.

The sharks had disappeared, and that too was an encouraging sign. They didn't like the oil slicks that were appearing in the water.

But presently the gulls left us, and we feared we were drifting away from land.

'Circles,' repeated Mr Muggeridge. 'Circles.'

We had sufficient food and water for another week at sea; but no one even wanted to think about spending another week at sea.

The sun was a ball of fire. Our water ration wasn't sufficient to quench our thirst. By noon, we were without much hope or energy.

My father had his pipe in his mouth. He didn't have any tobacco, but he liked holding the pipe between his teeth. He said it prevented his mouth from getting too dry.

The sharks came back.

Mr Muggeridge removed his other shoe and threw it at them.

'Nothing like a lovely wet English summer,' he mumbled.

I fell asleep in the well of the dinghy, my father's large handkerchief spread over my face. The yellow spots on the cloth seemed to grow into enormous revolving suns.

When I woke up, I found a huge shadow hanging over us. At first I thought it was a cloud. But it was a shifting shadow. My father took the handkerchief from my face and said, 'You can wake up now, lad. We'll be home and dry soon.'

A fishing boat was beside us, and the shadow came from its wide, flapping sail. A number of bronzed, smiling, chattering fishermen—Burmese, as we discovered later—were gazing down at us from the deck of their boat.

A few days later my father and I were in Bombay.

My father sold his rare stamps for over a thousand rupees, and we were able to live in a comfortable hotel. Mr Muggeridge was flown back to England. Later we got a postcard from him, saying the English rain was awful!

'And what about us?' I asked. 'Aren't we going back to England?'

'Not yet,' said my father. 'You'll be going to a boarding school in Shimla, until the war's over.'

'But why should I leave you?' I asked.

'Because I've joined the RAF,' he said. 'Don't worry, I'm being posted to Delhi. I'll be able to come up to see you sometimes.'

A week later I was on a small train which went chugging up the steep mountain track to Shimla. Several Indian, Anglo-Indian and English children tumbled around in the compartment. I felt quite out of place among them, as though I had grown out of their pranks. But I wasn't unhappy. I knew my father would be coming to see me soon. He'd promised me some books, a pair of roller-skates, and a cricket bat, just as soon as he got his first month's pay.

Meanwhile, I had the jade sea horse which Sono had given me.

And I have it with me today.

UNTOUCHABLE

&

THE SWEEPER-BOY SPLASHED WATER over the *khus* matting that hung in the doorway and for a while the air was cooled.

I sat on the edge of my bed, staring out of the open window, brooding upon the dusty road shimmering in the noon-day heat. A car passed and the dust rose in billowing clouds.

Across the road lived the people who were supposed to look after me while my father lay in hospital with malaria. I was supposed to stay with them, sleep with them. But except for meals, I kept away. I did not like them and they did not like me.

For a week, longer probably, I was going to live alone in the red-brick bungalow on the outskirts of the town, on the fringe of the jungle. At night the sweeper-boy would keep guard, sleeping in the kitchen. Apart from him, I had no company; only the neighbours' children, and I did not like them and they did not like me.

Their mother said, 'Don't play with the sweeper-boy, he is unclean. Don't touch him. Remember, he is a servant. You must come and play with my boys.'

Well, I did not intend playing with the sweeper-boy; but neither did I intend playing with her children. I was going to sit on my bed all week and wait for my father to come home.

Sweeper-boy . . . all day he pattered up and down between the house and the water-tank, with the bucket clanging against his knees.

Back and forth, with a wide, friendly smile.

I frowned at him.

He was about my age, ten. He had short-cropped hair, very white teeth, and muddy feet, hands, and face. All he wore was an old pair of khaki shorts; the rest of his body was bare, burnt a deep brown.

At every trip to the water tank he bathed, and returned dripping and glistening from head to toe.

I dripped with sweat.

It was supposedly below my station to bathe at the tank, where the gardener, water-carrier, cooks, ayahs, sweepers, and their children all collected. I was the son of a 'sahib' and convention ruled that I did not play with servant children.

But I was just as determined not to play with the other sahibs' children, for I did not like them and they did not like me.

I watched the flies buzzing against the window-pane, the lizards scuttling across the rafters, the wind scattering petals of scorched, long-dead flowers.

The sweeper-boy smiled and saluted in play. I avoided his eyes and said, 'Go away.'

He went into the kitchen.

I rose and crossed the room, and lifted my sun helmet off the hatstand.

A centipede ran down the wall, across the floor.

I screamed and jumped on the bed, shouting for help.

The sweeper-boy darted in. He saw me on the bed, the centipede on the floor; and picking a large book off the shelf, slammed it down on the repulsive insect.

I remained standing on my bed, trembling with fear and revulsion.

He laughed at me, showing his teeth, and I blushed and said, 'Get out!'

I would not, could not, touch or approach the hat or hatstand. I sat on the bed and longed for my father to come home.

A mosquito passed close by me and sang in my ear. Half-heartedly, I clutched at it and missed; and it disappeared behind the dressing-table.

That mosquito, I reasoned, gave the malaria to my father. And now it was trying to give it to me!

The next-door lady walked through the compound and smiled thinly from outside the window. I glared back at her.

The sweeper-boy passed with the bucket, and grinned. I turned away.

In bed at night, with the lights on, I tried reading. But even books could not quell my anxiety.

The sweeper-boy moved about the house, bolting doors, fastening windows. He asked me if I had any orders.

I shook my head.

He skipped across to the electric switch, turned off the light, and slipped into his quarters. Outside, inside, all was dark; only one shaft of light squeezed in through a crack in the sweeper-boy's door, and then that too went out.

I began to wish I had stayed with the neighbours. The darkness worried me—silent and close—silent, as if in suspense.

Once a bat flew flat against the window, falling to the ground outside; once an owl hooted. Sometimes a dog barked. And I tautened as a jackal howled hideously in the jungle behind the bungalow. But nothing could break the overall stillness, the night's silence . . .

Only a dry puff of wind . . .

It rustled in the trees, and put me in mind of a snake slithering over dry leaves and twigs. I remembered a tale I had been told not long ago, of a sleeping boy who had been bitten by a cobra.

I would not, could not, sleep. I longed for my father . . .

The shutters rattled, the doors creaked. It was a night for ghosts.

Ghosts!

God, why did I have to think of them?

My God! There, standing by the bathroom door . . .

My father! My father dead from the malaria, and come to see me!

I threw myself at the switch. The room lit up. I sank down on the bed in complete exhaustion, the sweat soaking my nightclothes.

It was not my father I had seen. It was his dressing-grown hanging on the bathroom door. It had not been taken with him to the hospital.

I turned off the light.

The hush outside seemed deeper, nearer. I remembered the centipede, the bat, thought of the cobra and the sleeping boy; pulled the sheet tight over my head. If I could see nothing, well then, nothing could see me.

A thunderclap shattered the brooding stillness.

A streak of lightning forked across the sky, so close that even through the sheet I saw a tree and the opposite house silhouetted against the flashing canvas of gold.

I dived deeper beneath the bedclothes, gathered the pillow about my ears.

But at the next thunderclap, louder this time, louder than I had ever heard, I leapt from my bed. I could not stand it. I fled, blundering into the sweeper-boy's room.

The boy sat on the bare floor.

'What is happening?' he asked.

The lightning flashed, and his teeth and eyes flashed with it. Then he was a blur in the darkness.

'I am afraid,' I said.

I moved towards him and my hand touched a cold shoulder. 'Stay here,' he said. 'I too am afraid.'

I sat down, my back against the wall; beside the untouchable, the outcaste . . . and the thunder and lightning ceased, and the rain came down, swishing and drumming on the corrugated roof.

'The rainy season has started,' observed the sweeper-boy, turning to me. His smile played with the darkness, and then he laughed. And I laughed too, but feebly.

But I was happy and safe. The scent of the wet earth blew in through the skylight and the rain fell harder.

(This was my first short story, written when I was sixteen.)

All Creatures Great and Small

❧

INSTEAD OF HAVING BROTHERS and sisters to grow up with in India, I had as my companions an odd assortment of pets, which included a monkey, a tortoise, a python and a Great Indian Hornbill. The person responsible for all this wildlife in the home was my grandfather. As the house was his own, other members of the family could not prevent him from keeping a large variety of pets, though they could certainly voice their objections; and as most of the household consisted of women—my grandmother, visiting aunts and occasional in-laws (my parents were in Burma at the time)—Grandfather and I had to be alert and resourceful in dealing with them. We saw eye to eye on the subject of pets, and whenever Grandmother decided it was time to get rid of a tame white rat or a squirrel, I would conceal them in a hole in the jackfruit tree; but unlike my aunts, she was generally tolerant of Grandfather's hobby, and even took a liking to some of our pets.

Grandfather's house and menagerie were in Dehra and I remember travelling there in a horse-drawn buggy. There were cars in those days—it was just over twenty years ago—but in the foothills a tonga was just as good, almost as fast, and certainly more dependable when it came to getting across the swift little Tons river.

During the rains, when the river flowed strong and deep, it was impossible to get across except on a hand-operated ropeway; but in the dry months, the horse went splashing through, the carriage wheels churning through clear mountain water. If the horse found the going difficult, we removed our shoes, rolled up our skirts or trousers, and waded across.

When Grandfather first went to stay in Dehra, early in the century, the only way of getting there was by the night mail-coach. Mail ponies, he told me, were difficult animals, always attempting to turn around and get into the coach with the passengers. It was only when the coachman used his whip liberally, and reviled the ponies' ancestors as far back as their third and fourth generations, that the beasts could be persuaded to move. And once they started, there was no stopping them. It was a gallop all the way to the first stage, where the ponies were changed to the accompaniment of a bugle blown by the coachman.

At one stage of the journey, drums were beaten; and if it was night, torches were lit to keep away the wild elephants who, resenting the approach of this clumsy caravan, would sometimes trumpet a challenge and throw the ponies into confusion.

Grandfather disliked dressing up and going out, and was only too glad to send everyone shopping or to the pictures—Harold Lloyd and Eddie Cantor were the favourites at Dehra's small cinema—so that he could be left alone to feed his pets and potter about in the garden. There were a lot of animals to be fed, including, for a time, a pair of great Danes who had such enormous appetites that we were forced to give them away to a more affluent family.

The Great Danes were gentle creatures, and I would sit astride one of them and go for rides round the garden. In spite of their size, they were very sure-footed and never knocked over people or chairs. A little monkey, like Toto, did much more damage.

Grandfather bought Toto from a tonga-owner for the sum of five rupees. The tonga-man used to keep the little red monkey tied to a feeding-trough, and Toto looked so out of place there—almost conscious of his own incongruity—that Grandfather immediately decided to add him to our menagerie.

Toto was really a pretty little monkey. His bright eyes sparkled with mischief beneath deep-set eyebrows, and his teeth, a pearly-white, were often on display in a smile that frightened the life out of elderly Anglo-Indian ladies. His hands were not those of a Tallulah Bankhead (Grandfather's only favourite actress), but were shrivelled and dried-up, as though they had been pickled in the sun for many years. But his fingers were quick and restless; and his tail, while adding to his good looks—Grandfather maintained that a tail would add to anyone's good looks—often performed the service of a third hand. He could use it to hang from a branch; and it was capable of scooping up any delicacy that might be out of reach of his hands.

Grandmother, anticipating an outcry from other relatives, always raised objections when Grandfather brought home some new bird or animal, and so for a while we managed to keep Toto's presence a secret by lodging him in a little closet opening into my bedroom wall. But in a few hours he managed to dispose of Grandmother's ornamental wall-paper and the better part of my school blazer. He was transferred to the stables for a day or two, and then Grandfather had to make a trip to neighbouring Saharanpur to collect his railway pension and, anxious to keep Toto out of trouble, he decided to take the monkey along with him.

Unfortunately I could not accompany Grandfather on this trip, but he told me about it afterwards.

A black kit-bag was provided for Toto. When the strings of the bag were tied, there was no means of escape from within, and the canvas was too strong for Toto to bite his way through. His initial efforts to get out only had the effect of making the bag roll about on the floor, or occasionally jump in the air—an exhibition that attracted a curious crowd of onlookers on the Dehra railway platform.

Toto remained in the bag as far as Saharanpur, but while Grandfather was producing his ticket at the railway turnstile, Toto managed to get his hands through the aperture where the bag was tied, loosened the strings, and suddenly thrust his head through the opening.

The poor ticket-collector was visibly alarmed; but with great presence of mind, and much to the annoyance of Grandfather, he said, 'Sir, you have a dog with you. You'll have to pay for it accordingly.'

In vain did Grandfather take Toto out of the bag to prove that a monkey was not a dog or even a quadruped. The ticket-collector, now thoroughly annoyed, insisted on classing Toto as a dog; and three rupees and four annas had to be handed over as his fare. Then Grandfather, out of sheer spite, took out from his pocket a live tortoise that he happened to have with him, and said, 'What must I pay for this, since you charge for all animals?'

The ticket-collector retreated a pace or two; then advancing again with caution, he subjected the tortoise to a grave and knowledgeable stare.

'No ticket is necessary, sir,' he finally declared. 'There is no charge for insects.'

When we discovered that Toto's favourite pastime was catching mice, we were able to persuade Grandmother to let us keep him. The unsuspecting mice would emerge from their holes at night to pick up any corn left over by our pony; and to get at it they had to run the gauntlet of Toto's section of the stable. He knew this, and would pretend to be asleep, keeping, however, one eye open. A mouse would make a rush—in vain; Toto, as swift as a cat, would have his paws upon him . . . Grandmother decided to put his talents to constructive use by tying him up one night in the larder, where a guerrilla-band of mice were playing havoc with our food supplies.

Toto was removed from his comfortable bed of straw in the stable, and chained up in the larder, beneath shelves of jam-pots and other delicacies. The night was a long and miserable one for Toto, who must have wondered what he had done to deserve such treatment. The mice scampered about the place, while he, most uncatlike, lay curled up in a soup tureen, trying to snatch some sleep. At dawn, the mice returned to their holes; Toto awoke, scratched himself, emerged from the soup tureen, and looked about for something to eat. The jam-pots attracted his notice, and it did not take him long to prise open the covers. Grandmother's treasured jams—she had made most of them herself—disappeared in an amazingly short time. I was present when she opened the door to see how many mice Toto had caught. Even the rain-god Indra could not have looked more terrible when planning a thunderstorm; and the imprecations Grandmother hurled at Toto were surprising coming from someone who had been brought up in the genteel Victorian manner.

The monkey was later reinstated in Grandmother's favour. A great treat for him on cold winter evenings was the large bowl of warm water provided by Grandmother for his bath. He would bathe himself, first of all gingerly testing the temperature of the water with his fingers. Leisurely he would step into the bath, first one foot, then the other, as he had seen me doing, until he was completely sitting down in it. Once comfortable, he would take the soap in his hands or feet, and rub himself all over. When he found the water becoming cold, he would get out and run as quickly as he could to the fire, where his coat soon dried. If anyone laughed at him during this performance, he would look extremely hurt, and refuse to go on with his ablutions.

One day Toto nearly succeeded in boiling himself to death.

The large kitchen kettle had been left on the fire to boil for tea; and Toto, finding himself for a few minutes alone with it, decided to take the lid off. On discovering that the water inside was warm, he got into the kettle with the intention of having a bath, and sat down with his head protruding from the opening. This was very pleasant for some time, until the water began to simmer. Toto raised himself a little, but finding it cold outside, sat down again. He continued standing and sitting for some time, not having the courage to face the cold air. Had it not been for the timely arrival of Grandmother, he would have been cooked alive.

If there is a part of the brain especially devoted to mischief, that part must have been largely developed in Toto. He was always tearing things to bits, and whenever one of my aunts came near him, he made every effort to get hold of her dress and tear a hole in it. A variety of aunts frequently came to stay with my grandparents, but during Toto's stay they limited their visits to a day or two, much to Grandfather's relief and Grandmother's annoyance.

Toto, however, took a liking to Grandmother, in spite of the beatings he often received from her. Whenever she allowed him the liberty, he would lie quietly in her lap instead of scrambling all over her as he did on most people.

Toto lived with us over a year, but the following winter, after too much bathing, he caught pneumonia. Grandmother wrapped him in flannel, and Grandfather gave him a diet of chicken soup and Irish stew; but Toto did not recover. He was buried in the garden, under his favourite mango tree.

Perhaps it was just as well that Toto was no longer with us when Grandfather brought home the python, or his demise might have been less conventional. Small monkeys are a favourite delicacy with pythons.

Grandmother was tolerant of most birds and animals, but she drew the line at reptiles. She said they made her blood run cold. Even a handsome, sweet-tempered chameleon had to be given up. Grandfather should have known that there was little chance of his being allowed to keep the python. It was about four feet long, a young one, when Grandfather bought it from a snake-charmer for six rupees, impressing the bazaar crowd by slinging it across his shoulders and walking home with it. Grandmother nearly fainted at the sight of the python curled round Grandfather's throat.

'You'll be strangled!' she cried. 'Get rid of it at once!'

'Nonsense,' said Grandfather. 'He's only a young fellow. He'll soon get used to us.'

'Will he, indeed?' said Grandmother. 'But I have no intention of getting used to him. You know quite well that your cousin Mabel is coming to stay with us tomorrow. She'll leave us the minute she knows there's a snake in the house.'

'Well, perhaps we ought to show it to her as soon as she arrives,' said Grandfather, who did not look forward to fussy Aunt Mabel's visits any more than I did.

'You'll do no such thing,' said Grandmother.

'Well, I can't let it loose in the garden,' said Grandfather with an innocent expression. 'It might find its way into the poultry house, and then where would we be?'

'How exasperating you are!' grumbled Grandmother. 'Lock the creature in the bathroom, go back to the bazaar and find the man you bought it from, and get him to come and take it back.'

In my awestruck presence, Grandfather had to take the python into the bathroom, where he placed it in a steep-sided tin tub. Then he hurried off to the bazaar to look for the snake-charmer, while Grandmother paced anxiously up and down the veranda. When he returned looking crestfallen, we knew he hadn't been able to find the man.

'You had better take it away yourself,' said Grandmother, in a relentless mood. 'Leave it in the jungle across the river-bed.'

'All right, but let me give it a feed first,' said Grandfather; and producing a plucked chicken, he took it into the bathroom, followed, in single file, by me, Grandmother, and a curious cook and gardener.

Grandfather threw open the door and stepped into the bathroom. I peeped round his legs, while the others remained well behind. We couldn't see the python anywhere.

'He's gone,' announced Grandfather. 'He must have felt hungry.'

'I hope he isn't too hungry,' I said.

'We left the window open,' said Grandfather, looking embarrassed.

A careful search was made of the house, the kitchen, the garden, the stable and the poultry shed; but the python couldn't be found anywhere.

'He'll be well away by now,' said Grandfather reassuringly.

'I certainly hope so,' said Grandmother, who was half way between anxiety and relief.

Aunt Mabel arrived next day for a three-week visit, and for a couple of days Grandfather and I were a little apprehensive in case the python made a sudden reappearance; but on the third day, when he didn't show up, we felt confident that he had gone for good.

And then, towards evening, we were startled by a scream from the garden. Seconds later, Aunt Mabel came flying up the veranda steps, looking as though she had seen a ghost.

'In the guava tree!' she gasped. 'I was reaching for a guava, when I saw it staring at me. The *look* in its eyes! As though it would *devour* me—'

'Calm down, my dear,' urged Grandmother, sprinkling her with eau-de-cologne. 'Calm down and tell us what you saw.'

'A snake!' sobbed Aunt Mabel. 'A great boa-constrictor. It must have been twenty feet long! In the guava tree. Its eyes were terrible. It looked at me in such a *queer* way . . .'

My grandparents looked significantly at each other, and

Grandfather said, 'I'll go out and kill it,' and sheepishly taking hold of an umbrella, sallied out into the garden. But when he reached the guava tree, the python had disappeared.

'Aunt Mabel must have frightened it away,' I said.

'Hush,' said Grandfather. 'We mustn't speak of your aunt in that way.' But his eyes were alive with laughter.

After this incident, the python began to make a series of appearances, often in the most unexpected places. Aunt Mabel had another fit of hysterics when she saw him admiring her from under a cushion. She packed her bags, and Grandmother made us intensify the hunt.

Next morning I saw the python curled up on the dressing-table, gazing at his reflection in the mirror. I went for Grandfather, but by the time we returned the python had moved elsewhere. A little later he was seen in the garden again. Then he was back on the dressing-table, admiring himself in the mirror. Evidently he had become enamoured of his own reflection. Grandfather observed that perhaps the attention he was receiving from everyone had made him a little conceited.

'He's trying to look better for Aunt Mabel,' I said; a remark that I instantly regretted, because Grandmother overheard it, and brought the flat of her broad hand down on my head.

'Well, now we know his weakness,' said Grandfather.

'Are you trying to be funny too?' demanded Grandmother, looking her most threatening.

'I only meant he was becoming very vain,' said Grandfather hastily. 'It should be easier to catch him now.'

He set about preparing a large cage with a mirror at one end. In the cage he left a juicy chicken and various other delicacies, and fitted up the opening with a trap-door. Aunt Mabel had already left by the time we had this trap ready, but we had to go on with the project because we couldn't have the python prowling about the house indefinitely.

For a few days nothing happened, and then, as I was leaving for school one morning, I saw the python curled up in the cage. He had eaten everything left out for him, and was relaxing in front of the mirror with something resembling a smile on his face—if you can imagine a python smiling . . . . I lowered the trap-door gently, but the python took no notice; he was in raptures over his handsome reflection. Grandfather and the gardener put the cage in the ponytrap, and made a journey to the other side of the river-bed. They left the cage in the jungle, with the trap-door open.

'He made no attempt to get out,' said Grandfather later. 'And I didn't have the heart to take the mirror away. It's the first time I've seen a snake fall in love.'

And the frogs have sung their old song in the mud . . . . This was Grandfather's favourite quotation from Virgil, and he used it whenever we visited the rain-water pond behind the house where there were quantities of mud and frogs and the occasional water buffalo. Grandfather had once brought a number of frogs into the house. He had put them in a glass jar, left them on a window-sill, and then forgotten all about them. At about four o'clock in the morning the entire household was awakened by a loud and fearful noise, and Grandmother and several nervous relatives gathered in their night-clothes on the veranda. Their timidity changed to fury when they discovered that the ghastly sounds had come from Grandfather's frogs. Seeing the dawn breaking, the frogs had with one accord begun their morning song.

Grandmother wanted to throw the frogs, bottle and all, out of the window; but Grandfather said that if he gave the bottle a good shaking, the frogs would remain quiet. He was obliged to keep awake, in order to shake the bottle whenever the frogs showed any inclination to break into song. Fortunately for all concerned, the next day a servant took the top off the bottle to see what was inside. The sight of several big frogs so startled him that he ran off without replacing the cover; the frogs jumped out and presumably found their way back to the pond.

It became a habit with me to visit the pond on my own, in order to explore its banks and shallows. Taking off my shoes, I would wade into the muddy water up to my knees, to pluck the water-lilies that floated on the surface.

One day I found the pond already occupied by several buffaloes. Their keeper, a boy a little older than me, was swimming about in the middle. Instead of climbing out on to the bank, he would pull himself up on the back of one of his buffaloes, stretch his naked brown body out on the animal's glistening wet hide, and start singing to himself.

When he saw me staring at him from across the pond, he smiled, showing gleaming white teeth in a dark, sun-burnished face. He invited me to join him in a swim. I told him I couldn't swim, and he offered to teach me. I hesitated, knowing that Grandmother held strict and old-fashioned views about mixing with village children; but, deciding that Grandfather—who sometimes smoked a hookah on the sly—would get me out of any trouble that might occur, I took the bold step of accepting the boy's offer. Once taken, the step did not seem so bold.

He dived off the back of his buffalo, and swam across to me. And I, having removed my clothes, followed his instructions until I was floundering about among the water-lilies. His name was Ramu, and he promised to give me swimming lessons every afternoon; and so it was during the afternoons—especially summer afternoons when everyone was asleep—that we usually met. Before long I was able to swim across the pond to sit with Ramu astride a contented buffalo, the great beast standing like an island in the middle of a muddy ocean.

Sometimes we would try racing the buffaloes, Ramu and I sitting on different mounts. But they were lazy creatures, and would leave one comfortable spot only to look for another; or, if they were in no mood for games, would roll over on their backs, taking us with them into the mud and green slime of the pond. Emerging in shades of green and khaki, I would slip into the house through the bathroom and bathe under the tap before getting into my clothes.

One afternoon Ramu and I found a small tortoise in the mud, sitting over a hole in which it had laid several eggs. Ramu kept the eggs for his dinner, and I presented the tortoise to Grandfather. He had a weakness for tortoises, and was pleased with this addition to his menagerie, giving it a large tub of water all to itself, with an island of rocks in the middle. The tortoise, however, was always getting out of the tub and wandering about the house. As it seemed able to look after itself quite well, we did not interfere. If one of the dogs bothered it too much, it would draw its head and legs into its shell and defy all their attempts at rough play.

Ramu came from a family of bonded labourers, and had received no schooling. But he was well-versed in folklore, and knew a great deal about birds and animals.

'Many birds are sacred,' said Ramu, as we watched a bluejay swoop down from a peepul tree and carry off a grasshopper. He told me that both the bluejay and the god Shiva were called Nilkanth. Shiva had a blue throat, like the bird, because out of compassion for the human race he had swallowed a deadly poison which was intended to destroy the world. Keeping the poison in his throat, he did not let it go any further.

'Are squirrels sacred?' I asked, seeing one sprint down the trunk of the pipal tree.

'Oh yes, Lord Krishna loved squirrels,' said Ramu. He would take them in his arms and stroke them with his long fingers. That is why they have four dark lines down their backs from head to tail. Krishna was very dark, and the lines are the marks of his fingers.

Both Ramu and Grandfather were of the opinion that we should be more gentle with birds and animals and should not kill so many of them.

'It is also important that we respect them,' said Grandfather. 'We must acknowledge their rights. Everywhere, birds and animals are finding it more difficult to survive, because we are trying to destroy both them and their forests. They have to keep moving as the trees disappear.'

This was especially true of the forests near Dehra, where the tiger and the pheasant and the spotted deer were beginning to disappear.

Ramu and I spent many long summer afternoons at the pond. I still remember him with affection, though we never saw each other again after I left Dehra. He could not read or write, so we were unable to keep in touch. And neither his people, nor mine, knew of our friendship. The buffaloes and frogs had been our only confidants. They had accepted us as part of their own world, their muddy but comfortable pond. And when I left Dehra, both they and Ramu must have assumed that I would return again like the birds.

COMING HOME TO DEHRA

ॐ

THE FAINT QUEASINESS I always feel towards the end of a journey probably has its origin in that first homecoming after my father's death.

It was the winter of '44—yes, a long time ago— and the train was running through the thick sal forests near Dehra, bringing me at every click of the rails nearer to the mother I hadn't seen for four years and the stepfather I had seen just once or twice before my parents were divorced.

I was eleven and I was coming home to Dehra.

Three years earlier, after the separation, I had gone to live with my father. We were very happy together. He was serving in the RAF, at New Delhi, and we lived in a large tent somewhere near Humayun's tomb. The area is now a very busy part of urban Delhi, but in those days it was still a wilderness of scrub jungle where black buck and nilgai roamed freely. We took long walks together, exploring the ruins of old tombs and forts; went to the pictures (George Formby comedies were special favourites of mine); collected stamps; bought books (my father had taught me to read and write before I started going to school); and made plans for going to England when the war was over.

Six months of bliss, even though it was summer and there weren't any fans, only a thick khus reed curtain which had to be splashed with water every hour by a *bhisti* (water-carrier) who did the rounds of similar tents with his goat-skin water bag. I remember the tender refreshing fragrance of the khus, and also the smell of damp earth outside, where the water had spilt.

A happy time. But it had to end. My father's periodic bouts of malarial fever resulted in his having to enter hospital for a week. The *bhisti's* small son came to stay with me at night, and during the day I took my meals with an Anglo-Indian family across the road.

I would have been quite happy to continue with this arrangement whenever my father was absent, but someone at Air Headquarters must have advised him to put me in a boarding school.

Reluctantly he came to the decision that this would be the best thing—'until the war is over'—and in the June of '43 he took me to Shimla, where I was incarcerated in a preparatory school for boys.

This is not the story of my life at boarding school. It might easily have been a public school in England; it did in fact pride itself on being the 'Eton of the East'. The traditions—such as ragging and flogging, compulsory games and chapel attendance, prefects larger than life, and Honour Boards for everything from school captaincy to choir membership—had all apparently been borrowed from *Tom Brown's Schooldays*.

My father wrote to me regularly, and his letters were the things I looked forward to more than anything else. I went to him for the winter holidays, and the following summer he came to Shimla during my mid-term break and took me out for the duration of the holidays. We stayed in a hotel called Craig-Dhu, on a spur north of Jacko Hill. It was an idyllic week; long walks; stories about phantom rickshaws; ice-creams in the sun; browsings in bookshops; more plans: 'We will go to England next year.'

School seemed a stupid and heartless place after my father had gone away. He had been transferred to Calcutta and he wasn't keeping well there. Malaria again. And then jaundice. But his last letter sounded quite cheerful. He'd been selling part of his valuable stamp collection so as to have enough money for the fares to England.

One day my class-teacher sent for me.

'I want to talk to you, Bond,' he said. 'Let's go for a walk.'

I knew immediately that something was wrong.

We took the path that went through the deodar forest, past Council Rock where Scout meetings were held. As soon as my unfortunate teacher (no doubt cursing the Headmaster for having given him this unpleasant task) started on the theme of 'God wanting your father in a higher and better place', as though there could be any better place than Jacko Hill in mid-summer, I knew my father was dead, and burst into tears.

They let me stay in the school hospital for a few days until I felt better. The Headmaster visited me there and took away the pile of my father's letters that I'd kept beside me.

'Your father's letters. You might lose them. Why not leave them with me? Then at the end of the year, before you go home, you can come and collect them.'

Unwillingly I gave him the letters. He told me he'd heard from my mother that I would be going home to her at the end of the year. He seemed surprised that I evinced no interest in this prospect.

At the end of the year, the day before school closed, I went to the HM's office and asked for my letters.

'What letters?' he said. His desk was piled with papers and correspondence, and he was irritated by my interruption.

'My father's letters,' I explained. 'I gave them to you to keep for me, Sir—when he died . . .'

'Letters. Are you sure you gave them to me?'

He grew more irritated. 'You must be mistaken, Bond. Why should I want to keep your father's letters?'

'I don't know, sir. You said I could collect them before going home.'

'Look, I don't remember any letters and I'm very busy just now, so run along. I'm sure you're mistaken, but if I find your letters, I'll send them to you.'

I don't suppose he meant to be unkind, but he was the first man who aroused in me feelings of hate . . .

As the train drew into Dehra. I looked out of the window to see if there was anyone on the platform waiting to receive me. The station was crowded enough, as most railway stations are in India, with overloaded travellers, shouting coolies, stray dogs, stray station-masters . . . . Pandemonium broke loose as the train came to a halt and people debouched from the carriages. I was thrust on the platform with my tin trunk and small attache case. I sat on the trunk and waited for someone to find me.

Slowly the crowd melted away. I was left with one elderly coolie who was too feeble to carry heavy luggage and had decided that my trunk was just the right size and weight for his head and shoulders. I waited another ten minutes, but no representative of my mother or stepfather appeared. I permitted the coolie to lead me out of the station to the tonga stand.

Those were the days when everyone, including high-ranking officials, went about in tongas. Dehra had just one taxi. I was quite happy sitting beside a rather smelly, paan-spitting tonga-driver, while his weary, underfed pony clip-clopped along the quiet tree-lined roads.

Dehra was always a good place for trees. The valley soil is very fertile, the rainfall fairly heavy; almost everything grows there, if given the chance. The roads were lined with neem and mango trees, eucalyptus, Persian lilac, jacaranda, amaltas (laburnum) and many others. In the gardens of the bungalows were mangoes, litchis and guavas; sometimes jackfruit and papaya. I did not notice all these trees at once; I came to know them as time passed.

The tonga first took me to my grandmother's house. I was under the impression that my mother still lived there.

A lovely, comfortable bungalow that spread itself about the grounds in an easygoing, old-fashioned way. There was even smoke coming from the chimneys, reminding me of the smoke from my grandfather's pipe. When I was eight, I had spent several months there with my grandparents. In retrospect it had been an idyllic interlude. But Grandfather was dead. Grandmother lived alone.

White-haired, but still broad in the face and even broader behind, she was astonished to see me getting down from the tonga.

'Didn't anyone meet you at the station?' she asked.

I shook my head. Grandmother said: 'Your mother doesn't live here any more. You can come in and wait, but she may be worried about you, so I'd better take you to her place. Come on, help me up into the tonga . . . . I might have known it would be a white horse. It always makes me nervous sitting in a tonga behind a white horse.'

'Why, Granny?'

'I don't know, I suppose white horses are nervous, too. Anyway, they are always trying to topple me out. Not so fast, driver!' she called out, as the tonga-man cracked his whip and the pony changed from a slow shuffle to a brisk trot.

It took us about twenty-five minutes to reach my stepfather's house which was in the Dalanwala area, not far from the dry bed of the seasonal Rispana river. My grandmother, seeing that I was in need of moral support, got down with me, while the tonga-driver carried my bedding roll and tin trunk on to the veranda. The front door was bolted from inside. We had to knock on it repeatedly and call out before it was opened by a servant who did not look pleased at being disturbed. When he saw my grandmother he gave her a deferential salaam, then gazed at me with open curiosity.

'Where's the memsahib?' asked grandmother.

'Out,' said the servant.

'I can see that, but where have they gone?'

'They went yesterday to Motichur, for shikar. They will be back this evening.'

Grandmother looked upset, but motioned to the servant to bring in my things. 'Weren't they expecting the boy?' she asked. 'Yes,' he said looking at me again. 'But they said he would be arriving tomorrow.'

'They'd forgotten the date,' said Grandmother in a huff. 'Anyway, you can unpack and have a wash and change your clothes.'

Turning to the servant, she asked, 'Is there any lunch?'

'I will make lunch,' he said. He was staring at me again, and I felt uneasy with his eyes on me. He was tall and swarthy, with oily, jet-back hair and a thick moustache. A heavy scar ran down his left cheek, giving him a rather sinister appearance. He wore a torn shirt and dirty pyjamas. His broad, heavy feet were wet. They left marks on the uncarpeted floor.

A baby was crying in the next room, and presently a woman (who turned out to be the cook's wife) appeared in the doorway, jogging the child in her arms.

'They've left the baby behind, too,' said Grandmother, becoming more and more irate. 'He is your young brother. Only six months old.' I hadn't been told anything about a younger brother. The discovery that I had one came as something of a shock. I wasn't prepared for a baby brother, least of all a baby half-brother. I examined the child without much enthusiasm. He looked healthy enough and he cried with gusto.

'He's a beautiful baby,' said Grandmother. 'Well, I've got work to do. The servants will look after you. You can come and see me in a day or two. You've grown since I last saw you. And you're getting pimples.'

This reference to my appearance did not displease me as Grandmother never indulged in praise. For her to have observed my pimples indicated that she was fond of me.

The tonga-driver was waiting for her. 'I suppose I'll have to use the same tonga,' she said. 'Whenever I need a tonga, they disappear, except for the ones with white ponies . . . . When your mother gets back, tell her I want to see her. Shikar, indeed. An infant to look after, and they've gone shooting.'

Grandmother settled herself in the tonga, nodded in response to the cook's salaam, and took a tight grip of the armrests of her seat. The driver flourished his whip and the pony set off at the same listless, unhurried trot, while my grandmother, feeling quite certain that she was going to be hurtled to her doom by a wild white pony, set her teeth and clung tenaciously to the tonga seat. I was sorry to see her go.

My mother and stepfather returned in the evening from their hunting trip with a pheasant which was duly handed over to the cook, whose name was Mangal Singh. My mother gave me a perfunctory kiss. I think she was pleased to see me, but I was accustomed to a more intimate caress from my father, and the strange reception I had received made me realize the extent of my loss. Boarding school life had been routine. Going home was something that I had always looked forward to. But going home had meant my father, and now he had vanished and I was left quite desolate.

I suppose if one is present when a loved one dies, or sees him dead and laid out and later buried, one is convinced of the finality of the thing and finds it easier to adapt to the changed circumstances. But when you hear of a death, a father's death, and have only the faintest idea of the manner of his dying, it is rather a lot for the imagination to cope with—especially when the imagination is a small boy's. There being no tangible evidence of my father's death, it was, for me, not a death but a vanishing. And although this enabled me to remember him as a living, smiling, breathing person, it meant that I was not wholly reconciled to his death, and subconsciously expected him to turn up (as he often did, when I most needed him) and deliver me from an unpleasant situation.

My stepfather barely noticed me. The first thing he did on coming into the house was to pour himself a whisky and soda. My mother, after inspecting the baby, did likewise. I was left to unpack and settle in my room.

I was fortunate in having my own room. I was as desirous of my own privacy as much as my mother and stepfather were desirous of theirs. My stepfather, a local businessman, was ready to put up with me provided I did not get in the way. And, in a different way, I was ready to put up with him, provided he left me alone. I was even willing that my mother should leave me alone.

There was a big window to my room, and I opened it to the evening breeze, and gazed out on to the garden, a rather unkempt place where marigolds and a sort of wild blue everlasting grew rampant among the litchi trees.

WHAT'S YOUR DREAM?

❧

AN OLD MAN, A beggar man bent double, with a flowing white beard and piercing grey eyes, stopped on the road on the other side of the garden wall and looked up at me, where I perched on the branch of a litchi tree.

'What's your dream?' he asked.

It was a startling question coming from that raggedy old man on the street. Even more startling that it should have been made in English. English-speaking beggars were a rarity in those days.

'What's your dream?' he repeated.

'I don't remember,' I said. 'I don't think I had a dream last night.'

'That's not what I mean. You know it isn't what I mean. I can see you're a dreamer. It's not the litchi season, but you sit in that tree all afternoon, dreaming.'

'I just like sitting here,' I said. I refused to admit that I was a dreamer. Other boys didn't dream, they had catapults.

'A dream, my boy, is what you want most in life. Isn't there something that you want more than anything else?'

'Yes,' I said promptly. 'A room of my own.'

'Ah! A room of your own, a tree of your own, it's the same thing. Not many people can have their own rooms, you know. Not in a land as crowded as ours.'

'Just a small room.'

'And what kind of room do you live in at present?'

'It's a big room, but I have to share it with my brothers and sisters and even my aunt when she visits.'

'I see. What you really want is freedom. Your own tree, your own room, your own small place in the sun.'

'Yes, that's all.'

'That's all? That's everything! When you have all that, you'll have found your dream.'

'Tell me how to find it!'

'There's no magic formula, my friend. If I was a godman, would I be wasting my time here with you? You must work for your dream and move towards it all the time, and discard all those things that come in the way of finding it. And then, if you don't expect too much too quickly, you'll find your freedom, a room of your own. The difficult time comes afterwards.'

'Afterwards?'

'Yes, because it's so easy to lose it all, to let someone take it away from you. Or you become greedy, or careless, and start taking everything for granted, and—poof!—suddenly the dream has gone, vanished!'

'How do you know all this?' I asked.

'Because I had my dream and lost it.'

'Did you lose everything?'

'Yes, just look at me now, my friend. Do I look like a king or a godman? I had everything I wanted, but then I wanted more and more . . . . You get your room, and then you want a building, and when you have your building you want your own territory, and when you have your own territory you want your own kingdom—and all the time it's getting harder to keep everything. And when you lose it—in the end, all kingdoms are lost—you don't even have your room any more.'

'Did you have a kingdom?'

'Something like that . . . . Follow your own dream, boy, but don't take other people's dreams, don't stand in anyone's way, don't take from another man his room or his faith or his song.' And he turned and shuffled away, intoning the following verse which I have never heard elsewhere, so it must have been his own—

Live long, my friend, be wise and strong,
But do not take from any man his song.

I remained in the litchi tree, pondering his wisdom and wondering how a man so wise could be so poor. Perhaps he became wise afterwards. Anyway, he was free, and I was free, and I went back to the house and demanded (and got) a room of my own. Freedom, I was beginning to realize, is something you have to insist upon.

THE LAST TONGA RIDE

❧

IT WAS A WARM spring day in Dehradun, and the walls of the
bungalow were aflame with flowering bougainvillaea. The
papayas were ripening. The scent of sweetpeas drifted across
the garden. Grandmother sat in an easy chair in a shady corner
of the veranda, her knitting needles clicking away, her head
nodding now and then. She was knitting a pullover for my
father. 'Delhi has cold winters,' she had said, and although the
winter was still eight months away, she had set to work on
getting our woollens ready.

In the Kathiawar states touched by the warm waters of the
Arabian Sea, it had never been cold. But Dehra lies at the foot
of the first range of the Himalayas.

Grandmother's hair was white and her eyes were not very
strong, but her fingers moved quickly with the needles and the
needles kept clicking all morning.

When Grandmother wasn't looking, I picked geranium leaves,
crushed them between my fingers and pressed them to my nose.

I had been in Dehra with my grandmother for almost a
month and I had not seen my father during this time. We had
never before been separated for so long. He wrote to me every
week, and sent me books and picture postcards, and I would
walk to the end of the road to meet the postman as early as
possible to see if there was any mail for us.

We heard the jingle of tonga-bells at the gate and a familiar
horse-buggy came rattling up the drive.

'I'll see who's come,' I said, and ran down the veranda
steps and across the garden.

It was Bansi Lal in his tonga. There were many tongas and tonga-drivers in Dehra but Bansi was my favourite driver. He was young and handsome and he always wore a clean white shirt and pyjamas. His pony, too, was bigger and faster than the other tonga ponies.

Bansi didn't have a passenger, so I asked him, 'What have you come for, Bansi?'

'Your grandmother sent for me, *dost.'* He did not call me *'chota sahib'* or 'baba', 'but *dost'* and this made me feel much more important. Not every small boy could boast of a tonga-driver for his friend!

'Where are you going, Granny?' I asked, after I had run back to the veranda.

'I'm going to the bank.'

'Can I come too?'

'Whatever for? What will you do in the bank?'

'Oh, I won't come inside, I'll sit in the tonga with Bansi.'

'Come along, then.'

We helped Grandmother into the back seat of the tonga, and then I joined Bansi in the driver's seat. He said something to his pony and the pony set off at a brisk trot, out of the gate and down the road.

'Now, not too fast, Bansi,' said Grandmother, who didn't like anything that went too fast—tonga, motor car, train, or bullock-cart.

'Fast?' said Bansi. 'Have no fear, memsahib. This pony has never gone fast in its life. Even if a bomb went off behind us, we could go no faster. I have another pony which I use for racing when customers are in a hurry. This pony is reserved for you, memsahib.'

There was no other pony, but Grandmother did not know this, and was mollified by the assurance that she was riding in the slowest tonga in Dehra.

A ten-minute ride brought us to the bazaar. Grandmother's bank, the Allahabad Bank, stood near the clock tower. She was gone for about half-an-hour and during this period Bansi and I sauntered about in front of the shops. The pony had been left with some green stuff to munch.

'Do you have any money on you?' asked Bansi.

'Four annas,' I said.

'Just enough for two cups of tea,' said Bansi, putting his arm round my shoulders and guiding me towards a tea stall. The money passed from my palm to his.

'You can have tea, if you like,' I said. 'I'll have a lemonade.'

'So be it, friend. A tea and a lemonade, and be quick about it,' said Bansi to the boy in the tea shop and presently the drinks were set before us and Bansi was making a sound rather like his pony when it drank, while I burped my way through some green, gaseous stuff that tasted more like soap than lemonade.

When Grandmother came out of the bank, she looked pensive and did not talk much during the ride back to the house except to tell me to behave myself when I leant over to pat the pony on its rump. After paying off Bansi, she marched straight indoors.

'When will you come again?' I asked Bansi.

'When my services are required, *dost*. I have to make a living, you know. But I tell you what, since we are friends, the next time I am passing this way after leaving a fare, I will jingle my bells at the gate and if you are free and would like a ride—a fast ride!—you can join me. It won't cost you anything. Just bring some money for a cup of tea.'

'All right—since we are friends,' I said.

'Since we are friends.'

And touching the pony very lightly with the handle of his whip, he sent the tonga rattling up the drive and out of the gate. I could hear Bansi singing as the pony cantered down the road.

Ayah was waiting for me in the bedroom, her hands resting on her broad hips—sure sign of an approaching storm.

'So you went off to the bazaar without telling me,' she said. (It wasn't enough that I had Grandmother's permission!) 'And all this time I've been waiting to give you your bath.'

'It's too late now, isn't it?' I asked hopefully.

'No, it isn't. There's still an hour left for lunch. Off with your clothes!'

While I undressed, Ayah berated me for keeping the company of tonga-drivers like Bansi. I think she was a little jealous.

'He is a rogue, that man. He drinks, gambles, and smokes

opium. He has T.B. and other terrible diseases. So don't you be too friendly with him, understand, baba?'

I nodded my head sagely but said nothing. I thought Ayah was exaggerating as she always did about people, and besides, I had no intention of giving up free tonga rides.

As my father had told me, Dehra was a good place for trees, and Grandmother's house was surrounded by several kinds— pipal, neem, mango, jackfruit, papaya, and an ancient banyan tree. Some of the trees had been planted by my father and grandfather.

'How old is the jackfruit tree?' I asked Grandmother.

'Now let me see,' said Grandmother, looking very thoughtful. 'I should remember the jackfruit tree. Oh yes, your grandfather put it down in 1927. It was during the rainy season. I remember because it was your father's birthday and we celebrated it by planting a tree—14 July 1927. Long before you were born!'

The banyan tree grew behind the house. Its spreading branches, which hung to the ground and took root again, formed a number of twisting passageways in which I liked to wander. The tree was older than the house, older than my grandparents, as old as Dehra. I could hide myself in its branches behind thick, green leaves and spy on the world below.

It was an enormous tree, about sixty feet high, and the first time I saw it I trembled with excitement because I had never seen such a marvellous tree before. I approached it slowly, even cautiously, as I wasn't sure the tree wanted my friendship. It looked as though it had many secrets. There were sounds and movements in the branches but I couldn't see who or what made the sounds.

The tree made the first move, the first overture of friendship. It allowed a leaf to fall.

The leaf brushed against my face as it floated down, but before it could reach the ground I caught and held it. I studied the leaf, running my fingers over its smooth, glossy texture. Then I put out my hand and touched the rough bark of the tree and this felt good to me. So I removed my shoes and socks as people do when they enter a holy place; and finding first a foothold and then a handhold on that broad trunk, I pulled myself up with the help of the tree's aerial roots.

As I climbed, it seemed as though someone was helping me. Invisible hands, the hands of the spirit in the tree, touched me and helped me climb.

But although the tree wanted me, there were others who were disturbed and alarmed by my arrival. A pair of parrots suddenly shot out of a hole in the trunk and with shrill cries, flew across the garden—flashes of green and red and gold. A squirrel looked out from behind a branch, saw me, and went scurrying away to inform his friends and relatives.

I climbed higher, looked up, and saw a red beak poised above my head. I shrank away, but the hornbill made no attempt to attack me. He was relaxing in his home, which was a great hole in the tree trunk. Only the bird's head and great beak were showing. He looked at me in rather a bored way, drowsily opening and shutting his eyes.

'So many creatures live here,' I said to myself. 'I hope none of them is dangerous!'

At that moment the hornbill lunged at a passing cricket. Bill and tree trunk met with a loud and resonant 'Tonk!'

I was so startled that I nearly fell out of the tree. But it was a difficult tree to fall out of! It was full of places where one could sit or even lie down. So I moved away from the hornbill, crawled along a branch which had sent out supports, and so moved quite a distance from the main body of the tree. I left its cold, dark depths for an area penetrated by shafts of sunlight.

No one could see me. I lay flat on the broad branch hidden by a screen of leaves. People passed by on the road below. A sahib in a sun-helmet, his memsahib twirling a coloured silk sun-umbrella. Obviously she did not want to get too brown and be mistaken for a country-born person. Behind them, a pram wheeled along by a nanny.

Then there were a number of Indians—some in white dhotis, some in western clothes, some in loincloths. Some with baskets on their heads. Others with coolies to carry their baskets for them.

A cloud of dust, the blare of a horn, and down the road, like an out-of-condition dragon, came the latest Morris touring car. Then cyclists. Then a man with a basket of papayas balanced on his head. Following him, a man with a performing monkey. This man rattled a little hand-drum, and children followed man and monkey along the road. They stopped in the shade of a mango tree on the other side of the road. The little red monkey wore a frilled dress and a baby's bonnet. It danced for the children, while the man sang and played his drum.

The clip-clop of a tonga pony, and Bansi's tonga came rattling down the road. I called down to him and he reined in with a shout of surprise, and looked up into the branches of the banyan tree.

'What are you doing up there?' he cried.

'Hiding from Grandmother,' I said.

'And when are you coming for that ride?'

'On Tuesday afternoon,' I said.

'Why not today?'

'Ayah won't let me. But she has Tuesdays off.'

Bansi spat red paan-juice across the road. 'Your ayah is jealous,' he said.

'I know,' I said. 'Women are always jealous, aren't they? I suppose it's because she doesn't have a tonga.'

'It's because she doesn't have a tonga-driver,' said Bansi, grinning up at me. 'Never mind. I'll come on Tuesday—that's the day after tomorrow, isn't it?'

I nodded down to him, and then started backing along my branch, because I could hear Ayah calling in the distance. Bansi leant forward and smacked his pony across the rump, and the tonga shot forward.

'What were you doing up there?' asked Ayah a little later.

'I was watching a snake cross the road,' I said. I knew she couldn't resist talking about snakes. There weren't as many in Dehra as there had been in Kathiawar and she was thrilled that I had seen one.

'Was it moving towards you or away from you?' she asked.

'It was going away.'

Ayah's face clouded over. 'That means poverty for the beholder,' she said gloomily.

Later, while scrubbing me down in the bathroom, she began to air all her prejudices, which included drunkards ('they die quickly, anyway'), misers ('they get murdered sooner or later') and tonga-drivers ('they have all the vices').

'You are a very lucky boy,' she said suddenly, peering closely at my tummy.

'Why?' I asked. 'You just said I would be poor because I saw a snake going the wrong way.'

'Well, you won't be poor for long. You have a mole on your tummy and that's very lucky. And there is one under your armpit, which means you will be famous. Do you have one on the neck? No, thank God! A mole on the neck is the sign of a murderer!'

'Do you have any moles?' I asked.

Ayah nodded seriously, and pulling her sleeve up to her shoulder, showed me a large mole high on her arm.

'What does that mean?' I asked.

'It means a life of great sadness,' said Ayah gloomily.

'Can I touch it?' I asked.

'Yes, touch it,' she said, and taking my hand, she placed it against the mole.

'It's a nice mole,' I said, wanting to make Ayah happy. 'Can I kiss it?'

'You can kiss it,' said Ayah.

I kissed her on the mole.

'That's nice,' she said.

Tuesday afternoon came at last, and as soon as Grandmother was asleep and Ayah had gone to the bazaar, I was at the gate, looking up and down the road for Bansi and his tonga. He was not long in coming. Before the tonga turned into the road, I could hear his voice, singing to the accompaniment of the carriage bells.

He reached down, took my hand, and hoisted me on to the seat beside him. Then we went off down the road at a steady jog-trot. It was only when we reached the outskirts of the town that Bansi encouraged his pony to greater efforts. He rose in his seat, leaned forward and slapped the pony across the haunches. From a brisk trot we changed to a carefree canter. The tonga swayed from side to side. I clung to Bansi's free arm, while he grinned at me, his mouth red with paan-juice.

'Where shall we go, *dost*?' he asked.

'Nowhere,' I said. 'Anywhere.'

'We'll go to the river,' said Bansi.

The 'river' was really a swift mountain stream that ran through the forests outside Dehra, joining the Ganga about fifteen miles away. It was almost dry during the winter and early summer; in flood during the monsoon.

The road out of Dehra was a gentle decline and soon we were rushing headlong through the tea gardens and eucalyptus forests, the pony's hoofs striking sparks off the metalled road, the carriage wheels groaning and creaking so loudly that I feared one of them would come off and that we would all be thrown into a ditch or into the small canal that ran beside the road. We swept through mango groves, through guava and litchi orchards, past broad-leaved sal and shisham trees. Once in the sal forest, Bansi turned the tonga on to a rough cart-track, and we continued along it for about a furlong, until the road dipped down to the stream bed.

'Let us go straight into the water,' said Bansi. 'You and I and the pony!' And he drove the tonga straight into the middle of the stream, where the water came up to the pony's knees.

'I am not a great one for baths,' said Bansi, 'but the pony needs one, and why should a horse smell sweeter than its owner?' saying which, he flung off his clothes and jumped into the water.

'Better than bathing under a tap!' he cried, slapping himself on the chest and thighs. 'Come down, *dost*, and join me!'

After some hesitation I joined him, but had some difficulty in keeping on my feet in the fast current. I grabbed at the pony's tail and hung on to it, while Bansi began sloshing water over the patient animal's back.

After this, Bansi led both me and the pony out of the stream and together we gave the carriage a good washing down. I'd had a free ride and Bansi got the services of a free helper for the long overdue spring-cleaning of his tonga. After we had finished the job, he presented me with a packet of *aam papar*—a sticky toffee made from mango pulp—and for some time I tore at it as a dog tears at a bit of old leather. Then I felt drowsy and lay down on the brown, sunwarmed grass. Crickets and grasshoppers were telephoning each other from tree and bush and a pair of bluejays rolled, dived, and swooped acrobatically overhead.

Bansi had no watch. He looked at the sun and said, 'It is past three. When will that ayah of yours be home? She is more frightening than your grandmother!'

'She comes at four.'

'Then we must hurry back. And don't tell her where we've been, or I'll never be able to come to your house again. Your grandmother's one of my best customers.'

'That means you'd be sorry if she died.'

'I would indeed, my friend.'

Bansi raced the tonga back to town. There was very little motor traffic in those days, and tongas and bullock-carts were far more numerous than they are today.

We were back five minutes before Ayah returned. Before Bansi left, he promised to take me for another ride the following week.

The house in Dehra had to be sold. My father had not left any money; he had never realized that his health would deteriorate so rapidly from the malarial fevers which had grown in frequency. He was still planning for the future when he died. Now that my father was gone, Grandmother saw no point in staying on in India; there was nothing left in the bank and she needed money for our passages to England, so the house had to go. Dr Ghose, who had a thriving medical practice in Dehra, made her a reasonable offer, which she accepted.

Then things happened very quickly. Grandmother sold most of our belongings, because as she said, we wouldn't be able to cope with a lot of luggage. The *kabaris* came in droves, buying up crockery, furniture, carpets and clocks at throwaway prices. Grandmother hated parting with some of her possessions such as the carved giltwood mirror, her walnut-wood armchair and her rosewood writing desk, but it was impossible to take them with us. They were carried away in a bullock-cart.

Ayah was very unhappy at first but cheered up when Grandmother got her a job with a tea-planter's family in Assam. It was arranged that she could stay with us until we left Dehra.

We went at the end of September, just as the monsoon

clouds broke up, scattered, and were driven away by soft breezes from the Himalayas. There was no time to revisit the island where my father and I had planted our trees. And in the urgency and excitement of the preparations for our departure, I forgot to recover my small treasures from the hole in the banyan tree. It was only when we were in Bansi's tonga, on the way to the station, that I remembered my top, catapult, and Iron Cross. Too late! To go back for them would mean missing the train.

'Hurry!' urged Grandmother nervously. 'We mustn't be late for the train, Bansi.'

Bansi flicked the reins and shouted to his pony, and for once in her life Grandmother submitted to being carried along the road at a brisk trot.

'It's five to nine,' she said, 'and the train leaves at nine.'

'Do not worry, memsahib. I have been taking you to the station for fifteen years, and you have never missed a train!'

'No,' said Grandmother. 'And I don't suppose you'll ever take me to the station again, Bansi.'

'Times are changing, memsahib. Do you know that there is now a taxi—a *motor car*—competing with the tongas of Dehra? You are lucky to be leaving. If you stay, you will see me starve to death!'

'We will all starve to death if we don't catch that train,' said Grandmother.

'Do not worry about the train, it never leaves on time, and no one expects it to. If it left at nine o'clock, everyone would miss it.'

Bansi was right. We arrived at the station at five minutes past nine, and rushed on to the platform, only to find that the train had not yet arrived.

The platform was crowded with people waiting to catch the same train or to meet people arriving on it. Ayah was there already, standing guard over a pile of miscellaneous luggage. We sat down on our boxes and became part of the platform life at an Indian railway station.

Moving among piles of bedding and luggage were sweating, cursing coolies; vendors of magazines, sweetmeats, tea and betel-leaf preparations; also stray dogs, stray people and sometimes a stray station-master. The cries of the vendors mixed with the general clamour of the station and the shunting of a steam engine in the yards. 'Tea, hot tea!' Sweets, papads, hot stuff, cold drinks, toothpowder, pictures of film stars, bananas, balloons, wooden toys, clay images of the gods. The platform had become a bazaar.

Ayah was giving me all sorts of warnings.

'Remember, baba, don't lean out of the window when the train is moving. There was that American boy who lost his head last year! And don't eat rubbish at every station between here and Bombay. And see that no strangers enter the compartment. Mr Wilkins was murdered *and* robbed last year!'

The station bell clanged, and in the distance there appeared a big, puffing steam engine, painted green and gold and black. A stray dog with a lifetime's experience of trains, darted away across the railway lines. As the train came alongside the platform, doors opened, window shutters fell, faces appeared in the openings, and even before the train had come to a stop, people were trying to get in or out.

For a few moments there was chaos. The crowd surged backward and forward. No one could get out. No one could get in. A hundred people were leaving the train, two hundred were getting into it. No one wanted to give way.

The problem was solved by a man climbing out of a window. Others followed his example and the pressure at the doors eased and people started squeezing into their compartments.

Grandmother had taken the precaution of reserving berths in a first-class compartment, and assisted by Bansi and half-a-dozen coolies, we were soon inside with all our luggage. A whistle blasted and we were off! Bansi had to jump from the running train.

As the engine gathered speed, I ignored Ayah's advice and put my head out of the window to look back at the receding platform. Ayah and Bansi were standing on the platform waving to me, and I kept waving to them until the train rushed into the darkness and the bright lights of Dehra were swallowed up in the night. New lights, dim and flickering, came into existence as we passed small villages. The stars too were visible and I saw a shooting star streaking through the heavens.

I remembered something that Ayah had once told me, that

stars are the spirits of good men, and I wondered if that shooting star was a sign from my father that he was aware of our departure and would be with us on our journey. And I remembered something else that Ayah had said—that if one wished on a shooting star, one's wish would be granted, provided of course that one thrust all five fingers into the mouth at the same time!

'What on earth are you doing?' asked Grandmother staring at me as I thrust my hand into my mouth.

'Making a wish,' I said.

'Oh,' said Grandmother.

She was preoccupied, and didn't ask me what I was wishing for; nor did I tell her.

CALYPSO CHRISTMAS

❧

My first Christmas in London had been a lonely one. My small bed-sitting-room near Swiss Cottage had been cold and austere, and my landlady had disapproved of any sort of revelry. Moreover, I hadn't the money for the theatre or a good restaurant. That first English Christmas was spent sitting in front of a lukewarm gas-fire, eating beans on toast, and drinking cheap sherry. My one consolation was the row of Christmas cards on the mantelpiece—most of them from friends in India.

But the following year I was making more money and living in a bigger, brighter, homelier room. The new landlady approved of my bringing friends—even girls—to the house, and had even made me a plum pudding so that I could entertain my guests. My friends in London included a number of Indian and Commonwealth students, and through them I met George, a friendly, sensitive person from Trinidad.

George was not a student. He was over thirty. Like thousands of other West Indians, he had come to England because he had been told that jobs were plentiful, that there was a free health scheme and national insurance, and that he could earn anything from ten to twenty pounds a week—far more than he could make in Trinidad or Jamaica. But, while it was true that jobs were to be had in England, it was also true that sections of local labour resented outsiders filling these posts. There were also those, belonging chiefly to the lower middle-classes, who were prone to various prejudices, and though these people were a minority, they were still capable of making themselves felt and heard.

In any case, London is a lonely place, especially for the stranger. And for the happy-go-lucky West Indian, accustomed to sunshine, colour and music, London must be quite baffling.

As though to match the grey-green fogs of winter, Londoners wore sombre colours, greys and browns. The West Indians couldn't understand this. Surely, they reasoned, during a grey season the colours worn should be vivid reds and greens— colours that would defy the curling fog and uncomfortable rain? But Londoners frowned on these gay splashes of colour; to them it all seemed an expression of some sort of barbarism. And then again Londoners had a horror of any sort of loud noise, and a blaring radio could (quite justifiably) bring in scores of protests from neighbouring houses. The West Indians, on the other hand, liked letting off steam; they liked holding parties in their rooms at which there was much singing and shouting. They had always believed that England was their mother country, and so, despite rain, fog, sleet and snow, they were determined to live as they had lived back home in Trinidad. And it is to their credit, and even to the credit of indigenous Londoners, that this is what they succeeded in doing.

George worked for British Railways. He was a ticket-collector at one of the underground stations. He liked his work, and received about ten pounds a week for collecting tickets. A large, stout man, with huge hands and feet, he always had a gentle, kindly expression on his mobile face. Amongst other accomplishments he could play the piano, and as there was an old, rather dilapidated piano in my room, he would often come over in the evenings to run his fat, heavy fingers over the keys, playing tunes that ranged from hymns to jazz pieces. I thought he would be a nice person to spend Christmas with, so I asked him to come and share the pudding my landlady had made, and a bottle of sherry I had procured.

Little did I realize that an invitation to George would be interpreted as an invitation to all George's friends and relations— in fact, anyone who had known him in Trinidad—but this was the way he looked at it, and at eight o'clock on Christmas Eve, while a chilly wind blew dead leaves down from Hampstead Heath, I saw a veritable army of West Indians marching down Belsize Avenue, with George in the lead.

Bewildered, I opened my door to them; and in streamed George, George's cousins, George's nephews and George's friends. They were all smiling and they all shook hands with me, making complimentary remarks about my room ('Man, that's some piano!' 'Hey, look at that crazy picture!' 'This rocking chair gives me fever!') and took no time at all to feel and make themselves at home. Everyone had brought something along for the party. George had brought several bottles of beer. Eric, a flashy, coffee-coloured youth, had brought cigarettes and more beer. Marian, a buxom woman of thirty-five, who called me 'darling' as soon as we met, and kissed me on the cheeks saying she adored pink cheeks, had brought bacon and eggs. Her daughter Lucy, who was sixteen and in the full bloom of youth, had brought a gramophone, while the little nephews carried the records. Other friends and familiars had also brought beer; and one enterprising fellow produced a bottle of Jamaican rum.

Then everything began to happen at once.

Lucy put a record on the gramophone, and the strains of *Basin Street Blues* filled the room. At the same time George sat down at the piano to hammer out an accompaniment to the record. His huge hands crushed down on the keys as though he were chopping up hunks of meat. Marian had lit the gas-fire and was busy frying bacon and eggs. Eric was opening beer bottles. In the midst of the noise and confusion I heard a knock on the door—a very timid, hesitant sort of knock—and opening it, found my landlady standing on the threshold.

'Oh, Mr Bond, the neighbours—' she began, and glancing into the room was rendered speechless.

'It's only tonight,' I said. 'They'll all go home after an hour. Remember, it's Christmas!'

She nodded mutely and hurried away down the corridor, pursued by something called *Be Bop A-Lula*. I closed the door and drew all the curtains in an effort to stifle the noise; but everyone was stamping about on the floorboards, and I hoped fervently that the downstairs people had gone to the theatre. George had started playing calypso music, and Eric and Lucy were strutting and stomping in the middle of the room, while the two nephews were improvising on their own. Before I knew what was happening, Marian had taken me in her strong arms and was teaching me to do the calypso. The song playing, I think, was *Banana Boat Song*.

Instead of the party lasting an hour, it lasted three hours. We ate innumerable fried eggs and finished off all the beer. I took turns dancing with Marian, Lucy, and the nephews. There was a peculiar expression they used when excited. 'Fire!' they shouted. I never knew what was supposed to be on fire, or what the exclamation implied, but I too shouted 'Fire!' and somehow it seemed a very sensible thing to shout.

Perhaps their hearts were on fire, I don't know; but for all their excitability and flashiness and brashness they were lovable and sincere friends, and today, when I look back on my two years in London, that Christmas party is the brightest, most vivid memory of all, and the faces of George and Marian, Lucy and Eric, are the faces I remember best.

At midnight someone turned out the light. I was dancing with Lucy at the time, and in the dark she threw her arms around me and kissed me full on the lips. It was the first time I had been kissed by a girl, and when I think about it, I am glad that it was Lucy who kissed me.

When they left, they went in a bunch, just as they had come. I stood at the gate and watched them saunter down the dark, empty street. The buses and tubes had stopped running at midnight, and George and his friends would have to walk all the way back to their rooms at Highgate and Golders Green.

After they had gone, the street was suddenly empty and silent, and my own footsteps were the only sounds I could hear. The cold came clutching at me, and I turned up my collar. I looked up at the windows of my house, and at the windows of all the other houses in the street. They were all in darkness. It seemed to me that we were the only ones who had really celebrated Christmas.

The Last Time I Saw Delhi

‎❧

I'D HAD THIS OLD and faded negative with me for a number of years and had never bothered to make a print from it. It was a picture of my maternal grandparents. I remembered my grandmother quite well, because a large part of my childhood had been spent in her house in Dehra after she had been widowed; but although everyone said she was fond of me, I remembered her as a stern, somewhat aloof person, of whom I was a little afraid.

I hadn't kept many family pictures and this negative was yellow and spotted with damp.

Then last week, when I was visiting my mother in hospital in Delhi, while she awaited her operation, we got talking about my grandparents, and I remembered the negative and decided I'd make a print for my mother.

When I got the photograph and saw my grandmother's face for the first time in twenty-five years, I was immediately struck by my resemblance to her. I have, like her, lived a rather spartan life, happy with my one room, just as she was content to live in a room of her own while the rest of the family took over the house! And like her, I have lived tidily. But I did not know the physical resemblance was so close—the fair hair, the heavy build, the wide forehead. She looks more like me than my mother!

In the photograph she is seated on her favourite chair, at the top of the veranda steps, and Grandfather stands behind her in the shadows thrown by a large mango tree which is not in the picture. I can tell it was a mango tree because of the pattern the leaves make on the wall. Grandfather was a slim, trim man, with a drooping moustache that was fashionable in the twenties. By all accounts he had a mischievous sense of humour, although he looks unwell in the picture. He appears to have been quite swarthy. No wonder he was so successful in dressing up 'native' style and passing himself off as a street-vendor. My mother tells me he even took my grandmother in on one occasion, and sold her a basketful of bad oranges. His character was in strong contrast to my grandmother's rather forbidding personality and Victorian sense of propriety; but they made a good match.

So here's the picture, and I am taking it to show my mother who lies in the Lady Hardinge Hospital, awaiting the removal of her left breast.

It is early August and the day is hot and sultry. It rained during the night, but now the sun is out and the sweat oozes through my shirt as I sit in the back of a stuffy little taxi taking me through the suburbs of Greater New Delhi.

On either side of the road are the houses of well-to-do Punjabis, who came to Delhi as refugees in 1947 and now make up more than half the capital's population. Industrious, flashy, go-ahead people. Thirty years ago, fields extended on either side of this road as far as the eye could see. The Ridge, an outcrop of the Aravallis, was scrub jungle, in which the black buck roamed. Feroz Shah's fourteenth century hunting lodge stood here in splendid isolation. It is still here, hidden by petrol pumps and lost in the sounds of buses, cars, trucks and scooter-rickshaws. The peacock has fled the forest, the black buck is extinct. Only the jackal remains. When, a thousand years from now, the last human has left this contaminated planet for some other star, the jackal and the crow will remain, to survive for years on all the refuse we leave behind.

It is difficult to find the right entrance to the hospital, because for about a mile along the Panchkuian Road the pavement has been obliterated by tea shops, furniture shops, and piles of accumulated junk. A public hydrant stands near the gate, and dirty water runs across the road.

I find my mother in a small ward. It is a cool, dark room, and a ceiling fan whirrs pleasantly overhead. A nurse, a dark pretty girl from the South, is attending to my mother. She says,

'In a minute,' and proceeds to make an entry on a chart.

My mother gives me a wan smile and beckons me to come nearer. Her cheeks are slightly flushed, due possibly to fever, otherwise she looks her normal self. I find it hard to believe that the operation she will have tomorrow will only give her, at the most, another year's lease on life.

I sit at the foot of her bed. This is my third visit since I flew back from Jersey, using up all my savings in the process; and I will leave after the operation, not to fly away again, but to return to the hills which have always called me back.

'How do you feel?' I ask.

'All right. They say they will operate in the morning. They've stopped my smoking.'

'Can you drink? Your rum, I mean?'

'No. Not until a few days after the operation.'

She has a fair amount of grey in her hair, natural enough at fifty-four. Otherwise she hasn't changed much; the same small chin and mouth, lively brown eyes. Her father's face, not her mother's.

The nurse has left us. I produce the photograph and hand it to my mother.

'The negative was lying with me all these years. I had it printed yesterday.'

'I can't see without my glasses.'

The glasses are lying on the locker near her bed. I hand them to her. She puts them on and studies the photograph.

'Your grandmother was always very fond of you.'

'It was hard to tell. She wasn't a soft woman.'

'It was her money that got you to Jersey, when you finished school. It wasn't much, just enough for the ticket.'

'I didn't know that.'

'The only person who ever left you anything. I'm afraid I've nothing to leave you, either.'

'You know very well that I've never cared a damn about money. My father taught me to write. That was inheritance enough.'

'And what did I teach you?'

'I'm not sure . . . . Perhaps you taught me how to enjoy myself now and then.'

She looked pleased at this. 'Yes, I've enjoyed myself between troubles. But your father didn't know how to enjoy himself. That's why we quarrelled so much. And finally separated.'

'He was much older than you.'

'You've always blamed me for leaving him, haven't you?'

'I was very small at the time. You left us suddenly. My father had to look after me, and it wasn't easy for him. He was very sick. Naturally I blamed you.'

'He wouldn't let me take you away.'

'Because you were going to marry someone else.'

I break off; we have been over this before. I am not here as my father's advocate, and the time for recrimination has passed.

And now it is raining outside, and the scent of wet earth comes through the open doors, overpowering the odour of medicines and disinfectants. The dark-eyed nurse comes in again and informs me that the doctor will soon be on his rounds. I can come again in the evening, or early morning before the operation.

'Come in the evening,' says my mother. 'The others will be here then.'

'I haven't come to see the others.'

'They are looking forward to seeing you.' 'They' being my stepfather and half-brothers.

'I'll be seeing them in the morning.'

'As you like . . . .'

And then I am on the road again, standing on the pavement, on the fringe of a chaotic rush of traffic, in which it appears that every vehicle is doing its best to overtake its neighbour. The blare of horns can be heard in the corridors of the hospital, but everyone is conditioned to the noise and pays no attention to it. Rather, the sick and the dying are heartened by the thought that people are still well enough to feel reckless, indifferent to each other's safety! In Delhi there is a feverish desire to be first in line, the first to get anything . . . . This is probably because no one ever gets round to dealing with second-comers.

When I hail a scooter-rickshaw and it stops a short distance away, someone elbows his way past me and gets in first. This epitomizes the philosophy and outlook of the Delhiwallah.

So I stand on the pavement waiting for another scooter, which doesn't come. In Delhi, to be second in the race is to be last.

I walk all the way back to my small hotel, with a foreboding of having seen my mother for the last time.

THE GOOD OLD DAYS

❧

I took Miss Mackenzie an offering of a tin of Malabar sardines, and so lessened the sharpness of her rebuke.

'Another doctor's visit, is it?' she said, looking reproachfully at me over her spectacles. 'I might have been dead all this time . . .'

Miss Mackenzie, at eighty-five, did not show the least signs of dying. She was the oldest resident of the hill station. She lived in a small cottage half way up a hill. The cottage, like Longfellow's village of Attri, gave one the impression of having tried to get to the top of the bill and failed halfway up. It was hidden from the road by oaks and maples.

'I've been away,' I explained. 'I had to go to Delhi for a fortnight. I hope you've been all right?'

I wasn't a relative of Miss Mackenzie's, nor a very old friend; but she had the knack of making people feel they were somehow responsible for her.

'I can't complain. The weather's been good, and the padre sent me some eggs.'

She set great store on what was given to her in the way of food. Her pension of forty rupees a month only permitted a diet of dal and rice; but the thoughtfulness of people who knew her and the occasional gift parcel from England lent variety to her diet and frequently gave her a topic of conversation.

'I'm glad you have some eggs,' I said. 'They're four rupees a dozen now.'

'Yes, I know. And there was a time when they were only six annas a dozen.'

'About thirty years ago, I suppose.'

'No, twenty-five. I remember, May Taylor's eggs were always the best. She lived in Fairville—the old house near the Raja's estate.'

'Did she have a poultry farm?'

'Oh no, just her own hens. Very ordinary hens too, not White Leghorns or Rhode Island Reds—but they gave lovely eggs; she knew how to keep her birds healthy . . . May Taylor was a friend of mine. She didn't supply eggs to just *anybody*, you know.'

'Oh, naturally not. Miss Taylor's dead now, I suppose?'

'Oh yes, quite dead. Her sister saw to that.'

'Oh!' I sensed a story. 'How did that happen?'

'Well, it was a bit of a mystery really. May and Charlotte never did get on with each other and it's a wonder they agreed to live together. Even as children they used to fight. But Charlotte was always the spoilt one—prettier, you see. May, when I knew her, was thirty-five, a *good* woman if you know what I mean. She saw to the house and saw to the meals and she went to church like other respectable people and everyone liked her. But Charlotte was moody and bad-tempered. She kept to herself—always had done, since the parents died. And she was a little too fond of the bottle.'

'Neither of them were married?'

'No—I suppose that's why they lived together. Though I'd rather live alone myself than put up with someone disagreeable. Still they were sisters. Charlotte had been a gay, young thing once, very popular with the soldiers at the convalescent home. She refused several offers of marriage and then when she thought it time to accept someone there were no more offers. She was almost thirty by then. That's when she started drinking—heavily, I mean. Gin and brandy, mostly. It was cheap in those days. Gin, I think, was two rupees a bottle.'

'What fun! I was born a generation too late.'

'And a good thing, too. Or you'd probably have ended up as Charlotte did.'

'Did she get delirium tremens?'

'She did nothing of the sort. Charlotte had a strong constitution.'

'And so have you, Miss Mackenzie, if you don't mind my saying so.'

'I take a drop when I can afford it—.' She gave me a meaningful look. 'Or when I'm offered . . .'

'Did you sometimes have a drink with Miss Taylor?'

'I did not! I wouldn't have been seen in her company. All over the place she was when she was drunk. Lost her powers of discrimination. She even took up with a barber! And then she fell down a *khud* one evening, and broke her ankle!'

'Lucky it wasn't her head.'

'No, it wasn't her own head she broke, more's the pity, but her sister May's—the poor, sweet thing.'

'She broke her sister's head, did she?' I was intrigued. 'Why, did May find out about the barber?'

'Nobody knows what it was, but it may well have been something like that. Anyway, they had a terrible quarrel one night. Charlotte was drunk, and May, as usual, was admonishing her.'

'Fatal,' I said. 'Never admonish a drunk.'

Miss Mackenzie ignored me and carried on.

'She said something about the vengeance of God falling on Charlotte's head. But it was May's head that was rent asunder. Charlotte flew into a sudden rage—she was given to these outbursts even when sober—and brought *something* heavy down on May's skull. Charlotte never said what it was. It couldn't have been a bottle, unless she swept up the broken pieces afterwards. It may have been a heavy—what writers sometimes call a blunt instrument.

'When Charlotte saw what she had done, she went out of her mind. They found her two days later wandering about near some ruins, babbling a lot of nonsense about how she might have been married long ago if May hadn't clung to her.'

'Was she charged with murder?'

'No, it was all hushed up. Charlotte was sent to the asylum at Ranchi. We never heard of her again. May was buried here. If you visit the old cemetery you'll find her grave on the second tier, third from the left.'

'I'll look it up some time. It must have been an awful shock for those of you who knew the sisters.'

'Yes, I was quite upset about it. I was very fond of May. And then, of course, the chickens were sold and I had to buy my eggs elsewhere and they were never so good. Still, those were the days, the good old days—when eggs were six annas a dozen and gin only two rupees a bottle!'

Binya Passes By

&

WHILE I WAS WALKING home one day, along the path through the pines, I heard a girl singing.

It was summer in the hills, and the trees were in new leaf. The walnuts and cherries were just beginning to form between the leaves.

The wind was still and the trees were hushed, and the song came to me clearly; but it was not the words—which I could not follow—or the rise and fall of the melody which held me in thrall, but the voice itself, which was a young and tender voice.

I left the path and scrambled down the slope, slipping on fallen pine needles. But when I came to the bottom of the slope the singing had stopped and there was no one there. 'I'm sure I heard someone singing,' I said to myself and then thought I might have been wrong. In the hills it is always possible to be wrong.

So I walked on home, and presently I heard another song, but this time it was the whistling thrush rendering a broken melody, singing a dark, sweet secret in the depths of the forest.

I had little to sing about myself. The electricity bill hadn't been paid, and there was nothing in the bank, and my second novel had just been turned down by another publisher. Still, it was summer and men and animals were drowsy, and so too were my creditors. The distant mountains loomed purple in the shimmering dust-haze.

I walked through the pines again, but I did not hear the singing. And then for a week I did not leave the cottage, as the novel had to be rewritten, and I worked hard at it, pausing only to eat and sleep and take note of the leaves turning a darker green.

The window opened on to the forest. Trees reached up to the window. Oak, maple, walnut. Higher up the hill, the pines started, and further on, armies of deodars marched over the mountains. And the mountains rose higher, and the trees grew stunted until they finally disappeared and only the black spirit-haunted rocks rose up to meet the everlasting snows. Those peaks cradled the sky. I could not see them from my windows. But on clear mornings they could be seen from the pass on the Tehri road.

There was a stream at the bottom of the hill. One morning, quite early, I went down to the stream, and using the boulders as stepping-stones, moved downstream for about half a mile. Then I lay down to rest on a flat rock in the shade of a wild cherry tree and watched the sun shifting through the branches as it rose over the hill called Pari Tibba (Fairy Hill) and slid down the steep slope into the valley. The air was very still and already the birds were silent. The only sound came from the water running over the stony bed of the stream. I had lain there ten, perhaps fifteen minutes, when I began to feel that someone was watching me.

Someone in the trees, in the shadows, still and watchful. Nothing moved; not a stone shifted, not a twig broke. But someone was watching me. I felt terribly exposed; not to danger, but to the scrutiny of unknown eyes. So I left the rock and, finding a path through the trees, began climbing the hill again.

It was warm work. The sun was up, and there was no breeze. I was perspiring profusely by the time I got to the top of the hill. There was no sign of my unseen watcher. Two lean cows grazed on the short grass; the tinkling of their bells was the only sound in the sultry summer air.

That song again! The same song, the same singer. I heard her from my window. And putting aside the book I was reading, I leant out of the window and started down through the trees. But the foliage was too heavy and the singer too far away for me to be able to make her out. 'Should I go and look for her?' I wondered. 'Or is it better this way—heard but not seen? For, having fallen in love with a song, must it follow that I will fall in love with the singer? No. But surely it is the voice and not the song that has touched me . . .' Presently the singing ended, and I turned away from the window.

A girl was gathering bilberries on the hillside. She was fresh-faced, honey-coloured. Her lips were stained with purple juice. She smiled at me. 'Are they good to eat?' I asked.

She opened her fist and thrust out her hand, which was full of berries, bruised and crushed. I took one and put it in my mouth. It had a sharp, sour taste. 'It is good,' I said. Finding that I could speak haltingly in her language, she came nearer, said, 'Take more then,' and filled my hand with bilberries. Her fingers touched mine. The sensation was almost unique, for it was nine or ten years since my hand had touched a girl's.

'Where do you live?' I asked. She pointed across the valley to where a small village straddled the slopes of a terraced hill.

'It's quite far,' I said. 'Do you always come so far from home?'

'I go further than this,' she said. 'The cows must find fresh grass. And there is wood to gather and grass to cut.' She showed me the sickle held by the cloth tied firmly about her waist. 'Sometimes I go to the top of Pari Tibba, sometimes to the valley beyond. Have you been there?'

'No. But I will go some day.'

'It is always windy on Pari Tibba.'

'Is it true that there are fairies there?'

She laughed. 'That is what people say. But those are people who have never been there. I do not see fairies on Pari Tibba. It is said that there are ghosts in the ruins on the hill. But I do not see any ghosts.'

'I have heard of the ghosts,' I said. 'Two lovers who ran away and took shelter in a ruined cottage. At night there was a storm, and they were killed by lightning. Is it true, this story?'

'It happened many years ago, before I was born. I have heard the story. But there are no ghosts on Pari Tibba.'

'How old are you?' I asked.

'Fifteen, sixteen, I do not know for sure.'

'Doesn't your mother know?'

'She is dead. And my grandmother has forgotten. And my brother, he is younger than me and he's forgotten his own age. Is it important to remember?'

'No, it is not important. Not here, anyway. Not in the hills. To a mountain, a hundred years are but as a day.'

'Are you very old?' she asked.

'I hope not. Do I look very old?'

'Only a hundred,' she said, and laughed, and the silver bangles on her wrists tinkled as she put her hands up to her laughing face.

'Why do you laugh?' I asked.

'Because you looked as though you believed me. How old are you?'

'Thirty-five, thirty-six, I do not remember.'

'Ah, it is better to forget!'

'That's true,' I said, 'but sometimes one has to fill in forms and things like that, and then one has to state one's age.'

'I have never filled a form. I have never seen one.'

'And I hope you never will. It is a piece of paper covered with useless information. It is all a part of human progress.'

'Progress?'

'Yes. Are you unhappy?'

'No.'

'Do you go hungry?'

'No.'

'Then you don't need progress. Wild bilberries are better.'

She went away without saying goodbye. The cows had strayed and she ran after them, calling them by name: 'Neelu, Neelu!' (Blue) and 'Bhuri!' (Old One). Her bare feet moved swiftly over the rocks and dry grass.

Early May. The cicadas were singing in the forest; or rather, orchestrating, since they make the sound with their legs. The whistling thrushes pursued each other over the tree-tops in acrobatic love-flights. Sometimes the langurs visited the oak trees to feed on the leaves. As I moved down the path to the stream, I heard the same singing, and coming suddenly upon the clearing near the water's edge I saw the girl sitting on a rock, her feet in the rushing water—the same girl who had given me bilberries. Strangely enough, I had not guessed that she was the singer. Unseen voices conjure up fanciful images. I had imagined a woodland nymph, a graceful, delicate, beautiful, goddess-like creature, not a mischievous-eyed, round-faced, juice-stained, slightly ragged pixie. Her dhoti—a rough, homespun sari—was faded and torn; an impractical garment, I thought, for running about on the hillside, but the village folk put their girls into dhotis before they are twelve. She'd compromised by hitching it up and by strengthening the waist with a length of cloth bound tightly about her, but she'd have been more at ease in the long, flounced skirt worn in the hills further away.

But I was not disillusioned. I had clearly taken a fancy to her cherubic, open countenance; and the sweetness of her voice added to her charms.

I watched her from the banks of the stream, and presently she looked up, grinned, and stuck her tongue out at me.

'That's a nice way to greet me,' I said. 'Have I offended you?'

'You surprised me. Why did you not call out?'

'Because I was listening to your singing. I did not wish to speak until you had finished.'

'It was only a song.'

'But you sang it sweetly.'

She smiled. 'Have you brought anything to eat?'

'No. Are you hungry?'

'At this time I get hungry. When you come to meet me you must always bring something to eat.'

'But I didn't come to meet you. I didn't know you would be here.'

'You do not wish to meet me?'

'I didn't mean that. It is nice to meet you.'

'You will meet me if you keep coming into the forest. So always bring something to eat.'

'I will do so next time. Shall I pick you some berries?'

'You will have to go to the top of the hill again to find the kingora bushes.'

'I don't mind. If you are hungry, I will bring some.'

'All right,' she said, and looked down at her feet, which were still in the water.

Like some knight-errant of old, I toiled up the hill again until I found the bilberry bushes, and stuffing my pockets with berries I returned to the stream. But when I got there I found she'd slipped away. The cowbells tinkled on the far hill.

Glow-worms shone fitfully in the dark. The night was full of sounds—the tonk-tonk of a nightjar, the cry of a barking deer, the shuffling of porcupines, the soft flip-fop of moths beating against the window-panes. On the hill across the valley, lights flickered in the small village—the dim lights of kerosene lamps swinging in the dark.

'What is your name?' I asked, when we met again on the path through the pine forest.

'Binya,' she said. 'What is yours?'

'I've no name.'

'All right, Mr No-name.'

'I mean I haven't made a name for myself. We must make our own names, don't you think?'

'Binya is my name. I do not wish to have any other. Where are you going?'

'Nowhere.'

'No-name goes nowhere! Then you cannot come with me, because I am going home and my grandmother will set the village dogs on you if you follow me.' And laughing, she ran down the path to the stream; she knew I could not catch up with her.

Her face streamed summer rain as she climbed the steep hill, calling the white cow home. She seemed very tiny on the windswept mountainside. A twist of hair lay flat against her forehead and her torn blue dhoti clung to her firm round thighs. I went to her with an umbrella to give her shelter. She stood with me beneath the umbrella and let me put my arm around her. Then she turned her face up to mine, wonderingly, and I kissed her quickly, softly on the lips. Her lips tasted of raindrops and mint. And then she left me there, so gallant in the blistering rain. She ran home laughing. But it was worth the drenching.

Another day I heard her calling to me—'No-name, Mister No-name!'—but I couldn't see her, and it was some time before I found her, halfway up a cherry tree, her feet pressed firmly against the bark, her dhoti tucked up between her thighs—fair, rounded thighs, and legs that were strong and vigorous.

'The cherries are not ripe,' I said.

'They are never ripe. But I like them green and sour. Will you come onto the tree?'

'If I can still climb a tree,' I said.

'My grandmother is over sixty, and *she* can climb trees.'

'Well, I wouldn't mind being more adventurous at sixty. There's not so much to lose then.' I climbed into the tree without much difficulty, but I did not think the higher branches would take my weight, so I remained standing in the fork of the tree, my face on a level with Binya's breasts. I put my hand against her waist, and kissed her on the soft inside of her arm. She did not say anything. But she took me by the hand and helped me to climb a little higher, and I put my arm around her, as much to support myself as to be close to her.

The full moon rides high, shining through the tall oak trees near the window. The night is full of sounds—crickets, the tonk-tonk of a nightjar, and floating across the valley from your village the sound of drums beating and people singing. It is a festival day, and there will be feasting in your home. Are you singing too, tonight? And are you thinking of me, as you sing, as you laugh, as you dance with your friends? I am sitting here alone, and so I have no one to think of but you.

Binya . . . I take your name again and again—as though by taking it I can make you hear me, and come to me, walking over the moonlit mountain . . .

There are spirits abroad tonight. They move silently in the trees; they hover about the window at which I sit; they take up with the wind and rush about the house. Spirits of the trees, spirits of the old house. An old lady died here last year. She'd lived in the house for over thirty years; something of her personality surely dwells here still. When I look into the tall, old mirror which was hers, I sometimes catch a glimpse of her pale face and long, golden hair. She likes me, I think, and the house is kind to me. Would she be jealous of you, Binya?

The music and singing grows louder. I can imagine your face glowing in the firelight. Your eyes shine with laughter. You have all those people near you and I have only the stars, and the nightjar, and the ghost in the mirror.

I woke early, while the dew was still fresh on the grass, and walked down the hill to the stream, and then up to a little knoll where a pine tree grew in solitary splendour, the wind going *hoo-hoo* in its slender branches. This was my favourite place, my place of power, where I came to renew myself from time to time. I lay on the grass, dreaming. The sky in its blueness swung round above me. An eagle soared in the distance. I heard her voice down among the trees; or I thought I heard it. But when I went to look, I could not find her.

I'd always prided myself on my rationality, had taught myself to be wary of emotional states, like 'falling in love', which turned out to be ephemeral and illusory. And although I told myself again and again that the attraction was purely physical, on my part as well as hers, I had to admit to myself that my feelings towards Binya differed from the feelings I'd had for others; and that while sex had often been for me a celebration, it had, like any other feast, resulted in satiety, a need for change, a desire to forget . . .

Binya represented something else—something wild, dream-like, fairy-like. She moved close to the spirit-haunted rocks, the old trees, the young grass. She had absorbed something from them—a primeval innocence, an unconcern with the passing of time and events, an affinity with the forest and the mountains, and this made her special and magical.

And so, when three, four, five days went by, and I did not find her on the hillside, I went through all the pangs of frustrated love: had she forgotten me and gone elsewhere? Had we been seen together, and was she being kept at home? Was she ill? Or had she been spirited away?

I could hardly go and ask for her. I would probably be driven from the village. It straddled the opposite hill, a cluster of slate-roof houses, a pattern of little terraced fields. I could see figures in the fields, but they were too far away, too tiny, for me to be able to recognize anyone.

She had gone to her mother's village a hundred miles away, or so, a small boy told me.

And so I brooded; walked disconsolately through the oak forest, hardly listening to the birds—the sweet-throated whistling thrush; the shrill barbet; the mellow-voiced doves. Happiness had always made me more responsive to nature. Feeling miserable, my thoughts turned inward. I brooded upon the trickery of time and circumstance; I felt the years were passing by, *had* passed by, like waves on a receding tide, leaving me washed up like a bit of flotsam on a lonely beach. But at the same time, the whistling thrush seemed to mock at me, calling tantalizingly from the shadows of the ravine: 'It isn't time that's passing by, it is you and I, it is you and I . . .'

Then I forced myself to snap out of my melancholy. I kept away from the hillside and the forest. I did not look towards the village. I buried myself in my work, tried to think objectively, and wrote an article on 'The inscriptions on the iron pillar at Kalsi'; very learned, very dry, very sensible.

But at night I was assailed by thoughts of Binya. I could not sleep. I switched on the light, and there she was, smiling at me from the looking glass, replacing the image of the old lady who had watched over me for so long.

As Time Goes By

Prem's boys are growing tall and healthy, on the verge of manhood. How can I think of death, when faced with the full vigour and confidence of youth? They remind me of Somi and Daljit, who were the same age when I knew them in Dehra during our schooldays. But remembering Somi and Dal reminds me of death again—for Dal had died a young man—and I look at Prem's boys again, haunted by the thought of suddenly leaving this world, and pray that I can be with them a little longer.

Somi and Dal . . . . I remember: it was going to rain. I could see the rain moving across the hills, and I could smell it on the breeze. But instead of turning back, I walked on through the leaves and brambles that grew over the disused path, and wandered into the forest. I had heard the sound of rushing water at the bottom of the hill, and there was no question of returning until I had found the water.

I had to slide down some smooth rocks into a small ravine, and there I found the stream running across a bed of shingle. I removed my shoes and socks and started walking up the stream. Water trickled down from the hillside, from amongst ferns and grass and wild flowers; and the hills, rising steeply on either side, kept the ravine in shadow. The rocks were smooth, almost soft, and some of them were grey and some yellow. The pool was fed by a small waterfall, and it was deep beneath the waterfall. I did not stay long, because now the rain was swishing over the sal trees, and I was impatient to tell the others about the pool.

Somi usually chose the adventures we were to have, and I would just grumble and get involved in them; but the pool was my own discovery, and both Somi and Daljit gave me credit for it.

I think it was the pool that brought us together more than anything else. We made it a secret, private pool, and invited no others. Somi was the best swimmer. He dived off rocks and went gliding about under the water, like a long, golden fish. Dal threshed about with much vigour but little skill. I could dive off a rock too, but I usually landed on my belly.

There were slim silverfish in the waters of the stream. At first we tried catching them with a line, but they usually took the bait and left the hook. Then we brought a bedsheet and stretched it across one end of the stream, but the fish wouldn't come near it. Eventually Somi, without telling us, brought along a stick of dynamite, and Dal and I were startled out of a siesta by a flash across the water and a deafening explosion. Half the hillside tumbled into the pool, and Somi along with it; but we got him out, as well as a good supply of stunned fish which were too small for eating.

The effects of the explosion gave Somi another idea, and that was to enlarge our pool by building a dam across one end. This he accomplished with Dal's and my labour. But one afternoon, when it rained heavily, a torrent of water came rushing down the stream, bursting the dam and flooding the ravine; our clothes were all carried away by the current, and we had to wait for night to fall before creeping home through the darkest alleyways, for we used to bathe quite naked; it would have been unmanly to do otherwise.

Our activities at the pool included wrestling and buffalo-riding. We wrestled on a strip of sand that ran beside the stream, and rode on a couple of buffaloes that sometimes came to drink and wallow in the more muddy parts of the stream. We would sit astride the buffaloes, and kick and yell and urge them forward, but on no occasion did we ever get them to move. At the most, they would roll over on their backs, taking us with them into a pool of slush.

But the buffaloes were always comfortable to watch. Solid, earthbound creatures, they liked warm days and cool, soft mud. There is nothing so satisfying to watch than buffaloes wallowing in mud, or ruminating over a mouthful of grass, absolutely oblivious to everything else. They watched us with sleepy, indifferent eyes, and tolerated the pecking of crows. Did they think all that time, or did they just enjoy the sensuousness of soft, wet mud, while we perspired under a summer sun . . . ? No, thinking would have been too strenuous for those supine creatures; to get neck-deep in water was their only aim in life.

It didn't matter how muddy we got ourselves, because we had only to dive into the pool to get rid of the muck. In fact, mud-fighting was one of our favourite pastimes. It was like playing snowballs, only we used mud balls.

If it was possible for Somi and Dal to get out of their houses undetected at night, we would come to the pool and bathe by moonlight, and at these time we would bathe silently and seriously, because there was something subduing about the stillness of the jungle at night.

I don't exactly remember how we broke up, but we hardly noticed it at the time. That was because we never really believed we were finally parting, or that we would not be seeing the pool again. After about a year, Somi passed his matriculation and entered the military academy. The last time I saw him, about twenty-five years ago, he was about to be commissioned, and sported a fierce and very military moustache. He remembered the pool in a sentimental, military way, but not as I remembered it.

Shortly after Somi had matriculated, Dal and his family left town, and I did not see him again, until after I returned from England. Then he was in Air Force uniform, tall, slim, very handsome, completely unrecognizable as the chubby little boy who had played with me in the pool. Three weeks after this meeting I heard that he had been killed in an air crash. Sweet Dal . . . I feel you are close to me now . . . I want to remember you exactly as you were when first we met. Here is my diary for 1951*, when I was sixteen and you thirteen or fourteen:

September 7: 'Do you like elephants?' Somi asked me.

---

* This diary formed the nucleus of my first novel, The Room on the Roof.

'Yes, when they are tame.'

'That's all right, then. Daljit!' he called. 'You can come up. Ruskin likes elephants.'

Dal is not exactly an elephant. He is one of us.

He is fat, oh yes he is fat, but it is his good nature that is so like an elephant's. His fatness is not grotesque or awkward; it is a very pleasant plumpness, and nothing could suit him better. If Dal were thin he would be a failure.

His eyes are bright and round, full of mischievousness and a sort of grumpy gaiety.

And what of the pool?

I looked for it, after an interval of more than thirty years, but couldn't find it. I found the ravine, and the bed of shingle, but there was no water. The stream had changed its course, just as we had changed ours.

I turned away in disappointment, and with a dull ache in my heart. It was cruel of the pool to disappear; it was the cruelty of time. But I hadn't gone far when I heard the sound of rushing water, and the shouting of children; and pushing my way through jungle, I found another stream and another pool and about half-a-dozen children splashing about in the water.

They did not see me, and I kept in the shadow of the trees and watched them play. But I didn't really see them. I was seeing Somi and Daljit and the lazy old buffaloes, and I stood there for almost an hour, a disembodied spirit, romping again in the shallows of our secret pool. Nothing had really changed. Time is like that.

From Small Beginnings

٭

*And the last puff of the day-wind brought from the
unseen villages the scent of damp wood-smoke, hot cakes,
dripping undergrowth, and rotting pine-cones. That is the
true smell of the Himalayas, and if once it creeps into the
blood of a man, that man will at the last, forgetting all
else, return to the hills to die.*

—*Rudyard Kipling*

On the first clear September day, towards the end of the rains,
I visited the pine-knoll, my place of peace and power.

It was months since I'd last been there. Trips to the plains,
a crisis in my affairs, involvements with other people and their
troubles, and an entire monsoon had come between me and the
grassy, pine-topped slope facing the Hill of Fairies (Pari Tibba
to the locals). Now I tramped through late monsoon foliage—
tall ferns, bushes festooned with flowering convolvulus—and
crossed the stream by way of its little bridge of stones before
climbing the steep hill to the pine slope.

When the trees saw me, they made as if to turn in my
direction. A puff of wind came across the valley from the
distant snows. A long-tailed blue magpie took alarm and flew
noisily out of an oak tree. The cicadas were suddenly silent.
But the trees remembered me. They bowed gently in the breeze
and beckoned me nearer, welcoming me home. Three pines, a
straggling oak and a wild cherry. I went among them and
acknowledged their welcome with a touch of my hand against

their trunks—the cherry's smooth and polished; the pine's patterned and whorled; the oak's rough, gnarled, full of experience. He'd been there longest, and the wind had bent his upper branches and twisted a few, so that he looked shaggy and undistinguished. But like the philosopher who is careless about his dress and appearance, the oak has secrets, a hidden wisdom. He has learnt the art of survival!

While the oak and the pines are older than me and have been here many years, the cherry tree is exactly seven years old. I know, because I planted it.

One day I had this cherry seed in my hand, and on an impulse I thrust it into the soft earth, and then went away and forgot all about it. A few months later I found a tiny cherry tree in the long grass. I did not expect it to survive. But the following year it was two feet tall. And then some goats ate its leaves and a grass cutter's scythe injured the stem, and I was sure it would wither away. But it renewed itself, sprang up even faster, and within three years it was a healthy, growing tree, about five feet tall.

I left the hills for two years—forced by circumstances to make a living in Delhi—but this time I did not forget the cherry tree. I thought about it fairly often, sent telepathic messages of encouragement in its direction. And when, a couple of years ago, I returned in the autumn, my heart did a somersault when I found my tree sprinkled with pale pink blossom. (The Himalayan cherry flowers in November.) And later, when the fruit was ripe, the tree was visited by finches, tits, bulbuls and other small birds, all come to feast on the sour, red cherries.

Last summer I spent a night on the pine-knoll, sleeping on the grass beneath the cherry tree. I lay awake for hours, listening to the chatter of the stream and the occasional tonk-tonk of nightjar, and watching through the branches overhead, the stars turning in the sky. And I felt the power of the sky and the earth, and the power of a small cherry seed . . . .

And so when the rains are over, this is where I come, that I might feel the peace and power of this place.

This is where I will write my stories. I can see everything from here—my cottage across the valley; behind and above me, the town and the bazaar, straddling the ridge; to the left, the high mountains and the twisting road to the source of the great river; below me, the little stream and the path to the village; ahead, the Hill of Fairies and the fields beyond; the wide valley below, and another range of hills and then the distant plains. I can even see Prem Singh in the garden, putting the mattresses out in the sun.

From here he is just a speck on the far hill, but I know it is Prem by the way he stands. A man may have a hundred disguises, but in the end it is his posture that gives him away. Like my grandfather, who was a master of disguise and successfully roamed the bazaars as fruit-vendor or basket-maker. But we could always recognize him because of his pronounced slouch.

Prem Singh doesn't slouch, but he has this habit of looking up at the sky (regardless of whether it's cloudy or clear), and at the moment he's looking at the sky.

Eight years with Prem. He was just a sixteen-year-old boy when I first saw him, and now he has a wife and child.

I had been in the cottage for just over a year . . . . He stood on the landing outside the kitchen door. A tall boy, dark, with good teeth and brown, deep-set eyes, dressed smartly in white drill—his only change of clothes. Looking for a job. I liked the look of him, but—

'I already have someone working for me,' I said.

'Yes, sir. He is my uncle.'

In the hills, everyone is a brother or an uncle.

'You don't want me to dismiss your uncle?'

'No, sir. But he says you can find a job for me.'

'I'll try. I'll make enquiries. Have you just come from your village?'

'Yes. Yesterday I walked ten miles to Pauri. There I got a bus.'

'Sit down. Your uncle will make some tea.'

He sat down on the steps, removed his white keds, wriggled his toes. His feet were both long and broad, large feet but not ugly. He was unusually clean for a hill boy. And taller than most.

'Do you smoke?' I asked.

'No, sir.'

'It is true,' said his uncle. 'He does not smoke. All my nephews smoke but this one. He is a little peculiar, he does not smoke—neither bidi nor hookah.'

'Do you drink?'

'It makes me vomit.'

'Do you take bhang?'

'No, sahib.'

'You have no vices. It's unnatural.'

'He is unnatural, sahib,' said his uncle.

'Does he chase girls?'

'They chase him, sahib.'

'So he left the village and came looking for a job.' I looked at him. He grinned, then looked away and began rubbing his feet.

'Your name is . . . ?'

'Prem Singh.'

'All right, Prem, I will try to do something for you.'

I did not see him for a couple of weeks. I forgot about finding him a job. But when I met him again, on the road to the bazaar, he told me that he had got a temporary job in the Survey, looking after the surveyor's tents.

'Next week we will be going to Rajasthan,' he said.

'It will be very hot. Have you been in the desert before?'

'No, sir.'

'It is not like the hills. And it is far from home.'

'I know. But I have no choice in the matter. I have to collect some money in order to get married.'

In his region there was a bride price, usually of two thousand rupees.

'Do you have to get married so soon?'

'I have only one brother and he is still very young. My mother is not well. She needs a daughter-in-law to help her in the fields and the house, and with the cows. We are a small family, so the work is greater.'

Every family has its few terraced fields, narrow and stony, usually perched on a hillside above a stream or river. They grow rice, barley, maize, potatoes—just enough to live on. Even if their produce is sufficient for marketing, the absence of roads makes it difficult to get the produce to the market towns. There is no money to be earned in the villages, and money is needed for clothes, soap, medicines, and for recovering the family jewellery from the moneylenders. So the young men leave their villages to find work, and to find work they must go to the plains. The lucky ones get into the army. Others enter domestic service or take jobs in garages, hotels, wayside tea shops, schools . . . .

In Mussoorie the main attraction is the large number of schools which employ cooks and bearers. But the schools were full when Prem arrived. He'd been to the recruiting centre at Roorkee, hoping to get into the army; but they found a deformity in his right foot, the result of a bone broken when a landslip carried him away one dark monsoon night. He was lucky, he said, that it was only his foot and not his head that had been broken.

He came to the house to inform his uncle about the job and to say goodbye. I thought, another nice person I probably won't see again; another ship passing in the night, the friendly twinkle of its lights soon vanishing in the darkness. I said 'come again', held his smile with mine so that I could remember him better, and returned to my study and my typewriter. The typewriter is the repository of a writer's loneliness. It stares unsympathetically back at him every day, doing its best to be discouraging. Maybe I'll go back to the old-fashioned quill pen and marble ink-stand; then I can feel like a real writer—Balzac or Dickens—scratching away into the endless reaches of the night . . . . Of course, the days and nights are seemingly shorter than they need to be! They must be, otherwise why do we hurry so much and achieve so little, by the standards of the past . . . .

Prem goes, disappears into the vast faceless cities of the plains, and a year slips by, or rather I do, and then here he is again, thinner and darker and still smiling and still looking for a job. I should have known that hill men don't disappear altogether. The spirit-haunted rocks don't let their people wander too far, lest they lose them forever.

I was able to get him a job in the school. The Headmaster's wife needed a cook. I wasn't sure if Prem could cook very well but I sent him along and they said they'd give him a trial. Three days later the Headmaster's wife met me on the road and started gushing all over me. She was the type who gushed.

'We're so grateful to you! Thank you for sending me that lovely boy. He's so polite. And he cooks very well. A little too hot for my husband, but otherwise delicious—just delicious! He's a real treasure—a lovely boy.' And she gave me an arch look—the famous look which she used to captivate all the good-looking young prefects who became prefects, it was said, only if she approved of them.

I wasn't sure that she didn't want something more than a cook, and I only hoped that Prem would give every satisfaction.

He looked cheerful enough when he came to see me on his off-day.

'How are you getting on?' I asked.

'Lovely,' he said, using his mistress's favourite expression.

'What do you mean—lovely? Do they like your work?'

'The memsahib likes it. She strokes me on the cheek whenever she enters the kitchen. The sahib says nothing. He takes medicine after every meal.'

'Did he always take medicine—or only now that you're doing the cooking?'

'I am not sure. I think he has always been sick.'

He was sleeping in the Headmaster's veranda and getting sixty rupees a month. A cook in Delhi got a hundred and sixty. And a cook in Paris or New York got ten times as much. I did not say as much to Prem. He might ask me to get him a job in New York. And that would be the last I saw of him! He, as a cook, might well get a job making curries off-Broadway; I, as a writer, wouldn't get to first base. And only my Uncle Ken knew the secret of how to make a living without actually doing any work. But then, of course, he had four sisters. And each of them was married to a fairly prosperous husband. So Uncle Ken divided his year among them. Three months with Aunt Ruby in Nainital. Three months with Aunt Susie in Kashmir. Three months with my mother (not quite so affluent) in Jamnagar. And three months in the Vet Hospital in Bareilly, where Aunt Mabel ran the hospital for her veterinary husband. In this way he never overstayed his welcome. A sister can look after a brother for just three months at a time and no more. Uncle K had it worked out to perfection.

But I had no sisters and I couldn't live forever on the royalties of a single novel. So I had to write others. So I came to the hills.

The hill men go to the plains to make a living. I had to come to the hills to try and make mine.

'Prem,' I said, 'why don't you work for me?'

'And what about my uncle?'

'He seems ready to desert me any day. His grandfather is ill, he says, and he wants to go home.'

'His grandfather died last year.'

'That's what I mean—he's getting restless. And I don't mind if he goes. These days he seems to be suffering from a form of sleeping sickness. I have to get up first and make his tea . . . .'

Sitting here under the cherry tree, whose leaves are just beginning to turn yellow, I rest my chin on my knees and gaze across the valley to where Prem moves about in the garden. Looking back over the seven years he has been with me, I recall some of the nicest things about him. They come to me in no particular order—just pieces of cinema—coloured slides slipping across the screen of memory . . . .

Prem rocking his infant son to sleep—crooning to him, passing his large hand gently over the child's curly head— Prem following me down to the police station when I was arrested,* and waiting outside until I reappeared, his smile, when I found him in Delhi, his large, irrepressible laughter, most in evidence when he was seeing an old Laurel and Hardy movie.

Of course there were times when he could be infuriating, stubborn, deliberately pig-headed, sending me little notes of resignation—but I never found it difficult to overlook these little acts of self-indulgence. He had brought much love and laughter into my life, and what more could a lonely man ask for?

---

* On a warrant from Bombay, charging me with writing an allegedly obscene short story!

It was his stubborn streak that limited the length of his stay in the Headmaster's household. Mr Good was tolerant enough. But Mrs Good was one of those women who, when they are pleased with you, go out of their way to help, pamper and flatter, but when displeased, become vindictive, going out of their way to harm or destroy. Mrs Good sought power—over her husband, her dog, her favourite pupils, her servant . . . . She had absolute power over the husband and the dog, partial power over her slightly bewildered pupils, and none at all over Prem, who missed the subtleties of her designs upon his soul. He did not respond to her mothering, or to the way in which she tweaked him on the cheeks, brushed against him in the kitchen and made admiring remarks about his looks and physique. Memsahibs, he knew, were not for him. So he kept a stony face and went diligently about his duties. And she felt slighted, put in her place. Her liking turned to dislike. Instead of admiring remarks, she began making disparaging remarks about his looks, his clothes, his manners. She found fault with his cooking. No longer was it 'lovely'. She even accused him of taking away the dog's meat and giving it to a poor family living on the hillside—no more heinous crime could be imagined! Mr Good threatened him with dismissal. So Prem became stubborn. The following day he withheld the dog's food altogether, threw it down the khud where it was seized upon by innumerable strays, and went off to the pictures.

That was the end of his job. 'I'll have to go home now,' he told me. 'I won't get another job in this area. The Mem will see to that.'

'Stay a few days,' I said.

'I have only enough money with which to get home.'

'Keep it for going home. You can stay with me for a few days, while you look around. Your uncle won't mind sharing his food with you.'

His uncle did mind. He did not like the idea of working for his nephew as well; it seemed to him no part of his duties. And he was apprehensive that Prem might get his job.

So Prem stayed no longer than a week.

Here on the knoll the grass is just beginning to turn October yellow. The first clouds approaching winter cover the sky. The trees are very still. The birds are silent. Only a cricket keeps singing on the oak tree. Perhaps there will be a storm before evening. A storm like the one in which Prem arrived at the cottage with his wife and child—but that's jumping too far ahead . . . .

After he had returned to his village, it was several months before I saw him again. His uncle told me he had taken up a job in Delhi. There was an address. It did not seem complete, but I resolved that when I was next in Delhi I would try to see him.

The opportunity came in May, as the hot winds of summer blew across the plains. It was the time of year when people who can afford it, try to get away to the hills. I dislike New Delhi at the best of times, and I hate it in summer. People compete with each other in being bad-tempered and mean. But I had to go down—I don't remember why, but it must have seemed very necessary at the time—and I took the opportunity to try and see Prem.

Nothing went right for me. Of course the address was all wrong, and I wandered about in a remote, dusty, treeless colony called Vasant Vihar (Spring Garden) for over two hours, asking all the domestic servants I came across if they could put me in touch with Prem Singh of Village Koli, Pauri Garhwal. There were innumerable Prem Singhs, but apparently none who belonged to Village Koli. I returned to my hotel and took two days to recover from heatstroke before returning to Mussoorie, thanking God for mountains!

And then the uncle gave notice. He'd found a better paid job in Dehra Dun and was anxious to be off. I didn't try to stop him.

For the next six months I lived in the cottage without any help. I did not find this difficult. I was used to living alone. It wasn't service that I needed but companionship. In the cottage it was very quiet. The ghosts of long dead residents were sympathetic but unobtrusive. The song of the whistling thrush was beautiful, but I knew he was not singing for me. Up the valley came the sound of a lute, but I never saw the flute player. My affinity was with the little red fox who roamed the hillside below the cottage. I met him one night and wrote these lines:

> As I walked home last night
> I saw a lone fox dancing
> In the cold moonlight.
> I stood and watched—then
> Took the low road, knowing
> The night was his by right.
> Sometimes, when words ring true,
> I'm like a lone fox dancing
> In the morning dew.

During the rains, watching the dripping trees and the mist climbing the valley, I wrote a great deal of poetry. Loneliness is of value to poets. But poetry didn't bring me much money, and funds were low. And then, just as I was wondering if I would have to give up my freedom and take a job again, a publisher bought the paperback rights of one of my children's stories, and I was free to live and write as I pleased—for another three months!

That was in November. To celebrate, I took a long walk through the Landour Bazaar and up the Tehri road. It was a good day for walking; and it was dark by the time I returned to the outskirts of the town. Someone stood waiting for me on the road above the cottage. I hurried past him.

> If I am not for myself,
> Who will be for me?
> And if I am not for others,
> What am I?
> And if not now, when?

I startled myself with the memory of these words of Hillel, the ancient Hebrew sage. I walked back to the shadows where the youth stood, and saw that it was Prem.

'Prem!' I said. 'Why are you sitting out here, in the cold? Why did you not go to the house?'

'I went, sir, but there was a lock on the door. I thought you had gone away.'

'And you were going to remain here, on the road?'

'Only for tonight. I would have gone down to Dehra in the morning.'

'Come, let's go home. I have been waiting for you. I looked for you in Delhi, but could not find the place where you were working.'

'I have left them now.'

'And your uncle has left me. So will you work for me now?'

'For as long as you wish.'

'For as long as the gods wish.'

We did not go straight home, but returned to the bazaar and took our meal in the Sindhi Sweet Shop—hot puris and strong sweet tea.

We walked home together in the bright moonlight. I felt sorry for the little fox dancing alone.

That was twenty years ago, and Prem and his wife and three children are still with me. But we live in a different house now, on another hill.

DEATH OF THE TREES

❧

THE PEACE AND QUIET of the Maplewood hillside disappeared
forever one winter. The powers that be decided to build another
new road into the mountains, and the PWD saw fit to take it
right past the cottage, about six feet from the large window
which had overlooked the forest.

In my journal I wrote:

'Already they have felled most of the trees. The walnut
was one of the first to go. A tree I had lived with for over ten
years, watching it grow just as I had watched Prem's little
son, Rakesh, grow up . . . . Looking forward to its new leaf-
buds, the broad, green leaves of summer turning to spears of
gold in September when the walnuts were ripe and ready to
fall. I knew this tree better than the others. It was just below
the window, where a buttress for the road is going up.

Another tree I'll miss is the young deodar, the only one
growing in this stretch of the woods. Some years back it was
stunted from lack of sunlight. The oaks covered it with their
shaggy branches. So I cut away some of the overhanging branches
and after that the deodar grew much faster. It was just coming
into its own this year; now cut down in its prime like my young
brother on the road to Delhi last month: both victims of the roads;
the tree killed by the PWD, my brother by a truck.

Twenty oaks have been felled. Just in this small stretch near
the cottage. By the time this bypass reaches Jabarkhet, about six
miles from here, over a thousand oaks will have been
slaughtered, besides many other fine trees—maples, deodars
and pines—most of them unnecessarily, as they grow some
fifty to sixty yards from the roadside.

The trouble is, hardly anyone (with the exception of the contractor who buys the felled trees) really believes that trees and shrubs are necessary. They get in the way so much, don't they? According to my milkman, the only useful tree is one which can be picked clean of its leaves for fodder! And a young man remarked to me: 'You should come to Pauri. The view is terrific, there are no trees in the way!'

Well, he can stay here now, and enjoy the view of the ravaged hillside. But as the oaks have gone, the milkman will have to look further afield for his fodder.

Rakesh calls the maples the butterfly trees because when the winged seeds fall they flutter like butterflies in the breeze. No maples now. No bright red leaves to flame against the sky. No birds!

That is to say, no birds near the house. No longer will it be possible for me to open the window and watch the scarlet minivets flitting through the dark green foliage of the oaks; the long-tailed magpies gliding through the trees; the barbet calling insistently from his perch on top of the deodar. Forest birds, all of them, they will now be in search of some other stretch of surviving forest. The only visitors will be the crows, who have learnt to live with, and off, humans and seem to multiply along with roads, houses and people. And even when all the people have gone, the crows will still be around.

Other things to look forward to: trucks thundering past in the night; perhaps a tea and pakora shop round the corner; the grinding of gears, the music of motor horns. Will the whistling thrush be heard above them? The explosions that continually shatter the silence of the mountains—as thousand-year-old rocks are dynamited—have frightened away all but the most intrepid of birds and animals. Even the bold langurs haven't shown their faces for over a fortnight.

Somehow, I don't think we shall wait for the tea shop to arrive. There must be some other quiet corner, possibly on the next mountain, where new roads have yet to come into being. No doubt this is a negative attitude, and if I had any sense I'd open my own tea shop. To retreat is to be a loser. But the trees are losers too; and when they fall, they do so with a certain dignity.

Never mind. Men come and go; the mountains remain.'

WOULD ASTLEY RETURN?

ॐ

THE HOUSE WAS CALLED 'Undercliff' because that's where it stood—under a cliff. The man who went away—the owner of the house—was Robert Astley. And the man who stayed behind—the old family retainer—was Prem Bahadur.

Astley had been gone many years. He was still a bachelor in his late thirties when he'd suddenly decided that he wanted adventure, romance and faraway places. And he'd given the keys of the house to Prem Bahadur—who'd served the family for thirty years—and had set off on his travels.

Someone saw him in Sri Lanka. He'd been heard of in Burma around the ruby mines at Mogok. Then he turned up in Java seeking a passage through the Sunda Straits. After that the trail petered out. Years passed. The house in the hill station remained empty.

But Prem Bahadur was still there, living in an outhouse.

Every day he opened up Undercliff, dusted the furniture in all the rooms, made sure that the bedsheets and pillowcases were clean and set out Astley's dressing-gown and slippers.

In the old days, whenever Astley had come home after a journey or a long tramp in the hills, he had liked to bathe and change into his gown and slippers, no matter what the hour. Prem Bahadur still kept them ready. He was convinced that Robert would return one day.

Astley himself had said so.

'Keep everything ready for me, Prem, old chap. I may be back after a year, or two years, or even longer, but I'll be back, I promise you. On the first of every month I want you to go to my lawyer, Mr Kapoor. He'll give you your salary and any money that's needed for the rates and repairs. I want you to keep the house tip-top!'

'Will you bring back a wife, Sahib?'

'Lord, no! Whatever put that idea in your head?'

'I thought, perhaps—because you wanted the house kept ready . . . .'

'Ready for me, Prem. I don't want to come home and find the old place falling down.'

And so Prem had taken care of the house—although there was no news from Astley. What had happened to him? The mystery provided a talking-point whenever local people met on the Mall. And in the bazaar the shopkeepers missed Astley because he had been a man who spent freely.

His relatives still believed him to be alive. Only a few months back a brother had turned up—a brother who had a farm in Canada and could not stay in India for long. He had deposited a further sum with the lawyer and told Prem to carry on as before. The salary provided Prem with his few needs. Moreover, he was convinced that Robert would return.

Another man might have neglected the house and grounds, but not Prem Bahadur. He had a genuine regard for the absent owner. Prem was much older—now almost sixty and none too strong, suffering from pleurisy and other chest troubles—but he remembered Robert as both a boy and a young man. They had been together on numerous hunting and fishing trips in the mountains. They had slept out under the stars, bathed in icy mountain streams, and eaten from the same cooking-pot. Once, when crossing a small river, they had been swept downstream by a flash flood, a wall of water that came thundering down the gorges without any warning during the rainy season. Together they had struggled back to safety. Back in the hill station, Astley told everyone that Prem had saved his life while Prem was equally insistent that he owed his life to Robert.

This year the monsoon had begun early and ended late. It dragged on through most of September and Prem Bahadur's cough grew worse and his breathing more difficult.

He lay on his charpai on the veranda, staring out at the garden, which was beginning to get out of hand, a tangle of dahlias, snake-lilies and convolvulus. The sun finally came out. The wind shifted from the south-west to the north-west and swept the clouds away.

Prem Bahadur had shifted his charpai into the garden and was lying in the sun, puffing at his small hookah, when he saw Robert Astley at the gate.

He tried to get up but his legs would not oblige him. The hookah slipped from his hand.

Astley came walking down the garden path and stopped in front of the old retainer, smiling down at him. He did not look a day older than when Prem Bahadur had last seen him.

'So you have come at last,' said Prem.

'I told you I'd return.'

'It has been many years. But you have not changed.'

'Nor have you, old chap.'

'I have grown old and sick and feeble.'

'You'll be fine now. That's why I've come.'

'I'll open the house,' said Prem and this time he found himself getting up quite easily.

'It isn't necessary,' said Astley.

'But all is ready for you!'

'I know. I have heard of how well you have looked after everything. Come then, let's take a last look around. We cannot stay, you know.'

Prem was a little mystified but he opened the front door and took Robert through the drawing-room and up the stairs to the bedroom. Robert saw the dressing-gown and the slippers and he placed his hand gently on the old man's shoulder.

When they returned downstairs and emerged into the sunlight Prem was surprised to see himself—or rather his skinny body—stretched out on the charpai. The hookah was on the ground, where it had fallen.

Prem looked at Astley in bewilderment.

'But who is that—lying there?'

'It was you. Only the husk now, the empty shell. This is the real you, standing here beside me.'

'You came for me?'

'I couldn't come until you were ready. As for me, I left *my* shell a long time ago. But you were determined to hang on, keeping this house together. Are you ready now?'

'And the house?'

'Others will live in it. But come, it's time to go fishing . . . .'

Astley took Prem by the arm, and they walked through the dappled sunlight under the deodars and finally left that place for ever.

THE GIRL FROM COPENHAGEN

❧

THIS IS NOT A love story but it is a story about love. You will know what I mean.

When I was living and working in London I knew a Vietnamese girl called Phuong. She studied at the Polytechnic. During the summer vacations she joined a group of students— some of them English, most of them French, German, Indian and African—picking raspberries for a few pounds a week and drinking in some real English country air. Late one summer, on her return from a farm, she introduced me to Ulla, a sixteen-year-old Danish girl who had come over to England for a similar holiday.

'Please look after Ulla for a few days,' said Phuong. 'She doesn't know anyone in London.'

'But I want to look after you,' I protested. I had been infatuated with Phuong for some time, but though she was rather fond of me, she did not reciprocate my advances and it was possible that she had conceived of Ulla as a device to get rid of me for a little while.

'This is Ulla,' said Phuong, thrusting a blonde child into my arms. 'Bye and don't get up to any mischief!'

Phuong disappeared, and I was left alone with Ulla at the entrance to the Charing Cross Underground Station. She grinned at me and I smiled back rather nervously. She had blue eyes and a smooth, tanned skin. She was small for a Scandinavian girl, reaching only to my shoulders, and her figure was slim and boyish. She was carrying a small travel-bag. It gave me an excuse to do something.

'We'd better leave your bag somewhere,' I said taking it from her.

And after depositing it in the left-luggage office, we were back on the pavement, grinning at each other.

'Well, Ulla,' I said, 'how many days do you have in London?'

'Only two. Then I go back to Copenhagen.'

'Good. Well, what would you like to do?'

'Eat. I'm hungry.'

I wasn't hungry but there's nothing like a meal to help two strangers grow acquainted. We went to a small and not very expensive Indian restaurant off Fitzroy Square and burnt our tongues on an orange-coloured Hyderabad chicken curry. We had to cool off with a Tamil Koykotay before we could talk.

'What do you do in Copenhagen?' I asked.

'I go to school. I'm joining the University next year.'

'And your parents?'

'They have a bookshop.'

'Then you must have done a lot of reading.'

'Oh, no, I don't read much. I can't sit in one place for long. I like swimming and tennis and going to the theatre.'

'But you have to sit in a theatre.'

'Yes, but that's different.'

'It's not sitting that you mind but sitting and reading.'

'Yes, you are right. But most Danish girls like reading— they read more books than English girls.'

'You are probably right,' I said.

As I was out of a job just then and had time on my hands, we were able to feed the pigeons in Trafalgar Square and while away the afternoon in a coffee-bar before going on to a theatre. Ulla was wearing tight jeans and an abbreviated duffle coat and as she had brought little else with her, she wore this outfit to the theatre. It created quite a stir in the foyer but Ulla was completely unconscious of the stares she received. She enjoyed the play, laughed loudly in all the wrong places, and clapped her hands when no one else did.

The lunch and the theatre had lightened my wallet and dinner consisted of baked beans on toast in a small snack-bar. After picking up Ulla's bag, I offered to take her back to Phuong's place.

'Why there?' she said. 'Phuong must have gone to bed.'

'Yes, but aren't you staying with her?'

'Oh, no. She did not ask me.'

'Then where are you staying? Where have you kept the rest of your things?'

'Nowhere. This is all I brought with me,' she said, indicating the travel-bag.

'Well, you can't sleep on a park bench,' I said. 'Shall I get you a room in a hotel?'

'I don't think so. I have only the money to return to Copenhagen.' She looked crestfallen for a few moments. Then she brightened and slipped her arm through mine. 'I know, I'll stay with you. Do you mind?'

'No, but my landlady—' I began, then stopped. It would have been a lie. My landlady, a generous, broad-minded soul, would not have minded in the least.

'All right,' I said. 'I don't mind.'

When we reached my room in Swiss Cottage Ulla threw off her coat and opened the window wide. It was a warm summer's night and the scent of honeysuckle came through the open window. She kicked her shoes off and walked about the room barefoot. Her toenails were painted a bright pink. She slipped out of her blouse and jeans and stood before the mirror in her lace pants. A lot of sunbathing had made her quite brown but her small breasts were white.

She slipped into bed and said, 'Aren't you coming?'

I crept in beside her and lay very still while she chattered on about the play and the friends she had made in the country. I switched off the bed-lamp and she fell silent. Then she said, 'Well, I'm sleepy. Goodnight!' And turning over, she immediately fell asleep.

I lay awake beside her, conscious of the growing warmth of her body. She was breathing easily and quietly. Her long, golden hair touched my cheek. I kissed her gently on the lobe of the ear but she was fast asleep. So I counted eight hundred and sixty-two Scandinavian sheep and managed to fall asleep.

Ulla woke fresh and frolicsome. The sun streamed in through the window and she stood naked in its warmth, performing calisthenics. I busied myself with the breakfast. Ulla ate three eggs and a lot of bacon and drank two cups of coffee. I couldn't help admiring her appetite.

'And what shall we do today?' she asked, her blue eyes shining. They were the bright blue eyes of a Siamese kitten.

'I'm supposed to visit the Employment Exchange,' I said.

'But that is bad. Can't you go tomorrow—after I have left?'

'If you like.'

'I like.'

And she gave me a swift, unsettling kiss on the lips.

We climbed Primrose Hill and watched boys flying kites. We lay in the sun and chewed blades of grass and then we visited the zoo where Ulla fed the monkeys. She consumed innumerable ices. We lunched at a small Greek restaurant and I forgot to phone Phuong and in the evening we walked all the way home through scruffy Camden Town, drank beer, ate a fine, greasy dinner of fish and chips and went to bed early— Ulla had to catch the boat-train the next morning.

'It has been a good day,' she said.

'I'd like to do it again tomorrow.'

'But I must go tomorrow.'

'But you must go.'

She turned her head on the pillow and looked wonderingly into my eyes, as though she were searching for something. I don't know if she found what she was looking for but she smiled and kissed me softly on the lips.

'Thanks for everything,' she said.

She was fresh and clean, like the earth after spring rain.

I took her fingers and kissed them, one by one. I kissed her breasts, her throat, her forehead. And, making her close her eyes, I kissed her eyelids.

We lay in each other's arms for a long time, savouring the warmth and texture of each other's bodies. Though we were both very young and inexperienced, we found ourselves imbued with a tender patience, as though there lay before us not just this one passing night but all the nights of a lifetime, all eternity.

There was a great joy in our loving and afterwards we fell asleep in each other's arms like two children who have been playing in the open all day.

The sun woke me the next morning. I opened my eyes to see Ulla's slim, bare leg dangling over the side of the bed. I smiled at her painted toes. Her hair pressed against my face and the sunshine fell on it making each hair a strand of burnished gold.

The station and the train were crowded and we held hands and grinned at each other, too shy to kiss.

'Give my love to Phuong,' she said.

'I will.'

We made no promises—of writing, or of meeting again. Somehow our relationship seemed complete and whole, as though it had been destined to blossom for those two days. A courting and a marriage and a living together had been compressed, perfectly, into one summer night . . . .

I passed the day in a glow of happiness. I thought Ulla was still with me and it was only at night, when I put my hand out for hers, and did not find it, that I knew she had gone.

But I kept the window open all through the summer and the scent of the honeysuckle was with me every night.

The Trouble with Jinns

ॐ

My friend Jimmy has only one arm. He lost the other when he was a young man of twenty-five. The story of how he lost his good right arm is a little difficult to believe, but I swear that it is absolutely true.

To begin with, Jimmy was (and presumably still is) a Jinn. Now a Jinn isn't really a human like us. A Jinn is a spirit creature from another world who has assumed, for a lifetime, the physical aspect of a human being. Jimmy was a true Jinn and he had the Jinn's gift of being able to elongate his arm at will. Most Jinns can stretch their arms to a distance of twenty or thirty feet. Jimmy could attain forty feet. His arm would move through space or up walls or along the ground like a beautiful gliding serpent. I have seen him stretched out beneath a mango tree, helping himself to ripe mangoes from the top of the tree. He loved mangoes. He was a natural glutton and it was probably his gluttony that first led time to misuse his peculiar gifts.

We were at school together at a hill station in northern India. Jimmy was particularly good at basketball. He was clever enough not to lengthen his arm too much because he did not want anyone to know that he was a Jinn. In the boxing ring he generally won his fights. His opponents never seemed to get past his amazing reach. He just kept tapping them on the nose until they retired from the ring bloody and bewildered.

It was during the half-term examinations that I stumbled on Jimmy's secret. We had been set a particularly difficult algebra paper but I had managed to cover a couple of sheets with correct answers and was about to forge ahead on another sheet when I noticed someone's hand on my desk. At first I thought it was the invigilator's. But when I looked up there was no one beside me. Could it be the boy sitting directly behind? No, he was engrossed in his question paper and had his hands to himself. Meanwhile, the hand on my desk had grasped my answer-sheets and was cautiously moving off. Following its descent, I found that it was attached to an arm of amazing length and pliability. This moved stealthily down the desk and slithered across the floor, shrinking all the while, until it was restored to its normal length. Its owner was of course one who had never been any good at algebra.

I had to write out my answers a second time but after the exam I went straight up to Jimmy, told him I didn't like his game and threatened to expose him. He begged me not to let anyone know, assured me that he couldn't really help himself, and offered to be of service to me whenever I wished. It was tempting to have Jimmy as my friend, for with his long reach he would obviously be useful. I agreed to overlook the matter of the pilfered papers and we became the best of pals.

It did not take me long to discover that Jimmy's gift was more of a nuisance than a constructive aid. That was because Jimmy had a second-rate mind and did not know how to make proper use of his powers. He seldom rose above the trivial. He used his long arm in the tuck-shop, in the classroom, in the dormitory. And when we were allowed out to the cinema, he used it in the dark of the hall.

Now the trouble with all Jinns is that they have a weakness for women with long black hair. The longer and blacker the hair, the better for Jinns. And should a Jinn manage to take possession of the woman he desires, she goes into a decline and her beauty decays. Everything about her is destroyed except for the beautiful long black hair.

Jimmy was still too young to be able to take possession in this way, but he couldn't resist touching and stroking long black hair. The cinema was the best place for the indulgence of his whims. His arm would start stretching, his fingers would feel their way along the rows of seats, and his lengthening limb would slowly work its way along the aisle until it reached the back of the seat in which sat the object of his admiration. His hand would stroke the long black hair with great tenderness and if the girl felt anything and looked round, Jimmy's hand would disappear behind the seat and lie there poised like the hood of a snake, ready to strike again.

At college two or three years later, Jimmy's first real victim succumbed to his attentions. She was a lecturer in Economics, not very good-looking, but her hair, black and lustrous, reached almost to her knees. She usually kept it in plaits but Jimmy saw her one morning, just after she had taken a head-bath, and her hair lay spread out on the cot on which she was reclining. Jimmy could no longer control himself. His spirit, the very essence of his personality, entered the woman's body and the next day she was distraught, feverish and excited. She would not eat, went into a coma, and in a few days dwindled to a mere skeleton. When she died, she was nothing but skin and bone but her hair had lost none of its loveliness.

I took pains to avoid Jimmy after this tragic event. I could not prove that he was the cause of the lady's sad demise but in my own heart I was quite certain of it. For since meeting Jimmy, I had read a good deal about Jinns and knew their ways.

We did not see each other for a few years. And then, holidaying in the hills last year, I found we were staying at the same hotel. I could not very well ignore him and after we had drunk a few beers together I began to feel that I had perhaps misjudged Jimmy and that he was not the irresponsible Jinn I had taken him for. Perhaps the college lecturer had died of some mysterious malady that attacks only college lecturers and Jimmy had nothing at all to do with it.

We had decided to take our lunch and a few bottles of beer to a grassy knoll just below the main motor-road. It was late afternoon and I had been sleeping off the effects of the beer when I woke to find Jimmy looking rather agitated.

'What's wrong?' I asked.

'Up there, under the pine trees,' he said. 'Just above the road. Don't you see them?'

'I see two girls,' I said. 'So what?'

'The one on the left. Haven't you noticed her hair?'

'Yes, it is very long and beautiful and—now look, Jimmy, you'd better get a grip on yourself!' But already his hand was out of sight, his arm snaking up the hillside and across the road.

Presently I saw the hand emerge from some bushes near the girls and then cautiously make its way to the girl with the black tresses. So absorbed was Jimmy in the pursuit of his favourite pastime that he failed to hear the blowing of a horn. Around the bend of the road came a speeding Mercedes-Benz truck.

Jimmy saw the truck but there wasn't time for him to shrink his arm back to normal. It lay right across the entire width of the road and when the truck had passed over it, it writhed and twisted like a mortally wounded python.

By the time the truck-driver and I could fetch a doctor, the arm (or what was left of it) had shrunk to its ordinary size. We took Jimmy to hospital where the doctors found it necessary to amputate. The truck-driver, who kept insisting that the arm he ran over was at least thirty feet long, was arrested on a charge of drunken driving.

Some weeks later I asked Jimmy, 'Why are you so depressed? You still have one arm. Isn't it gifted in the same way?'

'I never tried to find out,' he said, 'and I'm not going to try now.'

He is of course still a Jinn at heart and whenever he sees a girl with long black hair he must be terribly tempted to try out his one good arm and stroke her beautiful tresses. But he has learnt his lesson. It is better to be a human without any gifts than a Jinn or a genius with one too many.

TRIBUTE TO A DEAD FRIEND

❧

NOW THAT THANH IS dead, I suppose it is not too treacherous of me to write about him. He was only a year older than I. He died in Paris, in his twenty-second year, and Pravin wrote to me from London and told me about it. I will get more details from Pravin when he returns to India next month. Just now I only know that Thanh is dead.

It is supposed to be in very bad taste to discuss a person behind his back and to discuss a dead person is most unfair, for he cannot even retaliate. But Thanh had this very weakness of criticizing absent people and it cannot hurt him now if I do a little to expose his colossal ego.

Thanh was a fraud all right but no one knew it. He had beautiful round eyes, a flashing smile and a sweet voice and everyone said he was a charming person. He was certainly charming but I have found that charming people are seldom sincere. I think I was the only person who came anywhere near to being his friend for he had cultivated a special loneliness of his own and it was difficult to intrude on it.

I met him in London in the summer of '54. I was trying to become a writer while I worked part-time at a number of different jobs. I had been two years in London and was longing for the hills and rivers of India. Thanh was Vietnamese. His family was well-to-do and though the Communists had taken their home-town of Hanoi, most of the family was in France, well-established in the restaurant business. Thanh did not suffer from the same financial distress as other students whose homes were in Northern Vietnam. He wasn't studying anything in particular but practised assiduously on the piano, though the only thing he could play fairly well was Chopin's Funeral March.

My friend Pravin, a happy-go-lucky, very friendly Gujarati boy, introduced me to Thanh. Pravin, like a good Indian, thought all Asians were superior people, but he didn't know Thanh well enough to know that Thanh didn't like being an Asian.

At first, Thanh was glad to meet me. He said he had for a long time been wanting to make friends with an Englishman, a real Englishman, not one who was a Pole, a Cockney or a Jew; he was most anxious to improve his English and talk like Mr Glendenning of the BBC. Pravin, knowing that I had been born and bred in India, that my parents had been born and bred in India, suppressed his laughter with some difficulty. But Thanh was soon disillusioned. My accent was anything but English. It was a pronounced *chi-chi* accent.

'You speak like an Indian!' exclaimed Thanh, horrified. 'Are you an Indian?'

'He's Welsh,' said Pravin with a wink.

Thanh was slightly mollified. Being Welsh was the next best thing to being English. Only he disapproved of the Welsh for speaking with an Indian accent.

Later, when Pravin had gone, and I was sitting in Thanh's room drinking Chinese tea, he confided in me that he disliked Indians.

'Isn't Pravin your friend?' I asked.

'I don't trust him,' he said. 'I have to be friendly but I don't trust him at all. I don't trust any Indians.'

'What's wrong with them?'

'They are too inquisitive,' complained Thanh. 'No sooner have you met one of them than he is asking you who your father is, and what your job is, and how much money you have in the bank.'

I laughed and tried to explain that in India inquisitiveness is a sign of a desire for friendship, and that he should feel flattered when asked such personal questions. I protested that I was an Indian myself and he said if that was so he wouldn't trust me either.

But he seemed to like me and often invited me to his rooms. He could make some wonderful Chinese and French dishes. When we had eaten, he would sit down at his second-hand piano and play Chopin. He always complained that I didn't listen properly.

He complained of my untidiness and my unwarranted self-confidence. It was true that I appeared most confident when I was not very sure of myself. I boasted of an intimate knowledge of London's geography but I was an expert at losing my way and then blaming it on someone else.

'You are a useless person,' said Thanh, while with chopsticks I stuffed my mouth with delicious pork and fried rice. 'You cannot find your way anywhere. You cannot speak English properly. You do not know any people except Indians. How are you going to be a writer?'

'If I am as bad as all that,' I said, 'why do you remain my friend?'

'I want to study your stupidity,' he said.

That was why he never made any real friends. He loved to work out your faults and examine your imperfections. There was no such thing as a real friend, he said. He had looked everywhere but he could not find the perfect friend.

'What is your idea of a perfect friend?' I asked him. 'Does he have to speak perfect English?'

But sarcasm was only wasted on Thanh—he admitted that perfect English was one of the requisites of a perfect friend!

Sometimes, in moments of deep gloom, he would tell me that he did not have long to live.

'There is a pain in my chest,' he complained. 'There is something ticking there all the time. Can you hear it?'

He would bare his bony chest for me and I would put my ear to the offending spot. But I could never hear any ticking.

'Visit the hospital,' I advised. 'They'll give you an x-ray and a proper check-up.'

'I have had x-rays,' he lied. 'They never show anything.'

Then he would talk of killing himself. This was his theme song: he had no friends, he was a failure as a musician, there was no other career open to him, he hadn't seen his family for five years, and he couldn't go back to Indo-China because of the Communists. He magnified his own troubles and minimized other people's troubles. When I was in hospital with an old acquaintance, amoebic dysentery, Pravin came to see me every day. Thanh, who was not very busy, came only once and never again. He said the hospital ward depressed him.

'You need a holiday,' I told him when I was out of hospital. Why don't you join the students' union and work on a farm for a week or two? That should toughen you up.'

To my surprise, the idea appealed to him and he got ready for the trip. Suddenly, he became suffused with goodwill towards all mankind. As evidence of his trust in me, he gave me the key of his room to keep (though he would have been secretly delighted if I had stolen his piano and chopsticks, giving him the excuse to say 'never trust an Indian or an Anglo-Indian'), and introduced me to a girl called Vu-Phuong, a small, very pretty Annamite girl who was studying at the Polytechnic. Miss Vu, Thanh told me, had to leave her lodgings next week and would I find somewhere else for her to stay? I was an experienced hand at finding bed-sitting rooms, having changed my own abode five times in six months (that sweet, nomadic London life!). As I found Miss Vu very attractive, I told her I would get her a room, one not far from my own, in case she needed any further assistance.

Later, in confidence, Thanh asked me not to be too friendly with Vu-Phuong as she was not to be trusted.

But as soon as he left for the farm, I went round to see Vu in her new lodgings which were one tube-station away from my own. She seemed glad to see me and as she too could make French and Chinese dishes I accepted her invitation to lunch. We had chicken noodles, soya sauce and fried rice. I did the washing-up. Vu said: 'Do you play cards, Ruskin?' She had a sweet, gentle voice that brought out all the gallantry in a man. I began to feel protective and hovered about her like a devoted cocker spaniel.

'I'm not much of a card-player,' I said.

'Never mind, I'll tell your fortune with them.'

She made me shuffle the cards. Then scattered them about on the bed in different patterns. I would be very rich, she said. I would travel a lot and I would reach the age of forty. I told her I was comforted to know it.

The month was June and Hampstead Heath was only ten

minutes walk from the house. Boys flew kites from the hill and little painted boats scurried about on the ponds. We sat down on the grass, on the slope of the hill, and I held Vu's hand.

For three days I ate with Vu and we told each other our fortunes and lay on the grass on Hampstead Heath and on the fourth day I said, 'Vu, I would like to marry you.'

'I will think about it,' she said.

Thanh came back on the sixth day and said, 'You know, Ruskin, I have been doing some thinking and Vu is not such a bad girl after all. I will ask her to marry me. That is what I need—a wife!'

'Why didn't you think of it before?' I said. 'When will you ask her?'

'Tonight,' he said. 'I will come to see you afterwards and tell you if I have been successful.'

I shrugged my shoulders resignedly and waited. Thanh left me at six in the evening and I waited for him till ten o'clock, all the time feeling a little sorry for him. More disillusionment for Thanh! Poor Thanh . . . .

He came in at ten o'clock, his face beaming. He slapped me on the back and said I was his best friend.

'Did you ask her?' I said.

'Yes. She said she would think about it. That is the same as "yes".'

'It isn't,' I said, unfortunately for both of us. 'She told me the same thing.'

Thanh looked at me as though I had just stabbed him in the back. *Et tu* Ruskin was what his expression said.

We took a taxi and sped across to Vu's rooms. The uncertain nature of her replies was too much for both of us. Without a definite answer neither of us would have been able to sleep that night.

Vu was not at home. The landlady met us at the door and told us that Vu had gone to the theatre with an Indian gentleman.

Thanh gave me a long, contemptuous look.

'Never trust an Indian,' he said.

'Never trust a woman,' I replied.

At twelve o'clock I woke Pravin. Whenever I could not sleep, I went to Pravin. He knew the remedy for all ailments.

As on previous occasions, he went to the cupboard and produced a bottle of Cognac. We got drunk. He was seventeen and I was nineteen and we were both quite decadent.

Three weeks later I returned to India. Thanh went to Paris to help in his sister's restaurant. I did not hear of Vu-Phuong again.

And now, a year later, there is the letter from Pravin. All he can tell me is that Thanh died of some unknown disease. I wonder if it had anything to do with the ticking in his chest or with his vague threats of suicide. I doubt if I will ever know. And I will never know how much I hated Thanh, and how much I loved him, or if there was any difference between hating and loving him.

My First Love

❧

AYAH, MY CHILDHOOD GOVERNESS, was my first love. She was thirty and I was six. She was a tall, broad-limbed woman, and in my view extremely handsome. The west-coast fishing community to which she belonged, and the Arab and African blood she had inherited, were partly responsible for her magnificent build and colourful personality. Occasionally when one of my parents' guests called her ugly without really taking a proper look at her, I would exclaim, 'No, she is beautiful!' The vehemence of my reply would disconcert the guests and embarrass my parents.

We lived in a small Indian State on the Kathiawar coast, where my father had a job as guardian-tutor to the Maharaja's children. He conducted a small school in a corner of the palace, and was fully occupied most of the day. My mother would frequently be visiting other Anglo-Indian families. And I, being considered too much of a menace to be taken to other people's houses, was left in the charge of Ayah.

Most children who saw Ayah drew away from her in fright. Her size, her wrestler's arms, her broad quivering hips, were at first disconcerting to a child. She had thick, crinkly hair and teeth stained red with the juice of innumerable paan-leaves. Her hands were rough and heavy, as I knew from the number of times she had brought them down on my bottom. When she was angry, her face resembled a menacing thundercloud; but when she smiled with pleasure it was as though the sun had just emerged, lighting up her features with a great dazzle. Ayah frequently beat me, but soon afterwards she would be overcome by remorse, and then she would take me in her strong arms and plant heavy wet kisses on my eyes and cheeks and mouth. She was in love with my soft white skin, and often made believe that I was her own child, pressing my face to her great breasts, bathing and dressing me with infinite tenderness, and defending me against everyone, including my parents.

Sometimes, when my parents were out, I would insist that she bathe with me. We would wallow together in the long marble tub: I, small, pink and podgy; and Ayah like a benevolent hippopotamus, causing the bath-tub to overflow. She scrubbed and soaped me, while I relaxed and enjoyed the sensation of her rough hands moving over my back and tummy. And then, before she could heave herself out of the tub, I would leap from the water and charge out of the bathroom without my clothes. Ayah would come flapping after me, a sheet tied hurriedly about her waist and we would race through the rooms until finally she caught up with me, gave me several resounding slaps, watched me burst into tears, and then broke down herself and took me to her comfortable bosom.

Ayah taught me many things. One of these was the eating of paan—a betel leaf containing lime, finely-cut areca nut, and some cardamom.

It was the scarlet tinge in the mouth which came from eating paan that appealed most to me. I did not care much for the taste, which was bitter, but I was fascinated by the red juice which Ayah was able to spit so accurately about the garden. When my parents were out, she would share her paan with me, and we would sit in the kitchen and gossip with the cook. Before my parents came home, Ayah would make me rinse my mouth with warm water, and with her rough fingers she would scrub my teeth clean.

A number of snakes lived in the old walls surrounding both our bungalow and the palace grounds. They seldom ventured into the house, but when they did, Ayah was against killing them. She always maintained that they would not harm us provided we left them alone.

She once told me the story of a snake who married a poor but beautiful girl. At first the girl very naturally did not wish to marry the snake, whom she had met in a forest. But the snake insisted, saying, 'I will kill you if you refuse,' which of course left her with no alternative. Then the snake led his bride away, and took her to a great treasure. 'I was a prince in my former life,' explained the snake, 'and this is my treasure. Now it is all yours.' And then he very gallantly disappeared.

'Which goes to show that even snakes are good at heart,' said Ayah.

Sometimes she would leave a saucer of milk beneath an old pipal tree, and once I saw a young cobra glide up to the saucer and finish the milk. When I told Ayah about this, she was a little perturbed, and said she had actually left the milk out for the spirits who lived in the pipal tree.

'I haven't seen any spirits in the tree,' I told her.

'And I hope you never will, my son,' said Ayah. 'But they are there all the same. If you happen to be standing beneath the tree after dark, and feel like yawning, don't forget to snap your fingers in front of your mouth, otherwise the spirit will jump down your throat.'

'And what if it does?' I asked.

For a moment Ayah was at a loss for an answer; then she brightened and said, 'It will probably upset your tummy.'

The pipal was a cool tree to sit beneath. Its heart-shaped leaves spun round in the faintest breeze, sending currents of cool air down from its branches. The leaf itself was likened by Ayah to the perfect male torso—a broad chest tapering down to a very slim waist—and she told me I ought to be built that way when I grew up.

One day we strayed into the ruined palace, which had turrets and towers and winding passageways. And there we found a room with many small windows, each window-pane set with coloured glass. I was often to spend hours in this room, gazing out at the palace and lake and gardens through the coloured window-panes. When the sun came through the windows, the entire room was suffused with beams of red and gold and green and purple light, playing on the walls and on my face and clothes.

The State had a busy little port, and Arab dhows sailed to and fro across the Gulf of Kutch. My father was friendly with the captain of a steamer making trips to Aden and back. The captain was a jovial, whisky-drinking Scotsman, who stuffed me with chocolates and suggested that I join the crew of his ship. The idea appealed to me, and I made elaborate plans for the voyage, only to discover one day when I went down to the docks that the ship had sailed away for ever.

Ayah was more dependable. She hated seeing me disappointed. When I told her about the treachery of Captain MacWhir she consoled me with the promise of a ride in a tonga—a two-wheeled horse-drawn buggy. Apparently she had a friend who plied a tonga in the bazaar.

He came the next day, a young man sporting an orange waistcoat and a magnificent moustache. His name was Bansi Lal. Ayah put me on the front seat beside him, while she sat at the back to try and maintain some sort of equilibrium. We went out of the gate at a brisk trot, but as soon as we were on the open road circling the lake, Bansi Lal lashed his horse into a gallop, and we went tearing along the road at a furious and exhilarating pace. Ayah shouted to her friend to slow down, and I shouted to him to go faster. He grinned at both of us while a devil danced in his eyes, and he cracked his whip and called endearments to both Ayah and his horse.

When finally we reached open country, he slowed down and brought the tonga to rest in a mango-grove. Ayah struggled out and, after berating Bansi Lal, sank down on the grass while I went off to explore the mango-grove. The fruit on the trees was as yet unripe, but the crows and minas had already begun to feast on the mangoes. I wandered about for some time, returning to the clearing by a different route to find Ayah and Bansi Lal embracing each other. Ayah had her back to me, but the tonga-driver had a rapt, rather funny expression on his face. This changed to a look of confusion when he saw me watching them with undisguised curiosity, and he got up hurriedly, fumbling with his pyjama-strings. I threw myself gaily upon Ayah and asked her what she had been doing; but for once she gave me an evasive reply. I don't think the incident had any immediate effect on my innocence, but as I grew older I found myself looking back on it with a certain amount of awe.

Both Ayah and I—for different reasons, as it turned out—began looking forward to our weekly tonga rides. Bansi Lal took us to some very lonely places—scrub-jungle or ruins or abandoned brick-kilns—and he and Ayah were extraordinarily tolerant of where I wandered during these excursions.

But the tonga-rides really meant the end of my affair with Ayah. One day she informed my parents that she intended marrying Bansi Lal and going away with him. While my parents considered this a perfectly natural desire on Ayah's part, I looked upon it as an act of base treachery. For several days I went about the house in a rebellious and sulky mood, refusing to speak to Ayah no matter how much she coaxed and petted me.

On Ayah's last day with us, Bansi Lal arrived in his tonga to take her away. He had painted the woodwork, scrubbed his horse down, and changed his orange waistcoat for a green one. He gave me a cheerful salaam, but I scowled darkly at him from the veranda steps, and he looked guiltily away.

Ayah tossed her bedding and few belongings into the tonga, and then came to say goodbye to me. But I had hidden myself in the jasmine bushes, and though she called and looked for me, I would not emerge. Sadly she climbed into the tonga, weighing it down at the back. Bansi Lal cracked his whip, shouted to his horse, and the tonga went rattling away down the gravel path. Ayah still looked to left and right, hoping to see me; and at last, unable to bear my misery any longer, I came out from the bushes and ran after the tonga, waving to her. Bansi reined in his horse, and Ayah got down and gathered me up in her great arms; and when the tonga finally took her away, there was a dazzling smile on her sweet and gentle face—the face of the lover whom I was never to see again . . . .

MISS BUN AND OTHERS

৯

March 1, 1975

BEER IN THE SUN. HIGH in the spruce tree the barbet calls, heralding summer. A few puffy clouds drift lazily over the mountains. Is this the great escape?

I could sit here all day soaking up beer and sunshine, but at *some* time during the day I must wipe the dust from my typewriter and produce something readable. There's only Rs 800 in the bank, book sales are falling off, and magazines are turning away from fiction.

Prem spoils me, giving me rice and kofta curry for lunch, which means that I sleep till four when Miss Bun arrives with patties and samosas.

Miss Bun is the baker's daughter.

Of course that's not her real name. Her real name is very long and beautiful, but I won't give it here for obvious reasons and also because her brother is big and ugly.

I am seeing Miss Bun after two months. She's been with relatives in Bareilly.

She sits at the foot of my bed, absolutely radiant. Her raven-black hair lies loose on her shoulders, her eyelashes have been trimmed and blackened and so have her eyes, with kajal. Her eyes, so large and innocent—and calculating!

There are pretty glass bangles on her wrists and she wears a pair of new slippers. Her kameez is new too—green silk, with gold-embroidered sleeves.

'You must have a rich lover,' I remark, taking her hand and

gently pulling her towards me. 'Who gave you all this finery?'

'You did. Don't you remember? Before I went away, you gave me a hundred rupees.'

'That was for the train and bus fares, I thought.'

'Oh, my uncle paid the fares. So I bought myself these things. Are they nice?'

'Very pretty. And so are you. If you were ten years older and I ten years younger, we'd make a good pair. But I'd have been broke long before this!'

She giggles and drops a paper-bag full of samosas on the bedside table. I hate samosas and patties, but I keep ordering them because it gives Miss Bun a pretext for visiting me. It's all in the way of helping the bakery get by. When she goes, I give the lot to Bijju and Binya or whoever might be passing.

'You've been away a long time,' I complain. 'What if I'd got married while you were away?'

'Then you'd stop ordering samosas.'

'Or get them from that old man Bashir, who makes much better ones, and cheaper!'

She drops her head on my shoulder. Her hair is heavily scented with jasmine hair-oil, and I nearly pass out. They should use it instead of anaesthesia.

'You smell very nice,' I lie. 'Do I get a kiss?'

She gives me a long kiss, as though to make up for her long absence. Her kisses always have a nice wholesome flavour, as you would expect from someone who lives in a bakery.

'That was an expensive kiss.'

'I want to buy some face-cream.'

'You don't need face-cream. Your complexion is perfect. It must be the good quality flour you use in the bakery.'

'I don't put flour on my face. Anyway, I want the cream for my elder sister. She has pockmarks.'

I surrender and give her two fives, quickly putting away my wallet.

'And when will you pay for the samosas?'

'Next week.'

'I'll bring you something nice next week,' she says, pausing in the doorway.

'Well, thanks, I was getting tired of samosas.'

She was gone in a twinkling.

I'll say this for Miss Bun—she doesn't trouble to hide her intentions.

March 4

My policeman calls on me this morning. Ghanshyam, the constable attached to the Barlowganj outpost.

He is not very tall for a policeman, and he has a round, cheerful countenance, which is unusual in his profession. He looks smart in his uniform. Most constables prefer to hang around in their pyjamas most of the time.

Nothing alarming about Ghanshyam's visit. He comes to see me about once a week, and has been doing so ever since I spent a night in the police station last year.

It happened when I punched a Muzzaffarnagar businessman in the eye for bullying a rickshaw coolie. The fat slob very naturally lodged a complaint against me, and that same evening a sub-inspector called and asked me to accompany him to the *thana*. It was too late to arrange anything and in any case I had only been taken in for questioning, so I had to spend the night at the police post. The sub-inspector went home and left me in the charge of a constable. A wooden bench and a charpoy were the only items of furniture in my cell, if you could call it that. The charpoy was meant for the night-duty constable, but he very generously offered it to me.

'But where will you sleep?' I asked.

'Oh, I don't feel like sleeping. Usually I go to the night show at the Picture Palace, but I suppose I'll have to stay here because of you.'

He looked rather sulky. Obviously I'd ruined his plans for the night.

'You don't have to stay because of me,' I said. 'I won't tell the SHO. You go to the Picture Palace, I'll look after the *thana*.'

He brightened up considerably, but still looked a bit doubtful.

'You can trust me,' I said encouragingly. 'My grandfather was a private soldier who became a Buddhist.'

'Then I can trust you as far as your grandfather.' He was quite cheerful now, and sent for two cups of tea from the shop across the road. It came gratis, of course. A little later he left me, and I settled down on the cot and slept fitfully. The constable came back during the early hours and went to sleep on the bench. Next morning I was allowed to go home. The Muzzaffarnagar businessman had got into another fight and was lodged in the main *thana*. I did not hear about the matter again.

Ghanshyam, the constable, having struck up a friendship with me, was to visit me from time to time.

And here he is today, boots shining, teeth gleaming, cheeks almost glowing, far too charming a person to be a policeman.

'Hello, Ghanshyam bhai,' I welcome him. 'Sit down and have some tea.'

'No, I can't stop for long,' he says, but sits down beside me on the veranda steps. 'Can you do me a favour?'

'Sure. What is it?'

'I'm fed up with Barlowganj. I want to get a transfer.'

'And how can I help you? I don't know any *netas* or bigwigs.'

'No, but our SP will be here next week and he can have me transferred. Will you speak to him?'

'But why should he listen to me?'

'Well, you see, he has a weakness . . . .'

'We all have our weaknesses. Does your SP have a weakness similar to mine? Do we proceed to blackmail him?'

'Yes. You see, he writes poetry. And you are a *kavi*, a poet, aren't you?'

'At times,' I concede. 'And I have to admit it's a weakness, especially as no one cares to read my poetry.'

'No one reads the SP's poetry, either. Although we have to listen to it sometimes. When he has finished reading out one of his poems, we salute and say "*Shabash!*"'

'A captive audience. I wish I had one.'

Ignoring my sarcasm, Ghanshyam continues: 'The trouble is, he can't get anyone to publish his poems. This makes him bad-tempered and unsympathetic to applications for transfer. Can you help?'

'I am not a publisher. I can only salute like the rest of you.'

'But you know publishers, don't you? If you can get some of his poems published, he'd be very grateful. To you. To me. To both of us!'

'You really are an optimist.'

'Just one or two poems. You see, I've already told him about you. How you spent all night in the lock-up writing verses. He thinks you are a famous writer. He's depending on me now. If his poems get published he will give me a transfer. I'm sick of Barlowganj!' He gives me a hug and pinches me on the cheek.

Before he can go any further, I say: 'Well, I'll do my best' —I am thinking of a little magazine published in Bhopal where most of my rejects find a home. 'For your sake, I'll try. But first I must see the poems.'

'You shall even see the SP,' he promises. 'I'll bring him here next week. You can give him a cup of tea.'

He gets up, gives me a smart salute and goes up the path with a spring in his step. The sort of man who knows how to get his transfers and promotions in a perfectly honest manner.

March 7

It gets warmer day by day.

This morning I decided to sunbathe—quite modestly, of course. Retaining my old khaki shorts but removing all other clothing, I stretched out on a mattress in the garden. Almost immediately I was disturbed by the baker (Miss Bun's father for a change), who presented me with two loaves of bread and half a dozen chocolate pastries, ordered the previous day. Then Prem's small son, Raki, turned up, demanding a pastry, and I gave him two. He insisted on joining me on the mattress, where he proceeded to drop crumbs in my hair and on my chest. 'Good morning, Mr Bond!' came the dulcet tones of Mrs Biggs, leaning over the gate. Forgetting that she was short-sighted, I jumped to my feet, and at the same time my shorts slipped down over my knees. As I grabbed for them, Mrs Biggs's effusiveness reached greater heights. 'Why, what a lovely agapanthus you've got!' she exclaimed, referring no doubt to the solitary lily in the garden. I must confess I blushed. Then, recovering myself, I returned her greeting, remarking on the freshness of the morning.

Mrs Biggs, at eighty, was a little deaf as well, and replied, 'I'm very well, thank you, Mr Bond. Is that a child you're carrying?'

'Yes, Prem's small son.'

'Prem is your son? I didn't know you had a family.'

At this point Raki decided to pluck the spectacles off Mrs Biggs's nose, and after I had recovered them for her, she beat a hasty retreat. Later, the Rev. Mr Biggs came over to borrow a book.

'Just light reading,' he said. 'I can't concentrate for long periods.'

He has become extremely absent-minded and forgetful; one of the drawbacks of living to an advanced age. During a funeral last year at which he took the funeral service, he read out the service for Burial at Sea. It was raining heavily at the time, and no one seemed to notice.

Now he has borrowed two of my Ross Macdonalds—the same two he read last month. I refrained from pointing this out. If he has forgotten the books already, it won't matter if he reads them again.

Having spent the better part of his seventy-odd years in India, the Rev. Biggs has a lot of stories to tell, his favourite being the one about the crocodile he shot in Orissa when he was a young man. He'd pitched his tent on the banks of a river and gone to sleep on a camp-cot. During the night he felt his cot moving, and before he could gather his wits, the cot had moved swiftly through the opening of the tent and was rapidly making its way down to the river. Mr Biggs leapt for dry land while the cot, firmly wedged on the back of the crocodile, disappeared into the darkness.

Crocodiles, it seems, often bury themselves in the mud when they go to sleep, and Mr Biggs had pitched his tent and made his bed on top of a sleeping crocodile. Waking in the night, it had made for the nearest water.

Mr Biggs shot it the following morning—or so he would have us believe—the crocodile having reappeared on the river bank with the cot still attached to its back.

Now having told me this story for the umpteenth time, Biggs said he really must be going, and returning to the bookshelf, extracted Gibbons' *Decline and Fall of the Roman Empire*, having forgotten the Ross Macdonalds on a side-table.

'I must do some serious reading,' he said. 'These modern novels are so violent.'

'Lots of violence in *Decline and Fall*,' I remarked.

'Ah, but it's history, isn't it? Well, I must go now, Mr Macdonald. Mustn't waste your time.'

As he stepped outside, he collided with Miss Bun, who droped samosas all over the veranda steps.

'Oh, dear, I'm so sorry,' he apologized, and started picking up the samosas despite my attempts to prevent him from doing so. He then took the paper-bag from Miss Bun and replaced the samosas.

'And who is this little girl?' he said benignly, patting Miss Bun on the head. 'One of your nieces?'

'That's right, sir. My favourite niece.'

'Well, I must not keep you. Service as usual, on Sunday.'

'Right, Mr Biggs.'

I have never been to a local church service, but why disillusion Rev. Biggs? I shall defend everyone's right to go to a place of worship provided they allow me the freedom to stay away.

Miss Bun was staring after Rev. Biggs as he crossed the road. Her mouth was slightly agape. 'What's the matter?' I asked.

'He's taken all the samosas!'

When I kiss Miss Bun, she bites my lip and draws blood.

'What was that for?' I complain.

'Just to make you angry.'

'But I don't like getting angry.'

'That's why.'

I get angry just to please her, and we take a tumble on the carpet.

March 11

Does anyone here make money? Apart from the traders, of course, who tuck it all away . . . .

A young man turned up yesterday, selling geraniums. He had a bag full of geraniums—cuttings and whole plants.

'All colours,' he told me confidently. 'Only one rupee a cutting.'

'I can buy them much cheaper at the government nursery.'

'But you would have to walk there, sir—six miles! I have brought these to your very doorstep. I will plant them for you in your empty ghee tins at no extra cost!'

'That's all right, you can give me a few. But what makes you sell geraniums?'

'I have nothing to eat, sir. I haven't eaten for two days.'

He must have sold all his plants that day, because in the evening I saw him at the country liquor shop, tippling away— and all on an empty stomach, I presume!

March 12

Mrs Biggs tells me that someone slipped into her garden yesterday morning while she was out, and removed all her geraniums!

'The most honest of people won't hesitate to steal flowers— or books,' I remark carelessly. 'Never mind, Mrs Biggs, you can have some of my geraniums. I bought them yesterday.'

'That's extremely kind of you, Mr Bond. And you've only just put them down, I can tell,' she says, spotting the cuttings in the Dalda tins. 'No, I couldn't deprive you—'

'I'll get you some,' I offer, and generously surrender half the geraniums, vowing that if ever I come across that young man again, I'll get him to recover all the plants he sold elsewhere.

March 19

Vinod, now selling newspapers, arrives as I am pouring myself a beer under the cherry tree. It's a warm day and I can see he is thirsty.

'Can I have a drink of water?' he asks.

'Would you like some beer?'

'Yes, sir!'

As I have an extra bottle, I pour him a glass and he squats on the grass near the old wall and brings me up to date on the local gossip. There are about fifty papers in his shoulder-bag, yet to be delivered.

'You may feel drowsy after some time,' I warn. 'Don't leave your papers in the wrong houses.'

'Nothing to worry about,' he says, emptying the glass and gazing fondly at the bottle sparkling in the spring sunshine.

'Have some more,' I tell him, 'and go indoors to see what Prem is making for lunch. (Stuffed gourds, fried brinjal slices and pilaf. Prem is in a good mood, preparing my favourite dishes. When I upset him, he gives me string beans.) Returning to the garden, I find Vinod well into his second glass of beer. Half of Barlowganj and all of Jharipani (the next village) are snarling and cursing, waiting for their newspapers.

'Your customers must be getting impatient,' I remark. 'Surely they want to know the result of the cricket test.'

'Oh, they heard it on the radio. This is the morning edition. I can deliver it in the evening.'

I go indoors and have my lunch with little Raki, and ask Prem to give Vinod something to eat. When I come outside again, he is stretched out under the cherry tree, burping contentedly.

'Thank you for the lunch,' he says, and closes his eyes and goes to sleep.

He's gone by evening but his bag of papers rests against my front door.

'He's left his papers behind,' I remark to Prem.

'Oh, he'll deliver them tomorrow, along with tomorrow's paper. He'll say the mail-bus was late due to a landslide.'

In the evening I walk through the old bazaar and linger in front of a Tibetan shop, gazing at the brassware, coloured stones, amulets, masks. I am about to pass on, when I catch a glimpse of the girl who looks after the shop. Two soft brown eyes in a round jade-smooth face. A hesitant smile.

I step inside. I have never cared much for Tibetan handicrafts, but beautiful brown eyes are different.

'Can I look around? I want to buy a present for a friend.'

I look around. She helps me by displaying bangles, necklaces, rings—all on the assumption that my friend is a young lady.

I choose the more frightening of two devil masks, and promise to come again for the pair to it.

On the way home I meet Miss Bun.

'When shall I come?' she asks, pirouetting on the road.

'Next year.'

'Next year!' Her pretty mouth falls open.

'That's right,' I say. 'You've just lost the election.'

March 31

Miss Bun hasn't been for several days. This morning I find her washing clothes at the public tap. She gives me a quick smile as I pass.

'It's nice to see you hard at work,' I remark.

She looks quickly to left and right, then says, 'It's punishment, because I bought new bangles with the money you gave me.'

I hurry on down the road.

During the afternoon siesta I am roused by someone knocking on the door. A slim boy with thick hair and bushy eyebrows is standing there. I don't know him, but his eyes remind me of someone.

He tells me he is Miss Bun's older brother. At a guess, he would be only a year or two older than her.

'Come in,' I say. It's best to be friendly! What could he possibly want?

He produces a bag of samosas and puts them down on my bedside table.

'My sister cannot come this week. I will bring you samosas instead. Is that all right?'

'Oh, sure. Sit down, sit down. So you're Master Bun. It's nice to know you.'

He sits down on the edge of the bed and studies the picture on the wall—a print of Kurosawa's *Wave*.

'Shall I pay you now for the samosas?' I ask.

'No, no, whenever you like.'

'And do you go to school or college?'

'No, I help my father in the bakery. Are you ill, sir?'

'No. What makes you think so?'

'Because you were lying down.'

'Well, I like lying down. It's better than standing up. And I do get a headache if I read or write for too long.'

He offers to give me a head massage, and I submit to his ministrations for about five minutes. The headache is now much worse, but I pay for both massage and samosas and tell him he can come again—preferably next year.

My next visitor is Constable Ghanshyam Singh, who tells me that the SP has extracted confessions from a couple of thieves simply by making them stand for hours and listen to him reciting his poetry. I know our police have a reputation for torturing suspects, but I think this is carrying things a bit too far.

'And what about your transfer?' I ask.

'As soon as those poems are published in the *Weekly*.'

'I'll do my best,' I promise.

(They appeared in the Bhopal *Weekly*. And a year later, when I was editing *Imprint*, I was able to publish one of the SP's poems. He has always maintained that if I'd published more of them, the magazine would never have folded.)

A note on Miss Bun

> *Little Miss Bun is fond of bed,*
> *But she keeps a cash-box in her head.*

April 8

Rev. Biggs at the door, book in hand.

'I won't take up your time, Mr Bond. But I thought it was time I returned your butterfly book.'

'My butterfly book?'

'Yes, thank you very much. I enjoyed it a great deal.'

Mr Biggs hands me the book on butterflies, a handsomely illustrated volume. It isn't my book, but if Mr Biggs insists on giving me someone else's book, who am I to quibble? He'd never find the right owner, anyway.

'By the way, have you seen Mrs Biggs?' he asks.

'No, not this morning, sir.'

'She went off without telling me. She's always doing things like that. Very irritating.'

After he has gone, I glance at the fly-leaf of the book. It says W. Biggs. So it's one of his own . . . .

A little later Mrs Biggs comes by.

'Have you seen Will?' she asks.

'He was here about fifteen minutes ago. He was looking for you.'

'Oh, he knew I'd gone to the garden shed. How tiresome! I suppose he's wandered off somewhere.'

'Never mind, Mrs Biggs, he'll make his way home when he gets hungry. A good lunch will always bring a wanderer home. By the way, I've got his book on butterflies. Perhaps you'd return it to him for me? And he shouldn't lend it to just anyone, you know. It's a valuable book, you don't want to lose it.'

'I'm sure it was quite safe with you, Mr Bond.'

Books always are, of course. On principle, I never steal another man's books. I might take his geraniums or his old school tie, but I wouldn't deprive him of his books. Or the song or melody or dream he lives by. And here's a little lullaby for Raki:

> Little one, don't be afraid of this big river.
> Be safe in these warm arms for ever.
> Grow tall, my child, be wise and strong.
> But do not take from any man his song.
> Little one, don't be afraid of this dark night.
> Walk boldly as you see the truth and light.
> Love well, my child, laugh all day long,
> But do not take from any man his song.

April 16

Is there something about the air at this height that makes people light-headed, absent-minded? Ten years from now I will probably be as forgetful as Mr Biggs. I must climb the next mountain before I forget where it is.

Outline for a story.

Someone lives in a small hut near a spring, within sound of running water. He never leaves the place, except to walk into the town for books, post, and supplies. 'Don't you ever get bored here?' I ask. 'Do you never wish to leave?' 'No,' he replies, and tells me of his experience in the desert, when for two days and two nights (the limit of human endurance in regard to thirst), he went without water. On the second night, half dead, lying in the open beneath the stars, he dreamt of just such a spring in the mountains, and it was as though it gave him spiritual sustenance. So later, when he was fully recovered, he went in search of the spring (which he was sure existed), and found it while hiking in the Himalayas. He knew that as long as he remained by the spring he would never feel unsafe; it was where his guardian-spirit lived . . . .

And so I feel safe near my own spring, my own mountain, for this is where my guardian-spirit lives too.

April 16

Visited the Tibetan shop and bought a small brass vase encrusted with pretty stones.

I'd no intention of buying anything, but the girl smiled at me as I passed, and then I just had to go in; and once in, I couldn't just stand there, a fatuous grin on my face.

I had to buy something. And a vase is always a good thing to buy. If you don't like it, you can give it away.

If she smiles at me every time I pass, I shall probably build up a collection of vases.

She isn't a girl, really; she's probably about thirty. I suppose she has a husband who smuggles Chinese goods in from Nepal, while her children—'charity cases'—go to one of the posh public schools. But she's fresh and pretty, and then of course I don't have many young women smiling at me these days. I shall be forty-three next month.

April 17

Miss Bun still smiles at me, even though I frown at her when we pass.

This afternoon she brought me samosas and a rose.

'Where's your brother?' I asked gruffly. 'He has more to talk about.'

'He's busy in the bakery. See, I've brought you a rose.'

'How much did it cost?'

'Don't be silly. It's a present.'

'Thanks. I didn't know you grew roses.'

'I don't. It's from the school garden.'

'Well, thank you anyway. You actually stole something on my behalf!'

'Where shall I put it?'

I found my new vase, filled it with fresh water, placed the rose in it and set it down on my dressing-table.

'It leaks,' remarked Miss Bun.

'My vase?' I was incredulous.

'See, the water's spreading all over your nice table.'

She was right of course. Water from the bottom of the vase was running across the varnished wood of great-grandmother's old rosewood dressing-table. The stain, I felt sure, would be permanent.

'But it's a new vase!' I protested.

'Someone must have cheated you. Why did you buy it without looking properly?'

'Well, you see, I didn't buy it actually. Someone gave it to me as a present.'

I fumed inwardly, vowing never again to visit the brassware shop. Never trust a smiling woman! I prefer Miss Bun's scowl.

'Do you want the vase?' she asks.

'No. Take it away.'

She places the rose on my pillow, throws the water out of the window and drops the vase into her cloth shopping-bag.

'What will you do with it?' I ask.

'I'll seal the leak with flour,' she says.

April 21

A clear fresh morning after a week of intermittent rain. And what a morning for birds! Three doves courting, a cuckoo calling, a bunch of minas squabbling, and a pair of king-crows doing Swedish exercises.

I find myself doing exercises of an original nature, devised by Master Bun. These consist of various contortions of the limbs which, he says, are good for my sex drive.

'But I don't want a sex drive,' I tell him. 'I want something that will take my mind *off* sex.'

So he gives me another set of exercises which consist mostly of deep breathing.

'Try holding your breath for five minutes,' he suggests.

'I know of someone who committed suicide by doing just that.'

'Then hold it for two minutes.'

I take a deep breath and last only a minute.

'No good,' he says. 'You have to relax more.'

'Well, I am tired of trying to relax. It doesn't work this way. What I need is a good meal.'

And Prem obliges by serving up my favourite kofta curry and rice. Satiated, I have no problem in relaxing for the rest of the afternoon.

April 28

Master Bun wears a troubled expression.

'It's about my sister,' he says.

'What about her?' I ask, fearing the worst.

'She has run away.'

'That's bad. On her own?'

'No . . . . With a professor.'

'That should be all right. Professors are usually respectable people. Maths or English?'

'I don't know. He has a wife and children.'

'Then obviously he hasn't taken them along.'

'He has taken her to Roorkee. My sister is an innocent girl.'

'Well, there is a certain innocence about her,' I say, recalling Nobokov's *Lolita*. 'Maybe the professor wants to adopt her.'

'But she's a virgin.'

'Then she must be rescued! Why are you here, talking to me about it, when you should be rushing down to Roorkee?'

'That's why I've come. Can you lend me the bus fare?'

'Better still, I'll come with you. We must rescue the professor—sorry, I mean your sister!'

May 1

> —Roorkee, to Roorkee, to find a sweet girl,
> Home again, home again, oh what a whirl!

We did everything except find Miss Bun. Our first evening in Roorkee we roamed the bazaar and the canal banks; the second day we did the rounds of the University, the regimental barracks and the headquarters of the Boys' Brigade. We made enquiries from all the bakers in Roorkee (many of them known to Master Bun), but none of them had seen his sister. On the college campus we asked for the professor, but no one had heard of him either.

Finally we bought platform tickets and sat down on a bench at the end of the railway platform and watched the arrival and departure of trains, and the people who got on and off; we saw no one who looked in the least like Miss Bun. Master Bun bought an astrological guide from the station bookstall and studied his sister's horoscope to see if that might help, but it didn't. At the same bookstall, hidden under a pile of pirated Harold Robbins novels, I found a book of mine that had been published ten years earlier. No one had bought it in all that time. I replaced it at the top of the pile. Never lose hope!

On the third day we returned to Barlowganj and found Miss Bun at home.

She had gone no further than Dehra's Paltan Bazaar, it seemed, and had ditched the professor there, having first made him buy her three dress pieces, two pairs of sandals, a sandalwood hair brush, a bottle of scent, and a satchel for her school-books.

May 5

And now it's Mr Biggs's turn to disappear.

'Have you seen our Will?' asks Mrs Biggs at my gate.

'Not this morning, Mrs Biggs.'

'I can't find him anywhere. At breakfast he said he was going out for a walk, but nobody knows where he went, and he isn't in the school compound, I've just enquired. He's been gone over three hours!'

'Don't worry, Mrs Biggs. He'll turn up. Someone on the hillside must have asked him in for a cup of tea, and he's sitting there talking about the crocodile he shot in Orissa.'

But at lunchtime Mr Biggs hadn't returned; and that was alarming, because Mr Biggs had never been known to miss his favourite egg curry and pilaf.

We organized a search. Prem and I walked the length of the Barlowganj bazaar and even lodged an unofficial report with Constable Ghanshyam. No one had seen him in the bazaar. Several members of the school staff combed the hillside without picking up the scent.

Mid-afternoon, while giving my negative report to Mrs Biggs, I heard a loud thumping coming from the direction of her storeroom.

'What's all that noise downstairs?' I asked.

'Probably rats. I don't hear anything.'

I ran downstairs and opened the storeroom door, and there was Mr Biggs looking very dusty and very disgruntled. He wanted to know why the devil (the first time he'd taken the devil's name in vain) Mrs Biggs had shut him up for hours. He'd gone into the storeroom in search of an old walking-stick, and Mrs Biggs, seeing the door open, had promptly bolted it, failing to hear her husband's cries for immediate release. But for Mr Bond's presence of mind, he averred, he might have been discovered years later, a mere skeleton!

The cook was still out hunting for him, so Mr Biggs had his egg curry cold. Still in a foul mood, he sat down and wrote a letter to his sister in Tunbridge Wells, asking her to send over a hearing-aid for Mrs Biggs.

Constable Ghanshyam turned up in the evening to inform me that Mr Biggs had last been seen at Rajpur in the foothills, in the company of several gypsies!

'Never mind,' I said. 'These old men get that way. One last fling, one last romantic escapade, one last tilt at the windmill. If you have a dream, Ghanshyam, don't let them take it away from you.'

He looked puzzled, but went on to tell me that he was being transferred to Bareilly jail, where they keep those who have been found guilty but of unsound mind. It's a reward, no doubt, for his services in getting the SP's poems published.

These journal entries date back some twenty years. What happened to Miss Bun? Well, she finally opened a beauty parlour in New Delhi, but I still can't tell you where it is, or give you her name.

Two or three years later, Mrs Biggs was laid to rest near her old friends in the Mussoorie cemetery. Rev. Biggs was flown home to Tunbridge Wells and his sister gave him a solid tombstone, so that he wasn't tempted to get up and wander off somewhere, in search of crocodiles.

A lot can happen in twenty years, and unfortunately not all of it gets recorded. 'Little Raki' is today a married man!

THE DAFFODIL CASE

ॐ

IT WAS A FOGGY day in March that found me idling along Baker Street, with my hands in my raincoat pockets, a threadbare scarf wound round my neck, and two pairs of socks on my feet. The BBC had commissioned me to give a talk on village life in northern India, and, ambling along Baker Street in the fog, thinking about the talk, I realized that I didn't really know very much about village life in India or anywhere else.

True, I could recall the smell of cowdung smoke and the scent of jasmine and the flood waters lapping at the walls of mud houses, but I didn't know much about village electorates or crop rotation or sugarcane prices. I was on the point of turning back and making my way to India House to get a few facts and figures when I realized I wasn't on Baker Street any more.

Wrapped in thought, I had wandered into Regent's Park. And now I wasn't sure of the way out.

A tall gentleman wearing a long grey cloak was stooping over a flower-bed. Going up to him, I asked, 'Excuse me, sir— can you tell me how I get out of here?'

'How did you get in?' he asked in an impatient tone, and when he turned and faced me, I received quite a shock. He wore a peaked hunting-cap, and in one hand he held a large magnifying glass. A long curved pipe hung from his sensuous lips. He possessed a strong, steely jaw and his eyes had a fierce expression—they were bright with the intoxication of some drug.

'Good heavens!' I exclaimed. 'You're Sherlock Holmes!'

'And you, sir,' he replied, with a flourish of his cloak, 'are just out of India, unemployed, and due to give a lecture on the radio.'

'How did you know all that?' I stammered. 'You've never seen me before. I suppose you know my name, too?'

'Elementary, my dear Bond. The BBC notepaper in your hand, on which you have been scribbling, reveals your intentions. You are unsure of yourself, so you are not a TV personality. But you have a considered and considerate tone of voice. Definitely radio. Your name is on the envelope which you are holding upside down. It's Bond, but you're definitely not James—you're not the type! You have to be unemployed, otherwise what would you be doing in the Park when the rest of mankind is hard at work in office, field, or factory?'

'And how do you know I'm from India?' I asked, a little resentfully.

'Your accent betrays you,' said Holmes with a knowing smile.

I was about to turn away and leave him when he laid a restraining hand on my shoulder.

'Stay a moment,' he said. 'Perhaps you can be of assistance. I'm surprised at Watson. He promised to be here fifteen minutes ago but his wife must have kept him at home. Never marry, Bond. Women sap the intellect.'

'In what way can I help you?' I asked, feeling flattered now that the great man had condescended to take me into his confidence.

'Take a look at this,' said Holmes, going down on his knees near a flower-bed. 'Do you notice anything unusual?'

'Someone's been pulling out daffodils,' I said.

'Excellent, Bond! Your power of observation is as good as Watson's. Now tell me, what else do you see?'

'The ground is a little trampled, that's all.'

'By what?'

'A human foot. In high heels. And . . . a dog has been here too, it's been helping to dig up the bulbs!'

'You astonish me, Bond. You are quicker than I thought you'd be. Now shall I explain what this is all about? You see, for the past week someone has been stealing daffodils from the park, and the authorities have now asked me to deal with the matter. I think we shall catch our culprit today.'

I was rather disappointed. 'It isn't dangerous work, then?'

'Ah, my dear Bond, the days are past when Ruritanian princes lost their diamonds and Maharanis their rubies. There are no longer any Ruritanian princes and Maharanis cannot afford rubies—unless they've gone into the fast-food business. The more successful criminals now work on the stock exchange, and the East End has been cleaned up. Dr Fu Manchu has a country house in Dorset. And those cretins at Scotland Yard don't even believe in my existence!'

'I'm sorry to hear that,' I said. 'But who do you think is stealing the daffodils?'

'Obviously it's someone who owns a dog. Someone who takes a dog out regularly for a morning walk. That points to a woman. A woman in London is likely to keep a small dog— and, judging from the animal's footprints, it was a little Pekinese or a very young Pomeranian. If you observe the damp patch on that lamp-post, you will realize that it could not have been very tall. So what I propose, Bond, is that we conceal ourselves behind this herbaceous border and wait for the culprit to return to the scene of the crime. She is sure to come again this morning. She has been stealing daffodils for the past week. And stealing daffodils, like smoking opium, soon becomes a habit.'

Holmes and I concealed ourselves behind the hedge and settled down to a long wait. After half an hour, our patience was rewarded. An elderly but upright woman in a smart green hat, resembling Margaret Thatcher, came walking towards us across the grass, followed by a small white Pom on a lead. Holmes had been right! More than ever did I admire his brilliance. We waited until the woman began pulling daffodil bulbs out of the loose soil, then Holmes leapt from the bushes.

'Ah, we have you, madam!' he cried springing upon her so swiftly that she shrieked and dropped the daffodils. I bent over to gather the evidence, but my efforts were rewarded by a nip on the posterior from the outraged Pomeranian.

Holmes was restraining the woman simply by peering at her heaving bosom through his magnifying glass. I don't know what frightened her more—being caught, or being confronted by that grim-visaged countenance, with its pipe, cloak and hunting-cap.

'Now, madam,' he said firmly, 'why were you stealing Her Majesty's daffodils?'

She had begun to weep—always a woman's best defence—and I thought Holmes would soften. He always did when confronted by weeping women. And this wasn't Mrs Thatcher; she would have gone on the offensive.

'I would be obliged, Bond, if you would call the park attendant,' he said.

I hurried off to a distant greenhouse and after a brief search found a gardener. 'Stealing daffodils, is she?' he said, running up at the double, a wicked-looking rake in one hand.

But when he got to the daffodil-bed, we couldn't find the thief anywhere. Nor was Holmes to be seen. Apparently they'd gone off together, leaving me in the lurch. I was overcome by doubt and embarrassment. But then I looked at the ground and saw daffodil bulbs scattered about on the grass.

'Holmes must have taken her to the police,' I said.

'Holmes,' repeated the gardener. 'And who's Holmes?'

'Sherlock Holmes, of course. The celebrated detective. Haven't you heard of him?'

The gardener gave me a suspicious look.

'Sherlock Holmes, eh? And you'll be Dr Watson, I presume?'

'Well, no,' I said apologetically. 'The name is Bond.'

That was enough for the gardener. He'd seen madmen in the park before. He turned and disappeared in the direction of the greenhouse.

Eventually I found my way out of the park, feeling that Holmes had let me down a little. Then, just as I was crossing Baker Street, I thought I saw him on the opposite curb. He was alone, looking up at a lighted room, and his arm was raised as though he was waving to someone. I thought I heard him shout 'Watson!', but I couldn't be sure. I started to cross the road, but a big red bus came out of the fog in front of me and I had to wait for it to pass. When the road was clear, I dashed across. By that time, Mr Holmes had gone, and the rooms above were dark.

Novels and Novellas

THE ROOM ON THE ROOF

CHAPTER ONE

෮

THE LIGHT SPRING RAIN rode on the wind, into the trees, down the road; it brought an exhilarating freshness to the air, a smell of earth, a scent of flowers; it brought a smile to the eyes of the boy on the road.

The long road wound round the hills, rose and fell and twisted down to Dehra; the road came from the mountains and passed through the jungle and valley and, after passing through Dehra, ended somewhere in the bazaar. But just where it ended no one knew, for the bazaar was a baffling place, where roads were easily lost.

The boy was three miles out of Dehra. The further he could get from Dehra, the happier he was likely to be. Just now he was only three miles out of Dehra, so he was not very happy; and, what was worse, he was walking homewards.

He was a pale boy, with blue-grey eyes and fair hair; his face was rough and marked, and the lower lip hung loose and heavy. He had his hands in his pockets and his head down, which was the way he always walked, and which gave him a deceptively tired appearance. He was a lazy but not a tired person.

He liked the rain as it flecked his face, he liked the smell and the freshness; he did not look at his surroundings or notice them—his mind, as usual, was very far away—but he felt their atmosphere, and he smiled.

His mind was so very far away that it was a few minutes before he noticed the swish of bicycle wheels beside him. The cyclist did not pass the boy, but rode beside him, studying him, taking in every visible detail, the bare head, the open-necked shirt, the flannel trousers, the sandals, the thick hide belt round his waist. A European boy was no longer a common sight in Dehra, and Somi, the cyclist, was interested.

'Hallo,' said Somi, 'would you like me to ride you into town? If you are going to town?'

'No, I'm all right,' said the boy, without slackening his pace, 'I like to walk.'

'So do I, but it's raining.'

And to support Somi's argument, the rain fell harder.

'I like to walk in the rain,' said the boy. 'And I don't live in the town, I live outside it.'

Nice people didn't live *in* the town . . . .

'Well, I can pass your way,' persisted Somi, determined to help the stranger.

The boy looked again at Somi, who was dressed like him except for short pants and turban. Somi's legs were long and athletic, his colour was an unusually rich gold, his features were fine, his mouth broke easily into friendliness. It was impossible to resist the warmth of his nature.

The boy pulled himself up on the cross-bar, in front of Somi, and they moved off.

They rode slowly, gliding round the low hills, and soon the jungle on either side of the road began to give way to open fields and tea-gardens and then to orchards and one or two houses.

'Tell me when you reach your place,' said Somi. 'You stay with your parents?'

The boy considered the question too familiar for a stranger to ask, and made no reply.

'Do you like Dehra?' asked Somi.

'Not much,' said the boy with pleasure.

'Well, after England it must seem dull . . . .'

There was a pause and then the boy said, 'I haven't been to England. I was born here. I've never been anywhere else except Delhi.'

'Do you like Delhi?'

'Not much.'

They rode on in silence. The rain still fell, but the cycle moved smoothly over the wet road, making a soft, swishing sound.

Presently a man came in sight—no, it was not a man, it was a youth, but he had the appearance, the build of a man—walking towards town.

'Hey, Ranbir,' shouted Somi, as they neared the burly figure, 'want a lift?'

Ranbir ran into the road and slipped on to the carrier, behind Somi. The cycle wobbled a bit, but soon controlled itself and moved on, a little faster now.

Somi spoke into the boy's ear, 'Meet my friend Ranbir. He is the best wrestler in the bazaar.'

'Hallo, mister,' said Ranbir, before the boy could open his mouth.

'Hallo, mister,' said the boy.

Then Ranbir and Somi began a swift conversation in Punjabi, and the boy felt very lost; even, for some strange reason, jealous of the newcomer.

Now someone was standing in the middle of the road, frantically waving his arms and shouting incomprehensibly.

'It is Suri,' said Somi.

It was Suri.

Bespectacled and owlish to behold, Suri possessed an almost criminal cunning, and was both respected and despised by all who knew him. It was strange to find him out of town, for his interests were confined to people and their privacies; which privacies, when known to Suri, were soon made public.

He was a pale, bony, sickly boy, but he would probably live longer than Ranbir.

'Hey, give me a lift!' he shouted.

'Too many already,' said Somi.

'Oh, come on Somi, I'm nearly drowned.'

'It's stopped raining.'

'Oh, come on . . . .'

So Suri climbed on to the handlebar, which rather obscured Somi's view of the road and caused the cycle to wobble all over the place. Ranbir kept slipping on and off the carrier, and the boy found the cross-bar exceedingly uncomfortable. The cycle had barely been controlled when Suri started to complain.

'It hurts,' he whimpered.

'I haven't got a cushion,' said Somi.

'It is a cycle,' said Ranbir bitingly, 'not a Rolls Royce.'

Suddenly the road fell steeply, and the cycle gathered speed.

'Take it easy, now,' said Suri, 'or I'll fly off!'

'Hold tight,' warned Somi. 'It's downhill nearly all the way. We will have to go fast because the brakes aren't very good.'

'Oh, Mummy!' wailed Suri.

'Shut up!' said Ranbir.

The wind hit them with a sudden force, and their clothes blew up like balloons, almost tearing them from the machine. The boy forgot his discomfort and clung desperately to the crossbar, too nervous to say a word. Suri howled and Ranbir kept telling him to shut up, but Somi was enjoying the ride. He laughed merrily, a clear, ringing laugh, a laugh that bore no malice and no derision but only enjoyment, fun . . . .

'It's all right for you to laugh,' said Suri, 'if anything happens, *I'll* get hurt!'

'If anything happens,' said Somi, 'we *all* get hurt!'

'That's right,' shouted Ranbir from behind.

The boy closed his eyes and put his trust in God and Somi—but mainly Somi . . . .

'Oh, Mummy!' wailed Suri.

'Shut up!' said Ranbir.

The road twisted and turned as much as it could, and rose a little only to fall more steeply on the other side. But eventually it began to even out, for they were nearing the town and were almost in the residential area.

'The run is over,' said Somi, a little regretfully.

'Oh, Mummy!'

'Shut up'.

The boy said: 'I must get off now, I live very near.' Somi skidded the cycle to a standstill, and Suri shot off the handlebar into a muddy side-track. The boy slipped off, but Somi and Ranbir remained on their seats, Ranbir steadying the cycle with his feet on the ground.

'Well, thank you,' said the boy.

Somi said, 'Why don't you come and have your meal with us, there is not much further to go.'

The boy's shyness would not fall away.

'I've got to go home,' he said. 'I'm expected. Thanks very much.'

'Well, come and see us some time,' said Somi. 'If you come to the chaat shop in the bazaar, you are sure to find one of us. You know the bazaar?'

'Well, I have passed through it—in a car.'

'Oh.'

The boy began walking away, his hands once more in his pockets.

'Hey!' shouted Somi. 'You didn't tell us your name!'

The boy turned and hesitated and then said, 'Rusty . . . .'

'See you soon, Rusty,' said Somi, and the cycle pushed off.

The boy watched the cycle receding down the road, and Suri's shrill voice came to him on the wind. It had stopped raining, but the boy was unaware of this; he was almost home, and that was a miserable thought. To his surprise and disgust, he found himself wishing he had gone into Dehra with Somi.

He stood in the side-track and stared down the empty road; and, to his surprise and disgust, he felt immeasurably lonely.

CHAPTER TWO

WHEN A LARGE WHITE butterfly settled on the missionary's wife's palatial bosom, she felt flattered, and allowed it to remain there. Her garden was beginning to burst into flower, giving her great pleasure—her husband gave her none—and such fellow-feeling as to make her tread gingerly among the caterpillars.

Mr John Harrison, the boy's guardian, felt only contempt for the good lady's buoyancy of spirit, but nevertheless gave her an ingratiating smile.

'I hope you'll put the boy to work while I'm away,' he said. 'Make some use of him. He dreams too much. Most unfortunate that he's finished with school, I don't know what to do with him.'

'He doesn't know what to do with himself,' said the missionary's wife. 'But I'll keep him occupied. He can do some weeding, or read to me in the afternoon. I'll keep an eye on him.'

'Good,' said the guardian. And, having cleared his conscience, he made quick his escape.

Over lunch he told the boy: 'I'm going to Delhi tomorrow. Business.'

It was the only thing he said during the meal. When he had finished eating, he lit a cigarette and erected a curtain of smoke between himself and the boy. He was a heavy smoker, his fingers were stained a deep yellow.

'How long will you be gone, sir?' asked Rusty, trying to sound casual.

Mr Harrison did not reply. He seldom answered the boy's questions, and his own were stated, not asked; he probed and suggested, sharply, quickly, without ever encouraging loose conversation. He never talked about himself; he never argued: he would tolerate no argument.

He was a tall man, neat in appearance; and, though over forty, looked younger because he kept his hair short, shaving above the ears. He had a small ginger toothbrush moustache.

Rusty was afraid of his guardian.

Mr Harrison, who was really a cousin of the boy's father, had done a lot for Rusty, and that was why the boy was afraid of him. Since his parents had died, Rusty had been kept, fed and paid for, and sent to an expensive school in the hills that was run on 'exclusively European lines'. He had, in a way, been bought by Mr Harrison. And now he was owned by him. And he must do as his guardian wished.

Rusty was ready to do as his guardian wished: he had always obeyed him. But he was afraid of the man, afraid of his silence and of the ginger moustache and of the supple malacca cane that lay in the glass cupboard in the drawing-room.

Lunch over, the boy left his guardian giving the cook orders, and went to his room.

The window looked out on the garden path, and a sweeper boy moved up and down the path, a bucket clanging against his naked thighs. He wore only a loincloth, his body was bare and burnt a deep brown, and his head was shaved clean. He went to and from the water-tank, and every time he returned to it he bathed, so that his body continually glistened with moisture.

Apart from Rusty, the only boy in the European community of Dehra was this sweeper boy, the low-caste untouchable, the cleaner of pots. But the two seldom spoke to each other, one was a servant and the other a sahib and anyway, muttered Rusty to himself, playing with the sweeper boy would be unhygienic . . . .

The missionary's wife had said: 'Even if you were an Indian, my child, you would not be allowed to play with the sweeper boy.' So that Rusty often wondered: with whom, then, could the sweeper boy play?

The untouchable passed by the window and smiled, but Rusty looked away.

Over the tops of the cherry trees were mountains. Dehra lay in a valley in the foothills, and the small, diminishing European community had its abode on the outskirts of the town.

Mr John Harrison's house, and the other houses, were all built in an English style, with neat front gardens and nameplates on the gates. The surroundings on the whole were so English that the people often found it difficult to believe that they did live at the foot of the Himalayas, surrounded by India's thickest jungles. India started a mile away, where the bazaar began.

To Rusty, the bazaar sounded a fascinating place, and what he had seen of it from the window of his guardian's car had been enough to make his heart pound excitedly and his imagination soar; but it was a forbidden place—'full of thieves and germs,' said the missionary's wife—and the boy never entered it save in his dreams.

For Mr Harrison, the missionaries, and their neighbours, this country district of blossoming cherry trees was India. They knew there was a bazaar and a real India not far away, but they did not speak of such places, they chose not to think about them.

The community consisted mostly of elderly people, the others had left soon after independence. These few stayed because they were too old to start life again in another country, where there would be no servants and very little sunlight; and, though they complained of their lot and criticized the government, they knew their money could buy them their comforts: servants, good food, whisky, almost anything—except the dignity they cherished most . . . .

But the boy's guardian, though he enjoyed the same comforts, remained in the country for different reasons. He did not care who were the rulers so long as they didn't take away his business; he had shares in a number of small tea-estates and owned some land—forested land—where, for instance, he hunted deer and wild pig.

Rusty, being the only young person in the community, was the centre of everyone's attention, particularly the ladies'.

He was also very lonely.

Every day he walked aimlessly along the road, over the

hill-side; brooding on the future, or dreaming of sudden and perfect companionship, romance and heroics; hardly ever conscious of the present. When an opportunity for friendship did present itself, as it had the previous day, he shied away, preferring his own company.

His idle hours were crowded with memories, snatches of childhood. He could not remember what his parents were like, but in his mind there were pictures of sandy beaches covered with sea-shells of every description. They had lived on the west coast, in the Gulf of Kutch; there had been a gramophone that played records of Gracie Fields and Harry Lauder, and a captain of a cargo ship who gave the child bars of chocolate and piles of comics—*The Dandy, Beano, Tiger Tim*—and spoke of the wonderful countries he had visited. But the boy's guardian seldom spoke of Rusty's childhood, or his parents, and this secrecy lent mystery to the vague, undefined memories that hovered in the boy's mind like hesitant ghosts.

Rusty spent much of his time studying himself in the dressing-table mirror; he was able to ignore his pimples and see a grown man, worldly and attractive. Though only sixteen, he felt much older.

He was white. His guardian was pink, and the missionary's wife a bright red, but Rusty was white. With his thick lower lip and prominent cheek-bones, he looked slightly Mongolian, specially in a half-light. He often wondered why no one else in the community had the same features.

*

Mr John Harrison was going to Delhi.

Rusty intended making the most of his guardian's absence: he would squeeze all the freedom he could out of the next few days; explore, get lost, wander afar; even if it were only to find new places to dream in. So he threw himself on the bed and visualized the morrow . . . where should he go—into the hills again, into the forest? Or should he listen to the devil in his heart and go into the bazaar? Tomorrow he would know, tomorrow . . . .

Chapter Three

❧

It was a cold morning, sharp and fresh. It was quiet until the sun came shooting over the hills, lifting the mist from the valley and clearing the bloodshot from the sky. The ground was wet with dew.

On the maidan, a broad stretch of grassland, Ranbir and another youth wrestled each other, their muscles rippling, their well-oiled limbs catching the first rays of the sun as it climbed the horizon. Somi sat on his veranda steps; his long hair loose, resting on his knees, drying in the morning sun. Suri was still dead to the world, lost in his blanket; he cared not for the morning or the sun.

Rusty stood at the gate until his guardian was comfortably seated behind the wheel of the car, and did not move until it had disappeared round the bend in the road.

The missionary's wife, that large cauliflower-like lady, rose unexpectedly from behind a hedge and called: 'Good morning dear! If you aren't very busy this morning, would you like to give me a hand pruning this hedge?' The missionary's wife was fond of putting Rusty to work in her garden: if it wasn't cutting the hedge, it was weeding the flower-beds and watering the plants, or clearing the garden path of stones, or hunting beetles and ladybirds and dropping them over the wall.

'Oh, good morning,' stammered Rusty. 'Actually, I was going for a walk. Can I help you when I come back, I won't be long . . . .'

The missionary's wife was rather taken aback, for Rusty seldom said no; and before she could make another sally the boy was on his way. He had a dreadful feeling she would call him back; she was a kind woman, but talkative and boring, and Rusty knew what would follow the garden work: weak tea or lemonade, and then a game of cards, probably beggar-my-neighbour.

But to his relief she called after him: 'All right, dear, come back soon. And be good!'

He waved to her and walked rapidly down the road. And the direction he took was different from the one in which he usually wandered.

Far down this road was the bazaar. First Rusty must pass the rows of neat cottages, arriving at a commercial area— Dehra's Westernized shopping centre—where Europeans, rich Indians, and American tourists *en route* for Mussoorie, could eat at smart restaurants and drink prohibited alcohol. But the boy was afraid and distrustful of anything smart and sophisticated, and he hurried past the shopping centre.

He came to the Clock Tower, which was a tower without a clock. It had been built from public subscriptions but not enough money had been gathered for the addition of a clock. It had been lifeless five years but served as a good landmark. On the other side of the Clock Tower lay the bazaar, and in the bazaar lay India. On the other side of the Clock Tower began life itself. And all three—the bazaar and India and life itself—were forbidden.

Rusty's heart was beating fast as he reached the Clock Tower. He was about to defy the law of his guardian and of his community. He stood at the Clock Tower, nervous, hesitant, biting his nails. He was afraid of discovery and punishment, but hungering curiosity impelled him forward.

The bazaar and India and life itself all began with a rush of noise and confusion.

The boy plunged into the throng of bustling people; the road was hot and close, alive with cries of vendors and the smell of cattle and ripening dung. Children played hopscotch in alleyways or gambled with coins, scuffling in the gutter for a lost anna. And the cows moved leisurely through the crowd, nosing around for paper and stale, discarded vegetables; the more daring cows helping themselves at open stalls. And above the uneven tempo of the noise came the blare of a loudspeaker playing a popular piece of music.

Rusty moved along with the crowd, fascinated by the sight of beggars lying on the roadside: naked and emaciated half-humans, some skeletons, some covered with sores; old men dying, children dying, mothers with suckling babies, living and dying. But, strangely enough, the boy could feel nothing for these people; perhaps it was because they were no longer recognizable as humans or because he could not see himself in the same circumstances. And no one else in the bazaar seemed to feel for them. Like the cows and the loudspeaker, the beggars were a natural growth in the bazaar, and only the well-to-do—sacrificing a few annas to placate their consciences—were aware of the beggars' presence.

Every little shop was different from the one next to it. After the vegetable stand, green and wet, came the fruit stall; and, after the fruit stall, the tea and betel-leaf shop, selling trinkets of gay colours. And then, after the toy shop, another from whose doors poured clouds of smoke.

Out of curiosity Rusty turned to the shop from which the smoke was coming. But he was not the only person making for it Approaching from the opposite direction was Somi on his bicycle.

Somi, who had not seen Rusty, seemed determined to ride right into the smoky shop on his bicycle, but his way was blocked by Maharani, the queen of the bazaar cows, who moved aside for no one. But the cycle did not lose speed.

Rusty, seeing the cycle but not recognizing the rider, felt sorry for the cow, it was sure to be hurt. But, with the devil in his heart or in the wheels of his machine, Somi swung clear of Maharani and collided with Rusty and knocked him into the gutter.

Accustomed as Rusty was to the delicate scents of the missionary's wife's sweet-peas and the occasional smell of bathroom disinfectant, he was nevertheless overpowered by the odour of bad vegetables and kitchen water that rose from the gutter.

'What the hell do you think you're doing?' he cried, choking and spluttering.

'Hallo,' said Somi, gripping Rusty by the arm and helping him up, 'so sorry, not my fault. Anyway, we meet again!'

Rusty felt for injuries and, finding none, exclaimed: 'Look at the filthy mess I'm in!'

Somi could not help laughing at the other's unhappy condition. 'Oh, that is not filth, it is only cabbage water! Do not worry, the clothes will dry . . . .'

His laugh rang out merrily, and there was something about the laugh, some music in it perhaps, that touched a chord of gaiety in Rusty's own heart. Somi was smiling, and on his mouth the smile was friendly and in his soft brown eyes it was mocking.

'Well, I am sorry,' said Somi, extending his hand.

Rusty did not take the hand but, looking the other up and down, from turban to slippers, forced himself to say: 'Get out of my way, please.'

'You are a snob,' said Somi without moving. 'You are a very funny one too.'

'I am not a snob,' said Rusty involuntarily.

'Then why not forget an accident?'

'You could have missed me, but you didn't try.'

'But if I had missed you, I would have hit the cow! You don't know Maharani, if you hurt her she goes mad and smashes half the bazaar! Also, the bicycle might have been spoilt . . . . Now please come and have chaat with me.'

Rusty had no idea what was meant by the word chaat, but before he could refuse the invitation Somi had bundled him into the shop from which the smoke still poured.

At first nothing could be made out; then gradually the smoke seemed to clear and there in front of the boys, like some shining god, sat a man enveloped in rolls of glistening, oily flesh. In front of him, on a coal fire, was a massive pan in which sizzled a sea of fat; and with deft, practised fingers, he moulded and flipped potato cakes in and out of the pan.

The shop was crowded; but so thick was the screen of smoke and steam, that it was only the murmur of conversation which made known the presence of many people. A plate made of banana leaves was thrust into Rusty's hands, and two fried cakes suddenly appeared in it.

'Eat!' said Somi, pressing the novice down until they were both seated on the floor, their backs to the wall.

'They are tikkees,' explained Somi, 'tell me if you like them.'

Rusty tasted a bit. It was hot. He waited a minute, then

tasted another bit. It was still hot but in a different way; now it was lively, interesting; it had a different taste from anything he had eaten before. Suspicious but inquisitive, he finished the tikkee and waited to see if anything would happen.

'Have you had it before?' asked Somi.

'No,' said Rusty anxiously, 'what will it do?'

'It might worry your stomach a little at first, but you will get used to it the more often you eat. So finish the other one too.'

Rusty had not realized the extent of his submission to the other's wishes. At one moment he had been angry, ill-mannered; but, since the laugh, he had obeyed Somi without demur.

Somi wore a cotton tunic and shorts, and sat cross-legged, his feet pressed against his thighs. His skin was a golden brown, dark on his legs and arms but fair, very fair, where his shirt lay open. His hands were dirty; but eloquent. His eyes, deep brown and dreamy, had depth and roundness.

He said: 'My name is Somi, please tell me what is yours, I have forgotten.'

'Rusty . . . .'

'How do you do,' said Somi, 'I am very pleased to meet you, haven't we met before?'

Rusty mumbled to himself in an effort to sulk.

'That was a long time ago,' said Somi, 'now we are friends yes, best favourite friends!'

Rusty continued to mumble under his breath, but he took the warm muddy hand that Somi gave him, and shook it. He finished the tikkee on his leaf, and accepted another. Then he said: 'How do you do, Somi, I am very pleased to meet you.'

CHAPTER FOUR

𝓮❧

THE MISSIONARY'S WIFE'S HEAD projected itself over the garden
wall and broke into a beam of welcome. Rusty hurriedly
returned the smile.

'Where have you been, dear?' asked his garrulous neighbour.
'I was expecting you for lunch. You've never been away so
long, I've finished all my work now, you know . . . . Was it a
nice walk? I know you're thirsty, come in and have a nice cool
lemonade, there's nothing like iced lemonade to refresh one
after a long walk. I remember when I was a girl, having to
walk down to Dehra from Mussoorie, I filled my thermos with
lemonade . . . .'

But Rusty had gone. He did not wish to hurt the
missionary's wife's feelings by refusing the lemonade but, after
experiencing the chaat shop, the very idea of a lemonade
offended him. But he decided that this Sunday he would
contribute an extra four annas to the missionary's fund for
upkeep of church, wife and garden; and, with this good thought
in mind, went to his room.

The sweeper boy passed by the window, his buckets
clanging, his feet going slip-slop on the watery path.

Rusty threw himself on his bed. And now his imagination
began building dreams on a new-found reality, for he had
agreed to meet Somi again.

And so, the next day, his steps took him to the chaat shop
in the bazaar; past the Clock Tower, past the smart shops,
down the road, far from the guardian's house.

The fleshy god of the tikkees smiled at Rusty in a manner

that seemed to signify that the boy was now likely to become a Regular Customer. The banana plate was ready, the tikkees in it flavoured with spiced sauces.

'Hallo, best favourite friend,' said Somi, appearing out of the surrounding vapour, his slippers loose, chup-chup-chup; loose, open slippers that hung on to the toes by a strap and slapped against the heels as he walked. 'I am glad you come again. After tikkees you must have something else, chaat or gol-guppas, all right?'

Somi removed his slippers and joined Rusty, who had somehow managed to sit cross-legged on the ground in the proper fashion.

Somi said, 'Tell me something about yourself. By what misfortune are you an Englishman? How is it that you have been here all your life and never been to a chaat shop before?'

'Well, my guardian is very strict,' said Rusty. 'He wanted to bring me up in English ways, and he has succeeded . . . .'

'Till now,' said Somi, and laughed, the laugh rippling up in his throat, breaking out and forcing its way through the smoke.

Then a large figure loomed in front of the boys, and Rusty recognized him as Ranbir, the youth he had met on the bicycle.

'Another best favourite friend,' said Somi.

Ranbir did not smile, but opened his mouth a little, gaped at Rusty, and nodded his head. When he nodded, hair fell untidily across his forehead; thick black bushy hair, wild and uncontrollable. He wore a long white cotton tunic hanging out over his baggy pyjamas; his feet were bare and dirty; big feet, strong.

'Hallo, mister,' said Ranbir, in a gruff voice that disguised his shyness. He said no more for a while, but joined them in their meal.

They ate chaat, a spicy salad of potato, guava and orange; and then gol-guppas, baked flour cups filled with burning syrups. Rusty felt at ease and began to talk, telling his companions about his school in the hills, the house of his guardian, Mr Harrison himself, and the supple malacca cane. The story was listened to with some amusement: apparently Rusty's life had been very dull to date, and Somi and Ranbir pitied him for it.

'Tomorrow is Holi,' said Ranbir, 'you must play with me, them you will be my friend.'

'What is Holi?' asked Rusty.

Ranbir looked at him in amazement. 'You do not know about Holi! It is the Hindu Festival of Colour! It is the day on which we celebrate the coming of spring, when we throw colour on each other and shout and sing and forget our misery, for the colours mean the rebirth of spring and a new life in our hearts . . . . You do not know of it!'

Rusty was somewhat bewildered by Ranbir's sudden eloquence, and began to have doubts about this game; it seemed to him a primitive sort of pastime, this throwing of paint about the place.

'I might get into trouble,' he said. 'I'm not supposed to come here, anyway, and my guardian might return any day . . . .'

'Don't tell him about it,' said Ranbir.

'Oh, he has ways of finding out. I'll get a thrashing.'

'Huh!' said Ranbir, a disappointed and somewhat disgusted expression on his mobile face. 'You are afraid to spoil your clothes, mister, that is it. You are just a snob.'

Somi laughed. 'That's what I told him yesterday, and only then did he join me in the chaat shop. I think we should call him a snob whenever he makes excuses.'

Rusty was enjoying the chaat. He ate gol-guppa after gol-guppa, until his throat was almost aflame and his stomach burning itself out. He was not very concerned about Holi. He was content with the present, content to enjoy the new-found pleasures of the chaat shop, and said: 'Well, I'll see . . . if my guardian doesn't come back tomorrow, I'll play Holi with you, all right?'

Ranbir was pleased. He said, 'I will be waiting in the jungle behind your house. When you hear the drum-beat in the jungle, then it is me. Then come.'

'Will you be there too, Somi?' asked Rusty. Somehow, he felt safe in Somi's presence.

'I do not play Holi,' said Somi. 'You see, I am different from Ranbir. I wear a turban and he does not, also there is a bangle on my wrist, which means that I am a Sikh. We don't play it. But I will see you the day after, here in the chaat shop.'

Somi left the shop, and was swallowed up by smoke and steam, but the chup-chup of his loose slippers could be heard for some time, until their sound was lost in the greater sound of the bazaar outside.

In the bazaar, people haggled over counters, children played in the spring sunshine, dogs courted one another, and Ranbir and Rusty continued eating gol-guppas.

The afternoon was warm and lazy, unusually so for spring; very quiet, as though resting in the interval between the spring and the coming winter. There was no sign of the missionary's wife or the sweeper boy when Rusty returned, but Mr Harrison's car stood in the driveway of the house.

At the sight of the car, Rusty felt a little weak and frightened; he had not expected his guardian to return so soon and had, in fact, almost forgotten his existence. But now he forgot all about the chaat shop and Somi and Ranbir, and ran up the veranda steps in a panic.

Mr Harrison was at the top of the veranda steps, standing behind the potted palms.

The boy said, 'Oh, hallo, sir, you're back!' He knew of nothing else to say, but tried to make his little piece sound enthusiastic.

'Where have you been all day?' asked Harrison, without looking once at the startled boy. 'Our neighbours haven't seen much of you lately.'

'I've been for a walk, sir.'

'You have been to the bazaar.'

The boy hesitated before making a denial; the man's eyes were on him now, and to lie Rusty would have had to lower his eyes—and this he could not do . . . .

'Yes, sir, I went to the bazaar.'

'May I ask why?'

'Because I had nothing to do.'

'If you had nothing to do, you could have visited our neighbours. The bazaar is not the place for you. You know that.'

'But nothing happened to me . . . .'

'That is not the point,' said Mr Harrison, and now his normally dry voice took on a faint shrill note of excitement, and he spoke rapidly. 'The point is, I have told you never to visit the bazaar. You belong here, to this house, this road, these people. Don't go where you don't belong.'

Rusty wanted to argue, longed to rebel, but fear of Mr Harrison held him back. He wanted to resist the man's authority, but he was conscious of the supple malacca cane in the glass cupboard.

'I'm sorry, sir . . . .'

But his cowardice did him no good. The guardian went over to the glass cupboard, brought out the cane, flexed it in his hands. He said : 'It is not enough to say you are sorry, you must be made to feel sorry. Bend over the sofa.'

The boy bent over the sofa, clenched his teeth and dug his fingers into the cushions. The cane swished through the air, landing on his bottom with a slap, knocking the dust from his pants. Rusty felt no pain. But his guardian waited, allowing the cut to sink in, then he administered the second stroke, and this time it hurt, it stung into the boy's buttocks, burning up the flesh, conditioning it for the remaining cuts.

At the sixth stroke of the supple malacca cane, which was usually the last, Rusty let out a wild whoop, leapt over the sofa and charged from the room.

He lay groaning on his bed until the pain had eased.

But the flesh was so sore that he could not touch the place where the cane had fallen. Wriggling out of his pants, he examined his backside in the mirror. Mr Harrison had been most accurate : a thick purple welt stretched across both cheeks, and a little blood trickled down the boy's thigh. The blood had a cool, almost soothing effect, but the sight of it made Rusty feel faint.

He lay down and moaned for pleasure. He pitied himself enough to want to cry, but he knew the futility of tears. But the pain and the sense of injustice he felt were both real.

A shadow fell across the bed. Someone was at the window, and Rusty looked up.

The sweeper boy showed his teeth.

'What do you want?' asked Rusty gruffly.

'You hurt, Chotta Sahib?'

The sweeper boy's sympathies provoked only suspicion in Rusty.

'You told Mr Harrison where I went!' said Rusty.

But the sweeper boy cocked his head to one side, and asked innocently, 'Where you went, Chotta Sahib?'

'Oh, never mind. Go away.'

'But you hurt?'

'Get out!' shouted Rusty.

The smile vanished, leaving only a sad, frightened look in the sweeper boy's eyes.

Rusty hated hurting people's feelings, but he was not accustomed to familiarity with servants ; and yet, only a few minutes ago, he had been beaten for visiting the bazaar where there were so many like the sweeper boy.

The sweeper boy turned from the window, leaving wet finger-marks on the sill; then lifted his buckets from the ground and, with his knees bent to take the weight, walked away. His feet splashed a little in the water he had spilt, and the soft red mud flew up and flecked his legs.

Angry with his guardian and with the servant and most of all with himself, Rusty buried his head in the pillow and tried to shut out reality; he forced a dream in which he was thrashing Mr Harrison until the guardian begged for mercy.

CHAPTER FIVE

&

IN THE EARLY MORNING, when it was still dark, Ranbir stopped in the jungle behind Mr Harrison's house, and slapped his drum. His thick mass of hair was covered with red dust and his body, naked but for a cloth round his waist, was smeared green; he looked like a painted god, a green god. After a minute he slapped the drum again, then sat down on his heels and waited.

Rusty woke to the sound of the second drum-beat, and lay in bed and listened; it was repeated, travelling over the still air and in through the bedroom window. Dhum! . . . a double-beat now, one deep, one high, insistent, questioning . . . . Rusty remembered his promise, that he would play Holi with Ranbir, meet him in the jungle when he beat the drum. But he had made the promise on the condition that his guardian did not return; he could not possibly keep it now, after the thrashing he had received.

Dhum-dhum, spoke the drum in the forest; dhum-dhum, impatient and getting annoyed . . . .

'Why can't he shut up,' muttered Rusty, 'does he want to wake Mr Harrison . . . . '

Holi, the Festival of Colour, the arrival of spring, the rebirth of the new year, the awakening of love, what were these things to him, they did not concern his life, he could not start a new life, not for one day . . . and besides, it all sounded very primitive, this throwing of colour and beating of drums . . . .

Dhum-dhum!

The boy sat up in bed.

The sky had grown lighter.

From the distant bazaar came a new music, many drums and voices, faint but steady, growing in rhythm and excitement. The sound conveyed something to Rusty, something wild and emotional, something that belonged to his dream world, and on a sudden impulse he sprang out of bed.

He went to the door and listened; the house was quiet, he bolted the door. The colours of Holi, he knew, would stain his clothes, so he did not remove his pyjamas. In an old pair of flattened rubber-soled tennis shoes, he climbed out of the window and ran over the dew-wet grass, down the path behind the house, over the hill and into the jungle.

When Ranbir saw the boy approach, he rose from the ground. The long hand-drum, the dholak, hung at his waist. As he rose, the sun rose. But the sun did not look as fiery as Ranbir who, in Rusty's eyes, appeared as a painted demon, rather than as a god.

'You are late, mister,' said Ranbir, 'I thought you were not coming.'

He had both his fists closed, but when he walked towards Rusty he opened them, smiling widely, a white smile in a green face. In his right hand was the red dust and in his left the green dust. And with his right hand he rubbed the red dust on Rusty's left cheek, and then with the other hand he put the green dust on the boy's right cheek; then he stood back and looked at Rusty and laughed. Then, according to the custom, he embraced the bewildered boy. It was a wrestler's hug, and Rusty winced breathlessly.

'Come,' said Ranbir, 'let us go and make the town a rainbow.'

And truly, that day there was an outbreak of spring.

The sun came up, and the bazaar woke up. The walls of the houses were suddenly patched with splashes of colour, and just as suddenly the trees seemed to have burst into flower; for in the forest there were armies of rhododendrons, and by the river the poinsettias danced; the cherry and the plum were in blossom; the snow in the mountains had melted, and the streams were rushing torrents; the new leaves on the trees were full of sweetness, and the young grass held both dew and sun, and made an emerald of every dew-drop.

The infection of spring spread simultaneously through the world of man and the world of nature, and made them one.

Ranbir and Rusty moved round the hill, keeping at the fringe of the jungle until they had skirted not only the European community but also the smart shopping centre. They came down dirty little side-streets where the walls of houses, stained with the wear and tear of many years of meagre habitation, were now stained again with the vivid colours of Holi. They came to the Clock Tower.

At the Clock Tower, spring had really been declared open. Clouds of coloured dust rose in the air and spread, and jets of water—green and orange and purple, all rich emotional colours—burst out everywhere.

Children formed groups. They were armed mainly with bicycle pumps, or pumps fashioned from bamboo stems, from which was squirted liquid colour. And the children paraded the main road, chanting shrilly and clapping their hands. The men and women preferred the dust to the water. They too sang, but their chanting held a significance, their hands and fingers drummed the rhythms of spring, the same rhythms, the same songs that belonged to this day every year of their lives.

Ranbir was met by some friends and greeted with great hilarity. A bicycle pump was directed at Rusty and a jet of sooty black water squirted into his face.

Blinded for a moment, Rusty blundered about in great confusion. A horde of children bore down on him, and he was subjected to a pumping from all sides. His shirt and pyjamas, drenched through, stuck to his skin; then someone gripped the end of his shirt and tugged at it until it tore and came away. Dust was thrown on the boy, on his face and body, roughly and with full force, and his tender, under-exposed skin smarted beneath the onslaught.

Then his eyes cleared. He blinked and looked wildly round at the group of boys and girls who cheered and danced in front of him. His body was running mostly with sooty black, streaked with red, and his mouth seemed full of it too, and he began to spit.

Then, one by one, Ranbir's friends approached Rusty.

Gently, they rubbed dust on the boy's cheeks, and embraced him; they were so like many flaming demons that Rusty could not distinguish one from the other. But this gentle greeting, coming so soon after the stormy bicycle pump attack, bewildered Rusty even more.

Ranbir said: 'Now you are one of us, come,' and Rusty went with him and the others.

'Suri is hiding,' cried someone. 'He has locked himself in his house and won't play Holi!'

'Well, he will have to play,' said Ranbir, 'even if we break the house down.'

Suri, who dreaded Holi, had decided to spend the day in a state of siege; and had set up camp in his mother's kitchen, where there were provisions enough for the whole day. He listened to his playmates calling to him from the courtyard, and ignored their invitations, jeers, and threats; the door was strong and well-barricaded. He settled himself beneath a table, and turned the pages of the English nudists' journal, which he bought every month chiefly for its photographic value.

But the youths outside, intoxicated by the drumming and shouting and high spirits, were not going to be done out of the pleasure of discomfiting Suri. So they acquired a ladder and made their entry into the kitchen by the skylight.

Suri squealed with fright. The door was opened and he was bundled out, and his spectacles were trampled.

'My glasses!' he screamed. 'You've broken them!'

'You can afford a dozen pairs!' jeered one of his antagonists.

'But I can't see, you fools, I can't see!'

'He can't see!' cried someone in scorn. 'For once in his life Suri can't see what's going on! Now, whenever he spies, we'll smash his glasses!'

Not knowing Suri very well, Rusty could not help pitying the frantic boy.

'Why don't you let him go?' he asked Ranbir. 'Don't force him if he doesn't want to play.'

'But this is the only chance we have of repaying him for all his dirty tricks. It is the only day on which no one is afraid of him!'

Rusty could not imagine how anyone could possibly be afraid of the pale, struggling, spindly-legged boy who was almost being torn apart, and was glad when the others had finished their sport with him.

All day Rusty roamed the town and countryside with Ranbir and his friends, and Suri was soon forgotten. For one day, Ranbir and his friends forgot their homes and work and the problem of the next meal, and danced down the roads, out of the town and into the forest. And, for one day, Rusty forgot his guardian and the missionary's wife and the supple malacca cane, and ran with the others through the town and into the forest.

The crisp, sunny morning ripened into afternoon.

In the forest, in the cool dark silence of the jungle, they stopped singing and shouting, suddenly exhausted. They lay down in the shade of many trees, and the grass was soft and comfortable, and very soon everyone except Rusty was fast asleep.

Rusty was tired. He was hungry. He had lost his shirt and shoes, his feet were bruised, his body sore. It was only now, resting, that he noticed these things, for he had been caught up in the excitement of the colour game, overcome by an exhilaration he had never known. His fair hair was tousled and streaked with colour, and his eyes were wide with wonder.

He was exhausted now, but he was happy.

He wanted this to go on for ever, this day of feverish emotion, this life in another world. He did not want to leave the forest; it was safe, its earth soothed him, gathered him in, so that the pain of his body became a pleasure   .

He did not want to go home.   .

CHAPTER SIX

❧

MR HARRISON STOOD AT the top of the veranda steps. The house was in darkness, but his cigarette glowed more brightly for it. A road lamp trapped the returning boy as he opened the gate, and Rusty knew he had been seen, but he didn't care much; if he had known that Mr Harrison had not recognized him, he would have turned back instead of walking resignedly up the garden path.

Mr Harrison did not move, nor did he appear to notice the boy's approach. It was only when Rusty climbed the veranda steps that his guardian moved and said: 'Who's that?'

Still he had not recognized the boy; and in that instant Rusty become aware of his own condition, for his body was a patchwork of paint. Wearing only torn pyjamas he could, in the half-light, have easily been mistaken for the sweeper boy or someone else's servant. It must have been a newly acquired bazaar instinct that made the boy think of escape. He turned about.

But Mr Harrison shouted, 'Come here, you!' and the tone of his voice—the tone reserved for the sweeper boy—made Rusty stop.

'Come up here!' repeated Mr Harrison.

Rusty returned to the veranda, and his guardian switched on a light; but even now there was no recognition.

'Good evening, sir,' said Rusty.

Mr Harrison received a shock. He felt a wave of anger, and then a wave of pain: was this the boy he had trained and educated—this wild, ragged, ungrateful wretch, who did not know the difference between what was proper and what was improper, what was civilized and what was barbaric, what was decent and what was shameful—and had the years of training come to nothing? Mr Harrison came out of the shadows and cursed. He brought his hand down on the back of Rusty's neck, propelled him into the drawing-room, and pushed him across the room so violently that the boy lost his balance, collided with a table and rolled over on to the ground.

Rusty looked up from the floor to find his guardian standing over him, and in the man's right hand was the supple malacca cane, and the cane was twitching.

Mr Harrison's face was twitching too, it was full of fire. His lips were stitched together, sealed up with the ginger moustache, and he looked at the boy with narrowed, unblinking eyes.

'Filth!' he said, almost spitting the words in the boy's face. 'My God, what filth!'

Rusty stared fascinated at the deep yellow nicotine stains on the fingers of his guardian's raised hand. Then the wrist moved suddenly and the cane cut across the boy's face like a knife, stabbing and burning into his cheek.

Rusty cried out and cowered back against the wall; he could feel the blood trickling across his mouth. He looked around desperately for a means of escape, but the man was in front of him, over him, and the wall was behind.

Mr Harrison broke into a torrent of words. 'How can you call yourself an Englishman, how can you come back to this house in such a condition? In what gutter, in what brothel have you been! Have you seen yourself? Do you know what you look like?'

'You don't . . . well, I'll tell you what you look like! You look like the mongrel that you are!'

'That's a lie!' exclaimed Rusty.

'It's the truth. I've tried to bring you up as an Englishman, as your father would have wished. But, as you won't have it our way, I'm telling you that he was about the only thing English about you. You're no better than the sweeper boy!'

Rusty flared into a temper, showing some spirit for the first time in his life. 'I'm no better than the sweeper boy, but I'm as good as him! I'm as good as you! I'm as good as anyone!' And, instead of cringing to take the cut from the cane, he flung himself at his guardian's legs. The cane swished through the air, grazing the boy's back. Rusty wrapped his arms round his guardian's legs and pulled on them with all his strength.

Mr Harrison went over, falling flat on his back.

The suddenness of the fall must have knocked the breath from his body, because for a moment he did not move.

Rusty sprang to his feet. The cut across his face had stung him to madness, to an unreasoning hate, and he did what previously he would only have dreamt of doing. Lifting a vase of the missionary's wife's best sweet-peas off the glass cupboard, he flung it at his guardian's face. It hit him on the chest, but the water and flowers flopped out over his face. He tried to get up; but he was speechless.

The look of alarm on Mr Harrison's face gave Rusty greater courage. Before the man could recover his feet and his balance, Rusty gripped him by the collar and pushed him backwards, until they both fell over on to the floor. With one hand still twisting the collar, the boy slapped his guardian's face. Mad with the pain in his own face, Rusty hit the man again and again, wildly and awkwardly, but with the giddy thrill of knowing he could do it: he was a child no longer, he was nearly seventeen, he was a man. He could inflict pain, that was a wonderful discovery; there was a power in his body—a devil or a god—and he gained confidence in his power; and he was a man!

'Stop that, stop it!'

The shout of a hysterical woman brought Rusty to his senses. He still held his guardian by the throat, but he stopped hitting him. Mr Harrison's face was very red.

The missionary's wife stood in the doorway, her face white with fear. She was under the impression that Mr Harrison was being attacked by a servant or some bazaar hooligan. Rusty did not wait until she found her tongue but, with a new-found speed and agility, darted out of the drawing-room.

He made his escape from the bedroom window. From the gate he could see the missionary's wife silhouetted against the drawing-room light. He laughed out loud. The woman swivelled round and came forward a few steps. And Rusty laughed again and began running down the road to the bazaar.

It was late. The smart shops and restaurants were closed. In the bazaar, oil lamps hung outside each doorway; people were asleep on the steps and platforms of shopfronts, some huddled in blankets, others rolled tight into themselves. The road, which during the day was a busy, noisy crush of people and animals, was quiet and deserted. Only a lean dog still sniffed in the gutter. A woman sang in a room high above the street—a plaintive, tremulous song—and in the far distance a jackal cried to the moon. But the empty, lifeless street was very deceptive; if the roofs could have been removed from just a handful of buildings, it would be seen that life had not really stopped but, beautiful and ugly, persisted through the night.

It was past midnight, though the Clock Tower had no way of saying it. Rusty was in the empty street, and the chaat shop was closed, a sheet of tarpaulin draped across the front. He looked up and down the road, hoping to meet someone he knew; the chaat-wallah, he felt sure, would give him a blanket for the night and a place to sleep; and the next day when Somi came to meet him, he would tell his friend of his predicament, that he had run away from his guardian's house and did not intend returning. But he would have to wait till morning: the chaat shop was shuttered, barred and bolted.

He sat down on the steps; but the stone was cold and his thin cotton pyjamas offered no protection. He folded his arms and huddled up in a corner, but still he shivered. His feet were becoming numb, lifeless.

Rusty had not fully realized the hazards of the situation. He was still mad with anger and rebellion and, though the blood on his cheek had dried, his face was still smarting. He could not think clearly: the present was confusing and unreal and he could not see beyond it; what worried him was the cold and the discomfort and the pain.

The singing stopped in the high window. Rusty looked up and saw a beckoning hand. As no one else in the street showed any signs of life, Rusty got up and walked across the road until he was under the window. The woman pointed to a stairway, and he mounted it, glad of the hospitality he was being offered.

The stairway seemed to go to the stars, but it turned suddenly to lead into the woman's room. The door was slightly ajar, and he knocked and a voice said, 'Come . . . .'

The room was filled with perfume and burning incense. A musical instrument lay in one corner. The woman reclined on a bed, her hair scattered about the pillow; she had a round, pretty face, but she was losing her youth, and the fat showed in rolls at her exposed waist. She smiled at the boy, and beckoned again.

'Thank you,' said Rusty, closing the door. 'Can I sleep here?'

'Where else?' said the woman.

'Just for tonight.'

She smiled, and waited. Rusty stood in front of her, his hands behind his back.

'Sit down,' she said, and patted the bedclothes beside her.

Reverently, and as respectfully as he could, Rusty sat down. The woman ran little fair fingers over his body, and drew his head to hers; their lips were very close, almost touching, and their breathing sounded terribly loud to Rusty, but he only said: 'I'm hungry.'

A poet, thought the woman, and kissed him full on the lips; but the boy drew away in embarrassment, unsure of himself, liking the woman on the bed and yet afraid of her . . . .

'What is wrong?' she asked.

'I'm tired,' he said.

The woman's friendly smile turned to a look of scorn; but she saw that he was only a boy whose eyes were full of unhappiness, and she could not help pitying him.

'You can sleep here,' she said, 'until you have lost your tiredness.'

But he shook his head. 'I will come some other time,' he said, not wishing to hurt the woman's feelings. They were both pitying each other, liking each other, but not enough to make them understand each other.

Rusty left the room. Mechanically, he descended the staircase, and walked up the bazaar road, past the silent sleeping forms, until he reached the Clock Tower. To the right of the Clock Tower was a broad stretch of grassland where, during the day, cattle grazed and children played and young men like Ranbir wrestled and kicked footballs. But now, at night, it was a vast empty space.

But the grass was soft, like the grass in the forest, and

Rusty walked the length of the maidan. He found a bench and sat down, warmer for the walk. A light breeze was blowing across the maidan, pleasant and refreshing, playing with his hair. Around him everything was dark and silent and lonely. He had got away from the bazaar, which held the misery of beggars and homeless children and starving dogs, and could now concentrate on his own misery; for there was nothing like loneliness for making Rusty conscious of his unhappy state. Madness and freedom and violence were new to him: loneliness was familiar, something he understood.

Rusty was alone. Until tomorrow, he was alone for the rest of his life.

If tomorrow there was no Somi at the chaat shop, no Ranbir, then what would he do? This question badgered him persistently, making him an unwilling slave to reality. He did not know where his friends lived, he had no money, he could not ask the chaat-wallah for credit on the strength of two visits. Perhaps he should return to the amorous lady in the bazaar; perhaps . . . but no, one thing was certain, he would never return to his guardian . . . .

The moon had been hidden by clouds, and presently there was a drizzle. Rusty didn't mind the rain, it refreshed him and made the colour run from his body; but, when it began to fall harder, he started shivering again. He felt sick. He got up, rolled his ragged pyjamas up to the thighs and crawled under the bench.

There was a hollow under the bench, and at first Rusty found it quite comfortable. But there was no grass and gradually the earth began to soften: soon he was on his hands and knees in a pool of muddy water, with the slush oozing up through his fingers and toes. Crouching there, wet and cold and muddy, he was overcome by a feeling of helplessness and self-pity. Everyone and everything seemed to have turned against him; not only his people but also the bazaar and the chaat shop and even the elements. He admitted to himself that he had been too impulsive in rebelling and running away from home; perhaps there was still time to return and beg Mr Harrison's forgiveness. But could his behaviour be forgiven? Might he not be clapped into irons for attempted murder? Most certainly he would be given another beating—not six strokes this time, but nine.

His only hope was Somi. If not Somi, then Ranbir. If not Ranbir . . . well, it was no use thinking further, there was no one else to think of.

The rain had ceased. Rusty crawled out from under the bench, and stretched his cramped limbs. The moon came out from a cloud, and played with his wet, glistening body, and showed him the vast, naked loneliness of the maidan and his own insignificance. He longed now for the presence of people, be they beggars or women, and he broke into a trot, and the trot became a run, a frightened run, and he did not stop until he reached the Clock Tower.

CHAPTER SEVEN

❧

THEY WHO SLEEP LAST, wake first. Hunger and pain lengthen the
night, and so the beggars and dogs are the last to see the stars;
hunger and pain hasten the awakening, and beggars and dogs
are the first to see the sun. Rusty knew hunger and pain, but
his weariness was even greater, and he was asleep on the steps
of the chaat shop long after the sun had come striding down
the road, knocking on nearly every door and window.

Somi bathed at the common water-tank. He stood under
the tap and slapped his body into life and spluttered with the
shock of mountain water.

At the tank were many people: children shrieking with
delight—or discomfort—as their ayahs slapped them about
roughly and affectionately; the ayahs themselves, strong, healthy
hill-women, with heavy bracelets on their ankles; the *bhisti* —
the water-carrier—with his skin bag; and the cook with his pots
and pans. The ayahs sat on their haunches, bathing the children,
their saris rolled up to the thighs; every time they moved their
feet, the bells on their ankles jingled. There was a continuous
shrieking and jingling and slapping of buttocks. The cook
smeared his utensils with ash and washed them, and filled an
earthen *chatty* with water; the *bhisti* hoisted the water-bag over
his shoulder and left, dripping; a pye-dog lapped at water
rolling off the stone platform; and a baleful-looking cow nibbled
at wet grass.

It was with these people that Somi spent his mornings,
laughing and talking and bathing with them. When he had
finished his ablutions, dried his hair in the sun, dressed and

tied his turban, he mounted his bicycle and rode out of the compound.

At this advanced hour of the morning Mr Harrison still slept. In the half-empty church, his absence was noted: he seldom missed Sunday morning services; and the missionary's wife was impatiently waiting for the end of the sermon, for she had so much to talk about.

Outside the chaat shop Somi said, 'Hey, Rusty, get up, what has happened? Where is Ranbir? Holi finished yesterday, you know!'

He shook Rusty by the shoulders, shouting into his ear; and the pale boy lying on the stone steps opened his eyes and blinked in the morning sunshine; his eyes roamed about in bewilderment, he could not remember how he came to be lying in the sunshine in the bazaar.

'Hey,' said Somi, 'your guardian will be very angry!'

Rusty sat up with a start. He was wide awake now, sweeping up his scattered thoughts and sorting them out. It was difficult for him to be straightforward; but he forced himself to look Somi straight in the eyes and, very simply and without preamble, say: 'I've run away from home.'

Somi showed no surprise. He did not take his eyes off Rusty, nor did his expression alter. A half-smile on his lips, he said: 'Good. Now you can come and stay with me.'

Somi took Rusty home on the bicycle. Rusty felt weak in the legs, but his mind was relieved and he no longer felt alone. Once again, Somi gave him a feeling of confidence.

'Do you think I can get a job?' asked Rusty.

'Don't worry about that yet, you have only just run away.'

'Do you think I can get a job,' persisted Rusty.

'Why not? But don't worry, you are going to stay with me.'

'I'll stay with you only until I find a job. Any kind of job, there must be something.'

'Of course, don't worry,' said Somi, and pressed harder on the pedals.

They came to a canal; it was noisy with the rush of mountain water, for the snow had begun to melt. The road, which ran parallel to the canal, was flooded in some parts, but Somi steered a steady course. Then the canal turned left and the road kept straight, and presently the sound of water was but a murmur, and the road quiet and shady; there were trees at the road-sides covered in pink and white blossoms, and behind them more trees, thicker and greener; and in amongst the trees were houses.

A boy swung on a creaking wooden gate. He whistled out, and Somi waved back; that was all.

'Who's that?' asked Rusty.

'Son of his parents.'

'What do you mean?'

'His father is rich. So Kishen is somebody. He has money, and it is as powerful as Suri's tongue.'

'Is he Suri's friend or yours?'

'When it suits him, he is our friend. When it suits him, he is Suri's friend.'

'Then he's clever as well as rich,' deducted Rusty.

'The brains are his mother's.'

'And the money his father's?

'Yes, but there isn't much left now. Mr Kapoor is finished . . . . He looks like his father too. His mother is beautiful. Well, here we are!'

Somi rode the bicycle in amongst the trees and along a snaky path that dodged this way and that, and then they reached the house.

It was a small flat house, covered completely by a crimson bougainvillaea creeper. The garden was a mass of marigolds which had sprung up everywhere, even in the cracks at the sides of the veranda steps. No one was at home. Somi's father was in Delhi, and his mother was out for the morning, buying the week's vegetables.

'Have you any brothers?' asked Rusty, as he entered the front room.

'No. But I've got two sisters. But they're married. Come on, let's see if my clothes will fit you.'

Rusty laughed, for he was older and bigger than his friend; but he was thinking in terms of shirts and trousers, the kind of garments he was used to wearing. He sat down on a sofa in the front room, whilst Somi went for the clothes.

The room was cool and spacious, and had very little furniture. But on the walls were many pictures, and in the centre a large one of Guru Nanak, the founder of the Sikh religion: his body bare, the saint sat with his legs crossed and the palms of his hands touching in prayer, and on his face there was a serene expression. The serenity of Nanak's countenance seemed to communicate itself to the room. There was a serenity about Somi too; maybe because of the smile that always hovered near his mouth.

Rusty concluded that Somi's family were middle class people, that is, they were neither rich nor beggars, but managed to live all the same.

Somi came back with the clothes.

'They are mine,' he said, 'so maybe they will be a little small for you. Anyway, the warm weather is coming and it will not matter what you wear—better nothing at all!'

Rusty put on a long white shirt which, to his surprise, hung loose; it had a high collar and broad sleeves.

'It is loose,' he said, 'how can it be yours?'

'It is made loose,' said Somi.

Rusty pulled on a pair of white pyjamas, and they were definitely small for him, ending a few inches above the ankle. The sandals would not buckle; and, when he walked, they behaved like Somi's and slapped against his heels.

'There!' exclaimed Somi in satisfaction. 'Now everything is settled, chaat in your stomach, clean clothes on your body, and in a few days we find a job! Now is there anything else?'

Rusty knew Somi well enough now to know that it wasn't necessary to thank him for anything; gratitude was taken for granted; in true friendship there are no formalities and no obligations. Rusty did not even ask if Somi had consulted his mother about taking in guests; perhaps she was used to this sort of thing.

'Is there anything else?' repeated Somi.

Rusty yawned. 'Can I go to sleep now, please?'

CHAPTER EIGHT

☙

RUSTY HAD NEVER SLEPT well in his guardian's house because he had never been tired enough; also his imagination would disturb him. And since running away, he had slept very badly because he had been cold and hungry and afraid. But in Somi's house he felt safe and a little happy, and so he slept; he slept the remainder of the day and through the night.

In the morning Somi tipped Rusty out of bed and dragged him to the water-tank. Rusty watched Somi strip and stand under the jet of tap water, and shuddered at the prospect of having to do the same.

Before removing his shirt, Rusty looked around in embarrassment; no one paid much attention to him, though one of the ayahs, the girl with the bangles, gave him a sly smile; he looked away from the women, threw his shirt on a bush and advanced cautiously to the bathing place.

Somi pulled him under the tap. The water was icy cold and Rusty gasped with the shock. As soon as he was wet, he sprang off the platform, much to the amusement of Somi and the ayahs.

There was no towel with which to dry himself; he stood on the grass, shivering with cold, wondering whether he should dash back to the house or shiver in the open until the sun dried him. But the girl with the bangles was beside him holding a towel; her eyes were full of mockery, but her smile was friendly.

At the midday meal, which consisted of curry and curds and chapattis, Rusty met Somi's mother, and liked her.

She was a woman of about thirty-five; she had a few grey

hair at the temples, and her skin—unlike Somi's—was rough and dry. She dressed simply, in a plain white sari. Her life had been difficult. After the partition of the country, when hate made religion its own, Somi's family had to leave their home in the Punjab and trek southwards; they had walked hundreds of miles and the mother had carried Somi, who was then six, on her back. Life in India had to be started again right from the beginning, for they had lost most of their property. The father found work in Delhi, the sisters were married off, and Somi and his mother settled down in Dehra, where the boy attended school.

The mother said: 'Mister Rusty, you must give Somi a few lessons in spelling and arithmetic. Always, he comes last in class.'

'Oh, that's good!' exclaimed Somi. 'We'll have fun, Rusty!' Then he thumped the table. 'I have an idea! I know, I think I have a job for you! Remember Kishen, the boy we passed yesterday? Well, his father wants someone to give him private lessons in English.'

'Teach Kishen?'

'Yes, it will be easy. I'll go and see Mr Kapoor and tell him I've found a professor of English or something like that, and then you can come and see him. Brother, it is a first class idea, you are going to be a teacher!'

Rusty felt very sceptical about the proposal; he was not sure he could teach English or anything else to the wilful son of a rich man. But he was not in a position to pick and choose. Somi mounted his bicycle and rode off to see Mr Kapoor to secure for Rusty the post of Professor of English. When he returned he seemed pleased with himself, and Rusty's heart sank with the knowledge that he had got a job.

'You are to come and see him this evening,' announced Somi, 'he will tell you all about it. They want a teacher for Kishen, especially if they don't have to pay.'

'What kind of a job without pay?' complained Rusty.

'No pay,' said Somi, 'but everything else. Food—and no cooking is better than Punjabi cooking; water—'

'I should hope so,' said Rusty.

'And a room, sir!'

'Oh, even a room,' said Rusty ungratefully, 'that will be nice.'

'Anyway,' said Somi, 'come and see him, you don't have to accept.'

The house the Kapoors lived in was very near the canal; it was a squat, comfortable-looking bungalow, surrounded by uncut hedges, and shaded by banana and papaya trees. It was late evening when Somi and Rusty arrived, and the moon was up, and the shaggy branches of the banana trees shook their heavy shadows out over the gravel path.

In an open space in front of the house a log fire was burning; the Kapoors appeared to be giving a party. Somi and Rusty joined the people who were grouped round the fire, and Rusty wondered if he had been invited to the party. The fire lent a friendly warmth to the chilly night, and the flames leapt up, casting the glow of roses on people's faces.

Somi pointed out different people: various shopkeepers, one or two Big Men, the sickly looking Suri (who was never absent from a social occasion such as this) and a few total strangers who had invited themselves to the party just for the fun of the thing and a free meal. Kishen, the Kapoors' son, was not present; he hated parties, preferring the company of certain wild friends in the bazaar.

Mr Kapoor was once a Big Man himself, and everyone knew this; but he had fallen from the heights; and, until he gave up the bottle, was not likely to reach them again. Everyone felt sorry for his wife, including herself.

Presently Kapoor tottered out of the front door arm-in-arm with a glass and a bottle of whisky. He wore a green dressing-gown and a week's beard; his hair, or what was left of it, stood up on end; and he dribbled slightly. An awkward silence fell on the company; but Kapoor, who was a friendly, gentle sort of drunkard, looked round benevolently, and said: 'Everybody here? Fine, fine, they are all here, all of them . . . . Throw some more wood on the fire!'

The fire was doing very well indeed, but not well enough for Kapoor; every now and then he would throw a log on the flames until it was feared the blaze would reach the house. Meena, Kapoor's wife, did not look flustered, only irritated; she was a capable person, still young, a charming hostess; and, in her red sari and white silk jacket, her hair plaited and scented with jasmine, she looked beautiful. Rusty gazed admiringly at her; he wanted to compliment her, to say, 'Mrs Kapoor, you are beautiful'; but he had no need to tell her, she was fully conscious of the fact.

Meena made her way over to one of the Big Men, and whispered something in his ear, and then she went to a Little Shopkeeper and whispered something in his ear, and then both the Big Man and the Little Shopkeeper advanced stealthily towards the spot where Mr Kapoor was holding forth, and made a gentle attempt to convey him indoors.

But Kapoor was having none of it. He pushed the men aside and roared: 'Keep the fire burning! Keep it burning, don't let it go out, throw some more wood on it!'

And, before he could be restrained, he had thrown a pot of the most delicious sweetmeats on the flames.

To Rusty this was sacrilege. 'Oh, Mr Kapoor . . .' he cried, but there was some confusion in the rear, and his words were drowned in a series of explosions.

Suri and one or two others had begun letting off fireworks: fountains, rockets, and explosives. The fountains gushed forth in green and red and silver lights, and the rockets struck through the night with crimson tails; but it was the explosives that caused the confusion. The guests did not know whether to press forward into the fires, or retreat amongst the fireworks; neither prospect was pleasing, and the women began to show signs of hysterics. Then Suri burnt his finger and began screaming, and this was all the women had been waiting for; headed by Suri's mother, they rushed the boy and smothered him with attention; whilst the men, who were in a minority, looked on sheepishly and wished the accident had been of a more serious nature.

Something rough brushed against Rusty's cheek.

It was Kapoor's beard. Somi had brought his host to Rusty, and the bemused man put his face close to Rusty's and placed his hands on the boy's shoulders in order to steady himself. Kapoor nodded his head, his eyes red and watery.

'Rusty . . . so you are Mister Rusty . . . . I hear you are going to be my schoolteacher.'

'Your son's, sir,' said Rusty, 'but that is for you to decide.'

'Do not call me "sir",' he said, wagging his finger in Rusty's face, 'call me by my name. So you are going to England, eh?'

'No, I'm going to be your schoolteacher.' Rusty had to put his arm round Kapoor's waist to avoid being dragged to the ground; Kapoor leant heavily on the boy's shoulders.

'Good, good. Tell me after you have gone, I want to give you some addresses of people I know. You must go to Monte Carlo, you've seen nothing until you've seen Monte Carlo, it's the only place with a future . . . . Who built Monte Carlo, do you know?'

It was impossible for Rusty to make any sense of the conversation or discuss his appointment as Professor in English to Kishen Kapoor. Kapoor began to slip from his arms, and the boy took the opportunity of changing his own position for a more comfortable one, before levering his host up again. The amused smiles of the company rested on this little scene.

Rusty said: 'No, Mr Kapoor, who built Monte Carlo?'

'I did. I built Monte Carlo!'

'Oh yes, of course.'

'Yes, I built this house, I'm a genius, there's no doubt of it! I have a high opinion of my own opinion, what is yours?'

'Oh, I don't know, but I'm sure you're right.'

'Of course I am. But speak up, don't be afraid to say what you think. Stand up for your rights, even if you're wrong! Throw some more wood on the fire, keep it burning.'

Kapoor leapt from Rusty's arms and stumbled towards the fire. The boy cried a warning and, catching hold of the end of the green dressing-gown, dragged his host back to safety. Meena ran to them and, without so much as a glance at Rusty, took her husband by the arm and propelled him indoors.

Rusty stared after Meena Kapoor, and continued to stare even when she had disappeared. The guests chattered pleasantly, pretending nothing had happened, keeping the gossip for the next morning; but the children giggled amongst themselves, and the devil Suri shouted: 'Throw some more wood on the fire, keep it burning!'

Somi returned to his friend's side. 'What did Mr Kapoor have to say?'

'He said he built Monte Carlo.'

Somi slapped his forehead. 'Toba! Now we'll have to come again tomorrow evening. And then, if he's drunk, we'll have to discuss with his wife, she's the only one with any sense.'

They walked away from the party, out of the circle of fire-light, into the shadows of the banana trees. The voices of the guests became a distant murmur: Suri's high-pitched shout came to them on the clear, still air.

Somi said: 'We must go to the chaat shop tomorrow morning, Ranbir is asking for you.'

Rusty had almost forgotten Ranbir: he felt ashamed for not having asked about him before this. Ranbir was an important person, he had changed the course of Rusty's life with nothing but a little colour, red and green, and the touch of his hand.

CHAPTER NINE

❦

AGAINST HIS PARENTS' WISHES, Kishen Kapoor spent most of his time in the bazaar; he loved it because it was forbidden, because it was unhealthy, dangerous and full of germs to carry home.

Ranbir loved the bazaar because he was born in it; he had known few other places. Since the age of ten he had looked after his uncle's buffaloes, grazing them on the maidan and taking them down to the river to wallow in mud and water; and in the evening he took them home, riding on the back of the strongest and fastest animal. When he grew older, he was allowed to help in his father's cloth shop, but he was always glad to get back to the buffaloes.

Kishen did not like animals, particularly cows and buffaloes. His greatest enemy was Maharani, the Queen of the Bazaar, who like Kishen was spoilt and pampered and fond of having her own way. Unlike other cows, she did not feed at dustbins and rubbish heaps, but lived on the benevolence of the bazaar people.

But Kishen had no time for religion; to him a cow was just a cow, nothing sacred; and he saw no reason why he should get off the pavement in order to make way for one, or offer no protest when it stole from under his nose. One day, he tied an empty tin to Maharani's tail and looked on in great enjoyment as the cow pranced madly and dangerously about the road, the tin clattering behind her. Lacking in dignity, Kishen found some pleasure in observing others lose theirs. But a few days later, Kishen received Maharani's nose in his pants and had to pick himself up from the gutter.

Kishen and Ranbir ate mostly at the chaat shop; if they had no money they went to work in Ranbir's uncle's sugar-cane fields and earned a rupee for the day; but Kishen did not like work, and Ranbir had enough of his own to do, so there was never much money for chaat; which meant living on their wits—or, rather, Kishen' wits, for it was his duty to pocket any spare money that might be lying about in his father's house—and sometimes helping themselves at the fruit and vegetable stalls when no one was looking.

Ranbir wrestled. That was why he was so good at riding buffaloes. He was the best wrestler in the bazaar; not very clever, but powerful; he was like a great tree, and no amount of shaking could move him from whatever spot he chose to plant his big feet. But he was gentle by nature. The women always gave him their babies to look after when they were busy, and he would cradle the babies in his open hands, and sing to them, and be happy for hours.

Ranbir had a certain innocence which was not likely to leave him. He had seen and experienced life to the full, and life had bruised and scarred him, but it had not crippled him. One night he strayed unwittingly into the intoxicating arms of a local temple dancing girl; but he acted with instinct, his pleasure was unpremeditated, and the adventure was soon forgotten—by Ranbir. But Suri, the scourge of the bazaar, uncovered a few facts and threatened to inform Ranbir's family of the incident; and so Ranbir found himself in the power of the cunning Suri, and was forced to please him from time to time; though, at times such as the Holi festival, that power was scorned.

On the morning after the Kapoors' party Ranbir, Somi, and Rusty were seated in the chaat shop, discussing Rusty's situation. Ranbir looked miserable; his hair fell sadly over his forehead, and he would not look at Rusty.

'I have got you into trouble,' he apologized gruffly, 'I am too ashamed.'

Rusty laughed, licking sauce from his fingers and crumpling up his empty leaf bowl.

'Silly fellow,' he said, 'for what are you sorry? For making me happy? For taking me away from my guardian? Well, I am not sorry, you can be sure of that.'

'You are not angry?' asked Ranbir in wonder.

'No, but you will make me angry in this way.'

Ranbir's face lit up, and he slapped Somi and Rusty on their backs with such sudden enthusiasm that Somi dropped his bowl of alu chole.

'Come on, misters,' he said, 'I am going to make you sick with gol-guppas so that you will not be able to eat any more until I return from Mussoorie!'

'Mussoorie?' Somi looked puzzled. 'You are going to Mussoorie?'

'To school!'

'That's right,' said a voice from the door, a voice hidden in smoke. 'Now we've had it . . . . '

Somi said, 'It's that monkey-millionaire Kishen come to make a nuisance of himself.' Then, louder: 'Come over here, Kishen, come and join us in gol-guppas!'

Kishen appeared from the mist of vapour, walking with an affected swagger, his hands in his pockets; he was the only one present wearing pants instead of pyjamas.

'Hey!' exclaimed Somi, 'who has given you a black eye?'

Kishen did not answer immediately but sat down opposite Rusty. His shirt hung over his pants, and his pants hung over his knees; he had bushy eyebrows and hair, and a drooping, disagreeable mouth; the sulky expression on his face had become a permanent one, not a mood of the moment. Kishen's swagger, money, unattractive face and qualities made him—for Rusty, anyway—curiously attractive . . . .

He prodded his nose with his forefinger, as he always did when a trifle excited. 'Those damn wrestlers, they piled on to me.'

'Why?' said Ranbir, sitting up instantly.

'I was making a badminton court on the maidan, and these fellows came along and said they had reserved the place for a wrestling ground.'

'So then?'

Kishen's affected American twang became more pronounced. 'I told them to go to hell!'

Ranbir laughed. 'So they all started wrestling you.'

'Yeah, but I didn't know they would hit me too. I bet if you fellows were there, they wouldn't have tried anything. Isn't that so, Ranbir?'

Ranbir smiled; he knew it was so, but did not care to speak of his physical prowess. Kishen took notice of the newcomer.

'Are you Mister Rusty?' he asked.

'Yes, I am,' said the boy. 'Are you Mister Kishen?'

'I am Mister Kishen. You know how to box, Rusty?'

'Well,' said the boy, unwilling to become involved in a local feud, 'I've never boxed wrestlers.'

Somi changed the subject. 'Rusty's coming to see your father this evening. You must try and persuade your pop to give him the job of teaching you English.'

Kishen prodded his nose, and gave Rusty a sly wink.

'Yes, Daddy told me about you, he says you are a professor. You can be my teacher on the condition that we don't work too hard, and you support me when I tell them lies, and that you tell them I am working hard. Sure, you can be my teacher, sure . . . better you than a real one.'

'I'll try to please everyone,' said Rusty.

'You're a clever person if you can. But I think you are clever.'

'Yes,' agreed Rusty, and was inwardly amazed at the way he spoke.

As Rusty had now met Kishen, Somi suggested that the two should go to the Kapoors' house together. So, that evening Rusty met Kishen in the bazaar and walked home with him.

There was a crowd in front of the bazaar's only cinema, and it was getting restive and demonstrative.

One had to fight to get into this particular cinema, as there was no organized queuing or booking.

'Is anything wrong?' asked Rusty.

'Oh, no,' said Kishen, 'it is just Laurel and Hardy today, they are very popular. Whenever a popular film is shown, there is usually a riot. But I know of a way in through the roof, I'll show you some time.'

'Sounds crazy.'

'Yeah, the roof leaks, so people usually bring their umbrellas. Also their food, because when the projector breaks down or the electricity fails, we have to wait a long time. Sometimes, when it is a long wait, the chaat-wallah comes in and does some business.'

'Sounds crazy,' repeated Rusty.

'You'll get used to it. Have a chewing gum.'

Kishen's jaws had been working incessantly on a lump of gum that had been increasing in size over the last three days; he started on a fresh stick every hour or so, without throwing away the old ones. Rusty was used to seeing Indians chew paan, the betel leaf preparation which stained the mouth with red juices, but Kishen wasn't like any of the Indians Rusty had met so far. He accepted a stick of gum, and the pair walked home in silent concentration, their jaws moving rhythmically, and Kishen's tongue making sudden sucking sounds.

As they entered the front room, Meena Kapoor pounced on Kishen.

'Ah! So you have decided to come home at last! And what do you mean by asking Daddy for money without letting me know? What have you done with it, Kishen? Where is it?'

Kishen sauntered across the room and deposited himself on the couch. 'I've spent it.'

Meena's hands went to her hips. 'What do you mean, you've spent it!'

'I mean I've eaten it.'

He got two resounding slaps across his face, and his flesh went white where his mother's fingers left their mark. Rusty backed towards the door; it was embarrassing to be present at this intimate family scene.

'Don't go, Rusty,' shouted Kishen, 'or she won't stop slapping me!'

Kapoor, still wearing his green dressing-gown and beard, came in from the adjoining room, and his wife turned on him.

'Why do you give the child so much money?' she demanded. 'You know he spends it on nothing but bazaar food and makes himself sick.'

Rusty seized the opportunity of pleasing the whole family; of saving Mr Kapoor's skin, pacifying his wife, and gaining the affection and regard of Kishen.

'It is all my fault,' he said, 'I took Kishen to the chaat shop. I'm very sorry.'

Meena Kapoor became quiet and her eyes softened; but Rusty resented her kindly expression because he knew it was prompted by pity—pity for him—and a satisfied pride. Meena was proud because of the thought that her son had shared his money with one who apparently hadn't any.

'I did not see you come in,' she said.

'I only wanted to explain about the money.'

'Come in, don't be shy.'

Meena's smile was full of kindness, but Rusty was not looking for kindness; for no apparent reason, he felt lonely; he missed Somi, felt lost without him, helpless and clumsy.

'There is another thing,' he said, remembering the post of Professor in English.

'But come in, Mister Rusty . . . .'

It was the first time she had used his name, and the gesture immediately placed them on equal terms. She was a graceful woman, much younger than Kapoor; her features had a clear, classic beauty, and her voice was gentle but firm. Her hair was tied in a neat bun and laced with a string of jasmine flowers.

'Come in . . . .'

'About teaching Kishen,' mumbled Rusty.

'Come and play carom,' said Kishen from the couch. 'We are none of us any good. Come and sit down, pardner.'

'He fancies himself as an American,' said Meena. 'If ever you see him in the cinema, drag him out.'

The carom board was brought in from the next room, and it was arranged that Rusty partner Mr Kapoor. They began play, but the game didn't progress very fast because Kapoor kept leaving the table in order to disappear behind a screen, from the direction of which came a tinkle of bottles and glasses. Rusty was afraid of Kapoor getting drunk before he could be approached about the job of teaching Kishen.

'My wife,' said Kapoor in a loud whisper to Rusty, 'does not let me drink in public any more, so I have to do it in a cupboard.'

He looked sad; there were tear-stains on his cheeks; the tears were caused not by Meena's scolding, which he ignored, but by his own self-pity; he often cried for himself, usually in his sleep.

Whenever Rusty pocketed one of the carom men, Kapoor exclaimed: 'Ah, nice shot, nice shot!' as though it were a cricket match they were playing. 'But hit it slowly, slowly . . . .' And when it was his turn, he gave the striker a feeble push, moving it a bare inch from his finger.

'Play properly,' murmured Meena, who was intent on winning the game; but Kapoor would be up from his seat again, and the company would sit back and wait for the tune of clinking glass.

It was a very irritating game. Kapoor insisted on showing Rusty how to strike the men; and whenever Rusty made a mistake, Meena said 'thank you' in an amused and conceited manner that angered the boy. When she and Kishen had cleared the board of whites, Kapoor and Rusty were left with eight blacks.

'Thank you,' said Meena sweetly.

'We are too good for you,' scoffed Kishen, busily arranging the board for another game.

Kapoor took sudden interest in the proceedings: 'Who won, I say, who won?'

Much to Rusty's disgust, they began another game, and with the same partners; but they had just started when Kapoor flopped forward and knocked the carom board off the table. He had fallen asleep. Rusty took him by the shoulders and eased him back into the chair. Kapoor's breathing was heavy; saliva had collected at the sides of his mouth, and he snored a little.

Rusty thought it was time he left. Rising from the table, he said, 'I will have to ask another time about the job . . . .'

'Hasn't he told you as yet?' said Meena.

'What?'

'That you can have the job.'

'Can I!' exclaimed Rusty.

Meena gave a little laugh. 'But of course! Certainly there is no one else who would take it on, Kishen is not easy to teach. There is no fixed pay, but we will give you anything you need. You are not our servant. You will be doing us a favour by giving Kishen some of your knowledge and conversation and company, and in return we will be giving you our hospitality. You will have a room of your own, and your food you will have with us. What do you think?'

'Oh, it is wonderful!' said Rusty.

And it was wonderful, and he felt gay and light-headed, and all the troubles in the world scurried away; he even felt successful: he had a profession. And Meena Kapoor was smiling at him, and looking more beautiful than she really was, and

Kishen was saying: 'Tomorrow you must stay till twelve o'clock, all right, even if Daddy goes to sleep. Promise me?'

Rusty promised.

An unaffected enthusiasm was bubbling up in Kishen; it was quite different from the sulkiness of his usual manner. Rusty had liked him in spite of the younger boy's unattractive qualities, and now liked him more; for Kishen had taken Rusty into his home and confidence without knowing him very well and without asking any questions. Kishen was a scoundrel, a monkey—crude and spoilt—but for him to have taken a liking to Rusty (and Rusty held himself in high esteem), he must have some virtues . . . or so Rusty reasoned.

His mind, while he walked back to Somi's house, dwelt on his relationship with Kishen; but his tongue, when he loosened it in Somi's presence, dwelt on Meena Kapoor. And when he lay down to sleep, he saw her in his mind's eye, and for the first time took conscious note of her beauty, of her warmth and softness; and made up his mind that he would fall in love with her.

Chapter Ten

❧

Mr Harrison was back to normal in a few days, and telling everyone of Rusty's barbaric behaviour.

'If he wants to live like an animal, he can. He left my house of his own free will, and I feel no responsibility for him. It's his own fault if he starves to death.'

The missionary's wife said: 'But I do hope you will forgive him if he returns.'

'I will, madam. I have to. I'm his legal guardian. And I hope he doesn't return.'

'Oh, Mr Harrison, he's only a boy . . . .'

'That's what you think.'

'I'm sure he'll come back.'

Mr Harrison shrugged indifferently.

Rusty's thoughts were far from his guardian. He was listening to Meena Kapoor tell him about his room, and he gazed into her eyes all the time she talked.

'It is a very nice room,' she said, 'but of course there is no water or electricity or lavatory.'

Rusty was bathing in the brown pools of her eyes.

She said: 'You will have to collect your water at the big tank, and for the rest, you will have to do it in the jungle . . . .'

Rusty thought he saw his own gaze reflected in her eyes.

'Yes?' he said.

'You can give Kishen his lessons in the morning until twelve o'clock. Then no more, then you have your food.'

'Then?'

He watched the movement of her lips.

'Then nothing, you do what you like, go out with Kishen or Somi or any of your friends.'

'Where do I teach Kishen?'

'On the roof, of course.'

Rusty retrieved his gaze, and scratched his head. The roof seemed a strange place for setting up school.

'Why the roof?'

'Because your room is on the roof.'

Meena led the boy round the house until they came to a flight of steps, unsheltered, that went up to the roof. They had to hop over a narrow drain before climbing the steps.

'This drain,' warned Meena, 'is very easy to cross. But when you are coming downstairs be sure not to take too big a step because then you might bump the wall on the other side or fall over the stove which is usually there . . . .'

'I will be careful,' said Rusty.

They began climbing, Meena in the lead. Rusty watched Meena's long, slender feet. The slippers she wore consisted only of two straps that passed between her toes, and the backs of the slippers slapped against her heels like Somi's, only the music—like the feet—was different . . . .

'Another thing about these steps,' continued Meena, ' there are twenty-two of them. No, don't count, I have already done so . . . . But remember, if you are coming home in the dark, be sure you take only twenty-two steps, because if you don't, then'—and she snapped her fingers in the air—'you will be finished! After twenty-two steps you turn right and you find the door, here it is. If you do not turn right and you take *twenty-three* steps, you will go over the edge of the roof!'

They both laughed, and suddenly Meena took Rusty's hand and led him into the room.

It was a small room, but this did not matter much as there was very little in it: only a string bed, a table, a shelf and a few nails in the wall. In comparison to Rusty's room in his guardian's house, it wasn't even a room: it was four walls, a door and a window.

The door looked out on the roof, and Meena pointed through it, at the big round water-tank.

'That is where you bathe and get your water,' she said.

'I know, I went with Somi.'

There was a big mango tree behind the tank, and Kishen was sitting in its branches, watching them. Surrounding the house were a number of litchee trees, and in the summer they and the mango would bear fruit.

Meena and Rusty stood by the window in silence, hand in hand. Rusty was prepared to stand there, holding hands for ever. Meena felt a sisterly affection for him; but he was stumbling into love.

From the window they could see many things. In the distance, towering over the other trees was the Flame of the Forest, its flowers glowing red-hot against the blue of the sky. Through the window came a shoot of pink bougainvillaea creeper; and Rusty knew he would never cut it; and so he knew he would never be able to shut the window.

Meena said, 'if you do not like it, we will find another . . . .'

Rusty squeezed her hand and smiled into her eyes, and said: 'But I like it. This is the room I want to live in. And do you know why, Meena? Because it isn't a real room, that's why!'

The afternoon was warm, and Rusty sat beneath the big banyan tree that grew behind the house, a tree that was almost a house in itself; its spreading branches dropped to the ground and took new root, forming a maze of pillared passages. The tree sheltered scores of birds and squirrels.

A squirrel stood in front of Rusty. It looked at him from between its legs, its tail in the air, back arched gracefully and nose quivering excitedly.

'Hello,' said Rusty.

The squirrel brushed its nose with its forepaw, winked at the boy, hopped over his leg, and ran up a pillar of the banyan tree.

Rusty leant back against the broad trunk of the banyan, and listened to the lazy drone of the bees, the squeaking of the squirrels and the incessant bird talk.

He thought of Meena and of Kishen, and felt miserably happy; and then he remembered Somi and the chaat shop. The chaat-wallah, that god of the tikkees, handed Rusty a leaf bowl, and prepared allu chole: first sliced potatoes, then peas, then red and gold chilli powders, then a sprinkling of juices, then he shook it all up and down in the leaf bowl and, in a moment the alu chole was ready.

Somi removed his slippers, crossed his legs, and looked a question.

'It's fine,' said Rusty.

'You are sure?'

There was concern in Somi's voice, and his eyes seemed to hesitate a little before smiling with the mouth.

'It's fine,' said Rusty. 'I'll soon get used to the room.'

There was a silence. Rusty concentrated on the alu chole, feeling guilty and ungrateful.

'Ranbir has gone,' said Somi.

'Oh, he didn't even say goodbye!'

'He has not gone for ever. And anyway, what would be the use of saying goodbye . . . .'

He sounded depressed. He finished his alu chole and said: 'Rust, best favourite friend, if you don't want this job I'll find you another.'

'But I like it Somi, I want it, really I do. You are trying to do too much for me. Mrs Kapoor is wonderful, and Mr Kapoor is good fun, and Kishen is not so bad, you know . . . . Come on to the house and see the room. It's the kind of room in which you write poetry or create music.'

They walked home in the evening. The evening was full of sounds. Rusty noticed the sounds, because he was happy, and a happy person notices things.

Carriages passed them on the road, creaking and rattling, wheels squeaking, hoofs resounding on the ground; and the whip cracks above the horse's ear, and the driver shouts, and round go the wheels, squeaking and creaking, and the hoofs go clippety-clippety, clip-clop-clop . . . .

A bicycle came swishing through the puddles, the wheels purring and humming smoothly, the bell tinkling . . . . In the bushes there was the chatter of sparrows and seven-sisters, but Rusty could not see them, no matter how hard he looked.

And there were footsteps . . . .

Their own footsteps, quiet and thoughtful; and ahead of them an old man, with a dhoti round his legs and a black umbrella in his hand, walking at a clockwork pace. At each alternate step he tapped with his umbrella on the pavement; he wore noisy shoes, and his footsteps echoed off the pavement to the beat of the umbrella. Rusty and Somi quickened their own steps, passed him by, and let the endless tapping die on the wind.

They sat on the roof for an hour, watching the sun set; and Somi sang.

Somi had a beautiful voice, clear and mellow, matching the serenity of his face. And when he sang, his eyes wandered into the night, and he was lost to the world and to Rusty; for when he sang of the stars he was of the stars, and when he sang of a river he was a river. He communicated his mood to Rusty, as he could not have done in plain language; and, when the song ended, the silence returned and all the world fell asleep.

CHAPTER ELEVEN

❧

RUSTY WATCHED THE DAWN blossom into light.

At first everything was dark, then gradually objects began
to take shape—the desk and chair, the walls of the room—and
the darkness lifted like the raising of a veil, and over the tree-
tops the sky was streaked with crimson. It was like this for
some time, while everything became clearer and more
distinguishable; and then, when nature was ready, the sun
reached up over the trees and hills, and sent one tentative
beam of warm light through the window. Along the wall crept
the sun, across to the bed and up the boy's bare legs, until it
was caressing his entire body and whispering to him to get up
get up, it is time to get up . . . .

Rusty blinked. He sat up and rubbed his eyes and looked
around. It was his first morning in the room, and perched on
the window-sill was a small brown and yellow bird, a mina,
looking at him with its head cocked to one side. The mina was
a common sight, but this one was unusual—it was bald. All the
feathers had been knocked off its head in a series of fights.

Rusty wondered if he should get up and bathe, or wait for
someone to arrive. But he didn't wait long. Something bumped
him from under the bed.

He stiffened with apprehension. Something was moving
beneath him, the mattress rose gently and fell. Could it be a jackal
or a wolf that had stolen in through the open door during the
night? Rusty trembled, but did not move . . . . It might be
something even more dangerous, the house was close to the
jungle . . . . or it might be a thief . . . but what was there to steal?

Unable to bear the suspense, Rusty brought his fists down on the uneven lump in the quilt, and Kishen sprang out with a cry of pain and astonishment.

He sat on his bottom and cursed Rusty.

'Sorry,' said Rusty, 'but you frightened me.'

'I'm glad, because you hurt me, mister.'

'Your fault. What's the time?'

'Time to get up. I've brought you some milk, and you can have mine too, I hate it, it spoils the flavour of my chewing-gum.'

Kishen accompanied Rusty to the water-tank, where they met Somi. After they had bathed and filled their *sohrais* with drinking-water, they went back to the room for the first lesson.

Kishen and Rusty sat cross-legged on the bed, facing each other. Rusty fingered his chin, and Kishen played with his toes.

'What do you want to learn today?' asked Rusty.

'How should I know? That's your problem, pardner.'

'As it's the first day, you can make a choice.'

'Let's play noughts and crosses.'

'Be serious. Tell me, bhaiya, what books have you read?'

Kishen turned his eyes up to the ceiling. 'I've read so many I can't remember the names.'

'Well, you can tell me what they were about.'

Kishen looked disconcerted. 'Oh, sure . . . sure . . . let me see now . . . what about the one in which everyone went down a rabbit-hole?'

'What about it?'

'Called *Treasure Island*.'

'Hell!' said Rusty.

'Which ones have you read?' asked Kishen, warming to the discussion.

'*Treasure Island* and the one about the rabbit-hole, and you haven't read either. What do you want to be when you grow up, Kishen? A businessman, an officer, an engineer?'

'Don't want to be anything. What about you?'

'You're not supposed to be asking me. But if you want to know, I'm going to be a writer. I'll write books. You'll read them.'

'You'll be a great writer, Rusty, you'll be great . . . .'

'Maybe, who knows.'

'I know,' said Kishen, quite sincerely, 'you'll be a terrific writer. You'll be famous. You'll be a king.'

'Shut up . . . .'

The Kapoors liked Rusty. They didn't admire him, but they liked him. Kishen liked him for his company, Kapoor liked him for his flattering conversation, and Meena liked him because—well, because he liked her . . . .

The Kapoors were glad to have him in their house.

Meena had been betrothed to Kapoor since childhood, before they knew each other, and despite the fact that there was a difference of nearly twenty years between their ages. Kapoor was a promising young man, intelligent and beginning to make money; and Meena, at thirteen, possessed the freshness and promise of spring. After they were married, they fell in love.

They toured Europe, and Kapoor returned, a connoisseur of wine. Kishen was born, looking just like his father. Kapoor never stopped loving his wife, but his passion for her was never so great as when the warmth of old wine filled him with poetry. Meena had a noble nose and forehead ('Aristocratic,' said Kapoor; 'she has blue blood') and long raven-black hair ('Like seaweed,' said Kapoor, dizzy with possessive glory). She was tall, strong, perfectly formed, and she had grace and charm and a quick wit.

Kapoor lived in his beard and green dressing-gown, something of an outcast. The self-made man likes to boast of humble origins and initial poverty, and his rise from rags can be turned to effective publicity; the man who has lost much recalls past exploits and the good name of his family, and the failure at least publicizes these things. But Kapoor had gone full cycle: he could no longer harp on the rise from rags, because he was fast becoming ragged; and he had no background except the one which he himself created and destroyed; he had nothing but a dwindling bank balance, a wife and a son. And the wife was his best asset.

But on the evening of Rusty's second day in the room, no one would have guessed at the family's plight. Rusty sat with them in the front room, and Kapoor extolled the virtues of chewing-gum, much to Kishen's delight and Meena's disgust.

'Chewing gum,' declared Kapoor, waving a finger in the air, 'is the secret of youth. Have you observed the Americans, how young they look, and the English, how haggard? It has nothing to do with responsibilities, it is chewing gum. By chewing, you exercise your jaws and the muscles of your face. This improves your complexion and strengthens the tissues of your skin.'

'You're very clever, Daddy,' said Kishen.

'I'm a genius,' said Kapoor. 'I'm a genius.'

'The fool!' whispered Meena, so that only Rusty could hear.

Rusty said, 'I have an idea, let's form a club.'

'Good idea!' exclaimed Kishen. 'What do we call it?'

'Before we call it anything, we must decide what sort of club it should be. We must have rules, we must have a president, a secretary . . . .'

'All right, all right,' interrupted Kishen who was sprawling on the floor, 'you can be all those things if you like. But what I say is, the most important thing in a club is its name. Without a good name, what's the use of a club?'

'The Fools' Club,' suggested Meena.

'Inappropriate,' said Kapoor, 'inappropriate . . . .'

'Everyone shut up,' ordered Kishen, prodding at his nose, 'I'm trying to think.'

They all shut up and tried to think.

This thinking was a very complicated process, and it soon became obvious that no one had been thinking of the club; for Rusty was looking at Meena thinking, and Meena was wondering if Kishen knew how to think, and Kishen was really thinking about the benefits of chewing gum, and Kapoor was smelling the whisky bottles behind the screen and thinking of them.

At last Kapoor observed: 'My wife is a devil, a beautiful, beautiful devil!'

This seemed an interesting line of conversation, and Rusty was about to follow it up with a compliment of his own, when Kishen burst out brilliantly: 'I know! The Devil's Club? How's that?'

'Ah, ha! exclaimed Kapoor. 'The Devil's Club, we've got it! I'm a genius.'

They got down to the business of planning the club's

activities. Kishen proposed carom and Meena seconded, and Rusty looked dismayed. Kapoor proposed literary and political discussions and Rusty, just to spite the others, seconded the proposal. Then they elected officers of the club. Meena was given the title of Our Lady and Patroness, Kapoor was elected President, Rusty the Secretary, and Kishen the Chief Whip. Somi, Ranbir and Suri, though absent, were accepted as Honorary Members.

'Carom and discussions are not enough,' complained Kishen, 'we must have adventures.'

'What kind?' asked Rusty.

'Climb mountains or something.'

'A picnic,' proposed Meena.

'A picnic!' seconded Kishen, 'and Somi and the others can come too.'

'Let's drink to it,' said Kapoor, rising from his chair, 'let's celebrate.'

'Good idea,' said Kishen, foiling his father's plan of action, 'we'll go to the chaat shop!'

As far as Meena was concerned, the chaat shop was the lesser of the two evils, so Kapoor was bundled into the old car and taken to the bazaar.

'To the chaat shop!' he cried, falling across the steering-wheel. 'We will bring it home!'

The chaat shop was so tightly crowded that people were breathing each other's breath.

The chaat-wallah was very pleased with Rusty for bringing in so many new customers—a whole family—and beamed on the party, rubbing his hands and greasing the frying-pan with enthusiasm.

'Everything!' ordered Kapoor. 'We will have something of everything.'

So the chaat-wallah patted his cakes into shape and flipped them into the sizzling grease; and fashioned his gol-guppas over the fire, filling them with the juice of the devil.

Meena sat curled up on a chair, facing Rusty. The boy stared at her—she looked quaint, sitting in this unfamiliar posture. Her eyes encountered Rusty's stare, mocking it. In hot confusion, Rusty moved his eyes upward, up the wall, on to the ceiling, until they could go no further.

'What are you looking at?' asked Kishen.

Rusty brought his eyes to the ground, and pretended not to have heard. He turned to Kapoor and said, 'What about politics?'

The chaat-wallah handed out four big banana leaves.

But Kapoor wouldn't eat. Instead, he cried: 'Take the chaat shop to the house. Put it in the car, we must have it! We must have it, we must have it!'

The chaat-wallah, who was used to displays of drunkenness in one form or another, humoured Kapoor. 'It is all yours, lallaji, but take me with you too, or who will run the shop?'

'We will!' shouted Kishen, infected by his father's enthusiasm. 'Buy it, Daddy. Mummy can make the tikkees and I'll sell them and Rusty can do the accounts!'

Kapoor threw his banana leaf on the floor and wrapped his arms round Kishen. 'Yes, we will run it! Take it to the house!' And making a lunge at a bowl of chaat, fell to his knees.

Rusty helped Kapoor get up, then looked to Meena for guidance. She said nothing, but gave him a nod, and the boy found he understood the nod.

He said, 'It's a wonderful idea, Mr Kapoor, just put me in charge of everything. You and Meena go home and get a spare room ready for the supplies, and Kishen and I will make all the arrangements with the chaat-wallah.'

Kapoor clung to Rusty, the spittle dribbling down his cheeks. 'Good boy, good boy . . . we will make lots of money together, you and I . . . .' He turned to his wife and waved his arm grandiloquently. 'We will be rich again, Meena, what do you say?'

Meena, as usual, said nothing; but took Kapoor by the arm and bundled him out of the shop and into the car.

'Be quick with the chaat shop!' cried Kapoor.

'I will have it in the house in five minutes,' called Rusty. 'Get everything ready!'

He returned to Kishen, who was stuffing himself with chaat; his father's behaviour did not appear to have affected him, he was unconscious of its ridiculous aspect and felt no shame; he was unconscious too of the considerate manner of the chaat-wallah, who felt sorry for the neglected child. The chaat-wallah did not know that Kishen enjoyed being neglected.

Rusty said, 'Come, let's go . . . .'

'What's the hurry, Rusty? Sit down and eat, there's plenty of dough tonight. At least give Mummy time to put the sleeping-tablets in the whisky.'

So they sat and ate their fill, and listened to other people's gossip; then Kishen suggested that they explore the bazaar.

The oil lamps were lit, and the main road was bright and crowded; but Kishen and Rusty went down an alleyway, where the smells were more complicated and the noise intermittent; two women spoke to each other from their windows on either side of the road, a baby cried monotonously, a cheap gramophone blared. Kishen and Rusty walked aimlessly through the maze of alleyways.

'Why are you white like Suri?' asked Kishen.

'Why is Suri white?'

'He is Kashmiri; they are fair.'

'Well, I am English . . . .'

'English?' said Kishen disbelievingly. 'You? But you do not look like one.'

Rusty hesitated. He did not feel there was any point in raking up a past that was as much a mystery to him as it was to Kishen.

'I don't know,' he said. 'I never saw my parents. And I don't care what they were and I don't care what I am, and I'm not very interested . . . .'

But he couldn't help wondering, and Kishen couldn't help wondering, so they walked on in silence, wondering . . . . They reached the railway station, which was at the end of the bazaar; the gates were closed, but they peered through the railings at the goods wagons. A pleasure house did business near the station.

'If you want to have fun,' said Kishen, 'let's climb that roof. From the skylight you can see everything.'

'No fun in just watching,' said Rusty.

'Have you ever watched?'

'Of course,' lied Rusty, turning homewards; he walked with a distracted air.

'What are you thinking of?' asked Kishen.

'Nothing.'

'You must be in love.'

'That's right.'

'Who is it, eh?'

'If I told you,' said Rusty, 'you'd be jealous.'

'But I'm not in love with anybody. Come on, tell me, I'm your friend.'

'Would you be angry if I said I loved your mother?'

'Mummy!' exclaimed Kishen. 'But she's old! She's married. Hell, who would think of falling in love with Mummy? Don't joke, mister.'

'I'm sorry,' said Rusty.

They walked on in silence and crossed the maidan, leaving the bazaar behind. It was dark on the maidan, they could hardly see each other's faces; Kishen put his hand on Rusty's shoulder.

'If you love her,' he said, 'I'm not jealous. But it sounds funny . . . .'

Chapter Twelve

🐟

In his room, Rusty was a king. His domain was the sky and everything he could see. His subjects were the people who passed below, but they were his subjects only while they were below and he was on the roof; and he spied on them through the branches of the banyan tree. His close confidants were the inhabitants of the banyan tree; which, of course, included Kishen.

It was the day of the picnic, and Rusty had just finished bathing at the water-tank. He had become used to the people at the tank and had made friends with the ayahs and their charges. He had come to like their bangles and bracelets and ankle-bells. He liked to watch one of them at the tap, squatting on her haunches, scrubbing her feet, and making much music with the bells and bangles; she would roll her sari up to the knees to give her legs greater freedom, and crouch forward so that her jacket revealed a modest expanse of waist.

It was the day of the picnic, and Rusty had bathed, and now he sat on a disused chimney, drying himself in the sun.

Summer was coming. The litchis were almost ready to eat, the mangoes ripened under Kishen's greedy eye. In the afternoons the sleepy sunlight stole through the branches of the banyan tree, and made a patchwork of arched shadows on the walls of the house. The inhabitants of the trees knew that summer was coming; Somi's slippers knew it, and slapped lazily against his heels; and Kishen grumbled and became more untidy, and even Suri seemed to be taking a rest from his private investigations. Yes, summer was coming.

And it was the day of the picnic.

The car had been inspected, and the two bottles that Kapoor had hidden in the dickey had been found and removed; Kapoor was put into khaki drill trousers and a bush-shirt and pronounced fit to drive; a basket of food and a gramophone were in the dickey. Suri had a camera slung over his shoulders; Kishen was sporting a Gurkha hat; and Rusty had on a thick leather belt reinforced with steel knobs. Meena had dressed in a hurry, and looked the better for it. And for once, Somi had tied his turban to perfection.

'Everyone present?' said Meena. 'If so, get into the car.'

'I'm waiting for my dog,' said Suri, and he had hardly made the announcement when from around the corner came a yapping mongrel.

'He's called Prickly Heat,' said Suri. 'We'll put him in the back seat.'

'He'll go in the dickey,' said Kishen. 'I can see the lice from here.'

Prickly Heat wasn't any particular kind of dog, just a kind of dog; he hadn't even the stump of a tail. But he had sharp, pointed ears that wagged as well as any tail, and they were working furiously this morning.

Suri and the dog were both deposited in the dickey; Somi, Kishen and Rusty made themselves comfortable in the back seat, and Meena sat next to her husband in the front. The car belched and lurched forward, and stirred up great clouds of dust; then, accelerating, sped out of the compound and across the narrow wooden bridge that spanned the canal.

The sun rose over the forest, and a spiral of smoke from a passing train was caught by a slanting ray and spangled with gold. The air was fresh and exciting. It was ten miles to the river and the sulphur springs, ten miles of intermittent grumbling and gaiety, with Prickly Heat yapping in the dickey and Kapoor whistling at the wheel and Kishen letting fly from the window with a catapult.

Somi said: 'Rusty, your pimples will leave you if you bathe in the sulphur springs.'

'I would rather have pimples than Pneumonia,' replied Rusty.

'But it's not cold,' said Kishen. 'I would bathe myself, but I don't feel very well.'

'Then you shouldn't have come,' said Meena from the front.

'I didn't want to disappoint you all,' said Kishen.

Before reaching the springs, the car had to cross one or two river-beds, usually dry at this time of the year. But the mountains had tricked the party, for there was a good deal of water to be seen, and the current was strong.

'It's not very deep,' said Kapoor at the first river-bed, 'I think we can drive through easily.'

The car dipped forward, rolled down the bank, and entered the current with a great splash. In the dickey, Suri got a soaking.

'Got to go fast,' said Mr Kapoor, 'or we'll stick.'

He accelerated, and a great spray of water rose on both sides of the car. Kishen cried out for sheer joy, but at the back Suri was having a fit of hysterics.

'I think the dog's fallen out,' said Meena.

'Good,' said Somi.

'I think Suri's fallen out,' said Rusty.

'Good,' said Somi.

Suddenly the engines spluttered and choked, and the car came to a standstill.

'We have stuck,' said Kapoor.

'That,' said Meena bitingly, 'is obvious. Now I suppose you want us all to get out and push?'

'Yes, that's a good idea.'

'You're a genius.'

Kishen had his shoes off in a flash, and was leaping about in the water with great abandon. The water reached up to his knees and, as he hadn't been swept off his feet, the others followed his example.

Meena rolled her sari up to the thighs, and stepped gingerly into the current. Her legs, so seldom exposed, were very fair in contrast to her feet and arms, but they were strong and nimble, and she held herself erect. Rusty stumbled to her side, intending to aid her; but ended by clinging to her dress for support. Suri was not to be seen anywhere.

'Where is Suri?' asked Meena.

'Here,' said a muffled voice from the floor of the dickey. 'I've got sick. I can't push.'

'All right,' said Meena. 'But you'll clean up the mess yourself.'

Somi and Kishen were looking for fish. Kapoor tooted the horn.

'Are you all going to push?' he said, 'or are we going to have the picnic in the middle of the river?'

Rusty was surprised at Kapoor's unusual display of common sense; when sober, Mr Kapoor did sometimes have moments of sanity.

Everyone put their weight against the car and pushed with all their strength; and as the car moved slowly forward, Rusty felt a thrill of health and pleasure run through his body. In front of him, Meena pushed silently, the muscles of her thighs trembling with the strain. They all pushed silently, with determination; the sweat ran down Somi's face and neck, and Kishen's jaws worked desperately on his chewing gum. But Kapoor sat in comfort behind the wheel, pressing and pulling knobs, and saying 'harder, push harder', and Suri began to be sick again. Prickly Heat was strangely quiet, and it was assumed that the dog was sick too.

With one last, final heave, the car was moved up the opposite bank and on to the road. Everyone groaned and flopped to the ground. Meena's hands were trembling.

'You shouldn't have pushed,' said Rusty.

'I enjoyed it,' she said, smiling at him. 'Help me to get up.'

He rose, and taking her hand, pulled her to her feet. They stood together, holding hands. Kapoor fiddled around with starters and chokes and things.

'It won't go,' he said. 'I'll have to look at the engine. We might as well have the picnic here.'

So out came the food and lemonade bottles and, miraculously enough, out came Suri and Prickly Heat, looking as fit as ever.

'Hey,' said Kishen, 'we thought you were sick. I suppose you were just making room for lunch.'

'Before he eats anything,' said Somi, 'he's going to get wet. Let's take him for a swim.'

Somi, Kishen and Rusty caught hold of Suri and dragged him along the river-bank to a spot downstream where the current was mild and the water warm and waist-high. They disrobed Suri, took off their own clothes, and ran down the sandy slope to the water's edge. Feet splashed ankle-deep, calves thrust into the current, and then the ground suddenly disappeared beneath their feet.

Somi was a fine swimmer; his supple limbs cut through the water, and when he went under, he was almost as powerful; the chequered colours of his body could be seen first here and then there, twisting and turning, diving and disappearing for what seemed like several minutes, and then coming up under someone's feet.

Rusty and Kishen were amateurs. When they tried swimming underwater, their bottoms remained on the surface, having all the appearance of floating buoys. Suri couldn't swim at all, but though he was often out of his depth and frequently ducked, managed to avoid his death by drowning.

They heard Meena calling them for food and scrambled up the bank, the dog yapping at their heels. They ate in the shade of a poinsettia tree, whose red long-fingered flowers dropped sensually to the running water; and when they had eaten, lay down to sleep or drowse the afternoon away.

When Rusty awoke, it was evening and Kapoor was tinkering about with the car, muttering to himself, a little cross because he hadn't had a drink since the previous night. Somi and Kishen were back in the river, splashing away, and this time they had Prickly Heat for company. Suri wasn't in sight. Meena stood in a clearing at the edge of the forest.

Rusty went up to Meena, but she wandered into the thicket. The boy followed. She must have expected him, for she showed no surprise at his appearance.

'Listen to the jungle,' she said.

'I can't hear anything.'

'That's what I mean. Listen to nothing.'

They were surrounded by silence; a dark, pensive silence, heavy, scented with magnolia and jasmine.

It was shattered by a piercing shriek, a cry that rose on all sides, echoing against the vibrating air; and, instinctively, Rusty put his arm around Meena—whether to protect her or to protect himself, he did not really know—and held her tight.

'It is only a bird,' she said, 'what are you afraid of?'

But he was unable to release his hold, and she made no

effort to free herself. She laughed into his face, and her eyes danced in the shadows. But he stifled her laugh with his lips.

It was a clumsy, awkward kiss, but fiercely passionate, and Meena responded, tightening the embrace, returning the fervour of the kiss. They stood together in the shadows, Rusty intoxicated with beauty and sweetness, Meena with freedom and the comfort of being loved.

A monkey chattered shrilly in a branch above them, and the spell was broken.

'Oh, Meena . . . .'

'Shh . . . you spoil these things by saying them.'

'Oh, Meena . . . .'

They kissed again, but the monkey set up such a racket that they feared it would bring Kapoor and the others to the spot. So they walked through the trees, holding hands.

They were barefoot, but they did not notice the thorns and brambles that pricked their feet; they walked through heavy foliage, nettles and long grass, until they came to a clearing and a stream.

Rusty was conscious of a wild urge, a desire to escape from the town and its people, and live in the forest with Meena, with no one but Meena . . . .

As though conscious of his thoughts, she said: 'This is where we drink. In the trees we eat and sleep, and here we drink.'

She laughed, but Rusty had a dream in his heart. The pebbles on the bed of the stream were round and smooth, taking the flow of water without resistance. Only weed and rock could resist water; only weed or rock could resist life.

'It would be nice to stay in the jungle,' said Meena.

'Let us stay . . . .'

'We will be found. We cannot escape—from—others . . . .'

'Even the world is too small. Maybe there is more freedom in your little room than in all the jungle and all the world.'

Rusty pointed to the stream and whispered, 'Look!'

Meena looked, and at the same time a deer looked up. They looked at each other with startled, fascinated eyes, the deer and Meena. It was a spotted cheetal, a small animal with delicate, quivering limbs and muscles, and green antlers.

Rusty and Meena did not move, nor did the deer; they

might have gone on staring at each other all night if somewhere
a twig hadn't snapped sharply.

At the snap of the twig, the deer jerked its head up with a
start, lifted one foot pensively, sniffed the air; then leapt the
stream and in a single bound, disappeared into the forest.

The spell was broken, the magic lost. Only the water ran on
and life ran on.

'Let's go back,' said Meena.

They walked back through the dappled sunlight, swinging
their clasped hands like two children who had only just
discovered love.

Their hands parted as they reached the river-bed.

Miraculously enough, Kapoor had started the car and was
waving his arms and shouting to everyone to come home.
Everyone was ready to start back except for Suri and Prickly
Heat, who were nowhere to be seen. Nothing, thought Meena,
would have been better than for Suri to disappear for ever, but
unfortunately she had taken full responsibility for his well-
being, and did not relish the thought of facing his strangely
affectionate mother. So she asked Rusty to shout for him.

Rusty shouted, and Meena shouted, and Somi shouted, and
then they all shouted together; only Suri didn't shout.

'He's up to his tricks,' said Kishen. 'We shouldn't have
brought him. Let's pretend we're leaving, then he'll be scared.'

So Kapoor started the engine and everyone got in, and it
was only then that Suri came running from the forest, the dog
at his heels, his shirt-tails flapping in the breeze, his hair
wedged between his eyes and his spectacles.

'Hey, wait for us!' he cried. 'Do you want me to die?'

Kishen mumbled in the affirmative, and swore quietly.

'We thought you were in the dickey,' said Rusty.

Suri and Prickly Heat climbed into the dickey, and at the
same time the car entered the river with a determined splashing
and churning of wheels, to emerge the victor.

Everyone cheered, and Somi gave Kapoor such an
enthusiastic slap on the back that the pleased recipient nearly
caught his head in the steering-wheel.

It was dark now, and all that could be seen of the
countryside was what the headlights showed. Rusty had hopes
of seeing a panther or a tiger, for this was their territory, but

only a few goats blocked the road. However, for the benefit of Suri, Somi told a story of a party that had gone for an outing in a car and on returning home, had found a panther in the dickey.

Kishen fell asleep just before they reached the outskirts of Dehra, his fuzzy head resting on Rusty's shoulder. Rusty felt protective towards the boy, for a bond of genuine affection had grown between the two. Somi was Rusty's best friend, in the same way that Ranbir was a friend, and their friendship was on a high emotional plane. But Kishen was a brother more than a friend. He loved Rusty, but without knowing or thinking or saying it, and that is the love of a brother.

Somi began singing. Then the town came into sight, the bazaar lights twinkling defiance at the starry night.

Chapter Thirteen

❧

Rusty and Mr Harrison met in front of the town's main grocery store, the 'wine and general merchants'; it was part of the smart shopping centre, alien to the bazaar but far from the European community—and thus neutral ground for Rusty and Mr Harrison.

'Hello, Mr Harrison,' said Rusty, confident of himself and deliberately omitting the customary 'sir'.

Mr Harrison tried to ignore the boy, but found him blocking the way to the car. Not wishing to lose his dignity, he decided to be pleasant.

'This is a surprise,' he said, 'I never thought I'd see you again.'

'I found a job,' said Rusty, taking the opportunity of showing his independence. 'I meant to come and see you but didn't get the time.'

'You're always welcome. The missionary's wife often speaks of you, she'd be glad to see you. By the way, what's your job?'

Rusty hesitated; he did not know how his guardian would take the truth—probably with a laugh or a sneer ('you're *teaching*!')—and decided to be mysterious about his activities.

'Baby-sitting,' he replied with a disarming smile. 'Anyway, I'm not starving. And I've got many friends.'

Mr Harrison's face darkened and the corners of his mouth twitched; but he remembered that times had changed, and that Rusty was older and also free, and that he wasn't in his own house; and he controlled his temper.

'I can get you a job', he said. 'On a tea estate. Or, if you'd like to go abroad, I have friend in Guiana . . . .'

'I like baby-sitting,' said Rusty.

Mr Harrison smiled, got into the car, and lit a cigarette before starting the engine. 'Well, as I said, you're always welcome in the house.'

'Thanks,' said Rusty. 'Give my regards to the sweeper boy.'

The atmosphere was getting tense.

'Why don't you come and see him some time?' said Mr Harrison, as softly and as malevolently as he could.

It was just as well the engine had started.

'I will,' said Rusty.

'I kicked him out,' said Mr Harrison, putting his foot down on the accelerator and leaving Rusty in a cloud of dust.

But Rusty's rage turned to pleasure when the car almost collided with a stationary bullock-cart, and a uniformed policeman brought it to a halt. With the feeling that he had been the master of the situation, Rusty walked homewards.

The litchi trees were covered with their pink-skinned fruit, and the mangoes were almost ripe. The mango is a passionate fruit, its inner gold sensuous to the lips and tongue. The grass had not yet made up its mind, whether to remain yellow or turn green, and would probably keep its dirty colour until the monsoon rains arrived.

Meena met Rusty under the banana trees.

'I am bored,' she said, 'so I am going to give you a haircut. Do you mind?'

'I will do anything to please you. But don't take it all off.'

'Don't you trust me?'

'I love you.'

Rusty was wrapped up in a sheet and placed on a chair. He looked up at Meena, and their eyes met, laughing, blue and brown.

Meena cut silently, and the fair hair fell quickly, softly, lightly to the ground. Rusty enjoyed the snip of the scissors and the sensation of lightness; it was as though his mind was being given more room in which to explore.

Kishen came loafing round the corner of the house, still wearing his pyjamas which were rolled up to the knees. When he saw what was going on, he burst into laughter.

'And what is so funny?' asked Rusty.

'You!' spluttered Kishen. 'Where is your hair, your beautiful golden hair? Has Mummy made you become a monk? Or have you got ringworm? Or fleas? Look at the ground, all that beautiful hair!'

'Don't be funny, Kishen,' said Meena, 'or you will get the same treatment.'

'Is it so bad?' asked Rusty anxiously.

'Don't you trust me?' said Meena.

'I love you.'

Meena glanced swiftly at Kishen to see if he had heard the last remark, but he was still laughing at Rusty's haircut and prodding his nose for all he was worth.

'Rusty, I have a favour to ask you,' said Meena. 'Mr Kapoor and I may be going to Delhi for a few weeks, as there is a chance of him getting a good job. We are not taking Kishen, as he is only nuisance value, so will you look after him and keep him out of mischief? I will leave some money with you. About how much will you need for two weeks?'

'When are you going?' asked Rusty, already in the depths of despair.

'How much will you need?'

'Oh, fifty rupees . . . but when—'

'A hundred rupees!' interrupted Kishen. 'Oh boy, Rusty, we'll have fun!'

'Seventy-five,' said Meena, as though driving a bargain, 'and I'll send more after two weeks. But we should be back by then. There, Rusty, your haircut is complete.'

But Rusty wasn't interested in the result of the haircut; he felt like sulking; he wanted to have some say in Meena's plans, he felt he had a right to a little power.

That evening in the front room, he didn't talk much. Nobody spoke. Kishen lay on the ground, stroking his stomach, his toes tracing imaginary patterns on the wall. Meena looked tired; wisps of hair had fallen across her face, and she did not bother to brush them back. She took Kishen's foot and gave it a pull.

'Go to bed,' she said.

'Not tired.'

'Go to bed, or you'll get a slap.'

Kishen laughed defiantly, but got up from the floor and ambled out of the room.

'And don't wake Daddy,' she said.

Kapoor had been put to bed early, as Meena wanted him to be fresh and sober for his journey to Delhi and his interviews there. But every now and then he would wake up and call out for something—something unnecessary, so that after a while no one paid any attention to his requests. He was like an irritable invalid, to be humoured and tolerated.

'Are you not feeling well, Meena?' asked Rusty. 'If you like, I'll also go.'

'I am only tired, don't go . . . .'

She went to the window and drew the curtains and put out the light. Only the table lamp burned. The lampshade was decorated with dragons and butterflies—it was a Chinese lampshade—and as Rusty sat gazing at the light, the dragons began to move and the butterflies to flutter. He couldn't see Meena, but felt her presence across the room.

She turned from the window; and silently, with hardly a rustle, slipped to the ground. Her back against the couch, her head resting against the cushion, she looked up at the ceiling. Neither of them spoke.

From the next room came sounds of Kishen preparing for the night, one or two thumps and a muttered imprecation. Kapoor snored quietly to himself, and the rest was silence.

Rusty's gaze left the revolving dragons and prancing butterflies to settle on Meena, who sat still and tired, her feet lifeless against the table legs, her slippers fallen to the ground. In the lamplight, her feet were like jade.

A moth began to fly round the lamp, and it went round and round and closer, till—with a sudden plop—it hit the lampshade and fell to the ground. But Rusty and Meena were still silent, their breathing the only conversation.

Chapter Fourteen

❧

During the day, flies circled the room with feverish buzzing, and at night the mosquitoes came singing in one's ears; summer days were hot and sticky, the nights breathless. Rusty covered his body in citronella oil which had been given him by Somi's mother; its smell, while pleasant to his own senses, was repugnant to mosquitoes.

When Rusty rubbed the oil on his limbs he noticed the change in his physique. He had lost his puppy fat, and there was more muscle to his body; his complexion was a healthier colour, and his pimples had almost disappeared. Nearly everyone had advised him about his pimples: drink *dahi*, said Somi's mother, don't eat fat; eat carrots, said Somi; plenty of fruit; mangoes! said Kishen; not at all, oranges; see a doctor, said Meena; have a whisky, said Kapoor; but the pimples disappeared without any of these remedies, and Rusty put it down to his falling in love.

The bougainvillaea creeper had advanced further into the room and was now in flower; and watching Rusty oil himself was the bald mina bird; it had been in so many fights that the feathers on its head never got a chance to grow.

Suri entered the room without warning and wiping his spectacles on the bedsheet, said: 'I have written an essay, Mr Rusty, for which I am going to be marked in school. Correct it, if you please.'

'Let me finish with this oil . . . . It would be cheating, you know.'

'No, it wouldn't. It has to be corrected some time, so you

will save the master some trouble. Anyway, I'm leaving this rotten school soon. I'm going to Mussoorie.'

'To the same place as Ranbir? He'll be glad to see you.'

Suri handed Rusty the copy-book. On the cover was a pencil sketch of a rather over-developed nude.

'Don't tell me this is your school book!' exclaimed Rusty.

'No, only rough work.'

'You drew the picture?'

'Of course, don't you like it?'

'Did you copy it, or imagine it, or did someone pose for you?'

Suri winked. 'Someone posed.'

'You're a liar. And a pig.'

'Oh, look who's talking! You're not such a saint yourself, Mr Rusty.'

'Just what do you mean,' said Rusty, getting between Suri and the door.

'I mean, how is Mrs Kapoor, eh?'

'She is fine.'

'You get on well with her, eh?'

'We get on fine.'

'Like at the picnic?'

Suri rubbed his hands together, and smiled beatifically. Rusty was momentarily alarmed.

'What do you mean, the picnic?'

'What did you do together, Mister Rusty, you and Mrs Kapoor? What happened in the bushes?'

Rusty leant against the wall and returned Suri's smile, and said: 'I'll tell you what we did, my friend. There's nothing to hide between friends, is there? Well, Mrs Kapoor and I spent all our time making love. We did nothing but love each other. All the time. And Mr Kapoor only a hundred yards away, and you in the next bush . . . . Now what else do you want to know?'

Suri's smile was fixed. 'What if I tell Mr Kapoor?'

'You won't tell him,' said Rusty.

'Why not?'

'Because you are the last person he'll believe. And you'll probably get a kick in the pants for the trouble.'

Suri's smile had gone.

'Cheer up,' said Rusty. 'What about the essay, do you want me to correct it?'

That afternoon the old car stood beneath the banana trees with an impatient driver tooting on the horn. The dickey and bumpers were piled high with tin trunks and bedding-rolls as though the Kapoors were going away for a lifetime. Meena wasn't going to let Kapoor drive her all the way to Delhi and had taken on a professional instead.

Kapoor sat on the steps of the house, wearing his green dressing-gown and making a throaty noise similar to that of the motor-horn.

'The devil!' he exclaimed, gesticulating towards Meena, who was bustling about indoors. 'The devil of a wife is taking me to Delhi! Ha! The car will never get there.'

'Oh yes, it will,' said Meena, thrusting her head out of the window, 'and it will get there with you in it, whether or not you shave and dress. So you might as well take a seat.'

Rusty went into the house and found Meena locking rooms. She was looking a little tired and irritable.

'You're going sooner than I expected,' said Rusty. 'Has Kishen got the money?'

'No, you must keep it. I'll give it to you in five-rupee notes, wait a minute . . . . He'll have to sleep with you, I'm locking the house . . . .'

She opened a drawer and taking out an envelope, gave it to Rusty.

'The money,' she said. Rusty picked up a small suitcase and followed Meena outside to the car. He waited till she was seated before handing her the case, and when he did, their hands touched. She laced her fingers with his and gave him a quick smile, and squeezed his fingers.

From the front seat Kapoor beckoned Rusty. He grasped the boy's hand and slipped a key into it.

'My friend,' he whispered, 'these are the keys of the back door. In the kitchen you will find six bottles of whisky. Keep them safe until our return.'

Rusty shook Kapoor's hand, the hand of the man he laughed at, but whom he could not help loving as well.

In the confusion Kishen had gone almost unnoticed, but he was there all the time, and now he suffered a light kiss from his mother and a heavy one from his father.

The car belched and after narrowly missing a banana tree, rattled down the gravel path, bounced over a ditch, and disappeared in a cloud of dust.

Kishen and Rusty were flapping their handkerchiefs for all they were worth. Kishen was not a bit sorry that his parents had gone away, but Rusty felt like crying. He was conscious now of a sense of responsibility, which was a thing he did not like having, and of a sense of loss. But the depression was only momentary.

'Hey!' said Kishen. 'Do you see what I see?'

'I can see a lot of things that you can see, so what do you mean?'

'The clothes! Mummy's washing, it is all on the rose bushes!'

Meena had left without collecting her washing which, as always, had been left to dry on the rose bushes. Mr Kapoor's underwear spread itself over an entire bush, and another tree was decorated with bodices and blouses of all colours.

Rusty said: 'Perhaps she means them to dry by the time she comes back.'

He began to laugh with Kishen, so it was a good thing, Meena's forgetfulness; it softened the pain of parting.

'What if we hadn't noticed?' chuckled Kishen. 'They would have been stolen.'

'Then we must reward ourselves. What about the chaat shop, bhai?

At the risk of making himself unpopular, Rusty faced Kishen and with determination, said: 'No chaat shop. We have got seventy rupees to last a month, and I am not going to write for more once this finishes. We are having our meals with Somi. So, bhai, no chaat shop!'

'You are a swine, Rusty.'

'And the same to you.'

In this endearing mood they collected the clothes from the rose bushes, and marched upstairs to the room on the roof.

There was only one bed, and Kishen was a selfish sleeper;

twice during the night Rusty found himself on the floor. Eventually he sat in the chair with his feet on the table, and stared out of the window at the black night. Even if he had been comfortable, he would not have slept; he felt terribly lovesick. He wanted to write a poem, but it was too dark to write. He wanted to write a letter, but she hadn't been away a day. He wanted to run away with Meena into the hills, into the forests, where no one could find them, and he wanted to be with her for ever and never grow old . . . . neither of them must ever grow old . . . .

CHAPTER FIFTEEN

❧

IN THE MORNING THERE was a note from Suri. Rusty wondered how Suri had managed to leave it on the door-step without being seen. It went:

> Tomorrow I'm going up to Mussoorie. This is to request the pleasure of Misters Rusty and Kishen to my goodbye party, five o'clock sharp this same evening.

As soon as it became known that Suri was leaving, everyone began to love him. And everyone brought him presents, just so he wouldn't change his mind and stay.

Kishen bought him a pair of cheap binoculars so that he could look at the girls more closely, and the guests sat down at a table and Suri entertained them in grand style. And they tolerated everything he said and were particularly friendly and gave him three cheers, hooray, hooray, hooray, they were so glad he was going.

They drank lemonade and ate cream cakes (specially obtained from the smart restaurant amongst the smart shops) and Kishen said, 'We are so sorry you are leaving, Suri,' and they had more cream cakes and lemonade, and Kishen said, 'You are like a brother to us, Suri dear'; and when the cream cakes had all been finished, Kishen fell on Suri's neck and kissed him.

It was all very moving, those cream cakes and lemonade and Suri going away.

Kishen made himself sick, and Rusty had to help him back

to the room. Kishen lay prostrate on the bed, whilst Rusty sat in front of the window gazing blankly into the branches of the banyan tree.

Presently he said, 'It's drizzling. I think there'll be a storm, I've never seen the sky so black.'

As though to confirm this observation, there was a flash of lightning in the sky. Rusty's eyes lit up with excitement; he liked storms; sometimes they were an expression of his innermost feelings.

'Shut the window,' said Kishen.

'If I shut the window, I will kill the flowers on the creeper.'

Kishen snorted, 'You're a poet, that's what you are!'

'One day I'll write poems.'

'Why not today?'

'Too much is happening today.'

'I don't think so. Nothing ever happens in Dehra. The place is dead. Why don't you start writing now? You're a great writer, I told you so before.'

'I know.'

'One day . . . one day you'll be a king . . . but only in your dreams . . . . Meanwhile, shut the window!'

But Rusty liked the window open, he liked the rain flecking his face, and he liked to watch it pattering on the leaves of the banyan tree.

'They must have reached Delhi now,' he said, half to himself.

'Daddy's drunk,' said Kishen.

'There's nothing for him to drink.'

'Oh, he'll find something. You know, one day he drank up all the hair oil in the house. Hey, didn't he give you the keys to the back door? Let's drink one of the bottles ourselves . . . .'

Rusty didn't reply. The tense sky shuddered. The blanket of black cloud groaned aloud and the air, which had been still and sultry, trembled with electricity. Then the thunder gave a great clap, and all at once the hailstones came clattering down on the corrugated iron roof.

'What a noise!' exclaimed Kishen. 'You'd think a lot of skeletons were having a fight on the roof!'

The hailstones, as big as marbles, bounced in from the

doorway, and on the roof they were forming a layer of white ice. Through the window Rusty could see one of the ayahs tearing down the gravel path, the pram bouncing madly over the stones, the end of her head-cloth flapping wildly.

'Will you shut the window!' screamed Kishen.

'Why are you so cruel, bhai?'

'I'm not cruel, I'm *sick*! Do you want me to get sick all over the place?'

As gently as he could, Rusty pushed the creeper out of the window and laid it against the outside wall. Then he closed the window. This shut out the view, because the window was made of plywood and had no glass panes.

'And the door,' moaned Kishen.

With the door closed, the room was plunged into darkness.

'What a room,' complained Kishen, 'not even a light. You'll have to live downstairs when they come back.'

'But I like it here.'

The storm continued all night; it made Kishen so nervous that instead of pushing Rusty off the bed, he put his arms around him for protection.

The rain had stopped by morning, but the sky was still overcast and threatening. Rusty and Kishen lay in bed, too bored to bestir themselves. There was some dry fruit in a tin, and they ate the nuts continuously. They could hear the postman making his rounds below, and Rusty suddenly remembered that the postman wouldn't know the Kapoors had left. He leapt out of bed, opened the door and ran to the edge of the roof.

'Hey postman!' he called. 'Anything for Mr and Mrs Kapoor?'

'Nothing,' said the postman, 'but there is something for you, shall I come up?'

But Rusty was already on his way down, certain that it was a letter from Meena.

It was a telegram. Rusty's fingers trembled as he tore it open, and he had read it before he reached the room. His face was white when he entered the room.

'What's wrong,' said Kishen, 'you look sick. Doesn't Mummy love you any more?'

Rusty sat down on the edge of the bed, his eyes staring emptily at the floor.

'You're to go to Hardwar,' he said at last, 'to stay with your aunty.'

'Well, you can tell Mummy I'm staying here.'

'It's from your aunty.'

'Why couldn't Mummy say so herself?'

'I don't want to tell you.'

'But you have to tell me!' cried Kishen, making an ineffectual grab at the telegram. 'You have to tell me, Rusty, you have to!'

There was panic in Kishen's voice, he was almost hysterical.

'All right,' said Rusty, and his own voice was strained and hollow. 'The car had an accident.'

'And something happened to Daddy?'

'No.'

There was a terrible silence. Kishen looked helplessly at Rusty, his eyes full of tears and bewilderment; and Rusty could stand the strain no longer, and threw his arms around Kishen and wept uncontrollably.

'Oh, Mummy, Mummy,' cried Kishen, 'Oh, Mummy . . . .'

CHAPTER SIXTEEN

***

IT WAS LATE EVENING the same day, and the clouds had passed and the whole sky was sprinkled with stars. Rusty sat on the bed, looking out at the stars and waiting for Kishen.

Presently, bare feet sounded on the stone floor and Rusty could make out the sharp lines of Kishen's body against the faint moon in the doorway.

'Why do you creep in like a ghost?' whispered Rusty.

'So as not to wake you.'

'It's still early. Where have you been, I was looking for you.'

'Oh, just walking . . . .'

Kishen sat down beside Rusty, facing the same way, looking at the stars. The moonlight ran over their feet, but their faces were in darkness.

'Rusty,' said Kishen.

'Yes.'

'I don't want to go to Hardwar.'

'I know you don't, bhaiya. But you will not be allowed to stay here. You must go to your relatives. And Hardwar is a beautiful place, and people are kind . . . .'

'I'll stay with you.'

'I can't look after you, Kishen, I haven't got any money, any work . . . . you must stay with your aunt. I'll come to see you.'

'You'll never come.'

'I'll try.'

Every night the jackals could be heard howling in the

nearby jungle, but tonight their cries sounded nearer, much nearer the house.

Kishen slept. He was exhausted—he had been walking all evening, crying his heart out. Rusty lay awake his eyes wide open, brimming with tears. He did not know if the tears were for himself or for Meena or for Kishen, but they were for someone.

Meena is dead, he told himself, Meena is dead.If there is a god, then God will look after her; if God is Love, then my love will be with her. She loved me. I can see her so clearly, her face speckled with sun and shadow when we kissed in the forest, the black waterfall of hair, her tired eyes, her feet like jade in the lamplight, she loved me, she was mine . . . .

Rusty was overcome by a feeling of impotence and futility, and of unimportance of life. Every moment, he told himself, every moment someone is born and someone dies, you can count them one, two, three, a birth and a death for every moment . . . . what is this one life in the whole pattern of life, what is this one death but a passing of time . . . . And if I were to die now, suddenly and without cause, what would happen, would it matter . . . we live without knowing why or to what purpose.

The moon bathed the room in a soft, clear light. The howl of the jackals seemed to be coming from the field below, and Rusty thought, 'A jackal is like death, ugly and cowardly and mad . . . .' He heard a faint sniff from the doorway, and lifted his head.

In the doorway, a dark silhouette against the moonlight, stood the lean, craving form of a jackal, its eyes glittering balefully.

Rusty wanted to scream. He wanted to throw everything in the room at the snivelling, cold-blooded beast, or throw himself out of the window instead. But he could do none of these things.

The jackal lifted its head to the sky and emitted a long, blood-curdling howl that ran like an electric current through Rusty's body. Kishen sprang up with a gasp and threw his arms around Rusty.

And then Rusty screamed.

It was half shout, half scream, and it began in the pit of his stomach, was caught by his lungs, and catapulted into the empty night. Everything around him seemed to be shaking, vibrating to the pitch of the scream.

The jackal fled. Kishen whimpered and sprang back from Rusty and dived beneath the bedclothes.

And as the scream and its echo died away, the night closed in again with a heavy, petrifying stillness; and all that could be heard was Kishen sobbing under the blankets, terrified not so much by the jackal's howl as by Rusty's own terrible scream.

'Oh, Kishen bhai,' cried Rusty, putting his arms around the boy, 'don't cry, please don't cry. You are making me afraid of myself. Don't be afraid, Kishen. Don't make me afraid of myself . . . .'

And in the morning their relationship was a little strained.

Kishen's aunt arrived. She had a tonga ready to take Kishen away. She gave Rusty a hundred rupees, which she said was from Mr Kapoor. Rusty didn't want to take it, but Kishen swore at him and forced him to accept it.

The tonga pony was restless, pawing the ground and champing at the bit, snorting a little. The driver got down from the carriage and held the reins whilst Kishen and his aunt climbed on to their seats.

Kishen made no effort to conceal his misery.

'I wish you would come, Rusty,' he said.

'I will come and see you one day, be sure of that.'

It was very seldom that Kishen expressed any great depth of feeling; he was always so absorbed with comforts of the flesh that he never had any profound thoughts. But he did have profound feelings, though they were seldom thought or spoken.

He grimaced and prodded his nose.

'Inside of me,' he said, 'I am all lonely . . . .'

The driver cracked his whip, the horse snorted, the wheels creaked, and the tonga moved forward. The carriage bumped up in the ditch and it looked as though everyone would be thrown out; but it bumped down again without falling apart, and Kishen and his aunt were still in their seats. The driver jingled his bell and the tonga turned on to the main road that led to the station; the horse's hoofs clip-clopped and the carriage-wheels squeaked and rattled.

Rusty waved. Kishen sat stiff and upright, clutching the ends of his shirt.

Rusty felt afraid for Kishen, who seemed to be sitting on his own, apart from his aunt, as though he disowned or did not know her: it seemed as though he were being borne away to some strange, friendless world where no one would know or care for him; and, though Rusty knew Kishen to be wild and independent, he felt afraid for him.

The driver called to the horse, and the tonga went round the bend in the road and was lost to sight.

Rusty stood at the gate, staring down the empty road. He thought: 'I'll go back to my room and time will run on and things will happen but *this* will not happen again . . . there will still be sun and litchis, and there will be other friends, but there will be no Meena and no Kishen, for our lives have drifted apart . . . . Kishen and I have been going down the river together, but I have been caught in the reeds and he has been swept onwards; and if I do catch up with him, it will not be the same, it might be sad . . . . Kishen has gone, and part of my life has gone with him, and inside of me I am all lonely.'

CHAPTER SEVENTEEN

❧

IT WAS A STICKY, restless afternoon. The water-carrier passed below the room with his skin bag, spraying water on the dusty path. The toy-seller entered the compound, calling his wares in a high-pitched sing-song voice, and presently there was the chatter of children.

The toy-seller had a long bamboo pole, crossed by two or three shorter bamboos from which hung all manner of toys—little celluloid drums, tin watches, tiny flutes and whistles, and multi-coloured rag dolls—and when these ran out, they were replaced by others from a large bag, a most mysterious and fascinating bag, one in which no one but the toy-seller was allowed to took. He was a popular person with rich and poor alike, for his toys never cost more than four annas and never lasted longer than a day.

Rusty liked the cheap toys, and was fond of decorating the room with them. He bought a two-anna flute and walked upstairs, blowing on it.

He removed his shirt and sandals and lay flat on the bed staring up at the ceiling. The lizards scuttled along the rafters, the bald mina hopped along the window-ledge. He was about to fall asleep when Somi came into the room.

Somi looked listless.

'I feel sticky,' he said. 'I don't want to wear any clothes.'

He too pulled off his shirt and deposited it on the table, then stood before the mirror, studying his physique. Then he turned to Rusty.

'You don't look well,' he said, 'there are cobwebs in your hair.'

'I don't care.'

'You must have been very fond of Mrs Kapoor. She was very kind.'

'I loved her, didn't you know?'

'No. My own love is the only thing I know. Rusty, best favourite friend, you cannot stay here in this room, you must come back to my house. Besides, this building will soon have new tenants.'

'I'll get out when they come, or when the landlord discovers I'm living here.'

Somi's usually bright face was somewhat morose, and there was a faint agitation showing in his eyes.

'I will go and get a cucumber to eat,' he said, 'then there is something to tell you.'

'I don't want a cucumber,' said Rusty, 'I want a coconut.'

'I want a cucumber.'

Rusty felt irritable. The room was hot, the bed was hot, his blood was hot. Impatiently, he said: 'Go and eat your cucumber, I don't want any . . . .'

Somi looked at him with pained surprise; then, without a word, picked up his shirt and marched out of the room. Rusty could hear the slap of his slippers on the stairs, and then the bicycle tyres on the gravel path.

'Hey, Somi!' shouted Rusty, leaping off the bed and running out on to the roof. 'Come back!'

But the bicycle jumped over the ditch, and Somi's shirt flapped, and there was nothing Rusty could do but return to bed. He was alarmed at his own ill-temper. He lay down again and stared at the ceiling, at the lizards chasing each other across the rafters. On the roof two crows were fighting, knocking each other's feathers out. Everyone was in a temper.

What's wrong? wondered Rusty. I spoke to Somi in fever, not in anger, but my words were angry. Now I am miserable, fed up. Oh, hell . . . .

He closed his eyes and shut out everything.

He opened his eyes to laughter. Somi's face was close, laughing into Rusty's.

'Of what were you dreaming, Rusty, I have never seen you smile so sweetly!'

'Oh, I wasn't dreaming,' said Rusty, sitting up, and feeling better now that Somi had returned. 'I am sorry for being so grumpy, but I'm not feeling . . . .'

'Quiet,' admonished Somi, putting his finger to the other's lips. 'See, I have settled the matter. Here is a coconut for you, and here is a cucumber for me!'

They sat cross-legged on the bed, facing each other, Somi with his cucumber and Rusty with his coconut. The coconut milk trickled down Rusty's chin and on to his chest, giving him a cool, pleasant sensation.

Rusty said: 'I am afraid for Kishen. I am sure he will give trouble to his relatives, and they are not like his parents. Mr Kapoor will have no say, without Meena.'

Somi was silent. The only sound was the munching of the cucumber and the coconut. He looked at Rusty, an uncertain smile on his lips but none in his eyes; and in a forced conversational manner, said: 'I'm going to Amritsar for a few months. But I will be back in the spring, Rusty, you will be all right here . . . .'

This news was so unexpected that for some time Rusty could not take it in. The thought had never occurred to him that one day Somi might leave Dehra, just as Ranbir and Suri and Kishen had done. He could not speak. A sickening heaviness clogged his heart and brain.

'Hey, Rusty!' laughed Somi. 'Don't look as though there is poison in the coconut!'

The poison lay in Somi's words. And the poison worked, running through Rusty's veins and beating against his heart and hammering on his brain. The poison worked, wounding him.

He said, 'Somi . . .' but could go no further.

'Finish the coconut!'

'Somi,' said Rusty again, 'if you are leaving Dehra, Somi, then I am leaving too.'

'Eat the coco . . . what did you say?'

'I am going too.'

'Are you mad?'

'Not at all.'

Serious now, and troubled, Somi put his hand on his friend's wrist; he shook his head, he could not understand.

'Why, Rusty? Where?'

'England.'

'But you haven't got money, you silly fool!'

'I can get an assisted passage. The British Government will pay.'

'You are a British subject?'

'I don't know . . . .'

'*Toba!*' Somi slapped his thighs and looked upwards in despair. 'You are neither Indian subject nor British subject, and you think someone is going to pay for your passage! And how are you to get a passport?'

'How?' asked Rusty, anxious to find out.

'*Toba!* Have you a birth certificate?'

'Oh, no.'

'Then you are not born,' decreed Somi, with a certain amount of satisfaction. 'You are not alive! You do not happen to be in this world!'

He paused for breath, then waved his finger in the air. 'Rusty, you cannot go!' he said.

Rusty lay down despondently.

'I never really thought I would,' he said, 'I only said I would because I felt like it. Not because I am unhappy—I have never been happier elsewhere—but because I am restless as I have always been. I don't suppose I'll be anywhere for long . . . .'

He spoke the truth. Rusty always spoke the truth. He defined truth as feeling, and when he said what he felt, he said truth. (Only he didn't always speak his feelings.) He never lied. You don't have to lie if you know how to withhold the truth.

'You belong here,' said Somi, trying to reconcile Rusty with circumstance. 'You will get lost in big cities, Rusty, you will break your heart. And when you come back—if you come back—I will be grown up and you will be grown up—I mean more than we are now—and we will be like strangers to each other . . . . And besides, there are no chaat shops in England!'

'But I don't belong here, Somi. I don't belong anywhere. Even if I had papers, I don't belong. I'm a half-caste, I know it, and that is as good as not belonging anywhere.'

What am I saying, thought Rusty, why do I make my inheritance a justification for my present bitterness? No one has cast me out . . . of my own free will I run away from India . . . why do I blame inheritance?

'It can also mean that you belong everywhere,' said Somi. 'But you never told me. You are fair like a European.'

'I had not thought much about it.'

'Are you ashamed?'

'No. My guardian was. He kept it to himself, he only told me when I came home after playing Holi. I was happy then. So when he told me, I was not ashamed, I was proud.'

'And now?'

'Now? Oh, I can't really believe it. Somehow I do not really feel mixed.'

'Then don't blame it for nothing.'

Rusty felt a little ashamed, and they were both silent awhile, then Somi shrugged and said: 'So you are going. You are running away from India.'

'No, not from India.'

'Then you are running away from your friends, from me!'

Rusty felt the irony of this remark, and allowed a tone of sarcasm into his voice.

'*You*, Master Somi, *you* are the one who is going away. I am still here. *You* are going to Amritsar. I only *want* to go. And I'm here alone; everyone has gone. So if I do eventually leave, the only person I'll be running away from will be myself!'

'Ah!' said Somi, nodding his head wisely. 'And by running away from yourself, you will be running away from me and from India! Now come on, let's go and have chaat.'

He pulled Rusty off the bed, and pushed him out of the room. Then, at the top of the steps, he leapt lightly on Rusty's back, kicked him with his heels, and shouted: 'Down the steps, my *tutoo*, my pony! Fast down the steps!'

So Rusty carried him downstairs and dropped him on the grass. They laughed, but there was no great joy in their laughter—they laughed for the sake of friendship.

'Best favourite friend,' said Somi, throwing a handful of mud in Rusty's face.

CHAPTER EIGHTEEN

&

N<small>OW EVERYONE HAD GONE</small> from Dehra. Meena would never return, and it seemed unlikely that Kapoor could come back. Kishen's departure was final. Ranbir would be in Mussoorie until the winter months, and this was still summer and it would be even longer before Somi returned. Everyone Rusty knew well had left, and there remained no one he knew well enough to love or hate.

There were, of course, the people at the water-tank—the servants, the ayahs, the babies—but they were busy all day. And when Rusty left them, he had no one but himself and memory for company.

He wanted to forget Meena. If Kishen had been with him, it would have been possible; the two boys would have found comfort in their companionship. But alone, Rusty realized he was not the master of himself.

And Kapoor. For Kapoor, Meena had died perfect. He suspected her of no infidelity. And, in a way, she had died perfect; for she had found a secret freedom. Rusty knew he had judged Kapoor correctly when scoring Suri's threat of blackmail; he knew Kapoor couldn't believe a single disparaging word about Meena.

And Rusty returned to his dreams, that wonderland of his, where he walked in perfection. He spoke to himself quite often, and sometimes he spoke to the lizards.

He was afraid of the lizards, afraid and at the same time fascinated. When they changed their colours from brown to red to green, in keeping with their immediate surroundings, they fascinated him. But when they lost their grip on the ceiling and fell to the ground with a soft, wet, boneless smack, they repelled him. One night, he reasoned, one of them would most certainly fall on his face . . . .

An idea he conceived one afternoon nearly sparked him into sudden and feverish activity. He thought of making a garden on the roof, beside his room.

The idea took his fancy to such an extent that he spent several hours planning the layout of the flower beds, and visualizing the completed picture, with marigolds, zinnias and cosmos blooming everywhere. But there were no tools to be had, mud and bricks would have to be carried upstairs, seeds would have to be obtained; and who knows, thought Rusty, after all that trouble the roof might cave in, or the rains might spoil everything . . . and anyway, he was going away . . . .

His thoughts turned inwards. Gradually, he returned to the same frame of mind that had made life with his guardian so empty and meaningless; he began to fret, to dream, to lose his grip on reality. The full life of the past few months had suddenly ended, and the present was lonely and depressing; the future became a distorted image created out of his own brooding fancies.

One evening, sitting on the steps, he found himself fingering a key. It was the key Kapoor has asked him to keep, the key to the back door. Rusty remembered the whisky bottles—'let's drink them ourselves' Kishen had said—and Rusty thought, 'why not, why not . . . a few bottles can't do any harm . . .' and before he could have an argument with himself, the back door was open.

In his room that night he drank the whisky neat. It was the first time he had tasted alcohol, and he didn't find it pleasant. But he wasn't drinking for pleasure, he was drinking with the sole purpose of shutting himself off from the world, and forgetting.

He hadn't drunk much when he observed that the roof had a definite slant—it seemed to slide away from his door to the field below, like a chute. The banyan tree was suddenly swarming with bees. The lizards were turning all colours at once, like pieces of rainbow.

When he had drunk a little more, he began to talk—not to himself any more, but to Meena, who was pressing his head and trying to force him down on the pillows. He struggled against Meena, but she was too powerful, and he began to cry.

Then he drank a little more. And now the floor began to wobble, and Rusty had a hard time keeping the table from toppling over. The walls of the room were caving in. He swallowed another mouthful of whisky, and held the wall up with his hands. He could deal with anything now. The bed was rocking, the chair was sliding about, the table was slipping, the walls were swaying, but Rusty had everything under control. He was everywhere at once, supporting the entire building with his bare hands.

And then he slipped, and everything came down on top of him, and it was black.

In the morning when he awoke, he threw the remaining bottles out of the window and cursed himself for a fool, and went down to the water-tank to bathe.

Days passed, dry and dusty, every day the same. Regularly, Rusty filled his earthen *sohrai* at the water-tank and soaked the reed mat that hung from the doorway. Sometimes, in the field, the children played cricket, but he couldn't summon up the energy to join them. From his room he could hear the sound of ball and bat, the shouting, the lone voice raised in shrill disagreement with some unfortunate umpire . . . or the thud of a football, or the clash of hockey-sticks . . . but better than these sounds was the jingle of the bells and bangles on the feet of the ayahs, as they busied themselves at the water-tank.

Time passed, but Rusty did not know it was passing. It was like living in a house near a river, and the river was always running past the house, on and away. But to Rusty, living in the house, there was no passing of the river; the water ran on, the river remained.

He longed for something to happen.

CHAPTER NINETEEN

❧

DUST. IT BLEW UP in great clouds, swirling down the road, clutching and clinging to everything it touched—burning, choking, stinging dust.

Then thunder.

The wind dropped suddenly, there was a hushed expectancy in the air. And then, out of the dust came big black rumbling clouds.

Something was happening.

At first there was a lonely drop of water on the window-sill, then a patter on the roof. Rusty felt a thrill of anticipation, and a mountain of excitement. The rains had come to break the monotony of the summer months—the monsoon had arrived!

The sky shuddered, the clouds groaned, a fork of lightning struck across the sky, and then the sky itself exploded.

The rain poured down, drumming on the corrugated roof. Rusty's vision was reduced to about twenty yards; it was as though the room had been cut off from the rest of the world by an impenetrable wall of water.

The rains had arrived, and Rusty wanted to experience to the full the novelty of that first shower. He threw off his clothes and ran naked on to the roof, and the wind sprang up and whipped the water across his body so that he writhed in ecstasy. The rain was more intoxicating than the alcohol, and it was with difficulty that he restrained himself from shouting and dancing in mad abandon. The force and freshness of the rain brought tremendous relief, washed way the stagnation that had been settling on him, poisoning mind and body.

The rain swept over the town, cleansing the sky and earth. The trees bent beneath the force of wind and water. The field was a bog, flowers flattened to the ground.

Rusty returned to the room, exhilarated, his body weeping. He was confronted by a flood. The water had come in through the door and the window and the skylight, and the floor was flooded ankle-deep. He took to his bed.

The bed took on the glamour of a deserted island in the middle of the ocean. He dried himself on the sheets, conscious of a warm, sensuous glow. Then he sat on his haunches and gazed out through the window.

The rain thickened, the tempo quickened. There was the banging of a door, the swelling of a gutter, the staccato splutter of the rain rhythmically persistent on the roof. The drain-pipe coughed and choked, the curtain flew to its limit; the lean trees swayed, swayed, bowed with the burden of wind and weather. The road was a rushing torrent, the gravel path inundated with little rivers. The monsoon had arrived!

But the rain stopped as unexpectedly as it had begun. Suddenly it slackened, dwindled to a shower, petered out. Stillness. The dripping of water from the drain-pipe drilled into the drain. Frogs croaked, hopping around in the slush.

The sun came out with a vengeance. On leaves and petals, drops of water sparkled like silver and gold. A cat emerged from a dry corner of the building, blinking sleepily, unperturbed and unenthusiastic.

The children came running out of their houses.

'Barsaat, barsaat!' they shouted. 'The rains have come!'

The rains had come. And the roof became a general bathing-place. The children, the night-watchmen, the dogs, all trooped up the steps to sample the novelty of a freshwater shower on the roof.

The maidan became alive with footballs. The game was called monsoon football, it was played in slush, in mud that was ankle-deep; and the football was heavy and slippery and difficult to kick with bare feet. The bazaar youths played barefoot because, in the first place, boots were too cumbersome for monsoon football, and in the second place they couldn't be afforded.

But the rains brought Rusty only a momentary elation, just

as the first shower had seemed fiercer and fresher than those which followed; for now it rained every day . . . .

Nothing could be more depressing than the dampness, the mildew, and the sunless heat that wrapped itself round the steaming land. Had Somi or Kishen been with Rusty, he might have derived some pleasure from the elements; had Ranbir been with him, he might have found adventure. But alone, he found only boredom.

He spent an idle hour watching the slow dripping from the pipe outside the door. Where do I belong, he wondered, what am I doing, what is going to happen to me . . . .

He was determined to break away from the atmosphere of timelessness and resignation that surrounded him, and decided to leave Dehra.

'I must go,' he told himself. 'I do not want to rot like the mangoes at the end of the season, or burn out like the sun at the end of the day. I cannot live like the gardener, the cook and the water-carrier, doing the same task every day of my life. I am not interested in today, I want tomorrow. I cannot live in this same small room all my life, with a family of lizards, living in other people's homes and never having one of my own. I *have* to break away. I want to be either somebody or nobody. I don't want to be anybody.'

He decided to go to Delhi and see the High Commissioner for the United Kingdom, who was sure to give him an assisted passage to England, and he wrote to Somi, telling him of this plan. On his way he would have to pass through Hardwar, and there he would see Kishen. He had the aunt's address.

At night he slept brokenly, thinking and worrying about the future. He would listen to the vibrant song of the frog who wallowed in the drain at the bottom of the steps, and to the unearthly cry of the jackal, and questions would come to him, disturbing questions about loving and leaving and living and dying, questions that crowded out his sleep.

But on the night before he left Dehra, it was not the croaking of the frog or the cry of the jackal that kept him awake, or the persistent questioning, but a premonition of crisis and of an end to something.

CHAPTER TWENTY

THE POSTMAN BROUGHT A letter from Somi.

> Dear Rusty, best favourite friend,
>
> Do not ever travel in a third-class compartment. All the way to Amritsar I had to sleep standing up, the carriage was so crowded.
>
> I shall be coming back to Dehra in the spring, in time to watch you play Holi with Ranbir. I know you feel like leaving India and running off to England, but wait until you see me again, all right? You are afraid to die without having done something. You are afraid to die, Rusty, but you have hardly begun to live.
>
> I know you are not happy in Dehra, and you must be lonely. But wait a little, be patient, and the bad days will pass. We don't know why we live. It is no use trying to know. But we have to live, Rusty, because we really want to. And as long as we want to, we have got to find something to live for, and even die for it. Mother is keeping well and sends you her greetings. Tell me whatever you need.
>
> Somi

Rusty folded the letter carefully and put it in his shirt pocket—

he meant to keep it for ever. He could not wait for Somi's return, but he knew that their friendship would last a lifetime, and that the beauty of it would always be with him. In and out of Rusty's life, his turban at an angle, Somi would go; his slippers slapping against his heels for ever . . . .

Rusty had no case or bedding-roll to pack, no belongings at all—only the clothes he wore, which were Somi's, and about fifty rupees, for which he had to thank Kishen. He had made no preparations for the journey; he would slip away without fuss or bother, insignificant, unnoticed . . . .

An hour before leaving for the station, he lay down to rest. He gazed up at the ceiling where the lizards scuttled about, callous creatures, unconcerned with his departure: one human was just the same as any other. And the bald mina, hopping on and off the window-sill, would continue to fight and lose more feathers; and the crows and the squirrels in the mango tree, they would be missed by Rusty, but they would not miss him. It was true, one human was no different from any other— except to a dog or a human . . . .

When Rusty left the room, there was activity at the water-tank—clothes were being beaten on the stone, and the ayah's trinkets were jingling away. Rusty couldn't bear to say goodbye to the people at the water-tank, so he didn't close his door, lest they suspect him of leaving. He descended the steps—twenty-two of them, he counted for the last time—and crossed the drain, and walked slowly down the gravel path until he was out of the compound.

He crossed the maidan, where a group of students were playing cricket, whilst another group wrestled; prams were wheeled in and out of the sporting youths; young girls gossiped away the morning. And Rusty remembered his first night in the maidan, when he had been frightened and wet and lonely. And now, though the maidan was crowded, he felt the same loneliness, the same isolation. In the bazaar, he walked with a heavy heart. From the chaat shop came the familiar smell of spices and the crackle of frying fat. And the children bumped him, and the cows blocked the road, and though he knew they always did these things, it was only now that he noticed them. They all seemed to be holding him, pulling him back.

But he could not return. He was afraid of what lay ahead,

he dreaded the unknown, but it was easier to walk forwards than backwards.

The toy-seller made his way through the crowd, children clustering round him, tearing at his pole. Rusty fingered a two-anna piece, and his eye picked out a little plume of red feathers that seemed to have no useful purpose, and he was determined to buy it.

But before he could make the purchase, someone plucked at his shirt-sleeve.

'Chotta sahib, Chotta sahib,' said the sweeper boy, Mr Harrison's servant.

Rusty could not mistake the shaven head and the sparkle of white teeth, and wanted to turn away, to ignore the sweeper boy, who was linked up with a past that was distant and yet uncomfortably close. But the hand plucked at his sleeve and Rusty felt ashamed, angry with himself for trying to ignore someone who had never harmed him and who couldn't have been friendlier. Rusty was a sahib no longer, no one was his servant. He was not an Indian, he had no caste, he could not call another untouchable . . . .

'You are not at work?' asked Rusty.

'No work', the sweeper boy smiled, a flash of white in the darkness of his face.

'What of Mr Harrison, the sahib?'

'Gone.'

'Gone,' said Rusty, and was surprised at not being surprised. 'Where has he gone?'

'Don't know, but he gone for good. Before he go, I get sack. I drop the bathroom water on veranda, and the sahib, he hit me on the head with his hand, *put*! . . . I say, Sahib you are cruel, and he say cruelty to animals, no? Then he tell me I get sack, he leaving anyway. I lose two days pay.'

Rusty was filled with both relief and uncertainty, and for the same reason. Now there could never be a return—whether he wanted to or not, he could never go back to his old home.

'What about the others?' asked Rusty.

'They still there. Missionary's wife a fine lady, she give me five rupees before I go '

'And you? You are working now?'

Again the sweeper boy flashed his smile. 'No work . . . .'

Rusty didn't dare offer the boy any money, though it would probably have been accepted. In the sweeper boy he saw nobility, and he could not belittle nobility.

'I will try to get you work,' he said, forgetting that he was on his way to the station to buy a one-way ticket, and told the sweeper boy where he lived.

Instinctively, the sweeper boy did not believe him. He nodded his head automatically, but his eyes signified disbelief. And when Rusty left him, he was still nodding—to nobody in particular.

On the station platform the coolies pushed and struggled, shouted incomprehensibly, lifted heavy trunks with apparent ease. Merchants cried their wares, trundling barrows up and down the platform—soda-water, oranges, betel-nut, halwai sweets . . . . The files swarmed around the open stalls, clustered on glass-covered sweet boxes; the mongrel dogs, ownerless and unfed, roved the platform and railway lines, hunting for scraps of food and stealing at every opportunity.

Ignoring Somi's advice, Rusty bought a third-class ticket and found an empty compartment. The guard blew his whistle, but nobody took any notice. People continued about their business, certain that the train wouldn't start for another ten minutes—the Hardwar Mail never did start on time.

Rusty was the only person in the compartment until a fat lady, complaining volubly, oozed in through the door and spread herself across an entire bunk; her plan, it seemed, was to discourage other passengers from coming in. She had beady little eyes set in a big moon face, and they looked at Rusty in curiosity, darting away whenever they met his.

Others came in, in quick succession now, for the guard had blown his whistle a second time. A young woman with a baby, a soldier in uniform, a boy of about twelve . . . . they were all poor people except for the fat lady, who travelled third-class in order to save money.

The guard's whistle blew again, but the train still refused to start. Being the Hardwar Mail, this was but natural. No one ever expected the Hardwar Mail to start on time, for in all its history, it hadn't done so (not even during the time of the

British), and for it to do so now would be a blow to tradition. Everyone was for tradition, and so the Hardwar Mail was not permitted to arrive and depart at the appointed hour; though it was feared that one day some young fool would change the appointed hours. And imagine what would happen if the train did leave on time—the entire railway system would be thrown into confusion for, needless to say, every other train took its time from the Hardwar Mail . . . .

So the guard kept blowing his whistle, and the vendors put their heads in at the windows, selling oranges and newspapers and soda-water . . . .

'Soda-water!' exclaimed the fat lady. 'Who wants soda-water! Why, our farmer here has with him a *surahi* of pure cool water, and he will share it with us, will he not? Paan-wallah! Call the man, quick, he is not even stopping at the window!'

The guard blew his whistle again.

And they were off.

The Hardwar Mail, true to tradition, pulled out of Dehra station half an hour late.

Perhaps it was because Rusty was leaving Dehra for ever that he took an unusual interest in everything he saw and heard. Things that would not normally have been noticed by him, now made vivid impressions on his mind—the gesticulations of the coolies as the train drew out of the station, a dog licking a banana skin, a naked child alone amongst a pile of bundles, crying its heart out . . . .

The platform, fruit-stalls, advertisement boards, all slipped away.

The train gathered speed, the carriages groaned and creaked and rocked crazily. But as they left the town and the station behind, the wheels found their rhythm, beating time with the rails and singing a song.

It was a sad song, persistent and fatalistic.

Another life was finishing.

One morning, months ago, Rusty had heard a drum in the forest, a single drum-beat, dhum-tap; and in the stillness of the morning it had been a call, a message, an irresistible force. He had cut away from his roots, he had been replanted, had sprung to life, new life. But it was too quick a growth, rootless, and he had withered. And now he had run away again. No drum now—instead, the pulsating throb and tremor of the train rushing him away, away from India, from Somi, from the chaat shop and the bazaar. And he did not know why, except that he was lost and lonely and tired and old. Nearly seventeen, but old . . . .

The little boy beside him knelt in front of the window and counted the telegraph posts as they flashed by. They seemed, after a while, to be hurtling past whilst the train stood stationary. Only the rocking of the carriage could be felt.

The train sang through the forests, and sometimes the child waved his hand excitedly and pointed out a deer, the sturdy sambhar or delicate cheetal. Monkeys screamed from tree-tops or loped beside the train, mothers with their young clinging to their breasts. The jungle was heavy, shutting off the sky, and it was like this for half an hour. Then the train came into the open, and the sun struck through the carriage windows. They swung through cultivated land, maize and sugar-cane fields; past squat, mud-hut villages and teams of bullocks ploughing up the soil, leaving behind only a trail of curling smoke.

Children ran out from the villages—brown, naked children—and waved to the train, crying words of greeting. And the little boy in the compartment waved back and shouted merrily, and then turned to look at his travelling companions, his eyes shining with pleasure.

The child began to chatter about this and that, and the others listened to him good-humouredly—the farmer with simplicity and a genuine interest, the fat lady with a tolerant smile, and the soldier with an air of condescension. The young woman and the baby were both asleep. Rusty felt sleepy himself, and was unable to listen to the small boy. Vaguely, he thought of Kishen, and of how surprised and pleased Kishen would be to see him.

Presently he fell asleep.

When he awoke, the train was nearing Hardwar. He had slept for almost an hour, but to him it seemed like five minutes.

His throat was dry, and though his shirt was soaked with

perspiration, he shivered a little. His hands trembled and he had to close his fists to stop the trembling.

At midday the train steamed into Hardwar station and disgorged its passengers.

The fat lady, who was determined to be the first out of the compartment, jammed the doorway. But Rusty and the soldier outwitted her by climbing out of the window.

Rusty felt better once he was outside the station, but he knew he had a fever. The rocking of the train continued and the song of the wheels and the rails kept beating in his head. He walked slowly away from the station, comforted by the thought that at Kishen's aunt's house there would be food and rest. At night, he would catch the Delhi train.

CHAPTER TWENTY-ONE

❧

THE HOUSE WAS ON top of a hill, and from the road Rusty could see the river below, and the temples, and hundreds of people moving about on the long graceful steps that sloped down to the water. For the river was holy, and Hardwar sacred, a place of pilgrimage.

He knocked on the door, and presently there was the sound of bare feet on a stone floor. The door was opened by a lady, but she was a stranger to Rusty and they looked at each other with puzzled, questioning eyes.

'Oh . . . namaste ji,' faltered Rusty. 'Does—does Mr Kapoor or his sister live here?'

The lady of the house did not answer immediately. She looked at the boy with a detached interest, trying to guess at his business and intentions. She was dressed simply and well, she had a look of refinement, and Rusty felt sure that her examination of him was no more than natural curiosity.

'Who are you, please?' she asked.

'I am a friend from Dehra. I am leaving India and I want to see Mr Kapoor and his son before I go. Are they here?'

'Only Mr Kapoor is here,' she said. 'You can come in.'

Rusty wondered where Kishen and his aunt could be, but he did not want to ask this strange lady. He felt ill at ease in her presence, and the house seemed to be hers. Coming straight into the front room from bright sunshine, his eyes took a little time to get used to the dark, but after a moment or two he made out the form of Mr Kapoor, sitting in a cushioned armchair.

'Hello, Mister Rusty,' said Kapoor. 'It is nice to see you.'

There was a glass of whisky on the table, but Kapoor was not drunk. He was shaved and dressed, and looked a good deal younger than when Rusty had last seen him. But something else was missing. His jovial friendliness, his enthusiasm, had gone. This Kapoor was a different man from the Kapoor of the beard and green dressing-gown.

'Hello, Mister Kapoor,' said Rusty. 'How are you?'

'I am fine, jut fine. Sit down, please. Will you have a drink?'

'No thanks. I came to see you and Kishen before leaving for England. I wanted to see you again, you were very kind to me . . . .'

'That's all right, quite all right. I'm very glad to see you, but I'm afraid Kishen isn't here. By the way, the lady who just met you at the door—I haven't introduced you yet—this is my wife, Mister Rusty . . . I . . . I married again shortly after Meena's death.'

Rusty looked at the new Mrs Kapoor in considerable bewilderment, and greeted her quietly. It was not unusual for a man to marry again soon after his wife's death, and he knew it, but his heart was breaking with a fierce anger. He was revolted by the rapidity of it all. Hardly a month had passed, and here was Kapoor with another wife. Rusty remembered that it was for this man Kapoor—this weakling, this drunkard, this self-opinionated, selfish drunkard—that Meena had given her life, when there was no more fight in him and no more love in him and no more pride in him. Had she left then, she would be alive, and he—*he* would be dead . . . .

Rusty was not interested in the new Mrs Kapoor. For Kapoor, he had only contempt.

'Mister Rusty is a good friend of the family,' Kapoor was saying. 'In Dehra he was a great help to Kishen.'

'How did Meena die?' asked Rusty, determined to hurt Kapoor—if Kapoor could be hurt . . . .

'I thought you knew. We had an accident. Let us not talk of it, Mister Rusty . . . .'

'The driver was driving, of course?'

Kapoor did not answer immediately, but raised his glass and sipped from it.

'Of course,' he said.

'How did it all happen?'

'Please, Mister Rusty, I do not want to describe it. We were going too fast, and the car left the road and hit a tree. I can't describe it, Mister Rusty.'

'No, of course not,' said Rusty. 'Anyway, I am glad nothing happened to you. It is also good that you have mastered your natural grief and started a new life. I am afraid I am not as strong as you. Meena was wonderful, and I still can't believe she is dead.'

'We have to carry on . . . .'

'Of course. How is Kishen, I would like to see him.'

'He is in Lucknow with his aunt,' said Kapoor. 'He wished to stay with her.'

Mrs Kapoor had been quiet till now.

'Tell him the truth,' she said. 'There is nothing to hide.'

'You tell him then.'

'What do you mean?'

'He ran away from us. As soon as his aunt left, he ran away. We tried to make him come back, but it was useless, so now we don't try. But he is in Hardwar. We are always hearing about him. They say he is the most cunning thief on both sides of the river.'

'Where can I find him?'

'I don't know. He is wanted by the police. He robs for others, and they pay him. It is easier for a young boy to steal than it is for a man, and as he is quite a genius at it, his services are in demand. And I am sure he would not hesitate to rob us too . . . .'

'But you must know where I can find him,' persisted Rusty. 'You must have some idea.'

'He has been seen along the river and in the bazaar. I don't know where he lives. In a tree, perhaps, or in a temple, or in a brothel. He is somewhere in Hardwar, but exactly where I do not know . . . no one knows. He speaks to no one and runs from everyone. What can you want with him?'

'He is my friend,' said Rusty.

'He will rob you too.'

'The money I have is what he gave me.'

He rose to leave. He was tired, but he did not want to stay much longer in this alien house.

'You are tired,' said Mrs Kapoor. 'Will you rest, and have your meal with us?'

'No,' said Rusty, 'there isn't time.'

CHAPTER TWENTY-TWO

❧

ALL HOPE LEFT RUSTY as he staggered down the hill, weak and exhausted. He could not think clearly. He knew he hadn't eaten since morning, and cursed himself for not accepting Mrs Kapoor's hospitality.

He was hungry, he was thirsty, he was tormented by thoughts of what might have happened to Kishen, of what might happen . . . .

He stumbled down the long steps that led to the water. The sun was strong, striking up from the stone and shimmering against the great white temple that overlooked the river. He crossed the courtyard and came to the water's edge.

Lying on his belly on the river bank, he drank of the holy waters. Then he pulled off his shirt and sandals and slipped into the water. There were men and women on all sides, praying with their faces to the sun. Great fish swam round them, unafraid and unmolested, safe in the sacred waters of the Ganges.

When he had bathed and refreshed himself, Rusty climbed back on to the stone bank. His sandals and shirt had disappeared.

No one was near except a beggar leaning on a stick, a young man massaging his body with oil, and a cow examining an empty, discarded basket. And, of the three, the cow was the most likely suspect—it had probably eaten the sandals.

But Rusty no longer cared what happened to his things. His money was in the leather purse attached to his belt, and as long as he had the belt, he had both money and pyjamas.

He rolled the wet pyjamas up to his thighs, then, staring ahead with unseeing eyes, ignoring the bowls that were thrust before him by the beggars, he walked the length of the courtyard that ran parallel to the rising steps.

Children were shouting at each other, priests chanted their prayers, vendors with baskets on their heads—baskets of fruit and chaat—gave harsh cries, and the cows pushed their way around at will. Steps descended from all parts of the hill—broad, clean steps from the temple, and narrow, winding steps from the bazaars. A maze of alleyways zigzagged about the hill, through the bazaar, round the temples, along the river, and were lost amongst themselves and found again and lost . . . . .

Kishen, barefoot and ragged and thin, but with the same supreme confidence in himself, leant against the wall of an alleyway, and watched Rusty's progress along the river bank.

He wanted to shout to Rusty, go to him, embrace him, but he could not do these things. He did not understand the reason for his friend's presence, he could not reveal himself for fear of a trap. He was sure it was Rusty he watched, for who else was there with the same coloured hair and skin who would walk half-naked in Hardwar? It was Rusty, but why . . . was he in trouble, was he sick? Why, why . . . .

Rusty saw Kishen in the alleyway. He was too weak to shout. He stood in the sun and looked up the steps at Kishen standing in the alleyway.

Kishen did not know whether to run to Rusty, or run away. He too stood still at the entrance of the alley.

'Hallo Rusty,' he called.

And Rusty began to walk up the steps, slowly and painfully, his feet burning, his head reeling, his heart thundering with conflicting emotions.

'Are you alone?' called Kishen. 'Don't come if you are not alone.'

Rusty advanced up the steps until he was in the alleyway facing Kishen. Despite the haze before his eyes, he noticed Kishen's wild condition—the bones protruded from the boy's skin, his hair was knotted and straggly, his eyes danced, searching the steps for others.

'Why are you here, Rusty?'

'To see you . . . .'

'Why?'

'I am going away.'

'How can you go anywhere? You look sick enough to die.'

'I came to see you, anyway.'

'Why?'

Rusty sat down on a step. His wrists hung loose on his knees, and his head drooped forward.

'I'm hungry,' he said.

Kishen walked into the open, and approached a fruit-vendor. He came back with two large water-melons.

'You have money?' asked Rusty.

'No. Just credit. I bring them profits, they give me credit.'

He sat down beside Rusty, produced a small but wicked-looking knife from the folds of his shirt, and proceeded to slice the melons in half.

'You can't go away,' he said.

'I can't go back.'

'Why not?'

'No money, no job, no friends.'

They put their teeth into the water-melon and ate at terrific speed. Rusty felt much refreshed—he put his weakness and fever down to an empty stomach.

'I'll be no good as a bandit,' said Rusty. 'I can be recognized at sight, I can't go around robbing people, I don't think it's very nice anyway.'

'I don't rob poor people,' objected Kishen, prodding his nose. 'I only rob those who've got something to be robbed. And I don't do it for myself, that's why I'm never caught. People pay me to do their dirty work. Like that, they are safe because they are somewhere else when everything happens, and I am safe because I don't have what I rob, and haven't got a reason for taking it anyway . . . so it is quite safe. But don't worry, bhai, we will not do it in Dehra, we are too well-known there. Besides, I am tired of running from the police.'

'Then what will we do?'

'Oh, we will find someone for you to give English lessons. Not one, but many. And I will start a chaat shop.'

'When do we go?' said Rusty. And England and fame and riches were all forgotten, and would soon be dreams again.

'Tomorrow morning, early,' said Kishen. 'There is a boat crossing the river. We must cross the river, for on this side I am known, and there are many people who would not like me to leave. If we went by train, I would be caught at the station for sure. On the other side no one knows me, there is only jungle.'

Rusty was amazed at how competent and practical Kishen had become. Kishen's mind had developed far quicker than his body, and he was a funny cross between an experienced adventurer and a ragged urchin. A month ago he had clung to Rusty for protection; now Rusty looked to Kishen for guidance.

I wonder, thought Rusty, will they notice my absence in Dehra? After all, I have only been away a day, though it seems an age . . . the room on the roof will still be vacant when I return, no one but me could be crazy enough to live in such a room . . . . I will go back to the room as though nothing had happened, and no one will notice that anything has.

The afternoon ripened into evening.

As the sun sank, the temple changed from white to gold, from gold to orange, from orange to pink, and from pink to crimson, and all these colours were in turn reflected in the surrounding waters.

The noise subsided gradually, the night came on.

Kishen and Rusty slept in the open, on the temple steps. It was a warm night, the air was close and heavy. In the shadows lay small bundles of humanity—the roofless and the homeless, sleeping only to pass the time of night. Rusty slept in spasms, waking frequently with a nagging pain in his stomach. Poor stomach, it couldn't stand the unfamiliar strain of emptiness.

Chapter Twenty-three

❧

Before the steps and the river-tank came to life, Kishen and Rusty climbed into the ferry boat. It would be crossing the river all day, carrying pilgrims from temple to temple, charging nothing. And though it was very early, and this the first crossing, a free passage across the river made for a crowded boat.

The people who climbed in were even more diverse than those Rusty had met on the train. Women and children, bearded old men and wrinkled women, strong young peasants—not the prosperous or mercantile class, but the poor—who had come miles, mostly on foot, to bathe in the sacred waters of the Ganges.

On shore, the steps began to come to life. The previous day's cries and prayers and rites were resumed with the same monotonous devotion, at the same pitch, in the same spirit of timelessness, and the steps sounded to the tread of many feet, sandalled, slippered and bare.

The boat floated low in the water, it was so heavy, and the oarsmen had to strain upstream in order to avoid being swept down by the current. Their muscles shone and rippled under the grey iron of their weather-beaten skins. The blades of the oars cut through the water, in and out, and between grunts, the oarsmen shouted the time of the stroke.

Kishen and Rusty sat crushed together in the middle of the boat. There was no likelihood of their being separated now, but they held hands.

The people in the boat began to sing.

It was a low hum at first, but someone broke in with a song, and the voice—a young voice, clear and pure—reminded Rusty of Somi, and he comforted himself with the thought that Somi would be back in Dehra in the spring.

They sang in time to the stroke of the oars, in and out, and the grunts and shouts of the oarsmen throbbed their way into the song, becoming part of it.

An old woman, who had white hair and a face lined with deep furrows, said: 'It is beautiful to hear the children sing.'

'Then you too should sing,' said Rusty.

She smiled at him, a sweet, toothless smile.

'What are you, my son, are you one of us? I have never, on this river, seen blue eyes and golden hair.'

'I am nothing,' said Rusty. 'I am everything.'

He stated it bluntly, proudly.

'Where is your home, then?'

'I have no home,' he said, and felt proud of that too.

'And who is the boy with you?' asked the old woman, a genuine busybody. 'What is he to you?'

Rusty did not answer. He was asking himself the same question—what was Kishen to him? He was sure of one thing, they were both refugees, refugees from the world . . . . They were each other's shelter, each other's refuge, each other's help. Kishen was a *jungli* divorced from the rest of mankind, and Rusty was the only one who understood him—because Rusty too was divorced from mankind. And theirs was a tie that would hold, because they were the only people who knew each other and loved each other.

Because of this tie, Rusty had to go back. And it was with relief that he went back. His return was justified.

He let his hand trail over the side of the boat. He wanted to remember the touch of the water as it moved past them, down and away. It would come to the ocean, the ocean that was life.

He could not run away. He could not escape the life he had made, the ocean into which he had floundered the night he left his guardian's house. He had to return to the room, *his* room. He had to go back.

The song died away as the boat came ashore. They disembarked, walking over the smooth pebbles, and the forest rose from the edge of the river, and beckoned them.

Rusty remembered the forest on the day of the picnic, when he had kissed Meena and held her hands, and he remembered the magic of the forest and the magic of Meena.

'One day,' he said, 'we must live in the jungle.'

'One day,' said Kishen, and he laughed. 'But now we walk back. We walk back to the room on the roof! It is our room, we have to go back!'

They had to go back. To bathe at the water-tank and listen to the morning gossip, to sit in the fruit trees and eat in the chaat shop and perhaps make a garden on the roof; to eat and sleep; to work, to live, to die.

Kishen laughed.

'One day you'll be great, Rusty. A writer or an actor or a prime minister or something. Maybe a poet! Why not a poet, Rusty?'

Rusty smiled. He knew he was smiling, because he was smiling at himself.

'Yes,' he said, 'why not a poet?'

So they began to walk.

Ahead of them lay forest and silence—and what was left of time . . . .

Vagrants in the Valley

THE HOMELESS

❦

ON THE ROAD TO Dehra a boy played on a flute as he drove his flock of sheep down the road. He was barefoot and his clothes were old. A faded red shawl was thrown across his shoulders. It was December and the sun was up, pouring into the banyan tree at the side of the road where two boys where sitting on the great tree's gnarled, protruding roots.

The flute player passed the banyan tree and glanced at the boys, but did not stop playing. Presently he was only a speck on the dusty road, and the flute music was thin and distant, subdued by the tinkle of sheep-bells.

The boys left the shelter of the banyan tree and began walking in the direction of the distant hills.

The road stretched ahead, lonely and endless, towards the low ranges of the Siwalik hills. The dust was in their clothes and in their eyes and in their mouths. The sun rose higher in the sky, and as they walked, the sweat trickled down their armpits and down their legs.

The older boy, Rusty, was seventeen. He walked with his hands in the pockets of his thin cotton trousers, and he gazed at the ground. His far hair was matted with dust, and his cheeks and arms were scorched red by the fierce sun. His eyes were blue and thoughtful.

'We will be in Raiwala soon,' he said. 'Would you like to rest, bhaiya?'

Kishen shrugged his thin shoulders. 'We'll rest when we get to Raiwala. If I sit down now, I'll never be able to get up. I suppose we have walked about ten miles this morning.'

He was a slim boy, almost as tall as Rusty though he was two years younger. He had dark, rebellious eyes, and bushy eyebrows and thick black hair. His dusty white pyjamas were rolled up above his ankles, and he wore loose Peshawari chappals. An unbuttoned khaki shirt hung outside his pyjamas.

Like Rusty, he was without a home. Rusty had run away from an indifferent guardian a little over a year ago. Kishen had run away from a drunken father. He possessed distant relatives, but he preferred the risks and pleasures of vagrancy to the security of living with people he did not know. He had been with Rusty for a year, and his home was by his friend's side. He was Punjabi, Rusty was Anglo-Indian.

'From Raiwala we'll take the train,' said Rusty. 'It will cost us about five rupees.'

'Never mind,' said Kishen. 'We've done enough walking. And we've still got twelve rupees. Is there anything in our old rooms in Dehra that we can sell?'

'Let me see . . . . The table, the bed and the chair are not mine. There's an old tiger-skin, a bit eaten by rats, which no one will buy. There are one or two shirts and trousers.'

'Which we will need. These are all torn.'

'And some of my books . . . .'

'Which no one will buy.'

'I would not sell them. Well, those were the only things I got out of my guardian's house before I ran away.'

'Somi!' interrupted Kishen. 'Somi will be in Dehra—he'll help us! He got you a job once, he can do it again.'

Rusty was silent, remembering his friend Somi, who had won him with a smile and altered the course of his life. Somi, with his turban at an angle, a song on his lips . . . .

Kishen had left Dehra in a hurry and had been taken to Hardwar, a town on the banks of the sacred Ganges, by his aunt, and Rusty had followed him and his aunt. Only priests, beggars and shopkeepers could make a living in Hardwar, and the boys were soon back on the road to Dehra.

Now a cool breeze came across the plain, blowing down from the hills. In the fields there was a gentle swaying movement as the wind stirred the wheat. Then the breeze hit the road, and the dust began to swirl and eddy about the footpath. The boys moved into the middle of the road, holding their hands to their eyes, and stumbling forward. Out of the dust behind him came the rumbling of bullock-cart wheels.

'Ho there, out of my way!' shouted the driver of the cart. The bullocks snorted and came lumbering through the dust. The boys moved to the side of the road.

'Are you going to Raiwala?' called Rusty. 'Can you take us with you?'

'Climb up!' said the man, and the boys ran through the dust, and clambered on to the back of the moving cart.

The cart lurched and rattled and bumped, and they had to cling to its sides to avoid falling off. It smelt of dry grass and cowdung cakes. The driver had a red cloth tied around his head, and wore a tight vest and a dhoti around his waist. His feet and legs were bare, scorched black by the burning sun over the plains. He was smoking a bidi and shouting to his bullocks, cursing them at times, but sometimes speaking to them in endearing terms. He seemed to have forgotten the presence of the boys at the back, had dismissed them from his mind the moment they had climbed up. Rusty and Kishen were too busy clinging to the lopsided cart to bother about making conversation with the driver.

'I'd rather walk,' complained Kishen. 'Rusty, who suggested that we get into this silly old contraption? I am full of bumps and bruises already.'

'Beggars can't be choosers,' said Rusty.

'Please, we are not beggars—not yet, anyway . . . . And if we were, we'd be much better off financially, I can assure you! As far as the rest of the world is concerned, you are still the son of an English sahib, and I am still the distant relative of a distant maharaja.'

'A prince,' said Rusty derisively, 'and riding in a bullock-cart!'

'Well, not every prince can boast of the experience.'

A little later the bullock-cart rumbled across a canal and became involved in the traffic of Raiwala, a busy little market town. The boys jumped off and walked beside the cart.

'Should we give him something?' asked Rusty. 'We ought to offer him some money.'

'How can we?' said Kishen. 'Why didn't you think of that before we jumped on?'

'All right, we'll just thank him. Thank you, bhaiji!' he called, as the cart moved off. 'Thank you, bhaiji!' shouted Kishen.

But either the driver did not hear or did not bother to look around. He continued smoking his bidi and talking to his animals, and to all appearances had not even noticed that the boys had got down. He drove his bullock-cart away, leaving Rusty and Kishen standing on the road.

'I'm hungry,' said Kishen. 'We haven't eaten since last night.'

'Then we must eat,' said Rusty. 'Come on, bhaiya, we will eat.'

They walked through the narrow Raiwala bazaar, looking in at the tea and sweet shops until they found a place that looked dirty enough to be cheap. A servant boy brought them chappatis and dal and Kishen ordered an ounce of butter; this was melted and poured over the dal. The meal cost them a rupee, and for this amount they could eat as much as they liked. The butter was an extra, and cost six annas. They were left with a little over ten rupees.

When they came out, the sun was low in the sky and the day was cooler.

'We can't walk tonight,' said Rusty. 'We'll have to sleep at the railway station. Maybe we can get on the train without a ticket.'

'And if we are caught, we'll spend a month in jail. Free board and lodging.'

'And then the social workers will get you, or they'll put you in a remand home and teach you to make mattresses.'

'I think it's better to buy tickets,' said Kishen.

'I know what we'll do,' said Rusty. 'We won't get the train till past midnight, so let's not buy tickets. We'll get to Harrawala early in the morning. Then it's only about eight miles by road to Dehra.'

Kishen agreed, and they found their way to the railway station, where they made themselves comfortable in a first-class waiting-room.

'We don't have tickets,' said Kishen.

'But *we* are first class, aren't we?'

Kishen settled down in an armchair and covered his face

with a handkerchief. 'Wake me when the train comes in,' he said drowsily.

Rusty went to the bathroom. He put his head under a tap and allowed cold water to play over his neck. He washed his face, drying it with a handkerchief before returning to the waiting-room.

A man entered, setting out his belongings on the big table in the centre of the room. Rusty judged him to be in his thirties. The man was white, but he was too restless to be a European. He looked virile, but tired; he had a lean, sallow face, and pouches under the eyes. Rusty sat down on the edge of Kishen's armchair.

'Going to Delhi?' asked the stranger. His accent, though not very pronounced, was American.

'No, the other way,' replied Rusty. 'We live in Dehra.'

'I've often been there,' said the man. 'I've been trying to popularize a new steel plough in northern India, but without much success. Are you a student?'

'Not now. I finished with school two years ago.'

'And your friend?' He inclined his head towards the sleeping boy.

'He's with me,' said Rusty vaguely. 'We're travelling together.'

'Buddies.'

'Yes.'

The American took a flask from his bag and looked enquiringly at Rusty. 'Will you join me in a drink while we're waiting? There's almost an hour left for my train to arrive.'

'Well, I don't drink,' said Rusty, hesitating.

'A small one won't harm you. Just to keep me company.'

He took two small glasses from his bag, wiped them with a clean white handkerchief and set them down on the table. Then he poured some dark brown stuff from his flask.

'Brandy,' said Rusty, sniffing.

'So you recognize it. Yes, it's brandy.'

Rusty reached across the table and took the glass.

'Here's luck!' said the stranger.

'Thank you,' said Rusty, and gulped down a mouthful of neat liquor. He coughed and the tears came to his eyes. He put his head between his hands, but he was feeling better.

'You've come a long way,' said the American looking at the boy's clothes.

'On foot,' said Rusty. 'From Hardwar. Since morning.'

'Hardwar! That's a long walk. What made you do that?'

Rusty emptied his glass and set it down. The friendly stranger poured out more brandy. This is the way they do things in America, thought Rusty. When you meet a stranger, offer him a drink. He must go there one day.

'What made you walk?' asked the stranger again.

'Tomorrow we'll walk some more,' said Rusty.

'But why?'

'Because we have the time. We have all the time in the world.'

'How come?'

'Because we have no money. You can't have both time and money.'

'Oh, I agree. You are quite a philosopher. But what happened?' asked the American, looking at the sleeping boy. 'What is he to you?'

'He's with me,' said Rusty, ignoring the question. He was beginning to feel sleepy. The friendly stranger seemed to be getting further and further away and his voice came from a great distance.

'Tell me what happened.'

'I'll tell you,' said Rusty, leaning unsteadily across the table to see the other better, and speaking slowly. 'I ran away. I ran away from home, nearly a year ago. I had a guardian, an Englishman—my parents died when I was very small—and I lived in his house, in his own community, and it was a world of our own and I never went outside it. Then one day in the rain I met Somi. I became his friend and he took me to his home, and to the bazaar, and he showed me India and the world and life itself. My guardian beat me when I came back from the bazaar, and he beat me when I played Holi and came home drenched in colour. I returned the beating, though, and ran away.'

Rusty paused in order to finish the drink and to see if the man was interested.

'Go on,' said the stranger.

'Somi was my good friend, he did a lot for me. He found

a boy—Kishen over there—who needed English lessons, and his family took a liking to me and gave me a place to stay. She spent time with me often—I mean the boy's mother—Kishen's mother—and she was sweet and kind to me. She was beautiful. There will never be a woman as beautiful . . . .'

He lapsed into silence for about a minute, gazed into the glass as though he sought something there other than brandy, and continued: 'But then they went away. Somi went away, everyone went away. What could I do, but go away too? What could I do when Kishen's mother died, but go away? And if it wasn't for Kishen, I would never have come back. I tell you that straight, sir—I would never have come back. I wouldn't be here now, talking to you, if it wasn't for Kishen.'

'But I didn't know Kishen was alone. He had run away from his father, who was too drunk to care, and he had been living on his wits for weeks—he is good at that. But when I found him, I had to come back, we both had to come back. We have only got each other, you see.'

'I follow you a little,' said the stranger, and he filled Rusty's glass again. 'What are you going to do in Dehra, both of you? Do you have jobs to go to? I guess not. Well, if ever you find yourself in Delhi, look me up. Here's my card.'

A bell clanged on the station platform, and the stranger looked at his watch and said it was almost time for his train to arrive. He wiped the glasses with his handkerchief and returned them to his bag, then went outside and stood on the platform, waiting for the Delhi train.

Rusty leant against the waiting-room door, staring across the railway tracks. He heard the shriek of the whistle as the front light of an engine played over the rails. The train came in slowly, the hissing engine sending out waves of steam. At the same time, the carriage doors opened and people started pouring out.

There was a jam on the platform while men, women and children pushed and struggled, and it was several minutes before anyone could get in or out of the carriage doors. The American had been swallowed up by the crowd. Bundles of belongings were passed through windows, over the heads of bystanders. Several young men climbed in at the windows, heads first, assisted by pushes from behind. Rusty assumed that there was another religious fair at Hardwar, for the rush was even greater than usual.

When the train had gone, a calm descended on the platform. A few people waiting for the morning train to Dehra still slept near their bundles. Vendors selling soda-water, lemons, curds and cups of tea, pushed their barrows down the platform, still calling out their wares in desultory, sleepy voices. A baby cried, and the mother took the child to her bosom, but the baby kept on crying.

Rusty returned to the waiting-room. Kishen was still sound asleep in the armchair.

Rusty went to the light switch and turned it off, but the light from the platform streamed in through the gauze-covered doors. He did not think anyone would be coming in again that night. He sat down beside Kishen.

'Kishen, Kishen,' he whispered, touching the boy's shoulder.

Kishen stirred. 'What is it?' he mumbled drowsily. 'Why is it dark?'

'I put the light off,' said Rusty. 'You can sleep now.'

'I *was* sleeping,' said Kishen. 'But thank you all the same.'

THE FOREST ROAD

❧

AT DOIWALA NEXT MORNING, they had to leave the train. An inspector came round checking tickets, and Rusty and Kishen slipped out of the carriage from the side facing the jungle.

Doiwala stood just outside the Siwalik range, and already the fields were giving way to jungle. But there were maize-fields stretching away from the bottom of the railway banking, and the boys went in amongst the corn and waited in the field until the train had left. Kishen broke three or four corn-cobs from their stalks, stuffing them into his pockets.

'We might not get anything else to eat,' he said. 'Rusty, have you got matches so that we can light a fire and roast the corn?'

'We'll get some at the station.'

At Doiwala station they bought a box of matches, but they did not roast the corn until they had walked two miles up the road, into the jungle. Kishen collected dry twigs, and when they sat down at the side of the road he made a small fire. Kishen turned the corn-cobs over the fire until they were roasted a dark brown, burnt black in places. They dug their teeth into them, eating with relish.

'I wish we had some salt,' said Kishen.

'That would only make us thirsty, and we have no water. I hope we find a spring soon.'

'How far is Dehra now?' asked Kishen.

'About twelve miles, I think. It's funny how some miles seem longer than others. It depends on what you are thinking about, I suppose. What *you* are thinking and what I am thinking.

If our thoughts agree, the miles are not so long. We get on better when we are thinking together rather than when we are talking together!'

'All right then, stop talking.'

When they had finished eating they threw away the corn-cobs and began walking. They walked in silence; they had grown used to speaking only when they stopped to rest.

Rusty was thinking, I don't know how, but when we get to Dehra I've got to make a living for both of us. Kishen is too young to look after himself. He'll only get into trouble. I would not like to leave him alone even for a little while. Maybe I can get an English tuition. Or if I can write a story, a really good story, and sell it to a magazine, perhaps an American magazine . . . .

And Kishen was thinking, we will get money somehow. There are many ways of getting money. I don't mind anything as long as we are together. I don't mind anything as long as I am not alone.

Suddenly they heard the sound of rushing water. The road emerged from the jungle of sal trees and ended beside a river. There was a swift stream in the middle of the river-bed, coursing down towards the Ganges. A bridge had crossed this once, but it had been swept away during heavy monsoon rains, and the road ended at the river-bank.

They walked over sand and sharp rocks until they reached the water's edge, and they stood looking at the frothy water as it swirled below them.

'It's not deep,' said Kishen. 'I don't think it's above the waist anywhere.'

'It's not deep, but it's swift,' said Rusty. 'And the stones are slippery.'

'Shall we go back?'

'No, let's carry on—if it's too fast, we can turn back.'

They removed their shoes, tying them together by the laces and hanging them about their necks, then holding hands for security, they stepped into the water.

The stones were slippery underfoot, and the boys stumbled, hindering rather than helping each other. When they were half-way across, the water was up to their waists. They stopped in midstream, unwilling to go further for fear they would be swept off their feet.

'I can hardly stand,' said Kishen. 'It will be difficult to swim against the current.'

'It won't get deeper now,' said Rusty hopefully.

Just then, Kishen slipped and went over backwards into the water, bringing Rusty down on top of him. Kishen began kicking and threshing about, but eventually—by gripping on to Rusty's right foot—came spluttering out of the water.

When they found they were not being swept away by the current, they stopped struggling and cautiously dragged themselves across to the opposite bank. They came out of the water about thirty yards downstream.

The sun beat down on them as they lay exhausted on the warm sand. Kishen sucked at a cut in his hand, spitting the blood into the stream with a contemptuous gesture.

After some time they were walking again, though Kishen kept on bringing up mouthfuls of water.

'I'm getting hungry now,' he said, when he had emptied himself of water.

'We'll be in Dehra soon,' said Rusty. 'And then never mind the money, we'll eat like pigs.'

'Gourmets!' put in Kishen. 'I suppose there are still eight or ten miles left. Now I'm not even thinking. Are you?'

'I was thinking we should visit that river again one day, when we have plenty of food and nothing to worry about.'

'You won't get me coming here again,' said Kishen.

They shuffled along the forest path, tired and hungry, but quite cheerful. Then they rounded a bend and found themselves face to face with a tiger.

Well, not quite face to face. The tiger was about fifteen yards away from them, occupying the centre of the path. He was as surprised to see the boys as the boys were to see him. He lifted his head, and his tail swished from side to side, but he made no move towards them. The boys stood absolutely still in the middle of the path. They were too astonished to do anything else, which was just as well, because had they run or shouted or shown fear, the tiger might well have been provoked into attacking them. After a moment's hesitation, he crossed the path and disappeared into the forest without so much as a growl.

Still the boys did not move, but they found their voices.

'You didn't tell me there were tigers here,' said Kishen in a hoarse whisper.

'I didn't think about it,' said Rusty.

'Shall we go forwards or backwards?'

'Do you want to cross the stream again? Anyway, the tiger didn't seem to worry about us. Let's go on.'

And they walked on through the forest without seeing the tiger again, though they saw several splendid peacocks and a band of monkeys. It was not until they had left the forest behind and were on an open road with fields and villages on either side that they relaxed and showed their relief by bursting into laughter.

'I think we frightened that tiger more than it frightened us,' said Kishen. 'Why, it didn't even roar!'

'And a good thing it didn't, otherwise we might not have been here.'

They laughed at themselves, and when they laughed they were happy.

Rusty felt more at ease with Kishen than he did with anyone else—probably because Kishen had been one of his first friends, and they had grown swiftly together from childhood into adolescence. Rusty had never been at ease with anyone until he had met Somi and Kishen. His mother had died when he was very young, and his father had not lived much longer. His mother was a shadowy figure, and though he remembered her, she seemed, in his mind, to have less substance than his father. He had hated his guardian, who had looked after him when his father died.

Those early years had been very English, and the only Indians he had known were the servants. When he was five, and very proud, he had informed the cook that England was ten times as large as India, and the cook had believed him.

As he grew older, the forbidden India—the real India of bazaars and temples and sprawling villages—was discovered in bits and pieces; it was only when Rusty made Indian friends for the first time that he discovered it completely. His guardian had not liked his friends or his visits to the bazaars, and they had quarrelled, and Rusty had run away, living for a year with Kishen's family.

At first everything had been different, physically different—

wearing Indian clothes, eating Indian food, bathing Indian fashion—and then different in another, more subtle way, which had him thinking differently too. For though he was old enough to have already absorbed certain Western values, he was young enough and flexible enough to be able to adapt himself to his new and unfamiliar environment, and to absorb something of Indian values. He was not conscious of any division of loyalties in himself, but rather of a double inheritance.

For one year he had led an almost idyllic life. He had loved, almost worshipped, Kishen's mother, Meena—loved her with all the mute and helpless fervour of a sixteen-year-old—and she had loved him too, but only as a woman loves a homeless child. Then Meena was killed in a car accident, and Kishen's father returned to his whisky bottle and took another wife. Rusty had been on his way to Delhi to try and leave India, when he had met Kishen in Hardwar.

And together they were returning to Dehra which was their home.

The danger they had shared helped to revive their drooping spirits, and they grew light-hearted as they walked into the fertile valley that lay between the Siwaliks and the Himalayan foothills. Spreading over the valley were wheat and maize and sugar-cane fields, tea gardens and orchards of guava, litchi and mango.

There was a small village on the outskirts of Dehra, and the village lamps were lit when the boys, dusty and dishevelled, walked through with dragging feet. Now that their journey was almost over, they became more aware of their weariness and their aches, and the town which had been their home seemed suddenly strange and heartless, as though it did not recognize them any more.

A Place to Sleep

&

WHEN THEY GOT TO the Tandoori Fish Shop, Kishen and Rusty were too hungry and tired to think of going any further, so they sat down and ordered a meal. The fish came hot, surrounded by salad and lemon, and when they had finished it, they ate again, fish and salad and lemon, and drank glasses of hot, spiced tea.

'The best thing in life is food,' said Kishen. 'There is nothing to equal it.'

'I agree,' said Rusty. 'Bhaiya, you are absolutely right.'

Afterwards, they walked through the noisy, crowded bazaar which they knew so well, past the Clock Tower, up the steps of their old room. They were ready to flop down on the string cot and sleep for a week. But when they reached the top of the steps they found the door locked. It was not their lock, but a heavy, unfamiliar padlock, and its presence was ominous.

'Let's smash it!' said Kishen.

'That's no use,' said Rusty. 'The landlord doesn't want us to have the room. He's shut us out at the first opportunity. Well, let's go and see his agent. Perhaps he'll let us have the room back. Anyway, our things are inside.'

Rusty stood at the top of the steps, looking thoughtfully at the grounds—the gravel path, the litchee and mango trees, the grass badminton court, now overgrown with weeds—and half-expected to hear Kishen's mother calling to him from below, calling to him to come and play, while the father, in his green dressing-gown, sat on the steps clutching a bottle. They had gone now, and would never come back. Rusty was not sure that he wanted to stay in the old room.

'Would you like to wait here while I get the key?' he asked.
'No,' said Kishen. 'I'd be afraid to wait here alone.'
'Why?'
'Because,' he looked to Rusty for understanding, 'because this was our house once, and my mother and father lived here, and I'm afraid of the house when they are no longer in it. I'll come with you. I'd like to break the *munshi's* neck, anyway.'

The *munshi* met them at the door of his house. He was a slow, bent, elderly man, dressed in a black coat and white dhoti, a pair of vintage spectacles balanced precariously on his nose. He was in the service of the *seth* who owned a great deal of property in town, and his duties included the collection of rents, eviction of tenants—this had become increasingly difficult—and seeing to the repair and maintenance of the *seth's* property.

'Your room has been rented out,' explained the *munshi*.
'What do you mean, mister?' said Kishen, bristling.
'Why has it been rented when we haven't given it up?' asked Rusty.
'You were never a tenant,' said the *munshi*, with a shrug that almost unsettled his spectacles. 'Mr Kapoor let you use one of the rooms. Now he has vacated the house. When you went away, I thought you had gone permanently.' The *munshi* made a helpless gesture with his hands, and anticipated the imminent fall of his spectacles by taking them off and wiping them on his shirt.

Finally he said: '*Sethji* ordered me to let the room immediately.'
'But how could I have gone permanently,' argued Rusty, 'when my things are still in the room?'
The *munshi* scratched his head. 'There were not many things, I thought you had no need for them. I thought you were going to England. You can have your things tomorrow. They are in the storeroom, and the key is with the *seth*. But I cannot let you have the room again.'

Uncertain as to what he should do next, Rusty continued to stand in the light thrown from the *munshi's* front room. Kishen stepped forward.
'Give us another room, then,' he said belligerently.
'I cannot do that now,' said the *munshi*. 'It is too late. You

will have to come tomorrow, and even then I cannot promise you anything. All our rooms are full. Just now I cannot help you. There must be some place where you can stay . . . .'

'We'll find a place,' said Rusty, tired of the whole business. 'Come on, bhaiya. There's always the railway platform.'

Kishen hesitated, scowling at the *munshi*, before following Rusty out of the gate.

'What now?' he grumbled. 'Where do we go now?'

They stood uncertainly in the middle of the road.

'Let's sit down somewhere,' suggested Rusty. 'Then we can think of something. We can't come to a decision simply by standing stupidly on the road.'

'We'll sit in the tea shop,' said Kishen. 'We've had enough tea, but let's go there anyway.'

They found the tea shop at the end of the bazaar, a make-shift wooden affair built over a gully. There were only two tables in the shop, and most of the customers sat outside on a bench where they could listen to the shopkeeper, a popular storyteller.

Sitting on the ground in front of the shop was a thick-set youth with his head shaved, wearing rags. He was dumb—they called him the Goonga—and the customers often made sport of him, abusing him good-naturedly, and clouting him over the head from time to time. The Goonga did not mind this; he made faces at the others, and chuckled derisively at their remarks. He could say only one word, 'Goo' and he said it often. This kept the customers in fits of laughter.

'Goo!' he said, when he saw Kishen and Rusty enter the shop. He pointed at the boys, chuckled, and said 'Goo!' again. Everyone laughed. Someone got up from the bench and with the flat of his hand, whacked the Goonga over his naked head. The Goonga sprang at the man, making queer, gurgling noises. Someone tripped him and sent him sprawling on the ground, and there was more laughter.

Rusty and Kishen sat at an inside table. Everyone, except the Goonga, was drinking tea.

'Give the Goonga a glass of tea,' said Kishen to the shopkeeper.

The shopkeeper grinned and made the tea. The Goonga looked at Kishen and Rusty and said, 'Goo!'

'Now how much money is left?' asked Kishen, getting down to business.

'About nine rupees,' said Rusty. 'If we are careful, it will last us a few days.'

'More than a week,' said Kishen. 'We can get enough food for a rupee a day, as long as we don't start eating chicken. But you should find some work in a day or two.'

'Don't be too optimistic about that.'

'Well, it's no use worrying as yet.'

There was an interesting story being told by the shopkeeper, about a jinn who used his abnormally long reach to steal sweets, and the boys forgot about their 'conference' until the story was finished.

'Now it's someone else's turn,' said the shopkeeper.

'The fair boy will tell us one,' said a voice, and everyone turned to look at Rusty.

The person who had made the request was one of the boys who served tea to the customers. He could not have been more than twelve years old, but he had a worldly look about him, in spite of the dimples in his cheeks and the mischievous glint in his eyes. His fair complexion and high cheekbones showed that he came from the hills, from one of the border districts.

'I don't know any stories,' said Rusty.

'That isn't possible,' said the shopkeeper. 'Everyone knows at least one story, even if it is his own.'

'Yes, tell us,' said the hill boy.

'You find us a room for the night,' said Kishen, always ready to bargain in true Punjabi fashion, 'and he'll tell you a story.'

'I don't know of any place,' said the shopkeeper, 'but you are welcome to sleep in my shop. You won't sleep much, because there are people coming and going all night, especially the truck drivers.'

'Don't worry,' said the hill boy. 'I know of many places where you can stay. Now tell us the story.'

So Rusty embarked on a ghost story which held his audience enthralled.

'All right, now tell us,' said Rusty, after his story was over, 'where are we going to sleep tonight? You can't get a hotel room for less than two rupees.'

'It's not too cold,' said Kishen. 'We can sleep in the maidan. There's shelter there.'

Rusty gave a sigh of resignation and thought, a year ago when I ran away I slept in the maidan, and again I am going to sleep in the maidan. That's called 'Progress'.

He said, 'The last time I slept in the maidan, it rained. I woke up in a pool of mud.'

'But it won't rain today,' said Kishen cheerfully. 'There isn't a cloud in the sky.'

They looked out at the night sky. The moon was almost at the full, robbing the stars of their glory.

They left the shop and began walking towards the open grassland of the maidan. The bazaar was almost empty now, the shops closed, lights showing only from upper windows. Rusty became conscious of the sound of soft footfalls behind him, and looking over his shoulder, saw that they were being followed by the Goonga.

'Goo,' said the Goonga, on being noticed.

'Damn!' said Kishen. 'Why did we have to give him tea? He probably thinks we are rich and won't let us out of sight again.'

'He'll change his mind about us when he finds we're sleeping on the maidan.'

'Goo,' said the Goonga from behind, quickening his step.

They turned abruptly down an alleyway, trying to shake the Goonga off, but he padded after them, chuckling ghoulishly to himself. They cut back to the main road, but he was behind them at the Clock Tower. At the edge of the maidan Rusty turned and said: 'Go away, Goonga. We've got no money, no food, no clothes. We are no better off than you. Go away!'

'Yes, buzz off!' said Kishen, a master of Indo-Anglian slang.

But the youth said, 'Goo!' and took a step forward, and his shaved head glistened in the moonlight. Rusty shrugged and led Kishen to the maidan. The Goonga stood at the edge, shaking his head and chuckling. His dry black skin showed through his rags, and his feet were covered with mud. He watched the boys as they walked across the grass, watched them until they lay down, and then he shrugged his shoulders and said, 'Goo,' and went away.

THE OLD CHURCH

৯

'LETS LEAVE OUR THINGS with the *munshi*,' said Rusty, yawning and stretching his limbs. 'It's no use collecting them until we have somewhere to stay. But I *would* like to change my clothes.'

It had been cold in the maidan until the sun threw its first pink glow over the hills. On the grass lay yesterday's remnants— a damp newspaper, a broken toy, a kite hanging helplessly from the branches of a tree. The boys were sitting on the dew-sodden grass, waiting for the sun to seep through to their skin and drive the chill from their bones. They had not slept much, and their eyes were ringed and heavy. Rusty's hair looked like a small, untidy stack of hay. Kishen's legs were swollen with mosquito bites.

'Why is it that you haven't been bitten as much as I have?' complained Kishen.

'No doubt you taste better,' said Rusty. 'We had better split up now, I suppose.'

'But why?'

'We will get more done that way. You go to the *munshi* and see if you can persuade him to let us have another room. But don't pay anything in advance! Meanwhile, I'll call at the schools to see if I can get any English tuitions.'

'All right, Rusty. Where do we meet?'

'At the Clock Tower. At about twelve o'clock.'

'Then we can eat,' said Kishen with enthusiasm.

Rusty smiled. He had not smiled so brightly for a long time, and seeing the smile on Rusty's face, Kishen felt sure everything would come out all right.

'Eating is something we always agree upon,' said Rusty.

They washed their faces at the public tap at the edge of the maidan, where the wrestlers were usually to be found. The wrestlers had not assembled that morning, and the pit was empty, otherwise Rusty might have encountered a friend of his, called Hathi, who often came there to wrestle and use the weights. Scrubbing his back and shoulders at the tap, he realized that he needed a haircut and, worse still, a shave.

'I will have to get a shave,' he said ruefully. 'You're lucky to have only a little fluff on your cheeks so far. I have to shave at least once a week, do you know that?'

'How extravagant!' exclaimed Kishen. 'Can't you grow a beard? A shave will cost four annas.'

'Nobody will give me a tuition if they see this growth on my face.'

'Oh, all right,' grumbled Kishen, stroking the faint beginning of a moustache. 'You take four annas and have your shave, but I will keep the rest of the money with me in case I have to give the *munshi* something. It will be all right to let him have a rupee or two in advance if he can give us a room.'

He left Rusty at the tap and went straight to the *munshi's* house, but he had no luck there. The *munshi* asked for an advance of fifteen rupees before he would rent them a room. He was polite but firm. He was only the *seth's* servant, he insisted, and he had to carry out orders. Kishen made a few insulting remarks about the *seth* before leaving.

Disgruntled, but far from depressed (it was not in his nature to be easily depressed), Kishen sauntered off into the alleyways behind the bazaar. There were two hours ahead of him before he could meet Rusty; he was not sure what he should do with himself.

In a courtyard off one of the alleyways, three young men squatted in the sun, playing cards. Kishen watched them for a while, until one of the players beckoned to him, inviting him to join the game.

Kishen was with the card players till twelve o'clock.

Rusty went to the barber's shop and had his shave for four annas. And the barber, who was a special friend of his, and took great pleasure in running his fingers through Rusty's fair hair, gave him a head massage into the bargain.

It was a wonderful massage and included not only the head, but Rusty's eyes, neck and forehead. The barber was a dark, glistening man, with broad shoulders and a chest like a drum; he wore a fine white Lucknow shirt through which you could see his hard body. His strong fingers drummed and stroked and pressed, and with the palms and sides of his hands he thumped and patted Rusty's forehead. Rusty felt the blood rush to his temples, and when the massage was finished, he was hardly conscious of having a head, and walked into the street with a peculiar, elated, headless feeling.

He made a somewhat fruitless round of the three principal schools. At each of them he was told that if anything in his line turned up, they would certainly let him know. But they did not ask him where he could be found if he was wanted. The last school asked him to call again in a day or two.

On the outskirts of the town Rusty found the old church of St. Paul's, which had been abandoned for over a year due to meagre parish resources and negligible attendance. The Catholics of Dehra had been able to afford the upkeep of their church and convent, but nobody outside Dehra had bothered about St. Paul's, and eventually the padre had locked the building and gone away. Rusty regretted this, not because he had been fond of church-going—he had always disliked large gatherings of people—but because it was old, with historic and personal associations, and he hated to see old things, old people, suffer lonely deaths.

The plaster was crumbling, the paint peeling off the walls, moss growing in every crack. Wild creepers grew over the stained-glass windows. The garden, so well-kept once, was now a jungle of weeds and irrepressible marigolds.

Rusty leaned on the gate and gazed at the church. There had been a time when he hated visiting this place, for it had meant the uncomfortable presence of his guardian, the gossip of middle-aged women, the boredom of an insipid sermon. But, now, seeing the neglected church, he felt sorry for it—not only for the people who had been there, but for the place itself, and for those who were buried in the graves that kept each other silent company in the grounds. People he had known lay there, and some of them were people his father had known.

He opened the creaking wooden gate and walked up the overgrown path. The front door was locked. He walked around trying the side doors, finding them all closed. There was no lock on the vestry door, though it seemed to be bolted from within. Two panes of glass were set in the top portion of the door. Standing on his toes, Rusty reached up to them, pressing his fingers against the panes to test the thickness of the glass. He stood back from the door, took his handkerchief from his pocket and wrapped it round his hand. Standing on his toes again, he pushed his fist through one of the panes.

There was a tinkle of falling glass. Rusty groped around and found the bolt. Then he stepped back and kicked at the door.

The door opened. The handkerchief had fallen from his hand and one of his knuckles was bleeding. He picked up the handkerchief and wrapped it round the cut. Then he stepped into the vestry.

The place was almost empty. A cupboard door hung open on one hinge and a few old cassocks lay on a shelf in a dusty pile. An untidy heap of prayer books and hymnals was stacked in a packing-case, and a mouse sat on top of a half-eaten hymnal, watching the intruder.

Rusty went through the vestry into the church hall, where it was lighter. Sunlight poured through a stained-glass window, throwing patches of mellow orange and gold on the pews and on the frayed red carpet that ran down the aisle. The windows were full of cobwebs. As Rusty walked down the aisle, he broke through cordons of cobwebs, sending the frightened spiders scurrying away across the pews.

He left the church by the vestry door, closing it behind him, and removing the splintered glass from the window, he threw the pieces into the bushes.

Kishen could always find plenty to do in the bazaar, apart from gambling with cards. The bazaar was a mile long, stretching from the station to the Clock Tower. Little alleys led off the main road, winding towards the stench of the fish market or the wet freshness of the vegetable market.

Another alley led to the junk, or *kabari* market, which was always interesting. Here you could get anything from valuable antiques and rare books to old footballs, shoes, haversacks, tins and bottles. Most of the *kabaris* were Muslims, who had been either too old or too poor to leave Dehra after the partition of the country. They made up only a small part of the town's very mixed population which included sturdy little Gurkhas from Nepal, easygoing smiling Garhwalis from the hills, and bustling Punjabi Hindus and Sikhs.

The Punjabis had brought activity and noise to this once sleepy little town, and small shops and hotels and mushroomed up on all the roads. Skilled tailors and carpenters and businessmen who had lost nearly everything in their flight across the border when the country was divided, had set to work again, to make new livings and new fortunes. Only a Punjabi can make and lose a fortune with both speed and daring, and Kishen (who was Punjabi) could do it too, in his own small way.

He met Rusty at the Clock Tower, and together they went to the chaat shop to have a cheap meal of spiced fruits and vegetables. Kishen had been to the *munshi* again to get into the storeroom, and now carried a bundle of clothes. He had done this to please Rusty, as the matter of the card game would be difficult to explain.

'The *munshi* wouldn't give me a room without an advance of fifteen rupees,' he said. 'But I got some clothes anyway.'

'It doesn't matter about the room. I've found a place to stay.'

'Oh, good! What is it like?'

'Wait till you see it. I had no luck at the schools, though there may be something for me in a day or two. How much money did you say was left?'

'Eight rupees,' said Kishen, looking guilty and stuffing his mouth with potatoes to hide his confusion.

'I thought it was nine rupees,' said Rusty.

'It was nine,' said Kishen. 'But I lost one rupee. I was sure I could win, but those fellows had a trick I didn't know!'

'I see,' said Rusty resignedly. 'From now on I'll keep everything.'

Without any shame Kishen put the notes and coins on the table. Rusty separated the money into two piles, put the notes in his pocket, and pushed six annas across the table to Kishen.

Kishen grinned. 'So you are letting me keep something, after all?'

'That's to pay for the chaat,' said Rusty, and Kishen's grin turned into a grimace.

They walked to the church, Kishen grumbling a little, Rusty feeling very cheerful. Sometimes it would be the other way round. They were seldom cheerful together, and they never grumbled together, which was fortunate.

'I want a bath,' said Kishen unreasonably. 'How far is this place where you've got a room?'

'I didn't say anything about a room, and there's no place for a bath. But there's a stream not far away, in the jungle behind the road.'

Kishen looked puzzled and scratched his fuzzy head, but he did not say anything, reserving judgement till later.

'Hey, where are you going, Rusty?' he said, when Rusty turned in at the church gate.

'To the church,' said Rusty.

'What for—to pray?' asked Kishen anxiously. 'I never knew you were religious.'

'I'm not. But we're going to live in the place.'

Kishen slapped his forehead in astonishment, then burst into laughter. 'The places we stay at!' he exclaimed. 'Railway stations. Maidans. And now cathedrals!'

'It's not a cathedral, it's a church.'

'What's the difference? It's the same religion. A mosque can be different from a temple, but how is a cathedral different from a church?'

Rusty did not try to explain, but led Kishen in through the vestry door. Kishen crept cautiously into the quiet church, looking nervously at the dark, spidery corners, at the high windows, the bare altar, the gloom above the rafters.

'I can't stay here,' he said. 'There must be a ghost in the place.' He ran his fingers over the top of a pew, leaving tracks in the thick dust.

'We can sleep on the benches or on the carpet,' said Rusty. 'And we can cover ourselves with those old cassocks.'

'Why are they called cassocks?'

'I haven't the slightest idea.'

'Then don't lecture me about cathedrals. If someone finds out we are staying here, there will be trouble.'

'Nobody will find out. Nobody comes here any more. The place is not looked after, as you can see. Those who used to come have all gone away. Only I am left, and I never came here willingly.'

'Up till now,' said Kishen. 'Let some air in.'

Rusty climbed on a bench and opened one of the high windows. Fresh air rushed in/smelling sweet, driving away the mustiness of the closed hall.

'Now let's go to the stream,' said Rusty.

They left the church by the vestry door, passed through the unkempt garden and went into the jungle. A narrow path led through the sal trees, and they followed it for about a quarter of a mile. The path had not been used for a long time, and they had to push their way through thorny bushes and brambles. Then they heard the sound of rushing water.

They had to slide down a rock face into a small ravine, and there they found the stream running over a bed of shingle. Removing their shoes and rolling up their trousers, they crossed the stream. Water trickled down from the hillside, from amongst ferns and grasses and wild flowers; and the hills, rising steeply on either side, kept the ravine in shadow. The rocks were smooth, almost soft, and some of them were grey and some yellow. A small waterfall fell across them, forming a deep, round pool of apple-green water.

They removed their clothes and jumped into the pool. Kishen went too far out, felt the ground slipping away from beneath his feet, and came splashing back into the shallows.

'I didn't know it was so deep,' he said.

Soon they had forgotten the problem of making money, had forgotten the rigours of their journey. They swam and romped about in the cold mountain water. Kishen gathered the clothes together and washed them in the stream, beating them out on the smooth rocks, and spreading them on the grass to dry. When they had bathed, they lay down on the grass under a warm afternoon sun, talking spasmodically and occasionally falling into a light sleep.

'I am going to wire to Somi,' said Rusty, 'but I don't know his address.'

'Isn't his mother still here?' said Kishen.

Rusty sat up suddenly. 'I never thought of her. Somi said he was the only one leaving Dehra. She must be here.'

'Then let us go and see her,' said Kishen. 'She might be able to help us.'

'We'll go now,' said Rusty.

They waited until their clothes were dry, and then they dressed and went back along the forest path. The sun was setting when Rusty and Kishen arrived at Somi's house, which was about a mile from the church, in the direction of the station. It was an old yellow bungalow, almost lost amongst litchi and guava trees, and as Rusty passed beneath the trees he remembered a day when Somi, a golden boy singing in the sun, had sat on the limb of a guava tree, had fallen lightly on Rusty's shoulders, ruffling his hair and shouting, 'Run, my pony, my best favourite friend!'

He missed Somi's welcoming laughter as he walked up the veranda steps, but he found Somi's mother busy in the kitchen while the baby sister crawled about on the floor. Rusty took the child in his arms and lifted her high above his head; and the little girl screamed with delight as he tossed her in the air. Somi's mother, grey-haired, smiling, and dressed in a simple white sari, put her hands to her cheeks.

'Master Rusty!' she exclaimed. 'And Kishen bhaiya! Where have you been all these weeks?'

'Travelling,' said Rusty. 'We have been doing a world tour.'

'On foot,' added Kishen.

They sat in cane chairs on the veranda, and Rusty gave Somi's mother an account of their journey, deliberately omitting to mention that they were without work or money. But she had sensed their predicament.

'Are you having any trouble about your room?' she asked.

'We left it,' said Rusty. 'We are staying in a bigger place now.'

'Yes, much bigger,' said Kishen.

'What about that book you were going to write—is it published?'

'No, I'm still writing it,' said Rusty.

'How much have you done?'

'Oh, not much as yet. These things take a long time.'

'And what is it about?'

'Oh, everything I suppose,' said Rusty, feeling guilty and changing the subject, for his novel had not progressed beyond the second chapter. 'I'm starting another tuition soon. If you know of any people who want their children to learn English, please pass them on to me.'

'Of course I will. Somi would not forgive me if I did not do as you asked. But why don't you stay here? There is plenty of room.'

'Oh, we are quite comfortable in our place,' said Rusty.

'Oh, yes, very comfortable,' said Kishen, glaring at him.

Somi's mother made them stay for dinner, and they did not take much persuading, for the aroma of rich Punjabi food had been coming to them from the kitchen. They were prepared to sleep in churches and waiting-rooms all their lives, provided there was always good food to be had—rich, fleshy food, for they scorned most vegetables . . . .

Somi's mother gave them a feast of tandoor bread and buffalo's butter, meat cooked with spinach, vegetables with cheese, a sour pickle of turnip and lemon, and a jug of *lassi*. They did full justice to the meal, and Somi's mother watched them with satisfaction—the satisfaction of a mother and a good cook.

'Do you need any money?' she asked, when they had finished.

'Oh, no,' said Rusty, 'we have plenty of that.'

Kishen kicked him under the table.

'Enough for a week, anyway,' said Rusty.

After the meal, he took Somi's Amritsar address with the intention of writing to him the next day. He also stuffed his pockets with pencils and writing-paper. When they were about to leave, Somi's mother thrust a ten-rupee note into Rusty's hand, and he blushed, unable to refuse the money.

Once on the road, he said: 'We didn't come to borrow money, bhaiya.'

'But you can pay it back in a few days. What's the use

of having friends if you can't go to them for help?'

'I would have gone when there was nothing left. Until there is nothing left, I don't want to trouble anyone.'

They walked back to the church, buying two large candles on the way. Rusty lit one candle at the church gate and led the way down the dark, disused path.

New Encounters

&

'IT'S CREEPY,' SAID KISHEN, keeping close to Rusty. 'It's so quiet here. I think we should go back and stay at Somi's house. There must be something wrong with sleeping in a church.'

'It is no more wrong than sleeping in a tree.'

When they were inside, Rusty placed the burning candle on the altar steps. A bat swooped down from the rafters and Kishen ducked under a pew. 'I would rather sleep in the maidan,' he said.

'It's better here,' said Rusty. He came back from the vestry with a bundle of cassocks which he dumped on the floor. 'I'll do some writing,' he said, sitting down near the candle and producing pencil and paper from his pocket.

Kishen sat down on a bench and removed his shoes, rubbing his feet and playing with his toes. When he had got used to the bats diving overhead, he stood up and undressed. Long and bony in his vest and underpants, he sat down on the pile of cassocks, and with his elbows resting on his knees, and his chin cupped in the palms of his hands, he watched Rusty write.

He knew better than to interrupt when Rusty was writing or reading, particularly so when he was reading. Once Rusty was absorbed in a book, only something disastrous would get him away from it. He had been a bookworm ever since he had learnt to read, but the final commitment had been made at the age of twelve.

At this ripe and impressionable age he had been taken, by his guardian and several other sportsmen on a shikar expedition into the Terai jungles near Dehra. The prospect of a week in the jungle, as camp-follower to several egotistic adults with guns, filled Rusty with dismay. He knew that many long weary hours would be spent tramping behind tall, professional-looking huntsmen, who spoke in terms of bagging this tiger or that wild elephant, when all they ever got, if they were lucky, was a hare or a partridge. Tigers and excitement, it seemed, came to Jim Corbett. Rusty had been on several shikar trips and had always been overtaken by ennui.

That particular expedition had been different, but not because the hunters had been more than usually successful. At the end of the week all they had shot were two miserable, underweight wild fowl. But Rusty had contrived on the second day, to be left behind in the forest rest-house; and there he discovered a shelf of books half-hidden in a corner of the old bungalow.

Who had left them there? A literary forest officer? Some memsahib who had been bored with her husband's campfire boasting? Or someone who, pained at the prospect of slaughtering wild animals, insured himself against boredom by bringing his library along? But why leave it behind? For fellow sufferers, perhaps. Or possibly the poor fellow had gone into the jungle one day—as a sort of gesture to his more bloodthirsty companions—and been trampled by an elephant, or gored by a wild boar, or (more likely) accidentally shot by one of the shikaris, and his sorrowing friends had taken his remains away, but left his books behind.

Anyway, there they were—a shelf of some thirty volumes. The shelf was catholic in its contents—and Rusty had soaked up Dickens, Wodehouse, M. R. James, George Eliot, Maugham and Barrie, while the big-game hunters, instead of feasting on roast pig or venison, opened their tins of corned meat.

In the early hours of the morning a mouse nibbled at Kishen's toes and the boy woke with a yelp and shook Rusty.

'I've been bitten,' said Kishen urgently as Rusty surfaced from the cassocks. 'I've been bitten by a church mouse.'

'At least it isn't a cathedral rat,' said Rusty. 'I've had one crawling over me all night.' He shook out the cassocks, and with a squeak, a mouse leapt from the clothes and made a dash for safety.

Kishen put out his hand and touched Rusty's shoulder. The warmth of his friend's body reassured him, and he drew nearer and went to sleep with his arm around Rusty.

They rose before the sun was up, and went straight to the pool. It was a cold morning. They gasped and cried out from the shock of the ice-cold mountain water. Rusty was brown on his arms and legs where the sun had burnt him, and the rest of his body was pink from the slap of the water. Kishen had long loose limbs, and he threshed the water vigorously, but with little skill. They both tried diving off a rock, but landed on their bellies every time.

As they swam about, the sun came striking through the sal trees, making emeralds of the dewdrops, and pouring through the clear water till it touched the yellow sand. Rusty felt the sun touch his skin, felt it sink deep into his blood and bones and marrow, and, exulting in it, he hurled himself at Kishen. They tumbled over in the water, going down with a wild kicking of legs, and came spluttering to the surface, gasping and shouting. Then they lay on the rocks till they were dry.

When they left the pool, they walked to the maidan.

Every morning a group of young men wrestled at one end of the maidan, in a pit of soft, newly-dug earth. Hathi was one of the wrestlers. He was like a young bull, with a magnificent chest, and great broad thighs. His light brown hair and eyes were in startling contrast to the rest of his dark body.

Hathi relied more on strength than skill, and with a sweep of his broad hand he could level on opponent to the ground. Rusty had met him when he used to watch the wrestling with Somi and Kishen, and Hathi had always greeted them with a wide smile, inviting them to wrestle.

Kishen and Rusty found him at the tap, washing the mud and oil from his body, pummelling himself with resounding slaps. When he looked up and saw Rusty, he gave a shout of recognition, left the tap running, and gave Rusty an exuberant wet hug, transferring a fair amount of mud and oil on to his friend's already soiled shirt.

'My friend! Where have you been all these weeks? I thought you had forgotten me. And Kishen bhaiya, how are you?'

Kishen received the bear-hug with a grumble: 'I've already had my bath, Hathi.'

But Hathi continued talking while he put on his shirt and pyjamas. 'You are just in time to see me, as I am going away in a day or two,' he said.

'Where are you going?' asked Rusty.

'To my village in the hills. I have land there, you know— I am going back to look after it. Come and have tea with me— come! I wanted to make both of you wrestlers, but you disappeared, and now it is too late.'

He took them to the tea shop near the Clock Tower, where he mixed each of them a glass of hot milk, honey and beaten egg. The morning bath had refreshed them and they were feeling quite energetic.

'How do you get to your village?' asked Rusty. 'Is there a motor road?'

'No. The road ends at Landsdowne. From there one has to walk about thirty miles. It is a steep road, and you have to cross two mountains, but it can be done in a day if you start out early enough. Why don't you come with me?' he asked suddenly. 'There you will be able to write many stories. That is what you want to do, isn't it? There will be no noise or worry.'

'I can't come just now,' said Rusty. 'Maybe later, but not now.'

'You come too, Kishen,' pressed Hathi. 'Why not?'

'Kishen would be bored by mountains,' said Rusty.

'How do you know?' said Kishen, looking annoyed.

'Well, if you want to come later,' said Hathi, 'you have only to take the bus to Lansdowne, and then take the north-east road for the village of Manjari. You can come whenever you like. I will be living alone.'

'If we come,' said Rusty, 'we should be of some use to you there.'

'I will make farmers of you!' exclaimed Hathi, slapping himself on the thigh.

'Kishen is too lazy.'

'And Rusty too clumsy.'

'Well, maybe we will come,' said Rusty. 'But first I must see if I can get some sort of work here. I'm going to one of the schools again today. What will you do, Kishen?'

Kishen shrugged. 'I'll wait for you in the bazaar.'

'Stay with me,' said Hathi. 'I have nothing to do except

recover money from various people. If I don't get it now, I will never get it.'

While Hathi was engaged at the Sindhi Sweet Shop, arguing with a man about a certain amount of money, Kishen wandered off on his own, lounging about in front of the shops. He was standing in front of a clothes shop when he saw an old family friend, Mrs Bhushan, with her vixenish, fifteen-year-old daughter, Aruna, an old playmate of his. They were in the shop, haggling with the shopkeeper over the price of a sari. Mrs Bhushan was in the habit of going from shop to shop, like a bee sampling honey; she would have bales of cloth unfurled for inspection, but she seldom bought anything. Aruna was a dark, thin girl. She had pretty green eyes, and a mischievous smile, and she was not as innocent as she looked. Kishen would have liked to speak to her, but he did not relish the prospect of meeting Mrs Bhushan, who would make things awkward for him, so he turned his back on the shop and looked around for Hathi. He was about to walk away when he felt a heavy hand descend on his shoulder, and turning, found himself looking into the large, disagreeable eyes of Mrs Bhushan.

Mrs Bhushan was an imposing woman of some thirty-five years and she walked with a heavy determination that kept people, and even bulls, out of her way. Her dogs, her husband, and her servants were all afraid of her and submitted to her dictates without a murmur. A masculine woman, she bullied men and children, and lavished most of her affection on dogs. Her cocker spaniels slept on her bed, and her husband slept in the drawing-room.

'Kishen!' exclaimed Mrs Bhushan, pouncing upon the poor boy. 'What are you doing here?' And at the same time Aruna saw him, and her green eyes brightened, and she cried, 'Kishen! What are you doing here? We thought you were in Hardwar!'

Kishen was confused. To have Mrs Bhushan towering over him was like experiencing an eclipse of the sun. Moreover, he did not know how to explain his presence in Dehra. He contented himself with grinning sheepishly at Aruna.

'Where have you been, boy?' demanded Mrs Bhushan, getting business-like. 'Your clothes are all torn and you're a bundle of bones!'

'Oh, I've been on a walking-tour,' said Kishen unconvincingly.

'A walking-tour! Alone?'

'No, with a friend . . . .'

'You're too young to be wandering about like a vagrant. What do you think relatives are for? Now get into the car and come home with us.'

Kishen had not noticed the pre-war Hillman that stood beneath the tamarind tree. It had once belonged to a British magistrate, who had sold it cheap when he went away after Indian independence. Mrs Bhushan, in her aggressive way, had done her best to shorten the car's life, but it had lasted into the middle of the 1950s.

'What about my friend?' asked Kishen unhappily.

'You can see him later, can't you? Come on, Aruna, get in. There's something fishy about this walking-tour business, and I mean to get to the bottom of it!' And she trod on the accelerator with such ferocity that a lame beggar, who had been dawdling in the middle of the road, suddenly regained the use of both legs and sprang nimbly on to the pavement.

When they arrived at Mrs Bhushan's smart white bungalow, Kishen was placed in an armchair and subjected to Mrs Bhushan's own brand of third-degree, which consisted of snaps and snarls and snorts of disapproval. The cocker spaniels, disapproving of Kishen's ragged condition, snapped at his long-suffering legs, which had so far endured blisters, mosquito bites, and the nibbling of mice.

Before long, Kishen had told them the whole story of his journey from Hardwar with Rusty. Aruna listened to every word, full of admiration for the two boys, but Mrs Bhushan voiced her disapproval in strong terms.

'Well, this is the end of your wanderings, young man,' she said. 'You're staying here in this house. I won't have you wandering about the country with a lot of loafers.'

Mrs Bhushan, who was given to exaggeration, had visualized Rusty not as one person, but as several—an entire gang of tramps.

'Who would you rather stay with?' she demanded. 'Your father or me?'

'With you,' said Kishen hurriedly, certain that he had no choice.

'Then go and have a bath, while I get some clean clothes ready for you.'

Kishen spent half an hour under a hot shower, luxuriating in its warmth, while steam filled the room and his skin began to glow. It was weeks since he had used soap, and he lathered himself from head to foot, and watched the effect in the bathroom mirror. The water sent the soap scurrying down his legs, across the floor and down the drain and into the garden. He dried himself briskly, and hating the sight of his dusty old clothes, wrapped the towel around his waist and walked barefoot into the drawing-room.

Mrs Bhushan was searching for a pair of her husband's pyjamas to fit Kishen, and Aruna was alone in the room, reclining on the carpet. She pulled Kishen down beside her and held his hand.

'I wish I had been with you,' she said.

'Have you ever slept with a rat?' said Kishen. 'Because I did last night.'

'What about your friend Rusty? I can ask Mummy to let him stay with us for some time.'

'He won't come.'

'Why not?'

'He just won't come.'

'Is he too proud?'

'No, but you are proud. That's why he won't come.'

Aruna tossed the hair away from her face. 'Then let him stay where he is.'

'But I must go and tell him what has happened. He'll be waiting for me at the Clock Tower.'

'Not today, you won't,' said Mrs Bhushan, marching back into the room with a pink pyjama over her shoulder. 'You can see him tomorrow when we will drive you over in the car. I'm sure he can look after himself all right. If he had any sense, he'd have taken you home when he found you. The fellow must be an absolute rogue!'

And so, for the rest of the day, Kishen was held prisoner in Mrs Bhushan's comfortable drawing-room where Aruna kept him company, feeding him chicken curry and soft juicy papayas.

The school to which Rusty had been (the visit proved fruitless) stood near the dry riverbed of the Rispana, and on the other side of the riverbed lay mustard fields and tea gardens. As he had more than an hour left before meeting Kishen, he crossed the sandy riverbed and wandered through the fields. A peacock ran along the path with swift, ungainly strides.

A small canal passed through the tea gardens, and Rusty followed the canal, counting the horny grey lizards that darted in and out of the stones. He picked a tea leaf from a bush and holding it to his nose, found the smell sweet and pleasant. When he had walked about a mile, he came to a small clearing. There was a house in the clearing, surrounded by banana and poinsettia trees, the poinsettia leaves hanging down like long red tongues of fire. Bougainvillaea and other creepers covered the front of the house.

Sitting in a cane chair on the veranda was an Englishman. At least, Rusty assumed that the gentlemen he saw was an Englishman. He may have been a German or an American or a Russian, but the only Europeans Rusty had known were Englishmen, and he immediately took the white-haired gentleman in the cane chair to be English—and he happened to be right.

The gentleman was elderly, red-faced, dressed in a tweed coat and flannel shorts and thick woollen stockings. Sola-topees had gone out of fashion, otherwise he might have been wearing one. An unlit pipe was held between his teeth, and on his knees lay a copy of *The Times Literary Supplement*.

It was over a year since Rusty had seen an Englishman. The last one had been his guardian, and he had hated his guardian. But the old man in the chair seemed, somehow, bluff and amiable. Rusty advanced cautiously up the veranda steps, then waited for the old man to look up from his paper.

The old man did not look up, but he said, 'Yes, come in, boy. Pull up a chair and sit down.'

'I hope I'm not disturbing you,' said Rusty.

'You are, but it doesn't matter. Don't be so self-effacing.' The old man looked up at Rusty, and his grey eyes softened a little, but he did not smile; it was too much trouble to remove the pipe from his mouth.

Rusty pulled up a chair and sat down awkwardly, twiddling

his thumbs. The old man looked him up and down, said, 'Have a drink, I expect you're old enough,' and producing another glass from beneath the table, poured out two fingers of Solan whisky into Rusty's glass. He poured three fingers into his own glass. Then, from under the table, he produced two soda-water bottles and an opener. The bottle-tops flew out of the veranda with loud pops, and the golden liquid rose fuzzily to the top of the glass.

'Cheers,' said the old man, tossing down most of his drink.

'Pettigrew is the name,' said the old man. 'They used to call me Petty, though, down in Bangalore.'

'I'm pleased to meet you, Mr Pettigrew,' said Rusty politely. 'Is this your house?'

'Yes, the house is mine,' said Mr Pettigrew, knocking out his pipe on the table. 'It's all that is still mine—the house and my library. These gardens were mine once, but I only have a share in them now. It's third-grade tea, anyway. Only used for mixing.'

'Isn't there anyone to look after you?' asked Rusty, noticing the emptiness of the house.

'Look after me!' exclaimed Pettigrew indignantly. 'Whatever for? Do you think I'm a blooming invalid! I'm seventy, my boy, and I can ride a horse better than you can sit a bicycle!'

'I'm sure you can,' said Rusty hastily. 'And you don't look a year older than sixty. But I suppose you have a servant.'

'Well, I always thought I had one. But where the blighter is half the time, I'd like to know. Running after some wretched woman, I suppose.' A look of reminiscence passed over his face. 'I can remember the time when I did much the same thing. That was in the Kullu valley. There were two things Kullu used to be famous for—apples and pretty women!' He spluttered with laughter, and his face became very red. Rusty was afraid the old man's big blue veins were going to burst.

'Did you ever marry anyone?' he asked.

'Marry!' exclaimed Pettigrew. 'Are you off your head, young fellow? What do you think a chap like me would want to marry for? Only invalids get married, so that they can have someone look after them in their old age. No man's likely to be content with one woman in his life.'

He stopped then, and looked at Rusty in a peculiar defiant

way, and Rusty gathered that the old man was not really as cynical as he sounded.

'You're Harrison's boy, aren't you?' he asked suddenly.

'He was my guardian,' said Rusty. 'How did you know?'

'Never mind; I know. You ran off on your own a year ago, didn't you? Well, I don't blame you. Never could stand Harrison myself. Awful old bounder. Never bought a man a drink if he could help it. Guzzled other people's though. Don't blame you for running away. But what made you do it?'

'He was mean and he thrashed me and didn't allow me to make Indian friends. I was fed up. I wanted to live my own life.'

'Naturally. You're a man now. Your father was a fine man, too.'

'Did you know him?'

'Of course I knew him. He managed this estate for me once. I wanted to see you before, but Harrison never gave me the opportunity.'

'It was just chance that brought me this way.'

'I know. That's how everything happens.'

'Tell me about my father,' said Rusty. 'I was too small when he died, to remember much of him now.'

'Well, he was a good friend of mine, and we saw quite a lot of each other. He was interested in birds and insects and wild flowers—in fact, anything that had to do with natural history. Both of us were great readers and collectors of books, and that was what brought us together. But what I've been wanting to tell you was this. When he died, he had been living with an aunt of yours in the hills—near some village in Garhwal. Well, I may be wrong, but I think that if there was anything of value that your father may have wanted you to have, he'd have left in it the keeping of this aunt of yours. He trusted her—he trusted her a great deal more than he trusted Harrison, your legal guardian.'

'What was her name?' asked Rusty.

'I don't remember. I never saw her myself. But I do know she lived in the hills, where she had some land of her own.'

'Do you think I should look for her?' asked Rusty, surprised at his growing interest and enthusiasm.

'It might be a good idea,' said Mr Pettigrew. 'She must be

about forty, now. I think she lived in a small house on the banks of the river, about forty miles from Lansdowne. You'll have to walk much of the way from Lansdowne.'

'I'm used to walking. I have a Garhwali friend; perhaps he can help me.' Rusty was thinking of Hathi. He rose to go, anxious to tell Kishen and Hathi about this new development.

'Don't be in a hurry,' said Mr Pettigrew. 'Have you got any money?'

'A little.'

'Well, if you need any help, remember I'm here. I was your father's friend, you know.'

'Thank you, Mr Pettigrew. I'll see you again before I leave.'

After Rusty had gone, Mr Pettigrew refilled his pipe but did not bother to light it. Idly, he turned the pages of his paper, and when his servant same rushing up the path he forgot to reprimand the boy for being late. He was thinking of Rusty, and of how wonderful it was to be young, and regretting that he was now too old to climb mountains and look for lost friends.

'Damn!' he said in disgust, and threw the empty soda bottle into the bushes.

PROSPECT OF A JOURNEY

୬

Rusty waited at the Clock Tower for almost an hour, until it was nearly one o'clock. He had been feeling slightly impatient, not because he was anxious about Kishen, but because he wanted to tell him about Mr Pettigrew and the aunt in the hills. He presumed Kishen was loafing somewhere in the bazaar, or spending money at the Sindhi Sweet Shop. This did not worry him as he had kept most of the money; but one never knew what indiscretions Kishen might indulge in.

Rusty leant against the wall of the Clock Tower, watching the peddlers move lazily about the road, calling out their wares in desultory, afternoon voices; the toy-seller, waiting for the schools to close for the day and spill their children out into the streets; the fruit-vendor, with his basket of papayas, oranges, bananas and Kashmiri apples, which he continually sprinkled with water to make them look fresh; a cobbler drowsing in the shade of the tamarind tree, occasionally fanning himself with a strip of uncut leather. Rusty saw them all, without being very conscious of their existence, for his thoughts were far away, visualizing a strange person in the mountains.

A tall Sikh boy with a tray hanging by a string from his shoulders, approached Rusty. He wore a bright red turban, broad white pyjamas, and black Peshawari chappals which had been left unbuckled. He had long hands and feet, and if he was slim it was because he was still growing and had not had time to fill out. Though he was tall, he was upright, and his light brown eyes were friendly and direct. In the tray hanging from his neck lay an assortment of goods—combs, buttons, key-rings, reels of thread, bottles of cheap perfume, soaps and hair oils. He stopped near Rusty, but did not ask the boy if there was anything he wanted to buy. He stopped only to look at Rusty.

Rusty, feeling the other's gaze upon him, came out of his dreams and looked at the Sikh. They stared at each other for a minute with mutual interest; it was the first time they had set eyes on each other, but there was a compelling expression in the stranger's eyes, a haunting, half-sad, half-happy quality that held Rusty's attention, appealing to some odd quirk in his nature. The atmosphere was charged with this quality of sympathy.

A crow flapped down between them, and the significance of the moment vanished, and the bond of sympathy was broken.

Rusty turned away, and the Sikh boy wandered on down the road.

After waiting for another ten minutes, Rusty left the Clock Tower and began walking in the direction of the church, thinking that perhaps Kishen had gone there instead. He had not walked far when he found the Sikh boy sitting in the shade of a mango tree with his tray beside him and a book in his hands. Rusty paused to take a look at the book. It was Goldsmith's *The Traveller*. That was enough to make Rusty talk.

'Do you like the book?' he asked.

The Sikh looked up with a smile. 'It is in my Intermediate course. My exams begin next month. But I read other books, too,' he added.

'But when do you go to school?' asked Rusty, looking at the tray which was obviously the boy's means of livelihood.

'In the evening there are classes. During the day I sell this rubbish. I make enough to eat and to pay for my tuition. My name is Devinder.'

'My name is Rusty.'

Rusty leant against the trunk of the mango tree. 'What about your parents?' he asked. In India, when strangers meet, they must know each other's personal history before they can be friends. Rusty was well versed with the formalities.

'They are dead,' said Devinder. He spoke bluntly. 'They were killed during Partition in 1947, when we had to leave the Punjab. I was looked after in the refugee camp. But I prefer to be on my own, like this. I am happier this way.'

'And where do you stay?'

'Anywhere,' said Devinder, closing the book and standing up. 'In somebody's kitchen or veranda, or in the maidan. During the summer months it doesn't matter where I sleep, and in the winter people are kind and find some place for me.'

'You can sleep with us,' said Rusty impulsively. 'But I live in a church. I've been there since yesterday. It isn't very comfortable, but it's big.

'Are you a refugee too?' asked Devinder with a smile.

'Well, I'm a displaced person all right.'

They began waking down the road. They walked at a slow, easy pace, stopping now and then to sit on a wall or lean against a gate. They were not in a hurry to get anywhere. They had everywhere to go, and they could take their own time going there, and there was no one to hurry them on. Kishen would always have one foot in Rusty's world, and the other foot in a world of middle-class homes. Devinder had both his feet planted in the greater world, the open world, the world that is both lonely and free. He had been in it even longer than Rusty.

Rusty told Devinder about himself and about Kishen, and when he found that Kishen was not waiting at the church he really began to worry, but there was nothing he could do except wait for him. Devinder left his tray in the church and went with Rusty to the pool. They bathed and lay in the sun, and they were at the pool for about an hour.

The Goonga must have been following Rusty again, for he was sitting on the vestry steps when they returned to the church. 'Goo,' he said chuckling at his own cunning.

'Now I suppose he'll stay here too,' said Rusty.

In the company of Aruna, Kishen managed to forget Rusty for a few hours. They played carom and listened to the radio. Kishen took her hand and examining her palm, predicted misery; his predictions were made at length, for he enjoyed

holding Aruna's hand. Forgetting—or pretending to forget—
that they were almost grown-up people, they began wrestling
on the white Afghan carpet until Mrs Bhushan, who had been
visiting the neighbours to tell them about Kishen, came home
and lifted them off the carpet by the scruffs of their necks.

Aruna had to do her school homework, so she got Kishen
to help her with arithmetic. They carried a bench and table out
under a sweet-smelling pomalo tree.

As Kishen leant over Aruna, explaining sums which he did
not understand, he became acutely conscious of the scent of her
hair and the proximity of her right ear, and the sum gradually
lost its urgency. The right ear with its soft creamy lobe, was
excruciatingly near. Kishen was tempted to bite it.

'You have a nice ear, Aruna,' he said.

Aruna smiled at the sum.

But at night, lying in bed, he began to think of Rusty sitting
alone in the empty church, waiting for him. It was an intolerable
vision.

He was sleeping in a separate room. Mrs Bhushan and
Aruna slept together in the big bedroom. (Mr Bhushan was in
Delhi, enjoying a week's freedom.) Kishen had only to open his
window and slip out into the garden.

He crept quietly out of bed and slipped off Mr Bhushan's
pink pyjamas. Soft moonlight came in from the window, playing
on his naked legs. He hunted about the room until he found
his old pyjamas and then, taking his chappals in his hand, he
went slowly to the bedroom door. Opening it slowly, he peered
into the other room.

Mrs Bhushan lay flat on her back, her bosom heaving as
though it were in the throes of a minor earthquake, her breath
making strange, whistling sounds. There was no likelihood of
her waking up. But Aruna was wide awake. She sat up in bed,
staring at Kishen.

Kishen put a finger to his lips and approached the bed.

'I'm going to see Rusty,' he whispered. 'I will come back
before morning.'

His fingers found hers and squeezed them, then he left the
room, climbing out of the window and running down the path

to the gate. He kept running until he reached the church.

He was about to enter the vestry when he was almost startled out of his wits by a wild, frightening figure that suddenly loomed up before him.

'Goo!' said the Goonga.

'Oh, it's you!' gasped Kishen. 'I might have known it.'

He was even more taken aback to find Rusty sitting on the ground with Devinder, reading from *The Traveller*. The Sikh boy had removed his turban, and his long hair fell over his shoulders, giving him a wild, rather dangerous look.

Rusty looked up from the books as Kishen's shadow fell across the page.

'Where have you been, bhaiya?' he asked. 'You did not tell me you would be so late.'

'I was kidnapped,' said Kishen, sitting down on a bench and looking suspiciously at Devinder.

'He is our new member,' exclaimed Rusty lightly. 'He will be staying here too, from now on.'

Kishen gave Devinder a hostile nod. He was inclined to be possessive in his friendships, and resented anyone else being too close to Rusty.

'Is the Goonga staying here too?' he asked.

'He followed me again. We can use him as a chowkidar. But tell me, what happened to you?'

'I met Mrs Bhushan, an old friend of my mother's. I bluffed to her that I was on a walking-tour, but she didn't believe me. I had to go home with her, and it was only when she went to sleep that I managed to get away. But she will be sure to arrive here in the morning. What should I do then?'

'You never trouble to make up your own mind, do you, bhaiya?'

'I don't want to live with relatives.'

'But we can't wander about aimlessly for ever.'

'We have stopped wandering now,' said Kishen.

'You have. I think I must go away again. There is a relative of mine living in the hills. Perhaps she can help me.'

'I am definitely going with you!' exclaimed Kishen.

'And if I do not find her, what happens? We will both be stuck on a mountain without anything. If you stay here, you might be able to help me later.'

'Well, when you are going?' asked Kishen impatiently.

'As soon as I collect some money.'

'I will try to get some from Mrs Bhushan, she has plenty, but she is a miser. Will he go with you?' said Kishen, looking at Devinder.

'I cannot go,' said Devinder. 'I have my examinations in a month.'

Kishen kicked off his shoes and made himself comfortable on a pew. Rusty began reading aloud from *The Traveller*, and everyone listened—Kishen, with his feet stuck upon a pew-support; Devinder, with his chin resting on his knees and his eyes on Rusty; and the Goonga (not understanding a word) grinning in the candlelight.

Next morning the three boys went down to the pool to bathe. The smell of the neem trees, the sound of the water, the touch of the breeze, intoxicated them, filled them with a zest for living. They ran over the wild wood-sorrel, over the dew-drenched grass, down to the water.

The Goonga, who on principal refused to bathe, sat on top of the rocks and looked on with detached amusement at the others swimming in the pool and wrestling in the shallow water.

Devinder could stand in the deepest part of the pool and still have his head above water. To keep his long hair out of the way, he tied it in a knot, like a bun, on top of his head. His hair was almost auburn in colour, his skin was a burnished gold. He slipped about in the water like a long glistening fish.

Kishen began making balls from loose mud, which he threw at Devinder and Rusty. A mud fight developed. It was like playing snowballs, but more messy. At the height of the battle, the Goonga suddenly appeared on a buffalo.

They took turns mounting the buffalo, but only the Goonga managed to make it move. When Kishen or Rusty sat on it, kicking and shouting, the buffalo refused to budge; at the most, it would roll over on its side in the slush, taking the boys down as well. But it did not matter how muddy they got, because they had only to dive into the pool to be clean again.

They were a long time at the pool. When they returned to

the church they found the Hillman parked at the gate, with an impatient and irate Mrs Bhushan sitting at the wheel. She was in a mood to be belligerent, but seeing Kishen accompanied not only by Rusty but by two other dangerous looking youths, her worst fears were confirmed. Kishen was in the hands of cutthroats, and discretion would be the better part of valour.

'Kishen, my son,' she pleaded, 'we have been worrying about you very much. You should not have left without telling us! Aruna is very unhappy.'

Kishen stood sulkily near his friends.

'You had better go, Kishen,' said Rusty. 'You will be of more help to me if you stay with Mrs Bhushan.'

'But when will I see you?'

'As soon as I come back from the hills.'

Once Kishen was in the car, Rusty confronted Mrs Bhushan and said, 'He won't leave you now. But if he is not happy with you, we will come and take him away.'

'We are his *friends*,' said Mrs Bhushan.

'No, you are like a relative. *We* are his friends.'

Kishen said, 'If you don't come back soon, Rusty, I will start looking for you.' He scowled affectionately at Rusty and waved to Devinder and the Goonga as the car took him away.

'He might run back again tonight,' said Devinder.

'He will get used to Mrs Bhushan's house,' said Rusty. 'Soon he will be liking it. He will not forget us, but he will remember us only when he is alone. We are only something that happened to him once upon a time. But we have changed him a little. Now he knows there are others in the world besides himself.'

'I could not understand him,' said Devinder. 'But still I liked him.'

'I understood him,' said Rusty, 'and *still* I liked him.'

THE LAFUNGA

☙

'IF YOU HAVE NOTHING to do,' said Devinder, 'will you come with me on my rounds?'

'First we will see Hathi. If he has not left yet, I can accompany him to Lansdowne.'

Rusty set out with Devinder in the direction of the bazaar. As it was early morning, the shops were just beginning to open. Vegetable vendors were busy freshening their stock with liberal sprinklings of water, calling their prices and their wares. Children dawdled in the road on their way to school, playing hopscotch or marbles. Girls going to college chattered in groups like gay, noisy parrots. Men cycled to work, and bullock-carts came in from the villages, laden with produce. The dust, which had taken all night to settle, rose again like a mist.

Rusty and Devinder stopped at the tea shop to eat thickly buttered buns and drink strong, sweet tea. Then they looked for Hathi's room, and found it above a clothes shop, lying empty, with its doors open. The string bed leant against the wall. On shelves and window-ledges, in corners and on the floor, lay little coloured toys made of clay—elephants and bulls, horses and peacocks, and images of Krishna and Ganesha—a blue Krishna, with a flute to his lips, a jolly Ganesha with a delightful little trunk. Most of the toys were rough and unfinished, more charming than the completed pieces. Most of the finished products would now be on sale in the bazaar.

It came as a surprise to Rusty to discover that Hathi, the big wrestler, made toys for a living. He had not imagined there would be delicacy and skill in his friend's huge hands. The pleasantness of the discovery offset his disappointment at finding Hathi had gone.

'He has left already,' said Rusty. 'Never mind. I know he will welcome me even if I arrive unexpectedly.'

He left the bazaar with Devinder, making for the residential part of the town. As he would be leaving Dehra soon, there was no point in his visiting the school again. Later, though, he would see Mr Pettigrew.

When they reached the Clock Tower, someone whistled to them from across the street, and a tall young man came striding towards them.

He looked taller than Devinder, mainly because of his long legs. He wore a lose-fitting bush-shirt that hung open in front. His face was long and pale, but he had quick, devilish eyes, and he smiled disarmingly.

'Here comes Sudheer the Lafunga,' whispered Devinder. 'Lafunga means loafer. He probably wants some money. He is the most charming and the most dangerous person in town.' Aloud, he said, 'Sudheer, when are you going to return the twenty rupees you owe me?'

'Don't talk that way, Devinder,' said the Lafunga, looking offended. 'Don't hurt my feelings. You know your money is safer with me than it is in the bank. It will even bring you dividends, mark my words. I have a plan that will come off in a few days, and then you will get back double your money. Please tell me, who is your friend?'

'We stay together,' said Devinder, introducing Rusty. 'And he is bankrupt too, so don't get any ideas.'

'Please don't believe what he says of me,' said the Lafunga with a captivating smile that showed his strong teeth. 'Really, I am not very harmful.'

'Well, completely harmless people are usually dull,' said Rusty.

'How I agree with you! I think we have a lot in common.'

'No, he hasn't got anything,' put in Devinder.

'Well then, he must start from the beginning. It is the best way to make a fortune. You will come and see me, won't you, Mr Rusty? We could make a terrific combination, I am sure. You are the kind of person people trust! They take only one look at me and then feel their pockets to see if anything is missing!'

Rusty instinctively put his hand to his own pocket, and all three of them laughed.

'Well, I must go,' said Sudheer the Lafunga, now certain that Devinder was not likely to produce any funds. 'I have a small matter to attend to. It may bring me a fee of twenty or thirty rupees.'

'Go,' said Devinder. 'Strike while the iron is hot.'

'Not I,' said the Lafunga, grinning and moving off 'I make the iron hot by striking.'

'Sudheer is not too bad,' said Devinder as they walked away from the Clock Tower. 'He is a crook, of course—*Shree 420*— but he would not harm people like us. As he is quite well educated, he manages to gain the confidence of some well-to-do-people, and acts on their behalf in matters that are not always respectable. But he spends what he makes, and is too generous to be successful.'

They had reached a quiet, tree-lined road, and walked in the shade of neem, mango, jamun and eucalyptus trees. Clumps of tall bamboo grew between the trees. Nowhere but in Dehra had Rusty seen so many kinds of trees. Trees that had no names. Tall, straight trees, and broad, shady trees. Trees that slept or brooded in the afternoon stillness. And trees that shimmered and moved and whispered even when the winds were asleep.

Some marigolds grew wild on the footpath, and Devinder picked two of them, giving one to Rusty.

'There is a girl who lives at the bottom of the road,' he said. 'She is a pretty girl. Come with me and see her.'

They walked to the house at the end of the road and while Rusty stood at the gate, Devinder went up the path. Devinder stood at the bottom of the veranda steps, a little to one side, where he could be seen from a window, and whistled softly.

Presently a girl came out on the veranda. When she saw Devinder she smiled. She had a round, fresh face and long black hair, and she was not wearing any shoes.

Devinder gave her the marigold. She took it in her hand and not knowing what to say, ran indoors.

That morning Devinder and Rusty walked about four miles. Devinder's customers ranged from decadent maharanis and the wives of government officials to gardeners and sweeper women. Though his merchandise was cheap, the well-to-do were more finicky about the price than the poor. And there were a few who bought things from Devinder because they knew his circumstances and liked what he was doing.

A small girl with flapping pigtails came skipping down the road. She stopped to stare at Rusty as though he were something quite out of the ordinary, but not unpleasant.

Rusty took the other marigold from his pocket and gave it to the girl. It was a long time since he had been able to make anyone a gift.

After some time they parted, Devinder going back to the town, while Rusty crossed the river-bed. He walked through the tea gardens until he found Mr Pettigrew's bungalow.

The old man was not in the veranda, but a young servant salaamed Rusty and asked him to sit down. Apparently Mr Pettigrew was having his bath.

'Does he always bathe in the afternoon?' asked Rusty.

'Yes, the sahib likes his water to be put in the sun to get warm. He does not like cold baths or hot baths. The afternoon sun gives his water the right temperature.'

Rusty walked into the drawing-room and nearly fell over a small table. The room was full of furniture and pictures and bric-a-brac. Tiger-heads, stuffed and mounted, snarled down at him from the walls. On the carpet lay several cheetal skins, a bit worn at the sides. There were several shelves filled with books bound in morocco or calf. Photographs adorned the walls—one of a much younger Mr Pettigrew standing over a supine leopard, another of Mr Pettigrew perched on top of an elephant, with his rifle resting on his knees . . . . Remembering his own experiences, Rusty wondered how such an active shikari ever found time for reading. While he was gazing at the photographs, Pettigrew himself came in, a large bathrobe wrapped round his thin frame, his grizzly chest looking very raw and red from the scrubbing he had just given it.

'Ah, there you are!' he said. 'The bearer told me you were

here. Glad to see you again. Sit down and have a drink.'

Mr Pettigrew found the whisky and poured out two stiff drinks. Then, still in his bathrobe and slippers, he made himself comfortable in an armchair. Rusty said something complimentary about one of the mounted tiger-heads.

'Bagged it in Assam,' he said. 'Back in 1928, that was. I spent three nights on a machan before I got a shot at it.'

'You have a lot of books,' observed Rusty.

'A good collection, mostly flora and fauna. Some of them are extremely rare. By the way,' he said, looking around at the wall, 'did you ever see a picture of your father?'

'Have you got one?' asked Rusty. 'I've only a faint memory of what he looked like.'

'He's in that group photograph over there,' said Mr Pettigrew, pointing to a picture on the wall.

Rusty went over to the picture and saw three men dressed in white shirts and flannels, holding tennis rackets and looking very self-conscious.

'He's in the middle,' said Pettigrew. 'I'm on his right.'

Rusty saw a young man with fair hair and a fresh face. He was the only player who was smiling. Mr Pettigrew, sporting a fierce moustache, looked as though he was about to tackle a tiger with his racket. The third person was bald and uninteresting.

'Of course, he's very young in that photo,' said Pettigrew. 'It was taken long before you were ever thought of—before your father married.'

Rusty did not reply. He was trying to imagine his father in action on a tennis court, and wondered if he was a better player that Pettigrew.

'Who was the best player among you?' he asked.

'Ah, well, we were both pretty good, you know. Except for poor old Wilkie on the left. He got in the picture by mistake.'

'Did my father talk much?' asked Rusty.

'Well, we all talked a lot, you know, especially after a few drinks. He talked as much as any of us. He could sing, when he wanted to. His rendering of the "Kashmiri Love Song" was always popular at parties, but it wasn't often he sang, because he didn't like parties . . . . Do you remember it? "Pale hands I love, beside the Shalimar . . . ."'

Pettigrew began singing in a cracked, wavering voice, and Rusty was forced to take his eyes off the photograph. Half-way through the melody, Pettigrew forgot the words, so he took another gulp of whisky and began singing "The Rose of Tralee". The sight of the old man singing love songs in his bathrobe, with a glass of whisky in his hand, made Rusty smile.

'Well,' said Pettigrew, breaking off in the middle of the song, 'I don't sing as well as I used to. Never mind. Now tell me, boy, when are you going to Garhwal?'

'Tomorrow, perhaps.'

'Have you any money?'

'Enough to travel with. I have a friend in the hills with whom I can stay for some time.'

'And what about money?'

'I have enough.'

'Well, I'm lending you twenty rupees,' he said, thrusting an envelope into the boy's hands. 'Come and see me when you return, even if you don't find what you're looking for.'

'I'll do that, Mr Pettigrew.'

The old man looked at the boy for some time, as though summing him up.

'You don't really have to find out much about your father,' he said. 'You're just like him, you know.'

Returning to the bazaar, Devinder found Sudheer at a paan shop, his lips red with betel juice. Devinder went straight to the point.

'Sudheer,' he said, 'you owe me twenty rupees. I need it, not for myself, but for Rusty, who has to leave Dehra very urgently. You must get me the money by tonight.'

The Lafunga scratched his head.

'It will be difficult,' he said, 'but perhaps it can be managed. He really needs the money? It is not just a trick to get your own money back?

'He is going to the hills. There may be money for him there, if he finds the person he is looking for.'

'Well, that's different,' said the Lafunga, brightening up. 'That makes Rusty an investment. Meet me at the Clock Tower at six o'clock, and I will have the money for you. I am glad to find you making useful friends for a change.'

He stuffed another roll of paan into his mouth, and taking leave of Devinder with a bright red smile, strolled leisurely down the bazaar road.

As far as appearances went, he had little to do but loll around in the afternoon sunshine, frequenting tea shops and gambling with cards in small back rooms. All this he did very well—but it did not make him a living.

To say that he lived on his wits would be an exaggeration. He lived a great deal on other people's wits. There was the *seth* for instance, Rusty's former landlord, who owned much property and dabbled in many shady transactions and who was often represented by the Lafunga in affairs of an unsavoury nature.

Sudheer came originally from the Frontier, where little value was placed on human life; and while still a boy, he had wandered, a homeless refugee, over the border into India. A smuggler adopted him, taught him something of the trade, and introduced him to some of the best hands in the profession. But in a border-foray with the police, Sudheer's foster-father was shot dead, and the youth was once again on his own. By this time he was old enough to look after himself. With the help of his foster-father's connections, he soon attained the service and confidence of the *seth*.

Sudheer was no petty criminal. He practised crime as a fine art, and believed that thieves, and even murderers, had to have certain principles. If he stole, then he stole from a rich man who could afford to be robbed, or from a greedy man who deserved to be robbed. And if he did not rob poor men, it was not because of any altruistic motive—it was because poor men were not worth robbing.

He was good to those friends, like Devinder, who were good to him. Perhaps his most valuable friends, as sources of both money and information, were the dancing girls who followed their profession in an almost inaccessible little road in the heart of the bazaar. His best friends were Hastini and Mrinalini. He borrowed money from them very freely, and seldom paid back more than half of it.

Hastini could twang the sitar, dance—with a rather heavy tread—among various other accomplishments.

Mrinalini, a much smaller woman, had grown up in the profession. She was looked after by her mother, a former entertainer, who kept most of the money that Mrinalini made.

Sudheer woke Hastini in the middle of her afternoon siesta by tickling her under the chin with a feather.

'And who were you with last night, little brother?' she asked, running her fingers through his thick brown hair. 'You are smelling of some horrible perfume.'

'You know I do not spend my nights with anyone,' said Sudheer. 'The perfume is from yesterday.'

'Someone new?'

'No, my butterfly. I have known her for a week.'

'Too long a time,' said Hastini petulantly. 'A dangerously long time. How much have you spent on her?'

'Nothing so far. But that is not why I came to see you. Have you got twenty rupees?'

'Villain!' cried Hastini. 'Why do you always borrow from me when you want to entertain some stupid young thing? Are you so heartless?'

'My little lotus flower!' protested Sudheer, pinching her rosy cheeks. 'I am not borrowing for any such reason. A friend of mine has to leave Dehra urgently, and I must get the money for his train fare. I owe it to him.'

'Since when did you have a friend?'

'Never mind that. I have one. And I come to you for help because I love you more than any one else. Would you prefer that I borrow the money from Mrinalini?'

'You dare not,' said Hastini. 'I will kill you if you do.'

Between Hastini of the broad hips, and Mrinalini who was small and slender, there existed a healthy rivalry for the affections of Sudheer. Perhaps it was the great difference in their proportions that animated the rivalry. Mrinalini envied the luxuriousness of Hastini's soft body, while Hastini envied Mrinalini's delicacy, poise, slenderness of foot, and graceful walk. Mrinalini was the colour of milk and honey, she had the daintiness of a deer, while Hastini possessed the elegance of an elephant.

Sudheer could appreciate both these qualities.

He stood up, looking young even for his twenty-two years, and smiled a crooked smile. He might have looked effeminate had it not been for his hands—they were big, long-fingered, strong hands.

'Where is the money?' he asked.

'You are so impatient! Sit down, sit down. I have it here beneath the mattress.'

Sudheer's hand made its way beneath the mattress and probed about in search of the money.

'Ah, here it is! You have a fortune stacked away here. Yes, ten rupees, fifteen, twenty—and one for luck . . . . Now give me a kiss!'

About an hour later Sudheer was in the street again, whistling cheerfully to himself. He walked with a long, loping stride, his shirt hanging open. Warm sunshine filled one side of the narrow street and crept up the walls of shops and houses.

Sudheer passed a fruit stand where the owner was busy talking to a customer, and helped himself to a choice red Kashmiri apple. He continued on his way down the bazaar road, munching the apple.

The bazaar continued for a mile, from the Clock Tower to the railway station, and Sudheer could hear the whistle of a train. He turned off at a little alley, throwing his half-eaten apple to a stray dog. Then he climbed a flight of stairs— wooden stairs that were loose and rickety, liable to collapse at any moment . . . .

Mrinalini's half-deaf mother was squatting on the kitchen floor, making a fire in an earthen brazier. Sudheer poked his head round the door and shouted: 'Good morning, Mother, I hope you are making me some tea. You look fine today!' And then, in a lower tone, so that she could not hear: 'You look like a dried-up mango.'

'So it's you again,' grumbled the old woman. 'What do you want now?'

'Your most respectable daughter is what I want,' said Sudheer.

'What's that?' She cupped her hand to her ear and leaned forward.

'Where's Mrinalini?' shouted Sudheer.

'Don't shout like that! She is not here.'

'That's all I wanted to know,' said Sudheer, and he walked through the kitchen, through the living-room, and on to the veranda balcony, where he found Mrinalini sitting in the sun, combing out her long silken hair.

'Let me do it for you,' said Sudheer, and he took the comb from her hand and ran it through the silky black hair. 'For one so little, so much hair. You could conceal yourself in it and not be seen, except for your dainty little feet.'

'What are you after, Sudheer? You are so full of compliments this morning. And watch out for Mother—if she sees you combing my hair, she will have a fit!'

'And I hope it kills her.'

'Sudheer!'

'Don't be so sentimental about your mother. You are her little gold mine, and she treats you as such—soon I will be having to fill in application forms before I can see you! It is time you kept your earnings for yourself.'

'So that it will be easier for you to help yourself?'

'Well, it would be more convenient. By the way, I have come to you for twenty rupees.'

Mrinalini laughed delightedly and took the comb from Sudheer. 'What were you saying about my little feet?' she asked slyly.

'I said they were the feet of a princess, and I would be very happy to kiss them.'

'Kiss them, then.'

She held one delicate golden foot in the air, and Sudheer took it in his hands (which were as large as her feet) and kissed her ankle.

'That will be twenty rupees,' he said.

She pushed him away with her foot. 'But Sudheer, I gave you fifteen rupees only three days ago. What have you done with it?'

'I haven't the slightest idea. I only know that I must have more. It is most urgent, you can be sure of that. But if you cannot help me, I must try elsewhere.'

'Do that, Sudheer. And may I ask, whom do you propose to try?'

'Well, I was thinking of Hastini.'

'Who?'

'You know, Hastini, the girl with the wonderful figure . . . .'

'I should think I do! Sudheer, if you dare to take so much as a rupee from her, I'll never speak to you again!'

'Well then, what shall I do?'

Mrinalini beat the arms of the chair with her little fists and cursed Sudheer under her breath. Then she got up and went into the kitchen. A great deal of shouting went on in the kitchen before Mrinalini came back with flushed cheeks and fifteen rupees.

'You don't know the trouble I had getting it,' she said. 'Now don't come asking for more until at least a week has passed.'

'After a week, I will be able to supply you with funds. I am engaged tonight on a mission of some importance. In a few days I will place golden bangles on your golden feet.'

'What mission?' asked Mrinalini, looking at him with an anxious frown. 'If it is anything to do with the *seth*, please leave it alone. You know what happened to Satish Dayal. He was smuggling opium for the *seth*, and now he is sitting in jail, while the *seth* continues as always.'

'Don't worry about me. I can deal with the *seth*.'

'Then be off! I have to entertain a foreign delegation this evening. You can come tomorrow morning if you are free.'

'I may come. Meanwhile, goodbye!'

He walked backwards into the living-room, pivoted into the kitchen and bending over the old woman, kissed her on the forehead.

'You dried-up old mango,' he said. And went away whistling.

TO THE HILLS

❧

IN THE CHURCH, ON the night of his departure, Rusty felt the sadness of one leaving a familiar home and familiar faces. Up till now he had been with friends, people who had given him help and comradeship; but now he would be on his own, without Kishen or Devinder. That was the way it had always turned out.

He gave his spare clothes to the Goonga because he did not feel like carrying them with him. He left his books with Devinder.

'Stay here, Devinder,' he said. 'Stay here until I come back. I want to find you in Dehra.'

A breeze from the open window made the candles flutter, and the shadows on the walls leapt and gesticulated; but Devinder stood still, the candle-light playing softly on his face.

'I'm always here, Rusty,' he said.

The northern-bound train was not crowded, because in December few people went to the hills. Rusty had no difficulty in finding an empty compartment.

It was a small compartment with only two lower berths. Lying down on one of them, he stared out of the far window at the lights across the railway tracks. He fell asleep, and woke only when the train jerked into motion.

Looking out of the window, he saw the station platform slipping away, while the shouts of the coolies and vendors grew fainter until they were lost in the sound of the wheels and the rocking of the carriage. The town lights twinkled, grew distant, were swallowed up by the trees. The engine went panting through the jungle, its red sparks floating towards the stars.

There were four small stations between Dehra and Hardwar, and the train stopped for five or ten minutes at each station. At Doiwala he was woken from a light sleep by a tap at the window. It was dark outside, and he could not make out the face that was pressed against the glass. When he opened the door, a familiar, long-legged youth stepped into the carriage, swiftly shutting the door behind him. Before sitting down, he dropped all the shutters on the side facing the platform.

'We meet again,' said the youth, sitting down opposite Rusty as the train began to move. 'Don't you remember me? I'm Sudheer. I met you at the Clock Tower with Devinder.'

Rusty did not know that the money Devinder had given him had come through Sudheer, but it did not take him long to recognize the Lafunga.

'Of course I remember you,' he said. 'When I saw you just now, appearing suddenly out of the dark, I had the feeling you were someone I had seen seldom but knew quite well. But what are you doing on this train?'

'I'm going to Hardwar,' said Sudheer, a smile playing about the corners of his mouth. 'On business. Don't ask me for details.'

'Why didn't you get on the train at Dehra?'

'Because I have to use strategy, my friend.' He kicked off his shoes and put his feet on the opposite bunk. 'And where are you going now?'

'I'm going to the hills to see a friend.' Rusty was not sure if he should confide his plans to Sudheer, but if Devinder could trust him, why not?

'And when will you come back? I suppose you will come back.'

'I'm not sure what I'll do. I want to give myself a chance to be a writer, because I may succeed. It is the only kind of work I really want to do—if you can call it work.'

'Yes, it is work. Real work is what you want to do. It is only when you work for yourself that you really work. I use my eyes and my fingers and my wits. I have no morals and no scruples . . . .'

'But you have principles, I think.'

'I don't know about that.'

'You have feelings?'

'Yes, but I pay no attention to them.'

'I cannot do that.'

'You are too noble! Why don't you join me? I can guarantee money, excitement, friendship—my friendship, anyway . . . .'

Sudheer leant forward and took Rusty's hand. There was earnestness in his manner, and also a challenge.

'Come on. Be with me. The day I met you, I wanted you to be with me. I'm a crook, and I don't have any real friends. I don't ask you to be a crook. I ask you to be my friend.'

'I will be your friend,' said Rusty, taking a sudden liking to Sudheer. He almost said, 'I will be a crook, too,' but thought better of it.

'Why not get down at Hardwar?'

'Why not come with me to Lansdowne?'

'I have work in Hardwar.'

'And I in the hills.'

'That is why friends are so difficult to keep.' Sudheer smiled and leant back in the seat. 'All right, then. We will join up later. I will meet you in the hills. Wait for me, remember me, don't put me out of your mind.'

When the train drew into Hardwar, Sudheer got up and stood near the door.

'I have to go quickly,' he said. 'I will see you again.'

As the engine slowed down and the station lights became brighter, Sudheer opened the carriage door and jumped down to the railway banking.

Alarmed, Rusty ran to the open door and shouted, 'Are you all right, Sudheer?'

'Just worry about yourself!' called Sudheer, his voice growing faint and distant. 'Good luck!'

He was hidden from view by a signal box, and then the train drew into the brightly-lit, crowded station, and pilgrims began climbing into the compartments.

Two policemen came down the platform, looking in at carriage windows and asking questions. They stopped at Rusty's window and asked him if he had a companion during the journey, and gave him an unmistakable description of Sudheer.

'He got off the train long ago,' lied Rusty. 'At Doiwala, I think. Why, what do you want him for?'

'He has stolen one thousand rupees from a *seth* in Dehra,' said the policemen. 'If you see him again, please pull the alarm cord.'

Two days later, Rusty was in Hathi's house, sitting on a string cot out in the courtyard. There was snow on the tiled roof and in the fields, but the sun was quite warm. The mountains stretched away, disappearing into sky and cloud. Rusty felt he belonged there, to the hills and the pine and deodar forests, and the clear mountain streams.

There were about thirty families in the village. There were not many men about, and the few that could be found were either old or inactive. Most young men joined the army or took jobs in the plains, for the village economy was poor. The women remained behind to do the work. They fetched water, kept the houses clean, cooked meals, and would soon be ploughing the fields. The old men just sat around and smoked hookahs and gossiped the morning away.

It had been a long, lonely walk from the bus terminus at Lansdowne to Hathi's village. Rusty had walked fast, because there had been no one to talk to, and no food to be had on the way. But he had met a farmer coming from the opposite direction, and had shared the man's meal. All the farmer had were some onions and a few chappatis; but Rusty was hungry and he enjoyed the meal. When he had finished, he said goodbye and they went their different ways.

At first he walked along a smooth slippery carpet of pine needles; then the pine trees gave way to oak and rhododendron. It was cool and shady, but after Rusty had done about fifteen miles, the forest ended, the hills became bare and rocky, and the earth the colour of copper. He was thirsty, but there was nothing to drink. His tongue felt thick and furry and he could barely move his lips. All he could do was walk on mechanically, hardly conscious of his surroundings or even of walking.

When the sun went down, a cool breeze came whispering across the dry grass. And then, as he climbed higher, the grass grew greener, there were trees, water burst from the hillsides in small springs, and birds swooped across the path—bright green parrots, tree-pies and paradise flycatchers. He was walking beside a river, above the turbulent water rushing down a n arrow gorge. It was a steep climb to Hathi's village; and as it grew dark, he had to pick his way carefully along the narrow path.

As he approached Hathi's house on the outskirts of the village, he was knocked down by a huge Tibetan mastiff. He got up, and Hathi came out of the house and ran to greet Rusty and knocked him over again. Then he was in the house, drinking hot milk. And later he lay on a soft quilt, and a star was winking at him from the skylight.

The house was solid—built of yellow granite—and it had a black-tiled roof. There was an orange tree in the courtyard, and though there were no oranges on it at this time of the year, the young leaves smelt sweet. When Rusty looked around, he saw mountains, blue and white-capped, with dark clouds drifting down the valleys. Pale blue woodsmoke climbed the hill from the houses below, and people drifted about in the warm winter sunshine.

When Rusty and Hathi walked in the hills, they sometimes went barefoot. Once they walked a few miles upstream, and found a waterfall dashing itself down on to smooth rocks fifty feet below. Here the forest was dark and damp, and at night bears and leopards roamed the hillsides. When the leopards were hungry, they did not hesitate to enter villages and carry off stray dogs.

Once Rusty heard the hunting-cry of a leopard on the prowl. It was evening, and he was close to the village when he heard the harsh, saw-like cry, something between a grunt and a cough. Then the leopard appeared to his right, slinking through the trees, crouching low, a swift black shadow . . . .

There was only one shop in the village, and that was also the post office—it sold soap and shoes and the barest necessities. When Rusty passed it, he was hailed by the shopkeeper who was brandishing a postcard. Rusty was surprised that there should be a letter for him.

He was even more surprised when he discovered that the card was from Sudheer, the Lafunga.

It said: 'Join me at Landsdowne. I have news of your aunt. We will travel together. I have money for both of us, as I consider you a good investment.'

RUM AND CURRY

ॐ

SUDHEER AND RUSTY LEFT Lansdowne early one morning, and by the time they reached the oak and deodar forests of Kotli they were shivering with the cold.

'I am not used to this sort of travel,' complained Sudheer. 'If this is a wild goose chase, I will curse you, Rusty. At least we should have mules to sit on.'

'We are sure to find a village soon,' said Rusty. 'We can spend a night there. As for it being a wild goose chase, it was you who told me that my aunt lived somewhere here. If she is not in this direction, it is all your fault, Lafunga.'

There was little light in the Kotli forest, for the tall, crowded deodars and oaks kept out the moonlight. The road was damp and covered with snails.

They were relieved to find a few small huts clustered together in an open clearing. A light showed from only one of the houses. Rusty rapped on the hard oak door and called out: 'Is anyone there? We want a place to spend the night.'

'Who is it?' asked a nervous, irritable voice.

'Travellers,' said Sudheer. 'Tired, hungry and poor.'

'This is not a *dharamsala*,' grumbled the man inside. 'This is no place for pilgrims.'

'We are not pilgrims,' said Sudheer, trying a different approach. 'We are road inspectors, servants of the government— so open up, my friend!'

They heard much ill-natured muttering before the door opened, revealing an old and dirty man who had stubble on his chin, warts on his feet, and grease on his old clothes.

'Where do you come from?' he asked suspiciously.

'Lansdowne,' said Rusty. 'We have walked twenty miles since morning. Can we sleep in your house?'

'How do I know you are not thieves?' asked the old man, who did not look very honest himself.

'If we were thieves,' said Sudheer impatiently, 'we would not stand here talking to you. We would have cut your throat and thrown you to the vultures, and carried off your beautiful daughter.'

'I have no daughter here.'

'What a pity! Never mind. My friend and I will sleep in your house tonight. We are not going to sleep in the forest.'

Sudheer strode into the lighted room, but backed out almost immediately, holding his fingers to his nose.

'What dead animal are you keeping here?' he cried.

'They are sheepskins, for curing,' said the old man. 'What is wrong?'

'Nothing, nothing,' said Sudheer, not wishing to hurt their host's feelings so soon; but in an aside to Rusty, he whispered, 'There is such a stink, I doubt if we will wake up in the morning.'

They stumbled into the room, and Rusty dumped his bundle on the ground. The room was bare except for dilapidated sheep and deer skins hanging on the walls. There was a small fire in a corner of the room. Sudheer and Rusty got as close to it as they could, stamping their feet and chafing their hands. The old man sat down on his haunches and glared suspiciously at the intruders. Sudheer looked at him, and then at Rusty, and shrugged eloquently.

'May we know your name?' asked Rusty.

'It is Ram Singh,' said the old man grudgingly.

'Well, Ram Singh, my host,' said Sudheer solicitously, 'have you had your meal as yet?'

'I take it in the morning,' said Ram Singh.

'And in the evening?' Sudheer's voice held a note of hope.

'It is not necessary to eat more than once a day.'

'For a rusty old fellow like you, perhaps,' said Sudheer, 'but we have got blood in our veins. Is there nothing here to eat? Surely you have some bread, some vegetables?'

'I have nothing,' said the old man.

'Well, we will have to wait till morning,' said Sudheer. 'Rusty, take out the blanket and the bottle of rum.'

Rusty took the blanket from their bag, and a flask of rum slipped out from the folds. Ram Singh showed unmistakable signs of coming to life.

'Is that medicine you have?' asked the old man. 'I have been suffering from headaches for the last month.'

'Well, this will give you a worse headache,' said Sudheer, gulping down a mouthful of rum and licking his lips. 'Besides, for people who eat only once a day it is dangerous stuff.'

'We could get something to eat,' said the old man eagerly.

'You said you had nothing,' said Rusty, taking the bottle from Sudheer and putting it to his lips.

'There are some pumpkins on the roof,' said the old man. 'And I have a few potatoes and some spices. Shall I make a curry?'

And an hour later, warmed by rum and curry, they sat round the fire in a most convivial fashion. Rusty and Sudheer had gathered their only blanket about their shoulders, and Ram Singh had covered himself in sheepskins. He had been asking them questions about life in the cities—a life that was utterly foreign to him.

'You are men of the world,' said Ram Singh. 'You have been in most of the cities of India, you have known all kinds of men and women. I have never travelled beyond Lansdowne, nor have I seen the trains and ships which I hear so much about. I am seventy and I have not seen these things, though I have sons who have been away many years, and one who has even been out of India with his regiment. I would like to ask your advice. It is lonely living alone, and though I have had three wives, they are all dead.'

'If you have had three wives,' said Sudheer, 'you are a man of the world!'

He had his back to the wall, his feet stuck out towards the fire. Rusty was half-asleep, his head resting on Sudheer's shoulder.

'My daughters are all married,' continued Ram Singh. 'I would like to get married again, but tell me, how should I go about it?'

Sudheer laughed out loud. The old man in his youth must have been as crafty a devil as the Lafunga himself.

'Well, you would have to pay for her, of course,' said Sudheer.

'Tell me of a suitable woman. She should be young, of course. Her nose—what kind of nose should she have?'

'A flat nose,' said Sudheer, without the ghost of a smile. 'The nostrils should not be turned up.'

'Ah! And the shape of her body?'

'Not too manly. She should not be crooked. Do not expect too much, old man!'

'Her head?' asked the old man eagerly. 'What should her head be like?'

Sudheer gave this a moment's consideration. 'The head should not be bald,' he said.

'Ram Singh nodded his approval; his opinion of Sudheer was going up by leaps and bounds.

'And her colour, should it be white?'

'No, not very white.'

'Black?'

'Not too black. But she would have to be evil-smelling, otherwise she would not stay with you.'

A bear kept them awake during the early part of the night. It clambered up on the roof and made a meal of the old man's store of pumpkins.

'Can it get in?' asked Rusty.

'It comes every night,' said Ram Singh. 'But it is a vegetarian and eats only the pumpkins.'

There was a thud as a pumpkin rolled off the roof and landed on the ground. Then the bear climbed down from the roof and shambled off into the forest.

The fire was glowing feebly, but Sudheer and Rusty were warm beneath their blanket and, being very tired, were soon asleep, despite the efforts of an army of bugs to keep them awake. But at about midnight they were woken by a loud cry and starting up, found the lantern lit, and the old man throwing a fit.

Ram Singh was leaping about the room, waving his arms, going into contortions, and bringing up gurgling sounds from the back of his throat.

'What is the matter?' shouted Rusty, from under the blanket. 'Have you gone mad?'

For reply, the old man gurgled and shrieked, and continued his frenzied dance.

'A demon!' he shouted. 'A demon has entered me!'

Sudheer leapt to his feet. He had heard of the superstitions of some hill-people, of their belief in spirits, but he had never expected to witness such a performance.

'It's the medicine you gave me!' cried Ram Singh. 'The medicine was evil, it is all your doing!' And he continued dancing about the room.

'Should I throw the medicine away?' asked Sudheer.

'No, don't do that!' shouted Ram Singh, appearing normal for a moment. 'Throw yourself on the ground!'

Sudheer threw himself on the ground.

'On your back!' gasped the old man.

Sudheer turned over on to his back. Rusty had lifted a corner of the blanket and was watching, fascinated.

'Raise your left foot,' said the old man. 'Take it in your mouth. That will charm the demon away.'

'I will not put my foot in my mouth,' said Sudheer getting to his feet, having lost faith in the genuineness of the old man's fit. 'I don't think there is any demon in you. It is probably your curry. Have something more to drink, and you will be all right.'

He produced the all but empty flask of rum, made the old man open his mouth, and poured the rest of the spirit down his throat.

Ram Singh choked, shook his head violently, and grinned at Sudheer. 'The demon has gone now,' he said.

'I am glad to know it,' said Sudheer. 'But you have emptied the bottle. Now let us try to sleep again.'

The cold had come in through the blanket, and Rusty found sleep difficult. Instead, he began to think of the purpose of his journey, and wondered if it would not have been wiser to stay in Dehra. Outside, the air was still; the wind had stopped whistling through the pines. Only a jackal howled in the distance. The old man was tossing and turning on his sheepskins.

'Ram Singh,' whispered Rusty. 'Are you awake?'

Ram Singh groaned softly.

'Tell me,' said Rusty. 'Have you heard of a woman living alone in these parts?'

'There are many old women here.'

'No, I mean a well-to-do woman. She must be about forty. At one time she was married to a white sahib.'

'Ah, I have heard of such a woman . . . . She was beautiful when she was young, they tell me.'

Rusty was silent. He was afraid to ask any further questions, afraid to know too much, afraid of finding out too soon that there was nothing for him and nowhere to go.

'Ram Singh,' he whispered. 'Where does this woman live?'

'She had her house on the road to Rishikesh . . . .'

'And the woman, where is she? Is she dead?'

'I do not know, I have not heard of her recently,' said Ram Singh. 'Why do you ask of her? Are you related to the sahib?'

'No,' said Rusty. 'I have heard of her, that's all.'

Silence. The old man grumbled to himself, muttering quietly, and then began to snore. The jackal was silent, the wind was up again, the moon was lost in the clouds. Rusty felt Sudheer's hand slip into his own and press his fingers. He was surprised to find him awake.

'Forget it,' whispered Sudheer. 'Forget the dead, forget the past. Trouble your heart no longer. I have enough for both of us, so let us live on it till it is finished, and let us be happy, Rusty, my friend, let us be happy . . . .'

Rusty did not reply, but he held the Lafunga's hand and returned the pressure of his fingers to let him know that he was listening.

'This is only the beginning,' said Sudheer. 'The world is waiting for us.'

Rusty woke first, scratching and rubbing his legs. Looking up at the skylight, he saw the first glimmer of dawn. He slipped on his clothes and torn socks and without waking Sudheer or the old man, unlatched the door and stepped outside.

Before him lay a world of white.

It had snowed in the early hours of the morning while they had been sleeping. The snow lay thick on the ground, carpeting the hillside. There was not a breath of wind; the pine trees stood blanched and still, and a deep silence hung over the forest and the hills.

Rusty did not immediately wake the others. He wanted this all to himself—the snow and the silence and the coming of sun . . . .

Towards the horizon, the sky was red. And then the sun came over the hills and struck the snow, and Rusty ran to the top of the hill and stood in the dazzling sunlight, shading his eyes from the glare, taking in the range of mountains and the valley and the stream that cut its way through the snow like a dark trickle of oil. He ran down the hill and into the house.

'Wake up!' he shouted, shaking Sudheer. 'Get up and come outside!'

'Why—have you found your treasure?' complained Sudheer sleepily. 'Or has the old man had another fit?'

'More than that—it has snowed!'

'Then I shall definitely not come outside,' said Sudheer. And turning over, he went to sleep again.

LADY WITH A HOOKAH

ॐ

RUSTY GLIMPSED THE HOUSE as they came through the trees, and he knew at once that it was the place they had been looking for. It had obviously been built by an Englishman, with its wide veranda and sloping corrugated roof, like the house in Dehra where he had lived with his guardian. It stood in the knoll of a hill, surrounded by an orchard of apple and plum trees.

'This must be the place,' said Sudheer. 'Shall we just walk in?'

'Well, the gate is open,' said Rusty.

They had barely entered the gate when a huge black Tibetan mastiff appeared on the front veranda. It did not bark, but a low growl rumbled in its throat, and that was a more dangerous portent. The dog bounded down the steps and made for the gate, and Sudheer and Rusty scrambled back up the hillside, showing no sign of their weariness. The dog remained at the gate, growling as before.

A servant boy appeared on the veranda and called out, 'Who is it? What do you want?'

'We wish to see the lady who lives here,' replied Sudheer.

'She is resting,' said the boy. 'She cannot see anyone now.'

'We have come all the way from Dehra,' said Sudheer. 'My friend is a relative of hers. Tell her that, and she will see him.'

'She isn't going to believe that,' Rusty whispered fiercely.

The boy, with a doubtful glance at both of them, went indoors and was gone for some five minutes. When he reappeared on the veranda, he called the dog inside and chained it to the railing. Then he beckoned to Rusty and Sudheer to follow him. They went in cautiously through the gate.

He was a fair, lynx-eyed boy, and he stared appraisingly at them for a few moments before saying, 'She is at the back. Come with me.'

They went round the house along a paved path, and on to another veranda which looked out on the mountains. Rusty looked first at the view, and took his eyes away from the hills only when Sudheer tugged at his sleeve; then he looked into the veranda, but he could see nothing at first because of a difference in light. Only when he stepped into the shade was he able to make out someone—a woman reclining, barefoot and wearing a white sari, on a string cot. An elaborate hookah was set before her, and its long, pliable stem rose well above the level of the bed, so that she could manoeuvre it with comfort.

She looked surprisingly young. Rusty had expected to find an older woman. His aunt did not look over thirty-five; she was, in fact, forty. Having met an aged contemporary of his father's in Mr Pettigrew, he had expected his aunt to be an old woman; but now he remembered that she had been the wife of his father's younger brother. She came from a village in the higher ranges and this accounted for her good colour, her long black hair—and her hookah. She looked physically strong, and her face, though lacking femininity, was strikingly handsome.

'Please sit down,' she said; and Sudheer and Rusty, finding that chairs had materialized from behind while they stood staring at the lady, sank into them. The boy pattered away into the interior of the house.

'You have come a long way to see me,' she said. 'It must be important.' And she looked from Rusty to Sudheer, and back to Rusty, curious to know which of them concerned her. Her eyes rested on Rusty, on his eyes, and she said, 'You are *angrez*, aren't you?'

'Partly,' he said. 'I came to see you, because—because you knew my father—and I was told—I was told you would see me . . . .' Rusty did not quite know what he should say, or how to say it.

'Your father?' she said encouraging him, and he noticed a flicker of interest in her eyes. 'Who is your father?'

'He died when I was very young,' said Rusty. And when he told her his father's name, she thrust the hookah aside and leaned forward to look closely at the boy. 'You *are* his son, then . . . .'

Rusty nodded.

'Yes, you are his son. You have his eyes and nose and forehead. I would have known it without your telling me if it had not been so dark in here.' With an agility that was another surprise to Rusty, she sprang off the cot and pulled aside the curtains that covered one side of the veranda. Sunlight streamed in, bringing out the richness of her colouring.

'So you are only a boy,' she said, smiling at him indulgently. 'You must be sixteen—seventeen—I remember you only as a child, being taken up and down the Mall in Mussoorie. Fourteen, fifteen years ago . . . .' She put her hands to her cheeks, as though she would feel the lines of advancing age; but her cheeks were still smooth, her youth was still with her. It came of living in the hills, of not having had children, perhaps; of having just enough of everything and not too much.

'I came to you because you knew my father well.'

They were sitting again, and Sudheer's long legs stretched across the width of the veranda. Rusty sat beside his aunt's cot.

'I wish there was something of your father's that I could give you,' she said. 'He did not leave much money. I would have offered to look after you, but I was told you had a guardian, one of your father's relatives. You must have been in good hands. Later, after my husband's death, I tried to get news of you; but I lived far from any town and was out of touch with what was happening elsewhere. I am alone now. But I don't mind. Your uncle left me this house and the land around it. I have my dog.' She stroked the huge mastiff who sat devotedly beside her. 'And I have the boy. He is a good boy and looks after me well. You are welcome to stay with us, Rusty.'

'No, I did not come for that,' said Rusty. 'You are very generous, but I do not want to be a burden on anyone.'

'You will be no burden. And if you are, it doesn't matter.' She shook her head sadly. 'How was he to know? He was well and strong one day, dying the next. But let us not depress ourselves. Come, tell me about your tall friend, and what you propose to do, and where you are going from here. It is late, and you must take your meal with us and stay the night. You will need an entire day if you are going to Rishikesh. I have rooms and beds sufficient for several large families.'

They sat together in the twilight, and Rusty told his aunt about his quarrel with his guardian, of his friendship with Kishen and Devinder and Sudheer the Lafunga. When it was dark, his aunt drew a shawl around her shoulders and took them indoors; and Bisnu, the boy, brought them food on brass *thalis*, from which they ate sitting on the ground. Afterwards, they remained talking for about an hour, and the Lafunga expressed his admiration for a woman who could live alone in the hills without giving way to loneliness or despair. Rusty tried smoking the hookah, but it gave him a splitting headache, and when eventually he went to bed he could not sleep. Sudheer set up a rhythmic snoring, each snore gaining in tone and vibrancy, reminding Rusty of the brain-fever bird he often heard in Dehra.

He left his bed and walked out on the veranda. The moon showed through the trees, and he walked down the garden path where fallen apples lay rotting in the moonlight. When he turned at the gate to walk back towards the house, he saw someone standing in the veranda. Could it be a ghost? No, it was his aunt in her white sari, watching him.

'What is wrong, Rusty?' she asked, as he approached. 'Why are you wandering about at this time? I thought you were a ghost—and I was frightened, because I haven't seen one in years.'

'I've never seen one at all,' said Rusty. 'What are ghosts really like?'

'Oh, they are usually the spirits of immoral women, and they have their feet facing backwards. They are called *churels*. There are other kinds, too. But why are you out here?'

'I have a headache. I couldn't sleep.'

'All right. Come and talk to me.' And taking Rusty by the hand, she led him into her large moonlit room and made him lie down. Then she took his head in her hands, and with her strong cool fingers pressed his forehead and massaged his temples; and she began telling him a story, but her fingers were more persuasive than her tongue, and Rusty fell asleep before the tale could be finished.

Next morning while Sudheer slept late, she took Rusty around the house and grounds.

'I have some of your books,' she said, when they came indoors. 'You are probably too old for some of them now, but your father asked me to keep them for you. Especially *Alice in Wonderland*. He was particular about that one, I don't know why.'

She brought the books out, and the sight of their covers brought back the whole world of his childhood—lazy afternoons in the shade of a jackfruit tree, a book in his hand, while squirrels and magpies chattered in the branches above; the book-shelf in his grandfather's study—the books had not been touched for years when Rusty first discovered them. *Alice* had been there, and *Treasure Island*, and *Mister Midshipman Easy*— they had been Rusty's grandfather's, then his father's and finally his own. He had read them by the time he was eight; but he had been in boarding-school when his father died, and he did not see the books again after going to live in his guardian's house.

Now after ten years they had turned up once more, in the possession of his strange aunt who lived alone in the mountains.

He decided to take the books because they had once been part of his life. They were the only link between him and his father—they were his only legacy.

'Must you go back to Dehra?' asked his aunt.

'I promised my friends I would return. Later, I will decide what I should do and where I should go. During these last few months I have been a vagrant. And I used to dream of becoming a writer!'

'You can write here,' she said. 'And you can be a farmer, too.'

'Oh no, I will just be a nuisance. And anyway, I must stand on my own feet. I'm too old to be looked after by others.'

'You are old enough to look after me,' she said putting her

hand on his. 'Let us be burdens on each other. I am lonely, sometimes. I know you have friends, but they cannot care for you if you are sick or in trouble. You have no parents. I have no children. It is as simple as that.'

She looked up as a shadow fell across the doorway. Sudheer was standing there in his pyjamas, grinning sheepishly at them.

'I'm hungry,' he said. 'Aunty, will you feed us before we reluctantly leave your house?'

THE ROAD TO RISHIKESH

❧

SUDHEER AND RUSTY SET out on foot for Rishikesh, that small town straddling the banks of the Ganges where the great river emerges from the hills to stretch itself across the wide plains of northern India. In this town of saints and mendicants and pilgrims, Sudheer proposed to set up headquarters. Dehra was no longer safe, with the police and the *seth* still looking for him. He had already spent a considerable sum from the money he had appropriated, and he hoped that in Rishikesh, where all manner of men congregated, there would be scope for lucrative projects. And from Rishikesh, Rusty could take a bus to Dehra whenever he felt like returning. He had no immediate plan in mind, but was content to be on the road again with the Lafunga, as he had been with Kishen. He knew that he would soon tire of this aimless wandering, and wondered if he should return to his aunt. But for the time being he was content to wander; and with the Lafunga beside him, he felt carefree and reckless, ready for almost anything.

At noon, they arrived at a small village on the Rishikesh road. From here a bus went twice daily to Rishikesh, and they were just in time to catch the last one.

Through there was no snow, there had been rain. The road was full of slush and heaps of rubble that had fallen from the hillside. The bus carried very few passengers. Sacks of flour and potatoes took up most of the space.

The driver—unshaven, smoking a bidi—did not inspire confidence. Throughout the journey he kept up a heated political discussion with a passenger seated directly behind him. With one hand on the steering-wheel, he used the other hand to make his point, gesticulating and shouting in order to be heard above the rattle of the bus.

Nevertheless, Sudheer and Rusty enjoyed the ride. Rusty laughed whenever Sudheer's head hit the roof, and Sudheer sought comfort from the other passengers' discomfiture.

A stalwart, good-looking young farmer sitting opposite Sudheer said, 'I would feel safer if this was a government bus. Then, if we were killed, there would be some compensation for our families—or for us, if we were not dead!'

'Yes, let us be cheerful about these things,' said Sudheer. 'Take our driver, for instance. Do you think he is troubled at the thought of being reborn as a snake tomorrow? Not he!'

'Why should he be a snake?' asked the farmer. 'Why not a rat?'

'Well, he could be a rat,' said Sudheer. 'He's a political person, as you can see.'

They gazed out of the window, down a sheer two-hundred-foot cliff that fell to a boulder-strewn stream. The road was so narrow that they could not see the edge. Trees stood out perpendicularly from the cliff-face. A waterfall came gushing down from the hillside and sprayed the top of the bus, splashing in at the windows. The wheels of the bus turned up stones and sent them rolling downhill; they mounted the rubble of a landslip and went churning through a stretch of muddy water.

The driver was so immersed in his discussion that when he saw a boulder right in the middle of the road he did not have time to apply the brakes. It must be said to his credit that he did not take the bus over the cliff. Instead, he rammed it into the hillside, and there it stuck. Being quite used to accidents of this nature, the driver sighed, re-lit his bidi, and returned to his argument.

As there were only eight miles left for Rishikesh, the passengers decided to walk.

Sudheer once again got into conversation with the farmer, whose name he now knew to be Ganpat. Most of the produce in the bus was Ganpat's; no doubt the bus would take an extra day to arrive in Rishikesh, and that would give him an excuse for prolonging his stay in town and enjoying himself out of sight of his family.

'Is there any place in Rishikesh where we can spend the night?' asked Sudheer.

'There are many *dharamsalas* for pilgrims,' said Ganpat.

Finding some purpose to their enforced trek, they set out with even longer and more vigorous strides. Ganpat had a fine sun-darkened body, a strong neck set on broad shoulders, and a heavy, almost military, moustache. He wore his dhoti well; his strong ankles and broad feet were burnished by the sun, hardened by years of walking barefoot through the fields.

Soon he and the Lafunga had discovered something in common—they were both connoisseurs of beautiful women.

'I like them tall and straight,' said Ganpat, twirling his moustache. 'They must not be too fussy, and not too talkative. How does one please them?'

'Have you heard of the great sage Vatsayana? He had three wives. One he pleased with secret confidences, the other with secret respect, and the third with secret flattery.'

'You are a strange fellow,' said Ganpat.

Rusty had hurried on ahead of the others. Feeling fresh and exhilarated, he had an urge to reach the river before anyone else. He wanted to be waiting for Sudheer at Rishikesh; and he wanted to be alone for a while.

A thickly forested mountain hid the river, but Rusty knew it was there and where it was and what it looked like. He had heard from Hathi, of the fish in its waters, of its rocks and currents, and it only remained for him to touch the water and know it personally.

The path dropped steeply into a valley, then rose and went round a big mountain. Rusty passed a woodcutter and asked him how far it was to the river. The woodcutter was a short stocky man with a creased and weathered face.

'Seven miles,' he said, fairly accurately. 'Why do you want to know?'

'I am going to Rishikesh,' said Rusty.

'Alone?'

'The others are following, but I cannot wait for them. You will meet them on the way. When you see the Lafunga, the tall one, tell him I will be waiting at the river.'

'I will tell him,' said the woodcutter, and took his leave.

The path descended steeply, and Rusty had to run a little. It was a dizzy, winding path; he slipped once or twice. The hillside was covered with lush green ferns, and in the trees, unseen birds sang loudly. Soon he was in the valley, and the path straightened out. A girl was coming from the opposite direction. She held a long, curved knife with which she had been cutting grass and fodder. There were rings in her nose and ears, and her arms were covered with heavy bangles. She smiled innocently at Rusty—no girl in the plains had ever done that. The bangles made music when she moved her hands—it was as though her hands spoke a language of their own.

'How far is it to the river?' asked Rusty.

The girl had probably never been near the river, or she may have been thinking of another one, for she replied 'Twenty miles,' without any hesitation.

Rusty laughed and ran down the path. A parrot screeched suddenly and flew low over his head, a flash of blue and green. It took the course of the path, and Rusty followed its dipping flight, running until the path rose and the bird disappeared in the trees. He loved these hills which offered him their freedom, their own individual strength, allowing the boy to be himself, Rusty. Yes, he would want to come back to them . . . .

A trickle of water came out of the hillside, and Rusty stopped to drink. The water was cold and sharp and very refreshing. He had walked alone for nearly an hour. Presently he saw another boy ahead of him, driving a few goats down the path.

'How far is the river?' asked Rusty, when he had caught up with the boy.

The village boy said, 'Oh, not far, just round the next hill and then straight down.'

Rusty, feeling hungry, produced some dry bread from his pocket and breaking it in two, offered one half to the boy. They sat on the hillside and ate in silence. When they had finished, they walked on together and began talking. And talking, Rusty did not notice the smarting of his feet or the distance he had covered. But after some time his companion had to diverge along another path, and Rusty was once more on his own.

He missed the village boy; he looked up and down the path, but could see no one—no sign of Sudheer—and the river was not in sight either. He began to feel discouraged; he felt tired and isolated. But he walked on, along the dusty, stony path, past terraced fields and huts, until there were no more fields, only forest and sun and silence.

The silence was impressive and a little frightening—different from the silence of a room or an empty street. There was not much movement either, except for the bending of grass beneath his feet, and the circling of a hawk high above the pine trees.

And then, as he rounded a sharp bend, the silence broke into sound.

The sound of a river.

Far down in the valley, the river stretched and opened into broad, beautiful motion, and Rusty gasped and began to run. He slipped and stumbled, but still he ran. Then he was ankle-deep in the cold mountain water.

And the water was blue and white and wonderful.

END OF A JOURNEY

❧

IT WAS THE FESTIVAL of the Full Moon. The temples at Rishikesh lay bathed in a soft clear light. The broad, slow-moving Ganges caught the moonlight and held it, to become a river of liquid silver. Along the shore, devotees floated little lights downstream. The wicks were placed in earthen vessels, where they burned for a few minutes, a red-gold glow. Rusty lay on the sand and watched them float by, one by one, until they went out or were caught amongst rocks and shingle.

Sudheer and Ganpat had gone into the town to seek amusement, but Rusty preferred to stay by the river, at a little distance from the embankment where hundreds of pilgrims had gathered.

Had it been summer, he could have slept on the sand, but it was cold, and his blanket was no protection against the icy wind that blew down from the mountains. He went into a lighted *dharamsala* and settled down in a corner of the crowded room. Rolling himself into his blanket, he closed his eyes, listening to the desultory talk of pilgrims sheltering in the building.

The full moon does strange things to some people. In the hills, it is inclined to touch off a little madness. And its effect on those who are already a little mad—like Sudheer—is to make them madder.

When the moon is at the full, some converse with spirits, others lose all their inhibitions and dance in frenzied abandon; some love more ardently, and a few kill more readily. 'Do not sleep in the light of a full moon,' warn the pundits, 'it will bewitch you, and turn you to beautiful but evil thoughts.'

The moon made Sudheer the Lafunga a little drunk. But the moon not being enough, he consumed a bottle of country-made liquor with Ganpat. The drink had confused Ganpat and affected his judgement—was he dreaming, or did he really see Sudheer hopping about in the middle of the street, slapping himself on the buttocks?

'Sudheer,' he said, steadying himself. 'Are you dancing on the road, or am I drunk?'

'You are drunk,' said Sudheer. 'But it is true that I am dancing on the road.'

'Why do you do it?' asked Ganpat.

'Because I feel happy,' said Sudheer.

'Then I must try it,' said Ganpat. And he too began hopping about on the road, slapping himself on the buttocks.

Rishikesh comes to life at an early hour. The priests, sanyasis and their disciples rise at three, as soon as there is a little light in the sky, and begin their ablutions and meditation. From about five o'clock, pilgrims start coming down to the river to bathe. Along the bathing-steps walk saffron-robed sadhus and wandering mendicants, whilst the older and senior men sit on small edifices beneath shady trees, where they receive money and gifts from pilgrims, and dispense blessings in return.

Rusty had bathed early, leaving Sudheer and Ganpat asleep in the *dharamsala*. These two revellers had come in at two o'clock in the morning, disturbing others in the shelter. They did not get up until the sun had risen. The Ganpat crossed the river in a ferry boat in order to visit the temples on the other side, there to propitiate the gods with offerings of his own. Sudheer made his way outside to try and acquire a suitable disguise, as he had to visit Dehra for a few days. Dressed as he was, he would soon be spotted by the *seth's* informers. Later, he met Rusty at the bus-stand.

'I will be back tomorrow,' said Sudheer. 'I do not take you with me because in Dehra my company would be dangerous for you.'

'Why must you be going to Dehra, then?' asked Rusty.

'Well, there are one or two people who owe me money,' he said. 'And though, as you know, we have plenty to go on with, these people are not loved by me, so why should they keep my money? And another thing. There are two beautiful women in Dehra—one is Hastini and the other Mrinalini—and I must return the money I borrowed from them.'

'And why did you borrow money from them?' asked Rusty.

'Because I owed a debt to Devinder,' said Sudheer with a wide smile. 'And he wanted the money for you! Isn't life complicated?'

When the bus moved off in a cloud of dust, Rusty turned away. He sauntered through the bazaar, going from one sweet shop to another, assessing the quality of their different wares. Eventually he bought eight annas worth of hot, fresh, golden jalebis, and carrying them in a large plate made of banana leaves, went down to the river.

At the river-side grew a banyan tree, and Rusty sat in its shade and ate his sweets. The tree was full of birds—parrots and bulbuls and rosy pastors—feeding on the ripe red figs of the banyan. Rusty enjoyed leaning back against the trunk of the tree, listening to the chatter of the birds, studying their plumage.

When the sweets were finished, he rose and wandered along the banks of the river. On a stretch of sand two boys were wrestling. They were on their knees, arms interlocked, pressing forward like mad bulls, each striving to throw the other. The taller boy had the advantage at first; the smaller boy, who was dark and pockmarked, appeared to be yielding. But then there was a sudden flurry of arms and legs, and the small boy sat victorious across his opponent's chest.

When they saw Rusty watching them, the boys asked him if he would like to wrestle. But Rusty declined the invitation. He had eaten too many jalebis and felt sick.

He walked until the sickness had passed and he was hungry again (the trek to Rishikesh had increased his already healthy appetite), and returning to the bazaar, he feasted on puris and a well-spiced vegetable curry.

Well stuffed with puris, he returned to the banyan tree and slept right through the afternoon.

At midnight, in Dehra, Sudheer was paying a clandestine visit to Mrinalini. Knowing that he would have to stay away for some time, he wished to see her just once again, in order to make her a gift and a promise of his fidelity.

It took him a few seconds to climb the treacherous flight of stairs that led to Mrinalini's rooms. Every time he climbed those stairs, they swayed and plunged about more heavily.

Mrinalini was preparing herself for a visitor; she sat in front of a cracked, discoloured mirror which distorted her fine features into hideous dimensions. Whenever she looked into the distorting mirror and saw the bloated face, the crooked eyes, the smear of paint, she thought: One day I will look like that. One day, not long from now, I will be as ugly as that reflection . . . . And when she looked in the mirror again, it was always the reflection of her mother that she saw.

By contrast, Sudheer's reflection when it appeared beside hers in the mirror, reminded her of a horse—a horse with a rather long and silly face. And seeing it there, she laughed.

'What are you laughing at?' said Sudheer.

'At you, of course! You look so stupid in the mirror!'

'I did not know that,' said Sudheer, his vanity a little hurt. 'Hastini does not think so.'

'Hastini is a fool. She likes you because she thinks you are handsome. I like you because you have a face like a horse.'

'Well, your horse is going to be away from Dehra for some time. I hope you will not miss him.'

'You are always coming and going, but never staying.'

'That's life.'

'Doesn't it make you lonely?'

Mrinalini had moved away from the mirror, and now she went over to the bed where she made herself comfortable against a pillow.

'When I am lonely, I do something,' said Sudheer, standing over her, looking very tall. 'I go out and do something foolish or dangerous. When I am not doing things, I am lonely. But I was not made for loneliness.'

'I am lonely sometimes.'

'You! With your mother? She never leaves you alone. And you have visitors nearly every day, and many new faces.'

'Yes. The more people I see, the lonelier I get. You must have some companion, someone to talk to and quarrel with, if you are not to be lonely. You can find such a companion.

But who can I find? My mother is old and deaf and heartless.'

'One day I will come and take you away from here. I have some money now, Mrinalini. As soon as I have started a business in another town, I will call you there. Meanwhile, why not stay with Hastini?'

'I hate her.'

'You do not know her yet. When you know her, you will love her!'

'*You* love her.'

'I love her because she is so comfortable. I love you because you are so sweet. Can I help it if I love you both?'

'You are strange,' said Mrinalini with one of her rare smiles. 'Go now. Someone will be coming.'

'Then keep this for me,' said Sudheer.

He took a thin gold ring from his finger, and slipped it on to the third finger of Mrinalini's right hand.

'Keep it for me till I return,' he said. 'And if I do not return, then keep it for ever. Sell it only if you are in need. All right?'

Mrinalini stared at the ring for some time, turning it about on her finger so that the light fell on it in different places. She slipped it off her finger and hid it in her blouse.

'If I keep it on my hand, my mother will be sure to take it.'

Sudheer said, 'If only you would allow me, I'd finish off your mother for you.'

'Don't talk like that! She has not long to live . . . .'

'She is doing her best to outlive all of us. I will not be violent, I promise you. I will not even touch her. I will simply frighten her to death. I could pounce on her from a dark alley, or let off a firecracker . . . .'

'Sudheer!' cried Mrinalini. 'How can you be so cruel?'

'It would be a kindness.'

'Go now! Stay away from Dehra as long as you can.'

It was a wonderful morning in Rishikesh. There was a hint of spring in the air. Birds flashed across the water, and monkeys chased each other over the rooftops. Rusty lay on a stretch of sand, drinking in the crisp morning air, letting the sun sink into his body.

He had risen early and had gone down to the river to

bathe. Even before the *pujaris* had risen, he had run into the river, gasping with the shock of the cold water, threshing and embracing it until the sluggishness left his body, and he felt clean and fresh and happy.

The touch of the water brought memories of his own secret pool that lay in the forest behind the church. Perhaps Devinder would be there now; perhaps Kishen, too, had joined him for the morning dip; and the Goonga would be sitting on a buffalo.

Rusty sat on the sand, nostalgically thinking of his friends. But there was another pull now, from the house in the hills, and he was certain that his future did not lie in Dehra. He decided he would leave Rishikesh as soon as the Lafunga returned. After all, Sudheer was experienced in the ways of the world, and was never lacking in friends. Devinder and Kishen were of Rusty's age. He could understand and love them, and they could join him later. He could only love the Lafunga—he could not understand him.

Rusty lay on the white sand until the voices of distant bathers reached him, and the sun came hurrying over the hills. Slipping on his shirt and trousers, he went to the bazaar, where he found a little tea shop. And there he drank a glass of hot, sweet milky tea, and ate six eggs, to the amazement of the shopkeeper.

When he had finished eating, he strolled down to the bus-stand to see if Sudheer had returned. The second bus from Dehra had arrived, but Sudheer was not to seen anywhere. Rusty was about to go back when, turning, he found himself looking into the eyes of a distinguished-looking young sadhu, who had three vermilion stripes across his forehead, an orange robe wound about his thighs and shoulders, and an extremely unsaintly grin on his face. The disguise might have deceived Rusty, but not the grin.

'So now you have become a sadhu,' said Rusty. 'And for whose benefit is this?'

'It was for business in Dehra,' said Sudheer. 'I did not wish to be seen by the *seth* or his servants. Let us find a quiet place where we can talk. And let us get some fruit, I am hungry.'

Rusty bought six apples from a stall and took Sudheer to the banyan tree. They sat on the ground, talking and munching apples.

'Did you see your friends?' asked Rusty.

'Yes, I went to them first. The bus had made me tired and angry, and there is no one like Hastini for soothing and refreshing one. Then I went to Mrinalini and asked her to come to Rishikesh, but she is still waiting for her mother to die. In life, people do nothing but wait for other people to die.'

Sudheer was already making new plans. 'Do I look all right?' he asked.

'You look as handsome as ever.'

'I know that. But do I look like a sadhu?'

'Yes, a very handsome sadhu.'

'All the better. Come, let us go.'

'Where do we go?' asked Rusty.

'To look for disciples, of course. A sadhu such as I, must have disciples, and they should be rich disciples. There must be many fat, rich men in the world who are unhappy about their consciences. Come, we will be their consciences! We will be respectable, Rusty. There is more money to be made that way. Yes, we will be respectable—what an adventure that will be!'

They began walking towards the bazaar.

'Wait!' said Rusty. 'I cannot come with you, Sudheer!'

Sudheer came to an abrupt halt. He turned and faced Rusty, a puzzled and disturbed expression on his face.

'What do you mean, you cannot come with me?'

'I must return to Dehra. I may come this way again, if I want to live with my aunt.'

'But why? You have just left her. You came to the hills for money, didn't you? And she didn't have any money.'

'I wanted to see her, too. I wanted to know what she was like. It isn't just a matter of money.'

'Well, you saw her. And there is no future for you with her, or in Dehra. What's the use of returning?'

'I don't know, Sudheer. What's the use of anything, for that matter? What would be the use of staying with you? I want to give some direction to my life. I want to work, I want to be free, I want to be able to write. I can't wander about the hills and plains with you for ever.'

'Why not? There is nothing to stop you, if you like to wander. India has always been the home of wanderers.'

'I might join you again, if I fail at everything else.'

Sudheer looked sullen and downcast.

'You do not realize . . . .' he began, but stopped, groping for the right words; he had seldom been at a loss for words. 'I have got used to you, that is all,' he said.

'And I have got used to you, Sudheer. I don't think anyone else has ever done that.'

'That's why I don't want to lose you. But I cannot stop you from going.'

'I shall come to see you, I will, really . . . .'

Sudheer brightened up a little. 'Do you promise? Or do you say that just to please me?'

'Both.'

Sudheer was his old self again, smiling and digging his fingers into Rusty's arms. 'I'll be waiting for you,' he said. 'Whenever you want to look for treasure, come to me! Whenever you are looking for fun, come to me!'

Then he was silent again, and a shadow passed across his face. Did he, after all, know the meaning of loneliness? Perhaps Mrinalini had been right when she had said, 'You must have some companion, someone to talk to and quarrel with, if you are not to be lonely . . . .'

'Let us part now,' said Sudheer. 'Let us not prolong it. You go down the street to the bus-stand, and I'll go the other way.'

He held out his hand to Rusty. 'Your hand is not enough,' he said, and he put his arms around Rusty, and embraced him.

People stopped to stare; not because two youths were demonstrating their affection for each other—that was common enough—but because a sadhu in a saffron robe was behaving out of character.

When Sudheer realized this, he grinned at the passers-by; and they, embarrassed by his grin, and made nervous by his height, hurried on down the street.

Sudheer turned and walked away.

Rusty watched him for some time. The Lafunga stood out distinctly from the crowd of people in the bazaar, tall and handsome in his flowing robe.

FIRST AND LAST IMPRESSIONS

❧

Because he had told no one of his return, there was no one to meet Rusty at Dehra station when he stepped down from a third-class compartment. But on his way through the bazaar he met one of the tea shop boys who told him that Devinder might be found near the Clock Tower. And so he went to the Clock Tower, but he could not find his friend. Another familiar, a shoeshine boy, said he had last seen Devinder near the Courts, where business was brisk that day.

Rusty, feeling tired and dirty after his journey, decided he would look for Devinder later, and made his way to the church compound where he left his bag. Then he went through the jungle to the pool.

The Goonga was already there, bathing in the shallows, gesticulating and shouting incomprehensibles at a band of langur monkeys who were watching him from the sal trees. When the Goonga saw Rusty, he chortled with delight and rushed out of the water to give his friend and protector a hug.

'And how are you?' asked Rusty.

'Goo,' said the Goonga.

He was evidently very well. Devinder had been feeding him, and he no longer needed to prowl around tea shops and receive kicks and insults in exchange for a glass of tea or a stale bun.

Rusty took off his clothes and leapt into the cold, sweet, delicious water of the pool. He floated languidly on the water, gazing up through the branches of an overhanging sal, through a pattern of broad tree leaves, into a blind-blue sky. The

Goonga sat on a rock and grinned at the monkeys, making encouraging sounds. Looking from the Goonga to the monkeys and back to the hairy, long-armed youth, Rusty wondered how anyone could doubt Darwin's theories.

'And quite obviously, I belong to the same species,' he thought, joining the Goonga on the rock and making noises of his own. 'Oh, to be a langur, without a care in the world. Acorns and green leaves to feed on, lots of friends, and no romantic complications. But no books either. I suppose being human has its advantages. Not that it would make any difference to the Goonga.'

He was soon dry. He lay on his tummy, flat against the warm, smooth rock surface. He wanted to sink deep into that beautiful rock.

'Goo,' said the Goonga, as though he approved.

Then the sun was in the pool and the pool was in the sky and the rock had swallowed Rusty up, and when he woke he thought the Goonga was still beside him. But when he raised his head and looked, he saw that Devinder sat there—Devinder looking cool and clean in a white shirt and pyjamas, his tray lying on the ground a little way off.

'How long have you been here?' asked Rusty.

'I just came. It is good to see you. I was afraid you had left for good.'

'I'm hungry,' said Rusty.

'I'm glad you haven't lost your appetite. I have brought you something to eat.' He produced a paper bag filled with hot bazaar food, and a couple of oranges.

While Rusty ate, he told Devinder of his journey. Devinder was disappointed.

'So there was nothing for you, except a few books. I know money isn't everything, but it's time you had some of it, Rusty. How long can you carry on like this? You can't sell combs and buttons like me—you wouldn't know how to. You're a dreamer, a kind of poet, and you can't live on dreams. You don't have rich friends and relatives, like Kishen, to provide intervals of luxury. You're not like Sudheer, able to live on your wits. There's only this aunt of yours in the hills—and you can't spend the rest of your life lost in the mountains like a hermit. It will take you years to become a successful writer. Look at

Goldsmith—borrowing money all the time! And you haven't even started yet.'

'I know, Devinder. You don't have to tell me. Tomorrow I'll go and see Mr Pettigrew. Perhaps he can help me in some way—perhaps he can find me a job.'

They were silent, gazing disconsolately into the pool.

'Have you seen Kishen?' asked Rusty.

'Once, in the bazaar. He was with that girl, his cousin. They were on bicycles. I think they were going to the cinema. Kishen seemed happy enough. He stopped and spoke to me and asked me when you would be back. They will soon be sending him back to school. That's good, isn't it? He'll never be able to manage without a proper education. Degrees and things.'

'Well, Sudheer has managed well enough without one. You might call him self-educated. And Kishen is worldly enough. Also, he's a Punjabi. No one is likely to get the better of him. All the same, you're right. A couple of degrees behind your name could make all the difference, even if you can't put them down in the right order!'

Already the dream was fading. That's life, thought Rusty. You can't run away from it and survive. You can't be a vagrant for ever. You're getting nowhere, so you've got to stop somewhere. Kishen has stopped. He's thrown in his lot with the settled incomes—he had to. Even Mowgli left the wolf-pack to return to his own people. And India was changing. This great formless mass was taking some sort of shape at last. He had to stop now, and find a place for himself, or go forward to disaster.

'I'll see him tomorrow,' said Rusty. 'I'll see Kishen and say goodbye.'

Rusty decided he would leave his books with Mr Pettigrew instead of in the church vestry, a transient abode. So he put them in his bag, and after tea with Devinder near the Clock Tower, set out for the tea gardens.

He crossed the dry riverbed and yellow mustard fields which stretched away to the foothills, and found Mr Pettigrew sitting on his veranda as though he had not moved from his cane chair since Rusty had last visited him. Pettigrew gazed out across the flat tea bushes. He seemed to look through

Rusty, and at first the boy thought he had not been recognized. Perhaps the old man had forgotten him!

'Good morning,' said Rusty. 'I'm back.'

'The poinsettia leaves have turned red,' said Pettigrew. 'Another winter is passing.'

'Yes.'

'Full sixty hot summers have besieged my brow. I'm growing old so *slowly*. I wish there could be some action to make the process more interesting. Not that I feel very active, but I'd like to have something happening around me. A jolly old riot would be just the thing. You know what I mean, of course?'

'I think so,' said Rusty.

It was loneliness again. In a week Rusty had found two lonely people—his aunt and this elderly gentlemen, moving slowly through the autumn of their lives. It was beginning to affect him. He looked at Mr Pettigrew and wondered if he would be like that one day—alone, not very strong, living in the past, with a bottle of whisky to sustain him through the still, lonely evenings. Rusty had friends—but so had Pettigrew, in his youth. Rusty had books to read, and books to write—but Pettigrew had books, too. Did they make much difference? Weren't there any permanent flesh and blood companions to be found outside the conventions of marriage and business?

Pettigrew seemed suddenly to realize that Rusty was standing beside him. A spark of interest showed in his eyes. It flickered and grew into comprehension.

'Drinking in the mornings, that's my trouble. You've returned very soon. Sit down, my boy, sit down. Tell me—did you find the lady? Did she know you? Was it any good?'

Rusty sat down on a step, for there was no chair on the veranda apart from Mr Pettigrew's.

'Yes, she knew me. She was very kind and wanted to help me. But she had nothing of mine, except some old books which my father had left with her.'

'Books! Is that all? You've brought them with you, I see.'

'I thought perhaps you'd keep them for me until I'm properly settled somewhere.'

Mr Pettigrew took the books from Rusty and thumbed through them.

'Stevenson, Ballantyne, Marryat, and some early P.G.

Wodehouse. I expect you've read them. And here's *Alice in Wonderland*. "How doth the little crocodile . . . ." Tenniel's drawings. It's a first edition, methinks! It couldn't be—or *could* it?'

Mr Pettigrew fell silent. He studied the title page and the back of the title-leaf with growing interest and solicitude and then with something approaching reverence; for he knew something about books and printing and the value of the first edition. And a first edition of *Alice* would be a rare find.

'It could be, at that,' said Pettigrew, almost to himself, and Rusty was bewildered by the transformation on the old man's face. Ennui had given place to enthusiasm.

'Could be what, sir?'

'A first edition.'

'It was once my grandfather's book. His name is on the fly-leaf.'

'It *must* be a first. No wonder your father treasured it.'

'Is being a first edition very important?'

'Yes, from the book-collector's point of view. In England, on the Continent, and in America, there are people who collect rare works of literature—manuscripts, and the first editions of books that have since become famous. The value of a book depends on its literary worth, its scarcity, and its condition.'

'Well, *Alice* is a famous book. And this is a good copy. Is a first edition of it rare?'

'It certainly is. There are only two or three known copies.'

'And do you think this is one?'

'Well, I'm not an expert, but I do know something about books. This is the first printing. And it's in good condition, except for a few stains on the fly-leaf.'

'Let's rub them off.'

'No, don't touch a thing—don't tamper with its condition. I'll write to a bookseller friend of mine in London for his advice. I think this should be worth a good sum of money to you—several hundred pounds.'

'Hundreds!' exclaimed Rusty disbelievingly.

'Five or six hundred, maybe more. Your father must have known the book was valuable and meant you to have it one day. Perhaps this was his legacy.'

Rusty was silent, taking in the import of what Mr Pettigrew

had told him. He had never had much money in his life. A few hundred pounds would take him anywhere he wanted to go. It was also, he knew, quite easy to go through a sum of money, no matter how large the amount.

Pettigrew was glancing through the other books. 'None of these are firsts, except the Wodehouse novels, and you'll have to wait some time with those. But *Alice* is the real thing. My friend will arrange its sale.'

'It would be nice to keep it,' said Rusty.

Mr Pettigrew looked up in surprise. 'In other circumstances, my boy, I'd say keep it. Become a book-collector yourself. But when you're down on your beam-ends, you can't afford to be sentimental. Now leave this business in my hands, and let me advance you some money. Furthermore, this calls for a celebration!'

He poured himself a stiff whisky and offered Rusty a drink.

'I don't mind if I do,' said Rusty, bestowing his rare smile on the old man.

Later, after lunching with Mr Pettigrew, Rusty sat out on the veranda with the old man and discussed his future.

'I think you should go to England,' said Mr Pettigrew.

'I've thought of that before,' said Rusty, 'but I've always felt that India is my home.'

'But can you make a living here? After all, even Indians go abroad at the first opportunity. And you want to be a writer. You can't become one overnight, certainly not in India. It will take years of hard work, and even then—then if you're good— you may not make the reputation that means all the difference between failure and success. In the meantime, you've got to make a living at something. And what can you do in India? Let's face it, my boy, you've only just finished school. There are graduates who can't get jobs. Only last week a young man with a degree in the Arts came to me and asked my help in getting him a job as a petty clerk in the tea-estate manager's office. A clerk! Is that why he went to college—to become a clerk?'

Rusty did not argue the point. He knew that it was only people with certain skills who stood a chance. It was an age of specialization. And he did not have any skills, apart from some skill with words.

'You can always come back,' said Mr Pettigrew. 'If you are

successful, you'll be free to go wherever you please. And if you aren't successful, well then, you can make a go of something else—if not in England, then in some other English-speaking country, America or Australia or Canada or the Cook Islands!'

'Why didn't you leave India, Mr Pettigrew?'

'For reasons similar to yours. Because I'd lived many years in India and had grown to love the country. But unlike you, I'm at the fag-end of my life. And it's easier to fade away in the hot sun than in the cold winds of Blighty.'

He looked out rather wistfully at his garden, at the tall marigolds and bright clumps of petunia and the splurge of bougainvillaea against the wall.

'My journeyings are over,' he said. 'And yours have just begun.'

It was dark when Rusty slipped over a wall and moved silently round the porch of Mrs Bhushan's house. There was a light showing in the front room, and Rusty crept up to the window and looked in, pressing his face against the glass. He felt the music in the room even before he heard it. It came vibrating through the glass with a pulsating rhythm. Kishen and Aruna, both barefoot, were gyrating on the floor in a frenzy of hip-shivering movement. Their faces were blank. They did not sing. All expression was confined to their plunging torsos.

Rusty decided it was not a propitious moment for calling on his old friend. And was confirmed a few minutes later by the throaty blare of a horn and the glare of a car's headlights. Mrs Bhushan's Hillman was turning in at the gate. The music came to a sudden stop. Rusty dodged behind a rose-bush, stung his hands on nettle, and remained hidden until Mrs Bhushan had alighted from her car. He was moving cautiously through the shrubbery when one of the dogs started barking. Others took up the chorus.

Rusty was soon clambering over the wall, with two or three cockers snapping at his feet and trousers. He ran down the road until he found the entrance to a dark lane, down which he disappeared.

He slowed to a walk as he approached the crowded bazaar area. He was annoyed and a little depressed at not having been able to see Kishen, but he had to admit that Kishen appeared to be quite happy in Mrs Bhushan's house. Aruna had made all the difference; for Kishen was beginning to grow up.

Perhaps, thought Rusty, I'd better not see him at all.

START OF A JOURNEY

❧

Events moved swiftly—as they usually do, once a specific plan is set in motion—and within a few weeks Rusty was in possession of a passport, a rail ticket to Bombay, his boat ticket, an income tax clearance certificate (this had been the most difficult to obtain, in spite of the fact that he had no income), a smallpox vaccination certificate, various other bits and pieces of paper, and about fifty rupees in cash advanced by Mr Pettigrew. The money for *Alice* would not be realized for several months, and could be drawn upon in London.

He was late for his train. The tonga he had hired turned out to be the most ancient of Dehra's dwindling fleet of pony-drawn carriages. The pony was old, slow and dyspeptic. It stopped every now and then to pass quantities of wind. The tonga driver turned out to be a bhang addict who had not quite woken up from his last excursion into dreamland. The carriage itself was a thing of shreds and patches. It lay at an angle, and rolled from side to side. This motion seemed designed to suit the condition of the driver, who dozed off every now and then.

'If it hadn't been for your luggage,' said Devinder, 'we would have done better to walk.'

At their feet was a new suitcase and a spacious holdall given to Rusty by Mr Pettigrew. Devinder, Rusty and the tonga driver were the only occupants of the carriage.

'Please hurry,' begged Rusty of the tonga driver. 'I'll miss the train.'

'Miss the train?' mumbled the tonga driver, coming out of

his coma. 'No one ever misses the train—not when *I* take them to the station!'

'Why, does the train wait for you to arrive?' asked Devinder.

'Oh, no,' said the driver. 'But it waits.'

'Well, it should have left at seven,' said Rusty. 'And it's five past seven now. Even if it leaves on time, which means ten minutes late, we won't catch it at this speed.'

'You will be there in ten minutes, sahib.' And the man called out an endearment to his pony.

Neither Rusty nor Devinder could make out what the tonga driver said, but it did wonders to the pony. The beast came to life as though it had been injected with a new wonder hormone. Rusty and Devinder were jerked upright in their seats. The pony kicked up its hind legs and plunged forward, and cyclists and pedestrians scattered for safety. They raced through the town, followed by oaths and abuse from a vegetable-seller whose merchandise had been spilled on the road. Only at the station entrance did the pony slow down and then, as suddenly and unaccountably as it had come to life, it returned to its former dispirited plod.

Paying off the man, Rusty and Devinder grabbed hold of the luggage and tumbled on to the railway platform. Here they barged into Kishen who, having heard of Rusty's departure (from the barber, who had got it from an egg vendor, who had got it from Devinder), had come to see him off.

'You didn't tell me anything,' said Kishen with an injured look. 'You seem to have forgotten me altogether.'

'I hadn't forgotten you, bhaiya. I did come to see you once—but I couldn't bring myself to say goodbye. It seems so final, saying goodbye. I wanted to slip away quietly, that's all.'

'How selfish you are!' said Kishen.

A last-minute quarrel with Kishen was the last thing Rusty wanted.

'We must hurry,' said Devinder urgently. 'The train is about to leave.'

The guard was blowing his whistle, and there was a final scramble among the passengers. If sardines could take a look at the situation in a third-class railway compartment, they would not have anything to complain about. It is a perfect example of the individual being swallowed up by the mass, of a large number of identities merging into one corporate whole. Your leg, you discover, is not yours but your neighbour's; the growth of hair on your shoulder is someone's beard and the cold wind whistling down your neck is his asthmatic breath; a baby materializes in your lap and is reclaimed only after it has wet your trousers; and the corner of a seat which you had happily thought was your own green spot on this earth is suddenly usurped by a huge Sikh with a sword dangling at his side. Rusty knew from experience in third-class compartments that if he did not get into one of them immediately, his way would be permanently barred.

'There's no room anywhere,' said Kishen cheerfully. 'You'd better go tomorrow.'

'The boat sails in three days,' said Rusty.

'Then come on, let's squeeze you in somewhere.'

Managing the luggage themselves, and ignoring the protests of the station coolies, they hurried down the length of the platform looking for a compartment less crowded than most. They discovered an open door and a space within, and bundled Rusty and his worldly goods into it.

'It's empty!' said Rusty in delight. 'There's no one in it.'

'Of course not,' said Kishen. 'It's a first-class compartment.'

But the train was already in motion and there was no time to get out.

'You can shift into another compartment after Hardwar,' said Kishen. 'The train won't be so crowded then.'

Rusty closed the door and stuck his head out of the window. Perhaps this mad, confusing departure was the best thing that could have happened. It was impossible to say goodbye in dignified solemnity. And Rusty would have hated a solemn, tearful departure. Devinder and Kishen had time only to look relieved—relieved at having been able to get Rusty into the train. They would not realize, till later, that he was going forever out of their lives.

He waved to them from the window, and they waved back, smiling and wishing him luck. They were not dismayed at his departure. Rather, they were pleased that Rusty's life had taken a new direction; they were impressed by his good fortune, and they took it for granted that he would come back some day, with money and honours. Such is the optimism of youth.

Rusty waved until his friends were lost in the milling throng on the platform, until the station lights were a distant glow. And then the train was thundering through the swift-falling darkness of India. He looked in the glass of the window and saw his own face dimly reflected. And he wondered if he would ever come back.

There was someone else's reflection in the glass, and he realized that he was not alone in the compartment. Someone had just come out of the washroom and was staring at Rusty in some surprise. A familiar face, a foreigner. The man Rusty had met at the Raiwala waiting-room, when he had been travelling with Kishen to Dehra in different circumstances.

'We meet again,' said the American. 'Remember me?'

'Yes,' said Rusty. 'We seem to share a fondness for trains.'

'Well, I have to make this journey every week.'

'How is your work?'

'Much the same. I'm trying, but with little success, to convince farmers that a steel plough will pay greater dividends than a wooden plough.'

'And they aren't convinced?'

'Oh, they're quite prepared to be convinced. Trouble is, they find it cheaper and easier to *repair* a wooden plough. You see how complicated everything is? It's a question of parts. For want of a bolt, the plough was lost, for want of a plough the crop was lost, for want of a crop . . . . And where are *you* going, friend? I see you're alone this time.'

'Yes, I'm going away. I'm leaving India.'

'Where are you going? England?'

Rusty nodded. He looked out of the window in time to see a shooting star skid across the heavens and vanish. A bad omen; but he was defiant of omens.

'I'm going to England,' he said. 'I'm going to Europe and America and Japan and Timbuctoo. I'm going everywhere, and no one can stop me!'

DELHI IS NOT FAR

'Oh yes, I have known love, and again love, and many other kinds of love; but of that tenderness I felt then, is there nothing I can say?'

Andre Gide, *Fruits of the Earth*

'If I am not for myself, who will be for me?
And if I am not for others, what am I?
And if not now, when?'

Hillel (Ancient Hebrew sage)

DELHI IS NOT FAR

ॐ

I

MY BALCONY IS MY window on the world.

The room has one window, a square hole in the wall crossed by three iron bars.

The view from it is a restricted one. If I crane my neck sideways and put my nose to the bars, I can see the extremities of the building; below, a narrow courtyard where children—the children of all classes of people—play together. It is only when they are older that they become conscious of the barriers of class and caste.

Across the courtyard, on a level with my room, are three separate windows belonging to three separate rooms, each window barred in the same unimaginative way. During the day it is difficult to look into these rooms. The harsh, cruel sunlight fills the courtyard, making the windows patches of darkness.

My room is very small. I have paced about in it so often that I know its exact measurements. My foot, from heel to toe, is eleven inches. That makes the room just over fifteen feet in length; when I measure the last foot, my toes turn up against the wall. In breadth, the room is exactly eight feet.

The plaster has been peeling off the walls and there are many greasy stains and patches which are difficult to hide. I cover the worst stains with pictures cut from magazines, but as there is no symmetry about the stains, there is none about the pictures.

My personal effects are few, and none of them precious. On a shelf in the wall are a pile of paperbacks, in English, Hindi and Urdu; among them my two Urdu thrillers, *Khoon* (Blood) and *Jasoos* (Detective). They did not take long to write. Some passages were my own, some free translations from English authors. Having been brought up in a Hindu home in a Muslim city—and in an English school—I am fairly proficient in the three languages. The books have sold quite well—for my publisher . . . .

My publisher, who operated from a Meerut by-lane, paid me two hundred rupees for each book; a flat and final payment, no royalties. I could not get better terms from any other publisher. It is a good country for publishers but not for writers. To quote Byron: 'Now Barabbas was a publisher . . . .'

'If you want to make money,' my publisher confided in me when he handed me my last cheque, 'publish your own books. Not detective stories. They have a limited market. Haven't you realized that India is fuller than ever of young people trying to pass exams? It is a desperate matter, this race for academic qualifications. Half the entrants fall by the wayside. The other half are even more unfortunate. They pass their exams and then they fall by the wayside. The point is, millions are sitting for exams, for MA, BSc, Ph.D., and other degrees. They all want to get these degrees the easy way, without reading too many books or attending more than half a dozen lectures—and that's where a smart person like you comes in! Why should they wade through five volumes of political history when they can get a dozen model answer-papers? They are seldom wrong, the guess-papers. All you have to do is make friends with someone on the University Board, write your papers, print them cheaply—never mind a few printing errors—and flood the market. They'll sell like hot cakes,' he concluded, using an English expression.

I told him I would think about his proposal, but I never really liked the idea. I preferred spilling the blood of fictitious prostitutes to spoon-feeding the brains of misguided students.

Besides, it would have been very boring.

A friend who shall be nameless offered to teach me the art of pickpocketing. But I had to give up after a few clumsy attempts on his pocket. To pick someone's pocket successfully is definitely an art. My friend practised his craft at various railway stations and made a good living from it. I would have to stick to writing cheap thrillers.

II

The string of my charpai needs tightening. The dip in the middle of the bed is so pronounced that invariably I wake up in the morning with a backache. But I am hopeless at tightening charpai strings and will have to wait until one of the boys from the tea shop pays me a visit.

Under the charpai is my tin trunk. Its contents range from old, rejected manuscripts to photographs, clothes, newspaper cuttings and all that goes with the floating existence of an itinerant bachelor. I do not live entirely alone. Sometimes a beggar, if he is not diseased, spends the night on the balcony; during cold or rainy weather the boys from the tea shop, who normally sleep on the pavement, crowd into my room. But apart from them, there are the lizards on the walls—friends, these—and a large rat who gets in and out of the window and carries away manuscripts and clothing; definitely an enemy.

June nights are the most uncomfortable of all. Mosquitoes emerge from all the ditches and gullies and ponds, and take over control of Pipalnagar. Bugs, finding it uncomfortable inside the woodwork of the charpai, scramble out at night and find their way under my sheet. I wrap myself up in the sheet like a corpse, but the mosquitoes bite through the thin material, and the bugs get in at the tears and holes.

The lizards wander listlessly over the walls, impatient for the monsoon rains, when they will be able to feast off thousands of insects.

Everyone is waiting for the cool, quenching relief of the monsoon. But two months from now, when roofs have fallen in, the road is flooded, and the drinking water contaminated, we will be cursing the monsoon and praying for its speedy retreat.

To awake in the morning is not difficult, as sleep is fitful, uneasy, crowded with dreams and fantasies. I know it is five o'clock when I hear the first bus coming out of the shed. If I am to defecate in private, I must be up and away into the fields beyond the railway tracks. The public lavatory near the station hasn't been cleaned for over a week.

Afterwards I return to the balcony and, slipping out of my vest and pyjamas, rub down my body with mustard oil. If the boy from the tea shop is awake, I get him to massage me, while I lie flat on my back or on my belly, dreaming of things less mundane than life in Pipalnagar.

As the passengers alight from the first bus, I sit in the barber shop and talk to Deep Chand while he lathers my face with soap. The knife moves cleanly across my cheeks and throat, and Deep Chand's breath, smelling of cloves and cardamoms—he is a perpetual eater of paan—plays on my face. In the next chair the sweetmeat-seller is having the hair shaved from under his great flabby armpits. He is looked after by Deep Chand's younger brother, Ramu, who is deputed to attend to the less popular customers. Ramu flashes a smile at me when I enter the shop; we have had a couple of nature excursions together.

Deep Chand is a short, thick-set man, very compact, dark and smooth-skinned from his waist upwards. Below his waist, from his hips to his ankles, he is a mass of soft black hair. An extremely virile man, he is very attractive to women.

Deep Chand and Ramu know all there is to know about me—in fact, all there is to know about Pipalnagar.

'When are you going to get married, brother?' Deep Chand asked me recently.

'Oh, after five or ten years,' I replied. 'Unless I find a woman rich enough to support me.'

'You are twenty-five now,' he said. 'This is the time to marry. Once you are thirty, it will not be so easy to find a wife. In Pipalnagar, when you are thirty you are old.'

'I feel too old already,' I said. 'Don't talk to me of marriage, but give my head a massage. My brain is not functioning well these days. In my latest book I have killed three people in one chapter, and still it is dull.'

'Well, finish it soon,' said Deep Chand, beginning the ritual of the head massage. 'Then you can clear your debts. When you have paid your debts you will leave Pipalnagar, won't you?'

I could not answer because he had started thumping my skull with his hard, communicative fingers, tugging at the roots of my hair and squeezing my temples with the palms of his hands. No one gives a better massage than Deep Chand. Had his income been greater, he could have shifted his trade to another locality and made a decent living. Here, in our mohalla, his principal customers are shopkeepers, truck drivers, labourers from the railway station. He charges only two rupees for a haircut; in other places it is three rupees.

While Deep Chand ran his fingers through my hair, exerting a gentle pressure on my temples, I made a mental inventory of all the people who owed me money and to whom I was in debt. The amounts I had loaned out—to various bazaar acquaintances— were small compared to the amounts I owed others. There was my landlord, Seth Govind Ram, who was in fact the landlord of half Pipalnagar and the proprietor of the dancing-girls—they did everything but dance—living in a dormitory near the bus stop; I owed him six months' rent. Sixty rupees.

He does not bother me just now, but in six months' time he will be after my blood, and I will have to pay up somehow.

Seth Govind Ram possesses a bank, a paunch and, allegedly, a mistress. The bank and the paunch are both conspicuous landmarks in Pipalnagar. Few people have seen his mistress. She is kept hidden away in an enormous Rajput-style house outside the city, and continues to be a challenge to my imagination.

Seth Govind Ram is a prominent member of the municipality. Publicly, he is a staunch supporter of the ruling party; privately, he supports all parties with occasional contributions towards their funds. He owns most of the buildings in the Pipalnagar Mohalla; and though he is always promising to pull them down and build new ones, he finds it more profitable to leave them as they are.

III

MY efforts at making a fortune have been many and varied. I had, for three days, kept a vegetable stall. Then I invested in an imaginary tea shop. I even tried my hand as a palmist.

This last venture was a failure, not because I was a poor

palmist—I had intuition enough to be able to guess what a man or woman would be happy to know—but because prospective customers were few in Pipalnagar. My friends and neighbours had grown far too cynical of the future to expect any bonuses.

'When a child is born,' asserted Deep Chand, 'his fists are clenched. They have been clenched for so long that little creases form on his palms. That is the only meaning in our lines. What have they to do with our future?'

I agreed with Deep Chand, but I thought fortune-telling might be an easy way of making money. Others did it, from saffron-robed sadhus to BAs and BComs, and did it fairly successfully, so that I felt I should try it too. It did not take me long to read a book on the subject and to hang a board from my balcony, announcing my profession. That I did not succeed was probably due to the fact that I was too well-known in Pipalnagar. Half the mohalla thought it was a joke; the other half, quite understandably, didn't believe in my genuineness.

The vegetable stall was more exciting. Down the road, near the clock tower, a widow kept a grocery store. She sold rice, spices, pulses, almost everything except meat and vegetables. The widow did not think vegetables were worth the risk of an initial investment, but she was determined to try them out, and persuaded me to put up the money.

I found it difficult to refuse. She was a strong woman, ample-bosomed, known to fight in public with any man who tried to get the better of her. But she was a persuasive saleswoman, too, and soon had me conjuring up visions of a vegetable stall of my own, full of succulent fruits and fresh green vegetables.

Full it was, from beginning to end. I didn't sell a single cabbage or cauliflower or salad leaf. Before the vegetables went bad, I gave them away to Deep Chand, Pitamber, and other friends. The widow had insisted that I charge ten paise per kilo more than others charged, a disastrous thing to do in Pipalnagar, where the question of preferring quality to quantity does not arise. She said that for the extra ten paise customers would buy cleaner and greener vegetables. She was wrong. Customers wanted them cleaner and greener *and* cheaper.

Still, it had been exciting on the first morning, getting up at five (I hadn't done this in years) and walking down to the vegetable market near the railway station, haggling with the wholesalers, piling the vegetables into baskets, and leading the coolie back to the bazaar with a proprietorial air. The railway station, half a mile from the bus stop, had always attracted me. As a child I had been fascinated by trains (as I suppose most children are), and waved to the passengers as the trains flew through the fields, and was always delighted when one of them waved back to me. I had wondered about the people in the carriages—where they were going, and why . . . . Trains had meant romance, escape into another world.

'What you should do,' advised Deep Chand once, while he lathered my face with soap—(there are several reasons why I do not shave myself; laziness, the desire to gossip, the fact that Deep Chand uses his razor as an artist uses a brush)—'what you should do, is marry a wealthy woman. It would solve all your problems. She would be only too happy to possess a young man of sexual accomplishments. You could then do your writing at leisure, with slaves to fan you and press your legs.'

'Not a bad idea,' I said, but where does one find such a woman? I expect Seth Govind Ram has a wife in addition to a mistress, but I have never seen her; and the Seth doesn't look as though he is going to die.'

'She doesn't have to be a widow. Find a young woman who is married to a fat and important millionaire. She will support you.'

Deep Chand is a married man himself, with several children. I have never bothered to count them.

His children, and others', give one the impression that in Pipalnagar children outnumber adults five to one. This is really the case, I suppose. The census tells us that one in four of our population is in the age-group of five to fifteen years. They swarm over the narrow streets, appearing to belong to one vast family—a race of pot-bellied little men, half-naked, dusty, quarrelling and laughing and crying and having so little in common with the race of adults who have brought them into the world.

On either side of my room there are families, each with about a dozen members—each family living in a room a little bigger than mine, which is used for cooking, eating, sleeping and loving. The men work in the sugar factory and bring home about fifty rupees a month. The older children attend the Pipalnagar High School, and come home only for their food. The younger ones are in and out all day, their pockets full of stones and marbles and small coins.

Tagore wrote: 'Every child comes with the message that God is not yet discouraged of man.'

'I wonder why God ever bothered to make men, when he had the whole wide beautiful world to himself,' I had said. 'Why did he find it necessary to share it with others?'

'Perhaps he felt lonely,' said Suraj.

At noon, when the shadows shift and cross the road, a band of children rush down the empty, silent street, shouting and waving their satchels. They have been at their desks from early morning, and now, despite the hot sun, they will have their fling while their elders sleep on string charpais beneath leafy neem trees.

On the soft sand near the river-bed boys wrestle or play leap-frog. At alley-corners, where tall buildings shade narrow passages, the favourite game is *gulli-danda*.

The *gulli*—a small piece of wood about four inches long, sharpened to a point at each end—is struck with the *danda*, a short stout stick. A player is allowed three hits, and his score is the distance he hits the *gulli*, in *danda* lengths.

Boys who are experts at this game send the *gulli* flying far down the road; sometimes into a shop or through a window-pane, resulting in commotion, loud invective, and a dash for cover.

A game for both children and young men is kabaddi. It is a game that calls for good control of the breath and much agility. As it is essentially a village game, Pitamber excels at it; he is the Pipalnagar kabaddi champion.

As a wrestler, he knows all the holds and is particularly adept at capturing an opponent. He took me to his village where all the boys were long-limbed and sun-browned, erect and at the same time relaxed. There was a sense of vitality and confidence in Pitamber's village, which I have not seen in Pipalnagar.

In Pipalnagar there is not exactly despair, but resignation, an indifference to both living and dying. The town is almost truly reflected in the Pipalnagar Home, where in an open courtyard surrounded by mud walls a score of mental patients wander about, listless and bored. One man jabbers excitedly, but most of the inmates are quite sad and resentful—resentful because we do not try to understand their beautiful insane world.

Aziz visits me occasionally for a loan of two or three rupees, which he returns in kind whenever I visit his junk shop. He is a Muslim boy of eighteen. He lives in a small room behind the junk shop.

The shop has mud walls and a tin roof. The walls are always in danger of being washed away during the monsoon, and the roof of sailing away during a dust-storm. The rain comes in, anyway, and the floor is awash most of the time; bound copies of old English magazines gather mildew, and the pots and pans and spare parts grow rusty. Aziz, at eighteen, is beginning to collect dust and age and disease.

But he is an optimistic soul, even though there is nothing for him to be optimistic about, and he is always asking me when I intend keeping my vow of going to Delhi to make my fortune. I am to keep an eye out for a favourable shop-site near Chandni Chowk where he can open a more up-to-date junk shop. He is saving towards this end; but what he saves trickles away in paying for his wife's upkeep at the Home.

IV

I was walking through the fields beyond the railway tracks, when I saw someone lying on the footpath next to the wheat fields, his head and body hidden by the ripening wheat. The wheat was shaking where he lay, and as I came nearer I saw that one of his legs kept twitching convulsively.

Thinking that perhaps it was a case of robbery with violence, I prepared to run; but then, cursing myself for being a coward, I approached the agitated person.

He was a youth of about eighteen, and he appeared to be in the throes of a violent fit.

His face was white, except where a little blood had trickled from his mouth. His leg kept twitching, and his hands moved restlessly, helplessly amongst the wheat.

I spoke to him. 'What is wrong?' I asked, but he was obviously unconscious and could not answer. So I ran down the path to the well, and dipping the end of my shirt in a shallow trough of water, soaked it well, and ran back to the boy.

By that time he seemed to have recovered from the fit. The twitching had ceased, and though he still breathed heavily, his face was calm and his hands still. I wiped the blood from his mouth, and he opened his eyes and stared at me without any immediate comprehension.

'You have bitten your tongue,' I said. 'There's no hurry. I'll stay here with you.'

We rested where we were for some minutes without saying anything. He was no longer agitated. Resting his chin on his knees, he passed his hands around his drawn-up legs.

'I am all right now,' he said.

'What happened?'

'It was nothing, it often happens. I don't know why. I cannot stop it.'

'Have you seen a doctor?'

'I went to the hospital when it first began. They gave me some pills. I had to take them every day. But they made me so tired and sleepy that I couldn't do any work. So I stopped taking them. I get the attack about once a week, but I am useless if I take those pills.'

He got to his feet, smiling as he dusted his clothes.

He was a thin boy, long-limbed and bony. There was a little fluff on his cheeks and the promise of a moustache. His pyjamas were short for him, accentuating the awkwardness of his long, bony feet. He had beauty, though; his eyes held secrets, his mouth hesitant smiles.

He told me that he was a student at the Pipalnagar College, and that his terminal examination would be held in August. Apparently his whole life hinged on the result of the coming examination. If he passed, there was the prospect of a scholarship, and eventually a place for himself in the world. If he failed, there was only the prospect of Pipalnagar, and a living eked out by selling combs and buttons and little vials of perfume.

I noticed the tray of merchandise lying on the ground. It usually hung at his waist, the straps going round his neck. All day he walked about Pipalnagar, covering ten to fifteen miles a day, selling odds and ends to people at their houses. He made about two rupees a day, which gave him enough for his food. And he ate irregularly, at little tea shops, at the stalls near the bus stops, or on the roadside under shady jamun and mango trees. When the jamuns were ripe, he would sit in a tree, sucking the sour fruit till his lips were stained purple with their juice. There was always the fear that he would get a fit while sitting in a tree, and fall off; but the temptation to eat jamuns was too great for him, and he took the risk.

'Where do you stay?' I asked. 'I will walk back with you to your home.'

'I don't stay anywhere in particular. Sometimes in a dharamsala, sometimes in the gurudwara, sometimes in the maidan. In the summer months I like to sleep in the maidan, on the grass.'

'Then I'll walk with you to the maidan,' I said.

There was nothing extraordinary about his being a refugee and an orphan. During the communal holocaust of 1947 thousands of homes had been destroyed, women and children killed. What was extraordinary was his sensitivity—or should I say sensibility—a rare quality in a Punjabi youth who had been brought up in the Frontier Provinces during one of the most cruel periods in the country's history. It was not his conversation that impressed me—though his attitude to life was one of hope, while in Pipalnagar people were too resigned even to be desperate—but the gentle persuasiveness of his voice, eyes, and also of his hands, long-fingered, gliding hands, and his smile which flickered with amusement and sometimes irony.

V

One morning, when I opened the door of my room, I found Suraj asleep at the top of the steps. His tray lay a short distance away. I shook him gently, and he woke up immediately, blinking in the bright sunlight.

'Why didn't you come in?' I said. 'Why didn't you tell me?'

'It was late,' he said. 'I didn't want to disturb you.'

'Someone could have stolen your things while you slept.'

'So far no one has stolen from me.'

I made him promise to sleep in my room that night, and he came in at ten, curled up on the floor and slept fitfully, while I lay awake worrying if he was comfortable enough.

He came several nights, and left early in the morning, before I could offer him anything to eat. We would talk into the early hours of the morning. Neither of us slept much.

I liked Suraj's company. He dispelled some of my own loneliness, and I found myself looking forward to the sound of his footsteps on the stairs. He liked my company because I was full of stories, even though some of them were salacious; and because I encouraged his ambitions and gave him confidence.

I forget what it was I said that offended him and hurt his feelings—something unintentional, and, of course, silly. One of those things that you cannot remember afterwards but which seem terribly important at the time. I had probably been giving him too much advice, showing off my knowledge of the world and women, and joking about his becoming the Prime Minister one day; because the next night he didn't come to my room.

I waited till eleven o'clock for the sound of his footsteps, and then when he didn't come, I left the room and went in search of him. I couldn't bear the thought of an angry and unhappy Suraj sleeping alone in the maidan. What if he should have another fit? I told myself that he had been through scores of fits without my being around to help him, but already I was beginning to feel protective towards him.

The shops had closed and lights showed only in upper windows. There were many sleeping on the sidewalk, and I peered into the face of each, but I did not find Suraj. Eventually I found him in the maidan, asleep on a bench.

'Suraj,' I said, and he awoke and sat up.

'What is it?'

'I've been looking for you for the last two hours. Come on home,'

'Why don't you spend the night here?' he said. 'This is my home.'

I felt angry at first, but then I felt ashamed of my anger.

I said, 'Thank you for your kind offer, dear friend, it will be a privilege to be your guest,' and sat down on the bench beside him.

We were silent for some time, while a big yellow moon played hide-and-seek with the clouds. Then it began to drizzle.

It's raining,' I said. 'Why didn't you make a roof over your house? Now let us go back to mine.'

I thought he might still refuse to return with me, but he got up, smiling; perhaps it was my own sudden humility, or perhaps it was the rain . . . . I think it was my own humility, because it made him feel he had wronged me.

In the afternoon Pipalnagar is empty. The temperature has touched 106°F! To walk barefoot on the scorching pavement is possible only for the beggars and labourers whose feet have developed several layers of hard protective skin. And even they lie stretched out in the shade given by shops and walls, their open sores festering in the hot sun.

Suraj will be asleep in the shade of a peepul or banyan tree, a book lying open beside him, his tray a few feet away. Sometimes the crows are fascinated by his many coloured combs and come down from the trees to inspect them.

At this hour of the day I lie naked on the stone floor of my room because the floor is the coolest place of all. And as I am too listless to work or sleep, I study my navel, the hairs on my belly, the languid aspect of my genitals, and the hair on my legs and thighs. I study my toes and with the dust that has accumulated on my feet, I trace patterns on the walls and disturb the flaking plaster which in itself has formed a score of patterns—birds and snakes and elephants . . . . With a little imagination I can conjure up the entire world of the *Panchatantra* . . . .

Of all the joys of the senses, I think it is the sense of touch I relish most—contact with the cool floor on a hot day. That is why I lie naked in my room so that all my flesh is in touch with the cool stones.

The touch of the earth—soft earth, stony earth, grass, mud. Sometimes the road is so hot that it scorches the most hardened feet. Sometimes it is cold and hard and cruel. Grass is good, especially dew-drenched grass; then the feet are stained with juices and the sap seems to pass into the body. Wet earth is soft and sensuous and when the mud cakes on one's feet it is interesting to bathe at a tap and watch the muddy water run away. Splashing through puddles and streams . . . .

There are days and there are nights and then there are other days and other nights and all the days and nights in Pipalnagar are the same.

A few things reassure me . . . .

The desire to love and be loved. The beauty and ugliness of the human body, the intricacy of its design. These things fascinate me. Sometimes I make love as a sort of exploration of all that is physical. Falling in love becomes an exploration of the mind.

VI

It is difficult to fall asleep some nights. Apart from the mosquitoes and the oppressive atmosphere, there are the loudspeakers blaring all over Pipalnagar—at cinemas, marriages and religious gatherings. There is a continuous variety of fare—religious music and film music. I do not care much for either and yet I am compelled to listen, both repelled and fascinated by the sounds that permeate the midnight air.

Strangely enough, it does not trouble Suraj. He is immune to noise. Once he is asleep, it would take a bomb to disturb him. At the first blare of the loudspeaker, he pulls a pillow or towel over his head and falls asleep. He has been in Pipalnagar longer than I and has grown accustomed to living against a background of noise. And yet he is a silent person, silent in his movements and in his moods. And I, who love silence so much—I am clumsy and garrulous.

Suraj does not know if his parents are dead or alive. He lost them, literally, when he was seven.

His father had been a cultivator, a dark unfathomable man, who spoke little, thought perhaps even less, and was vaguely aware that he possessed a son—a weak boy, who resembled his mother to a disconcerting degree in that he not only looked like her but was given to introspection and dawdling at the river-bank when he should have been at work in the fields.

The boy's mother was a subdued, silent woman—frail and consumptive. Her husband did not expect that she would live long. Perhaps the separation from her son put an end to her interest in life—or perhaps it has urged her to live on somewhere, in the hope that she will find him again.

Suraj lost his parents at Amritsar railway station, where trains coming over the border disgorged themselves of thousands of refugees—or pulled into the station half-empty, drenched with blood and piled with corpses.

Suraj and his parents were lucky to escape the massacre. Had they been able to travel on an earlier train (they had tried desperately to get into one) they might easily have been killed. But circumstances favoured them then, only to trick them later.

Suraj was clinging to his mother's sari while she kept close to her husband who was elbowing his way through the frightened, bewildered throng of refugees. Looking over his shoulder at a woman sobbing on the ground, Suraj collided with a burly Sikh and lost his grip on his mother's sari.

The Sikh had a long, curved sword at his waist and Suraj stared up at him in terror and fascination—at his long hair, which had fallen loose, and his wild black beard and the bloodstains on his white shirt. The Sikh pushed him out of the way and when Suraj looked around for his mother she was not to be seen.

He could hear her calling to him, 'Suraj, where are you, Suraj?' and he tried to force his way through the crowd, in the direction of her voice, but he was carried the other way.

VII

At a certain age a boy is like young wheat, growing, healthy, on the verge of manhood. His eyes are alive, his mind quick, his gestures confident. You cannot mistake him.

This is the most fascinating age, when a boy becomes a man—it is interesting both physically and mentally. The growth of the boy's hair, the toning of the muscles, the consciousness of growing and changing and maturing—never again will there be so much change and development in so short a period of time. The body exudes virility, is full of currents and counter-currents.

For a girl, puberty is a frightening age when alarming things begin to happen to her body. For a boy it is an age of self-assertion, of a growing confidence in himself and in his attitude to the world. His physical changes are a source of happiness and pride.

There were no inhibitions in my friendship with Suraj. We spoke of bodies as we spoke of minds, and discussed the problems of one as we would discuss those of the other, for they are really the same problems.

He was beautiful, with the beauty of the short-lived, a transient, sad beauty. It made me sad even to look at his pale slim limbs. It hurt me to look into his eyes. There was death in his eyes.

He told me that he was afraid of women, that he constantly felt the urge to possess a woman, but that when confronted with one he might just as well have been a eunuch.

I told him that not every woman was made for every man, and that I would bring him a girl with whom he would be happy.

This was Kamla, a very friendly person from the house run by Seth Govind Ram. She was very small and rather delicate but more skilled in love-making than any of her colleagues. She was patient and particularly fond of the young and inexperienced. She was only twenty-three but had been four years in the profession.

Kamla's hands and feet are beautiful. That in itself is satisfying. A beautiful face leaves me cold if the hands and feet are ugly. Perhaps this is some sort of phobia with me.

Kamla first met me when I came up the stairs shortly after I had moved into the room above the bus stop. She was sitting on the steps, eating a melon. And when she saw me, she smiled and held out a slice.

'Will you eat melon, bhai sahib?' she asked and her voice was so appealing and her eyes so mischievous that I couldn't help taking the melon from her hands.

'Sit down,' she said, patting the step. I had never come

across a girl so openly friendly and direct. As I sat down, I discovered the secret of her smile. It lay in the little scar on her right cheek. When she smiled the scar turned into a dimple.

'Don't you do any work?' she asked.

'I write stories and things,' I said.

'Is that work?'

'Well, I live by it.'

'Show me,' she demanded.

I brought her a magazine and began turning the pages for her. She could read a little if the words were simple enough. But she didn't get as far as my story because her attention was arrested by a picture of a girl with an urchin haircut.

'Is it a girl?' she asked. And, when I assured her it was: 'But her hair, how is it like that?'

'That's the latest fashion,' I protested. 'Thousands of women keep hair like that. At least they did a year ago,' I added, looking at the date on the magazine.

'Is it easy to make?'

'Yes, you just take a pair of scissors and cut away until it looks untidy enough.'

'I like it. You give it to me. I'll go and get scissors.'

'No, no!' I said. 'You can't do that. Your family will be most upset.'

She stamped her bare foot on the step. 'I have no family, silly man! I have a husband who is happy only if I can make myself attractive to others. He is skinny and smells of garlic and he has given my father five acres of land for the favour of having a wife half his age. But it is Seth Govind Ram who really owns me. My husband is only his servant.'

'Why are you telling me all this?'

'Why shouldn't I tell you?' she said and gave me a dark, defiant look. 'You like me, do you not?'

'Of course I like you,' I hastened to assure her.

I think I hate families. I am jealous of them. Their sense of security, of interdependence infuriates me. To every family I am an outsider because I have no family. A man without a family is a social outcast. He has no credentials. A man's credentials are his father and his father's property. His mother is of no consequence either; it is her family—her father—that matters.

So I am glad that I do not belong to a family and at the same time sad because in our country if you do not belong to a family you are a piece of driftwood. And so two pieces of driftwood come together and finding themselves caught in the same current move along with it until they are trapped in a counter-current and dispersed.

And that is the way it is with me. I must cling to someone as long as circumstances will permit it.

Having no family of our own, it was odd and even touching that Kamla should have adopted us both as her brothers during the Raksha Bandhan festival.

This is the time of year when sisters tie the sacred thread to the wrists of their brothers. As a token of affection, the brother makes her a small gift of money and promises her his protection.

It was a change to have Kamla visiting us early in the morning instead of late at night. And we were surprised, and rather disconcerted, to be treated as her brothers.

She tied the silver tinsel round our wrists and I said, 'Kamla, we are proud to be your brothers and we would like to make you some gift. But at the moment there is no money with us.'

'I want your protection, not your money,' said Kamla. 'I want to feel that I am not alone in the world.'

So that made three of us. But we could hardly call ourselves a family.

Kamla visited us about once a week when she found time to spare from her professional duties.

Though I was the more accomplished lover, I think she preferred Suraj. He was gentle and he was beautiful and I think she felt, as I did, that he would not live very long. She wanted to give him as much of herself as she could in so short a time.

Suraj was always a bit embarrassed with her. At first I thought it was because of my presence in the room. But when

I offered to leave, he protested. He told me that he would have been completely helpless if I was not present all the time. In fact, I think he slept with Kamla only in order to please me.

VIII

The beggars on the whole are a thriving community and it came as no surprise to me when the municipality decided to place a tax on begging.

I know that some beggars earned, on an average, more than a chaprasi or a clerk. I knew for certain that the one-legged man, who had been hobbling about town on crutches long before I came to Pipalnagar, sent money orders home every month. Begging had become a profession, and so perhaps the municipality felt justified in taxing it and, besides, the municipal coffers needed replenishing.

Shaggy old Ganpat Ram, who was bent double and couldn't straighten up, didn't like it at all and told me so. 'If I had known this was going to happen,' he mumbled, 'I would have chosen some other line of work.'

Ganpat Ram was an aristocrat among beggars. I had heard that he had once been a man of property with several houses and a European wife. When his wife packed up and returned to Europe, together with all their savings, Ganpat had a nervous breakdown from which he never recovered. His health became steadily worse until he had to hobble about with a stick. He never made a direct request for money but greeted you politely, commented on the weather or the price of things, and stood significantly beside you.

I suspected his story to be half true because whenever he approached a well-dressed person, he used impeccable English. He had a white beard and twinkling eyes and was not the sort of beggar who invokes the names of the gods and calls on the mercy of the passer-by. Ganpat would rely more on a good joke. Some said he was a spy or a policeman in disguise, but so, devoted to his work that he would probably remain a beggar for five more years.

I don't know how blind the blind man was because he always recognized me in the street even when he was alone. He would invoke blessings on my head, or curses, as the occasion demanded. I didn't like the blind man, because he made too much capital out of his affliction. There were opportunities for him to work with other blind people but he found begging more profitable. The boy who sometimes led him around town didn't beg from me but would ask, 'Have you got an anna on you?' as though he were merely borrowing the money, or needed it only for a minute or two. He was quite friendly and even came up to my room to see how I was getting on. He was very solicitous about my welfare. If he saw me from a hundred yards down the street, he would run all the way up to enquire about my health and borrow an anna. He had a crafty, healthy face and wore a long, dirty cloak draped over his shoulders, and very little else. He didn't care about the tax on begging. That was the blind man's problem.

In fact, the tax didn't affect the boys at all. With them, begging was a pastime and not a profession. They had big watery eyes and it was difficult to resist their appeal.

'I haven't any small change,' I would say defensively.

'I'll change your note,' offers the boy.

'It's not a note. It's a fifty-paise coin.'

'What do you want to change that for? Give me the coin and I won't trouble you for the rest of the week.'

'That's very kind of you.' But even if I gave him the two annas, he would accost me again at the first opportunity and wheedle something more from my pocket. There was a time when beggars asked for one or two pice but these days, what with the rise in the cost of living, they never ask for anything less than an anna.

Friday is Lepers' day.

There is a leper colony a little way out of town, on the banks of a muddy, mosquito-ridden ditch, the other side of the railway station. They come into Pipalnagar once a week to beg and wander through the town in small groups making for wealthy-looking individuals who give them something if only to avoid being followed down the road. (Of course the danger of contagion is there, but if the municipal authorities do not let the lepers beg they will have to support them and that would prove expensive).

Some of the leper girls have good faces but their hands are withered stumps or their arms and legs are eaten away. The older ones have lost their ears and noses and the men shuffle about with one or two limbs missing. Most of the sufferers belong to the hill areas where it is still widely believed that leprosy is punishment for sins committed in a former life. The victim is ostracized and often driven out by his family. He goes into the towns and, in order to get work, makes a secret of his affliction. It is only when it can no longer be concealed that he goes for treatment and then it is too late. The few who get into the hospitals are soldiers and policemen who are looked after by the state and a few others whose families have not disclaimed responsibility for them.

But the tax didn't affect the boys or the lepers. It was aimed at the professionals, those who had made a business of begging over the past few years. It was rumoured that one beggar, after spending the day on the pavement calling for alms, would have a taxi drawn up beside him in the evening and would be driven off to his residence outside town. And when, some months back, news got around that the Pipalnagar Bank was ready to crash, one beggar, who had never been seen to stand on his own two feet, leapt from the pavement and sprinted for the bank. The professionals are usually crippled or maimed in one way or another—many of them have maimed themselves, others have gone through rigorous training schools in their youth, where they are versed in the fine art of begging. A few cases are genuine and those are not so loud in their demands for charity with the result that they don't make much. There are some who sing for their money and I do not class these as beggars unless they sing badly.

Well, when the municipality decided to place a tax on begging, you should have seen the beggars get together. Anyone would have thought they had a union. About a hundred of them took a procession down the main road to the municipal offices, shouting slogans and even waving banners to express the injustice felt by the beggar fraternity over this high-handed action of the authorities. They came with sticks and in carts, a dirty, ragged bunch, one or two of them stark naked; and they stood for two hours outside the municipal office, to the embarrassment of the working staff and anyone who tried to enter the building.

Eventually somebody came out and told them it was all a

rumour and that no such tax had been contemplated. It would be far too impractical for one thing. The beggars could all go home and hoard their earnings without any fear of official interference.

So the beggars returned jubilant, feeling they had won a moral victory, conscious of the power of group action. They went out of their way to develop their union and now there is a full-fledged Beggars' Union. Different districts are allotted to different beggars and woe betide the trespasser! Beggars are becoming more demanding than ever and it is rumoured that they intend staging demonstrations outside the houses of those who refuse to be charitable!

But my own personal beggars, old Ganpat Ram and the boys, don't take advantage of their growing power. They treat me with due respect and affection. They do not consider me just another member of the public who has to be blackmailed into charity but look upon me as a friend who can be counted upon to make them a small loan from time to time without expecting any immediate return.

IX

Should I go to Delhi, Suraj?'

'Why not? You are always talking about it. You should go.'

'I would like you to come with me. Perhaps they can make you better there, even cure you of your fits.'

'Not now. After my examinations.'

'Then I will wait . . . .'

'Go now, if there is a chance of making a living in Delhi.'

'There is nothing definite. But I know the chance will not come until I leave this place and make my chances. There are one or two editors who have asked me to look them up. They could give me some work. And if I find an honest publisher I might be encouraged to write an honest book.'

'Write the book, even if you don't find a publisher.'

'I will try.'

We decided to save a little money from his small earnings and from my occasional erratic payments which came by money-order. I would need money for my trip to Delhi. Sometimes there were medicines to be paid for and we had no warm clothes for the cold weather. We managed to put away twenty rupees one week but withdrew it the next as Pitamber needed a loan for repairs on his cycle-rickshaw. He returned the money in three instalments and it disappeared in meeting various small bills.

Pitamber and Deep Chand and Ramu and Aziz all had plans for visiting Delhi. Only Kamla could not foresee such a move for herself. She was a woman and she had no man.

Deep Chand dreamt of his barber shop. Pitamber planned to own a scooter-rickshaw, which would involve no physical exertion and would bring in more money. Ramu had a hundred and one different dreams, all of which featured beautiful women. He was a sweet boy with little intelligence but much good nature.

Once, when he had his arm gashed by a knife in a street fight, he came to me for treatment. The hospital would have had to report the matter to the police. I washed his wound, poured benzedrine over it to stop the bleeding, and bandaged his arm rather crudely. He was very grateful and rewarded me with the story of his life. It was a chronicle of disappointed females, all of whom had been seduced by Ramu in fantastic circumstances and had been discarded by him after he had slept with each but once. Ramu boasted that he did not go twice to the same woman.

All this was good-natured lying, as it was well-known that a girl-teaser like Ramu had never seen anything more than a well-shaped ankle. But apparently Ramu believed in many of his own adventures, which in his mind had acquired a legendary aspect.

I did not ask him how he got his arm cut because I knew he would have given me a fantastic explanation involving his honour and a lady's dishonour. Later I discovered that an irate brother had stabbed him for spreading discreditable rumours about his sister.

Ramu slept in my room that night. It was the sweet sleep of childhood. Suraj read his books and Kamla came and went while Ramu dreamt—he told us about it in the morning—of a woman with three breasts.

X

'Look, Ganpat,' I said one day, 'I've heard a lot of stories about you and I don't know which is true. How did you get your crooked back?'

'That's a very long story,' he said, flattered by my interest in him. 'And I don't know if you will believe it. Besides, it is not to everyone that I would speak freely.'

He had served his purpose of whetting my appetite. I said, 'I'll give you four annas if you tell me your story. How about that?'

He stroked his beard, considering my offer. 'All right,' he said, squatting down on his haunches in the sunshine, while I pulled myself up on a low wall. 'But it happened more than twenty years ago and you cannot expect me to remember very clearly.'

In those days (said Ganpat) I was quite a young man and had just been married. I owned several acres of land and, though we were not rich, we were not very poor. When I took my produce to the market, five miles away, I harnessed the bullocks and drove down the dusty village road. I would return home at night.

Every night, I passed a pipal tree, and it was said this tree was haunted. I had never met the ghost and did not believe in him but his name, I was told, was Bippin, and long ago he had been hanged from the pipal tree by a band of dacoits. Ever since, his ghost had lived in the tree, and was in the habit of pouncing upon any person who resembled a dacoit and beating him severely. I suppose I must have looked dishonest, for one night Bippin decided to pounce on me. He leapt out of the tree and stood in the middle of the road, blocking the way.

'You, there!' he shouted. 'Get off your cart. I am going to kill you!'

I was, of course, taken aback, but saw no reason why I should obey.

'I have no intention of being killed,' I said. 'Get on the cart yourself!'

'Spoken like a man!' cried Bippin, and he jumped up on the cart beside me. 'But tell me one good reason why I should not kill you?'

'I am not a dacoit,' I replied.

'But you look like one. That is the same thing.'

'You would be sorry for it later if you killed me. I am a poor man with a wife to support.'

'You have no reason for being poor,' said Bippin angrily.

'Well, make me rich if you can.'

'So you think I don't have the power to make you rich? Do you defy me to make you rich?'

'Yes,' I said. 'I defy you to make me rich.'

'Then drive on!' cried Bippin. 'I am coming home with you.' I drove the bullock-cart into the village with Bippin sitting beside me.

'I have so arranged it,' he said, 'that no one but you will be able to see me. And another thing. I must sleep beside you every night and no one must know of it. If you tell anyone about me, I'll kill you immediately!'

'Don't worry,' I said. 'I won't tell anyone.'

'Good. I look forward to living with you. It was getting lonely in that pipal tree.'

So Bippin came to live with me, and he slept beside me every night and we got on very well together. He was as good as his word and money began to pour in from every conceivable and inconceivable source until I was in a position to buy more land and cattle. Nobody knew of our association though of course my friends and relatives wondered where all the money was coming from. At the same time, my wife was rather upset at my refusing to sleep with her at night. I could not very well keep her in the same bed as a ghost and Bippin was most particular about sleeping beside me. At first, I had told my wife I wasn't well, that I would sleep on the veranda. Then I told her that there was someone after our cows, and I would have to keep an eye on them at night. Bippin and I slept in the barn.

My wife would often spy on me at night, suspecting infidelity, but she always found me lying alone with the cows. Unable to understand my strange behaviour, she mentioned it to her family. They came to me demanding an explanation.

At the same time, my own relatives were insisting that I tell them the source of my increasing income. Uncles and aunts and distant cousins all descended on me one day, wanting to know where the money was coming from.

'Do you want me to die?' I said, losing patience with them. 'If I tell you the cause of my wealth, I will surely die.'

But they laughed, taking this for a half-hearted excuse. They suspected I was trying to keep everything for myself. My wife's relatives insisted that I had found another woman. Eventually, I grew so exhausted with their demands that I blurted out the truth.

They didn't believe the truth either (who does?), but it gave them something to think and talk about and they went away for the time being.

But that night, Bippin didn't come to sleep beside me. I was all alone with the cows. And he didn't come the following night. I had been afraid he would kill me while I slept but it appeared that he had gone his way and left me to my own devices. I was certain that my good fortune had come to an end and so I went back to sleeping with my wife.

The next time I was driving back to the village from the market, Bippin leapt out of the pipal tree.

'False friend!' he cried, halting the bullocks. 'I gave you everything you wanted and still you betrayed me!'

'I'm sorry,' I said. 'You can kill me if you like.'

'No, I cannot kill you,' he said. 'We have been friends for too long. But I will punish you all the same.'

Picking up a stout stick, he struck me three times across the back, until I was bent up double.

'After that,' Ganpat concluded, 'I could never straighten up again and, for over twenty years, I have been a crooked man. My wife left me and went back to her family and I could no longer work in the fields. I left my village and wandered from one city to another, begging for a living. That is how I came to Pipalnagar where I decided to remain. People here seem to be more generous than they are in other towns, perhaps because they haven't got so much.'

He looked up at me with a smile, waiting for me to produce the four annas.

'You can't expect me to believe that story,' I said. 'But it was a good invention. So here is your money.'

'No, no!' said Ganpat, backing away and affecting indignation. 'If you don't believe me, keep the money. I would not lie to you for a mere four annas!'

He permitted me to force the coin into his hand and then went hobbling away, having first wished me a pleasant afternoon.

I was almost certain he had been telling me a very tall

story; but you never can tell . . . . Perhaps he really had met Bippin the ghost. And it was wise to give him the four annas, just in case, after all, he was a CID man.

XI

Pitamber is a young lion. A shaggy mane of black hair tumbles down the nape of his neck. His body, though, is naked and hairless, burnt a rich chocolate by the summer sun. His only garment is a pair of knickers. When he pedals his cycle-rickshaw through the streets of Pipalnagar, the muscles of his calves and thighs stand out like lumps of grey iron. He has carried in his rickshaw fat baniyas and their fat wives and this has given him powerful legs, a strong back and hollow cheeks. His thighs are magnificent, solid muscle, not an ounce of surplus flesh. They look as though they have been carved out of teak.

His face, though, is gaunt and hollow, his eyes set deep in their sockets. But there is a burning intensity about his eyes and sometimes I wonder if he, too, is tubercular, like many in Pipalnagar. You cannot tell just by looking at a person if he is sick. Sometimes the weak will last for years while the strong will suddenly collapse and die.

Pitamber has a wife and three children in his village five miles from Pipalnagar. They have a few acres of land on which they grow maize and sugarcane. One day he made me sit in his rickshaw and we cycled out of the town along the road to Delhi. Then we had to get down and push the rickshaw over a rutted cart-track until we reached his village.

This visit to Pitamber's village had provided me with an escape route from Pipalnagar. I persuaded Suraj to put aside his tray and his books and hiring a cycle from a stand near the bus stop (on credit), I seated Suraj in front of me on the cross-bar and rode out of Pipalnagar.

It was then that I made the amazing discovery that by exerting my legs a little I could get out of Pipalnagar and that, except for the cycle-hire, it did not involve any expense or great sacrifice.

It was a hot, sunny morning and I was perspiring by the time we had gone two miles but a fresh wind sprang up suddenly and I could smell rain in the air, though there were no clouds to be seen.

When Suraj began to feel cramped on the saddle-bar, we got down and walked along the side of the road.

'Let us not go to the village,' said Suraj. 'Let us go where there are no people at all. I am tired of people.'

We pushed the cycle off the road and took a path through a paddy-field and then a field of young maize, and in the distance we saw a tree, a crooked tree, growing beside a well.

I do not know the name of that tree. I had never seen one of its kind before. It had a crooked trunk and crooked branches, and it was clothed in thick, broad crooked leaves, like the leaves on which food is served in the bazaars.

In the trunk of the tree was a hole and when I set my cycle down with a crash, two green parrots flew out of the hole and went dipping and swerving across the fields.

There was grass around the well, cropped short by grazing cattle, so we sat in the shade of the crooked tree and Suraj untied the red cloth in which he had brought our food.

We ate our bread and spiced vegetables and meanwhile the parrots returned to the tree.

'Let us come here every week,' said Suraj, stretching himself out on the grass and resting his head against my shoulder.

It was a drowsy day, the air humid, and soon Suraj fell asleep. I, too, stretched myself out on the grass and closed my eyes but did not sleep. I was aware instead of a score of different sensations.

I heard a cricket singing in the crooked tree; the cooling of pigeons which dwelt in the walls of the old well; the quiet breathing of Suraj; a rustling in the leaves of the tree; the distant hum of an aeroplane.

I smelt the grass and the old bricks round the well and the promise of rain.

I felt Suraj's fingers touching my arm and the sun creeping over my cheek.

I opened my eyes and saw the clouds on the horizon and Suraj still asleep, his arm thrown across his eyes to keep away the glare.

Being thirsty, I went to the well and, putting my shoulders to it, turned the wheel, walking around the well four times, while cool clean water gushed out over the stones and along the channel to the fields.

I drank from one of the trays and the water was sweet with age.

Suraj was sitting up, looking at the sky.

'It is going to rain,' he said. When he had taken his fill of water we pushed the cycle back to the main road and began cycling homewards, but we were still two miles out of Pipalnagar when it began to rain.

A lashing wind swept the rain across our faces but we exulted in it and sang at the top of our voices until we reached the bus stop.

I left the cycle at the hire-shop. Suraj and I ran up the ricketty, swaying steps to my room.

Soon there were puddles on the floor where we had left our soaking clothes and Suraj was sitting on the bed, a sheet wrapped round his chest.

He became feverish that evening and I pulled out an old blanket and covered him with it. I massaged his scalp with mustard oil and he fell asleep while I did this.

It was dark by then and the rain had stopped and the bazaar was lighting up. I curled up at the foot of the bed and slept for a little while but at midnight I was woken by the moon shining full in my face: a full moon, shedding its light exclusively on Pipalnagar and peeping and prying into every room, washing the empty streets, silvering the corrugated tin roof.

People are restless tonight, with the moon shining through their windows. Suraj turns restlessly in his sleep. Kamla, having sent away a drunken customer, will be bathing herself, as she always does before she finally sleeps . . . . Deep Chand is tossing on his cot, dreaming of electric razors and a plush haircutting saloon in the capital, with the Prime Minister as his client. And Seth Govind Ram, unable to sleep because of the accusing moonlight, paces his veranda, worrying about his rent, counting up his assets, and wondering if he should stand for election to the Legislative Assembly.

In the temple the moonlight rests gently on the generous Ganesh, and in the fields Krishna is playing his flute and Radha is singing . . . . 'I follow you, devoted . . . . How can you deceive me, so tortured by love's fever as I am . . . .'

XII

In June, the lizards hang listlessly on the walls, scanning their horizon in vain. Insects seldom show up—either the heat has killed them, or they are sleeping and breeding in cracks in the plaster. The lizards wait—and wait . . . .

All Pipalnagar is waiting for its release from the oppressive heat of June.

One day clouds loom up on the horizon, growing rapidly into enormous towers. A faint breeze springs up. Soon it is a wind which brings with it the first raindrops. This is the moment everyone is waiting for. People run out of their chawls and houses to take in the fresh breeze and the scent of those first raindrops on the parched, dusty earth.

Underground, in their cracks and holes the insects are moving. Termites and white ants, which have been sleeping through the hot season, emerge from their lairs. They have work ahead of them.

Now, on the second or third night of the monsoon, comes the great yearly flight of the insects into the cool brief freedom of the night. Out of every crack, from under the roots of trees, huge winged ants emerge, at first fluttering about heavily, on this the first and last flight of their lives. At night there is only one direction in which they can fly—towards the light; towards the electric bulbs and smoky kerosene lamps that illuminate Pipalnagar.

The street lamp opposite the bus stop, beneath my room, attracts a massive quivering swarm of clumsy termites which give the impression of one thick, slowly revolving body.

The first frog has arrived and comes hopping on to the balcony to pause beneath the electric bulb. All he has to do is gobble as the insects fall about him.

This is the hour of the lizards. Now there are rewards for those days of patient waiting. Plying their sticky pink tongues, they devour the insects as fast as they come. For hours they cram their stomachs, knowing that such a feast will not be theirs again for another year. How wasteful nature is . . . . Through the whole hot season the insect world prepares for this flight out of darkness into light and not one of them survives its freedom.

As most of my writing is done at night, and much of my

sleeping by day, it often happens that at about midnight I put down my pen and go out for a walk. In Pipalnagar this is a pleasant time for a walk provided you are not taken for a burglar. There is the smell of jasmine in the air, the moonlight shining on sandy stretches of wasteland, and a silence broken only by the hideous bellow of the chowkidar, or night-watchman.

This is the person who, employed by the residents of our mohalla, keeps guard over us at night and walks the roads calling like a jackal: 'Khabardar!' (Beware) for the benefit of prospective evil-doers. Apart from keeping half the population awake, he is successful in warning thieves of his presence.

The other night, in the course of a midnight stroll, I encountered our chowkidar near a dark cavern and wished him a good evening. He leapt into the air like a startled rabbit and immediately shouted 'Khabardar!' as though this were some magic word that would bring me down on my knees begging for mercy.

'It's quite all right,' I assured him. 'I'm only one of your clients.'

The chowkidar laughed nervously and said he was glad to hear it. He hoped I didn't mind his shouting 'Khabardar' at me, but these were grim times and robbers were on the increase.

I said yes, there were probably quite a few of them at work this very night. Had he ever tried creeping up on them quietly? He might catch a few that way.

But why should he catch them, the chowkidar wanted to know. It was his business to frighten them away. He could do that better by roaring defiantly on the roads than by accosting them on someone's premises—violence must be avoided, if he could help it.

'Besides,' he said, 'the people who live here like me to shout at night. It makes them feel safe, knowing that I am on guard. And if I didn't shout 'Khabardar' every few minutes they would think I had fallen asleep and I would be dismissed.'

This was a logical argument. I asked him what he would do if, by accident, he encountered a gang of thieves. He said he would keep shouting 'Khabardar' until the people came out of their houses to help him. I said I doubted very much if they would come out of their houses, but wished him luck all the same and continued with my walk.

Every five minutes or so I heard his cry, followed by a 'Khabardar' which grew fainter until the chowkidar had reached the far side of the mohalla. I thought it would be a good idea to give him a helping hand from my side, so I cupped my hands to my mouth and shouted, 'Khabardar, Khabardar!'

It worked like magic.

Three dark figures scrambled over a neighbouring wall and fled down the empty road. I shouted 'Khabardar' a second time and they ran faster. Imagine the thieves' confusion when they were met by more 'khabardars' in front, coming from the chowkidar, and realized that there were now two chowkidars operating in the mohalla.

On those nights when sleep was elusive we left the room and walked for miles around Pipalnagar. It was generally about midnight that we became restless. The walls of the room would give out all the heat they had absorbed during the day, and to lie awake sweating in the dark only gave rise to morbid and depressing thoughts.

In our singlets and pyjamas Suraj and I would walk barefoot through the empty mohalla, over the cooling brick pavements, until we were out of the bazaar and crossing the maidan, our feet sinking into the springy dew-fresh grass. The maidan was broad and spacious and the star-swept sky seemed to meet each end of the plain.

Then out of the town, through lantana scrub, till we came to the dry riverbed, where we walked amongst rocks and boulders, sitting down occasionally, while great horny lizards watched us from between the stones.

Across the riverbed, fields of maize stretched away for a few miles until there came a dry region where thorns and a few bent trees grew, the earth splitting up in jagged cracks like a jigsaw puzzle; and where water had been, the skin was peeling off the earth in great flat pancakes. Dotting the landscape were old abandoned brick kilns, and it was said that thieves met there at nights, in the trenches around the kilns; but we never saw any.

When it rained heavily the hollows filled up with water. Suraj and I came to one of these places to bathe and swim.

There was an island in the middle of one of the hollows and on this small mound stood the ruins of a hut where a night-watchman once lived and looked after the bricks at night.

We swam out to the island which was only a few yards away. There was a grassy patch in front of the hut and here we lay and sunned ourselves in the early morning until it became too hot. We would oil and massage each other's bodies and wrestle on the grass.

Through I was heavier than Suraj and my chest was as sound as a new drum, he had a lot of power in his long arms and legs and often pinioned me about the waist with his bony knees or fastened me with his strong fingers.

Once while we wrestled on the new monsoon grass I felt his body go tense as I strained to press his back to the ground. He stiffened, his thigh jerked against me and his legs began to twitch. I knew that he had a fit coming on but was unable to extricate myself from his arms, which gripped me more tightly as the fit took possession of him. Instead of struggling, I lay still and tried desperately to absorb some of his anguish by embracing him. I felt my own body might draw some of the agitation to itself. It was only a strange fancy but I felt that it made a difference, that by consciously sharing his unconscious condition I was alleviating it. At other times, I have known this same feeling. When Kamla was burning with a fever, I had thought that by taking her in my arms I could draw the fever from her, absorb the heat of her body, transfer to hers the coolness of my own.

Now I pressed against Suraj and whispered soothingly and lovingly into his ear, though I knew he had no idea what I could be saying. And then when I noticed his mouth working, I thrust my hand in sideways to prevent him from biting his tongue.

But so violent was the convulsion that his teeth bit into the flesh of my palm and ground against my knuckles. I gasped with pain and tried to jerk my hand away but it was impossible to loosen the grip of his teeth. So I closed my eyes and counted one, two, three, four, five, six, seven—until I felt his body relax again and his jaws give way slowly.

My hand had blood on it and was trembling. I bound it in a handkerchief before Suraj came to himself.

We walked back to the town without talking much. He looked depressed and hopeless though I knew he would be buoyant again before long. I kept my hand concealed beneath my singlet but he was too dejected to notice this. It was only at night, when he returned from his classes, that he noticed it was bandaged, and then I told him I had slipped on the road, cutting my hand on some broken glass.

XIII

Rain upon Pipalnagar and until the rain stops, Pipalnagar is fresh and clean and alive. The children run out of their houses glorying in their nakedness. They are innocent and unashamed. Older children, by no means innocent, but by all means unashamed, romp through the town, inviting the shocked disapproval of their elders and, presumably, betters.

Before we are ten, we are naked and free and unafraid; after ten, we must cloak our manhood, for we are no longer certain that we are men.

The gutters choke and the mohalla becomes a mountain stream, coursing merrily down towards the bus stop. And it is at the bus stop that pandemonium breaks loose for newly-arrived passengers panic at sight of the sea of mud and rain water that surrounds them on all sides, and about a hundred tongas and cycle-rickshaws try all at once to take care of a score of passengers. Result: only half the passengers find a conveyance, while the other half find themselves knee-deep in Pipalnagar mire.

Pitamber has, of course, succeeded in acquiring as his passenger the most attractive and frightened young woman on the bus, and proceeds to show off his skill and daring by taking her home by the most devious and uncomfortable route. And when she gets her feet covered with mud, wipes them with the seedy red cloth that he ties about his neck.

The rain swirls over the trees and roofs of the town and the parched earth soaks it up, exuding a fragrance that comes only once in a year, the fragrance of quenched earth, the most exhilarating of all smells.

And in my room, too, I am battling against the elements, for the door will not shut against the breeze, and the rain is sweeping in through the opening and soaking my cot.

When eventually I succeed in barricading the floor, I find the roof leaking and the water trickling down the walls, obliterating the dusty designs I have made on the plaster with my foot. I place a tin here and a mug there, and then, satisfied that everything is under control, sit on my cot and watch the roof-tops through my window.

But there is a loud banging on the door. It flies open with the pressure, and there is Suraj, standing on the threshold, shaking himself like a wet dog. Coming in, he strips off all his clothes and then dries himself with a torn threadbare towel and sits shivering on the bed while I make frantic efforts to close the door again.

'You are cold, Suraj, I will make you some tea.'

He nods, forgetting to smile for once, and I know his mind is elsewhere, in one of a thousand places and all of them dreams.

When I have got the fire going and have placed the kettle on the red hot coals, I sit down beside Suraj and put my arm around his bony shoulders and dream a little with him.

'One day I will write a book,' I tell him. 'Not a murder story, but a real book, about real people. Perhaps it will be about you and me and Pipalnagar. And then we will break away from Pipalnagar, fly away like eagles, and our troubles will be over and fresh new troubles will begin. I do not mind difficulties, as long as they are new difficulties.'

'First I must pass my exams,' said Suraj. 'Without a certificate one can do nothing, go nowhere.'

'Who taught you such nonsense? While you are preparing for your exams, I will be writing my book. That's it! I will start tonight. It is an auspicious night, the first night of the monsoon. Let us start tonight.'

And by the time we had drunk our tea it was evening and growing dark. The light did not come on. A tree must have fallen across the wires. So I lit a candle and placed it on the window-sill (the rain and wind had ceased), and while the candle spluttered in the steady stillness, Suraj opened his books and with one hand on a book, and the other playing with his toes—this helped him to read—he began his studies.

I took the ink down from the shelf, and finding the bottle

empty, added a little rain-water to it from one of the mugs. I sat down beside Suraj and began to write but the pen was no good and made blotches all over and I didn't really know what to write about, though I was full of writing just then.

So I began to look at Suraj instead; at his eyes, hidden in the shadows, his hands in the candle light; and felt his breathing and the slight movement of his lips as he read softly to himself.

A gust of wind came through the window and the candle went out. I swore softly in Punjabi.

'Never mind,' said Suraj, 'I was tired of reading.'

'But I was writing.'

'Your book?'

'No, a letter . . . .'

'I have never known you to write letters, except to publishers asking them for money. To whom were you writing?'

'You,' I said. 'And I will send you the letter one day, perhaps when we are no longer together.'

'I will wait for it, then. I will not read it now.'

XIV

At ten o'clock on a wet night Pipalnagar had its first earthquake in thirty years. It lasted exactly five seconds. A low, ominous rumble was followed by a few quick shudders, and the water surahi jumped off the window-ledge and crashed on the floor.

By the time Suraj and I had tumbled out of the room the shock was over but panic prevailed, and the entire population of the mohalla was out on the street. One old man of seventy had leapt from a first-floor balcony and broken his neck; a large crowd had gathered round his body. Several women had fainted. On the other hand, astrologers had predicted the end of the world and everyone was convinced that this was only the first of a series of earthquakes.

At temples and other places of worship prayer meetings were held. People moved about the street, pointing out the cracks that had appeared in their houses. Some of these cracks had, of course, been there for years and were only now being discovered.

At midnight, men and women were still about; and, as though to justify their prudence, another, milder tremor, made itself felt. The roof of an old house, weakened by many heavy monsoons, was encouraged to give way, and fell with a suitably awe-inspiring crash. Fortunately no one was beneath it. Everyone was soaking wet by now, as the rain had come down harder, but no one dared venture indoors, especially after a roof had fallen in.

Worse still, the electricity failed and the entire mohalla plunged into darkness. People huddled together fearing the worst, while the rain came down incessantly.

'More people will die of pneumonia than earthquake,' observed Suraj. 'Let's go for a walk. It is better than standing about doing nothing.'

We rolled up our pyjamas and went splashing through the puddles. On the outskirts of the town we met Pitamber dancing in the middle of the road. He was very merry, and quite drunk.

'Why are you dancing on the road?' I asked.

'Because I am happy, that's why,' said Pitamber.

'And what makes you so happy, my friend?'

'Because I am dancing on the road,' he replied.

We began walking home again. The rain had stopped. There was a break in the clouds and a pale moon appeared. The neem trees gave out a strong, sweet smell.

There were no more tremors that night. When we got back to the mohalla, the sky was lighter, and people were beginning to move into their houses again.

We lay on our island in the shade of a thorn bush, watching a pair of sarus cranes on the opposite bank prancing and capering around each other. Tall, stork-like birds, with naked red heads and long red legs.

'We might be saruses in some future life,' I said.

'I hope so,' said Suraj. 'Even if it means being born on a lower level. I would like to be a beautiful white bird. I am tired of being a man but I do not want to leave the world altogether. It is very lovely, sometimes.'

'I would like to be a sacred bird,' I said. 'I don't wish to be shot at.'

'Aren't saruses sacred? Look how they enjoy themselves.'

'They are making love. That is their principal occupation apart from feeding themselves. And they are so devoted to each other that if one bird is killed the other will haunt the scene for weeks, calling distractedly. They have even been known to pine away and die of grief. That's why they are held in such affection by people in villages.'

'So many birds are sacred.'

We saw a bluejay swoop down from a tree—a flash of blue—and carry off a grasshopper.

Both the bluejay and Lord Siva are called Nilkanth. Siva has a blue throat, like the bluejay, because out of compassion for the human race he swallowed a deadly poison which was meant to destroy the world. He kept the poison in his throat and would not let it go any further.

'Are squirrels sacred?' asked Suraj, curiously watching one fumbling with a piece of bread which we had thrown away.

'Krishna loved them. He would take them in his arms and stroke them with his long, gentle fingers. That is why they have four dark lines down their backs from head to tail. Krishna was very dark-skinned and the lines are the marks of his fingers.'

'We should be gentle to animals . . . . Why do we kill so many of them?'

'It is not so important that we do not kill them—it is important that we respect them. We must acknowledge their right to live on this earth. Everywhere, birds and animals are finding it more difficult to survive, because we are destroying their homes. They have to keep moving as the trees and the green grass keep disappearing.'

Flowers in Pipalnagar—do they exist?

I have known flowers in poetry and as a child I knew a garden in Lucknow where there were fields of flowers and another garden where only roses grew. In the fields round Pipalnagar I have seen dandelions that evaporate when you breathe on them, and sometimes a yellow buttercup nestling among thistles. But in our mohalla, there are no flowers except one. This is a marigold growing out of a crack in my balcony.

I have removed the plaster from the base of the plant and filled in a little earth which I water every morning. The plant is healthy and sometimes it produces a little orange marigold which I pluck and give away before it dies.

Sometimes Suraj keeps the flower in his tray, among the combs and scent bottles and buttons that he sells. Sometimes he offers the flower to a passing child—to a girl who runs away; or it might be a boy who tears the flower to shreds. Some children keep it. Others give flowers to Suraj when he passes their houses.

Suraj has a flute which he plays whenever he is tired of going from house to house.

He will sit beneath a shady banyan or pipal, put his tray aside, and take out his flute. The haunting little notes travel down the road in the afternoon stillness and children come to sit beside him and listen to the flute music. They are very quiet when he plays because there is a little sadness about his music, and children especially can sense that sadness.

Suraj has made flutes cut of pieces of bamboo but he never sells them. He gives them away to the children he likes. He will sell anything, but not his flutes.

Sometimes Suraj plays his flute at night when I am lying awake on the cot, unable to sleep. And even when I fall asleep, the flute plays in my dreams. Sometimes he brings it with him to the crooked tree and plays it for the benefit of the birds but the parrots only make harsh noises and fly away.

Once, when Suraj was playing his flute to a group of children, he had a fit. The flute fell from his hands and he began to roll about in the dust on the roadside. The children were frightened and ran away.

But they did not stay away for long. The next time they heard the flute play, they came to listen as usual.

XV

As Suraj and I walked over a hill near the limestone quarries, past the shacks of the Rajasthani labourers, we met a funeral procession on its way to the cremation ground. Suraj placed his hand on my arm and asked me to wait until the procession had passed. At the same time a cyclist dismounted and stood at the side of the road. Others hurried on, without glancing at the little procession.

'I was taught to respect the dead in this way,' said Suraj. 'Even if you do not respect a man in life, you should respect him in death. The body is unimportant but we should honour it out of respect for the man's mind.'

'It is a good custom,' I said.

'It must be difficult to live on after the one you have loved has died.'

'I don't know. It was not happened to me. If a love is strong, I cannot see its end . . . . It cannot end in death, I feel . . . . Even physically, you would exist for me somehow.'

He was asleep when I returned late at night from a card game in which I had lost fifty rupees. I was a little drunk and when I tripped near the doorway, he woke up and though he did not open his eyes, I felt he was looking at me.

I felt very guilty and ashamed, because he had been ill that day, and I had forgotten it. Now there was no point in saying I was sorry. Drunkenness is really a vice because it degrades a man and humiliates him.

Prostitution is degrading but a prostitute can still keep her dignity. Thieving is degrading according to the character of the theft. Begging is degrading but it is not as undignified as drunkenness. We lose our pride, our heads, and above all, our natural dignity. We become so obviously and helplessly 'human' that we lose our glorious animal identity.

I sat down at the side of the bed and bending over Suraj, whispered, 'I got drunk and lost fifty rupees. What am I to do about it?'

He smiled but still he didn't open his eyes, and I kicked off my sandals and pulled off my shirt and lay down across the foot of the bed. He was still burning with fever; I could feel it radiating through the sheet.

We were silent for a long time and I didn't know if he was awake or asleep so I pressed his foot and said, 'I'm sorry,' but he was asleep by then and did not hear me.

Moonlight.

Pipalnagar looks clean in the moonlight and my thoughts are different from my daytime thoughts.

The streets are empty and the moon probes the alley-ways and there is a silver dustbin and even the slush and the puddles near the bus stop shimmer and glisten.

Kisses in the moonlight. Hungry kisses. The shudder of bodies clinging to each other on the moonswept floor.

A drunken quarrel in the street. Voices rise and fall. The night-watchman waits for the trouble to pass and then patrols the street once more, banging his lathi on the pavement.

Kamla asleep. She sleeps like an angel. I go downstairs and walk in the moonlight. I meet Suraj coming home, his books under his arm; he has been studying late with Aziz, who keeps a junk shop near the station. Their exams are only a month off. I am confident that Suraj will be successful. I am only afraid that he will work himself to a standstill. With his weak chest and the uncertainty of his fits, he should not walk all day and read all night.

When I wake up in the early hours of the morning and Kamla stirs beside me in her sleep (her hair so laden with perfume that my own sleep has been fitful and disturbed), Suraj is still squatting on the floor, reading by the light of the kerosene lamp.

And even when he has finished reading he does not sleep, but asks me to walk with him before the sun rises, and, as women were not made to get up before the sun, we leave Kamla stretched out on the cot, relaxed and languid, small breasts and a boy's waist; her hair tumbling about the pillow; her mouth slightly apart, her lips still swollen and bruised with kisses.

I have been seeking through sex something beyond sex—a union with all mankind.

XVI

It was Lord Krishna's birthday, and the rain came down as heavily as it must have done the day Krishna was born in Brindaban. Krishna is the best beloved of all the gods. Young mothers laugh and weep as they read of or hear the pranks of his childhood. Young men pray to be as tall and strong as Krishna was when he killed Kamsa's elephant and Kamsa's wrestlers. Young girls dream of a lover as daring as Krishna to carry them off like Rukmani in a war chariot. Grown-up men envy the wisdom and statesmanship with which he managed the affairs of his kingdom.

The rain came suddenly and took everyone by surprise. In a few seconds people were drenched to the skin, and within ten minutes the mohalla was completely flooded. The temple tank overflowed, the railway lines disappeared, and the old wall near the bus stop shivered and fell silently, the noise of the collapse drowned by the rain.

Children shrieked with excitement and five naked young men with a dancing bear cavorted in the middle of the vegetable market.

Wading knee-deep down the road, I saw roadside vendors salvaging what they could. Plastic toys, cabbages and utensils floated away and were seized upon by urchins. The water had risen to the level of the shop-fronts and the floors were awash. Aziz was afloat in his junk shop. Deep Chand, Ramu and a customer were using buckets to bail the water out of their premises. Pitamber churned through the stream in his cycle-rickshaw, offering free lifts to the women in the bazaar with their saris held high above their knees.

The rain stopped as suddenly as it had begun. The sun came out. The water began to find an outlet, flooding other low-lying areas, and a paper-boat came sailing between my legs.

'When did you last go out of Pipalnagar?' I asked Suraj. 'I mean far out, to another part of the country?'

'Not since I came here,' he said. 'I have never had the funds. And you?'

'I don't remember. I have been stagnating in Pipalnagar for five years without a break. I would like to see the hills again. Once, when I was a child, my parents took me to the hills. I remember them vividly—pine trees, the wind at night, men carrying loads of wood up the steep mountain paths—yes, I would like to see the hills again . . . .'

'I have never seen them,' said Suraj.

'How strange! I don't think that a man can be complete until he has lived in the hills. Of course we are never complete but there is something about a mountain that adds a new dimension to life. The change in air and altitude makes one think and feel and act differently. Suraj, we must go to the hills! This is the time to go. Let's get away from this insufferable heat, from these drains and smells and noises—even if it is only for a few days . . . .'

'But my exams are only a few weeks off.'

'Good. The change will help. Bring your books along. You will study much better there. You will feel better. I can guarantee that you will not have a single fit all the time we are away!'

I was carried away in a flood of enthusiasm. I waved my arms about and described the splendour of the sun rising—or setting—behind Nanda Devi, and talked about the book I could write if I stayed a few weeks in the hills.

'But what about money?' interrupted Suraj breaking in on my oration. 'How do we go there?'

'Money?' I said contemptuously. 'Money?' I said again, more respectfully. And then doubtfully, 'Money.'

'Yes, money,' I muttered to myself and sat down on the string cot, suddenly deflated and discouraged.

Suraj burst into laughter.

'What are you laughing about?' I hissed.

'I can't help it,' he said, holding his sides with mirth. 'It's your face. One minute it was broad with smiles, now it is long and mournful, like the face of a horse.'

'We'll get money!' I shouted springing up again. 'How much do we need—two hundred, five hundred—it's easy! My gold ring can be pawned. On our return we shall retrieve it. The book will see to that.'

I was never to see my ring again but that did not matter. We managed to raise a hundred rupees and with it we prepared ourselves feverishly for our journey, afraid that at the last moment something would prevent us from going.

We were to travel by train to the railway terminus, a night's journey, then take the bus. Though we hoped to be away for at least a week, our funds did not in fact last more than four days.

808 • RUSKIN BOND

We locked our room, left the key with Kamla, and asked Deep Chand to keep an eye on both her and our things.

In the train that night Suraj had a mild fit. It helped reduce the numbers in our compartment. Some, thinking he suffered from a communicable disease, took themselves and their belongings elsewhere. Others, used to living with illness, took no notice. But Suraj was not to have any more fits until we returned to Pipalnagar.

We slept fitfully that night, continually shifting our positions on the hard bench of the third-class compartment; Suraj with his head against my shoulder, I with my feet on my bedding roll. Above us, a Sikh farmer slept vigorously, his healthy snores reverberating through the compartment. A woman with her brood of four or five children occupied the bunk opposite. They had knocked over their earthen surahi, smashing it and flooding the compartment. Two young men in the corner played cards and exchanged lewd jokes. No general companionship was evident, but whenever the train drew into a station everyone cooperated in trying to prevent people on the outside from entering the already crowded compartment. And if someone did manage to get in, usually by crawling through a window, he would fall in with the same policy of keeping others out.

We awoke in the early hours of the morning and looked out of the window at the changing landscape. It was so long since I had seen trees—not trees singly or in clumps, but forests of trees, thick and dark and broody, commencing at the railway tracks and stretching away to the foothills. Trees full of birds and monkeys; and in the forest clearing we saw a deer, it's head raised, scenting the wind . . . .

XVII

There were many small hotels in the little town that straddled two or three hills but Suraj and I went to a dharamsala, where we were given a small room overlooking the valley.

We did not spend much time there. There were too many hills and streams and trees inviting us on all sides. It seemed as though they had been waiting all these years for our arrival. Each tree has an individuality of its own—perhaps more individuality than a man—and if you look at a tree with a personal eye, it will give you something of itself, something deep and personal: its smell, its sap, its depth and wisdom.

So we mingled with the trees. We felt and understood the dignity of the pine, the weariness of the willow, the resignation of the oak. The blossoms had fallen from the plum and apricot trees and the branches were bare, touched with the light green of new foliage. Pine needles made the ground soft and slippery and we went sliding downhill on our bottoms.

Then we took paper and pencil and some mangoes and went among some rocks and there I wrote odd things that came into my head, about the hills and the sounds we heard.

The silence of the mountains was accentuated by the occasional sounds around us—a shepherd boy shouting to his mate, a girl singing to her cattle, the jingle of cow bells, a woman pounding clothes on a flat stone . . . . Then, when these sounds stopped , there were quieter, subtler sounds—the singing of crickets, the whistling of anonymous birds, the wind sighing in the pine trees . . . .

It was hot in the sun until a cloud came over, and then it was suddenly cool and our shirts flapped against us in the breeze.

The hills went striding away into the distance. The nearest hill was covered with oak and pine, the next was brown and naked and topped with a white temple, like a candle on a fruit-cake. The furthest hill was a misty blue.

XVIII

The 'season' as they called it, was just beginning in the hills. Those who had money came to the hill station for a few weeks, to parade up and down the Mall in a variety of costumes ranging from formal dinner jackets to cowboy jeans. There were the anglicized élite, models of English gentry, and there was the younger set, imitating western youth as depicted in films and glossy magazines. Suraj and I felt out of place walking down the Mall in kameez and pyjamas. We were foreigners on our own soil. Where these really Indians exhibiting themselves or were they ghastly caricatures of the West?

The town itself had gone to seed. English houses and cottages, built by unimaginative Victorians to last perhaps fifty years, were now over a hundred years old, all in a state of immediate collapse. No one repaired them, no one tore them down. Some had been built to look like Swiss chateaux, others like *Arabian Nights* castles, most like homely English cottages—all were out of place, incongruous oddities desecrating a majestic mountain.

Though the sahibs had gone long ago, coolie-drawn rickshaws still plied the steep roads, transporting portly Bombay and Delhi businessmen and their shrill, quarrelsome wives from one end of the hill station to the other. It was as though a community of wealthy Indians had colonized an abandoned English colony and had gone native, adopting English clothes and attitudes.

A lonely place on a steep slope hidden by a thicket of oaks through which the sun filtered warmly. We lay on crisp dry oak leaves, while a cool breeze fanned our naked bodies.

I wondered at the frail beauty of Suraj's body, at the transient beauty of all flesh, the vehicle of our consciousness. I thought of Kamla's body—firm, supple, economical, in spite of the indignities to which it had been put; of the body of a child, soft and warm and throbbing with vigour; the bodies of pot-bellied glandular males; and bodies bent and deformed and eaten away . . . . The armours of our consciousness, every hair from the head to the genitals a live and beautiful thing . . . .

I believe in the death of flesh but not in the end of living.

When, at the age of six, I saw my first mountain, it did not astonish me. It was something new and exhilarating, but all the same I felt I had known mountains before. Trees and flowers and rivers were not strange things. I had lived with them, too. In new places, new faces, we see the familiar. Even as children we are old in experience. We are not conscious of a beginning, only of an eternity.

Death must be an interval, a rest for a tired and misused body, which has to be destroyed before it can be renewed. But consciousness is a continuing thing.

Our very thoughts have an existence of their own. Are we so unimaginative as to presume that life is confined to the shells that are our bodies? Science and religion have not even touched upon the mysteries of our existence.

Let me not confine myself to the few years between this birth and this death—which is, after all, the only period I can remember well . . . .

In moments of rare intimacy two people are of one mind and one body, speaking only in thoughts, brilliantly aware of each other.

I have felt this way about Suraj even when he is far away; his thoughts hover about me, as they do now.

He lies beside me with his eyes closed and his head turned away, but all the time we are talking, talking, talking . . . .

To a temple on the spur of a hill. Scrambling down a slippery hillside, getting caught in thorny thickets among sharp rocks; along a dry water-course, where we saw the skeleton of a jungle-cat, its long, sharp teeth still in perfect condition.

A footpath, winding round the hills to the temple; a forest of silver oaks shimmering in the breeze. Cool, sweet water bubbling out of the mountain side, the sweetest, most delicious water I have ever tasted, coming through rocks and ferns and green grasses.

Then up, up, up the steep mountain, where long-fingered cacti point to the sloping sky and pebbles go tumbling into the valley below. A giant langur, with a five-foot long tail, leaps from tree to jutting boulder, anxious lest we invade its domain among the unattended peach trees.

On top of the hill, a little mound of stones and a small cross. I wondered what lonely, romantic foreigner, so different from his countrymen, could have been buried here, where sky and mountain meet . . . .

XIX

Though we had lost weight in the hills, through climbing and riding, the good clean air had sweetened our blood and we felt like spartans on our return to Pipalnagar.

That Suraj was gaining in strength I knew from the way he pinned me down when we wrestled on the sand near the old brick kilns. It was no longer necessary for me to yield a little to him.

Though his fits still occurred from time to time as they would continue to do, the anxiety and the death had gone from his eyes . . . .

Suraj passed his examinations. We never doubted that he would. Still, neither of us could sleep the night before the results appeared. We lay together in the dark and spoke of many things—of living and dying and the reason for all striving—we asked each other the same questions that thousands have asked themselves—and like those thousands, we had no answers, we could not even comfort ourselves with religion because God eluded us.

Only once had I felt the presence of God. I awoke one morning and, finding Suraj asleep beside me, was overcome by a tremendous happiness, and kept saying, 'Thank you, God, thank you for giving me Suraj . . . .'

The newspapers came with the first bus at six in the morning. A small crowd of students had gathered at the bus stop, joking with each other and hiding their nervous excitement with a hearty show of indifference.

There were not many passengers on the first bus and there was a mad grab for the newspapers as the bundle landed with a thud on the pavement. Within half an hour the newsboy had sold all his copies. It was the only day of the year when he had a really substantial sale.

Suraj did not go down to meet the bus but I did. I was more nervous than he, I think. And I ran my eye down the long columns of roll numbers so fast that I missed his number the first time. I began again, in a panic, then found it at the top of the list, among the successful ones.

I looked up at Suraj who was standing on the balcony of my room and he could tell from my face that he had passed, and he smiled down at me. I joined him on the balcony and we looked down at the other boys comparing newspapers, some of them exultant, some resigned, a few still hopeful, still studying the columns of roll numbers—each number representing a year's concentration on dull, ill-written text books.

Those who had failed had nothing to be ashamed of. They had failed through sheer boredom.

I had been called to Delhi for an interview and I needed a shirt. The few I possessed were either torn at the shoulders or frayed at the collars. I knew writers and artists were not expected to dress very well but I felt I was not in a position to indulge in eccentricities. Why display my poverty to an editor of all people . . . .

Where was I to get a shirt? Suraj generally wore an old redstriped T-shirt. He washed it every second evening and by morning it was dry and ready to wear again but it was tight even for him. What I needed was something white, something respectable.

I went to Deep Chand. He had a collection of shirts. He was only too glad to lend me one. But they were all brightly coloured things—yellow and purple and pink . . . . They would not impress an editor. No editor could possibly take a liking to an author who wore a pink shirt. They looked fine on Deep Chand when he was cutting people's hair.

Pitamber was also unproductive. He had only someone's pyjama coat to offer.

In desperation, I went to Kamla.

'A shirt?' she said. 'I'll soon get a shirt for you. Why didn't you ask me before? I'll have it ready for you in the morning.'

And not only did she produce a shirt next morning, but a pair of silver cuff-links as well.

'Whose are these?' I asked.

'One of my visitors,' she replied with a shrug. 'He was about your size. As he was quite drunk when he went home, he did not realize that I had kept his shirt. He had removed it to show me his muscles, as I kept telling him he hadn't any to show. Not where it really mattered.'

I laughed so much that my belly ached (laughing on a half empty stomach is painful) and kissed the palms of Kamla's hands and told her she was wonderful.

Freedom.

The moment the bus was out of Pipalnagar, and the fields opened out on all sides, I knew I was free; that I had always been free; held back only by my own weakness, lacking the impulse and the imagination to break away from an existence that had become habitual for years.

And all I had to do was sit in a bus and go somewhere.

It had never occurred to me before. Only by leaving Pipalnagar could I help Suraj. Brooding in my room, I was no good to anyone.

I sat near the open window of the bus and let the cool breeze freshen my face. Herons and snipe waded among the lotus on flat green ponds; bluejay swooped around the telegraph poles; and children jumped naked into the canals that wound through the fields.

Because I was happy, it seemed that everyone else was happy—the driver, the conductor, the passengers, the farmers in their fields, on their bullock-carts. When two women began quarrelling over a coat behind me, I intervened, and with tact and sweetness soothed their tempers. Then I took a child on my knee and pointed out camels and buffaloes and vultures and pariah dogs.

And six hours later the bus crossed the swollen Yamuna, passed under the great red walls of the fort built by Shahjahan, and entered the old city of Delhi.

XX

The editor of the Urdu weekly had written asking me if I would care to be his literary editor. He was familiar with some of my earlier work—poems and stories—and had heard that my circumstances and the quality of my work had deteriorated. Though he did not promise me a job and did not offer to pay my fare to Delhi or give me any ideas of what my salary might be, there was the offer and there was the chance—an opportunity to escape, to enter the world of the living, to write, to read, to explore . . . .

On my second night in Delhi I wrote to Suraj from the station waiting-room, resting the pad on my knee as I sat alone with my suitcase in one corner of the crowded room. Women chattered amongst themselves, or slept silently; children wandered about on the platform outside; babies cried or searched for their mothers' breasts . . . .

Dear Suraj

It is strange to be in a city again, after so many years of Pipalnagar. It is a little frightening, too. You suffer a loss of identity as you feel your way through the indifferent crowds in Chandni Chowk late in the evening. You are an alien amongst the Westernized who frequent the restaurants and shops at Connaught Place; a stranger amongst one's fellow refugees who have grown prosperous now and live in the flat treeless colonies that have mushroomed around the city. It is only when I am near an old tomb or in the garden of long-forgotten kings, that I become conscious of my identity again.

I wish you had accompanied me. That would have made this an exciting, not an intimidating experience! Anyway, I shall see you in a day or two. I think I have the job. I saw my editor this morning. He is from Hyderabad. Just imagine the vastness of our country, that it should take almost half a lifetime for a North Indian to meet a South Indian for the first time in his life.

I don't think my editor is very fond of North Indians, judging from some of his remarks about Punjabi traders and taxi-drivers in Delhi; but he liked what he called my unconventionality (I don't know if he meant my work or myself). I said I thought he was the unconventional one. This always pleases, and he asked me what salary I would expect if he offered me a position on his staff. I said three hundred. He said he might not manage to get me so much, but if they offered me one-fifty, would I accept? I said I would think about it and let him know the next day.

Now I am cursing myself for not having accepted it there and then but I did not want to appear too eager or desperate, and I must not give the impression that a job is indispensable to me. I told him that I had actually come to Delhi to do some research for a book I intended writing about the city. He asked me the title and I thought quickly

*and said, 'Delhi Is Still Far—Nizamuddin's comment
when told that Tughlaq Saha was marching to Delhi' and
he was suitably impressed.*

*Thinking about it now, perhaps it would be a good idea to
do a book about Delhi—its cities and kings, poets and
musicians . . . . I walked the streets all day, wandering
through the bazaars, down the wide shady roads of the
capital, resting under the jamun trees near Humayun's
tomb, and thinking all the time of what you and I can do
here; and while I wander about Delhi, you must be
wandering around Pipalnagar, with that wonderful tray
of yours . . . .*

Chandni Chowk has not changed in character even if its face
has a different look. It is still the heart of Delhi, still throbbing
with vitality—more so perhaps, with the advent of the
enterprising Punjabi. The old buildings and landmarks are still
there, the lanes and alleys are as torturous and mysterious as
ever. Travellers and cloth merchants and sweetmeat-sellers may
have changed in name and character but their professions have
not given place to new ones. And if on a Sunday the shops
must close, they merely spill out on the pavement and across
the tram-lines—toys, silks and cottons, glassware, china, basket-
work, furniture, carpets and perfumes—it is as busy as on any
market-day and the competition louder and more fierce.

In front of the town hall the statue of Queen Victoria still
frowns upon the populace, as ugly as all statues, flecked with
white pigeons droppings. The pigeons, hundreds of them, sit
on the railing and the telegraph wires, their drowsy murmuring
muted by the sounds of the street, the cries of vendors and
tonga drivers and the rattle of the tram.

The tram is a museum piece. I don't think it has been
replaced since it was first installed over fifty years ago. It
crawls along the crowded thoroughfare, clanging at an impatient
five miles an hour, bursting at the seams with its load of
people, while urchins hang on by their toes and eyebrows.

An ash-smeared ascetic sits at the side of the road and
cooks himself a meal; a juggler is causing a traffic jam; a man

has a lotus tattooed on his forearm. From the balcony of the Sonehri the invader Nadir Shah watched the slaughter of Delhi's citizens. I walk down the Dariba, famed street of the silversmiths, and find myself at the steps of the Jama Masjid, surrounded by bicycle shops, junk shops, fish shops, bird shops, and fat goats ready for slaughter.

Cities and places have risen and fallen on the plains of Delhi but Chandni Chowk is indestructible, the heart of both old and new . . . .

All night long I hear the shunting and whistling of engines and like a child I conjure up visions of places with sweet names like Kumbekonam, Krishnagiri, Mahabalipuram and Polonnarurawa; dreams of palm-fringed beanches and inland lagoons; of the echoing chambers of some deserted city, red sandstone and white marble; of temples in the sun and elephants crossing wide, slow-moving rivers . . . .

Ours is a land of many people, many races; their diversity gives it colour and character. For all Indians to be alike would be as dull as for all sexes to be the same, or for all humans to be normal. In Delhi, too, there is a richness of race, though the Punjabi predominates—in shops, taxis, motor workshops and carpenters' sheds. But in the old city there are still many Muslims following traditional trades—butchers, painters, makers of toys and kites. South Indians have filled our offices; Rajasthanis move dexterously along the scaffolding of new buildings springing up everywhere; and in the surrounding countryside nomadic Gujjars still graze their cattle, while settled villagers find their lands selected for trails of new tubewells, pumps, fertilizers and ploughs.

The city wakes early. The hour before sunrise is the only time when it is possible to exercise. Once the sun is up, people must take refuge beneath fans or in the shade of jamun and neem trees. September in Delhi is sultry and humid, relieved only by an occasional monsoon downpour. In the old city there is always the danger of cholera. In the new capital, people fall ill from sitting too long in air-conditioned cinemas and restaurants.

At noon the streets are almost empty; but early in the morning everyone is about—young and old, shopkeeper and clerk, taxi driver and shoeshine boy—flooding the maidans and open spaces in their vests and underwear. Some sprint around the maidans; some walk briskly down the streets, swinging their arms like soldiers; young men wrestle or play volleyball or kabaddi; others squat on their haunches, some stand on their heads; some pray, facing the sun; some study books, mumbling to themselves, or make speeches to vast, invisible audiences; scrub their teeth with neem twigs, bathe at public taps, wash clothes, tie dhotis or turbans and go about their business.

The sun is up, clerks are asleep with their feet up on their desks, government employees drink innumerable cups of tea and the machinery of bureaucracy and civilization runs on as smoothly as ever.

XXI

Suraj was on the platform when the Pipalnagar Express steamed into the station in the early hours of a warm late September morning. I wanted to shout to him from the carriage window, to tell him that everything was well, that the world was wonderful, and that I loved him and the world and everything in it.

But I couldn't say anything until we had left the station and I was drinking hot tea on the string bed in our room.

'It is three hundred a month,' I said, 'but we should be able to manage on that, if we are careful. And now that you have done your matriculation, you will be able to join the Polytechnic. So we will both be busy. And when we are not working, we shall have all Delhi to explore. It will be better in the city. One should live either in a city or in a village. In a village, everyone knows you intimately. In a city, no one has the slightest interest in you. But in a town like Pipalnagar everyone knows you, nobody loves you. When you die, you are forgotten; while you live, you are only a subject for malicious conversation. Poor Pipalnagar . . . . Will you be sorry to leave the place, Suraj?'

'Yes, I will be sorry. This is where I have lived.'

'This is where I've existed. I only began to live when I realized I could leave the place.'

'When we went to the hills?'

'When I met you.'

'How did I change anything? I am still an additional burden.'

'You have made me aware of who and what I am.'

'I don't understand.'

'I don't want you to. That would spoil it.'

There was no rent to be paid before we left, as Seth Govind Ram's *munshi* had taken it in advance, and there were five days to go before the end of the month; there was little chance of the balance being returned to us.

Deep Chand was happy to know that we were leaving. 'I shall follow you soon,' he said. 'There is money to be made in Delhi, cutting hair. Why, even girls are beginning to keep short hair. I shall keep a special saloon for ladies which Ramu can attend. Women feel safe with him. He looks so pretty and innocent.'

Ramu winked at me in the mirror. I could not imagine anyone less innocent. Girls going to school and college still complained that he harassed them and threatened to remove their pigtails with his razor.

The snip of Deep Chand's scissors lulled me to sleep as I sat in his chair; his fingers beat a rhythmic tattoo on my scalp; his razor caressed my cheeks. It was my last shave and Deep Chand did not charge me anything. I promised to write to him as soon as I had settled down in Delhi.

Kamla had gone home for a few days. Her village was about five miles from Pipalnagar in the opposite direction to Pitamber's, among the mustard and wheat fields that sloped down to the banks of the little water-course. I worked my way downstream until I came to the fields.

I waited behind some trees on the outskirts of the village until I saw her playing with a little boy. Then I whistled and stepped out of the trees but when she saw me she motioned me back and took the child into one of the small mud houses.

I waited amongst the sal trees until I heard footsteps a short distance away.

'Where are you?' I called but received no answer. I walked in the direction of the door steps and found a small path going through the trees. After a short distance the path turned to meet a stream and Kamla was waiting there.

'Why didn't you wait for me?' I asked.

'I wanted to see if you would follow me.'

'Well, I am good at it,' I said, sitting down beside her on the banks of the stream. The water was no more than ankle-deep, cool and clear. I took off my shoes, rolled up my trousers, and put my feet in the water. Kamla was barefoot and so she had to tuck up her sari a little, before slipping her feet in.

With my feet I churned up the mud at the bottom of the stream. As the mud subsided, I saw her face reflected in the water and looking up at her again, into her dark eyes, I wanted to care for her and protect her. I wanted to take her away from Pipalnagar; I wanted her to live like other people. Of course, I had forgotten all about my poor finances.

I kissed the tips of her fingers, then her neck. She ran her fingers through my hair. The rain began splatting down and Kamala said, 'Let us go.'

We set off. Soon the rain began pelting down. Kamala shook herself free and we dashed for cover. She was breathing heavily and I kissed her again. Kamla's hair came loose and streamed down her body. We had to hop over pools and avoid the soft mud. And then I thought she was crying, but I wasn't sure, it might have been the raindrops on her cheeks, and her heavy breathing.

'Come with me,' I said. 'Come away from Pipalnagar.'

She smiled.

'Why can't you come?'

'Because you do not really want me to. For you a woman would only be a liability. You are free like birds, you and Suraj, you can go where you like and do as you like. I cannot help you in any way. And what use is a woman to a man if she cannot help him? I have helped you pass your time in Pipalnagar. That is something. I am part of this place. Neither Pipalnagar nor I can change. But you can, simply by going away.'

'Will you come later, once I have started making a living in Delhi?'

'I am married. It is as simple as that . . . .'

'If it is that simple, you can come.'

'I have to think of my parents, you know. It would ruin them if I ran away.'

'Yes, but they do not care that they have broken your heart.'

She shrugged and looked away towards the village. 'I am not so unhappy. He is an old fool, my husband, and I get some fun out of teasing him. He will die one day and so will the Seth and then I will be free.'

'Will you?'

'Why not? And anyway, you can always come to see me, and nobody will be made unhappy by it.'

I felt sad and frustrated but I couldn't take my frustration out on anyone or anything.

'It was Suraj, not I, who stole your heart,' she said.

She touched my face softly and then abruptly ran towards her little hut. She waved once and then was gone.

XXII

At six every morning the first bus arrives and the passengers alight, looking sleepy and dishevelled and rather depressed at the sight of our mohalla. When they have gone their various ways, the bus is driven into the shed and the road is left clear for the arrival of the municipal van. The cows congregate at the dustbin, and the pavement dwellers come to life, stretching their dusty limbs on the hard stone steps. I carry the bucket up three steps to my room and bathe for the last time in the open balcony. Our tin trunks are packed and Suraj's tray is empty.

At Pitamber's village the buffaloes are wallowing in green ponds while naked urchins sit astride them, scrubbing their backs, and a crow or water-bird perches on a glistening neck. The parrots are busy in the crooked tree, and a slim green snake basks in the sun on our island near the brick kiln. In the hills, the mists have lifted and the distant mountains are covered with snow.

It is autumn and the rains are over. The earth meets the sky in one broad sweep of the creator's brush.

A land of thrusting hills. Terraced hills, wood-covered and windswept. Mountains where the gods speak gently to the lonely heart. Hills of green and grey rock, misty at dawn, hazy at noon, molten at sunset; where fierce fresh torrents rush to the valleys below.

A quiet land of fields and ponds, shaded by ancient trees and ringed with palms, where sacred rivers are touched by temples; where temples are touched by the southern seas.

This is the real land, the land I should write about. My mohalla is but a sickness, a wasting disease, and I should turn aside from it to sing instead of the splendours of tomorrow. But only yesterdays are splendid . . . . There are other singers, sweeter than I, to sing of tomorrow. I can only sing of today, of Pipalnagar, where I have lived and loved.

Yesterday I was sad and tomorrow I may be sad again, but today I know that I am happy. I want to live on and on, delighting like a pagan in all that is physical; and I know that this one lifetime, however long, cannot satisfy my heart.

A Flight of Pigeons

A Flight of Pigeons

*

Prologue

The revolt broke out at Meerut on the 10th of May, at the beginning of a very hot and oppressive summer. The sepoys shot down their English officers; there was rioting and looting in the city; the jail was broken open, and armed convicts descended on English families living in the city and cantonment, setting fire to houses and killing the inmates. Several mutinous regiments marched to Delhi, their principal rallying-point, where the peaceable, poetry-loving Emperor Bahadur Shah suddenly found himself the figurehead of the revolt.

The British Army, which had been cooling off in Shimla, began its long march to Delhi. But meanwhile, the conflict had spread to other cities. And on the 30th of May there was much excitement in the magistrate's office at Shahjahanpur, some 250 miles east of Delhi.

A bungalow in the cantonment, owned by the Redmans, an Anglo-Indian family, had been set on fire during the night. The Redmans had been able to escape, but most of their property was looted or destroyed. A familiar figure had been seen flitting around the grounds that night; and Javed Khan, a Rohilla Pathan, well-known to everyone in the city, was arrested on suspicion of arson and brought before the magistrate.

Javed Khan was a person of some importance in the bazaars of Shahjahanpur. He had a reputation for agreeing to undertake any exploit of a dangerous nature, provided the rewards were high. He had been brought in by the authorities for a number of offences. But Javed knew the English law, and challenged the court to produce witnesses. None came forward to identify him as the man who had been seen running from the blazing bungalow. The case was adjourned until further evidence could be collected. When Javed left the courtroom, it was difficult to tell whether he was being escorted by the police or whether he was escorting them. Before leaving the room, he bowed contemptuously to Mr Ricketts, the magistrate, and said: '*My* witnesses will be produced tomorrow, whether you will have them or not.'

The burning of the Redmans' bungalow failed to alert the small English community in Shahjahanpur to a sense of danger. Meerut was far away, and the *Moffusilite*, the local news sheet, carried very little news of the disturbances. The army officers made their rounds without noticing anything unusual, and the civilians went to their offices. In the evening they met in the usual fashion, to eat and drink and dance.

On the 30th of May it was Dr Bowling's turn as host. In his drawing-room, young Lieutenant Scott strummed a guitar, while Mrs Bowling sang a romantic ballad. Four army officers sat down to a game of whist, while Mrs Ricketts, Mr Jenkins, the Collector, and Captain James, discussed the weather over a bottle of Exshaw's whisky.

Only the Labadoors had any foreboding of trouble. They were not at the party.

Mr Labadoor was forty-two, his wife thirty-eight. Their daughter, Ruth, was a pretty girl, with raven black hair and dark, lustrous eyes. She had left Mrs Shield's school at Fatehgarh only a fortnight before, because her mother felt she would be safer at home.

Mrs Labadoor's father had been a French adventurer who had served in the Maratha army; her mother came from a well-known Muslim family of Rampur. Her name was Mariam. She and her brothers had been brought up as Christians. At eighteen, she married Labadoor, a quiet, unassuming man, who was a clerk in the magistrate's office. He was the grandson of a merchant from Jersey (in the Channel Islands), and his original Jersey name was Labadu.

While most of the British wives in the cantonment thought it beneath their dignity to gossip with servants, Mariam Labadoor, who made few social calls, enjoyed these conversations of hers. Often they enlivened her day by reporting the juiciest scandals, on which they were always well-informed. But from what Mariam had heard recently, she was convinced that it was only a matter of hours before rioting broke out in the city. News of the events at Meerut had reached the bazaars and sepoy lines, and a fakir, who lived near the River Khannaut, was said to have predicted the end of the English East India Company's rule in the coming months. Mariam made her husband and daughter stay at home the evening of the Bowling's party, and had even suggested that they avoid going to church the next day, Sunday: a surprising request from Mariam, a regular church-goer.

Ruth liked having her way, and insisted on going to church the next day; and her father promised to accompany her.

The sun rose in a cloudless, shimmering sky, and only those who had risen at dawn had been lucky enough to enjoy the cool breeze that had blown across the river for a brief spell. At seven o'clock the church bell began to toll, and people could be seen making their way towards the small, sturdily built cantonment church. Some, like Mr Labadoor, and his daughter, were on foot, wearing their Sunday clothes. Others came in carriages, or were borne aloft in *dolies* manned by sweating *dolie*-bearers.

St Mary's, the little church in Shahjahanpur, was situated on the southern boundary of the cantonment, near an ancient mango-grove. There were three entrances: one to the south, facing a large compound known as Buller's; another to the west, below the steeple; and the vestry door opening to the north. A narrow staircase led up to the steeple. To the east there were open fields sloping down to the river, cultivated with melon; to the west, lay an open plain bounded by the city; while the parade ground stretched away to the north until it reached the barracks of the sepoys. The bungalows scattered about the side of the parade ground belonged to the regimental officers, Englishmen who had slept soundly, quite unaware of an atmosphere charged with violence.

I will let Ruth take up the story . . .

At The Church

Father and I had just left the house when we saw several sepoys crossing the road, on their way to the river for their morning bath. They stared so fiercely at us that I pressed close to my father and whispered, 'Papa, how strange they look!' But their appearance did not strike him as unusual: the sepoys usually passed that way when going to the River Khannaut, and I suppose Father was used to meeting them on his way to office.

We entered the church from the south porch, and took our seats in the last pew to the right. A number of people had already arrived, but I did not particularly notice who they were. We had knelt down, and were in the middle of the Confession, when we heard a tumult outside and a lot of shouting, that seemed nearer every moment. Everyone in the church got up, and Father left our pew and went and stood at the door, where I joined him.

There were six or seven men on the porch. Their faces were covered up to their noses, and they wore tight loincloths as though they had prepared for a wrestling bout; but they held naked swords in their hands. As soon as they saw us, they sprang forward, and one of them made a cut at us. The sword missed us both and caught the side of the door where it buried itself in the wood. My father had his left hand against the door, and I rushed out from under it, and escaped into the church compound.

A second and third cut were made at my father by the others, both of which caught him on his right cheek. Father tried to seize the sword of one of his assailants, but he caught it high up on the blade, and so firmly, that he lost two fingers from his right hand. These were the only cuts he received; but though he did not fall, he was bleeding profusely. All this time I had stood looking on from the porch, completely bewildered and dazed by what had happened. I remember asking my father what had happened to make him bleed so much.

'Take the handkerchief from my pocket and bandage my face,' he said.

When I had made a bandage from both our handkerchiefs and tied it about his head, he said he wished to go home. I took him by the hand and tried to lead him out of the porch; but we had gone only a few steps when he began to feel faint, and said, 'I can't walk, Ruth. Let us go back to the church.'

The armed men had made only one rush through the church, and had then gone off through the vestry door. After wounding my father, they had run up the centre of the aisle, slashing right and left. They had taken a cut at Lieutenant Scott, but his mother threw herself over him and received the blow on her ribs; her tight clothes saved her from a serious injury. Mr Ricketts, Mr Jenkins, the Collector, and Mr MacCullam, the Minister, ran out through the vestry.

The rest of the congregation had climbed up to the belfry, and on my father's urging me to do so, I joined them there. We saw Captain James riding up to the church, quite unaware of what was happening. We shouted him a warning, but as he looked up at us, one of the sepoys, who were scattered about on the parade ground, fired at him, and he fell from his horse. Now two other officers came running from the Mess, calling out to the sepoys: 'Oh! children, what are you doing?' They tried to pacify their men, but no one listened to them. They had, however, been popular officers with the sepoys, who did not prevent them from joining us in the turret with their pistols in their hands.

Just then we saw a carriage coming at full speed towards the church. It was Dr Bowling's, and it carried him, his wife and child, and the nanny. The carriage had to cross the parade ground, and they were halfway across when a bullet hit the doctor who was sitting on the coach box. He doubled up in his seat, but did not let go of the reins, and the carriage had almost reached the church, when a sepoy ran up and made a slash at Mrs Bowling, missing her by inches. When the carriage reached the church, some of the officers ran down to help Dr Bowling off the coach box. He struggled in their arms for a while, and was dead when they got him to the ground.

I had come down from the turret with the officers, and now ran to where my father lay. He was sitting against the wall, in a large pool of blood. He did not complain of any pain, but his lips were parched, and he kept his eyes open with an effort. He told me to go home, and to ask Mother to send someone with a cot, or a *dolie*, to carry him back. So much had happened so quickly that I was completely dazed, and though Mrs Bowling and the other women were weeping, there wasn't a tear in my eye. There were two great wounds on my father's face, and I was reluctant to leave him, but to run home and fetch a *dolie* seemed to be the only way in which I could help him.

Leaving him against the stone wall of the church, I ran round to the vestry side and almost fell over Mr Ricketts, who was lying about twelve feet from the vestry door. He had been attacked by an expert and powerful swordsman, whose blow had cut through the trunk from the left shoulder separating the head and right hand from the rest of the body. Sick with horror, I turned from the spot and began running home through Buller's compound.

Nobody met me on the way. No one challenged me, or tried to intercept or molest me. The cantonment seemed empty and deserted; but just as I reached the end of Buller's compound, I saw our house in flames. I stopped at the gate, looking about for my mother, but could not see her anywhere. Granny, too, was missing, and the servants. Then I saw Lala Ramjimal walking down the road towards me.

'Don't worry, my child,' he said. 'Mother, Granny and the others are all safe. Come, I will take you to them.'

There was no question of doubting Lala Ramjimal's intentions. He had held me on his knee when I was a baby, and I had grown up under his eyes. He led me to a hut some thirty yards from our old home. It was a mud house, facing the road, and its door was closed. Lala knocked on the door, but received no answer; then he put his mouth to a chink and whispered, '*Missy-baba* is with me, open the door.'

The door opened, and I rushed into my mother's arms.

'Thank God!' she cried. 'At least one is spared to me.'

'Papa is wounded at the church,' I said. 'Send someone to fetch him.'

Mother looked up at Lala and he could not resist the appeal in her eyes.

'I will go,' he said. 'Do not move from here until I return.'

'You don't know where he is,' I said. 'Let me come with you and help you.'

'No, you must not leave your mother now,' said Lala. 'If you are seen with me, we shall both be killed.'

He returned in the afternoon, after several hours. 'Sahib is dead,' he said, very simply. 'I arrived in time to see him die. He had lost so much blood that it was impossible for him to live. He could not speak and his eyes were becoming glazed, but he looked at me in such a way that I am sure he recognized me . . .'

Lala Ramjimal

Lala left us in the afternoon, promising to return when it grew dark, then he would take us to his own house. He ran a grave risk in doing so, but he had promised us his protection, and he was a man who, once he had decided on taking a certain course of action, could not be shaken from his purpose. He was not a Government servant and owed no loyalties to the British; nor had he conspired with the rebels, for his path never crossed theirs. He had been content always to go about his business (he owned several *dolies* and carriages, which he hired out to Europeans who could not buy their own) in a quiet and efficient manner, and was held in some respect by those he came into contact with; his motives were always personal and if he helped us, it was not because we belonged to the ruling class—my father was probably the most junior officer in Shahjahanpur—but because he had known us for many years, and had grown fond of my mother, who had always treated him as a friend and equal.

I realized that I was now fatherless, and my mother, a widow; but we had no time to indulge in our private sorrow. Our own lives were in constant danger. From our hiding place we could hear the crackling of timber coming from our burning house. The road from the city to the cantonment was in an uproar, with people shouting on all sides. We heard the tramp of men passing up and down the road, just in front of our door; a moan or a sneeze would have betrayed us, and then we would have been at the mercy of the most ruffianly elements from the bazaar, whose swords flashed in the dazzling sunlight.

There were eight of us in the little room: Mother, Granny, myself; my cousin, Anet; my mother's half-brother, Pilloo, who was about my age, and his mother; our servants, Champa and Lado; as well as two of our black and white spaniels, who had followed close on Mother's heels when she fled from the house.

The mud hut in which we were sheltering was owned by Tirloki, a mason who had helped build our own house. He was well-known to us. Weeks before the outbreak, when Mother used to gossip with her servants and others about the possibility of trouble in Shahjahanpur, Tirloki had been one of those who had offered his house for shelter should she ever be in need of it. And Mother, as a precaution, had accepted his offer, and taken the key from him.

Mother afterwards told me that as she sat on the veranda that morning one of the gardener's sons had come running to her in great haste and had cried out: 'Mutiny broken out, sahib and *missy-baba* killed!' Hearing that we had both been killed, Mother's first impulse was to throw herself into the nearest well; but Granny caught hold of her, and begged her not to be rash, saying, 'And what will become of the rest of us if you do such a thing?' And so she had gone across the road, followed by the others, and had entered Tirloki's house and chained the door from within.

We were shut up in the hut all day, expecting, at any moment, to be discovered and killed. We had no food at all, but we could not have eaten any had it been there. My father gone, our future appeared a perfect void, and we found it difficult to talk. A hot wind blew through the cracks in the door, and our throats were parched. Late in the afternoon, a *chatty* of cold water was let down to us from a tree outside a window at the rear of the hut. This was an act of compassion on the part of a man called Chinta, who had worked for us as a labourer when our bungalow was being built.

At about ten o'clock, Lala returned, accompanied by Dhani, our old bearer. He proposed to take us to his own house. Mother hesitated to come out into the open, but Lala assured her that the roads were quite clear now, and there was little fear of our being molested. At last, she agreed to go.

We formed two batches. Lala led the way with a drawn sword in one hand, his umbrella in the other. Mother and Anet and I followed, holding each other's hands. Mother had thrown over us a counterpane which she had been carrying with her when she left the house. We avoided the main road, making our way round the sweeper settlement, and reached Lala's house after a fifteen-minute walk. On our arrival there, Lala offered us a bed to sit upon, while he squatted down on the ground with his legs crossed.

Mother had thrown away her big bunch of keys as we left Tirloki's house. When I asked her why she had done so, she pointed to the smouldering ruins of our bungalow and said: 'Of what possible use could they be to us now?'

The bearer, Dhani, arrived with the second batch, consisting of dear Granny, Pilloo and his mother, and Champa and Lado, and the dogs. There were eight of us in Lala's small house; and, as far as I could tell, his own family was as large as ours.

We were offered food, but we could not eat. We lay down for the night—Mother, Granny and I on the bed, the rest on the ground. And in the darkness, with my face against my mother's bosom, I gave vent to my grief and wept bitterly. My mother wept, too, but silently, and I think she was still weeping when at last I fell asleep.

In Lala's House

Lala Ramjimal's family consisted of himself, his wife, mother, aunt and sister. It was a house of women, and our unexpected arrival hadn't changed that. It must indeed have been a test of the Lala's strength and patience, with twelve near-hysterical females on his hands!

His family, of course, knew who we were, because Lala's mother and aunt used to come and draw water from our well, and offer bel leaves at the little shrine near our house. They were at first shy of us; and we, so immersed in our own predicament, herded together in a corner of the house, looked at each other's faces and wept. Lala's wife would come and serve us food in platters made of stitched leaves. We ate once in twenty-four hours, a little after noon, but we were satisfied with this one big meal.

The house was an ordinary mud building, consisting of four flat-roofed rooms, with a low veranda in the front, and a courtyard at the back. It was small and unpretentious, occupied by a family of small means.

Lala's wife was a young woman, short in stature, with a fair complexion. We didn't know her name, because it is not customary for a husband or wife to call the other by name; but her mother-in-law would address her as *dulhan*, or bride.

Ramjimal himself was a tall, lean man, with a long moustache. His speech was always very polite, like that of most Kayasthas but he had an air of determination about him that was rare in others.

On the second day of our arrival, I overhead his mother speaking to him: 'Lalaji, you have made a great mistake in bringing these *Angrezans* into our house. What will people say? As soon as the rebels hear of it, they will come and kill us.'

'I have done what is right,' replied Lala very quietly. 'I have not given shelter to *Angrezans*. I have given shelter to friends. Let people say or think as they please.'

He seldom went out of the house, and was usually to be seen seated before the front door, either smoking his small hookah, or playing chess with some friend who happened to drop by. After a few days, people began to suspect that there was somebody in the house about whom Lala was being very discreet, but they had no idea who these guests could be. He kept a close watch on his family, to prevent them from talking too much; and he saw that no one entered the house, keeping the front door chained at all times.

It is a wonder that we were able to live undiscovered for as long as we did, for there were always the dogs to draw attention to the house. They would not leave us, though we had nothing to offer them except the leftovers from our own meals. Lala's aunt told Mother that the third of our dogs, who had not followed us, had been seen going round and round the smoking ruins of our bungalow, and that on the day after the outbreak, he was found dead, sitting up—waiting for his master's return!

One day, Lala came in while we were seated on the floor

talking about recent events. Anxiety for the morrow had taken the edge off our grief, and we were able to speak of what had happened without becoming hysterical.

Lala sat down on the ground with a foil in his hand—the weapon had become his inseparable companion, but I do not think he had yet had occasion to use it. It was not his own, but one that he had found on the floor of the looted and ransacked courthouse.

'Do you think we are safe in your house, Lala? asked Mother. 'What is going on outside these days?'

'You are quite safe here,' said Lala, gesturing with the foil. 'No one comes into this house except over my dead body. It is true, though, that I am suspected of harbouring *kafirs*. More than one person has asked me why I keep such a close watch over my house. My reply is that as the outbreak has put me out of employment, what would they have me do except sit in front of my house and look after my women? Then they ask me why I have not been to the Nawab, like everyone else.'

'What Nawab, Lala?' asked Mother.

'After the sepoys entered the city, their leader, the Subedar-Major, set up Qadar Ali Khan as the Nawab, and proclaimed it throughout the city. Nizam Ali, a pensioner, was made Kotwal, and responsible posts were offered to Javed Khan and to Nizam Ali Khan, but the latter refused to accept office.'

'And the former?'

'He has taken no office yet, because he and Azzu Khan have been too busy plundering the sahibs' houses. Javed Khan also instigated an attack on the treasurer. It was like this . . .

'Javed Khan, as you know, is one of the biggest ruffians in the city. When the sepoys had returned to their lines after proclaiming the Nawab, Javed Khan paid a visit to their commander. On learning that the regiment was preparing to leave Shahjahanpur and join the Bareilly brigade, he persuaded the Subedar-Major, Ghansham Singh, to make a raid on the Rosa Rum Factory before leaving. A detachment, under Subedar Zorawar Singh, accompanied Javed Khan, and they took the road which passes by Jhunna Lal, the treasurer's house. There they halted, and demanded a contribution from Jhunna Lal. It so happened that he had only that morning received a sum of six thousand rupees from the Tehsildar of Jalalabad, and this the Subedar seized at once. As Jhunna Lal refused to part with any more, he was tied hand and foot and suspended from a tree by his legs. At the same time Javed Khan seized all his account books and threw them into a well, saying, "Since you won't give us what we need, there go your accounts! We won't leave you with the means of collecting money from others!"

'After the party had moved on, Jhunna Lal's servants took him down from the tree. He was half-dead with fright, and from the rush of blood to his head. But when he came to himself, he got his servants to go down the well and fish up every account book!'

'And what about the Rosa Factory?' I asked.

'Javed Khan's party set fire to it, and no less than 70,000 gallons of rum, together with a large quantity of loaf sugar, were destroyed. The rest was carried away. Javed Khan's share of loaf sugar was an entire cartload!'*

The next day when Lala came in and sat beside us—he used to spend at least an hour in our company every day—I asked him a question that had been on my mind much of the time, but the answer to which I was afraid of hearing: the whereabouts of my father's body.

'I would have told you before, *missy-baba*,' he said, 'but I was afraid of upsetting you. The day after I brought you to my house I went again to the church, and there I found the body of your father, of the Collector-Sahib, and the doctor, exactly where I had seen them the day before. In spite of their exposure and the great heat they had not decomposed at all, and neither the vultures nor the jackals had touched them. Only their shoes had gone.

'As I turned to leave I saw two persons, Muslims, bringing in the body of Captain James, who had been shot at a little distance from the church. They laid it beside that of your father and Dr Bowling. They told me that they had decided to bury the mortal remains of those Christians who had been killed. I told them that they were taking a risk in doing so, as they might be accused by the Nawab's men of being in sympathy

---

* *The Rosa Rum Factory survives to this day.*

with the *Firangis*. They replied that they were aware of the risk, but that something had impelled them to undertake this task, and that they were willing to face the consequences.

'I was put to shame by their intentions, and, removing my long coat, began to help them carry the bodies to a pit they had dug outside the church. Here I saw, and was able to identify, the bodies of Mr MacCullam, the *Padri*-Sahib, and Mr Smith, the Assistant Collector. All six were buried side-by-side, and we covered the grave with a masonry slab upon which we drew parallel lines to mark each separate grave. We finished the work within an hour, and when I left the place I felt a satisfaction which I cannot describe . . .'

Later, when we had recovered from the emotions which Ramjimal's words had aroused in us, I asked him how Mr MacCullam, the chaplain, had met his death; for I remembered seeing him descending from his pulpit when the ruffians entered the church, and running through the vestry with Mr Ricketts' mother.

'I cannot tell you much,' said Lala. 'I only know that while the sepoys attacked Mr Ricketts, Mr MacCullam was able to reach the melon field and conceal himself under some creepers. But another gang found him there, and finished him off with their swords.'

'Poor Mr MacCullam!' sighed Mother. 'He was such a harmless little man. And what about Arthur Smith, Lala?' Mother was determined to find out what had happened to most of the people we had known.

'Assistant-Sahib was murdered in the city,' said Lala. 'He was in his bungalow, ill with fever, when the trouble broke out. His idea was to avoid the cantonment and make for the city, thinking it was only the sepoys who had mutinied. He went to the courts, but found them a shambles, and while he was standing in the street, a mob collected round him and began to push him about. Somebody prodded him with the hilt of his sword. Mr Smith lost his temper and, in spite of his fever, drew his revolver and shot at the man. But alas for Smith-Sahib, the cap snapped and the charge refused to explode. He levelled again at the man, but this time the bullet had no effect, merely striking the metal clasp of the man's belt and falling harmlessly to the ground. Mr Smith flung away his revolver in disgust, and now the man cut at him with his sword and brought him to his knees. Then the mob set upon him. Fate was against Smith-Sahib. The Company Bahadur's prestige had gone, for who ever heard of a revolver snapping, or a bullet being resisted by a belt?'

A Change of Name

According to the reports we received from Lala Ramjimal, it seemed that by the middle of June every European of Shahjahanpur had been killed—if not in the city, then at Muhamdi, across the Khannaut, where many, including Mrs Bowling and her child, had fled. The only survivors were ourselves and (as we discovered later) the Redmans. And we had survived only because the outer world believed that we, too, had perished. This was made clear to us one day when a woman came to the door to sell fish.

Lala's wife remarked: 'You have come after such a long time. And you don't seem to have sold anything today?'

'Ah, Lalain!' said the woman. 'Who is there to buy from me? The *Firangis* are gone. There was a time when I used to be at the Labadoor house every day, and I never went away without making four or five annas. Not only did the memsahib buy from me, but sometimes she used to get me to cook the fish for her, for which she used to pay me an extra two annas.'

'And what has become of them?' asked Lalain.

'Why, the sahib and his daughter were killed in the church, while the memsahib went and threw herself in the river.'

'Are you sure of this?' asked Lalain.

'Of course!' said the woman. 'My husband, while fishing next morning, saw her body floating down the Khannaut!'

We had been in Lala Ramjimal's house for two weeks, and our clothes had become dirty and torn. There had been no time to bring any clothing with us, and there was no possibility of changing, unless we adopted Indian dress. And so Mother borrowed a couple of petticoats and light shawls from Lalain, and altered them to our measurements. We had to wash them in the courtyard whenever they became dirty, and stand around wrapped in sheets until they were half-dry.

Mother also considered it prudent to take Indian names. I was given the name of Khurshid, which is Persian for 'sun', and my cousin Anet, being short of stature, was called Nanni. Pilloo was named Ghulam Husain, and his mother automatically became known as Ghulam Husain's mother. Granny was, of course, Bari-bi. It was easier for us to take Mohammedan names, because we were fluent in Urdu, and because Granny did in fact come from a Muslim family of Rampur. We soon fell into the habits of Lala's household, and it would have been very difficult for anyone, who had known us before, to recognize us as the Labadoors.

Life in Lala's house was not without its touches of humour. There lived with us a woman named Ratna, wife to Imrat Lal, a relative of Lala's. He was a short, stout man. She was tall, and considered ugly. He had no children by her, and after some time, had become intimate with a low-caste woman who used to fill water for his family and was, like himself, short and stout. He had two sons by her, and though his longing for children was now satisfied, his peace of mind was soon disturbed by the wranglings of his two wives. He was an astrologer by profession; and, one day, after consulting the stars, he made up his mind to desert his family and seek his fortune elsewhere. His wives, left to themselves, now made up their differences and began to live together. The first wife earned a living as a seamstress, the second used to grind. Occasionally, there would be outbreaks of jealousy. The second wife would taunt the first for being barren, and the seamstress would reply, 'When you drew water, you had corns on your hands and feet. Now grinding has given you corns on your fingers. Where next are you going to get corns?'

Imrat Lal had, meanwhile, become a yogi and soothsayer and began to make a comfortable living in Haridwar. Having heard of his whereabouts, the second wife had a petition writer draw up a letter for her, which she asked me to read to her, as I knew Urdu. It went something like this:

'O thou who hast vanished like mustard oil which, when

absorbed by the skin, leaves only its odour behind; thou with the rotund form dancing before my eyes, and the owl's eyes which were wont to stare at me vacantly; wilt thou still snap thy fingers at me when this letter is evidence of my unceasing thought of thee? Why did you call me your *lado*, your loved one, when you had no love for me? And why have you left me to the taunts of that stick of a woman whom you in your perversity used to call a precious stone, your Ratna? Who has proved untrue, you or I? Why have you sported thus with my feelings? Drown yourself in a handful of water, or return and make my hated rival an ornament for your neck, or wear her effigy nine times round your arm as a charm against my longings for you.'

But she received no reply to this letter. Probably when Imrat Lal read it, he consulted the stars again, and decided it was best to move further on into the hills, leaving his family to the care of his generous relative, Lala Ramjimal.

As the hot weather was now at its height everyone slept out in the courtyard, including Lala and the female members of his household. We had become one vast family. Everyone slept well, except Mother, who, though she rested during the day, stayed awake all night, watching over us. It was distressing to see her sit up night after night, determined not to fall asleep. Her forebodings of danger were as strong as before. Lala would fold his hands to her and say, 'Do sleep, Mariam. I am no Mathur if I shirk my duty.' But her only reply was to ask him for a knife that she could keep beside her. He gave her a rusty old knife, and she took great pains to clean it and sharpen its edges.

A day came when mother threatened to use it.

It was ten o'clock and everyone had gone to bed, except Mother, who still sat at the foot of my cot. I was just dozing off when she remarked that she could smell jasmine flowers, which was strange, because there was no jasmine bush near the house. At the same time a clod of earth fell from the high wall, and looking up, we saw in the dark the figure of a man stretched across it. There was another man a little further along, concealed in the shadows of a neem tree that grew at the end of the yard. Mother drew her knife from beneath her pillow, and called out that she would pierce the heart of the first man who attempted to lay his hands on us. Impressed by her ferocity, which was like that of a tigress guarding her young, the intruders quietly disappeared into the night.

This incident led us to believe that we were still unsafe, and that our existence was known to others. A few days later something else happened that made us even more nervous.

Lado, one of the two servants who had followed us, had been permitted by Lala to occupy a corner of the house. She had a daughter married to a local sword-cleaner, who had been going about looking for Lado ever since the outbreak. Hearing the rumour that there were *Firangis* hiding in Lala's house, he appeared at the front door on the 23rd of June, and spoke to Lala.

'I am told that my mother-in-law is here,' he said. 'I have enquired everywhere and people tell me that she was seen to come only as far as this. So, Lalaji, you had better let me take her away, or I shall bring trouble upon you.'

Lala denied any knowledge of Lado's whereabouts, but the man was persistent, and asked to be allowed to search the house.

'You will do no such thing,' said Ramjimal. 'Go your way, insolent fellow. How dare you propose to enter my zenana?'

The man left in a huff, threatening to inform the Nawab, and to bring some sepoys to the house. When Lado heard of what had happened, she came into the room and fell at Mother's feet, insisting that she leave immediately, lest her son-in-law brought us any trouble. She blessed me and my cousin, and left the house in tears. Poor Lado! She had been with us many years, and we had all come to like her. She had touched our hearts with her loyalty during our troubles.

In the evening, when Lala came home, he told us of what had befallen Lado. She had met her son-in-law in the city.

'Where have you been, Mother?' he had said. 'I have been searching for you everywhere. From where have you suddenly sprung up?'

'I am just returning from Fatehgarh,' she said.

'Why, Mother, what took you to Fatehgarh? And what has become of the *Angrezans* you were serving?'

'Now how am I to know what became of them?' replied Lado. 'They were all killed, I suppose. Someone saw Labadoor-Mem drowned in the Khannaut.'

The Nawab heard of the sudden reappearance of our old servant. He sent for her and had her closely questioned; but Lado maintained that she did not know what had happened to us.

The Nawab swore at her. 'This "dead one " tries to bandy words with me,' he said. 'She knows where they are, but will not tell. On my oath, I will have your head chopped off, unless you tell me everything you know about them. Do you hear?'

'My Lord!' answered Lado, trembling from head to foot, 'how can I tell you what I do not know myself? True, I fled with them from the burning house, but where they went afterwards, I do not know.'

'This she-devil!' swore the Nawab. 'She will be the cause of my committing a violent act. She evades the truth. All right, let her be dealt with according to her desserts.'

Two men rushed up, and, seizing Lado by the hair, held a naked sword across her throat. The poor woman writhed and wriggled in the grasp of her captors, protesting her innocence and begging for mercy.

'I swear by your head, My Lord, that I know nothing.'

'So you swear by my head, too?' raged the Nawab. 'Well, since you are not afraid even of the sword, I suppose you know nothing. Let her go.'

And poor Lado, half-dead through fright, was released and sent on her way.

Another Nawab

On the 24th of June there was a great beating of drums, and in the distance we heard the sound of fife and drum. We hadn't heard these familiar sounds since the day of the outbreak, and now we wondered what could be happening. There was much shouting on the road, and the trample of horses, and we waited impatiently for Lala to come home and satisfy our curiosity.

'A change of Nawabs today?' enquired Mother. 'How will it affect us?'

'It isn't possible to say as yet. Ghulam Qadar Khan is the

same sort of man as his predecessor, and they come from the same family. Both of them were opposed to the Company's rule. There is this difference, though: whereas Qadar Ali was a dissolute character and ineffective in many ways, Ghulam Qadar has energy, and is said to be pious—but he, too, has expressed his determination to rid this land of all *Firangis* . . .

'When the Mutiny first broke out, he was in Oudh, where he had been inciting the rural population to throw off the foreign yoke. He would have acted in unison with Qadar Ali had they not already disagreed; for Ghulam Qadar was against the murder of women and children. However, Qadar Ai's counsels prevailed, and Ghulam Qadar withdrew for a while, to watch the course of events. Now several powerful landholders have thrown their lot in with him, including Nizam Ali Khan, Vittal Singh, Abdul Rauf, and even that ruffian, Javed Khan. Yesterday he entered Shahjahanpur and without any opposition took over the government. This morning the leading rebels attended the durbar of the new Nawab. And tonight the Nawab holds an entertainment.'

'Do you think he will trouble us, Lala?' asked Granny anxiously. 'What has he to gain by killing such harmless people as us?'

'I cannot say anything for certain, Bari-Bi,' said Lala. 'He might wish to popularize his reign by exterminating a few *kafirs* as his predecessor did. But there is a rumour in the city that he has been afflicted with some deep sorrow . . .'

'What could it be?' asked Mother. 'Is his wife dead? Surely he can get another, especially now that he is the Nawab. And how can his grief affect us?'

'It could influence his actions,' said Lala. 'The rumour is that his daughter Zinat, a young and beautiful girl, has been abducted by a lover. Where she has been taken, no one knows.'

And the lover?' asked Mother, displaying for a moment her habitual curiosity about other people's romantic affairs.

'They say that Farhat, one of Qadar Ali's sons, disappeared at the same time. They suspect that he has eloped with the girl.'

'Ah, I remember Farhat,' said Mother. 'A handsome young fellow who often passed in front of our house, showing off on a piebald nag. Still, what has all this to do with us?'

'I was coming to that, Mariam,' said Lala. 'No sooner had the Nawab taken his seat at the durbar, than some informers came to him with the story about Lado, and suggested that my house be searched for your family. Well, the Nawab wanted to know that had happened to Labadoor-Sahib who, he remarked, had always been a harmless and inoffensive man. When told that he had been killed along with the others in the church, the Nawab said, "So be it. Then we need not go out of our way to look for his women. I will have nothing to do with the murder of the innocent . . ." '

'How far can we trust his present mood?' asked Mother.

'I was told by Nizam Ali Khan that the Nawab once gave his daughter a certain promise—that he would not lift his hand against the women and children of the *Firangis*. It sounds very unlikely, I know. But I think Nizam Ali's information is usually reliable.'

'That is true,' said Mother. 'My husband knew him well. We had the lease of his compound for several years, and we paid the rent regularly.'

'Well, the Nawab likes him,' said Lala. 'He has given him orders to begin casting guns in his private armoury. If the Nawab sticks to men like Nizam Ali, public affairs will be handled more efficiently than they would have been under Qadar Ali Khan.'

We had all along been dependent upon Lala Ramjimal for our daily necessities and though Mother had a little money in her jewel box, which she had brought with her, she had to use it very sparingly.

One day, folding his hands before her, Lala said, 'Mariam, I am ashamed to say it, but I have no money left. Business has been at a standstill, and the little money I had saved is all but finished.'

'Don't be upset, Lala,' said Mother, taking some leaf-gold from her jewel box and giving it to him. 'Take this gold to the bazaar, and sell it for whatever you can get.'

Lala was touched, and at the same time overjoyed at this unexpected help.

'I shall go to the bazaar immediately and see what I can get

for it,' he said. 'And I have a suggestion, Mariam. Let us all go
to Bareilly. I have my brother there, and some of your relatives
are also there. We shall at least save on house rent, which I am
paying here. If you agree, I will hire two carts which should
accommodate all of us.'

We readily agreed to Lala's suggestion, and he walked off
happily to the bazaar, unaware that his plans for our safety
were shortly to go awry.

Caught!

We had been with Lala almost a month, and this was to be our
last day in his house.

We were, as usual, huddled together in one room, discussing
our future prospects, when our attention was drawn to the
sound of men's voices outside.

'Open the door!' shouted someone, and there was a loud
banging on the front door.

We did not answer the summons, but cast nervous glances
at each other. Lalain, who had been sitting with us, got up and
left the room, and chained our door from the other side.

'Open up or we'll force your door in!' demanded the voice
outside, and the banging now became more violent.

Finally, Ratna went to the front door and opened it, letting in
some twenty to thirty men, all armed with swords and pistols.
One of them, who had done all the shouting and seemed to be the
leader, ordered the women to go up to the roof of the house, as
he intended searching all the rooms for the fugitive *Firangis*. Lala's
family had no alternative but to obey him, and they went up to
the roof. The men now approached the door of our room, and we
heard the wrench of the chain as it was drawn out. The leader,
pushing the door open violently, entered the room with a naked
sword in his hand.

'Where is Labadoor's daughter?' he demanded of Mother,
gripping her by the arm and looking intently into her face. 'No,
this is not her,' he said, dropping her hand and turning to look
at me.

'This is the girl!' he exclaimed, taking me by the hand and
dragging me away from Mother into the light of the courtyard.
He held his uplifted sword in his right hand.

'No!' cried Mother in a tone of anguish, throwing herself in front of me. 'If you would take my daughter's life, take mine before hers, I beg of you by the sword of Ali!'

Her eyes were bloodshot, starting out of their sockets, and she presented a magnificent, and quite terrifying sight. I think she frightened me even more than the man with the raised sword; but I clung to her instinctively, and tried to wrest my arm from the man's grasp. But so impressed was he by Mother's display that he dropped the point of his sword and in a gruff voice commanded us both to follow him quietly if we valued our lives. Granny sat wringing her hands in desperation, while the others remained huddled together in a corner, concealing Pilloo, the only boy, beneath their shawls. The man with the sword led Mother and me from the house, followed by his band of henchmen.

It was the end of June, and the monsoon rains had not yet arrived. It was getting on for noon, and the sun beat down mercilessly. The ground was hard and dry and dusty. Barefooted and bareheaded, we followed our captor without a murmur, like lambs going to slaughter. The others hemmed us in, all with drawn swords, their steel blades glistening in the sun. We had no idea where we were being taken, or what was in store for us.

After walking half a mile, during which our feet were blistered on the hot surface of the road, our captor halted under a tamarind tree, near a small mosque, and told us to rest. We told him we were thirsty, and some water was brought to us in a brass jug. A crowd of curious people had gathered around us.

'These are the *Firangans* who were hiding with the Lala! How miserable they look. But one is young—she has fine eyes! They are her mother's eyes—notice!'

A pir, a wandering hermit, who was in the group, touched our captor on the shoulder and said, 'Javed, you have taken away these unfortunates to amuse yourself. Give me your word of honour that you will not ill treat or kill them.'

'So this is Javed Khan,' whispered Mother.

Javed Khan, his face still muffled, brought his sword to a

slant before his face. 'I swear by my sword that I will neither kill nor ill-treat them!'

'Take care for your soul, Javed,' said the pir. 'You have taken an oath which no Pathan would break and still expect to survive. Let no harm come to these two, or you may expect a short lease of life!'

'Have no fear for that!' said Javed Khan, signalling us to rise.

We followed him as before, leaving the crowd of gazers behind, and taking the road that led into the narrow mohalla of Jalalnagar, the Pathan quarter of the city.

Passing down several lanes, we arrived at a small square, at one end of which a horse was tied. Javed Khan slapped the horse on the rump, and opening the door of his house, told us to enter. He came in behind us. In the courtyard, we saw a young woman sitting on a swing. She seemed astonished to see us.

'These are the *Firangans*,' said Javed Khan, closing the front door behind him and walking unconcernedly across the courtyard.

An elderly woman approached Mother.

'Don't be afraid,' she said. 'Sit down and rest a little.'

Javed Khan

When Javed Khan returned to his zenana after and a wash a change of clothes, he addressed his wife.

'What do you think of my *Firangans*? Didn't I say I would not rest until I found them? A lesser man would have given up the search long ago!' And chuckling, he sat down to his breakfast, which was served to him on a low, wooden platform.

His aunt, the elderly woman who had first welcomed us, and who was known as Kothiwali, spoke gently to Mother.

'Tell me,' she said, 'tell me something of your story. Who are you?'

'You see us for what we are,' replied Mother. 'Dependent on others, at the mercy of your relative who may kill us whenever it takes his fancy.'

'Who is going to take your miserable lives?' interrupted Javed Khan.

'No, you are safe while I am here,' said Kothiwali. 'You may speak to me without fear. What is your name, and that of the girl with you?'

'The girl is Khurshid, my only daughter. My name is Mariam, and my family is well-known in Rampur, where my father was a minister to the Nawab.'

'Which Rampur?' asked Khan-Begum, Javed's wife.

'Rohelon-ka-Rampur,' replied Mother.

'Oh, that Rampur!' said Khan-Begum, evidently impressed by Mother's antecedents.

'This, my only child,' continued Mother bestowing an affectionate glance at me, 'is the offspring of an Englishman. He was massacred in the church, on the day the outbreak took place. So I am now a widow, and the child, fatherless. Our lives were saved through the kindness of Lala Ramjimal, and we were living at his house until your relative took us away by force. My mother and others of our family are still there. Only Allah knows what will become of us all, for there is no one left to protect us.'

Mother's feelings now overcame her, and she began weeping. This set me off too, and hiding my face in Mother's shawl, I began to sob.

Kothiwali was touched. She place her hand on my head and said, 'Don't weep, child, don't weep,' in a sympathetic tone.

Mother wiped the tears from her eyes and looked up at the older woman. 'We are in great trouble, Pathani!' she said. 'Spare our lives and don't let us be dishonoured, I beg of you.'

Javed Khan, quite put out by all this weeping, now exclaimed, 'Put your mind at rest, good woman. No one will kill you, I can assure you. On the contrary, I have saved your daughter from dishonour at the hands of others. I intend to marry her honouraby, whenever you will.'

The plate dropped from Javed Khan's wife's hand. He gave her a fierce look. 'Don't be such a fool, Qabil!' he said.

Before Mother could say anything, Kothiwali said, 'Javed, you should not have done this thing. These two are of good birth, and they are in distress. Look how faded and careworn they are! Be kind to them, I tell you, and do not insult them in their present condition.'

'Depend on it, Chachi,' he replied. 'They will receive nothing but kindness from my hands. True, now they have fallen from their former greatness!'

'I should like to know how you became acquainted with them?' enquired Kothiwali. 'Is not your Khan-Begum as good a wife as any? Mark her fine nose!'

'Who says anything to the contrary? But, oh Chachi!' he exclaimed. 'How can I make you understand the fascination this girl exerted over me when she was in her father's house! The very first time I saw her, I was struck by her beauty. She shone like Zohra, the morning star. Looking at her now, I realize the truth of the saying that a flower never looks so beautiful as when it is on its parent stem. Break it, and it withers in the hand. Would anyone believe that this poor creature is the same angelic one I saw only a month ago?'

I was full of resentment, but could say nothing and do nothing, except press closer to my mother and look at Javed Khan with all the scorn I could muster. Khan-Begum, too, must have been seething with indignation; but she too was helpless, because Javed was well within his rights to think in terms of a second wife.

'The greater fool you, Javed, for depriving the child of her father, and breaking the flower from its stem before it had bloomed!' said Khan-Begum.

'What did you say, Qabil?' he asked sharply. 'No, don't repeat it again. The demon is only slumbering in my breast, and it will take little to rouse it.'

He gave me a scorching look, and I could not take my eyes from his face; I was like a doomed bird, fascinated by the gaze of a rattlesnake. But Mother was staring at him as though she would plumb his dark soul to its innermost depths, and he quailed under her stern gaze.

'Don't put me down for a common murderer,' he said apologetically. 'If I have taken lives, they have been those of infidels, enemies of my people. I am deserving of praise rather than blame.'

'Now don't excite yourself,' said Kothiwali, coming to the rescue again. 'What I wanted to bring home to you is that if you are such an admirer of beauty, your Khan-Begum is neither ugly nor dark. I should have thought *Firangi* women had blue eyes and fair hair, but these poor things—how frightened they look!— would pass off as one of us!'

'All right, all right,' grumbled Javed Khan in a harsh voice. 'Don't carry on and on about Qabil's beauty, as if she ever possessed any. Let us drop the subject. But Chachi,' and his eyes softened as he glanced at me, 'you should have judged this girl at the time I first set eyes on her. She was like a rose touched by a breath of wind, a doe-like creature . . .'

'Will you not stop your rubbish?' interrupted Kothiwali. 'Look at her now, and tell me if she answers the same description.'

'*W'allah!* A change has come over them!' exclaimed Javed Khan wonderingly, becoming poetical again. 'She is not what she used to be. Within a month she has aged twenty years. When I seized the girl by her arm at the Lala's house, she was ready to faint. But oh, how can I describe the terror which seized me at the sight of her mother! Like an enraged tigress, whose side has been pierced by a barbed arrow, she hurled herself at me and presented her breast to my sword. I shall never forget the look she gave me as she thrust me away from the girl! I was awed. I was subdued. I was unmanned. The sword was ready to fall from my hand. Surely the blood of a hero runs in her veins! This is no ordinary female!' And bestowing a kindly glance on Mother, he exclaimed: 'A hundred mercies to thee, woman!'

Guests of the Pathan

'I think you and I will be good friends,' said Kothiwali to Mother. 'I already love your daughter. Come, *beti*, come nearer to me,' she said, caressing my head.

Javed Khan had finished his meal and had gone out into the courtyard, leaving his wife and aunt alone to eat with us. Though we were hungry and thirsty, we did not have the heart to eat much with Granny's, and cousin Anet's, fate still unknown to us. But we took something, enough to keep up our strength, and when Javed Khan came in again, he seemed pleased that we had partaken of his food.

'Having tasted salt under my roof,' he said, 'you are no longer strangers in the house. You must make my house your home for the future.'

'It is very good of you to say so,' replied Mother. 'But there are others who are dependent on me, my mother and my niece, and without them everything I eat tastes bitter in my mouth.'

'Don't worry, they shall join you,' said Javed Khan. 'I had seen your daughter a long time before the outbreak, when I took a fancy to her. A ruffian had intended to carry her off before and would have done so had I not anticipated him. I have brought you here with the best of intentions. As soon as I have your consent, I propose to marry Khurshid, and will give her a wife's portion.'

'But how can you do that?' asked Mother. 'You have a wife already.'

'Well, what is there to prevent me having more wives than one? Our law allows it.'

'That may be,' rejoined Mother, 'but how can you, a Muslim, marry a Christian girl?'

'There is no reason why I may not,' replied Javed Khan. 'We Pathans can take a wife from any race or creed we please. And—' pausing as his wife let fall a petulant 'oh!'—'I dare my wife to object to such a proceeding on my part. Did not my father take in a low-caste woman for her large, pretty eyes, the issue of that union being the brat, Saifullah—a plague on him!—and Kothiwali, whom you see here, was a low-caste Hindu who charmed my uncle out of his wits. So what harm can there be if I take a Christian for a wife?'

My mother had a quiver full of counter arguments, but the time was not favourable for argument; it was safer to dissemble.

'I trust you will not expect an immediate answer to your request,' she said. 'I have just lost my husband, and there is no one to guide or advise me. Let us speak again on this subject at some other time.'

'I am in no hurry,' said Javed Khan. 'A matter of such importance cannot be settled in a day. Take a week, good woman. And do not forget that this is no sudden infatuation on my part. The girl has been in my mind for months. I am not Javed if I let the opportunity pass me by. Be easy in your mind—there is no hurry . . .'

And he went out again into the courtyard.

All that had happened to us that morning, and Javed Khan's proposal of marriage, gave me food for thought for the rest of the day. A bed was put down for us in the veranda, and I lay down on my back, staring up at the ceiling where two small lizards darted about in search of flies. Mother was engrossed in a conversation with Kothiwali. Her perfect Urdu, her fine manners, and her high moral values, all took Kothiwali by storm. She was in raptures over Mother, and expressed every sympathy for us. She had come to Javed's house on a short visit, and did not feel like leaving.

'You must let Mariam come and spend a few days with me,' she said to her niece.

'And what is to become of her daughter?' replied Khan-Begum. 'Is she to be left here alone?'

'Of course not. She must come with her mother. And, Qabil, don't allow all this to upset you. Javed's head is a little befuddled nowadays, but he will be all right soon. As for these poor things, they are in no way to blame. You will come, Mariam, won't you?'

'With pleasure,' said Mother. 'If we are allowed to.'

We were worrying about Granny and the others when the sound of an altercation at the front door reached us. We recognized the voice of our friend and protector, Lala Ramjimal, who had tracked us down, and now insisted on seeing us.

'Khan Saheb!' we heard him say to Javed Khan. 'It was very wrong of you to enter my house during my absence and bring away my guests without my permission. Had I been there, you could only have done so by making your way over my dead body.'

'That is exactly why I came when you were not there,' replied Javed Khan. 'I had no wish to end your life.'

'I would not be a Mathur if I had not defended them. Well, what is done is done. I cannot force you to return them to my house. But let me be permitted to see if they need anything. I will also say goodbye to them.'

Mother went to the door and spoke to Lala, thanking him for taking the risk in coming to see us.

'What Vishnu ordered has come to pass,' said Lala resignedly. 'No skill of ours could have prevented it. But be comforted, for better days must lie ahead. I have brought your jewel box back for you.'

She took the jewel box from his hand, but did not bother to examine its contents, knowing that nothing would be missing.

'I have sold the gold you gave me,' said Lala, 'and I have brought the price of it—thirty rupees. I shall bring Bari-Bi and Nani to you this evening. The others can stay with me a little longer.'

'Oh, Lala!' said Mother. 'How are we to repay you for all your kindness?'

'I shall be repaid in time to come,' said Lala. 'But what is to become of your dogs?'

'Keep them, Lala, or do what you like with them. It is going to be difficult enough for us to look after ourselves.'

'True,' he said. 'I shall take them with me to Bareilly and keep them for you.'

He made a low bow to Mother and left us, and that was the last we saw of him.

We heard later that Lala had taken his family to Bareilly, along with our old servant, Dhani. We never knew what become of the dogs. That evening, Javed Khan had himself gone to Lala's house and brought away Granny and Anet, who were overjoyed to see us. According to the laws of hospitality, food was immediately put before them.

Our party of eight had now been thinned to four. Pilloo and his mother, and Champa, had been left at Lala's house, and we were not to know what became of them until some time afterwards. Javed Khan did not fancy introducing into his household a *Firangi* boy of fourteen. It was fortunate for Pilloo that he was left behind, otherwise he would surely have been killed by one of the cutthroats who lived in the mohalla near Javed's house.

Pilloo's Fate

In order to preserve some sort of sequence, I must record what happened to the three members of our household who were left at Lala's house.

No sooner had he and Javed Khan left the house with Granny and cousin Anet, than it was beset again by another band of Pathans, headed by one Mangal Khan. He forced his way into the house, the Lala's womenfolk retired to the roof as before, and Pilloo, his mother, and Champa, their servant, shut themselves in their room.

'Where is the *Firangi* youth?' shouted Mangal Khan. 'Bring him out, so that we may deal with him as we have dealt with others of his kind.'

Seeing that there was no means of escape, Pilloo's mother came out, and falling at Mangal Khan's feet, begged him to spare her son's life.

'*Your* son!' he said, eyeing her disbelievingly from head to foot, for she had a swarthy complexion. 'Let's see what sort of fellow he is.'

Pilloo now came out dressed fantastically, a perfect caricature of a Kayastha boy—pantaloons and shirt; no socks or shoes or headdress—all but his face and fair complexion, which could not be disguised.

'This fellow does not even reach my shoulders,' said Mangal Khan, standing over him. 'How old are you?' he asked sternly.

Pilloo was trembling all over with fright and was unable to answer; instead, he looked at his mother.

She folded her hands and replied, 'Your slave is not more than fourteen, Khan Saheb! I beg of you, spare his life for the Prophet's sake! Do what you like with me, but spare the boy.' And Pilloo's mother rained tears, and fell at his feet again.

The Pathan was moved by these repeated appeals to his feelings.

'Get up, woman!' he said. 'I can see the boy is young and harmless. Will both of you come with me? Remember, if you don't, there are others who will not be as soft-hearted as I.'

Lala's house was obviously no longer safe as a hiding-place, and Pilloo's mother agreed to accompany Mangal Khan. So off they were marched, together with Champa, to another mohalla inhabited chiefly by Pathans, where they were hospitably received at Mangal Khan's house.

Mangal Khan was at heart a generous man. After he had

taken the fugitives under his roof, he showed them every kindness and consideration. He called Pilloo by his new name, Ghulam Husain, and his mother continued to be known as Ghulam Husain's mother. Champa, of course, remained Champa. She was a Rajput girl, and there was no mistaking her for anything else.

Pilloo and his mother continued to live under the protection of Mangal Khan. What their subsequent fortunes were we did not know until much later, many months after we had left Lala Ramjimal's house.

Further Alarms

It was in our interests to forget that we had European blood in our veins, and that there was any advantage in the return of the British to power. It was also necessary for us to *seem* to forget that the Christian God was our God, and we allowed it to be believed that we were Muslims. Kothiwali often offered to teach us the *Kalma*, but Mother would reply that she knew it already, which was perfectly true. When she was asked to attend prayers with the others, her excuse would be: 'How can we? Our clothes are unclean and we have no others.'

The only clothes we had were those acquired in Lala Ramjimal's house, and, on our third day in Javed's house, he seemed to notice them for the first time.

'Mariam,' he said. 'It won't do to wear such clothes in my house. You must get into a pyjama.'

'Where have I the means to make pyjamas?' asked Mother.

And the same day Javed went and bought some black chintz in the bazaar, and handed it over to Mother. She made us pyjamas and kurta-dupattas, cutting the material, while Anet and I did the sewing. Khan-Begum was astonished to find that Mother could cut so well, and that Anet and I were so adept with our needles.

Before we changed into our new clothes, Mother suggested that we be given facilities for bathing. I think we had not bathed for a month, for in Lala's house there was no water close at hand; his womenfolk would bathe every morning at the river, but it had been too dangerous for us to go out.

There was a well right in the middle of the courtyard of

Javed Khan's house, and so it was quite possible for us to take a cold bath. Mother told Zeban, the female barber of the house, to draw water for us and help us bathe, and that she would reward this service with a payment of four pice—a pice per person—and Zeban was overjoyed at the prospect of this little windfall. She set up a couple of beds at right angles to one another in the courtyard, covering them with sheets to form a screen. Kothiwali had heard that we were going to change our clothes and bathe, and this being quite an event, she arrived at the house in a great fluster, determined to assist us in the mysteries of the bath.

It was the 2nd of July, a day memorable in our lives from a hygienic point of view.

Kothiwali offered to pour water over us with her own hands. To this, however, Mother strenuously objected. She pointed out that it was not customary among her people to be seen undressed by others, even by members of the same sex, and that she would not therefore, give Kothiwali the trouble.

Kothiwali was dismayed. 'But how can you take the sacred bath and be purified,' she urged, 'unless at least three tumblers of sanctified water are poured on you?'

Mother was ready with her reply. She said that each of us knew the *Kalma*, and that doubtless we would remember the last three tumblers when we came to them. And this embarrassment being overcome, we had the satisfaction of washing our bodies with fresh water from the well, and afterwards, putting on our new clothes, which fitted us perfectly.

After this, we opened our hair to dry, and instantly there were loud exclamations of admiration from the women who were present. Such lovely, long hair! And looking at my curls— my hair was not very long but quite wavy—exclaimed at my pretty 'ghungarwala'. Mother and Granny did indeed have beautiful heads of hair. Granny's reached down to her heels; Mother's, to a little below the knees. Anet's hair, like mine, reached only to the waist, but it was very bushy, and when made into a plait, was as thick as a fat woman's arm. As we sat about drying our hair, the women gazed at us with their mouths open. We explained that the family from which my mother came was distinguished for the long and bushy hair of its females.

We were also faced with the problem of oiling so much hair, and Khan-Begum asked us what oil we used. Mother said we used coconut oil, but no one knew where so much coconut oil could be had. So Khan-Begum gave a pice to Zeban, and had her fetch us some sweet oil from the bazaar. She also sent for a small fine-tooth comb made of horn. Granny got up and oiled and combed Mother's hair, while Mother dressed mine and Anet's, as well as Granny's.

Next morning we felt buoyant and refreshed. We busied ourselves in sewing a second suit of clothes, which we intended trying on after taking another bath the following Friday, the day of the week on which most Pathan women bathe.

At ten o'clock, Javed Khan received a visitor in the person of Sarfaraz Khan, his wife's brother-in-law. This man had been a constable in the police service, and had retired to his home on the outbreak of the Mutiny. In accordance with the costume of the time, he was armed with sword, pistol, knife and a double-barrelled gun. He appeared excited as he met Javed Khan at the door.

'You have brought some *Firangans* into the house, Javed?' he said. 'Wouldn't you like to show them to me?'

'You shall see them,' replied Javed, 'and be given the opportunity of appreciating my taste for the beautiful.'

With his hand on his pistol and a menacing look on his bearded face, Sarfaraz Khan strode into the veranda. Khan-Begum stood up and made him a salaam, and we did the same. He sat down on a cot, resting the butt of his gun on the ground, while with one hand he held the barrel—a typical Pathan attitude.

'So these are the *Firangans* who have made such a stir in the mohalla!' he observed.

Javed Khan had gone into the house, and Mother spoke up for us.

'What stir can we make?' she said. 'We are poor, helpless people.'

'And yet everyone is saying that you have come into this house to find a husband for your daughter, and that Javed Khan is going to marry her! Why have you brought trouble to this good woman?' he said, pointing towards Khan-Begum.

Though Mother was indignant at the insinuation, she restrained her feelings, and answered him quietly.

'What are you saying, brother? Surely you know that we would not have entered this house unless we had been compelled to. Javed Khan brought us here by force, from a house where we had received every kindness, in order to please himself. We are grateful for his hospitality, but as to marrying my daughter to him or to anyone else, that is a matter which I am not in a position to discuss, and we are grateful to your brother for not forcing us to agree to his wishes.'

'And yet it is the talk of the mohalla,' said Sarfaraz Khan, 'that Javed intends marrying your daughter, and this talk has put Khan-Begum in a great state of mind!'

'In what way are we responsible for what people say?' replied Mother. 'We would do anything to save Khan-Begum from unhappiness.'

Javed, who had overheard much of the conversation, now stamped in, looking quite ruffled.

'Brother, what is your motive in questioning this good woman and treating these people as though they were intruders? By my head, they are in no way to blame! It was I who brought them to my house, and only I am answerable for their actions.'

'Why have you brought trouble to your good wife?' asked Sarfaraz Khan. 'You have spoilt the good name of our family by your foolish conduct.'

'I know who has sent you here,' remarked Javed, folding his arms across his chest.

'Yes, Abdul Rauf has sent me here to take the women to the riverside, and there strike their heads off, in order that the fire raging in your wife's bosom may be quenched.'

'No one has the right to tell me what I should do in my own house,' said Javed fiercely, drawing himself up to his full height and towering over Sarfaraz Khan. 'If Abdul Rauf is wise, he will look to his own house and family, instead of prying into other people's affairs. I will have none of his interference. As to Qabil, she is a fool for talking too much to the neighbours. I shall have to restrict her liberty.'

The two enraged Pathans would have come to blows, or worse, had not Mother put herself forward again.

'As to cutting off our heads,' she said, 'you have the power, Khan Saheb, and we cannot resist. If it should be Allah's will that we die by your hand, let it be so. There is but one favour, however, that I would ask of you, and that is that you kill every one of us, without exception. I shall not allow you to kill one or two only!'

Sarfaraz Khan was touched, both by Mother's courage, and because she had spoken in the name of Allah. He warmed towards her, as others had done.

'Great is your faith, and great your spirit,' he said. 'Well, I wash my hands off this business. To have been sent on a fool's errand, and to be put off by the calm persuasiveness of a woman!'

'It was Allah's will,' said Javed. 'You will not be so foolish again. Why poison your heart on behalf of your relatives? It was their doing, I knew that all along.'

Another Proposal

Two or three days after the visit of Sarfaraz Khan, when we had taken our evening meal, Javed Khan entered the room and made himself comfortable on the low, wooden platform.

'Mariam, you promised to speak to me again on a certain subject which you know is close to my heart,' he said, addressing Mother. 'Now that you have had time to think it over, perhaps you can give me a definite answer.'

'What subject do you mean?' asked Mother, feigning ignorance.

'I mean my original proposal to marry your daughter.'

'I have hardly had time to argue the matter with myself,' said Mother, 'or to give it the attention it deserves. It was only the other day that your brother-in-law came here to kill us without a moment's notice. If we are likely to be killed even while under your protection, what use is there in discussing the subject of marriage? If I am to lose my life, my daughter's life must go too. She and I are inseparable. Someone like Sarfaraz may be on his way here even now!'

'Upon my head, you make me angry when you talk like that!' exclaimed Javed. 'I tell you that had he lifted his hand against either of you, he would have lost his own life. As long as you are under Javed's roof, there is not a man who would dare to raise his finger against you. I shall strike off the heads of half a dozen before a hair on my *Firangan's* head can be touched.' And he gave me a look of such passion and ferocity, that I trembled with fright, and hid my face behind Mother's back.

He was terribly excited, and to calm him Mother said, 'I am sure you are strong enough to protect us. But why do you bring up this subject again?'

'Because it is always on my mind. Why delay it any longer?'

'If you knew our circumstances and the history of my family,' said Mother, 'you would see that I am not in a position to give her way.'

'Why so?' asked Javed.

'I have my brothers living. What shall I answer them when they find out that I have given you my daughter in marriage, and the girl still only a child? And moreover, my husband's younger brother is still alive. I have to consult them before I can decide anything.'

'That may be so,' said Javed. 'But they are not likely to question you, as in all probability they have been killed along with the other *Firangis*.'

'I hope not. But would it not be wiser to wait and make certain they are dead before we come to any definite decision?'

'I am an impatient man, Mariam, and life is not so long that I can wait an eternity to quench my desires. I have restrained myself out of respect for your wishes, and out of respect for you. But my desire to call your girl my wife grows stronger daily, and I am prepared to take any risk to have her for my own.'

'Suppose the English Government is restored to power—what shall we do then? Your life will be worth little, and with you dead, my daughter will be a widow at thirteen. Cannot you wait a few months, until we are certain as to who will remain masters of this country?'

'True, if the English retook Shahjahanpur, they would show little mercy to the leaders of the revolt. They would hang me from the nearest tree. And no doubt you are hoping for their return, or you would not talk of such a possibility. But how many of them are left? Only a few thousand struggling to hold their own before the walls of Delhi, and they too will soon be disposed of, please God!'

'Then let Delhi decide our future,' said Mother, seizing at a straw. 'If the British army now besieging Delhi is destroyed, that will be the time to talk of such matters. Meanwhile, are we not your dependents and in your power? You have only to await the outcome of the war.'

'You point a long way off, Mariam, and seem to forget that I have the power to marry her against your will and the will of everyone else, including'—and he gave his wife a defiant look—'the owner of a pair of jealous eyes now gazing at me!'

'Did I say you did not have that power?' asked Mother. 'If you take her by force, we have no power to resist. But it would be unmanly of you to compel a fatherless child to gratify your desires. What merit would there be in that? Whereas, if you were to wait until the British are driven from Delhi, my argument would no longer carry any weight. And by that time, my daughter would be more of an age for marriage.'

'It is fortunate for you that I am a man. No one shall take her away from Javed, and Javed's wife she shall be, and I will give her a handsome dowry. And if you were to take my advice, Mariam, you ought to take a husband as well and settle down again in life. You are still young.'

'Why would I marry now?'

'You should marry, if it be only to find a home of your own and bread with it.'

'Why would I marry?' asked Mother again. 'What would become of my girls?'

'Why, your daughter shall be mine,' said Javed brightly. 'And as to your niece, she too will fit in somewhere! She is not unattractive, you know!'

We did not speak much for the rest of the evening. Javed Khan settled himself before a hookah, puffing contentedly, blissfully unaware of the agitation he had set up in everyone's minds. No one spoke. Khan-Begum went about with a long face, and sighed whenever she looked at me. Mother, too, sighed when she looked at me, and Anet and I stared at each other in bewilderment.

As we rose to go to our part of the house, Khan-Begum seized Mother's hand, and in a choking voice, whispered, 'Mariam, you are my mother. Do not help him to inflict greater torment on me than I have already suffered. Promise me that you won't give your daughter to him.'

Mother replied, 'Bibi, you have seen and heard everything that has happened. I am truly a dead one in the hands of the living. You distress yourself for nothing. If I have my way, he shall never get my consent. But will he wait for my consent?'

'Allah bless you!' exclaimed Khan-Begum. 'Your daughter deserves a better fate than to play second fiddle in this family. I will pray that your wishes are granted.'

I could not sleep much that night. The light from the full moon came through the high, barred window, and fell across the foot of the bed. I dozed a little, but the insistent call of the brain-fever bird kept waking me. I opened my eyes once, and saw Javed Khan standing in the doorway, the moonlight shining on his face. He stood there a long while, staring at me, and I was too afraid to move or call out. Then he turned and walked quietly away; and shivering with fright, I put my arms around Mother, and lay clinging to her for the remainder of the night.

On Show

When Khan-Begum had last visited her husband's sister, the latter had made her promise to come again soon; and on a Thursday, a servant came to her with a message, saying, 'Your sister sends her salaams, and wishes to know when you are going to fulfil your promise of calling on her?'

'Give my respects to my sister,' answered Khan-Begum, 'and tell her I cannot come now. There are some *Firangans* staying with us, brought into the house by my husband.'

Later, another messenger arrived with the suggestion that Khan-Begum take her guests along with her, as her relatives were most anxious to see them too. And so our hostess proposed that we accompany her to her sister Qamran's house the next morning.

Four of us set out in one *meana:* Khan-Begum, Mother, Anet and myself. Granny was left behind.

A *meana* is something like a palanquin of old, but smaller, and used exclusively for the conveyance of women. It has short, stubby legs to rest on the ground, the floor is interlaced with string, and the top is covered with red curtains, hanging down the sides. The bearers fix two bamboo poles on either side, by which they lift the *meana* from the ground.

Supported by four perspiring bearers, we arrived at Qamran's house, where we were kindly received. Qamran had at first been prejudiced against us, but the report taken to her by Sarfaraz Khan had made her change her views. She was eager to make our acquaintance and pressed us to stay with her; and during the weeks to come, we were to be her showpieces, on display for those who wanted to see us.

Sarfaraz Khan had come to Javed's house with the intention of striking off our heads, but Mother's charm had baffled him and won him over. Returning home, he had said, 'Who can lift his hand against such harmless things? The girl is like a frightened doe, and the mother—she is a perfect nightingale!' And so, among those who came to see us at Qamran's house was Sarfaraz Khan's wife, Hashmat. She, too, fell a victim to Mother's charm. 'Oh sister!' she exclaimed to Khan-Begum. 'My husband was quite right in his opinion of them. Mariam's lips, like the bee, distil nothing but honey.'

As to Qamran herself, her soft, sympathetic nature was roused by the story of our bereavement and our trials. Her large, pretty black eyes would fill with tears as she listened to Mother, and once she placed her head on Mother's shoulder and sobbed aloud.

She was about thirty-five, and on the verge of becoming stout; but she had fine feature and a clear complexion. We were told that when she was dressed for her marriage, her father passed by, and was so struck by her beauty, that he exclaimed: 'Couldn't we have reserved so much beauty for someone who did not have to go out of our family!'

Qamran's husband, a much older man, was a cavalry lieutenant in the army at Bhopal. At their first meeting, she had felt a repugnance for his person. She repelled his advances, and would not allow him even to touch her, with the result that her mother and others began to believe that she was in love with a jinn, or spirit. It suited her to encourage them in this belief. Her husband was disgusted, and returned to his cavalry regiment, but continued to keep her supplied with funds. Eventually, through the good offices of mutual friends, they were reconciled, and were blessed with a daughter, whom they named Badran.

Badran's beauty was different from her mother's. At the time we saw her she was sixteen or seventeen; she was slightly darker than her mother, and her eyes, though large, lacked the liquid softness which gave such serenity to Qamran's face. But a pink birthmark on her left cheek gave her an interesting face. She did not have her mother's liveliness or enquiring nature, and we did not see much of her.

Qamran had heard of our skill with the needle. She had made up her mind to make a present to her sister-in-law's small son, and asked us if we would help make the kurta-topi, which would consist of miniature trousers, coat and cap. Mother offered to cut and sew them.

She gave the kurta, which was of purple cloth, a moghlai neck; that is, it had one opening, buttoning to the side over the left shoulder. It was finished off with gold lace round the edges, the sleeves and the neck. She also gave it a crescent-shaped, gold-embroidered band round the neck, and epaulettes on the shoulders. The trousers were made of rich, green satin, and also finished off with gold lace. The cap was made of the same stuff as the coat, and had several gold pendants tacked round in front, so that it formed a kind of fillet, resting on the forehead. The three garments cost Qamran something like forty rupees—a sumptuous suit for a child!

Mother was pleased with the result of her work, and all who saw the suit were in raptures, and Qamran made Mother a present of a new set of bangles made of glass and enamelled blue.

We soon established ourselves as favourites in Qamran's house, and members of the household vied with each other in showing us kindness. Whereas they had formerly believed that, as *Firangi* women, we would be peeping out of doors and windows in order to be seen by men, without whose society European women were supposed to be unable to live, they were agreeably surprised to find that we delighted in hard work, that we loved needles and thread, and that, far from seeking the company of men, we did our best to avoid them.

'You are like one of us,' said Qamran to Mother one day. 'I would not exchange you for half a dozen women of my own race. Who could possibly ever tire of you?'

Politics seldom entered the four walls of the zenana—wars and deeds of violence were considered the prerogative of men. Seldom was any reference made to the disturbances that were taking place throughout the country, or to our own troubles. Only once was the even tenor of our lives disturbed, and that was due to the woman, Umda, who had taken a jealous dislike to us from the beginning.

I do not know in what way she was related to Qamran, but they addressed each other as 'sister', and Badran called her 'aunt'. She was a spiteful young woman, with a sharp, lashing tongue, very hostile towards all foreign races. She had been very displeased at our introduction into the family, always gave us angry looks, and never missed an opportunity to speak ill of us.

It pleased Umda to hear of the British reverses, and she was convinced that they would be swept from the walls of Delhi. Occasionally, she would leave aside generalities and give her attention to individuals.

Once Mother, Anet and I sat quietly together, sewing a pair of pyjamas for Badran, while Badran herself sat at the end of the veranda, whispering nonsense to her good-natured young husband, Hafizullah Khan. He, however, had his eyes on Umda, for he knew her well.

She began by changing the conversation with a contemptuous reference to the *Firangi* race, bringing up the old story of the hunger of European women for male company.

'Those wantons!' she said. 'They cannot live without the society of men.' 'Perhaps not, Chachi,' observed Hafizullah Khan from the other end of the veranda, 'and perhaps they are quite right in doing so. They have so much of male company that their appetite for it is probably less than yours. And then not all their men are opium eaters like your husband, who, beyond rolling in the dust like a pig, has little time for anything else.'

'That may be so,' she said haughtily, 'but what has it to do with *Firangi* women? You cannot deny that they enjoy laughing and joking with strange men, that they dance and sing, sometimes half-nude, with the arms of strange men round their waists. Then they retire into dark corners where they kiss and are kissed by men other than their husbands!'

Badran's bright eyes had grown wide with astonishment at this recital of the ways of the *Firangi* female.

'I did not know all that,' said Hafizullah Khan. 'From where do you obtain your deep knowledge, Chachi?'

'Never mind where,' she replied impatiently. 'It is true, what I have said, and that's why I say these *Firangans* will prove troublesome.'

'Now you are going too far, Chachi,' said Hafizullah. 'Upon my head, you are very careless in what you say. What charge can you bring against our guests here?'

'Well, when they first entered Javed's house, there was some excitement among the men in the neighbourhood.'

'Quite possibly,' said Hafizullah with sarcasm, 'your good husband was a little excited too, I suppose. Well, what came of it?'

'You are a funny boy, Hafiz!' she said mischievously, giving him a knowing wink in full sight of us. 'What are your intentions, eh?'

'You are behaving very stupidly today, Chachi!' said Hafizullah, growing impatient. 'What do you insinuate by that shake of your unbalanced head? I tell you again, be careful how you speak of Mariam and her daughter!'

'The boy stands as a champion of the white brood! Well, I have no patience with them.'

There was a pause in the contention. Mother, Anet and I had remained absolutely silent during this heated conversation; we were not in a position to say anything in our own defence, for we were in Qamran's house only on sufferance, and had no right to quarrel with anyone; and at the same time, we could not have improved on Hafizullah's performance.

Umda was bent on mischief and would not change the subject. 'My son has gone with the expedition. I hope and pray that he does not bring a *Firangi* female back with him.'

Hafizullah was ready for her. 'No doubt your son will perform deeds of great valour on his expedition, but considering that it is only a few refractory landowners that they have been sent to quell, I don't think there is any chance of his finding any *Firangans* to come back with.'

Before Umda could take up the cudgels again, Hafizullah got to his feet and told her that it was time she returned to her own house; that he did not intend sitting by to hear us abused by her. But Umda was determined to have the last word.

'Great is the power of prayer,' she said. 'I have advised Khan-Begum to take ashes in her hand, and blow them towards these women so that they might fly away like this.' And throwing a pinch of dust towards us, she mumbled something under her breath.

It was too much for Hafizullah Khan. He rushed at Umda and dragged her out of the veranda. Then telling her to be gone, or he would be more rough with her, he returned and sat down near his wife, in a great rage.

The Rains

'It does not surprise me,' said Qamran, when she came home and heard of the quarrel between Umda and her son-in-law. 'Umda has too long and too venomous a tongue altogether. What business is it of hers that you should be my guests? She might have taken a lesson from you in patience and forbearance. Son!' she said, addressing Hafizzullah. 'You need not have dragged her out. Nevertheless, it was noble of you to have taken the side of these unfortunate ones. Mariam, forgive her for her foolishness. She has only succeeded in giving the young an opportunity to jeer at her. In my house you will always be welcome.'

It was now the height of the rainy season, and heavy clouds were banking in the west. A breeze brought us the fresh scent of approaching rain, and presently we heard the patter of raindrops on the jasmine bushes that grew in the courtyard.

It was the day of the monsoon festival observed throughout

northern India by the womenfolk, who put on their most colourful costumes, and relax on innumerable swings, giving release to feelings of joy and abandon. Double ropes are suspended from a tree, and the ends are knotted together and made to hold narrow boards painted in gay colours. Two women stand facing each other, having taken each other's ropes by catching them between their toes. They begin to swing gently, gradually moving faster and higher, until they are just a brightly coloured blur against the green trees and grey skies. Sometimes, a small bed is fixed between the ropes, on which two or three can sit while two others move the swing, singing to them at the same time.

A swing having been put up from an old banyan tree that grew just behind the house, Badran and Hashmat, both dressed in red from head to foot, climbed on to it. Anet and I swung them, while Gulabia, the servant-girl, sang. When they came down we had our turn, and I found it an exhilarating experience, riding through the air, watching the racing clouds above me at one moment, and Anet's dark curls below me at the next. Removed for a while from the world below, I felt again that life could be gay and wonderful.

Mother's memory was stored with an incredible amount of folklore, and she would sometimes astonish our hosts with her references to sprites and evil spirits. One day Badran, having taken her bath, came out into the courtyard with her long hair lying open.

'My girl, you ought not to leave your hair open,' said Mother. 'It is better to make a knot in it.'

'But I have not yet oiled it,' said Badran. 'How can I put it up?'

'It is not wise to leave it open when you sit outside in the cool of the evening.'

'Do tell me why,' said Badran. 'See, I will do as you say and give it a knot for the present.' And she pressed Mother to tell her why it was unsafe to leave her hair open in the evening.

'There are aerial beings called jinns, who are easily attracted by long hair and pretty black eyes like yours,' said Mother.

Badran blushed, her mother and husband both being present; and Qamran smiled at the recollection of her own youthful waywardness, when she made everyone believe that she was the object of a jinn's passion.

'Do the jinns visit human beings?' asked Hafizullah Khan.

'So it is said,' said Mother. 'I have never seen a jinn myself, but I have noticed the effect they have on others.'

'Oh, please tell us what you have seen,' begged Qamran.

'There was once a lovely girl who had a wealth of black hair,' said Mother. 'Quite unexpectedly she became seriously ill, and inspite of every attention and the best medical advice, she grew worse every day. She became as thin as a whipping-post and lost all her beauty, with the exception of her hair, which remained beautiful and glossy until her dying day. Whenever she fell asleep, she would be tormented by dreams. A young jinn would appear to her, and tell her that he had fallen in love with her beautiful hair one evening as she was drying it after a bath, and that he intended to take her away. She was in great pain, yet in the midst of her sufferings her invisible tormentor never ceased to visit her; and though her body became shrivelled, there shone in her eyes an unearthly light; and when her body decayed and died, her gorgeous head of hair remained as beautiful as ever.'

'What a dreadful story!' said Badran, hurriedly tying another knot in her hair.

Conversation then turned upon different types of ghosts and spirits, and Qamran told us about the *Munjia*—the disembodied spirit of a Brahmin youth who has died before his marriage—which is supposed to have its abode in a pipal tree. When the *Munjia* gets annoyed, it rushes out from the tree and upsets bullock-carts, *meanas* and even horse-driven carriages. Should anyone be passing beneath a lonely pipal tree at night, advised Qamran, one should not make the mistake of yawning without snapping one's fingers in front of one's mouth.

'If you don't remember to do this,' said Qamran, 'the *Munjia* will dash down your throat and completely ruin you.'

Mother then launched into an account of the various types of ghosts she was acquainted with: the ghosts of immoral women—*churels*—who appear naked, with their feet facing backwards; ghosts with long front teeth, which suck human blood; and ghosts which take the form of animals. In some of the villages near Rampur (according to Mother), people have a means by which they can tell what form a departed person has taken in the next life. The ashes are placed in a basin and left outside at night, covered with a heavy lid. Next morning, a footprint can be seen in the ashes. It may be the footprint of a man or a bird or an elephant, according to the form taken by the departed spirit.

By ten o'clock we were feeling most reluctant to leave each other's company on the veranda. It did not make us feel any better to be told by mother and Qamran to recite certain magical verses to keep away evil spirits. When I got into bed I couldn't lie still, but kept twisting and turning and looking at the walls for moving shadows. After some time, we heard a knocking on our door, and the voices of Badran and Hashmat. Getting up and opening it, we found them looking pale and anxious. Qamran had succeeded in frightening them, too.

'Are you all right, Khurshid?' they asked. 'Wouldn't you like to sleep in our room? It might be safer. Come, we'll help you to carry your bed across.'

'We are quite all right here,' protested Mother, but we were hustled along to the next room, as though a band of ghosts was conspiring against us. Khan-Begum had been absent during all this activity (though she had been present during the story-telling), and the first we heard of her was a loud cry. We ran towards the sound and found her emerging from our room.

'Mariam has disappeared!' she cried. 'Khurshid and Anet have gone too!'

And then, when she saw us come running out of her own room, our hair loose and disordered, she gave another cry and fainted on the veranda.

White Pigeons

'You are bearing your troubles very well,' said Hafizullah to Mother one evening. 'You are so cheerful and patient, and you seem to look forward to the future with hope. And after all, what is the good of mourning for a past which can never return?'

'I doubt if there can be any improvement in their situation,' said Khan-Begum. 'Only yesterday the fakir was saying that the Firangis had been wiped off the face of the land.'

'I am not so sure of that,' remarked Hafizullah.

'Nor I,' said Qamran. 'The fact is, we do not get much news here.'

'Well, I can tell you something,' said Hafizullah. 'Though my uncle did boast the other day that there were no Firangis left, I overheard him whispering to Sarfaraz Khan that they were not yet totally extinct. The hills are full of them. My uncle was relating how Abdul Rauf Khan had gone on the morning of Id to pay his respects to Mian Saheb, the same fakir you speak of, and he was astounded by what the old man told him.'

'What was it?' urged Khan-Begum.

'Abdul Rauf said that Mian Saheb was in a strange mood. He cast off the white clothes which he had been wearing during the past three months and, very suddenly, and without apparent reason, put on a black robe. Abdul Rauf and the others had gone to him to ask that he pray for the defeat of the Firangis before Delhi, but what do you think he told them?'

Hafizullah paused dramatically, and both Qamran and Khan-Begum said at the same time, 'What did he tell them?'

'He told them that the restoration of the Firangi rule was as certain as the coming of doomsday. It would be another hundred years, he said, before the foreigners could be made to leave. "See, here they come!" he cried, pointing to the north where a flock of white pigeons could be seen hovering over the city. "They come flying like white pigeons which, when disturbed, fly away, and circle, and come down to rest again. White pigeons from the hills!" Abdul Rauf folded his hands and begged Mian Saheb to say no more. But the Mian is no respecter of persons, and his words are not to be taken lightly.'

Our stay with Qamran was drawing to a close. We had passed almost the entire rainy season in the company of her agreeable household, and time had passed swiftly. We could not have received greater kindness or sympathy than we had been given by Qamran, and her son-in-law, Hafizullah. Javed Khan had been several times to see us—or rather, to see his wife and sister. Once or twice he had pressed Qamran to shorten our stay, but she did not want us to leave, and kept us on the pretext that we were sewing some things for her, which were not quite ready. He did not press her too much, as he knew that having both his wife and us under his roof did not make things easier for him.

Though appointed by the Nawab to a military command, we did not hear that Javed had engaged in any new or daring enterprise. His sacking of the Rosa Rum Factory had been his chief exploit to date, and that too had been done more for personal gain than from any other motive. He had shown no enthusiasm for the massacre at Muhamdi, where a company of sepoys had finished off the few Europeans who had managed to get away from Shahjahanpur. Now he limited his services to attending the Nawab's receptions, and to keeping him informed of news from Delhi and the whereabouts of stray refugees and survivors like ourselves. We heard, for instance, of the hiding-place of the Redmans. A beggar woman happened to be passing before the house of the Redmans' old washerwoman, and stopping there to beg, recognized the tall, fair woman sitting in the yard.

'Who are you, eh?' she cackled. 'I know who you are! And where are your white husband and son?'

'Be off, *churel*!' said Mrs Redman. 'Go about your begging, and do not interfere with my affairs.'

Meanwhile the dhobi came home and, taking in the situation, told the beggar woman, 'How do you know she is a *Firangan*? She happens to be my sister-in-law.'

'Very fair for one of your caste!' said the old woman slyly.

'Ask any more questions and my washing-board will descend on your head!' threatened the dhobi. 'Be off, dead one!'

The beggar woman hobbled off, cursing both the dhobi's family and the Redmans, and made her way to Abdul Rauf Khan's house, where she informed him of what she had discovered. Abdul Rauf took his information to the Nawab, and suggested that he be permitted to capture the *Firangan*.

'That would be an adventure worthy of you,' said the amused Nawab. 'No doubt you would need an armed detachment to capture her. But I prefer not to hound these refugees, Khan Saheb. They have not done our cause any harm.' And he showed them the same forbearance that he had shown us.

The season of Moharram had come and gone. We did not even notice that it was over, for there were very few Shia families in Shahjahanpur, and the festival was not kept up with the same zeal that was shown in other towns. Unlike the Shia women, the Pathan women do not go into mourning during the ten days of fasting, nor do they remove their ornaments. Food and clothing were, however, sent to the nearest mosque to be distributed among the poor of the city.

Moharram over, it was decided that we should return to Javed Khan's house on Friday, the 4th of September.

The Impatience of Javed Khan

Poor Khan-Begum was to suffer many more pangs of jealousy before she could be done with us. On the same day that we returned to her house, Javed Khan took the opportunity to question Mother again, regarding her plans for my marriage.

'Tell me, Mariam, how much longer am I to wait?' he asked after dinner.

'What can I say?' sighed Mother. 'You ask me so often. I have already told you that I cannot give my daughter away without consulting my brothers. You had agreed to wait until the contest before Delhi was decided.'

'May the *Firangi* name perish, I say!' he exclaimed furiously. 'Surely your brothers have all been exterminated by now!' Then, his mood changing suddenly from anger to a brooding sullenness, he muttered to himself: 'Perhaps the fellow spoke the truth when he said, "Subedarji, will you reach Delhi at all?" For Ghansham Singh was not fated to set foot within the walls of the city. He fell at the Hindan bridge, when the *Firangi* army attacked the Bareilly brigade. He could not tell the King of our achievements here on the 31st of May. Well, I have done my part—and the sugar loaf solved my sherbet problem at Moharram. I would also have dealt well with that boy at Mangal Khan's, but the fool, Mangal, came between us and said he had adopted the boy as his own son. I never heard of a true believer adopting an infidel—a plague on them all!'

His face was dark and threatening as he went out of the house, and after a few minutes, we were startled by the screams of the boy Saifulla, Javed's half-brother, who had bumped into Javed in the lane and upon whom the Pathan was now venting his rage and frustration.

Javed Khan had stripped the boy to the waist, and taking out his horsewhip, had lashed the boy so severely, that the skin was actually torn from his back. Saifulla was laid up for several days, yelling from the pain which the festered parts gave him; but instead of softening toward him, Javed Khan threatened to repeat the flogging if the boy didn't stop groaning.

I have no doubt that it was Mother's disappointing answer that had driven Javed into a frenzy, and I suppose I should have been grateful that his passion had found an outlet on the back of his brother. Javed hated the boy for being the offspring of an illicit affair of his father's.

The same evening, Javed gave a further display of his savage disposition. Having enquired from the syce whether his horse had received its gram, and having been informed that Rupia, the servant-woman, had not yet ground it, he called the woman and demanded to know why the gram had not yet been ground.

'I was busy with other things,' she explained.

'Were you, you dead one?' he shouted fiercely, and seizing his whip again, laid it on her so violently, that she was literally made black and blue, and her torn and scanty clothes were cut to rags. She was bedridden for several days. Every one in the house went about in apprehension, wondering what Javed's next outburst would be like, but Mother could not bear to hear the groans of the woman and the boy. She had Zeban fetch some ground turmeric, which she heated on the fire and applied to the bruises. She attended to them for three days until their wounds began to heal.

One day Javed approached Mother again, and we were afraid there would be a repetition of his earlier display of temper; but he looked crestfallen, and was probably a little ashamed of his behaviour. He complained of having pains all over his body, and begged Mother to tell him of a remedy.

'You have been prescribing for those two wretches,' he said. 'Can't you give me something too?'

'What can I give you?' replied Mother. 'I am not a hakim. When I was in my senses I might have been able to think of something for your pain. You look very well, I must say.'

'I am not well,' said Javed. 'I cannot sit on my horse as well as usual. It is all due to my disregard for the wisdom of my betters: "Don't shoot on a Thursday." Last Thursday when I went out shooting, I saw a black buck and fired at it, but I missed, and instead, I hit a white pigeon sitting on a tomb. The pigeon flew into a bush, and I could not find it; but it must have been killed. I got nothing that day, and when I returned home in the evening, I felt exhausted and quite unable to use my limbs. I was as stiff as a dead one. Abdul Rauf was informed, and when he heard of what had happened he came to see me, very angry, because I had fired on the bird. "Pigeons," he said, "are people who come out of their graves on Thursdays for a little fresh air." Well, Abdul Rauf had me treated, shut me in a room, and eventually I came to myself. But I have this swelling on my face, where the dead one must have slapped me.'

His face did appear to be slightly swollen; but, before Mother could take a closer look, Javed started at the sound of music in the street. His face underwent a violent change and, taking down his whip, he rushed out of the house.

There was a great deal of commotion outside, and then we heard the sound of someone shouting: '*Hai! Hai!* Save me, I am being murdered!'

We all looked at each other in wonder, and Khan-Begum said, 'It must be that boy who passes this way sometimes, singing and playing love songs on his flute. My husband swore, by the soul of his dead father, to flog the fellow within an inch of his life if he caught him singing before this house.'

'But what harm is done by his singing?' asked Mother.

'None that I know of. But in a Pathan settlement, no one is allowed to sing or play any instrument in the streets. Music is supposed to excite all sorts of passions, and so it is discouraged.'

'Still, I do not see what right our protector has to assault another in the street merely because he is singing and playing his flute. Is Javed not afraid that he might have to answer to the Nawab for his high-handedness?'

Khan-Begum began to laugh. 'The Nawab?' she said. 'Of what are you thinking, Mariam? Why should the Nawab care about it?'

A Visit from Kothiwali

It was the 13th of September, a Sunday morning, when the family barber brought a message from Kothiwali for Javed Khan. 'Your Chachi sends you her salaams, and says she intends to pay you a visit tomorrow.' To this Javed Khan sent the reply: 'It is my Chachi's house, let her come and throw the light of her presence on it.' Messages of this sort were always couched in extremely polite language.

The following morning Kothiwali arrived in her *meana*, attended by her servants. We were glad to see her again, as she was always so friendly.

'Now, Mariam, I have come to ask you to spend some time with me. I am seething with jealousy because you spent so much time at Qamran's house. Javed, you have no objection to my taking them with me?'

'It is all the same to me whether they stay here or go with you,' said Javed Khan with a shrug of his shoulders.

'Why so?' asked Kothiwali mischievously. 'I thought you were unhappy unless they were under your own roof?'

'True, but what good is it?' he said. 'My ambition was to possess the girl.'

'Well, she is in your possession now, isn't she?' said Kothiwali.

'Upon my head, you are exasperating!' exclaimed Javed. 'So far as her presence in my house goes, she is in my possession, but what of that? I would marry her today, if it were not for her mother's procrastinations! Sometimes it is: "I have not consulted my brothers," as if she had any brothers left to consult. Sometimes it is: "Wait until the fighting before Dilli is over," as if, even when it is over, it will make any great difference to people like us. It is foolish to expect that the *Firangis* will be victorious. Have I not seen a score of them running for their lives pursued by one of our soldiers?'

'Perhaps, but it is not always like that,' said Kothiwali.

'I wonder why your sympathies are with them, Chachi?'

'Well, they have always been quite good to me,' she replied. 'When my husband was killed by his enemies, it was the Collector who came to my house to condole with me, and it was he who saw to it that our fields were not taken from us. True, that was a long time ago. But I have no reason to wish them ill. At the same time, don't think I wish to run down the cause you have made your own—the rebel cause, I mean.'

'The *rebel* cause! Why do you always call it the rebel cause, Chachi?' Javed Khan looked very upset. 'Rebels against whom? Against aliens! Are they not to be expelled from the land? To fight them is not rebellion, but a meritorious act, surely!'

'Maybe, if it doesn't involve the murder of innocent women and children. But see how the *Firangis* are holding out before Delhi!'

'Enough, Chachi. Say no more, or you will rouse the demon in me. Let us not anticipate events. Delhi still stands, and Bahadur Shah reigns!'

'Nevertheless, I would advise you to take Mariam's suggestion and wait until the siege is raised. Be cautious, Javed, in your designs on this girl.'

'I have need to be, no doubt, after hearing about the example set by the Kanpur girl.'

'Oh! And who was she?'

'The General's daughter. A girl still beautiful at the age of twenty. She was saved from the massacre by Jamadar Narsingh, one of Nana Saheb's bodyguards, who would have liked to make her his wife. His intentions, like mine, were probably quite honourable, but Zerandaz Khan, another officer, stole the girl one night from the Jamadar's house, and treated her so savagely, that he roused in her all the pride and resentment of her race. For some time she concealed her feelings, but one night, when he was asleep, she drew his scimitar from under his pillow and plunged it into his breast. She then went and threw herself in a well. That was pluck and daring, wasn't it, Chachi? But,'—pointing at me, though looking away—'I have not even looked her full in the face, believe me!'

'Ah, you sly man!' said Kothiwali jestingly.

There was a pause at the end of which Kothiwali said, 'They may come with me, Javed, mayn't they? You are in a surly mood this morning.'

'Oh yes, take them with you,' he muttered sulkily. 'If they are happier with you, they may go with you.'

Seated in the same *meana* as Kothiwali, we were carried along to her house. I should really call it a mansion, because it was a large brick building with a high entrance and a spacious courtyard. There was also a set of glass-roofed chambers over the gateway, which the men used as retiring rooms; while the women's apartments were situated on the ground floor, and were cool and spacious.

The family consisted of Kothiwali, her daughter and two sons, one daughter-in-law, one son-in-law, and innumerable grandchildren. Kothiwali was the widow of a landed proprietor in the District, and must have been about forty years old when we knew her. She was tall, with black hair and eyes, a large mouth, small teeth, coloured black with *missi* and paan. She wore no trinkets except for a round silver bangle on each hand, and a plain silver ring on her right small finger. Her face was always cheerful, and she possessed great spirit. She commanded great respect from the rest of her community, who often came to consult her when in difficulty.

Mother soon became a favourite in the household, and so did Anet and I, but to a lesser degree. Kothiwali paid special attention to us. 'What quiet girls they are!' she would sometimes say. 'They never waste their time in idle talk.'

'Why not have the girls' ears and noses pierced?' she said to Mother one day.

'What would be the good when I have nothing to make them wear,' replied mother.

The lobes of our ears were already pierced, and I was glad I did not have to submit to having my nose pierced as well.

'I am glad you did not submit to Javed's request for your daughter's hand in marriage,' said Kothiwali. 'Had she been my daughter, I would never have agreed. Javed is very inconstant.'

'It would have been an incongruous match,' said Mother.

'My poor husband could never have imagined that she would be sought for by a Pathan as his second wife!'

Kothiwali's elder son, Wajihullah Khan, came in and sat down while we were talking. He was a young man of twenty-five, a hafiz—one who knows the *Quran* by heart—and regular at his prayers: it was he who gave the call to prayer in the neighbouring mosque. He was fair, of medium height, and quiet and respectful in his manner.

His usual haunt was the bungalow over the gateway, where he spent most of his time reading or playing chess—a game which is now losing much of its popularity. He came in with a friend named Kaddu Khan, a very handsome young man, who called Kothiwali Chachi I think I recognized him as one of the band who had forced us to leave Lala Ramjimal's house. He was suffering from consumption in its first stage, and Wajihullah joined Kothiwali in begging Mother to prescribe something for him.

'I am not a doctor,' said Mother. 'I know the remedies for some minor ailments, but I very much doubt if I could help this boy.'

'No, do not refuse to do something for him,' urged Wajihullah. 'He is really a man of an adventurous spirit, though he has yet to gain fame for his achievements.'

'Do not make fun of the poor fellow,' said Kothiwali. 'He looks sufficiently depressed already.'

'No, I shall relate his worthy deeds to Mausi, before I ask her to give him something to improve his condition.'

Kaddu Khan now looked more dejected than ever and hung his handsome head in acute embarrassment.

'To begin with, Mausi, this is the gentleman who proposed to Nawab Qadar Ali to dig up the Christian graves for the treasure which, he was sure, was buried there.'

Kaddu Khan looked up and said, 'So I was made to believe. And the fox who gave me that information also told me that when a *Firangi* dies, two bags of money are buried with him.'

'And of course you believed that absurd story, and went about digging up their bones? Tell us what treasure you found!'

'We began digging at night,' said Kaddu Khan, deciding it would be better if he told the story himself. 'It was a moonlit night. There were three of us. I volunteered to go down into the grave and bring up anything valuable that I could find. To keep in touch with my comrades, we hammered a peg in the ground above and fastened a rope to it, and with its help, I slipped down. But imagine my horror when, instead of touching firm ground, I found myself hanging between heaven and earth! I let out a cry of distress. My comrades, instead of helping me out, thought the *Firangi* devils were after us, and instantly took to their heels, leaving me dangling over the grave.'

'A situation you had merited,' observed Wajihullah. 'But tell us how you got out.'

'I hung on to the rope and with a great deal of effort managed to raise myself to the bank. And now I tried to follow the example of my brave companions by making a run for it, but as I got up to do so, I felt a violent jerk around my waist and fell down again. Again I tried to get up and run, and again I was pulled to the ground. I was half-dead through fright, but I made one last lunge forward, and this time the wooden peg came up too, and I lost no time in taking to my heels. Chachi, that graveyard is full of *Firangi* devils!'

'What a thick-headed fellow you are!' said Wajihullah, enjoying himself immensely. 'One would think there would be some sense beneath that beautiful brow of yours. It was your waistband, Kaddu, that got hammered down with the peg. It left you dangling over the grave, and when you tried to run, it pulled you down again. It was only when you pulled the peg up that your cummerbund was loosened.'

Kothiwali and the rest of us had a good laugh at Kaddu Khan's discomfiture.

'It should serve as a lesson to you,' said Kothiwali, 'that all men are alike when the time comes to die. When you are dead would you like somebody to disturb your body in search of treasure? Treasure indeed! Even kings go empty-handed when they die. A child, when it is born, comes into the world with a closed fist, and the same hand lies open and flat at the time of death. We bring nothing into the world and we take nothing out!' At this juncture, Kaddu Khan's mother and sister joined us and, folding their hands to Mother, entreated her to do something for the youth.

They had conceived an exaggerated idea of Mother's powers

of healing. All she told Kaddu to do was to take a dose of *khaksir* tea every six hours, and to abstain from acidic and hot food; and she told him to chew some fresh coconut every morning, drinking the juice as well. Kaddu Khan tried these simple remedies, and we heard that he eventually got better.

The Fall of Delhi

We were sitting in the veranda with Kothiwali when there was a disturbance in the next porch, where most of the men were sitting. Javed Khan had just ridden up, and had whispered something in Sarfaraz Khan's ear. Sarfaraz got up immediately and came and whispered something to Kothiwali. As soon as he had gone, Kothiwali turned to Mother and said, 'Well, Mariam, Delhi has been taken by the *Firangis*. What great changes will take place now . . .'

Our hearts leapt at the news, and tears came to our eyes, for a British victory meant a release from our confinement and state of dependence; but Delhi was a far cry from Shahjahanpur, and we did not give any expression to our feelings.

On the contrary, Mother took Kothiwali's hand and said, 'May you have peace out of it, too, Pathani.'

'Javed Khan will look quite small now, won't he?' said Kothiwali merrily. Apparently the news did not affect her one way or the other: she dealt in individuals, not in communities. 'But he has good reason to be worried. The *Firangis* will have heavy scores to settle in this city.'

The next day the menfolk held a long discussion. Some spoke of fleeing the city, others suggested that it would be better to wait and watch the course of events.

Sarfaraz Khan: 'Though Delhi has fallen to the *Firangi* army, it will be a long time before a small town like ours can be reoccupied. Our soldiers, who have been driven from Delhi, will make a stand at some other important place, Lucknow perhaps, and it will be months before we see a *Firangi* uniform in Shahjahanpur. Do not be in a hurry to run away, unless, of course, you have special reasons to be afraid of an avenging army . . .'

Javed: 'True, very true, *bhai*. I have done nothing to be afraid of. Have I, now? It's fellows like Abdul Rauf, who served under the *Firangis* and then threw in their lot with the sepoys, that are sure to be hanged. As for me, I never did take salt with the *Firangis*. If it comes to the worst, I shall ride across the border into Nepal, or take service in the Gwalior brigade.'

Sarfaraz: 'Oh, I'm sure you will. But why leave the city at all if there is nothing to be afraid of?'

Hafizullah: 'I saw some of our men who had returned from Delhi. They were lucky to get away. They had on only their tattered tunics and shorts.'

'Did they say anything of the fighting in Delhi?' asked Sarfaraz Khan.

'They told me that our army was not able to make much impression on the *Angrez* lines entrenched on the Ridge. There were many sorties, and during the last one, only a few days before the city was stormed, our men performed great feats of valour, but they were repulsed and cut down to the last man. The *Firangis* lost many men, too, but the victory gave them great confidence. When their storming parties approached the walls and blew open the Kashmiri Gate, their leader, Nikalsein, was seen waving his handkerchief on the point of his sabre from an elevated site. A ball struck him, and he fell. But his men forced their way through the city at the point of the bayonet, and Delhi is in *Firangi* hands again.'

'And what became of the King?' enquired Sarfaraz.

'He was made a prisoner, and his sons, who fled with him, were shot.'

'And so much for the rebellion,' said Sarfaraz Khan philosophically. 'The city of Delhi was a garden of flowers, and now it is a ruined country; the stranger is not my enemy, nor is anyone my friend . . .'

'Don't grow sentimental and poetic, Sarfaraz,' said Javed Khan irritably. 'Who was it who came to my house to kill certain people?'

'It was I,' said Sarfaraz. 'But did I kill anyone?'

Behind the Curtain

It was now winter, though the cold winds had not yet begun

to blow. Mother sold two of the silver spoons from the jewel box which she had rescued from our burning house, and used the money to make quilts and some warm clothing to keep away the cold.

Ever since we had heard of the fall of Delhi, a change had come over our outlook and our expectations. We began to look forward to the time when Shahjahanpur would be reoccupied by the British—it would mean the end of our captivity which, though it had been made pleasant by Kothiwali and Qamran and their households, was not a state to which we could resign ourselves for ever; it would—we hoped—mean a reunion with other members of my mother's and father's families; and it would put an end to Javed Khan's plans to marry me. Our motives in hoping for the restoration of British authority were, therefore, entirely personal. We had, during the past months, come to understand much of the resentment against a foreign authority, and we saw that the continuation of that authority could only be an unhappy state of affairs for both sides; but for the time being it was in our interests to see it restored. Our lives depended on it.

But as yet there was no sign of the approach of British soldiers. We had no doubt that they would arrive sooner or later, but of course we did not speak on the subject, nor did we consider it prudent to show too great an interest in what was happening elsewhere. Of Kothiwali's sympathy we were sure, but we were afraid Javed Khan, in his defeat and frustration, might try to inflict some injury on us.

One day the mohalla sweeper, having taken ill, sent another girl to carry out her duties. The new girl recognized us as soon as she saw us, and a look of understanding passed between her and Mother. I remembered that she was called Mulia, and that she was the elder sister of a girl with whom I used to play when I was younger.

The latrine was the one place where we could manage any sort of privacy, and when Mulia went behind its curtain wall, Mother followed her.

'Mausi, you have no need to worry any more,' whispered Mulia. 'Delhi is taken, and your own people will be among us again. And I am to tell you that your brother is safe at Bharatpur. If you wish to send him a message, there is a person going on a pilgrimage to Mathura, and he will take your letter.'

Overjoyed at having met someone whom she knew and could trust, Mother agreed to make use of the messenger.

'But what am I to write the letter with?' she asked.

'Don't worry,' said Mulia. 'Tomorrow I will bring paper and pencil. Meet me here again.'

We did not betray our feelings at this fortunate meeting, nor did anyone notice anything unusual about our behaviour. We did not even tell Anet or Granny about it, for fear that our hopes might be disappointed.

Next morning, keeping her promise, Mulia came again and waited for Mother behind the curtain wall. She handed her a scrap of paper and a small pencil, upon which Mother scribbled these words: 'I, Ruth, Anet, Mother, alive and well and hiding here. Do your best to take us away.'

She handed the note to Mulia, who slipped it into her bodice, Mulia then slipped away, leaving us in a state of suppressed excitement.

It was early January, and we had been with Kothiwali for over three months. We had wanted for nothing but had, on the contrary, been treated with great kindness and consideration. We were rather disappointed when it was suggested that we should return to Javed Khan's house. He came himself and asked Kothiwali to let us go. Perhaps he still hoped that Mother might be persuaded to give her consent to my marriage—months had passed since the British had taken Delhi, but there were still no signs of their arrival in Shahjahanpur.

Khan-Begum was not exactly overjoyed at our return, and was still subject to fits of jealousy. There must have been a heated argument between her and Javed, because the morning after our arrival we heard him exclaiming to her angrily: 'I hate this constant nagging of yours.' She gave him some reply, which was followed by the slash of Javed's whip and a long silence.

He left the house without speaking to anyone, and only came back in the evening for his dinner. He asked Khan-Begum if she had had anything to eat.

She replied: 'No, I am not hungry.'

'Then you had better sit down and eat,' he said, 'and don't put on any more of your airs.' She knew he was in a bad temper and had no wish to feel his whip again; so she did what he told her, though she remained glum and unfriendly until Kothiwali came and took us away again.

The Battle of Bichpuri

We were now in the middle of April 1858, and the hot winds of approaching summer brought the dust eddying into Kothiwali's veranda. The gulmohar tree outside the gate was aflame with scarlet flowers, and the mango trees were in blossom, promising fruit in abundance. The visits of Javed Khan to Kothiwali's house had of late become more frequent, and there were many whispered conversations between him and Kothiwali. We had no idea how we would fit in with their future plans should the British reoccupy Shahjahanpur.

One day Kothiwali received a visitor, a stranger whom we had not seen before. His name was Faizullah, and he too addressed Kothiwali as Chachi, though he was not related to her. He was a brash young man, and gave a vivid account of his experiences at Fatehgarh, from where he had just returned.

'So you were present at the battle of Bichpuri?' asked Kothiwali.

'Yes, Chachi' he replied, 'and what a great battle it was! We fought the *Firangis* hand to hand, and made them feel the strength of our arms. I made a heap of the slain, and have brought with me a string of heads to present to the Nawab!'

'What a liar you are!' exclaimed Kothiwai.

'I swear by my head, Chachi!'

'How did a thin fellow like you manage to carry so many heads?'

'Why, I slung them over my saddle, and rode home in triumph.'

'And who was it who got the worst of the fight?'

'Why, the *kafirs*, of course, Chachi We made a clean sweep of them,' and he passed the palm of his right hand over his left.

'Indeed!' said Kothiwali.

'There was not one man left, Chachi, so do you know what they did? They sent their women out to fight us!'

'This becomes more intriguing,' said Kothiwali. 'You are a gifted boy, Faizullah—you have a wonderful imagination! Tell us, what did their women look like?'

'Well, they were rather big for women. Some of them wore false beards and moustaches. But each one of them had a high skirt with a metal disc hanging down in front.' (It suddenly dawned on me that Faizullah was describing a Scots regiment of Highlanders.) 'Such horrid-looking women, I assure you. Of course, there was no question of fighting them. I don't lift my hand against women, and out of sheer disgust I left the camp and came away.'

'You did right,' said Kothiwali. 'But will you not show us one of the *Firangi* heads you obtained?'

'I would be delighted to, Chachi but believe me, I have made a present of the whole string to the Nawab!'

Judging by the fact that Faizullah was safe at home instead of with a victorious army, we were fairly certain that they had been defeated by the British at Fatehgarh, and that it would not be long before Shahjahanpur was entered. This surmise was confirmed by Sarfaraz Khan who arrived at that moment and, giving Faizullah a look of scorn, said, 'So this warrior has been telling you of the *Firangi* heads he cut off! Is he able to tell us who cut off Nizam Ali Khan's head?'

This announcement produced quite a sensation, and Kothiwali jumped up, exclaiming: 'Nizam Ali killed! You don't mean it!'

Nizam Ali Khan was probably the Nawab's most valued official, a moderate and widely respected man. We had once had the lease of his compound, and had always found him courteous and friendly.

'But I do mean it,' said Sarfaraz. 'I have it on better authority than the chatter of this bragging lout. There is mourning in Nizam Ali's family, and both his sons have been wounded—one in the head, the other in the leg.'

Faizullah, abashed at being found out, sat gazing at the ground while his hands, which had been busy with the slings of his rifle, now lay motionless.

'The Nawab sent out a strong force under Nizam Ali with instructions to prevent the *Firangi* army from crossing the Ganga. But they were too slow and cumbrous, and the enemy had made two marches towards our city before Nizam Ali sighted them. The *Firangi* troops had just reached their camping ground when they noticed a cloud of dust rising on the horizon. Their scouts brought them the intelligence that the Nawab's army was marching upon them, and the cavalry was immediately ordered to remount and prepare for action. They attacked the Nawabi force before the latter had time to form, while the light guns raked them in the flank. Taken by surprise, our soldiers were demoralized. They were seized by panic, and broke and fled.'

'And what about Nizam Ali?' asked Kothiwali impatiently.

'He made a desperate attempt to keep his men together and to put up some sort of resistance, but his efforts were in vain. He could not bring any of his men together to make a stand. His gunners could not fire, as the fugitive soldiers surged from one part of the field to the other. Resolved not to survive this disgrace, Nizam Ali dismounted, and requested his servant to pass his sword through his body. But the servant would not. Then Nizam Ali rushed about madly and put his head into the mouth of a cannon, and ordered a gunner to apply a match and blow him to pieces. But the gunner refused. Poor Nizam Ali! He was about to stab himself with his poignard when the *Firangi* cavalry came thundering down like a torrent, sweeping all before them. A *sawar* belonging to De Kantzow's Horse recognized him—Nizam Ali's distinctive appearance could not be mistaken—and wheeling round, charged at him at full gallop and pinned him with his lance to the ground. And so ended the life of a man who possessed more determination and character than Abdul Rauf Khan, and who was the mainstay of the Nawabi. With Nizam Ali gone, I doubt if the Nawab's government will last another week.'

'I am truly sorry to hear of his fate,' said Kothiwali with a sigh. 'But what became of his sons? You said that two of them were wounded.'

'Better that they had been killed by the side of their noble father. Why, they joined in the stampede and fled from the field of battle as fast as their horses could carry them, following the example of my friend Faizullah here. I have just left them beating their heads and yelling like old women over their fallen fortunes.'

'You are the bearer of serious news,' said Kothiwali. 'Unless I am very much mistaken, the *Firangi* army will soon be here. What will become of us, then?'

'They are marching this way, that is certain,' said Sarfaraz. 'There can be no doubt that the city will soon be reoccupied. We must think of how to save ourselves, because it is certain that they will order the city to be sacked, as was done at Delhi. It has become the custom now.'

'Allah forbid!' cried Kothiwali. 'Let us all meet this evening at my house and discuss measures for our safety. No time must be lost, because tomorrow the *Firangi* army is sure to be in the district, and the day after they will enter the city.'

And so Kothiwali, who had remained quietly at home all through the most violent stages of the revolt, now showed her qualities as a leader. She ordered these rough, disorderly men about as though they were children, and brought about a sense of organization where otherwise panic might have prevailed.

In Flight Again

That evening Kothiwali said to Mother, 'Well, Mariam, the *Firangis* are coming. I am glad that you are with me. Should it be necessary for us to flee the city, you will come with us, won't you?'

'Yes,' said Mother, 'for how will they know us for what we are? We have no one among them who would receive and protect us. From our complexions and our clothes they would take us for Mohammedan women, and we will receive the same treatment as your women. No, for the present we are identified with you all, and we must go where you go.'

When it was decided by Kothiwali that she and her family should flee Shahjahanpur, it was agreed by everyone that the rendezvous would be Javed Khan's house. We left for his house that same evening. There was Kothiwali's family; Qamran's family; and a doctor and his family, whom we had never seen before. Including Javed and his family, there were about thirty persons gathered at his house that evening, the 28th of April 1858. It was almost a year since we had left our own burning house behind. Before long, Javed Khan's house would be burning too. It did not make any sense at all; but I suppose war never has made sense to ordinary individuals.

There was, of course, no sleeping that night, for *meana* after *meana* kept dropping in till late, and there were whispers and secret consultations. The decision arrived at was that we should make our flight in a northerly direction, as the British force was marching from the south. And so, early on the morning of the 29th, long before dawn, the *meanas* began to fill up.

We had expected to get a seat in one of the *meanas* but soon they were all full and there was no room left.

Javed Khan came up to us and said, 'Mariam, you had better get into the doctor's bullock-cart. You will be quite comfortable there.'

There was no other choice; and so the four of us—Granny, Mother, Anet and myself—took our seats in the cart. Beside us were the doctor's wife, her brothers' wives, and their children. The party set off at once, the men riding ahead on their horses, while the *meana*-bearers trotted along at a brisk pace, and our bullock-cart trundled along in the rear.

After about two hours we reached the village of Indarkha, some eight miles out of Shahjahanpur. The sun was up, and when we raised the cloth which formed the roof of our cart, we were astonished to find ourselves alone, for the *meanas* and horsemen had all disappeared. It seemed that our driver had taken a circuitous route, and we had been left well behind. And there we were, in a strange village, and with companions who were unknown to us.

The doctor enquired for a vacant house where we could rest, but there was none to be had. The villagers were quite indifferent to our plight, and told us that we could not put up in the village. But the doctor grew bold, and brought them round to the notion that it was their duty to accommodate us all, whoever we were. Finally they told him: 'There really is no vacant house in the village, but there is one thing you can do. At the southern end of the village, just opposite the big banyan tree, a new house is being built. It is not yet complete, but it is habitable. You may occupy it and remain in it for a short time.' And so we gladly got down from our cart and entered a mud structure which consisted of a line of rooms at one end, a courtyard in front, and a wall all round.

We were, in a way, the guests of the doctor and his wife,

and they were very kind to us. He was a Bengali Muslim, and had belonged to the Shahjahanpur regiment, but had severed his connection with it when it had marched out to Bareilly on the 1st of June 1857. Renting a house in the city, he soon acquired a reputation for possessing a healing hand and his practice flourished.

The doctor's sisters-in-law now busied themselves with digging and setting up an oven. One of them lighted it and set a pot of dal on the fire, while the other kneaded flour and began to make chapattis.

That evening, after everyone had eaten, the doctor came in and sat down, and in very civil language asked Mother to tell him who she was and what her circumstances were. Mother told him our story, which aroused his sympathy and compassion.

'Do you think,' asked Mother, 'do you think that British authority will be restored again?'

'I do not know about the distant future,' he replied, 'but certainly their authority will be restored. But, I was going to say that now you are with us, I hope you will make yourself at home and command me in any way you please. We are all in the same boat at present, so let us help each other as best we can.'

Mother was touched by his expression of goodwill, and we remained with him that night and the next day. Long after sunset, when everything was still and the noisy birds in the banyan tree were silent, the doctor came to Mother and said, 'Javed Khan has come and he wants to speak to you.'

'Why has he come?' asked Mother. 'What further business has he with us?'

'He seems most anxious to see you,' said the doctor. 'He cannot come in here, but you can speak to him at the door.'

Mother went out to meet Javed Khan and I, being curious, followed her and stood in the shadow of the wall.

'Mariam,' said Javed, 'I have come to say that the *Firangis* have reoccupied Shahjahanpur. You will not, of course, go to them, but don't forget the protection you have received from me.'

'I will not forget it,' said Mother. 'I am grateful to you for giving us shelter. And I will never forget the kindness shown to me by Kothiwali and Qamran.'

'I have only one request to make,' said Javed, uneasily shifting his weight from one foot to the other.

'Yes, what is it?' asked Mother.

'I know that the time has passed when I could speak of marrying your daughter,' he said. 'It is too late now to do anything about that. But will you permit me to see her once more, before I leave?'

'What good will that do?' began Mother; but impelled by some odd impulse, I stepped forward into the light and stood before Javed Khan.

He gazed at me in silence for about a minute, and for the first time I did not take my eyes away from his; then, without a smile or a word, he turned away and mounted his horse and rode away into the night.

The Final Journey

The doctor spoke to Mother the next morning: 'I have heard that yesterday the British army entered Shahjahanpur and that a civil government has already been established. Won't you go to them now that order has been restored?'

'A good suggestion,' said Mother, 'but whom will we know among them?'

The doctor said, 'You will be known at once by your voice, your accent and your manner, and perhaps you will find that some of your own relatives have arrived and are looking for you.'

The doctor then went to the village elders and told them that Mother was a European lady who had escaped during the massacre, and that she and her family wished to go into Shahjahanpur. Now that civil authority had been restored, would anyone undertake to carry them into town on his cart?

'You are not telling us anything we don't know,' said the headman. 'As soon as they stepped down from your bullock-cart we knew who they were.'

'How did you know?' asked the doctor.

'You must take me for a pumpkin,' said the old man. 'Why,

their very walk and their carriage indicated who they were. I marked their legs particularly. Those are not the feet, thought I, of women who go about barefoot. The way they treaded gingerly on the hot sand was proof enough. So they want to return to Shahjahanpur, do they? Well, I, Gangaram, shall take them in my own cart, and will reach them to any spot in Shahjahanpur where they wish to go. Tomorrow, in the morning, I shall be ready.'

We put our few belongings together and the next day, at about ten, we got into Gangaram's bullock-cart and set out for Shahjahanpur.

Our journey was uneventful. We reached the town late in the afternoon, and asked Gangaram to take us to our old house, for we did not know where else we could go. As we halted before the ruins of our old house, Mr Redman came up and told Mother briefly of his own escape and his family's. He informed us that the British Commander-in-Chief had reoccupied the district, but had since then continued his march to Bareilly, leaving a small force under Colonel Hall to guard Shahjahanpur. He said the town was not quite safe yet, as the Maulvi of Faizabad was still in control of the eastern boundary of the district; and he advised us to take shelter in the quarters he was occupying with his family. Mother was reluctant to accept his invitation, but we were still homeless and without any male protection, and so we stopped for the night in the building in which the Redmans had taken shelter. Here we met a party of three men whom my uncle had sent from Bharatpur to escort us to him. One was a mounted orderly named Nasim Khan, and the other two were servants of the Maharaja of Bharatpur. We came to know that the note sent through Mulia had actually been delivered to my uncle, and he took immediate steps for our rescue. Mother wept to see the familiar handwriting of her brother, and to read his letter which was full of affection and anxiety for our welfare, and contained a pressing invitation to come to him at Bharatpur where, he said, she would find a home for the rest of her life.

This was on Sunday, the 3rd of May 1858. Next morning we were surprised to see Pilloo's mother arrive in our midst— without Pilloo! She looked so upset that we felt certain Pilloo had been killed; but when at last we got her to speak coherently, we discovered that Pilloo had decided to remain behind of his own accord! He had grown so attached to Mangal Khan that he refused to come away, and his mother had to leave without him, hoping he would relent and follow her. But he never did. He preferred the companionship of the Pathan, and continued to live with him and his family. We never did understand his behaviour.

While we were listening to Pilloo's mother's tale of woe, Mr Redman returned from a visit to Colonel Hall's camp and invited us all to sit down to breakfast. We had, however, scarcely eaten anything, when an alarm was raised that the rebel army, under the Maulvi of Faizabad, was crossing the Khannaut by the bridge of boats. Nasim Khan, my uncle's man, who had gone to bathe his horse at the river, came running back at the same time, with the report that the enemy had driven in the vedettes of the little force led by the Colonel, who had entrenched himself in the old jail. There was a smell of battle in the air. The sound of bugles, the neighing of horses, the clatter of riderless mounts dashing across the plain, the dull thump of guns, and the confused noise of men running in different directions; all these were unmistakable signs that a considerable force had attacked the small British garrison.

We had no time to lose if we were to save ourselves. Gangaram's cart was still at our disposal. Though Mr Redman assured Mother that there was no danger, she was determined to make for the countryside where she thought we would be safer. We all climbed into the cart: Granny, Mother, myself, Anet, Pilloo's mother, and Vicky, the Redman's daughter. We were scarcely out of the compound gate when we heard shouts, and, amidst a cloud of dust, some ten or twelve troopers of the rebel cavalry came riding at full gallop, flourishing their sabres in the air, and surrounded our cart. We heard one of them say: 'Here are some of them, let us finish them off!' We expected that at any moment they would tear the covering from over our heads and bury their shining blades in our bosoms. Little Vicky held her neck with both her hands, saying: 'Let us all put our hands round our necks so that only our fingers will be cut off and our heads will be safe!'

Everyone was unnerved except for Mother. With her eyes almost starting out of their sockets, her face haggard and lined after months of sorrow and uncertainty, she grasped the handle of her knife, while with her free hand she removed the covering and put out her head. Her expression was enough to frighten even these ruffians who were thirsting for our blood. They reined back.

'What do you want with us, young fellows?' said Mother. 'Is there anything unusual about seeing so many helpless females fleeing from the city to escape dishonour and death?'

They did not stop to hear any more. Believing us to be Muslim women escaping from the city, they turned about and tackled Nasim Khan, who was riding behind us. But he had the presence of mind to tell them that he was a soldier of the faith, and that the women in the cart were his relatives, leaving the city as the *Firangis* had occupied it.

After the troopers had gone, Gangaram came down from the cart, and folding his hands before Mother, exclaimed: 'Well done! You are weak in body, but you have the spirit of a goddess! I do not know of any other woman who could have dealt so well with those men.'

Our adventures did not end there. Scarcely had we started moving again when, with a heavy thud, the cart fell down on its side. The axle had broken. There was no possibility of repairing it on the spot. We had to push on somehow, if we did not wish to fall in with another detachment of the enemy. The whirring and crashing of shells, the rattle of musketry, and the shouts of soldiers could be distinctly heard. We got down from the cart and, bidding goodbye to Gangaram, began to walk. We had no idea where we were walking, but it was our intention to get as far away as possible from the fighting.

After an hour of walking under the hot sun, we met a number of baggage carts passing along the highway. They belonged to the British army and were going, like ourselves, in the direction of Bareilly. One of the Sikh escorts saw us, and took pity on our condition. Mother had a high fever, and kept asking to be left alone by the wayside while we went on and found a place of safety. Nasim Khan dismounted and put her up on his horse, while he walked alongside, supporting Mother with his hands. At this moment another accident took place.

As Nasim Khan was dismounting, his pistol went off. This threw us all into a panic once more.

Nasim Khan looked puzzled and turned round several times before he realized what had happened. 'Oh, how stupid of me!' he exclaimed. 'I had cocked it when we met the maulvi's men. But, as usual, it goes off only when the enemy is out of sight!'

The Sikh soldiers burst into laughter, and we could not help joining in, though our own laughter was rather hysterical. Then the Sikhs offered us a lift in one of the baggage carts, and Anet, Vicky and I gratefully accepted it, for we were completely tired out.

We journeyed on like this for another three or four miles until we reached a small village where we were offered shelter. As it was now afternoon, and there was no shelter in the baggage cart from the blazing sun, we were only too glad to accept the villagers' hospitality.

Two days later, having hired a cart, we proceeded towards the south and, avoiding the main highways, reached Fatehgarh after four days. There we joined up with Mr Redman's party; and Mother called on the Collector, who gave her some 'succour-money', which enabled us to continue our journey to Bharatpur in comparative comfort.

Ten days later we were in the home of my uncle, where we found rest, shelter and comfort, until a rumour that a rebel force was about to cross the territory threw us all into a panic again. It was only a rumour. But the trials of the past year had made such an impression on my mind, that I was often to wake up terrified from nightmares in which I saw again those fierce swordsmen running through the little church, slashing at anyone who came in their way. However, our troubles were really over when we arrived at Bharatpur, and we settled down to a quiet and orderly life, though it was never to be the same again without my father.

We did not hear again of Lala Ramjimal and his family. We would have liked to thank him for his kindness to us, and for risking his own life in protecting us; but beyond the knowledge that he had settled with his family in Bareilly, we received no further news of him.

We heard that Kothiwali and Qamran and their families eventually returned to Shahjahanpur, after life had returned to normal. But Javed Khan disappeared and was never seen again. Perhaps he had escaped into Nepal. It is more probable that he was caught and hanged with some other rebels. Secretly, I have always hoped that he succeeded in escaping. Looking back on those months when we were his prisoners, I cannot help feeling a sneaking admiration for him. He was very wild and muddle-headed, and often cruel, but he was also very handsome and gallant, and there was in him a streak of nobility which he did his best to conceal. But perhaps I really admire him because he thought I was beautiful.

NOTES

Pathans formed thirty per cent of the Muslim population of Shahjahanpur (Muslims forming twenty-three per cent of the entire population) according to the 1901 census. Most were cultivators, although many were landed proprietors of the district. (True Pathans are descendants of Afghan immigrants.) 'Their attitude during the Mutiny cost them dear, as many estates were forfeited for rebellion.' (*Gazetteer*)

Most of the rebel leaders were either killed or brought to trial, and in all cases their property was confiscated. Ghulam Qadir Khan died shortly after the reoccupation and his estates were seized.

'The number of Muslims whose services (to the British) were recognized was extremely small, as, apart from the two men who sheltered their European kinsman, Mr Maclean, in pargana Tilhar, the only persons recognized were Nasir Khan and Amir Ali of Shahjahanpur, who buried the bodies of the Englishmen murdered on the occasion of the outbreak, and Ghulam Husain, who saved the commissariat buildings from destruction and for some time protected several Hindus on the district staff.' (p. 150, *Gazetteer*, 1900)

'At Jalalabad, the tehsildar Ahmed Yar Khan at once showed his sympathy with the rebels by releasing several criminals under arrest. On the arrival of Ghulam Qadir at Shahjahanpur, the tehsildar was raised to the dignity of *nezim*, but his tyranny aroused the resistance of the Rajputs of Khandar and other villages.' (p. 248, *Gazetteer*)

'Mr Lemaistre, a clerk in the Collector's office, was killed in the church, and the fate of his daughter is unknown.'

(*The Meerut Mofussilite*, 1858)

The city was populated by a large body of Afghans sent there by Bahadur Khan (a soldier of fortune in the service of Jehangir and later Shahjahan), at that time serving beyond the Indus. The story goes that these Afghans belonged to fifty-two tribes and that each had its own mohalla, many quarters of the city to this day being named after Pathan clans . . . . The history of the town and of Bahadur Khan's family is told in an anonymous work called the *Shahjahanpurnama* or the *Anhar-ul-bahr*, written in 1839, and also in the *Akbar-i-Muhabbat* of Nawab Muhabbat Khan.

I first heard the story of Mariam and her daughter from my father, who was born in the Shahjahanpur military cantonment a few years after the Mutiny. That, and my interest in the accounts of those who had survived the 1857 uprising, took me to Shahjahanpur on a brief visit in the late 1960s. It was one of those small U.P. towns that had resisted change, and there were no high-rise buildings or blocks of flats to stifle the atmosphere. I found the old church of St Mary's without any difficulty, and beside it a memorial to those who were killed there on that fateful day. It was surrounded by a large, open parade ground, bordered by mango groves and a few old bungalows. It couldn't have been very different in Ruth Labadoor's time. The little River Khannaut was still crossed by a bridge of boats.

THE SENSUALIST

THE SENSUALIST

❧

'When you hold him in your two hands, you should first
honour him duly and then devour him. You will find him
with flesh upon his bones, but leave him as the remnants of
a fish, which are spines and skin. But what am I saying?
Even when there is no fish left, you shall by no means cast
the bones aside till you have cracked them and sucked the
marrow. He must be left incapable of work, unable even to
stumble, with wandering glances, emptied, broken,
finished . . .'

Damodaragupta, The Lessons of a Bawd,
8th century A.D.)

I

THIS RANGE IS BARE and rocky, with steep hillsides suddenly
rearing up in front of the tired, discouraged traveller. The grass
is short and almost colourless. An eagle circles high overhead
and the burning sun, striking through the rarefied atmosphere,
is reflected from the granite rocks. Caves of banded light
shimmer along the dusty mountain path. I walk alone and I am
thirsty.

The last stream disappeared into the valley ten miles back,
and this region seems to be devoid of any kind of moisture. The
villages, the terraced fields, have been left behind. The pine
forests are a purple blanket on the next mountain. I have a long

way to go to reach the river and the town. I must have taken the wrong path sometime back, but this doesn't worry me very much. I have lost my way in the hills before and found it again simply by following the line of a valley; but I will not reach the river tonight. It is already half-past three and the September sun is low in the sky.

I have a strong desire to sit down and rest but there is no shade anywhere except under the big boulders which look as though they might topple over at any moment. Huge lizards bask on the rocks, scuttling away at my approach. Where do they get their moisture? Some subterranean pocket of water must exist here to sustain these creatures, because except for the eagle, I find no other sign of life.

But this path must lead somewhere. There are no mule-tracks, no imprint of human feet to give me confidence, but no mountain path can exist without someone to wear down the sharp rocks and prevent the grass from growing. Someone, at some time, must pass this way, and beyond the next hill there should be a village and grass that is green; perhaps a lime tree with a patch of fragrant shade and a glass of sour curds and a draw at the hookah.

Even while I dream of it, I find a patch of emerald grass at my feet, and trickling through it a sliver of clear water. It comes from a rock in the hillside. Just below the rock the water runs into a small pool made by the human hand, and it is the overflow from this that runs across the path. I drink from the little pool and find the water cool and sweet. I splash my face and let the water run down my neck and arms. Then, looking up, I notice a cave high up on the hillside, with the narrowest of paths leading up to it. There will be shade there and a place to rest.

I clamber up the steep path. The dazzling sun leaps on me like a beast of prey, but I climb higher with the aid of rocks and tufts of grass. The sky turns round and round. Never has it looked so blue.

There is someone squatting, crouching at the entrance to the cave. As the sun is in my eyes, I cannot be sure if the creature is human or animal. It doesn't move. It is black and almost formless.

But as I come nearer, it takes the shape of a man.

He is naked except for a tightly wound loincloth. Long, matted hair falls below his shoulders. The ribs show through his chest. His skin has been burnt black by the sun and toughened into old leather by the dry wind that sweeps across the mountains. The eyes are bright black pinpoints in a cavernous face.

'It is some time since I had a visitor.' His voice is deep, sonorous.

I stare at this creature who looks like primitive man but speaks like an angel.

'I lost my way,' I explain.

'I had intended that you should. In a moment of weakness I felt a need for human company, and sent my thoughts abroad to confuse the mind of the first traveller who rounded the bend of the next mountain!'

'I was certainly confused. I hope you will be able to set me on the right path again.'

'All in good time. Will you not sit down here in the shade? I assure you that I am perfectly harmless. I am not even an eccentric, as you might think. For that matter, I am not even lonely. It was just a whim that made me desire your company. I hope you don't mind?'

'No.'

I do not know what to make of him as yet. Here is a recluse who has obviously spent a long time far from the haunts of men. I do not expect him to think or speak like other men. I realize that my norm is not his, and that, living entirely within himself, he must have attained dimensions of thought that are beyond my reach. The question that troubles me is, 'Can he harm me physically?' I am not afraid of the power of his thoughts, for I have confidence in my own.

He sits in the dust, and as there is no sign of anything resembling a comfortable seat, I drop to the ground, some five feet away from him. It is hot sitting there in the sun, but the only shade is inside the cave, and I do not feel inclined to enter that place. Besides, it will soon be evening and it will be cooler.

II

The recluse looks at me, sizing me up, and I recognize the eyes of one with hypnotic gifts. I look away from him, although I know that it is not necessary for him to look at me in order to enter my mind. This is purely a defensive reaction on my part. I can feel the weight of his consciousness and I am immediately aware that he bears no hostility towards me. No action or word of his can make me feel easier than the aura of hopelessness that emanates from his mind, communicating itself to me.

'I suppose you practise many austerities,' I say. 'I admire men who can withdraw from the world, from a life of the senses. But I am not sure that I would want to do the same.'

'You haven't had enough of the senses, perhaps.'

'Did you have too much?'

'Yes, but that was not the only reason . . . .' He gives me an enigmatic half-smile and I wonder, how long has he been here, and how old is he? It is impossible to tell from his appearance. He might have been here five years or an eternity.

'Perhaps you are hungry?' he asks.

'No. I ate at noon. I was very thirsty, but the spring at the bottom of the hill quenched my thirst. What do you get to eat here?'

'I eat very little. My existence is not entirely supernatural—not yet, anyway—and I must sustain this body of mine a little longer. But I have managed to destroy my former interest in food, and my body gets along quite well on the nourishment it receives. It is a question of conditioning, I suppose.'

'At some stage in your life you received formal education,' I observe.

'Oh yes, a fairly good education, although I never completed a single course. The learning I acquired has made it all the more difficult for me to accept this life. I love books. Therefore I do not keep books.'

'But why? Why give up what you love?'

'One can't give up some things and keep others. To reject the materialism of this life one must reject even the pleasures of the intellect. Otherwise, accept it fully—as I did once—and savour the delights of the senses to the full. Don't do things by half-measures. I never believed in the middle way, in moderation in all things. It never satisfied me. I took every pleasure there was to take, and then, satiated, I took my leave of the world and all that it meant to me.'

'With no regrets?'

'With every regret.'

'Then, I ask again—why?'

'I can give you a hundred answers to your question, and all of them would be right, and yet none of them would be right. For there is not one answer, but many.'

He rises to stretch himself. He does so with a single elastic movement, without the help of his hands. There is hardly any flesh between his skin and his bones, but his skin is as tough as buffalo-hide. He must be impervious to wind and weather.

He looks out over the bare rolling hills and the valley and at the silver river twisting across the distant plain like some mythological serpent. It is the great river we see, most sacred of rivers. To bathe in its waters is to wash away all sin.

'Have you come from Kapila?'

'I am on my way there.'

Kapila lies on the banks of the river where it emerges from a gorge in the mountains. It is an ancient city, much favoured by the sages of old.

'The stones by the river are beautifully smooth,' he says. 'Once, picking one up I took it between my hot hands, polishing it with care. I did not find it round enough, and I threw it far into the river so that the water might rub away its angles for a few thousand years longer. To me, as to a stone, a thousand years are but a day.'

He sinks to his haunches again and his long hair falls across his shoulders hiding his face from me. Although he has rejected the past, he cannot help brooding upon it. We cannot destroy our memories until we have succeeded in destroying ourselves.

'Are you comfortable?' he asks.

'Not very, but I did not expect to find comfort here.'

'There are some old rugs and skins inside.'

'I am all right. It is cool out here.'

'The nights are cold. You will sleep in the cave with me?'

'I should be on my way.'

'You cannot reach Kapila tonight. There is no shelter between this place and the river.'

I do not say anything. I have a feeling that the cave will not welcome me. It has about it an aura of damp and decay, the sweetness of a corpse soaked in scented water. But at the same time I feel that if this recluse really wants me to stay, I will find it difficult to resist his will. Those who live alone can be very strong. Having mastered their own minds (or gone mad in the attempt), they have little difficulty in mastering the minds of others.

I see the pine-tops dipping gently on the next mountain, and a little later I feel the evening breeze on my cheeks. I am still young, and a cool uplifting breeze always stirs me to the marrow. It is the best aphrodisiac in the world.

III

'The body of a woman,' he says, as though something of what I have been musing on has reached him, 'the body of a woman is an inexhaustible source of wonder and delight.'

I look at him with unfeigned surprise.

'Oh, of course I have finished with all that,' he says. 'That is obvious, isn't it? But, looking at me, you might get the impression that I have always been celibate. Nothing could be further from the truth. As a youth, I had an insatiable appetite for pleasure. It overrode all other considerations. I moved from one conquest to another in the single-minded pursuit of sexual pleasure. I suppose it was partly due to the woman servant who looked after me as a boy. She had some crazy idea that I was gifted with supernatural powers in these matters. She gave me strange potions and concoctions to drink!

'She was a big woman with broad hips and fleshy buttocks that quivered at every stride. Early every morning, even before the sun was up, she took me down the steps to bathe in the cold waters of the river. There was hardly anyone about at that time. Her huge, heavy breasts smelling of musk brushed against my cheeks as she poured the powerful waters over my head. She held me firmly between her thighs and laved my back with her rough hands. Later, in the small courtyard of our house she would massage my limbs with mustard oil and with her fingers she would press at the root of my penis, a sensation both painful and pleasurable.

'Sometimes, when my parents were away, she would make me lie down with her, lie down upon her naked and mountainous flesh, and she would take my mouth between her heavy lips and thrust her tongue against mine. This kissing was always pleasurable and I never tired of it. I was a merry monkey, full of good intentions, trying to satisfy an elephant!'

'Stop!' I say, unable to control my laughter. 'Why do you tell me all this?'

'I thought you wanted to hear my story.'

'Did I say so? Well, I didn't think you would be so explicit.'

'Would you like a more romantic tale?'

'No. Carry on. Just so you finish it quickly and let me go my way.'

'Would you hear more of this woman who instructed me in the hidden arts of pleasure?'

'If she is relevant . . .'

'Oh, but she is relevant. She was the sorceress who helped me become, not a god, but a satyr! There has been no romance in my life, no "falling in love" as you call it—except, perhaps, once, oh yes, once! From the beginning I was trained in the art of seduction, in the art of extracting from a woman all that she had to give—exhausting her, drawing on her hidden resources, feeding on her like a vampire, until she had nothing to give and was completely destroyed. Of course I did not reach this stage at that early age; but already at puberty, I was working towards it, I felt certain powers growing within me. It was power that I sought, not simply the appeasement of lust.

'A man who lived beside the river taught me to concentrate, to channelise my thoughts in such a way that I could gain a measure of mastery over the minds of others . . . every day, for an hour, I sat cross-legged on a smooth earthen floor and gazed steadily at a small black phallus placed a few feet away from me. As I gazed upon the stone, it seemed to grow before me, swelling and throbbing, and I experienced the sensation of having discarded my own sack of a body to enter the substance of the stone. It was only momentary. A spider crawling over my foot brought me back to the reality of my material self. Many hours of concentration were to pass before I could ignore the movements of spiders or insects.

'At home I practised before a mirror, concentrating on the space between my eyebrows. This was strenuous at first, and a throbbing headache would often result. But after a few weeks

I found I could stand before the glass for an indefinite period, concentrating on the space between my eyes.

'I concentrated on sounds. I could close my eyes, admit into my mind one sound—the tinkling of a bell, or the drip of a tap—and live with that sound, to the exclusion of all else. After some time, the tinkle would become the clanging of many great bells or the drip of the tap would be a thunderous waterfall. I had to be shaken out of trances I had entered. My mother was worried about my strange behaviour. My father, whose many business interests absorbed his own sexual drive, could not be bothered. Only the woman servant, my mentor and aide, was pleased. Who was she and where did she come from? Nobody seemed to know. She had come to our house soon after I was born and had made herself so useful that my parents kept her even after I was long past my childhood. She had no children of her own but it was said that she had been married once, that her husband had died and left her very rich, and that she had squandered her money on some obscure cult. The more orthodox did not recognize this cult and associated it with sorcery.

'Well, it was sorcery of a kind.

'Slowly I was developing my adolescent will to a point where I could impose it on others. I found it easier to do this when I closed my eyes. Then I could shut out all visual distractions and direct my thoughts towards the person I wished to influence. The first time I succeeded in doing this I thought it was purely accidental. Perhaps it was, that first time; but its success gave me confidence in my growing powers.

'It was a warm, languid afternoon and I felt the slow turning of desire as I lay on the string cot in the bedroom. Through the half-open door I could see our servant stretched out on her cot, her waist bare, her hair loose, her lips slightly parted, her eyes only half-closed. (Even when she was sound asleep, her eyes were never completely closed.) Desire welled up within me. I longed for her harsh kisses and rough caresses. But nothing was possible with my mother present, and I found myself wishing that I could be so gifted with magic powers that I would be able to make people disappear (or appear) at will! This, I knew, could only be achieved after hundreds of years of training, and one had first to learn to live a hundred years! Our thoughts are so tame and timid to begin with that we seldom realize, until it is too late, what concentrated powers lie untapped in our minds. And for those who learn too quickly, there is madness . . . .

'But I turned towards my mother, and closing my eyes, directed my thoughts at her, willing her to leave the room, the house—go anywhere, do anything, until I willed her back again. For five minutes I assaulted her in this way, and when I opened my eyes I found her staring at me with a rather bewildered expression.

"What time is it?" I asked.

She glanced at the small gold watch on her wrist and said, "It is only three . . . . Is there anything you want?"

' "No, but you asked me to remind you to go out at three o'clock." She had not made such a request but did not seem surprised at the suggestion. She got up slowly, stretched herself and went to the mirror to arrange her hair.

' "I have to go out at three," she said. "But I forget what I wanted . . ."

' "You were to visit someone."

' "Yes, that's it. Thank you for reminding me. It's your cousin Samyukta's birthday. Would you like to accompany me? They are always asking about you."

' "No. I do not like them. Besides, I have a headache."

' "Then I will wake Mulia and tell her to press your forehead."

' "It's all right, Mother. I will wake her myself when you have gone. Let her sleep a little longer."

'Mulia had been awake for some time and she came to me as soon as my mother left the house and began pressing my forehead, rubbing her thumbs over my eyelids and then pressing gently down on my temples. I let her do this for some time. I did have a headache, due perhaps to the effort I had made in shifting my mother from the house! It soon went, however, thanks to Mulia's ministrations.

'The voluptuous creature soon stood before me in all her monstrous beauty, a feast for the eye, a mountain worthy of conquest. I have never understood the misguided attitude of most people to heavy, fleshy women, who are generally considered ugly. Surely, in the generous abundance of their flesh, their broad dips and curves and gradual inclines—bodies where the questing lover may wander freely and unhindered; where he can stop and rest, or turn a corner and discover some hidden recess—surely these magnificent women have a marked superiority over those of a more conventional build? They have so much more to offer!

'Why go into detail? The memory no longer excites me and would only disturb your own peace of mind. I'm only trying to give you some idea of my development as a destructive force. Suffice it to say that my former governess was as thrilled as I at the achievement, and now declared herself to be my devoted paramour.

'Nor was it simply a matter of having qualified as a lover. The physical conquest was only half the victory. It could not have been achieved so completely without my having gained some command over her personality. Mulia had of course always intended that I should be hers. In spite of her imposing proportions, the strength of her arm, and her delightful witchcraft, her instincts were truly feminine. She had sought to conquer me only in order that she might be conquered. I had yet to impose my will on someone who resisted it. I had yet to enslave someone who held me in hatred and contempt. That would be the real challenge—the conquest, the ego-destruction of someone who had so far remained inviolate!'

IV

'I must go now,' I say. 'It is not yet dark. I can be at the river before ten o'clock.'

'I advise you to stay,' urges my 'host'. 'It is not safe to walk these hills at night.'

'I am not afraid of wild animals.'

'Nor should you be, by day. But at night who is to tell which is beast and which is demon? For the evil spirits of these mountains, chained to the rocks by day, move abroad at night.'

'Do they trouble you, then?'

'They do not trouble me. I am too powerful for any kind of spirit save one—the spirit of an innocent! But come inside, it is getting cold out here.'

'It is dark in the cave.'

'I have a lamp. You have nothing to fear if you are pure at

heart. Have you ever destroyed the soul of another human?'

'No.'

'Then what have you to fear?'

'Those who destroy souls.'

'Ah! Then you need not fear me, because I destroyed my last soul, my own, a long time ago.'

It is cold but dry inside the cave, which extends for some twenty feet into the side of the mountain. I sit down on a goat-skin and watch the recluse making a fire at the entrance to the cave.

'I will prepare some food for you,' he says.

'No, don't bother. I am not hungry.'

'As you wish. But I will light the fire to keep the animals away. Sometimes I am visited by a leopard or a hyena.'

The fire throws a warm red glow over his emaciated frame, and for a moment or two, as his shadow leaps across the walls of the cave, he seems a little larger than life. When he turns to me, his body comes between me and the fire, and he is now a crouching black phantom, featureless, faceless, formless, who might at any moment leap upon me in the dark to suck the blood from my fingers and feet. But his voice, as always, reassures me.

'Do you mind if I talk?' he asks.

'Not at all. I have no desire to sleep.'

'Nor have I. When I sleep, I am defenceless. Then my mind is invaded by sirens and beautiful women with twisted feet, and young maidens covered with boils, and they ravish me and I am helpless against them. By day, I am master of my own mind, and remembered flesh cannot touch me.'

'So you have not entirely escaped the world you left behind?'

'It is another world that invades my soul. Sometimes I sit up into the early hours of the morning, so that I may avoid these visitations. For when they possess me, they drain me of all my strength, as I once drained others of their life-blood. But I will not trouble you with a tale of torment. I will tell you instead, of the powers I developed as a youth, and what use I put them to! Did I mention my cousin Samyukta?

'I did not like her and she did not like me. We bore each other hatred and malice—and that was enough to make us physically attractive to each other.

'She was a pretty girl, but coy and very aloof, and I resented her airs and graces. I was never much to look at, and whenever we were in the same room she behaved as though I did not exist, although she was perfectly aware of my presence. She did her best to humiliate me. If she said anything, it was to comment on the careless way in which I dressed. But I was indifferent to my appearance. People were not impressed with me until I spoke to them or until they came within the ambit of my questing mind. Once I was certain of my powers, I could dominate most individuals; but certain barriers had first to be broken down.

'Samyukta and I were of the same age, and at the time I am telling you about, we were seventeen or eighteen. Mulia now called me her young stallion. But cousin Samyukta, unaware of my gifts, treated me with contempt and laughed at me whenever we passed each other on the road.

'I had always looked away at her approach, and that had been my mistake. But my joustings with Mulia had given me a new confidence in the presence of women, and I knew that my cousin, for all her supercilious ways, was not very sure of herself. One day I saw her walking along the opposite pavement, accompanied by two girls, school friends. Before she could notice me, I crossed the road and was standing in her way. She gave a start, but before she could speak (and her words were to be avoided, for they were as poisoned barbs), I fixed her eye with mine and held her motionless, while her expression changed from scorn to bewilderment to fear. At that moment, I am sure she felt I was capable of doing her violence. Later when we grew intimate, she swore that during that unexpected encounter she had seen a small yellow flame spring up in my right eye. I remember that she went pale, and when I saw her colour change I knew I had gained the ascendancy. I was so thoroughly aroused that I had difficulty in restraining myself from touching her on the street, in the presence of her friends. When I stood aside to let them pass, the colour flooded back to Samyukta's face, and she went strutting up the street, head in the air, as though she had just given me the snub of a lifetime.

'I smiled inwardly and walked home to Mulia. I told her of my intentions. She was not jealous. Knowing that she possessed my heart, she was prepared for others to possess my flesh.

' "But how do we arrange this?" I asked. "How do we get her here?"

' "We do not get her here. You go there, prince."

' "But she has a mother and an aunt."

' "They go out together on Saturday mornings. And on Saturday mornings Samyukta does not go to school. She prepares the midday meal, while her mother and aunt relax in the bazaar."

' "You are well informed, Mulia."

'She gave me a look of slavish devotion, took my hand and put my fingers to her lips. "You will never tire of me, will you?"

' "I will tire of you when you are old."

' "Ah! at least you do not try to deceive me."

' "You are not to be deceived."

' "No, but I am happy that you have told me the truth. I will preserve my burden of a body for another five, perhaps ten years, for as long as you desire it, and then I will go away."

'The next day Samyukta and her mother visited us. I did not make my presence felt, but sat quietly in a corner of the room, while tea was served. The women talked about other women, the price of vegetables, and the horoscope of a certain young man who might be a suitable match for Samyukta. My cousin sat between her mother and mine, saying very little, but occasionally casting a glance in my direction. Outwardly, I paid no attention to her, but after some time I closed my eyes, and conjuring up a vision of her face, dwelt upon it for some time, turning my thoughts towards her, creating a flow of mental energy that I hoped would reach her in waves of telepathic power! My intention, of course, was to impose my will on her in such a way that she would be absolutely receptive when the right opportunity brought us together. I wanted to be sure of her response well in advance.

'When I opened my eyes, I gazed full upon Samyukta. Her eyes were drawn inexorably to mine, and for more than a minute we gazed intensely at each other, until even our mothers could not help noticing.

' "Why are you staring so?" asked Samyukta's mother, who was facing her daughter and had her back to me.

'And my mother, who could not see Samyukta's face said, "Do not stare like that, my son. You frighten me."

'My mother, a nervous creature, had in fact grown afraid of me during the past year or two. She could sense certain changes taking place in me without being able to understand them. She knew that Mulia and I were very close, and while she was relieved that I did not make too many demands on her, she was uneasy because I went to the servant woman with my confidences. Already dominated by my father, my mother was not one to assert herself in any way. She was content to put away money for my "future" and to make occasional donations to the temples. She was certain that there was only one way into the hearts of the gods, and that was through the hands of the priests.

'And so, because my mother was frightened by my look, I turned my face to the window. A band of hermaphrodites was passing by in the street. Just then I longed to be one of them, the perfect synthesis of man and woman.

'Could Samyukta and I uniting lose our genders in each other and be as perfect as the hermaphrodites? For a few moments, perhaps; and then, uncoupled, would lose ourselves again until guided by the itching of desire, we took refuge once more in each other's embrace.'

'When the confrontation did take place about a week later, it came as something of an anti-climax. She was no novice. There was no pearl to prise loose from its shell, no citadel to lay waste. Even so, it must have been a novel experience for her, because she did not expect an assault as fierce as mine. She swooned away before the hour was up. I waited until she opened her eyes, and then I assaulted her again, until she moaned and scratched and bit. I had expected to stain her bed crimson with my lust. Instead it was she who drew blood. My arms and shoulders bore the wounds for weeks. Men have nothing to teach women. We can subdue women but we cannot teach them anything!

'Are you listening? Good. I am not trying to lecture you, nor do I wish to titillate you with an erotic tale. There is a principle contained in life that is more powerful than life itself. The body's rapture cannot be divorced from the rapture of the soul. It took me a long time to realize this. Certainly, at the age of sixteen, I had no thought for my soul. I believed in nothing, only love and its pleasures; and the strengthening of my mind and will was carried out with the object of gratifying my senses. I had no ambitions other than to glory in the delights that are there for all those who seek them—I was not interested in power or position. My father had money, and I was his only son. Therefore my first duty was to spend his fortune.

'My father, a man I hardly knew, had spent a lifetime in amassing wealth. He manufactured electric bulbs, shoe polish, and a hair-darkening cream. (The same ingredients went into both polish and cream.) On those rare occasions when he entertained his friends, he liked to tell them about the struggles of his youth and how he hawked his wares on the streets of Delhi. Although he had never been to school, he was determined that his son should receive the best possible education. After I had taken my degree, he would send me to Oxford!

'The thought of spending half my life in college horrified me. I was determined to fail my exams in order that I might discourage my parents from sending me to college. My father had lakhs of rupees, and competent managers to run his factories. I would be quite happy to take the money and leave the factories in the capable hands of his managers—they would see to it that the business continued to bring in profits. I could see no point in hoarding wealth and believed it to be a son's first duty to spend money as fast as his father could make it.

'My mother seemed to think so too, because though she was frugal by nature, she tried to get me the money I needed for my clothes, rings, watches, entertainments, and wines. She always gave me what I wanted, even if it meant dipping into her own allowance.

'My affair with cousin Samyukta was to last for over a year. But in the course of it I was to have several other adventures, some of them rather expensive. But I cannot dismiss Samyukta so quickly. She was a girl of some character, and when I look back on that wild and wilful time I realize that she had more to offer than most of the professional courtesans whom I visited from time to time. She did not give herself to me for mercenary reasons. I was a challenge to her own strong sensuous nature, and she matched my aggressive skills with her own passionate and fevered response. She was one of those restless women whose physical demand can never be wholly satisfied. If I was with her, she was happy and satisfied; but if a few days passed and I could not visit her, she grew pensive, irritable, burning up in the fever of her own desire. We grew to like each other. That's strange, isn't it? Because we had never liked each other before.

'But of course there were a few other adventures.

'A youth of eighteen who suddenly finds himself a sexual warrior becomes quite rampant, and pursues his prey indiscriminately. Too indiscriminately for his own good. The pleasure houses of Kapila were few, and did not offer any very startling attractions. Most of the painted trollops were past their prime, and their patrons had first of all to be bemused with bhang or opium so that they did not look too closely at their battle-scarred partners.

'But there was one who was different . . .'

V

'One evening I pushed open the door of an old house teetering over the riverbank, and looked into a narrow passage dimly lighted by a green paper lantern. From within came the sounds of flute and sitar. A curtain was drawn back and an old woman came towards me. She was a withered old crone who glanced at me with an enticing leer and led me to the top of a staircase where she took my money with a swooping, gull-like movement. She then led me into a small, dark room where I was able to make out a wide couch, raised just above the floor and decorated with a gay but tattered rug.

' "I will fetch Shankhini for you," she said. "You will be happy with her."

'My eyes gradually grew accustomed to the dim light, and I was able to see the girl who entered the room and closed and bolted the door behind her. She drew near with a composed and friendly manner, as if I was an old acquaintance. And in some ways I suppose I must have been, for to the prostitute, all men are one—unity in diversity!

'Except for a diaphanous wrap of silk and a narrow girdle, the girl was completely naked. She wore white jasmine blossoms in her black hair. She looked little more than a child, although her hips were graceful and well-rounded.

' "Shall I dance?" she asked. "Tell me what you would like me to do."

' "Dance," I said. I had been unprepared for her youthfulness.

'And so she danced beneath the greenish moon of the paper lantern, and the only sound was the soft fall of her feet upon the mat. The heavy door shut out the music downstairs, the street-cries, the hollow boom of the river. It was a dance without music, without sound, and I felt as though those small feet were dancing gently on my heart, on the very source of my life. When the dancing ceased the girl smiled at me with an expression simultaneously wise, childlike, and passionate. Looking like a sleek green-gold cat in the light from the lantern, she subsided softly on to the couch beside me. She had been trained in the art of making love. And yet beneath it all lay an undercurrent of innocence. I think this was because she suffered from no feelings of guilt. She had been brought up to please men as though this was her sole duty in life. She had not known and did not seek any other kind of existence.

'She did not let a moment pass in which she did not seem to be giving herself. Her aspect was continually changing. She did not surrender even one of her secrets without giving me an inkling that another still remained to be disclosed.

' "Do you find me beautiful?" she asked. It was her stock question. And I gave her the expected answer: "You are the most beautiful girl I have ever seen."

'She smiled at me with her large, childlike eyes. Then her head came between me and the lantern, and her face seemed to be framed in a halo of green light.

' "Forget everything," she said. "Here there is no time, neither night nor day."

' "Let me do something for you," I said, feeling suddenly generous towards this girl. "Let me give you something."

' "I take nothing," she answered. "It is for the old woman to take. You must only tell me that I am beautiful and that I have made you happy."

' "You are very beautiful. You make me very happy."

' "I have heard it a hundred times. But I still like to hear it." And then, drawing close to me and gazing into my eyes she said, "You are very important to yourself, are you not?" She raised her hand to my brow, and tapping my temples with her painted fingers, said: "There is a cold fire there! It is stronger than all other flames, and seems brighter. It fights against the warmth of the heart, and will quench the fire of many hearts. So you must always move from one to another. What are you looking for? There is nothing to find. Forget everything. Love me, and forget!" '

'Forget? Can mind forget? It was written by a sage of old: "Remember past deeds, O my mind, remember!" But the injunction is unnecessary, because we are remembering all the time—even when we say we have forgotten. And can the memory of past deeds really shape the nature of future deeds? Man cannot help but live in conformity with his nature; his subconscious is more powerful than his conscious mind, and he cannot deny his body until he removes himself from the scene of all physical activity. It is useless to struggle against one's nature. Some believe that there is salvation in struggle—they are merely showing that they do not know what salvation is.

'At first I sought to assuage my restlessness by communing with nature. I searched for truth in the rippling of streams and the rustling of leaves; in the blue heavens or the wilderness of the jungle; in the behaviour of men, beasts and plants; in the superabundance of sunshine that pours down in India. But our bodies germinate as the resurrections of nature. Each bubbling spring, swelling fruit or bursting blossom, reminded me that I too was part of this burgeoning process, so that it was not long before the throb in my loins was as tenderly painful as the unfolding of a rosebud.

'I am not trying to give you the impression that those years of youthful dissipation were interspersed with a vague searching for my inner self. Once again, I have anticipated . . . . The search, if you can call it that, came later. I am merely trying to tell you how I came to be here. This cave is the end of all searching but before the search there was the indulgence, and the indulgence was a part of the process that brought me to this place.'

VI

'And meanwhile, I grew in Mulia's love.

'She tended me as a gardener tends a favourite plant, giving it all the water and nourishment it needs. Special sweets were made for me. Ancient recipes were turned up, and sherbets of many hues and flavours were given to me morning, noon and night. I had given up asking what they contained. I left everything to Mulia. She tried each potion before passing it to me, to make sure that the brew was not too potent. I was convinced that one day I would find her lying dead on the floor, poisoned by one of her own concoctions.

'But I was not the sort of person who could give anything in return for love. As soon as I found someone growing tender towards me, I withdrew into myself, became remote and cold, so that the love that might have been mine was squandered in an empty void. I was determined to leave them with a feeling of insufficiency. Those who gave themselves to me suffered for it. I became cruel and callous towards them. Was it victory I wanted, or the chance to spurn victory? Samyukta was made to suffer in this way. But Mulia, twenty years older than me, was an exception. I seldom withheld my affections from her, I knew that she was wholly for me and with me. My wealth, strength, welfare and happiness were her sole concern. I was the ruling passion of her life and I knew that if I was taken from her, she would lose the impetus for living.

'Shankhini, the woman who lived by night, was in a different category altogether. All men had immersed themselves in her, and she could not be expected to love an individual man any more than a man could be expected to love her. But what was the mysterious attraction that drew me back to her again and again? She had no hold over me. And the old crone who ran the house, certain that I was enamoured with the lithe and boyish figure of this unusual girl, put the price up at every visit. I did not care, I could afford it—or rather my father could afford it. It even gave me a sensuous thrill to hand over the money to the old woman. Not that the old woman excited me in any way; she would have found it hard to arouse a camel! But the business of handing over the money in exchange for an hour or two of personal possession, ownership, of the girl who lived always in green shadows, was a thrill in itself.

'But would I ever be able to arouse her to any degree of rapture? Although I restrained myself, and took the time and trouble to create in her some crisis of response, she seemed incapable of reaching a state of ecstasy and abandonment. There had been too many men, she told me. Coupling with them had become a mechanical process, and there was no intensity or pleasurable sensation in it. She went through the motions, expertly and in order to satisfy those who had paid for the pastime, but she could not be expected to enjoy the game herself.'

'So perhaps she was a challenge to me, and that was why I went to her. I wanted to elicit from her a genuine, not a trained response. I think she preferred me to most of her customers, many of whom were pot-bellied businessmen whose overburdened waistlines gave their manhood a shrivelled aspect. Obesity is not conducive to effective love-making.

'It may seem strange, but I liked to talk to Shankhini. In those days, there were few to whom I could talk freely. Mulia was illiterate, and her talk was confined to practical affairs, my needs and bodily functions. She had no other interests outside her small world of service. My mother was old-fashioned and superstitious and so we had very little to say to each other. I hardly ever saw my father. Fellow students at school and college considered me a snob, a wealthy aristocrat, a privileged member of a feudal society. They envied me, and were a little afraid of me too, because unlike others from affluent families, I made no attempt to ingratiate myself with them. Had I lavished money on a few young men, I would soon have had a following, but I had no need of sycophants. I could live with myself, and within myself, provided there were always these women to bear the burden of my ego.

'Samyukta was intelligent, but there was no real meeting of our minds—the relationship was purely sensual in nature. I gave her the satisfaction she needed after she had exhausted herself intellectually. She was studying medicine, and had to work very hard. Whenever she stopped working, she wanted to stop thinking. I could supply no intellectual need, nor was that what she wanted. But when I moved within her, she cried with ecstasy, she was convulsed with joy; but afterwards she had little or nothing to say. She turned over, lay flat on her belly, and slept.

'And so in the evenings, as the lights were lit in the bazaar, and pilgrims placed little leaf-boats filled with rose petals on the waters of the river, I made my way to the tall old house with the green paper-lanterns, and asked for Shankhini.

'She was not always available in the evenings. So I took to visiting her in the afternoons, when other men were busy earning a living.

'The old woman told Shankhini I paid well, and so she went out of her way to make me comfortable, to please me, and to persuade me to come again. She did this as part of her duty; but it wasn't all commercial enterprise. As familiarity grew between us, we spent some time in talk. What did we have to say to each other? I don't remember much of it, but this strange girl had evolved a philosophy of her own to deal with the situation she found herself in. It was all a question of doing one's duty, she said. Death was a duty, just as much as life was just another way of dying.'

VII

It has grown cold in the cave. While my ascetic host has been talking, using me as his confessor, the fire has died down. Outside, a jackal complains loudly, and the wind grows restless and rushes up and down the hillside, seeking entry into the cave. But we are well protected by rocks and overhang, and when this twentieth-century cave-dweller adds more sticks to the embers, the flames shoot up again, and the warmth reaches out to me and I reach out to the warmth, move closer, get up and stretch my limbs and then sit down again, while the man's eyes follow me with a bright, probing look.

'So far,' I say, 'so far, you have not told me anything very startling about yourself. You did nothing that would account for your giving up the pleasures you have described. I envy you some of your exploits, but they are not in themselves extraordinary. Many young men have visited prostitutes and have even found sensitive souls among them. And many young men have sought to go through their father's money. Some have sunk by stages into a hell of squalor and have been quite happy wallowing in their own filth. You did not sink very low. Your obsessions were not those of the pervert or psychopath.

You were perhaps slightly more obsessed with sex than most, but apart from that your sex life appears to have been remarkably normal! Many young men would have done the same, given the opportunity.'

'I made my opportunities. I imposed my will on others. I cared for no one but myself.'

'I concede that.'

'And I am not even half-way through the story.'

'Ah, well, in that case . . . . I have no desire to sleep, and it isn't midnight yet. You were talking of Shankhini, the girl with the green-gold body.'

'Yes. She preserved a perfect body, almost as a challenge and a taunt to the shapeless creatures who came to her by day and by night. She gave them their money's worth like a true professional. She was well-versed in all the technicalities of love-making. She gave her customers her body but not her soul. She could not love men. Her love went to another, a dark girl from the coast who was also owned by the old woman. One day, entering the room unannounced, I found them in each other's arms, tenderly kissing each other. When they saw me standing there, they drew apart, unhurriedly and without any sense of guilt. Without a glance at me, the dark girl left the room.

' "You should not have come in without calling or knocking," said Shankhini.

' "There was no one about, and your door wasn't locked. Where's the old lady?"

' "She had to go out to collect some money. Sit down, and I will prepare some tea for you."

'I stretched myself out on the couch and asked, "Who was the girl with you?"

' "My friend. Why, did you like her? Would you like to go to her?"

' "I hardly saw her . . . ."

' "She is very beautiful. If you would like to go to her, I will tell the old one."

' "All right. If you don't mind, that is."

' "Why should I mind? It is my business to persuade you to keep coming here. If you tire of one of us, there is always another."

' "I haven't tired of you. I do not even know you as yet. But I thought you would mind because you seemed to like the girl."

' "I love her, but that does not interfere with our work. Men like you will come and go. Nalini and I will still be here."

' "Men like me . . . . Am I like other men?"

' "You want the same things, don't you?"

' "No. Most men only want to possess you physically. I want both your mind and your soul."

' "I do not have these things to offer you. I think, I feel, but I cannot share my thoughts and feelings with any man."

' "You can share them with Nalini?"

' "Here is the tea. Drink it, and tell me your pleasure."

'But after drinking tea, I got up to go. "You are very irritable today," I said. "I will come again." She looked dismayed and urged me to stay. Perhaps she was afraid that I might not come again and that her mistress would be annoyed. The old woman was just outside the door.

' "He would like to see Nalini," said Shankhini.

' "No," I said. "Not today. Some other time."

'It was a frustrating day. Mulia was out shopping. Samyukta's house was full of people. It was as though, for a few hours, I had ceased to exist for them! Although I knew that they were completely unconscious of my restlessness, I harboured feelings of resentment towards them. I was being neglected! I suppose it's the lot of the only son to feel that way.'

'I must have given you the impression that as a youth I was obsessed with sex to the exclusion of all else, and that I was devoid of finer feelings. It is true there was a time when I believed that although all men were born equal, some men turned out to be more virile than others!

'As for falling in love, I had no idea what it was about. Loving (I was told) is giving, but at the time I was interested only in taking.

'Have I given you the impression that my life was spent entirely in the company of women? I had not made friends at college, but then, I seldom attended college. I found the lectures boring and a waste of time. I had nothing against books and even read some poetry, but I did not want life second hand, from books. Mine was not a reflective nature—not then, anyway—and I could not reconcile mental pursuits with the pursuit of physical delight. And what would be the use of a degree in the Arts if I was going to spend the rest of my life helping my father to manufacture electric bulbs?

'When my father asked me to go to Delhi on his behalf, to attend an industrial exhibition that was being held in the capital, I agreed to do so. It was my father's intention to get me involved in the business. I was not interested in industrial exhibitions but I felt like a change from my confined life in Kapila and I set out with a sense of impending adventure. I had no idea where the adventure, if it came, would lead me. My father had given me five hundred rupees, and I would follow my fancy in seeing where it would take me and what I could do with it.'

VIII

'My train rushed into the darkness, the carriage wheels beating out a steady rhythm on the rails. The bright lights of Kapila were swallowed up in the night, and new lights—dim and flickering—came into existence as we passed small villages. A star falls, a person dies. I used to wonder why I did not see more shooting stars, because in India someone is dying every minute. And then I realized that with someone being born every half-minute, falling stars must be in short supply.

'The people in the carriage were settling down, finding places for themselves. There were about fifty of us in that compartment sharing the same breathing space, sharing each other's sweaty odours.

'At four in the morning I woke from a fitful sleep to find the train at a standstill. There was no noise or movement on the platform outside. It was a very small station, and the train for some mysterious reason of its own had stopped there longer than usual, so that those in the train who had woken up had gone to sleep again, and those few who had been spending the night on the platform slept on as though nothing had happened. This was not their train.

'I watched them from the window. A very small boy was curled up in a large basket. His mother had stretched herself out on the platform beside him. A coolie slept on a platform bench. The tea-stall was untenanted. A dim light from the assistant stationmaster's office revealed a pair of sandalled feet propped up against a mountain of files. A bedraggled crow perched on the board which gave the station its name: Deoband. The crow cawed disconsolately, as if to imply that this dismal wayside station was none of its doing. And yet—Deoband!—the name struck a chord. Wasn't this, by tradition, the most ancient town in India?

'The engine hissed, sending waves of hot steam into the fresh early morning air. My shirt clung to me. We were all smelling of perspiration. There had been no rain for a month but the atmosphere was humid, there were clouds overhead, dark clouds burgeoning with moisture. Thunder blossomed in the air.

'The monsoon was going to break that day. I knew it, the birds knew it, the grass knew it. There was the smell of rain in the air. And the grass, the birds and I responded to this odour with the same sensuous longing. We would welcome the rain as a woman welcomes a lover's embrace, his kiss, the fierce, fresh thrust of his loins after a period of abstinence.

'Suddenly I felt the urge to get out of that stuffy, overcrowded compartment, away from the sweat and smoke and smells, away from the commonplaces of life, from the certainty of my destination and predestined future. I would be a free wanderer, the last in a world where even the poets had retreated into the sculleries of their minds.

'I knew where I was supposed to be going: Delhi. I knew what I was supposed to do there—take the fatal step towards respectability. To be respectable—what an adventure that would be! And this prospect of an ordered, organized life frightened me. I knew that I could not put it off forever, but perhaps it could be postponed. I had five hundred rupees in my vest pocket. It would provide me with freedom for two weeks, perhaps three if I was not too extravagant. Five hundred rupees; the smell of coming rain; and outside, an unknown town. The combination was too strong for my wayward spirit.

'I clambered over my fellow passengers, my suitcase striking heads, shoulders, backsides. Grunts and curses followed me to the door. And then the train began to move. I was seized with panic. If I didn't get off quickly, I would never get off. I would be frozen forever into a respectable bulb manufacturer!

'I flung the door open and tumbled on to the platform. My suitcase spun away, hit the corner of a bench, burst open. The crow flew off in alarm. A dog began barking.

'The train moved on to Delhi, carrying with it six hundred souls in bondage, while I stood alone on the platform, in temporary possession of my own soul.

'The suitcase, which never locked properly, was soon closed. I looked furtively around. The coolie was still asleep—obviously no one ever got off at Deoband at that hour—or he would have grabbed my insignificant burden, carried it for a distance of twenty feet, and charged me a rupee. I needed my rupees. I could no longer scatter them about at random or live on credit as I did in my home town.

'I walked quietly to the turnstile. There was no one there to ask me for my ticket. I walked out of the station and found myself in a wasteland of nondescript shacks—some of them labourer's huts, some warehouses, one or two of them uninviting tea shops. The scene was a dismal one, and if the train had still been at the station I would have returned to it and gone to Delhi. But so far in my defiance of the gods, I had done quite well, and it would have been admitting defeat to have returned to the station to hang around waiting for another train.

'By evening I was sitting disconsolately on a small hotel balcony overlooking the street, telling myself that I was a fool. For three hours nothing had happened to me, and now it looked as though nothing was going to happen. There was no Mulia to press my aching limbs, no Samyukta to ravish, no Shankhini to battle with my ego. My only acquisition was a headache from drinking too much of the local beer and sleeping too long under the electric fan.

'The camel had gone from across the street, but in its place was a buffalo. The traffic had increased, there were more people in the street. There were also more flies on the balcony, and one of them came buzzing into my half-empty glass in an effort to drown itself in what remained of my drink. It was a suicidal kind of evening. I rescued the fly from my glass, placed it gently on the balcony railing and watched it crawl groggily away. But my compassion was wasted. As the fly neared the wall, a gecko, chuckling greedily, swooped on the insect and gobbled it up.

'There was no one to talk to. The hotel manager was a moron, and the bearer's thoughts dwelt on the contents of my suitcase. A large drop of water hit the balcony railing, darkening the thick dust on the woodwork. A faint breeze sprang up, and again I felt the moisture, closer and warmer.

'Then the rain approached like a dark curtain. I could see it marching down the street, heavy and remorseless. It drummed on the corrugated tin roof and swept across the road and over the balcony. I sat there without moving, letting the rain wet my sticky shirt and gritty hair.

'Outside, the street rapidly emptied. The crowd dissolved in the rain. Stray cows continued to rummage in dustbins, buses and tongas ploughed through the suddenly rushing water. A group of small boys, now gloriously naked, came romping along the street which was like a river in spate. When they came to a gutter choked with rain water, they plunged in, shouting their delight to whoever cared to listen. A garland of marigolds, swept from the steps of a temple, came floating down the middle of the road.

'The rain stopped as suddenly as it had begun. The day was dying, and the breeze remained cool and moist. In the brief twilight that followed, I was a witness to the great yearly flight of insects into the cool brief freedom of the night.

'It was the hour of the geckos. They had their reward for weeks of patient waiting. Plying their sticky pink tongues, they devoured insects as swiftly and methodically as Americans devour popcorn. For hours they crammed their stomachs, knowing that such a feast would not be theirs again. Throughout the entire hot season the insect world prepared for this flight out of darkness into light, and not one survived its bid for freedom.'

'I had walked the streets of the town for over three hours, and it was past midnight. Shop fronts were shuttered, the cinema was silent and deserted. The people living on either side of the narrow street could hear my footsteps, and I could hear their casual remarks, music, a burst of laughter.

'A three-quarter moon was up, shining through drifting, breaking clouds, and the roofs and awnings of the bazaar, still wet, glistened in the moonlight. From a few open windows fingers of light reached out into the night. Who could still be up? A shopkeeper going through his accounts, a college student preparing for his exams, a prostitute extricating herself from the arms of a paramour who had suddenly fallen asleep . . . .

'Three stray dogs were romping in the middle of the road. It was their road now, and they abandoned themselves to a wild chase, almost knocking me down. A jackal slunk across the road, looking to right and left to make sure the dogs had gone. A field rat wriggled its way through a hole in a rotting plank, on its nightly foray among sacks of grain and pulses.

'As I passed along the deserted street under the shadow of the clock tower, I found a young man, or a boy (I couldn't tell which) sleeping in a small recess under a rickety wooden staircase. He was wearing nothing but a pair of torn, dirty shorts—his shirt, or what was left of it, had been rolled into a pillow. He was sleeping with his mouth open; his cheeks were hollow, and his body, which looked as though it had been strong and vigorous at one time, was emaciated.

'There was no corruption, no experience on his face. He looked quite vulnerable, although I suppose he had nothing much to lose in the material sense.

'I passed by, my head down, my thoughts elsewhere—that is how we of the towns and cities usually behave when we see a fellow human lying in the gutter.

'And then I stopped. It was almost as though the bright moonlight had stopped me. And I startled myself with the question, "Why do I leave him there? And what am I doing here anyway?"

'I walked back to the shadows where the boy slept and looked at him again. He seemed a very heavy sleeper, the sort of person who can fall asleep anywhere, at any time, oblivious to all that goes on around him. I coughed loudly, but nothing happened; I whistled, but still he slept; I picked up an empty can and dropped it beside him, but the noise had no effect on the sleeper. In his dreams he was elsewhere, moving among the spirit-haunted mountains, while his material body lay in this town. I found myself wishing that I could sleep like that—

it was the sleep of one who was protected by his own innocence.

'I went down on my knees and touched the boy's shoulder. But he must have been touched often in his sleep. His lips moved slightly, but there was no alteration in the rhythm of his breathing.

'One arm was thrown back, and I noticed a scar under his armpit where the hair began. Looking at that scar, all the warnings of Mulia and my mother crowded in upon me—tales of crime by night, of assault and robbery. But when I looked again at the untroubled face, I saw nothing there to disturb me.

'And since he did not wake, and seemed comfortable, why did I not stand up and walk away and take the morning train to Delhi? I still do not know. Something was pressing me on, urging me to shake the boy out of his slumber.

'I took him by the shoulders and gave him a good shaking. He woke with a loud cry, as from a nightmare, and stared at me with something like terror. He sat up, cringing away, holding his hands before his face. But then, when he realized that I was a man and not the demon of his dream, his fear turned to indignation.

' "Who are you? What do you want?"

' "Nothing," I said, standing up and moving away. "I did not see you there. I am sorry to wake you."

'I moved a few steps away, then stopped and looked back at the youth. He was still crouching on the steps, still staring at me, but he had lost both his fear and his anger, and he was only a little puzzled by this apparition in the middle of the night.

' "Haven't you anywhere to stay?"

'He shook his head.

'Perhaps the tone of voice I used gave him some confidence, because the hostility left his face and in its place I saw a glimmer of hope.

'I had committed myself. I could not pass on.

' "Do you want a job?" I asked.

' "No."

' "You have money?"

' "No."

' "Do you want some money?"

' "No, babuji."

' "Then what do you want?"

' "I want to go home."

' "Where is your home?"

' "In the hills."

' "Far away?"

' "Yes, babuji. In the Jalan hills."

' "And how much does it cost to get there?"

' "Twenty rupees."

' "And how much have you got?"

' "One rupee."

'He held his torn shirt in his hands. It was his only possession. I liked his open look, the way he returned mine without any attempt at evasion.

' "I'll see that you get home," I said. "On one condition."

'A shadow of doubt passed across his mobile face. (It was no mask, that face.)

' "Babuji—I have never done anything—anything shameful."

' "Shameful? You have not heard my condition. What did you think I was going to ask you to do—sleep with me?"

'He laughed and looked embarrassed.

'I said, "Don't be an ass. I have always taken my pleasure with women. Listen to my condition before you start getting nervous."

'He did not say anything but kept twisting his shirt in his hands—he was no longer looking me in the eye.

' "I was about to say that I'd help you to get home provided you took me with you. I would like to see your hills."

'His dark, sombre face lit up. He smiled like an angel. All the latent hospitality of his tribe welled up and burst through the barrier of his poverty.

' "Oh, I will take you to my home, babuji. I have nothing here, but in the hills I have a house, fields, a buffalo! Yes! I will take you to my home."

'No longer hesitating, he came to me, brimming over with a simple trust and joy. I could not betray that trust, nor could I fail to trust him. I was committed to a stranger in the night. I had sought him out deliberately, imposed my will on him, and the consequences of the meeting would be entirely of my own making.

'And so there were two of us on that lonely street. The rain had held off just long enough for the encounter. Soon it began to drizzle.

' "We will go to my hotel," I said. "Have you anything to bring with you?"

' "Nothing," he said. "Yesterday I sold my shoes."

"Never mind. Let us get some sleep while the night remains with us. Tomorrow, in the morning, we will leave this place. It has served its purpose, and now there is nothing to keep me here. Nothing to bring me back again."

'The boy lay on the mattress which I had removed from the bed and placed on the floor. His face was in darkness but the light from the veranda bulb fell across his legs. There was no escape from my father's bulbs! I lay flat on my belly on the string cot, while the ceiling-fan hummed in the moist air immediately above me.

' "Are you awake?" I called.

' "Yes," said the boy.

' "The mosquitoes make it difficult to sleep. So let us talk. Tell me, how do we get to your village?"

' "It is a difficult place to reach," he said.

' "Well, if it was easy to reach, there would be no point in my going there. Will we have to walk a lot? I have not done much walking."

' "We must walk about thirty miles. But first we must take a train or a bus. Later we walk."

' "Good. And now tell me your name."

' "Roop."

' "You have brothers and sisters?"

' "A brother, no sisters. My brother is younger than me and goes to school. I never went to school. There was another brother, but he died—he was attacked by a leopard, and the wounds were so bad that he died after several days."

' "After a brief silence, he asked, "Why do you wish to visit my home, babuji?"

' "Because it is far away. Because I am bored with my own home. I have a mother and father and servants, but I am bored with all of them."

'Roop was one of those people blessed with the gift of being able to sleep sweetly and soundly through cannon-fire and earthquake. Once he fell asleep, there was little that could wake him. The morning sun embraced him, moved lovingly over his dark gleaming body, touched his eyelids, settled on his untidy hair. Still he did not wake. He slept on as though drugged. I called him, I shouted, I reached out and shook him by the shoulder, but he did not stir. A fly settled on his lips, but although his mouth twitched, he did not open his eyes.

' "One of us will have to get up," I muttered, looking at my expensive smuggled watch which showed nine o'clock. "Otherwise we won't get anywhere today."

'And I wanted to get away as soon as possible. The urge to stop at Deoband had been strong, but the urge to move on was stronger. During the night I had dreamt of pine forests and mountain streams, pale pink flowers growing in the clefts of rocks and fair hill maidens bathing beneath pellucid waterfalls.

'I got up and sprinkled water on Roop's face. Nothing happened. I placed my foot on his broad heavy thigh and shook him vigorously. But he simply smiled. He was still dreaming—of a girl, perhaps; or possibly of the chicken we had eaten on returning to the hotel the previous night.

'I decided that I would have to use some more positive method of rousing Roop. Shaking him was of no use, slapping his face would have been impolite. So I compromised—held the water-jug over his head and kept pouring until he awoke, spluttering and shaking his head and greeting the day (and me) with foul language.

'An hour later—my purse considerably lightened by our short stay at the hotel—we were sitting in a bus and moving hopefully in the direction of the hills.'

IX

'It had been raining all morning, and whenever there were dips in the road, the bus sent up sprays of muddy water. Sometimes the rain came in at the windows and wet my shirt. But I did not close the window, it was too stuffy in the bus, and the reek of cigarettes and bidis added to my discomfort.

'Let us be grateful for neem trees. Their pods had fallen on the roadside, and these, bursting or being crushed against the wet earth by passing vehicles, emitted a powerful but pleasant odour which drifted in through the window on the breeze.

'The road was straight, but the bus was continually having to swerve or brake to avoid coming into collision with the slow and ponderous bullock-carts that came lumbering and creaking down the middle of the highway. In the fields, the ploughing had begun. Long wooden ploughs yoked between two bullocks raked crooked furrows in the softened earth. A heron stood on one leg in a rice field. An egret perched behind a buffalo's ear, searching there for tender insects.

'The buffaloes were of course in their element. With tanks and ditches overflowing, they did not have to search for muddy water in which to wallow through the long hot days. Some were already knee-deep among the water-lilies. Their dung, as always, was precious, and I remember the quaint spectacle of a farmer, realizing that one of his buffaloes was about to give forth riches, taking up his position behind the heaving beast and collecting a generous amount of dung in his arms, even as it fell. Hot and fresh it must have been! A second later, and this precious product would have been lost forever in the lily-pond.

'Yes, I remember that bus ride. Who remembers bus journeys? They are always so monotonous. But I remember that one, because it was a monsoon day and I was moving towards the unknown.

'The bus moved past a score of naked children romping in the rain; past a tonga-load of villagers, drenched but merry; past a young man with a dancing bear; past a sugar factory; past a railway crossing, mercifully open; past a dead cow, dense with vultures; past tiny huts and huge factory buildings.'

'I woke to what sounded like the din of a factory buzzer but was in fact the voice of a single cicada emerging from the lime tree near my bed. A faint light was breaking over the mountains. The morning air was quite chill, and I moved closer to Roop for warmth. We had slept out of doors, sharing the same bed.

'His mother and young brother, who slept indoors, had thought me a little strange for wanting to sleep outside. Most hill people prefer to sleep inside the small stuffy rooms of their rough stone houses, even when the nights are warm. It has something to do with their fear of the dark, their belief in demons and malignant spirits who dwell in trees or take possession of the bodies of leopards and sometimes humans. Roop told me that he had seen the ghost of a woman who had been at least ten feet tall, and whose feet faced backwards. His strong belief in demonlore made him reluctant to join me outside; at the same time, he did not want to have his guest spirited off in the night. It would have been impolite on his part to leave me to the tree-spirits. His natural sense of hospitality overcame his naturally superstitious nature, and he joined me on the cot in the bright moonlight. No electric bulbs in his village—I had escaped my father at last!

'Once Roop was asleep, he was immune to all the spirits of the dead, being even more comatose than a corpse. The shrieking cicada had no effect on him. He slept with abandon, one leg thrown over my thigh, an arm hanging down from the side of the bed, his head thrown back, his mouth open in disregard of his own warning that spirits enter people through the mouth.

'As the sky grew lighter, I could see through the pattern of glossy lime-leaves the outlines of the mountains as they strode away into an immensity of sky. I could see the small house, standing in the middle of its narrow terraced fields. I could see the other houses, standing a little apart from each other in their own bits of land.

'I could see trees and bushes, and a path leading up the hill to the deodar forest on the summit. A couple of fruit trees grew behind the house.

'The tops of the distant mountains suddenly lit up as the sun touched the snow peaks. A door banged open. The house was stirring. A cock belatedly welcomed the daylight and elsewhere in the village dogs were barking. A magpie flew with a whirring sound as it crossed the courtyard and then glided downhill. Everyone, everything—except Roop beside me—came to life.'

'I was conscious of being observed. There was no one behind me, no one at the foot of the bed. But there was a soft footfall close by. I closed my eyes, pretended I was asleep. When I opened them, I found myself gazing into light brown eyes flecked with green—the fair complexioned face of Roop's younger brother. He had been looking at me with considerable curiosity because the night before, when I had arrived, it had been dark and he had not been able to see me properly.

'When I returned his gaze, he smiled. He did not resemble Roop Singh at all, except in the sturdiness of his physique. He looked sensitive, reserved. The smile was shy, self-protective.

' "Is it time for us to get up?"

'He shook his head. "No, you can sleep. I have to go to school."

' "Your school starts very early."

' "It is very far," he said. "Five miles." And then, anxious to avoid further questioning, he ran off.

'The sun was up. It slipped across the courtyard and into the newly ploughed field and ran over the tips of the young maize that had come up with the first rain. It was time to get up.

'Roop's mother was a strong, handsome woman of about thirty-five. Those with conventional notions of beauty would not have called her good-looking. Some would have thought her ugly. Huge silver ear-rings passed through the tops of her ears, turning them inwards, elongating them, twisting them out of their natural shape. Those huge, imprisoned ears were inclined to divert one's attention from the rest of her face. The forehead was narrow, but the eyes were large and attractive. The nose was a strong one, having withstood the weight of another large silver ring. She wore a silver bracelet and silver bangles clashed at her ankles. All her savings had gone into silver ornaments. It wasn't safe to wear or keep gold.

'Her voice was deep and resonant without actually being masculine in tone. She had strong hands, large heavy feet—she walked barefoot even on the rocky hillsides.

'Roop was rather afraid of her. The younger brother loved her deeply.

'She gave us a heavy breakfast of curds and black mandwa bread and hot sweet tea.

'She did not look directly at me, but all the time I felt that she was watching me.'

X

'I was to be enslaved by this woman in a way that no woman had ever been enslaved by me. As the days passed, I became aware of her strange and powerful matriarchal passion. It was not the passive worship of Mulia, but something quite different.

'Strangely enough, I had not at first thought of her in terms of passion. Her physique did not attract me. True, Mulia was strong too, but that was because she was heavy, a mountain of flesh; otherwise she was a soft, feminine creature. But there was no surplus flesh on this woman of the mountains. She was hard, even muscular. Her feet were longer and much broader than mine. Her legs, which I glimpsed whenever she climbed the steep path to the fields, were the legs of an athlete. She had strong arms and lifted stacks of grass or bags of grain with an ease and facility that would have been the envy of most men.

'There was nothing delicate or pretty about her, but her face was strong and handsome, and her eyes, although lacking tenderness, were expressive and of dark spiritual intensity. She laboured more like a pack-mule than a man, but there were powerful, unquenched fires smouldering within her.

'Three days passed before she spoke to me, and then it was to ask me if I felt tired. Roop and I had returned after a long walk to a famous waterfall. We came back very hungry and with our limbs aching from the effort of climbing up two steep valleys. His mother prepared tea for us and when she handed my glass to me, she looked straight into my eyes and asked, "Are you tired?"

' "Yes," I said. "Very tired."

' "Tomorrow you will rest."

'It rained heavily that night and all next morning.

'Only at noon did the clouds begin to break up and then the sun came through, gleaming gold on the green slopes. I remember a flock of parrots swooping low over the house, their wings flashing red and gold and blue. They settled in the oak trees. Roop Singh had gone to the next village, where there was a shop, to buy salt and soap.

'I walked through the fields till I came to a grassy slope. Then the sun seduced me, and I took off my clothes and lay stretched out on the grass. I fell asleep—for how long, I could not tell—but when I woke, I felt curiously relaxed, languid, even light-headed. I passed my hand over my forehead and felt something sticky; then, looking at my hand, I found it was covered with bright red blood.

'I sat up, and got the fright of my life. My entire body was covered with leeches.

'They had crawled on to me while I was sleeping, had fastened on to my succulent flesh—as you must know, the bite of the leech can hardly be felt—and had then proceeded to gorge themselves on my blood. I now had about thirty leeches on my face, arms, chest, belly, backside and legs. One or two had had their fill and fallen off, leaving tiny punctures from which the blood trickled freely. One particularly fat leech—it was about two inches long—was feeding near my navel. I tried to pull it away, but it was stuck fast.

'I remembered being told that it was a mistake to remove leeches by force. The bite sometimes became septic. They would fall away and dissolve if a little salt was applied.

'I sprang to my feet, gathered up my clothes, and ran naked through the ploughed field until I reached the house. Seeing no one about I rushed indoors, surprising Roop's mother who was lighting a fire.

'If she was surprised at my condition, she did not show it.

' "Look, mother of Roop," I said, addressing her directly for the first time. "I'm covered with leeches. Give me salt."

'She got up from the fire, came nearer to examine me (it was always dark indoors) and said, "There are too many. Come into the other room, I will remove them for you."

'Armed with a container of salt, she led me into the next room and then started applying salt to the leeches. One by one, they squirmed and twisted and fell off.

'As they fell, they burst open and my blood oozed out of their slowly dissolving bodies, staining the floor. Little rivulets of blood kept trickling down from the open wounds on my body, which took a long time to close up.

' "I must have a bath," I said.

' "No. Let the blood dry on you. Only then will the bleeding stop."

'So I sat down on the floor feeling rather foolish, while Roop's mother watched me gravely from the doorway. If only she'd smiled or laughed, I would not have felt so uneasy. But she watched me intently, her seemingly dispassionate gaze taking everything in.

'It was an unusual situation for me. I had been in the habit of gazing upon the attributes of women. Now the positions were reversed, and a woman, fully clad, was studying my anatomy. I felt defenceless, rather as though I was a male spider or scorpion about to be first mated and then devoured by the female.'

'She came to me that night. I had been feeling the humidity and slept on the veranda, while Roop, afraid of the early morning chill, slept indoors with his brother.

'I woke from a sound sleep to find someone lying beside me. Automatically, and from force of habit, I moved to one side. I stretched out an arm and my hand encountered those heavy ear-rings and twisted ears. Hastily, I drew my hand away; but I could not leave the bed. The woman's strong arms were around me, her powerful legs held me in a vice. Her breath, smelling of cloves, almost overpowered me.

'She did not attempt to kiss me. Kissing was obviously something foreign to her nature. But she began to stroke me with her large, rough hands; and roused, I could not help but respond.

'This was a reversal of the usual role. She was active rather than passive in her attitude.

'Her breasts were huge pendulous things. Her arms and legs were much stronger than mine. Always proud of my virility, I now felt as though I would be inadequate for this woman who did not flinch, but who took me in her powerful arms and pressed upon me until I gasped for breath and wanted to cry for help.

'She did not give me any rest. She worked on me with her hands until I was roused again, and then she mastered me with complacent efficiency. Nothing seemed to happen to her. She could not be satisfied. She was some kind of vampire, a succubus—I swear to it—and she was determined to drain me of my last ounce of manhood.

'Only towards morning, when first light showed in the sky, did she leave me, returning to her own room. I lay limp and exhausted. I had done nothing to quench her passion and I knew that she could overpower me again at the first opportunity.'

XI

During our long vigil in the cave, the fire has gradually died down. It is about four in the morning, and a faint light appears on the snow of the Bandarpoonch massif. I am feeling cold; but with sunrise only two hours away, I am able to summon enough patience and fortitude to bear the gnawing discomfort that has crept over me.

'Well—and then what did you do?' I ask.

'I ran away. Oh, not immediately. That would not have been possible. She watched over me wherever I went. She fattened me up with chicken and gave me strange sherbets to revive my flagging virility. It was Mulia all over again, but I was not the man who had tamed Mulia. I was in the hands of a lioness, a woman far stronger, both mentally and physically, then Mulia had ever been. Whereas once I had imposed my will on others, I now found myself squirming under another's will. Roop's mother fed me on reviving herbs and fluids only in order that she might drain me of my strength. She was a rakshasni prepared to reduce me to skin and bone, to suck me dry!'

'And what of Roop—did he know what was happening?'

'He was too simple to comprehend. And he was too busy wenching with the village girls. He was a randy fellow, poor Roop. But the younger brother, he knew . . . . He would wake up in the night, and tossing about restlessly, he would hope to disturb us, to put an end to the ravishing of my body. But she was in no mood to be bothered by minor distractions.

'And yet, there was a tremendous innocence about the way in which this single-minded woman had stripped me of my manhood and pretensions. Hers was the overpowering innocence of the mountains—I was helpless before it, just a computer lover overpowered by natural forces. She was not a scheming woman. She sought to appease a basic hunger, and she did so without a civilized veneer, without the cover of sophisticated talk. We who have grown up in the cities cannot understand the innocence of mountain people, because we cannot understand the innocence of mountains, high places which have retained their power over the minds of men because they still remain aloof from the human presence, barely touched by human greed. In the cities it is easy to despise those who live in awe of the mountains, because in the cities there are vehicles and noise and lights to hold at bay that fear of the dark which is the beginning of religion; but on the far hills the darkness is still terrible.

'And mountain people still keep some of their primal innocence. It can be disconcerting to one who is accustomed to the corruption of the cities, but unaccustomed to the simple terror and solitude of the hills. I was used to being the ravisher. I was now being ravished.'

'Had another man violated me, I would not have found it as humiliating as the experience of being violated by this unlettered woman with the heavy feet and long twisted ears. It was not only my manhood that she stripped; it was my beloved ego.

'Roop's younger brother helped me get away. He had been in sympathy with me from the first, had sensed my predicament, my helplessness.

'Roop's mother had the custody of my suitcase which was locked in the storeroom. Having no need of any money in the village—there was nothing to spend it on—I had kept my remaining cash, about three hundred rupees, in the suitcase. I knew I wouldn't get very far without any money, and I was equally certain that Roop's mother would not give it to me—she had no intention of letting me get away.

'When the boy asked me, "Will you walk with me to my school?", I almost said no. The pleasures of walking did not appeal to me just then. But something in his expression told me that his intentions went deeper than what his words implied. He was not asking me to accompany him, he was urging me to do so.

'Puzzled, I said I'd come. His mother did not try to restrain me—she was confident that I would be back.

'We took the path to the stream, then followed the watercourse for a mile or two until the path forked, one branch twisting up the mountain on our right, the other keeping to the stream and running straight up the valley.

' "I will leave you here," said the boy.

' "Don't you want me to come as far as the school?"

'He shook his head. "No. You should go now." He opened the satchel which contained his school books, and took out my wallet. "The money is all there," he said.

'I took the wallet and thanked him; then I offered him a hundred-rupee note.

' "That is not why I brought it," he said.

'He smiled and started climbing the steeper path. Where the path went round the hillside he turned and waved to me. Then he disappeared round the bend and went out of my life— my first and only friend.'

XII

'Soon it began to rain. But I did not seek shelter. I walked ten miles in pouring rain until I reached the bus terminus. I was very tired when I got there and was tempted to spend the night in one of those seedy little hotels that spring up like mushrooms near every bus-stand; but I was afraid that Roop may have been sent after me, to try and persuade me to return. I sought the last bus to the plains, and the following day I was back in Kapila, secure among the anonymous thousands who throng the waterfront.

'My parents did not ask me too many questions. They were glad enough to see me back. At least, my mother was glad. She did not have long to live and I think she knew it. She had suckled and spoilt me and wanted to see me happy. My father would probably not have minded if I had disappeared for ever. He hadn't much confidence in me, and knew I would never be of any help to him in the business. I've no doubt he was furious with me for having wandered off on my own instead of going to Delhi, but to humour my mother, he said nothing. She thought I'd run away from home. Now that I was back, she was ready to indulge my every whim. Instead of getting less money, I was given more. And if I did not attend college, no questions were asked. No prodigal son ever had it better. And in this way young men are ruined for life.

'Although my mother adored me, under the delusion that I was a favourite of the gods, Mulia fussed over me more like a mother—or rather, like a brooding hen. Who would have thought that I was in my twenties . . . .

'Strangely enough, I found that I had grown indifferent to Mulia. Had she changed, or had I? Had she grown older, flabbier, heavier, uglier—or was it that I looked now only for the ugliness instead of for the beauty? The strong odour of her body, which formerly had aroused me so easily, now failed to excite me. Instead I found myself disliking the odour. Strange, isn't it, how things that attract us become, after a period of time, the things that repel us . . . .

'I spoke to Mulia as before, but I avoided being alone with her. If my mother went out, I found some excuse for going out too. Mulia was constantly seeking opportunities for being alone with me; I was over alert, ready to slip away.

'Still, the confrontation had to come.

'I slept late one morning and did not know that my mother had gone out early. The air of September was warm and humid, and I lay on my bed in singlet and shorts, watching the lizards scuttle about on the walls. Then the door opened and Mulia entered the room.

'She had bathed, she had perfumed her hair, and she looked quite magnificent as she stood there before me, with the sun from the open window slanting across her great quivering breasts. She lay down beside me and began to caress and stroke my limbs almost as though she worshipped my body. And although you may not believe it now, my body once had all the attributes of the perfect male physique. I was slim-waisted like a pipal leaf, with fine broad shoulders; and my thighs were like plantains, long and smooth and powerful. That was—how many years ago—five, ten, I don't remember . . . . But it doesn't take long for a man to lose his vigour and freshness. Women and trees last longer.

'Anyway, to return to what I was saying, Mulia began caressing me, but I was totally unresponsive to her ministrations.

' "What is wrong?" she asked.

' "Nothing" I said. "I am unwell, that is all. I will be all right in a day or two."

'And I got up from the bed and went to the tap to refresh myself with a cold bath.

'That evening I bathed in the river. I felt listless and ill at ease, and perhaps I was hoping that the icy water would instil new life in me. Thousands bathed daily in the river. Each person sought his own care, his own solutions, his own personal benediction; and that surging mass of human flesh appeared to me as one living entity, a shapeless jelly of throbbing amoeba, struggling for life on the banks of a timeless river. Was I a distinct and sacred individual, or was I just a part of the quivering jelly that sought cohesion in the swirling waters? And did help come from within or from without? Did it come from the mind, as my teacher once said, or was there really a potency, a magic, in the waters of the river? Bathing should be a rite, not a routine, I thought.

'Mulia was worried about me. She made me one of her concoctions, a bitter brew of senna leaves, rose petals, pomegranate-bark and laburnum seeds. The result was diarrhoea.

'I placed more reliance on Samyukta. A few hours with her, I thought, and I would soon be myself again. I had spent too much time with older women, and I needed the challenge of someone my own age. Or so I tried to convince myself.'

XIII

'Since my return, I had seen Samyukta occasionally but had not found an opportunity to be alone with her. Then one day her mother decided to visit a fair on the other side of the river, and Samyukta, pleading a headache, remained at home. I found her combing her long black hair in front of the mirror. I knew that she spent many hours at the mirror, and suspected that she was deeply in love with her own beauty.

'I began kissing her on her lips and throat, and presently she got up and undressed and came to bed with me. She had blossomed in the past year, and I think there were few women who could match her physical attractions. She had never failed to rouse me, to meet my challenge. She was prepared to do so now—even eager to please—for in pleasing me, homage would be paid to her own beauty.

'But something terrible had happened to me. My failure with Mulia was not a thing of the moment. There I was, lying beside a girl with whom at one time I had been brutal in my lovemaking. And now, though there was no diminishing of desire, I found myself helpless, unable to take possession of her. For the first time in my life I found myself up against forces beyond my control. Fear crept over me. Had the woman of the hills completely destroyed my manhood? Or had my own body rebelled against me?

'The unfocussed stare of desire faded from Samyukta's eyes. She looked at me in surprise, and then in anger. My inadequacy was an insult to her beauty and womanhood. And she asked the same question that Mulia had asked: "What is wrong?"

' "I don't know," I said. "I must be ill. Or it's the evil eye."

'She got up and began to dress. She said nothing. But her silence was more eloquent than speech.

' "I'll come again," I said, "When I feel better."

How pathetic it sounded!

'And of course she said nothing. After all, what was there to say? A woman can hide her frigidity, but a man's impotence is obvious.'

'I primed myself on strong country liquor, and when evening came on and the sun sank in the river, and night crept up to cover our imperfections, I walked unsteadily towards the house with the green lantern and made my way upstairs. Shankhini's door was open. I walked in, but she was not to be seen anywhere. Feeling giddy and sick, I stumbled into the bathroom and supporting myself against the sink, began retching. Then, exhausted, I lent back against the wall. And while I stood there trying to pull myself together, I heard the voices of two people who had entered the room.

'One voice was Shankhini's—I recognized it immediately. The other was a man's voice.

'They spoke together for a few minutes, then the bed creaked under their combined weight. I couldn't resist moving to the bathroom door and looking through the curtains. The bathroom was in darkness, but Shankhini's bedroom was brightly lit. She lay on her bed, a fragile figure, while her guest for the night took his pleasure.

'The man, a stranger in town had close-cropped grey hair, hollow cheeks, and skinny legs; he must have been at least sixty. But he went about the whole business with all the verve and vigour of a young stallion.

'I watched in fear and fascination. Fear for myself, fascination at the old man. I had fancied myself the world's most accomplished lover. And there I stood, finished before I was thirty, while a man who was more than twice my age performed wonders on a bed. My ego was shattered. My self-esteem lay in the washbasin.

'There was a door leading from the bathroom to the passageway and, unable to face Shankhini, I departed ignominiously, stumbling into the street and being sick again on the pavement.'

XIV

The clear light of a September dawn has spread across the mountains, and from outside the cave comes the call of the whistling-thrush, a song sweet and haunting, recalling for me a different kind of joy. But inside the cave it is dark and clammy, a home for those who despise the light—bats, rodents and hollow men.

All the awe I had at first felt for the recluse disappeared at the very moment that the sun came shouting over the hills. There is nothing more beautiful than daylight. I want to flee from the cave, from all within it. Renunciation? He has not renounced the world, he has hidden from it. And I wonder how many thousands there are like him—men who have run, not simply from the world but from themselves; men who, hating themselves, cannot bear to see their own reflections in the faces of other men.

He has produced a small chilum—a clay pipe—and filled it with the dried leaves of the cannabis plant.

'No wonder you eat so little,' I say.

'It is mental food I require. Those few or many years ago, of which I have told you, when I thought that by strengthening my mental powers I might regain my manhood, I went again to the man who had taught me to concentrate, to bend others to my will. But he could do nothing for me. Perhaps he had lost his hypnotic powers in the same way that I had lost my physical powers—a failure of conservation!'

'And yet this weed which grows all about me, has made life tolerable. It has so solaced me that in my fantasies I can experience all those sensual pleasures without my miserable body having to do anything! Surely that's an achievement—surely that's victory for mind over matter!'

'I wouldn't call it that,' I say, now ready to refute. 'If it's the plant that brings you mental ease, that makes it a victory of matter over mind. Surely the only victory comes when the mind is free.'

'Perhaps, perhaps. But nothing else, human or divine, could help me. I had only one talent, you know. Misuse a gift, and you destroy it. And when I lost mine, I turned my back on the world and all it stood for.'

'But the world isn't exclusively a place for the pursuit of sensual pleasure.'

'No. But I was a sensualist. There was nothing else I could pursue.'

Before I go, I ask him where I can find the woman who had stolen his manhood—the hill-woman who had overpowered him with her own much stronger sensuality.

'Why?' he asks. 'Do you wish to lose your manhood too?'

'No. I wish to regain it. Or rather, I wish to discover it. And only a woman who can give so much of herself can revive true passion in a man.'

'You are wrong. A woman of great passion can only diminish a man.'

'That is because you were in love with your ego, you were too concerned about your self-esteem. You took the love but spurned the lover. And so you had to lose both. I hope to find them yet . . .'

And I leave him in the cave with his cold thoughts, and the cold ashes of his dead fire, and the cold corpse he still inhabits.

I leave my dead self in the cave and continue my search for the perfect stranger in the night.